THE OXFORD BOOK OF AMERICAN SHORT STORIES

THE OXFORD BOOK OF AMERICAN SHORT STORIES

SECOND EDITION

Edited by

Joyce Carol Oates

Oxford University Press is a department of the University of Oxford. It furthers the University's objective of excellence in research, scholarship, and education by publishing worldwide.

Oxford New York
Auckland Cape Town Dar es Salaam Hong Kong Karachi
Kuala Lumpur Madrid Melbourne Mexico City Nairobi
New Delhi Shanghai Taipei Toronto

With offices in
Argentina Austria Brazil Chile Czech Republic France Greece
Guatemala Hungary Italy Japan Poland Portugal Singapore
South Korea Switzerland Thailand Turkey Ukraine Vietnam

Published in the United States of America by Oxford University Press
198 Madison Avenue, New York, New York 10016
www.oup.com

Library of Congress Cataloging-in-Publication Data

The Oxford book of American short stories / edited by Joyce Carol Oates.
p. cm.

Includes index.
1. Short stories, American. I. Oates, Joyce Carol, 1938-
PS648.S5O94 2012
813'.0108--dc23
2012012423

ISBN 978-0-19-974439-8

1 3 5 7 9 8 6 4 2

Printed in the United States of America
on acid-free paper

ACKNOWLEDGMENTS

The editor and publisher gratefully acknowledge permission to reprint the following material.

James Baldwin: "Sonny's Blues," copyright © 1957 by James Baldwin, was originally published in *Partisan Review*. Copyright renewed. Collected in *Going to Meet the Man,* published by Vintage Books. Used by arrangement with the James Baldwin Estate.

Russell Banks: "The Child Screams and Looks Back at You" (pp. 139–48) from *The Angel on the Roof: Stories* by Russell Banks. Copyright © 2000 by Russell Banks. Reprinted by permission of HarperCollins Publishers.

Donald Barthelme: "The School" from *Amateurs* by Donald Barthelme, currently collected in *Sixty Stories*. Copyright © 1981, 1982 by Donald Barthelme, used with permission of The Wylie Agency LLC.

Pinckney Benedict: "Mercy" from *Miracle Boy and Other Stories* by Pinckney Benedict, copyright © 2010 by Pinckney Benedict. Used by permission of the author.

Paul Bowles: "A Distant Episode" copyright © 1948 by Paul Bowles from *The Stories of Paul Bowles* by Paul Bowles. Copyright © 2001 by the Estate of Paul Bowles. Introduction copyright © 2001 by Robert Stone. Reprinted by permission of HarperCollins Publishers.

T. C. Boyle: "Filthy with Things" from *Without a Hero* by T. Coraghessan Boyle, copyright © 1994 by T. Coraghessan Boyle. Used by permission of Viking Penguin, a division of Penguin Group (USA) Inc.

Ray Bradbury: "There Will Come Soft Rains." Reprinted by permission of Don Congdon Associated, Inc. Copyright © 1950 by the Crowell Collier Publishing Company, renewed 1977 by Ray Bradbury.

Raymond Carver: "Are These Actual Miles?" from *Where I'm Calling From*, copyright © 1976, 1988 by Raymond Carver. Used by permission of Grove/Atlantic, Inc.

John Cheever: "The Country Husband" from *The Stories of John Cheever* by John Cheever, copyright © 1978 by John Cheever. Used by permission of Alfred A. Knopf, a division of Random House, Inc.

Junot Díaz: "Edison, New Jersey" from *Drown* by Junot Díaz, copyright © 1996 by Junot Díaz. Used by permission of Riverhead Books, an imprint of Penguin Group (USA) Inc.

Ralph Ellison: "Battle Royal," copyright © 1948 by Ralph Ellison, from *Invisible Man* by Ralph Ellison. Used by permission of Random House, Inc.

Louise Erdrich: "Fleur," originally published by *Esquire*, August 1986, copyright © 1986 by Louise Erdrich, reprinted with permission of The Wylie Agency LLC.

William Faulkner: "That Evening Sun," copyright © 1931 and renewed 1959 by William Faulkner, from *Collected Stories of William Faulkner* by William Faulkner. Used by permission of Random House, Inc.

F. Scott Fitzgerald: "An Alcoholic Case." Reprinted with the permission of Scribner, a division of Simon & Schuster, Inc., from *The Stories of F. Scott Fitzgerald* edited by Malcolm Cowley. Copyright © 1937 by Esquire, Inc. Copyright renewed 1964 by Frances Scott Fitzgerald Lanahan. All rights reserved.

Jeffrey Ford: "The Drowned Life" from *The Drowned* by Jeffrey Ford, copyright © 2008 by Jeffrey Ford. Used by permission of HarperCollins Publishers.

Richard Ford: "Under the Radar" from *A Multitude of Sins* by Richard Ford, copyright © 2001 by Richard Ford. Used by permission of Alfred A. Knopf, a division of Random House, Inc.

Ernest Hemingway: "Hills Like White Elephants." Reprinted with the permission of Scribner, a division of Simon & Schuster, Inc., from *Men Without Women* by Ernest Hemingway. Copyright © 1927 by Charles Scribner's Sons. Copyright renewed © 1955 by Ernest Hemingway. All rights reserved.

Amy Hempel: "Today Will Be a Quiet Day." Reprinted with the permission of Scribner, a division of Simon & Schuster, Inc., from *The Collected Stories of Amy Hempel* by Amy Hempel. Copyright © 1985 by Amy Hempel. All rights reserved.

Langston Hughes: "Red-Headed Baby" from *The Ways of White Folks* by Langston Hughes, copyright © 1934 and renewed 1962 by Langston Hughes. Used by permission of Alfred A. Knopf, a division of Random House, Inc.

Shirley Jackson: "The Lottery" from *The Lottery* by Shirley Jackson. Copyright © 1948, 1949 by Shirley Jackson. Copyright renewed 1976, 1977 by Laurence Hyman, Barry Hyman, Mrs. Sarah Webster and Mrs. Joanne Schnurer. Reprinted by permission of Farrar, Straus and Giroux, LLC.

Ha Jin: "Children as Enemies" from *A Good Fall* by Ha Jin, copyright © 2009 by Ha Jin. Used by permission of Pantheon Books, a division of Random House, Inc.

Stephen King: "The Reach" from *Skeleton Crew* by Stephen King, copyright © 1985 by Stephen King, reprinted by permission of the author c/o Darhansoff & Verrill, Literary Agents. All rights reserved.

Jhumpa Lahiri: "Hell-Heaven" from *Unaccustomed Earth* by Jhumpa Lahiri, copyright © 2008 by Jhumpa Lahiri. Used by permission of Alfred A. Knopf, a division of Random House, Inc.

H. P. Lovecraft: "The Rats in the Walls" used by permission of Lovecraft Holdings, LLC.

Bernard Malamud: "My Son the Murderer" from *Rembrandt's Hat* by Bernard Malamud. Copyright © 1968, 1973 by Bernard Malamud. Reprinted by permission of Farrar, Straus and Giroux, Inc., and Russell & Volkening, Inc., as agents for the author.

Lorrie Moore: "How to Become a Writer," copyright © 1985 by M. L. Moore, from *Self-Help* by Lorrie Moore. Used by permission of Alfred A. Knopf, a division of Random House, Inc.

Joyce Carol Oates: "Heat" from *Heat*. Copyright © 1991 by The Ontario Review, Inc. Published by NAL/Dutton and reprinted by permission of The Ontario Review, Inc.

Tim O'Brien: "The Things They Carried" from *The Things They Carried* by Tim O'Brien. Copyright © 1990 by Tim O'Brien. Reprinted by permission of Houghton Mifflin Harcourt Publishing Company. All rights reserved.

Flannery O'Conner: "A Late Encounter with the Enemy" from *A Good Man is Hard to Find and Other Stories* copyright © 1953 by Flannery

O'Connor and renewed 1981 by Regina O'Connor, reprinted by permission of Houghton Mifflin Harcourt Publishing Company.

Cynthia Ozick: "The Shawl" from *The Shawl* by Cynthia Ozick, copyright © 1980, 1983 by Cynthia Ozick. Used by permission of Alfred A. Knopf, a division of Random House, Inc.

Annie Proulx: "The Mud Below." Reprinted with the permission of Scribner, a division of Simon & Schuster, Inc., from *Close Range: Wyoming Stories* by Annie Proulx. Copyright © 1999 by Dead Line Ltd. All rights reserved.

Philip Roth: "Defender of the Faith" from *Goodbye, Columbus* by Philip Roth. Copyright © 1959, renewed 1987 by Philip Roth. Reprinted by permission of Houghton Mifflin Harcourt Publishing Company. All rights reserved.

Jean Toomer: "Blood-Burning Moon" from *Cane* by Jean Toomer. Copyright © 1923 by Boni & Liveright, renewed 1951 by Jean Toomer. Used by permission of Liveright Publishing Corporation.

John Updike: "The Persistence of Desire" from *Pigeon Feathers and Other Stories* by John Updike, copyright © 1962 and renewed 1990 by John Updike. Used by permission of Alfred A. Knopf, a division of Random House, Inc.

David Foster Wallace: "Good People" from *The Pale King* by David Foster Wallace. Originally published in *The New Yorker*. Copyright © 2007, David Foster Wallace. Used by permission of the David Foster Wallace Literary Trust.

Eudora Welty: "Where is the Voice Coming From?" Reprinted by permission of Russell & Volkening, Inc., as agents for the author's estate. Copyright © 1963 by Eudora Welty, renewed 1991 by Eudora Welty. "Where is the Voice Coming From?" originally appeared in *The New Yorker*, July 6th, 1963.

Edmund White: "Give It Up for Billy" used by permission of the author.

William Carlos Williams: "The Girl with a Pimply Face" from *The Collected Stories of William Carlos Williams,* copyright © 1938 by William Carlos Williams. Reprinted by permission of New Directions Publishing Corp.

Tobias Wolff: "Hunters in the Snow" (pp. 9–26) from *In the Garden of the North American Martyrs* by Tobias Wolff. Copyright © 1981 by Tobias Wolff. Reprinted by permission of HarperCollins Publishers.

Richard Wright: "The Man Who Was Almost a Man" from *Eight Men* by Richard Wright. Copyright © 1940, © 1961 by Richard Wright; renewed © 1989 by Ellen Wright. Introduction © 1996 by Paul Gilroy. Reprinted by permission of HarperCollins Publishers.

CONTENTS

PREFACE

Perhaps the most profound change in the American short story, from the early nineteenth century (Washington Irving, William Austin, Nathaniel Hawthorne) to the early twenty-first century (a dazzling array of mainstream and "ethnic minority" writers of whom the youngest in this anthology is Junot Díaz, born 1968) is the movement from the mythic to the anecdotal, from a mode of impersonal storytelling in which the narrator is likely to be invisible, anonymous, and even irrelevant to the tale, to a mode of storytelling that is intensely personal, self-conscious, and narrated in a distinctive "voice." Perhaps more significantly, the change has been gradual from a literature that assumed a singular general, homogeneous audience educated in the classics, the Christian Bible, even (possibly) in Latin and Greek, to numerous particularized audiences that may have very little in common except the English language—which might not be, for many readers, their primary language.

In the Colonies and in the young United States, there were relatively few densely populated cities, of course; through the nineteenth-century, the readership for what we now call "nineteenth-century American literature" was far smaller than it is now, but, among this readership, writers like Irving, Hawthorne, Melville, and their contemporaries could assume a unified cultural community, predominantly Christian and "Anglo." Poets as radically different from one another as Henry Wadsworth Longfellow, Emily Dickinson, and Walt Whitman could nonetheless assume a common overlapping readership; their literary and Biblical allusions were part of a commonly shared vocabulary. Similarly, writers as radically different as Nathaniel Hawthorne, Herman Melville, Mark Twain, and Henry James could assume a common overlapping readership. Now, in the twenty-first century, our vast country has become populated—unevenly, in scattered regions of the continent—with countless ethnic minorities and sub-minorities, each bearing its own significant history: that of the "old world," and that of the "immigrant" and the immigrant's children. Here the crucial drama is the struggle to be assimilated into American society—unless it's the struggle to resist assimilation. "Identity politics" has carried over into the arts with enormous, unprecedented popular success for certain of its practitioners: JhumpaLahiri, Ha Jin, and Junot Díaz, to name just three new "transcultural" writers, can expect their books to be bestsellers, appealing to both their ethnic-minority constituents and a larger, mainstream readership, like the novels of Isabel Allende, Salman Rushdie, and Gary Shteyngart. Issues of gender, women's rights, gay rights, New Age, and cult sensibilities are now unifying issues for large segments of the reading population, a situation that would have been inconceivable in the literary United States of decades ago. With the meteoric rise of the Internet, online blogging and online publication of writers' works, including even the publication of full-length novels, clearly the older, hierarchical structure of a mainstream Literary Establishment is disintegrating; where publications like the *Saturday Evening Post, Redbook, Atlantic, Harper's,* and the *New Yorker* once dominated the literary culture, now there is an unmappable diversity—egalitarian and, in a sense, quality-blind. The Internet is the very emblem of the "buzzing, blooming confusion" of which William James spoke in his attempt to define the Universe.

Indeed, this edition of the Oxford anthology may be the last to reasonably claim any sort of national "American" identity, let alone unity.

Our obsessive concerns in twenty-first century America have to do with identity of a specific sort. Where earlier literature took for granted an Everyman-reader—male, white, educated, English-speaking—there is now a highly particularized reader. In Edmund White's "Give It Up for Billy," for instance, we are taken immediately into the confidence of a middle-aged gay man whose unsentimental perspective allows us an unnervingly frank, revealing portrait of "straight, heterosexual" individuals, as Junot Díaz's "Edison, New Jersey" presents a world seen with vivid particularity from the perspective of working-class Dominicans living in New Jersey. And the Chinese-American Ha Jin's entertainingly narrated but poignant "Children as Enemies"—so aptly titled!—dramatizes the pain of an immigrant group's cultural loss of identity in the indifference of an "Americanized" third generation. (This theme, too, could not have been explored before the 1950s, for it wasn't until that decade that children began to exist as a category of autonomous individuals with their own willful, even subversive wishes; and in that decade, in a wave of postwar prosperity, "children" and "teenagers" began to be identified as consumers, as they had not ever before in history.)

Within a literary culture so shifting, as the larger culture is continually shifting, it seems necessary to look both forward and back, to include new work by young and emerging writers like those mentioned above, but also to retrieve from the past writers who were not, for one reason or another, included in the original *Oxford Book of American Short Stories*, whose work has endured through the decades:

H. P. Lovecraft, whose influence upon "gothic" fiction and film has been inestimable; Nelson Algren, poet of Chicago slum-life; Shirley Jackson, author of an American gothic classic, "The Lottery"; and Philip Roth, whose "Defender of the Faith," startling and controversial when it was first published more than a half-century ago, has become, in the ongoing American drama of the anxiety of immigrant "identity," a classic as well.

THE OXFORD BOOK OF AMERICAN SHORT STORIES

Introduction

Familiar names, unfamiliar titles: this, in part, was my initial inspiration in assembling *The Oxford Book of American Short Stories*. The challenge was to discover, wherever possible, short stories by our finest writers that were less known than the stories by these writers usually found in anthologies, yet of equal merit and interest—stories that, while reflecting authors' characteristic styles, visions, and subjects, suggested other aspects of sensibility. We Americans are justly proud of our literature, and a good deal of that pride stems from our awareness of the crucial role of the short story—in its earliest manifestations, the short tale or romance—as a form ideally suited to the expression of the imagination.

In my reading of many months I was enormously pleased to discover virtually unknown yet fascinating work by certain of our classic American writers, whose famous titles recur from anthology to anthology with dismaying predictability. Certainly, Nathaniel Hawthorne's "Young Goodman Brown" and "The Birthmark" are brilliant moral parables—but what of the more psychologically realistic "The Wives of the Dead, " of which no one seems to have heard? Melville's "Bartleby the Scrivener" has entered our literary consciousness, deservedly, but what of "The Paradise of Bachelors and the Tartarus of Maids," with its eerily contemporary theme of sexual/class exploitation? (I first read this unclassifiable prose piece—hardly a "tale" in any conventional sense, still less a "story"—when I was an undergraduate at Syracuse University, and I have been haunted by its images ever since. Herman Melville, our first native feminist?—can it be so?) Henry James's aesthetic is nowhere more perfectly realized than in "The Beast in the Jungle," anthologized virtually everywhere; yet what of "The Middle Years," so much more direct, more human, more personal in its statement of the isolate's (or the artist's) life? It is in this lesser-known story that The Master speaks with painful candor, giving voice to what all artists know, yet perhaps would not want to express in such raw, unmediated terms:

> We work in the dark—we do what we can—we give what we have. Our doubt is our passion and our passion is our task. The rest is the madness of art.

As schoolchildren we read and admired Mark Twain's early, frankly derivative tall tale, "The Celebrated Jumping Frog of Calaveras County," but the darker, more sinister, yes and funnier Twain, as represented in the mordant "Cannibalism in the Cars," is virtually unknown. (And why, in most general anthologies, is there no representation at all of Twain's great contemporary Harriet Beecher Stowe, whose popularity as a writer was by no means confined to her most famous work, *Uncle Tom's Cabin?*) So too with such familiar classics as Stephen Crane's "The Open Boat," Jack London's "To Build a Fire," Edith Wharton's "Roman Fever," Hemingway's "The Snows of Kilimanjaro" and "The Short Happy Life of Francis Macomber," Willa Cather's "Paul's Case," William Carlos Williams's "The Use of Force." These are certainly great works of art; at the very least, they have helped to define the range and depth of the short story in America. But the reader begins to feel frustration when they are encountered repeatedly, alternated now and then with a very few other titles of almost equal familiarity. Though among them, F. Scott Fitzgerald, Eudora Welty, Flannery O'Connor, John Cheever, and John Updike have written literally hundreds of short stories, the same two or three titles by each writer are recycled continuously. Why, given such plenitude, is this so? Do editors of anthologies consult only other anthologies, instead of reading original collections of stories? But isn't the implicit promise of an anthology that it will, or aspires to, present something different, unexpected?

How ironic, it seemed to me, yet, perhaps, how symbolic, that in our age of rapid mass production and the easy proliferation of consumer products, the richness and diversity of the American literary imagination should be so misrepresented in most anthologies and textbooks!

Of course, I must confess that, despite months of reading and rereading, I could not avoid reprinting certain very familiar favorites.

Washington Irving's "Rip Van Winkle," Edgar Allan Poe's "The Tell-Tale Heart," Charlotte Perkins Gilman's "The Yellow Wallpaper," Ernest Hemingway's "Hills Like White Elephants," William Faulkner's "That Evening Sun"—the consequence of an ideal conjunction of quality of prose and quantity of pages. (All anthologies are compromises when a finitude of space is an issue.) James Baldwin's and Ralph Ellison's much-reprinted "Sonny's Blues" and "Battle Royal" are works by major American writers who did not cultivate the short story form, and so offer very few titles. Other old favorites which the scanning eye will note as absent—Ring Lardner's "Haircut," James Thurber's "The Secret Life of Walter Mitty,"—were reluctantly excluded because they are so readily available elsewhere, and because, with space restrictions, I thought it more important to present outstanding titles by writers representing a broad spectrum of cultural traditions: Mary E. Wilkins Freeman, Jean Toomer, Langston Hughes, Paul Bowles, Nelson Algren, Philip Roth, Louise Erdrich, Jhumpa Lahiri, Junot Díaz, to name but a few.

"No creative writer can swallow another contemporary," Virginia Woolf once noted, as a way, perhaps, of rationalizing her own highly subjective tastes, "—the reception of living work is too coarse and partial if you're doing the same thing yourself." Even if one is not doing the same thing oneself, or anything approaching it, there remains an obvious difficulty in attempting an overview of the very landscape one inhabits.

As we move through the post-War era and into contemporary times, the proliferation of published stories and the immense diversities of talent make selection enormously difficult. What riches here, and what sorrow for the editor in having to exclude so much! Here indeed is American plenitude—not solely of talent but of distinct aesthetic agendas; distinct ethnic and minority voices; distinct regional themes. It will be evident that, beginning with Harriet Beecher Stowe, I have sought to include more women writers than commonly appear in such volumes; yet, in the past two decades, so many outstanding women writers have emerged, and are emerging still, often as "ethnic" voices, that a proportional representation of their work, in such limited space, is all but impossible. Ethnic and minority fiction has revitalized our contemporary literature and constitutes, it might be argued, a new regionalism. (Or is American literature at its core a literature of *regions?* Note how, in this volume, works by writers so seemingly diverse as Annie Proulx and Russell Banks, Louise Erdrich and Stephen King, as well as T.C. Boyle, Edmund White, the late John Cheever, and the late John Updike are related along lines that have less to do with traditional American themes than with stories set in highly specific, vividly realized American *places.* Indeed, in writers so clearly linked to an idiomatic oral tradition as Flannery O'Connor and the young West Virginian Pinckney Benedict, place *is* voice.)

Because my emphasis in this anthology is on storytelling, often with a social and/or political theme, and not on literary experimentation, I have included, of the celebrated "meta-fictionalists" of the 1960s and 1970s, only Donald Barthelme, whose principal mode of fiction was the short story. Had I more space, I would have wished to include such dazzlingly inventive talents as John Barth, William Gass, John Hawkes, Robert Coover, Paul West, and Steven Millhauser, among others. Of writers associated with issues of "gender," I have included only Edmund White, whose most representative fiction, though generally concerned with gay Caucasian men of an educated middle class, transcends any labels; of the controversial "minimalists" of recent decades I have included only Raymond Carver, Tobias Wolff, Amy Hempel—with the immediate qualification that I, personally, don't consider these writers minimalists any more than Sherwood Anderson, Ernest Hemingway, and William Carlos Williams are minimalists. Even to classify them as "realists" is reductive and misleading.

Other editors have remarked in print of a problem arguably unique to our time and nation, of the proliferation of published stories by serious, committed, highly gifted writers who are carving out careers for themselves that will, in time, not only rest upon a few distinguished works, but upon solid bodies of work, which will, in turn, help to define our increasingly diversified and heterogeneous American literature. Obviously, I could include only a sampling of this richness. To do justice to the remarkable fecundity of the American short story would require not a single volume of this size, but a second.

> Not that the story need be long,
> but it will take a long while
> to make it short.
>
> Henry David Thoreau

Formal definitions of the short story are commonplace, yet there is none quite democratic enough to accommodate an art that includes so much variety and an art that so readily lends itself to experimentation and idiosyncratic voices. Perhaps length alone should be the sole criterion? Whenever critics try to impose other, more subjective strictures on the genre (as on any genre) too much work is excluded.

Yet length itself is problematic. No more than 10,000 words? Why not then 10,500? 11,000? Where, in fact, does a short story end and a novella begin? (Tolstoy's "The Death of Ivan Ilych" can be classified as both.) And there is the reverse problem, for, as short stories condense, they are equally difficult to define. What is the short-short story, precisely? What is that most teasing of prose works, the prose-poem? We can be guided by critical intuition in distinguishing between a newspaper article or an anecdote and a fully realized story, but intuition is notoriously difficult to define (or depend upon). Since the cultivation of the aesthetically subtle, minimally resolved short story by such masters as Chekhov, Lawrence, Joyce, and Hemingway, the definition of the "fully realized" story has become problematic as well.

My personal definition of the form is that it represents a concentration of imagination, and not an expansion; it is no more than 10,000 words; and, no matter its mysteries or experimental properties, it achieves closure—meaning that, when it ends, the attentive reader understand why.

That is to say, the short story is a prose piece that is not a mere concatenation of events, as in a news account or an anecdote, but an intensification of meaning by way of events. Its "plot" may be wholly interior, seemingly static, a matter of the progression of a character's thought. Its resolution need not be a formally articulated statement, as in many of Hawthorne's more didactic tales, or, in this collection, William Austin's once-famous cautionary tale, "Peter Rugg, the Missing Man," but it signals a tangible change of some sort; a distinct shift in consciousness; a deepening of insight. In the most elliptical of stories, a characteristic of the modern and contemporary story, the actual resolution frequently occurs in the reader's, and not the fictional characters', consciousness. To read stories as disparate as Paul Bowles's "A Distant Episode," Ray Bradbury's "There Will Come Soft Rains," Raymond Carver's "Are These Actual Miles?" and Tobias Wolff's "Hunters in the Snow," among others in this volume, is to read stories so structured as to provide the reader, and not the characters themselves, with insight. Because the meaning of a story does not lie on its surface, visible and self-defining, does not mean that meaning does not exist. Indeed, the ambiguity of meaning, its inner, private quality, may well be part of the writer's vision.

In addition to these qualities, most short stories (but hardly all) are restricted in time and place; concentrate upon a very small number of characters; and move toward a single ascending dramatic scene or revelation. And all are generated by conflict.

The artist *is* the focal point of conflict. Lovers of pristine harmony, those who dislike being upset, shocked, made to think and to feel, are not naturally suited to appreciate art, at least not serious art, which, unlike television dramas and situation comedies, for instance, does not evoke conflict merely to solve it within a brief space of time. Rather, conflict is the implicit subject itself, as conflict, the establishment of disequilibrium, is the impetus for the evolution of life, so is conflict the genesis, the prime mover, the secret heart of all art.

Discord, then, and not harmony, is the subject our writers share in common, though the quelling of discord and the re-establishment of harmony may well be the point of the art.

The "literary" short story, the meticulously constructed short story, descends to us by way of the phenomenon of magazine publication, beginning in the nineteenth century, but has as its ancestor the oral tale.

We must assume that storytelling is as old as mankind, at least as old as spoken language. Reality is not enough for us—we crave the imagination's embellishments upon it. *In the beginning. Once upon a time. A long time ago there lived a princess who.* How the pulse quickens, hearing such beginnings! such promises of something new, strange, unexpected! The epic poem, the ballad, the parable, the beast-fable, sacred narratives, visionary prophecies—the fabulous mythopoetic "histories" of ancient cultures—the "divinely inspired" books of the Old and New Testament: all are forms of storytelling, expressions of the human imagination.

Like a river fed by countless small streams, the modern short story derives from a multiplicity of sources. Historically, the earliest literary documents of which we have knowledge are Egyptian papyri dating from 4000–3000 B.C., containing a work called, most intriguingly, *Tales of the Magicians.* The Middle Ages revered such secular works as fabliaux, ballads, and verse romances; the Arabian *Thousand and One Nights* and the Latin tales and anecdotes of the *Gesta Romanorum,* collected before the end of the thirteenth century, as well as the one hundred tales of Boccaccio's *The Decameron,* and Chaucer's *Canterbury Tales,* were enormously popular for centuries. Storytelling as an oral art, like the folk ballad, was, or is, characteristic of nonliterate cultures, for obvious reasons. Even the prolongation of light (by artificial means) had an effect upon the storytelling tradition of our ancestors. The rise in literacy marked the ebbing of interest in old fairy tales and ballads, as did the gradual stabilization of languages and the cessation of local dialects in which the tales and ballads had been told most effectively. (The Brothers Grimm noted this phenomenon: if, in High German, a fairy tale gained in superficial clarity, it "lost in flavor, and no longer had such a firm hold of the kernel of meaning.")

One of the signal accomplishments of American literature, most famously exemplified by the great commercial and critical success of Samuel Clemens, is the reclamation of that "lost" flavor—the use, as style, of dialect, regional, and strongly (often comically) vernacular language. Of course, before Samuel Clemens cultivated the ingenuous-ironic persona of "Mark Twain," there were dialect writers and tale-tellers in America (for instance, Joel Chandler Harris, creator of the popular "Uncle Remus" stories); but Mark Twain was a phenomenon of a kind previously unknown here—our first American writer to be avidly read, coast to coast, by all classes of Americans, from the most high-born to the least cultured and minimally literate. The development of mass-market newspapers and subscription book sales made this success possible, but it was the brilliant reclamation of the vernacular in Twain's work (the early "The Celebrated Jumping Frog of Calaveras County," for instance) that made him into so uniquely *American* a writer, our counterpart to Dickens.

Twain's rapid ascent was by way of popular newspapers, which syndicated features coast to coast, and his crowd-pleasing public performances, but the more typical outlet for a short story writer, particularly of self-consciously "literary" work, was the magazine. Virtually every writer in this volume, from Washington Irving and Nathaniel Hawthorne onward, began his or her career publishing short fiction in magazines before moving on to book publication; in the nineteenth century, such highly regarded, and, in some cases, high-paying magazines as *The North American Review, Harper's Monthly, Atlantic Monthly, Scribner's Monthly* (later *The Century*), *The Dial,* and *Graham's Magazine* (briefly edited by Edgar Allan Poe) advanced the careers of writers who would otherwise have had financial difficulties in establishing themselves. In post–World War II America, the majority of short story writers publish in small-circulation "literary" magazines throughout their careers. It is all but unknown for a writer to publish a book of short stories without having published most of them in magazines beforehand.

Edgar Allan Poe's famous review–essay of Hawthorne's *Twice-Told Tales* (*Graham's Magazine,* 1842) is justly celebrated as one of the crucial documents in the establishment of the short story as a distinct literary genre. Poe's aesthetic is a curious admixture of the romantic and the classic: the intention of the art-work is to move the reader's soul deeply, but the means to this intention is coolly, if not chillingly, cerebral. Poe in his philosophy as in his practice is both visionary and manipulator:

> A skillful literary artist has constructed his tale. If wise, he has not fashioned his thoughts to accommodate his incidents; but having conceived, with deliberate care, a certain unique or single *effect* to be wrought out, he then invents such incidents—he then combines such events as may best aid him in establishing this preconceived effect.

Magazine publication is the ideal outlet for Poe's hypothesized tale, where works "requiring from a half-hour to one or two hours in [their] perusal" appeared. Indeed, the emphasis in Poe's review-essay is on the reader's experience of the work, and not upon the work itself; as if—can this be genius speaking? in the very language of the hack?—it scarcely matters *what* has been written, only *that* it has been written to a certain pre-conceived effect. (It should be noted too, and not incidentally, that Poe was a man of vast literary ambitions, and not simply, or not exclusively, a tormented Romantic driven to the composition of uncanny poetry and prose: he wrote for magazines, and he edited magazines, and it was his professional obsession from 1836 to his death in 1849 to found and edit a magazine, to be called *The Penn Magazine*.)

As the literary short story derives from the oral tale, so, in Poe's aesthetic, the meticulously constructed short story relates to the poem. While the highest genius, arguably, is best employed in poetry ("not to exceed in length what might be perused in an hour"), the "loftiest talent" may turn to the prose tale, as exemplified by Nathaniel Hawthorne. Poe elevates the prose tale above much of poetry, in fact, and above the novel, for poetry brings the reader to too high a pitch of excitement to be sustained, and the novel is objectionable because of its "undue" length. By contrast, the brief tale enables the writer "to carry out the fulness of his intention.... During the hour of perusal the soul of the reader is at the writer's control. There are no external or extrinsic influences—resulting from weariness or interruption."

In Poe's somewhat Aristotelian terms, the secret of the short story's composition is its unity. Yet, within this, as within a well-made play, a multiplicity of modes or inflections of thought and expression—"the ratiocinative, for example, the sarcastic, or the humorous"—are available to the writer, as they are not available, apparently, to the poet. This concept, dogmatic even for its time, relates only incidentally to the stories Poe himself wrote, but provides an aesthetic anticipating the work of such masters of the genre as Chekhov, Joyce, Henry James, and Hemingway, in which everything is excluded that does not contribute to the general effect, or design, of the story. (Like most critics who are also artists, Poe was formulating an aesthetic to accommodate his own practice and his own limitations. Temperamentally, Poe was probably incapable of the sustained effort of the novelist; this helps to explain his envious disparagement of Charles Dickens, who, for all his apparent flaws in Poe's judgment, enjoyed the enormous popular success denied to Poe during his own lifetime.)

The American short story, however, has had no more thoughtful, visionary, and influential an early critic than Poe, just as the history of the short story itself in America is bound up with the unique work Poe published in 1840, *Tales of the Grotesque and Arabesque.*

A predominant vein connecting the majority of the stories in this volume, from Washington Irving and William Austin through to our contemporaries, is the quest, in some cases a distinctly *American* quest, for one's place in the world, one's cultural and spiritual identity, in terms of self and others.

For ours is the nation, so rare in human history, of self-determination—a theoretical experiment in newness, exploration, discovery. In theory at least, who our ancestors have been, what languages they have spoken, in what religions they believed—these factors cannot really help to define *us.* And it has been often noted that, in the New World, history itself has moved with extraordinary rapidity. Each generation constitutes a beginning-again, a new discovery, sometimes of language itself.

Washington Irving, who begins most volumes of American short fiction, was, in much of his work, a chronicler of tumultuous political change. Though English-oriented in his education, and immensely influenced by eighteenth-century English writers of the didactic and satirical sort, Irving's genius was to appropriate, in his most famous tales, a theme out of folklore: the comedy of the dislocated citizen, who, visited by the supernatural, ends up not knowing who he is. In "Rip Van Winkle," the theme is brilliantly applied to the hapless Rip who falls asleep in colonial America and wakes in post-Revolutionary America: waking to an irrevocably altered world.

Irving was born in 1783, at the end of the American Revolution. But, like Hawthorne, he derived great imaginative inspiration from the history of the region in which he lived. Not Irving's contemporary America, that vital, seething young nation, but Colonial America, in the quaintly sequestered world of the Kaatskill Mountains, is the setting for the robustly tall tale "Rip Van Winkle," a parable of dislocation. Rip, a descendant of Dutch settlers of the early eighteenth century, falls into an enchanted sleep, and, when he wakes, finds himself in post-Revolutionary

America, where, to his astonishment, a new political language is spoken. The likeness of old King George has been metamorphosed into a dapper military portrait of someone called General Washington; Rip is no longer a subject of British rule, but a "free citizen of the United States"—which means nothing to him. It is a concept simply beyond his comprehension, as, Irving suggests, it is a concept beyond the comprehension of many citizens who had lived through the Revolution but were incapable of "revolutionizing" themselves. So, too, perhaps with the majority of men and women, in periods of violent social upheaval?

Where Irving's tone is jocular, tongue-in-cheek, William Austin's is grimly serious in his parable of "Peter Rugg, the Missing Man." Here, the enchantment is clearly a curse, and Peter Rugg is a Flying Dutchman of sorts, doomed to ceaseless motion. Austin may have intended his archetypal hero to represent a newer species of man—a "lost" man—an atheist—who utters an oath that offends God, thus sealing his doom. Like certain of Hawthorne's similarly accursed heroes Rugg is dislocated yet more radically than Rip Van Winkle. To Rugg, the "new generation" of Bostonians are his enemies, and his home, his family, his very identity have been stripped from him. (Compare the equally desperate fate of the elderly Major Molineux in Hawthorne's "My Kinsman, Major Molineux.")

Another aspect of identity, that of "gendered" fate, at least as linked with the vicissitudes of social class, is taken up, with characteristic irony, by Melville in his linked sexual allegories "The Paradise of Bachelors and the Tartarus of Maids." The vision of sexual determinism—for the working-class female, her doom—strikes us as disturbingly contemporary. (Melville, in his great, brooding, idiosyncratic prose works, is *always* our contemporary.) How like the nightmare fate of Charlotte Perkins Gilman's heroine, trapped in her femaleness as in the yellow wallpaper of her confinement, these young factory workers: blank-looking girls, with blank, white folders in blank hands, blankly folding blank paper. Biological destiny and the position of the individual in a burgeoning industrial society are memorably linked in Melville's vision of hell, where Cupid himself is an overseer, and where the production of blank white soulless pulp is an image of the blankness—and inevitability—of human reproduction. Melville's protagonist–observer becomes spellbound—"What made the thing I saw so specially terrible to me was the metallic necessity, the unbudging fatality which governed it." Only Herman Melville could have fashioned out of "real" events (his visits to a gentleman's club in London and to a paper mill in Dalton, Massachusetts) such harrowing and dreamlike allegorical fiction.

By Poe's criteria, "The Paradise of Bachelors and the Tartarus of Maids" is perhaps not a successful tale, lacking unity. Yet it is as horrific an image of man's (and woman's) fate as Poe himself created.

Questions of sexual and racial identity are taken up in more realistic terms by writers of subsequent generations, like Charles W. Chesnutt (whose "The Sheriff's Children" anticipates the obsessive father–son theme of Langston Hughes's work), Mary E. Wilkins Freeman (whose "Old Woman Magoun" anticipates radical feminist texts of our time), and Charlotte Perkins Gilman (whose "The Yellow Wallpaper," a Poe-inspired narration of lyric madness, has become in fact a celebrated feminist text of our time). Edith Wharton's unusually frank "A Journey" is a naturalistic allegory dramatizing a young wife's experience of her husband's dying; her resentment and terror of the burden his very body represents to her in death—as if she, yearning to live, will be stigmatized by his death, forced to disembark prematurely from the train (of life?). A similar moment of crisis is experienced—and transcended—by the hysterically repressed Presbyterian minister of Sherwood Anderson's "The Strength of God" (from *Winesburg, Ohio*): "God has appeared to me," the minister announces, "—in the person of Kate Swift, the school teacher, kneeling naked on a bed."

Arguably, most African-American writing is about racial identity: black cohesiveness and dispersion in a rapidly industrialized country; black experience (suffering, resignation, rebellion, rage, accommodation, integration, self-determination) in the face of historical white oppression. In broad theoretical images, the "white father's black son"—the unacknowledged progeny of the "white master"—is an emblem of the misbegotten and the rejected who returns as a powerful threat. The "Jesus" of William Faulkner's "That Evening Sun" is a bitter sort of savior: the degraded black man, the probable son of slaves, who revenges himself against the only victim available to him in his powerlessness—the black woman who is his wife. Faulkner's depiction of this tragedy is the more wrenching in that it is told to us obliquely, through the chattering and arguing of a self-absorbed white Mississippian family.

Striking a distinctly ominous note is Richard Wright's "The Man Who Was Almost a Man" (the black youth who is "almost" a murderer, and on his way to being one)—a story as disturbing to white readers as the author's controversial *Native Son,* one of the seminal novels of black American experience. The young black men of Jean Toomer's "Blood-Burning Moon" and Ralph Ellison's "Battle Royal" inhabit a society divided along indisputably racist lines; Eudora Welty's "Where Is the Voice Coming From?" presents a deranged white murderer, the very voice of a retrograde Southern society of the 1960s. Only James Baldwin's "Sonny's Blues" ends with an image of transcendence and hope, however painfully won: "Then they all gathered around Sonny, and Sonny played.... Sonny's fingers filled the air with life, his life. But that life contained so many others."

Among those writers with whom we associate literary Modernism (Ernest Hemingway, for instance) and those writers who are our contemporaries, questions of identity have become all-absorbing. The quintessential Hemingway hero is a paradigm for the hero (or heroine) of much twentieth-century fiction, whose predicament is: once one has stripped oneself of superfluities of identity, what remains? Scott Fitzgerald's cartoonist-hero of the painfully autobiographical "An Alcoholic Case" looks into a comer of the hotel bathroom and sees death awaiting him: and nothing more. Perhaps the most extreme (and unforgettable) image of twentieth-century existential dislocation is the brutalized, tongueless American professor (of linguistics) of Paul Bowles's nightmare parable, "A Distant Episode."

In our contemporaries, the burden of history and politics as *personal* fate, weighing, at times, almost physically upon the shoulders of survivors and descendants, is dramatized in stories encompassing a wide range of subject matter, style, and vision—from Flannery O'Connor's mordant "A Late Encounter with the Enemy" (an aged Civil War veteran's hallucinatory descent into death, and into his identity) to Bernard Malamud's "My Son the Murderer" (generational conflict in the radicalized, despairing sixties), and Louise Erdrich's "Fleur" (a Native American "witch" resists the fete that would make her a victim). The highly distilled "Children as

Enemies" by Ha Jin and the conversationally colloquial "Edison, New Jersey" by Junot Díaz take for granted a dominant Caucasian world in which the protagonists find themselves living—here, such abstractions as history and politics are realized in the experience of seemingly ordinary—"average"—individuals. And the nightmare surrealism of Jeffrey Ford's "The Drowned Life" suggests a spiritual apocalypse of the present, political era.

As Tolstoy said, talent is the capacity to direct concentrated attention upon the subject: "the gift of seeing what others have not seen."

Though it is hardly necessary, I suggest that the reader read this volume as it is assembled, more or less chronologically. A tale will unfold, by way of numerous tales, that is uniquely and wonderfully American.

WASHINGTON IRVING
(1783–1859)

Born in New York City on April 3, 1783, the last of eleven children of a wealthy Scottish merchant and an Englishwoman, Washington Irving is our first American writer to achieve a distinguished international reputation, and the first to become a "classic" during his own lifetime. Well educated, cosmopolitan, imbued with a deep admiration for English literature and an interest in adapting such seemingly primitive forms as the ballad and the folklore for serious literary purposes, Irving strikes us as a highly conscious, even rather scholarly craftsman—an "imitator," as Melville would characterize him, rather than a "creative genius." Yet, so vividly rendered are certain of his fictitious characters (notably Rip Van Winkle and Ichabod Crane, of "The Legend of Sleepy Hollow"), so deeply imprinted have they become in the popular imagination, they strike us as mythopoetic figures—timeless, archetypal, transcending the circumstances of their own creation.

Rip Van Winkle and Ichabod Crane spring from the pages of The Sketch Book *(1820), Irving's most famous title, published under the pseudonym "Geoffrey Crayon." In an earlier phase of his long career, Irving had achieved remarkable celebrity, aged twenty-five, as "Diedrich Knickerbocker," the comically pedantic author of* A History of New York *(1809). Irving was a writer of sketches rather than fully realized stories, and his characters, like the luckless Rip Van Winkle, have an emblematic quality, illuminated by the hearty glare of comedy. He was a superb stylist, not a psychologist, for whom, as he said, a story is "merely a frame on which to sketch my materials."*

But what rich materials, and how elegantly constructed a frame.

Rip Van Winkle

A Posthumous Writing of
Diedrich Knickerbocker

By Woden, God of Saxons,
From whence comes Wensday, that is Wodensday,
Truth is a thing that ever I will keep
Unto thylke day in which I creep into
My sepulchre

—Cartwright

Whoever has made a voyage up the Hudson must remember the Kaatskill Mountains. They are a dismembered branch of the great Appalachian family, and are seen away to the west of the river, swelling up to a noble height, and lording it over the surrounding country. Every change of season, every change of weather, indeed, every hour of the day, produces some change in the magical hues and shapes of these mountains, and they are regarded by all the good wives, far and near, as perfect barometers. When the weather is fair and settled, they are clothed in blue and purple, and print their bold outlines on the clear evening sky; but, sometimes, when the rest of the landscape is cloudless, they will gather a hood of gray vapors about their summits, which, in the last rays of the setting sun, will glow and light up like a crown of glory.

At the foot of these fairy mountains, the voyager may have descried the light smoke curling up from a village, whose shingle-roofs gleam among the trees, just where the blue tints of the upland melt away into the fresh green of the nearer landscape. It is a little village of great antiquity, having been founded by some of the Dutch colonists, in the early times of the province, just about the beginning of the government of the good Peter Stuyvesant, (may he rest in peace!) and there were some of the houses of the original settlers standing within a few years, built of small yellow bricks brought from Holland, having latticed windows and gable fronts, surmounted with weather-cocks.

In that same village, and in one of these very houses (which, to tell the precise truth, was sadly time-worn and weather-beaten), there lived many years since, while the country was yet a province of Great Britain, a simple good-natured fellow of the name of Rip Van Winkle. He was a descendant of the Van Winkles who figured so gallantly in the chivalrous days of Peter Stuyvesant, and accompanied him to the siege of Fort Christina. He inherited, however, but little of the martial character of his ancestors. I have observed that he was a simple, good-natured man; he was, moreover, a kind neighbor, and an obedient, hen-pecked husband. Indeed, to the latter circumstance might be owing that meekness of spirit which gained him such universal popularity; for those men are most apt to be obsequious and conciliating abroad, who are under the discipline of shrews at home. Their tempers, doubtless, are rendered pliant and malleable in the fiery furnace of domestic tribulation; and a curtain lecture is worth all the sermons in the world for teaching the virtues of patience and long-suffering. A termagant wife may, therefore, in some respects, be considered a tolerable blessing; and if so, Rip Van Winkle was thrice blessed.

Certain it is, that he was a great favorite among all the good wives of the village, who, as usual, with the amiable sex, took his part in all family squabbles; and never failed, whenever they talked those matters over in their evening gossipings, to lay all the blame on Dame Van Winkle. The children of the village, too, would shout with joy whenever he approached. He assisted at their sports, made their playthings, taught them to fly kites and shoot marbles, and told them long stories of ghosts, witches, and Indians. Whenever he went dodging about the village, he was surrounded by a troop of them, hanging on his skirts, clambering on his back, and playing a thousand tricks on him with impunity; and not a dog would bark at him throughout the neighborhood.

The great error in Rip's composition was an insuperable aversion to all kinds of profitable labor. It could not be from the want of assiduity or perseverance; for he would sit on a wet rock, with a rod as long and heavy as a Tartar's lance, and fish all day without a murmur, even though he should not be encouraged by a single nibble. He would carry a fowling-piece on his shoulder for hours together, trudging through woods and swamps, and up hill and down dale, to shoot a few squirrels or wild pigeons. He would never refuse to assist a neighbor even in the roughest toil, and was a foremost man at all country frolics for husking Indian corn, or building stone fences; the women of the village, too, used to employ him to run their errands, and to do such little odd jobs as their less obliging husbands would not do for them. In a word Rip was ready to attend to anybody's business but his own; but as to doing family duty, and keeping his farm in order, he found it impossible.

In fact, he declared it was of no use to work on his farm; it was the most pestilent little piece of ground in the whole country; everything about it went wrong, and would go wrong, in spite of him. His fences were continually falling to pieces; his cow would either go astray, or get among the cabbages; weeds were sure to grow quicker in his fields than anywhere else; the rain always made a point of setting in just as he had some out-door work to do; so that though his patrimonial estate had dwindled away under his management, acre by acre, until there was little more left than a mere patch of Indian corn and potatoes, yet it was the worst conditioned farm in the neighborhood.

His children, too, were as ragged and wild as if they belonged to nobody. His son Rip, an urchin begotten in his own likeness, promised to inherit the habits, with the old clothes of his father. He was generally seen trooping like a colt at his mother's heels, equipped in a pair of his father's cast-off galligaskins, which he had much ado to hold up with one hand, as a fine lady does her train in bad weather.

Rip Van Winkle, however, was one of those happy mortals, of foolish, well-oiled dispositions, who take the world easy, eat white bread or brown, whichever can be got with least thought or trouble, and would rather starve on a penny than work for a pound. If left to himself, he would have whistled life away in perfect contentment; but his wife kept continually dinning in his ears about his idleness, his carelessness, and the ruin he was bringing on his family. Morning, noon, and night, her tongue was incessantly going, and everything he said or did was sure to produce a torrent of household eloquence. Rip had but one way of replying to all lectures of the kind, and that, by frequent use, had grown into a habit. He shrugged his shoulders, shook his head, cast up his eyes, but said nothing. This, however, always provoked a fresh volley from his wife; so that he was fain to draw off his forces, and take to the outside of the house—the only side which, in truth, belongs to a hen-pecked husband.

Rip's sole domestic adherent was his dog Wolf, who was as much hen-pecked as his master; for Dame Van Winkle regarded them as companions in idleness, and even looked upon Wolf with an evil eye, as the cause of his master's going so often astray. True it is, in all points of spirit befitting an honorable dog, he was as courageous an animal as ever scoured the woods—but what courage can withstand the ever-during and all-besetting terrors of a woman's tongue? The moment Wolf entered the house his crest fell, his tail drooped to the ground, or curled between his legs, he sneaked about with a gallows air, casting many a sidelong glance at Dame Van Winkle, and at the least flourish of a broomstick or ladle, he would fly to the door with yelping precipitation.

Times grew worse and worse with Rip Van Winkle as years of matrimony rolled on; a tart temper never mellows with age, and a sharp tongue is the only edged tool that grows keener with constant use. For a long while he used to console himself, when driven from home, by frequenting a kind of perpetual club of the sages, philosophers, and other idle personages of the village; which held its sessions on a bench before a small inn, designated by a rubicund portrait of His Majesty George the Third. Here they used to sit in the shade through a long lazy summer's day, talking listlessly over village gossip, or telling endless sleepy stories about nothing. But it would have been worth any statesman's money to have heard the profound discussions that sometimes took place, when by chance an old newspaper fell into their hands from some passing traveller. How solemnly they would listen to the contents, as drawled out by Derrick Van Bummel, the schoolmaster, a dapper learned little man, who was not to be daunted by the most gigantic word in the dictionary; and how sagely they would deliberate upon the public events some months after they had taken place.

The opinions of this junto were completely controlled by Nicholas Vedder, a patriarch of the village, and landlord of the inn, at the door of which he took his seat from morning till night, just moving sufficiently to avoid the sun and keep in the shade of a large tree; so that the neighbors could tell the hour by his movements as accurately as by a sun-dial. It is true he was rarely heard to speak, but smoked his pipe incessantly. His adherents, however (for every great man has his adherents), perfectly understood him, and knew how to gather his opinions. When any thing that was read or related displeased him, he was observed to smoke his pipe vehemently, and to send forth short, frequent and angry puffs; but when pleased, he would inhale the smoke slowly and tranquilly, and emit it in light and placid clouds; and sometimes, taking the pipe from his mouth, and letting the fragrant vapor curl about his nose, would gravely nod his head in token of perfect approbation.

From even this stronghold the unlucky Rip was at length routed by his termagant wife, who would suddenly break in upon the tranquillity of the assemblage and call the members all to naught; nor was that august personage, Nicholas Vedder himself, sacred from the daring tongue of this terrible virago, who charged him outright with encouraging her husband in habits of idleness.

Poor Rip was at last reduced almost to despair; and his only alternative, to escape from the labor of the farm and clamor of his wife, was to take gun in hand and stroll away into the woods. Here he would sometimes seat himself at the foot of a tree, and share the contents of his wallet with Wolf, with whom he sympathized as a fellow-sufferer in persecution. "Poor Wolf," he would say, "thy mistress leads thee a dog's life of it; but never mind, my lad, whilst I live thou shalt never want a friend to stand by thee!" Wolf would wag his tail, look wistfully in his master's face, and if dogs can feel pity I verily believe he reciprocated the sentiment with all his heart.

In a long ramble of the kind on a fine autumnal day, Rip had unconsciously scrambled to one of the highest parts of the Kaatskill mountains. He was after his favorite sport of squirrel shooting, and the still solitudes had echoed and re-echoed with the reports of his gun. Panting and fatigued, he threw himself, late in the afternoon, on a green knoll, covered with mountain herbage, that crowned the brow of a precipice. From an opening between the trees he could overlook all the lower country for many a mile of rich woodland. He saw at a distance the lordly Hudson, far, far below him, moving on its silent but majestic course, with the reflection of a purple cloud, or the sail of a lagging bark, here and there sleeping on its glassy bosom, and at last losing itself in the blue highlands.

On the other side he looked down into a deep mountain glen, wild, lonely, and shagged, the bottom filled with fragments from the impending cliffs, and scarcely lighted by the reflected rays of the setting sun. For some time Rip lay musing on this scene; evening was gradually advancing; the mountains began to throw their long blue shadows over the valleys; he saw that it would be dark long before he could reach the village, and he heaved a heavy sigh when he thought of encountering the terrors of Dame Van Winkle.

As he was about to descend, he heard a voice from a distance, hallooing, "Rip Van Winkle! Rip Van Winkle!" He looked round, but could see nothing but a crow winging its solitary flight across the mountain. He thought his fancy must have deceived him, and turned again to descend, when he heard the same cry ring through the still evening air: "Rip Van Winkle! Rip Van Winkle!"—at the same time Wolf bristled up his back, and giving a low growl, skulked to his master's side, looking fearfully down into the glen. Rip now felt a vague apprehension stealing over him; he looked anxiously in the same direction, and perceived a strange figure slowly toiling up the rocks, and bending under the weight of something he carried on his back. He was surprised to see any human being in this lonely and unfrequented place, but supposing it to be some one of the neighborhood in need of his assistance, he hastened down to yield it.

On nearer approach he was still more surprised at the singularity of the stranger's appearance. He was a short square-built old fellow, with thick bushy hair, and a grizzled beard. His dress was of the antique Dutch fashion—a cloth jerkin strapped round the waist—several pair of breeches, the outer one of ample volume, decorated with rows of buttons down the sides, and bunches at the knees. He bore on his shoulder a stout keg, that seemed full of liquor, and made signs for Rip to approach and assist him with the load. Though rather shy and distrustful of this new acquaintance, Rip complied with his usual alacrity; and mutually relieving one another, they clambered up a narrow gully, apparently the dry bed of a mountain torrent. As they ascended, Rip every now and then heard long rolling peals, like distant thunder, that seemed to issue out of a deep ravine, or rather cleft, between lofty rocks, toward which their rugged path conducted. He paused for an instant, but supposing it to be the muttering of one of those transient thunder-showers which often take place in mountain heights, he proceeded. Passing through the ravine, they came to a hollow, like a small amphitheatre, surrounded by perpendicular precipices, over the brinks of which impending trees shot their branches, so that you only caught glimpses of the azure sky and the bright evening cloud. During the whole time Rip and his companion had labored on in silence; for though the former marvelled greatly what could be the object of carrying a keg of liquor up this wild mountain, yet there was something strange and incomprehensible about the unknown, that inspired awe and checked familiarity.

On entering the amphitheatre, new objects of wonder presented themselves. On a level spot in the centre was a company of odd-looking personages playing at ninepins. They were dressed in a quaint outlandish fashion; some wore short doublets, others jerkins, with long knives in their belts, and most of them had enormous breeches, of similar style with that of the guide's. Their visages, too, were peculiar: one had a large beard, broad face, and small piggish eyes; the face of another seemed to consist entirely of nose, and was surmounted by a white sugar-loaf hat set off with a little red cock's tail. They all had beards, of various shapes and colors. There was one who seemed to be the commander. He was a stout old gentleman, with a weather-beaten countenance; he wore a laced doublet, broad belt and hanger, high-crowned hat and feather, red stockings, and high-heeled shoes, with roses in them. The whole group reminded Rip of the figures in an old Flemish painting, in the parlor of Dominie Van Shaick, the village parson, and which had been brought over from Holland at the time of the settlement.

What seemed particularly odd to Rip was, that though these folks were evidently amusing themselves, yet they maintained the gravest faces, the most mysterious silence, and were, withal, the most melancholy party of pleasure he had ever witnessed. Nothing interrupted the stillness of the scene but the noise of the balls, which, whenever they were rolled, echoed along the mountains like rumbling peals of thunder.

As Rip and his companion approached them, they suddenly desisted from their play, and stared at him with such fixed statue-like gaze, and such strange, uncouth, lack-lustre countenances, that his heart turned within him, and his knees smote together. His companion now emptied the contents of the keg into large flagons, and made signs to him to wait upon the company. He obeyed with fear and trembling; they quaffed the liquor in profound silence, and then returned to their game.

By degrees Rip's awe and apprehension subsided. He even ventured, when no eye was fixed upon him, to taste the beverage, which he found had much of the flavor of excellent Hollands. He was naturally a thirsty soul, and was soon tempted to repeat the draught. One taste provoked another; and he reiterated his visits to the flagon so often that at length his senses were overpowered, his eyes swam in his head, his head gradually declined, and he fell into a deep sleep.

On waking, he found himself on the green knoll whence he had first seen the old man of the glen. He rubbed his eyes—it was a bright sunny morning. The birds were hopping and twittering among the bushes, and the eagle was wheeling aloft, and breasting the pure mountain breeze. "Surely," thought Rip, "I have not slept here all night." He recalled the occurrences before he fell asleep. The strange man with a keg of liquor—the mountain ravine—the wild retreat among the rocks—the woe-begone party at ninepins—the flagon—"Oh! that flagon! that wicked flagon!" thought Rip—"what excuse shall I make to Dame Van Winkle!"

He looked round for his gun, but in place of the clean well-oiled fowling-piece, he found an old firelock lying by him, the barrel incrusted with rust, the lock falling off, and the stock worm-eaten. He now suspected that the grave roysterers of the mountain had put a trick upon him, and, having dosed him with liquor, had robbed him of his gun. Wolf, too, had disappeared, but he might have strayed away after a squirrel or partridge. He whistled after him and shouted his name, but all in vain; the echoes repeated his whistle and shout, but no dog was to be seen.

He determined to revisit the scene of the last evening's gambol, and if he met with any of the party, to demand his dog and gun. As he rose to walk, he found himself stiff in the joints, and wanting in his usual activity. "These mountain beds do not agree with me," thought Rip, "and if this frolic should lay me up with a fit of the rheumatism, I shall have a blessed time with Dame Van Winkle." With some difficulty he got down into the glen: he found the gully up which he and his companion had ascended the preceding evening; but to his astonishment a mountain stream was now foaming down it, leaping from rock to rock, and filling the glen with babbling murmurs. He, however, made shift to scramble up its sides, working his toilsome way through thickets of birch, sassafras, and witch-hazel, and sometimes tripped up or entangled by the wild grapevines that twisted their coils or tendrils from tree to tree, and spread a kind of network in his path.

At length he reached to where the ravine had opened through the cliffs to the amphitheatre; but no traces of such opening remained. The rocks presented a high impenetrable wall, over which the torrent came tumbling in a sheet of feathery foam, and fell into a broad deep basin, black from the shadows of the surrounding forest. Here, then, poor Rip was brought to a stand. He again called and whistled after his dog; he was only answered by the cawing of a flock of idle crows, sporting high in air about a dry tree that overhung a sunny precipice; and who, secure in their elevation, seemed to look down and scoff at the poor man's perplexities. What was to be done? The morning was passing away, and Rip felt famished for want of his breakfast. He grieved to give up his dog and gun; he dreaded to meet his wife; but it would not do to starve among the mountains. He shook his head, shouldered the rusty firelock, and, with a heart full of trouble and anxiety, turned his steps homeward.

As he approached the village he met a number of people, but none whom he knew, which somewhat surprised him, for he had thought himself acquainted with everyone in the country round. Their dress, too, was of a different fashion from that to which he was accustomed. They all stared at him with equal marks of surprise, and whenever they cast their eyes upon him, invariably stroked their chins. The constant recurrence of this gesture induced Rip, involuntarily, to do the same, when, to his astonishment, he found his beard had grown a foot long!

He had now entered the skirts of the village. A troop of strange children ran at his heels, hooting after him, and pointing at his gray beard. The dogs, too, not one of which he recognized for an old acquaintance, barked at him as he passed. The very village was altered; it was larger and more populous. There were rows of houses which he had never seen before, and those which had been his familiar haunts had disappeared. Strange names were over the doors—strange faces at the windows—everything was strange. His mind now misgave him; he began to doubt whether both he and the world around him were not bewitched. Surely this was his native village, which he had left but the day before. There stood the Kaatskill mountains—there ran the silver Hudson at a distance—there was every hill and dale precisely as it had always been. Rip was sorely perplexed—"That flagon last night," thought he, "has addled my poor head sadly!"

It was with some difficulty that he found the way to his own house, which he approached with silent awe, expecting every moment to hear the shrill voice of Dame Van Winkle. He found the house gone to decay—the roof fallen in, the windows shattered, and the doors off the hinges. A half-starved dog that looked like Wolf was skulking about it. Rip called him by name, but the cur snarled, showed his teeth, and passed on. This was an unkind cut indeed—"My very dog," sighed poor Rip, "has forgotten me!"

He entered the house, which, to tell the truth, Dame Van Winkle had always kept in neat order. It was empty, forlorn, and apparently abandoned. This desolateness overcame all his connubial fears—he called loudly for his wife and children—the lonely chambers rang for a moment with his voice, and then all again was silence.

He now hurried forth, and hastened to his old resort, the village inn—but it too was gone. A large rickety wooden building stood in its place, with great gaping windows, some of them broken and mended with old hats and petticoats, and over die door was painted, "the Union Hotel, by Jonathan Doolittle." Instead of the great tree that used to shelter the quiet little Dutch inn of yore, there now was reared a tall naked pole, with something on the top that looked like a red night-cap, and from it was fluttering a flag, on which was a singular assemblage of stars and stripes—all this was strange and incomprehensible. He recognized on the sign, however, the ruby face of King George, under which he had smoked so many a peaceful pipe; but even this was singularly metamorphosed. The red coat was changed for one of blue and buff, a sword was held in the hand instead of a sceptre, the head was decorated with a cocked hat, and underneath, was painted in large characters, GENERAL WASHINGTON.

There was, as usual, a crowd of folk about the door, but none that Rip recollected. The very character of the people seemed changed. There was a busy, bustling, disputatious tone about it, instead of the accustomed phlegm and drowsy tranquillity. He looked in vain for the sage Nicholas Vedder, with his broad face, double chin, and fair long pipe, uttering clouds of tobacco-smoke instead of idle speeches; or Van Bummel, the schoolmaster, doling forth the contents of an ancient newspaper. In place of these, a lean, bilious-looking fellow, with his pockets full of handbills, was haranguing vehemently about rights of citizens—elections—members of Congress—liberty—Bunker's Hill—heroes of seventy-six—and other words, which were a perfect Babylonish jargon to the bewildered Van Winkle.

The appearance of Rip, with his long grizzled beard, his rusty fowling-piece, his uncouth dress, and an army of women and children at his heels, soon attracted the attention of the tavern politicians. They crowded round him, eying him from head to foot with great curiosity. The orator bustled up to him, and, drawing him partly aside, inquired "On which side he voted?" Rip stared in vacant stupidity. Another short but busy little fellow pulled him by the arm, and, rising on tiptoe, inquired in his ear, "Whether he was Federal or Democrat?" Rip was equally at a loss to comprehend the question; when a knowing, self-important old gentleman, in a sharp cocked hat, made his way through the crowd, putting them to the right and left with his elbows as he passed, and planting himself before Van Winkle, with one arm akimbo, the other resting on his cane, his keen eyes and sharp hat penetrating, as it were, into his very soul, demanded in an austere tone, "What brought him to the election with a gun on his shoulder, and a mob at his heels, and whether he meant to breed a riot in the village?"—"Alas! gentlemen," cried Rip, somewhat dismayed, "I am a poor quiet man, a native of the place, and a loyal subject of the king, God bless him!"

Here a general shout burst from the bystanders—"A tory! a tory! a spy! a refugee! hustle him! away with him!" It was with great difficulty that the self-important man in the cocked hat restored order; and, having assumed a tenfold austerity of brow, demanded again of the unknown culprit, what he came there for, and whom he was seeking? The poor man humbly assured him that he meant no harm, but merely came there in search of some of his neighbors, who used to keep about the tavern.

"Well—who are they?—name them."

Rip bethought himself a moment, and inquired. "Where's Nicholas Vedder?"

There was a silence for a little while, when an old man replied in a thin piping voice, "Nicholas Vedder! why, he is dead and gone these eighteen years! There was a wooden tombstone in the churchyard that used to tell all about him, but that's rotten and gone too."

"Where's Brom Dutcher?"

"Oh, he went off to the army in the beginning of the war; some say he was killed at the storming of Stony Point—others say he was drowned in a squall at the foot of Antony's Nose. I don't know—he never came back again."

"Where's Van Bummel, the schoolmaster?"

"He went off to the wars too, was a great militia general, and is now in Congress."

Rip's heart died away at hearing of these sad changes in his home and friends, and finding himself thus alone in the world. Every answer puzzled him too, by treating of such enormous lapses of time, and of matters which he could not understand: war—congress—Stony Point;—he had no courage to ask after any more friends, but cried out in despair, "Does nobody here know Rip Van Winkle?"

"Oh, Rip Van Winkle!" exclaimed two or three, "Oh, to be sure! that's Rip Van Winkle yonder, leaning against the tree."

Rip looked, and beheld a precise counterpart of himself, as he went up the mountain; apparently as lazy, and certainly as ragged. The poor fellow was now completely confounded. He doubted his own identity, and whether he was himself or another man. In the midst of his bewilderment, the man in the cocked hat demanded who he was, and what was his name?

"God knows," exclaimed he, at his wit's end; "I'm not myself— I'm somebody else—that's me yonder—no—that's somebody else got into my shoes—I was myself last night, but I fell asleep on the mountain, and they've changed my gun, and every thing's changed, and I'm changed, and I can't tell my name, or who I am!"

The bystanders began now to look at each other, nod, wink significantly, and tap their fingers against their foreheads. There was a whisper, also, about securing the gun, and keeping the old fellow from doing mischief, at the very suggestion of which the self-important man in the cocked hat retired with some precipitation. At this critical moment a fresh, comely woman pressed through the throng to get a peep at the gray-bearded man. She had a chubby child in her arms, which, frightened at his looks, began to cry. "Hush, Rip," cried she, "hush, you little fool; the old man won't hurt you." The name of the child, the air of the mother, the tone of her voice, all awakened a train of recollections in his mind. "What is your name, my good woman?" asked he.

"Judith Gardenier."

"And your father's name?"

"Ah, poor man. Rip Van Winkle was his name, but it's twenty years since he went away from home with his gun, and never has been heard of since—his dog came home without him; but whether he shot himself, or was carried away by the Indians, nobody can tell. I was then but a little girl."

Rip had but one question more to ask; but he put it with a faltering voice:

"Where's your mother?"

"Oh, she too had died but a short time since; she broke a blood-vessel in a fit of passion at a New England peddler."

There was a drop of comfort, at least, in this intelligence. The honest man could contain himself no longer. He caught his daughter and her child in his arms. "I am your father!" cried he—"Young Rip Van Winkle once—old Rip Van Winkle now!—Does nobody know poor Rip Van Winkle?"

All stood amazed, until an old woman, tottering out from among the crowd, put her hand to her brow, and peering under it in his face for a moment, exclaimed, "Sure enough! it is Rip Van Winkle—it is himself! Welcome home again, old neighbor—Why, where have you been these twenty long years?"

Rip's story was soon told, for the whole twenty years had been to him but as one night. The neighbors stared when they heard it; some were seen to wink at each other, and put their tongues in their cheeks; and the self-important man in the cocked hat, who, when the alarm was over, had returned to the field, screwed down the corners of his mouth, and shook his head—upon which there was a general shaking of the head throughout the assemblage.

It was determined, however, to take the opinion of old Peter Vanderdonk, who was seen slowly advancing up the road. He was a descendant of the historian of that name, who wrote one of the earliest accounts of the province. Peter was the most ancient inhabitant of the village, and well versed in all the wonderful events and traditions of the neighborhood. He recollected Rip at once, and corroborated his story in the most satisfactory manner. He assured the company that it was a fact, handed down from his ancestor the historian, that the Kaatskill mountains had always been haunted by strange beings. That it was affirmed that the great Hendrick Hudson, the first discoverer of the river and country, kept a kind of vigil there every twenty years, with his crew of the *Half-Moon;* being permitted in this way to revisit the scenes of his enterprise, and keep a guardian eye upon the river, and the great city called by his name. That his father had once seen them in their old Dutch dresses playing at ninepins in a hollow of the mountain; and that he himself had heard one summer afternoon, the sound of their balls, like distant peals of thunders.

To make a long story short, the company broke up, and returned to the more important concerns of the election. Rip's daughter took him home to live with her; she had a snug, well-furnished house, and a stout cheery farmer for a husband, whom Rip recollected for one of the urchins that used to climb upon his back. As to Rip's son and heir, who was the ditto of himself, seen leaning against the tree, he was employed to work on the farm; but evinced an hereditary disposition to attend to anything else but his business.

Rip now resumed his old walks and habits; he soon found many of his former cronies, though all rather the worse for the wear and tear of time, and preferred making friends among the rising generation, with whom he soon grew into great favor.

Having nothing to do at home, and being arrived at that happy age when a man can be idle with impunity, he took his place once more on the bench at the inn door, and was reverenced as one of the patriarchs of the village, and a chronicle of the old times "before the war." It was some time before he could get into the regular track of gossip, or could be made to comprehend the strange events that had taken place during his torpor. How that there had been a revolutionary war—that the country had thrown off the yoke of old England—and that, instead of being a subject of his Majesty George the Third, he was now a free citizen of the United States. Rip, in fact, was no politician; the changes of states and empires made but little impression on him; but there was one species of despotism under which he had long groaned, and that was—petticoat government. Happily that was at an end; he had got his neck out of the yoke of matrimony, and could go in and out whenever he pleased, without dreading the tyranny of Dame Van Winkle. Whenever her name was mentioned, however, he shook his head, shrugged his shoulders, and cast up his eyes; which might pass either for an expression of resignation to his fate, or joy at his deliverance.

He used to tell his story to every stranger that arrived at Mr. Doolittle's hotel. He was observed, at first, to vary on some points every time he told it, which was, doubtless, owing to his having so recently awaked. It at last settled down precisely to the tale I have related, and not a man, woman, or child in the neighborhood, but knew it by heart. Some always pretended to doubt the reality of it, and insisted that Rip had been out of his head, and that this was one point on which he always remained flighty. The old Dutch inhabitants, however, almost universally gave it full credit. Even to this day they never hear a thunderstorm of a summer afternoon about the Kaatskill, but they say Hendrick Hudson and his crew are at their game of ninepins; and it is a common wish of all hen-pecked husbands in the neighborhood, when life hangs heavy on their hands, that they might have a quieting draught out of Rip Van Winkle's flagon.

WILLIAM AUSTIN
(1778–1841)

Now forgotten, his most famous story virtually unread, William Austin was a prominent literary figure of his time, trained in the law, and an acute critic of law and politics of the early nineteenth century. He was born in Lunenburg, Massachusetts, graduated from Harvard University in 1798, and wrote "Strictures on Harvard University" soon after graduation. He was also the author of the critical Letters from London *(1804), viewing English law and politics from the perspective of a New Englander. Not a prolific writer, Austin's concerns were with the social and moral condition of the America of his time, a newly formed, incompletely defined nation "cut off from the last age," like Peter Rugg, the Missing Man.*

It is difficult to believe today that this long-forgotten story, a parable reminiscent of the most characteristic work of Nathaniel Hawthorne, was one of the most famous stories of its time; and Peter Rugg, its doomed, self-deluded hero, one of the best-known fictitious figures of his time. Contemporary readers will be struck by the eerie foreshadowing of themes to be taken up, with greater psychological intensity, by a number of subsequent writers—not only Hawthorne, Melville, and Poe, but Franz Kafka and Borges. Presented as a document by an impartial witness, the nightmare tale of Peter Rugg reads as folktale and allegory; Ruggs' damnation springs from a seemingly simple source—his profanity, which defies Heaven and sets him apart from the human community. How like the ending of Kafka's "A Country Doctor," these damning words out of nowhere: "There is nothing strange here but yourself, Mr. Rugg. . . .You were cut off from the last age, and you can never be fitted to the present. Your home is gone, and you can never have another home in this world."

Peter Rugg, the Missing Man

From Jonathan Dunwell of New York to Mr. Harman Krauff

Sir,—Agreeably to my promise, I now relate to you all the particulars of the lost man and child which I have been able to collect. It is entirely owing to the humane interest you seemed to take in the report, that I have pursued the inquiry to the following result.

You may remember that business called me to Boston in the summer of 1820. I sailed in the packet to Providence, and when I arrived there I learned that every seat in the stage was engaged. I was thus obliged either to wait a few hours or accept a seat with the driver, who civilly offered me that accommodation. Accordingly, I took my seat by his side, and soon found him intelligent and communicative. When we had travelled about ten miles, the horses suddenly threw their ears on their neck, as flat as a hare's. Said the driver, "Have you a surtout with you?"

"No," said I; "why do you ask?"

"You will want one soon," said he. "Do you observe the ears of all the horses?"

"Yes; and was just about to ask the reason."

"They see the storm-breeder, and we shall see him soon."

At this moment there was not a cloud visible in the firmament. Soon after, a small speck appeared in the road.

"There," said my companion, "comes the storm-breeder. He always leaves a Scotch mist behind him. By many a wet jacket do I remember him. I suppose the poor fellow suffers much himself,—much more than is known to the world."

Presently a man with a child beside him, with a large black horse, and a weather-beaten chair, once built for a chaise-body, passed in great haste, apparently at the rate of twelve miles an hour. He seemed to grasp the reins of his horse with firmness, and appeared to anticipate his speed. He seemed dejected, and looked anxiously at the passengers, particularly at the stage-driver and myself. In a moment after he passed us, the horse's ears were up, and bent themselves forward so that they nearly met.

"Who is that man?" said I; "he seems in great trouble."

"Nobody knows who he is, but his person and the child are familiar to me. I have met him more than a hundred times, and have been so often asked the way to Boston by that man, even when he was travelling directly from that town, that of late I have refused any communication with him; and that is the reason he gave me such a fixed look."

"But does he never stop anywhere?"

"I have never known him to stop anywhere longer than to inquire the way to Boston; and let him be where he may, he will tell you he cannot stay a moment, for he must reach Boston that night."

We were now ascending a high hill in Walpole; and as we had a fair view of the heavens, I was rather disposed to jeer the driver for thinking of his surtout, as not a cloud as big as a marble could be discerned.

"Do you look," said he, "in the direction whence the man came; that is the place to look. The storm never meets him; it follows him."

We presently approached another hill; and when at the height, the driver pointed out in an eastern direction a little black speck about as big as a hat. "There," said he "is the seed-storm. We may possibly reach Polley's before it reaches us, but the wanderer and his child will go to Providence through rain, thunder, and lightning."

And now the horses, as though taught by instinct, hastened with increased speed. The little black cloud came on rolling over the turnpike, and doubled and trebled itself in all directions. The appearance of this cloud attracted the notice of all the passengers, for after it had spread itself to a great bulk it suddenly became more limited in circumference, grew more compact, dark, and consolidated. And now the successive flashes of chain lightning caused the whole cloud to appear like a sort of irregular net-work, and displayed a thousand fantastic images. The driver bespoke my attention to a remarkable configuration in the cloud. He said every flash of lightning near its centre discovered to him, distinctly, the form of a man sitting in an open carriage drawn by a black horse. But in truth I saw no such thing; the man's fancy was doubtless at fault. It is a very common thing for the imagination to paint for the senses, both in the visible and invisible world.

In the mean time the distant thunder gave notice of a shower at hand; and just as we reached Polley's tavern the rain poured down in torrents. It was soon over, the cloud passing in the direction of the turnpike toward Providence. In a few moments after, a respectable-looking man in a chaise stopped at the door. The man and child in the chair having excited some little sympathy among the passengers, the gentleman was asked if he had observed them. He said he had met them; that the man seemed bewildered, and inquired the way to Boston; that he was driving at great speed, as though he expected to outstrip the tempest; that the moment he had passed him, a thunder-clap broke directly over the man's head, and seemed to envelop both man and child, horse and carriage. "I stopped," said the gentleman, "supposing the lightning had struck him, but the horse only seemed to loom up and increase his speed; and as well as I could judge, he travelled just as fast as the thundercloud."

While this man was speaking, a pedlar with a cart of tin merchandise came up, all dripping; and on being questioned, he said he had met that man and carriage, within a fortnight, in four different States; that at each time he had inquired the way to Boston; and that a thunder-shower like the present had each time deluged his wagon and his wares, setting his tin pots, etc., afloat, so that he had determined to get a marine insurance for the future. But that which excited his surprise most was the strange conduct of his horse, for long before he could distinguish the man in the chair, his own horse stood still in the road, and flung back his ears. "In short," said the pedlar, "I wish never to see that man and horse again; they do not look to me as though they belonged to this world."

This was all I could learn at that time; and the occurrence soon after would have become with me, "like one of those things which had never happened," had I not, as I stood recently on the doorstep of Bennett's hotel in Hartford, heard a man say, "There goes Peter Rugg and his child! he looks wet and weary, and farther from Boston than ever." I was satisfied it was the same man I had seen more than three years before; for whoever has once seen Peter Rugg can never after be deceived as to his identity.

"Peter Rugg!" said I; "and who is Peter Rugg?"

"That," said the stranger, "is more than any one can tell exactly. He is a famous traveller, held in light esteem by all innholders, for he never stops to eat, drink, or sleep. I wonder why the government does not employ him to carry the mail."

"Ay," said a by-stander, "that is a thought bright only on one side; how long would it take in that case to send a letter to Boston, for Peter has already, to my knowledge, been more than twenty years travelling to that place."

"But," said I, "does the man never stop anywhere; does he never converse with any one? I saw the same man more than three years since, near Providence, and I heard a strange story about him. Pray, sir, give me some account of this man."

"Sir," said the stranger, "those who know the most respecting that man, say the least. I have heard it asserted that Heaven sometimes sets a mark on a man, either for judgment or a trial. Under which Peter Rugg now labors, I cannot say; therefore I am rather inclined to pity than to judge."

"You speak like a humane man," said I; "and if you have known him so long, I pray you will give me some account of him. Has his appearance much altered in that time?"

"Why, yes. He looks as though he never ate, drank, or slept; and his child looks older than himself, and he looks like time broken off from eternity, and anxious to gain a resting-place."

"And how does his horse look?" said I.

"As for his horse, he looks fatter and gayer, and shows more animation and courage than he did twenty years ago. The last time Rugg spoke to me he inquired how far it was to Boston. I told him just one hundred miles."

"'Why,' said he, 'how can you deceive me so? It is cruel to mislead a traveller. I have lost my way; pray direct me the nearest way to Boston.'"

I repeated, it was one hundred miles.

"'How can you say so?' said he; 'I was told last evening it was but fifty, and I have travelled all night.'

"'But,' said I, 'you are now travelling from Boston. You must turn back.'

"'Alas,' said he, 'it is all turn back! Boston shifts with the wind, and plays all around the compass. One man tells me it is to the east, another to the west; and the guide-posts too, they all point the wrong way.'

"'But will you not stop and rest?' said I; 'you seem wet and weary.'

"'Yes,' said he, 'it has been foul weather since I left home.'

"'Stop, then, and refresh yourself.'

"'I must not stop; I must reach home to-night, if possible: though I think you must be mistaken in the distance to Boston.'

"He then gave the reins to his horse, which he restrained with difficulty, and disappeared in a moment. A few days afterward I met the man a little this side of Claremont, winding around the hills in Unity, at the rate, I believe, of twelve miles an hour."

"Is Peter Rugg his real name, or has he accidentally gained that name?"

"I know not, but presume he will not deny his name; you can ask him,—for see, he has turned his horse, and is passing this way."

In a moment a dark-colored, high-spirited horse approached, and would have passed without stopping, but I had resolved to speak to Peter Rugg, or whoever the man might be. Accordingly I stepped into the street; and as the horse approached, I made a feint of stopping him. The man immediately reined his horse. "Sir," said I, "may I be so bold as to inquire if you are not Mr. Rugg? For I think I have seen you before."

"My name is Peter Rugg," said he. "I have unfortunately lost my way; I am wet and weary, and will take it kindly of you to direct me to Boston."

"You live in Boston, do you; and in what street?"

"In Middle Street."

"When did you leave Boston?"

"I cannot tell precisely; it seems a considerable time."

"But how did you and your child become so wet? It has not rained here to-day."

"It has just rained a heavy shower up the river. But I shall not reach Boston to-night if I tarry. Would you advise me to take the old road or the turnpike?"

"Why, the old road is one hundred and seventeen miles, and the turnpike is ninety-seven."

"How can you say so? You impose on me; it is wrong to trifle with a traveller; you know it is but forty miles from Newburyport to Boston."

"But this is not Newburyport; this is Hartford."

"Do not deceive me, sir. Is not this town Newburyport, and the river that I have been following the Merrimack?"

"No, sir; this is Hartford, and the river the Connecticut."

He wrung his hands and looked incredulous. "Have the rivers, too, changed their courses, as the cities have changed places? But see! the clouds are gathering in the south, and we shall have a rainy night. Ah, that fatal oath!"

He would tarry no longer; his impatient horse leaped off, his hind flanks rising like wings: he seemed to devour all before him, and to scorn all behind.

I had now, as I thought, discovered a clew to the history of Peter Rugg; and I determined, the next time my business called me to Boston, to make a further inquiry. Soon after, I was enabled to collect the following particulars from Mrs. Croft, an aged lady in Middle Street, who has resided in Boston during the last twenty years. Her narration is this:

Just at twilight last summer a person stopped at the door of the late Mrs. Rugg. Mrs. Croft on coming to the door perceived a stranger, with a child by his side, in an old weather-beaten carriage, with a black horse. The stranger asked for Mrs. Rugg, and was informed that Mrs. Rugg had died at a good old age, more than twenty years before that time.

The stranger replied, "How can you deceive me so? Do ask Mrs. Rugg to step to the door."

"Sir, I assure you Mrs. Rugg has not lived here these twenty years; no one lives here but myself, and my name is Betsy Croft."

The stranger paused, looked up and down the street, and said, "Though the paint is rather faded, this looks like my house."

"Yes," said the child, "that is the stone before the door that I used to sit on to eat my bread and milk."

"But," said the stranger, "it seems to be on the wrong side of the street. Indeed, everything here seems to be misplaced. The streets are all changed, the people are all changed, the town seems changed, and what is strangest of all, Catherine Rugg has deserted her husband and child. Pray," continued the stranger, "has John Foy come home from sea? He went a long voyage; he is my kinsman. If I could see him, he could give me some account of Mrs. Rugg"

"Sir," said Mrs. Croft, "I never heard of John Foy. Where did he live?"

"Just above here, in Orange-tree Lane."

"There is no such place in this neighborhood."

"What do you tell me! Are the streets gone? Orange-tree Lane is at the head of Hanover Street, near Pemberton's Hill."

"There is no such lane now."

"Madam, you cannot be serious! But you doubtless know my brother, William Rugg. He lives in Royal Exchange Lane, near King Street."

"I know of no such lane; and I am sure there is no such street as King Street in this town."

"No such street as King Street! Why, woman you mock me! You may as well tell me there is no King George. However, madam, you see I am wet and weary, I must find a resting-place. I will go to Hart's tavern, near the market."

"Which market, sir? for you seem perplexed; we have several markets."

"You know there is but one market near the town dock."

"Oh, the old market; but no such person has kept there these twenty years."

Here the stranger seemed disconcerted, and uttered to himself quite audibly: "Strange mistake; how much this looks like the town of Boston! It certainly has a great resemblance to it; but I perceive my mistake now. Some other Mrs. Rugg, some other Middle Street.—Then," said he, "madam, can you direct me to Boston?"

"Why, this is Boston, the city of Boston; I know of no other Boston."

"City of Boston it may be; but it is not the Boston where I live. I recollect now, I came over a bridge instead of a ferry. Pray, what bridge is that I just came over?"

"It is Charles River bridge."

"I perceive my mistake: there is a ferry between Boston and Charlestown; there is no bridge. Ah, I perceive my mistake. If I were in Boston my horse would carry me directly to my own door. But my horse shows by his impatience that he is in a strange place. Absurd, that I should have mistaken this place for the old town of Boston. It is a much finer city than the town of Boston. It has been built long since Boston. I fancy Boston must lie at a distance from this city, as the good woman seems ignorant of it."

At these words his horse began to chafe, and strike the pavement with his forefeet. The stranger seemed a little bewildered, and said, "No home to-night;" and giving the reins to his horse, passed up the street, and I saw no more of him.

It was evident that the generation to which Peter Rugg belonged has passed away.

This was all the account of Peter Rugg I could obtain from Mrs. Croft; but she directed me to an elderly man, Mr. James Felt, who lived near her, and who had kept a record of the principal occurrences for the last fifty years. At my request she sent for him; and after I had related to him the object of my inquiry, Mr. Felt told me he had known Rugg in his youth, and that his disappearance had caused some surprise; but as it sometimes happens that men run away,—sometimes to be rid of others, and sometimes to be rid of themselves,—and Rugg took his child with him, and his own horse and chair, and as it did not appear that any creditors made a stir, the occurrence soon mingled itself in the stream of oblivion; and Rugg and his child, horse, and chair were soon forgotten.

"It is true," said Mr. Felt, "sundry stories grew out of Rugg's affair, whether true or false I cannot tell; but stranger things have happened in my day, without even a newspaper notice."

"Sir," said I, "Peter Rugg is now living. I have lately seen Peter Rugg and his child, horse, and chair; therefore I pray you to relate to me all you know or ever heard of him."

"Why, my friend," said James Felt, "that Peter Rugg is now a living man, I will not deny; but that you have seen Peter Rugg and his child, is impossible, if you mean a small child; for Jenny Rugg, if living, must be at least—let me see—Boston massacre, 1770—Jenny Rugg was about ten years old. Why, sir, Jenny Rugg, if living, must be more than sixty years of age. That Peter Rugg is living, is highly probable, as he was only ten years older than myself, and I was only eighty last March; and I am as likely to live twenty years longer as any man."

Here I perceived that Mr. Felt was in his dotage, and I despaired of gaining any intelligence from him on which I could depend.

I took my leave of Mrs. Croft, and proceeded to my lodgings at the Marlborough Hotel.

"If Peter Rugg," thought I, "has been travelling since the Boston massacre, there is no reason why he should not travel to the end of time. If the present generations know little of him, the next will know less, and Peter and his child will have no hold on this world."

In the course of the evening, I related my adventure in Middle Street.

"Ha!" said one of the company, smiling, "do you really think you have seen Peter Rugg? I have heard my grandfather speak of him, as though he seriously believed his own story."

"Sir," said I, "pray let us compare your grandfather's story of Mr. Rugg with my own."

"Peter Rugg, sir,—if my grandfather was worthy of credit,—once lived in Middle Street, in this city. He was a man of comfortable circumstances, had a wife and one daughter, and was generally esteemed for his sober life and manners. But unhappily, his temper, at times, was altogether ungovernable, and then his language was terrible. In these fits of passion, if a door stood in his way, he would never do less than kick a panel through. He would sometimes throw his heels over his head, and come down on his feet, uttering oaths in a circle; and thus in a rage, he was the first who performed a somerset, and did what others have since learned to do for merriment and money. Once Rugg was seen to bite a ten-penny nail in halves. In those days everybody, both men and boys, wore wigs; and Peter, at these moments of violent passion, would become so profane that his wig would rise up from his head. Some said it was on account of his terrible language; others accounted for it in a more philosophical way, and said it was caused by the expansion of his scalp, as violent passion, we know, will swell the veins and expand the head. While these fits were on him, Rugg had no respect for heaven or earth. Except this infirmity, all agreed that Rugg was a good sort of man; for when his fits were over, nobody was so ready to commend a placid temper as Peter.

"One morning, late in autumn, Rugg, in his own chair, with a fine large bay horse, took his daughter and proceeded to Concord. On his return a violent storm overtook him. At dark he stopped in Menotomy, now West Cambridge, at the door of a Mr. Cutter, a friend of his, who urged him to tarry the night. On Rugg's declining to stop, Mr. Cutter urged him vehemently. 'Why, Mr. Rugg,' said Cutter, 'the storm is overwhelming you. The night is exceedingly dark. Your little daughter will perish. You are in an open chair, and the tempest is increasing.' *'Let the storm increase,'* said Rugg, with a fearful oath, 'I *will see home to-night, in spite of the last tempest, or may I never see home!'* At these words he gave his whip to his high-spirited horse and disappeared in a moment. But Peter Rugg did not reach home that night, nor the next; nor, when he became a missing man, could he ever be traced beyond Mr. Cutter's, in Menotomy.

"For a long time after, on every dark and stormy night the wife of Peter Rugg would fancy she heard the crack of a whip, and the fleet tread of a horse, and the rattling of a carriage passing her door. The neighbors, too, heard the same noises, and some said they knew it was Rugg's horse; the tread on the pavement was perfectly familiar to them. This occurred so repeatedly that at length the neighbors watched with lanterns, and saw the real Peter Rugg, with his own horse and chair and the child sitting beside him, pass directly before his own door, his head turned toward his house, and himself making every effort to stop his horse, but in vain.

"The next day the friends of Mrs. Rugg exerted themselves to find her husband and child. They inquired at every public house and stable in town; but it did not appear that Rugg made any stay in Boston. No one, after Rugg had passed his own door, could give any account of him, though it was asserted by some that the clatter of Rugg's horse and carriage over the pavements shook the houses on both sides of the streets. And this is credible, if indeed Rugg's horse and carriage did pass on that night; for at this day, in many of the streets, a loaded truck or team in passing will shake the houses like an earthquake. However, Rugg's neighbors never afterward watched. Some of them treated it all as a delusion, and thought no more of it. Others of a different opinion shook their heads and said nothing.

"Thus Rugg and his child, horse, and chair were soon forgotten; and probably many in the neighborhood never heard a word on the subject.

"There was indeed a rumor that Rugg was seen afterward in Connecticut, between Suffield and Hartford, passing through the country at headlong speed. This gave occasion to Rugg's friends to make further inquiry; but the more they inquired, the more they were baffled. If they heard of Rugg one day in Connecticut, the next they heard of him winding round the hills in New Hampshire; and soon after a man in a chair, with a small child, exactly answering the description of Peter Rugg, would be seen in Rhode Island inquiring the way to Boston.

"But that which chiefly gave a color of mystery to the story of Peter Rugg was the affair at Charlestown bridge. The toll-gatherer asserted that sometimes, on the darkest and most stormy nights, when no object could be discerned, about the time Rugg was missing, a horse and wheel-carriage, with a noise equal to a troop, would at midnight, in utter contempt of the rates of toll, pass over the bridge. This occurred so frequently that the toll-gatherer resolved to attempt a discovery. Soon after, at the usual time, apparently the same horse and carriage approached the bridge from Charlestown square. The toll-gatherer, prepared, took his stand as near the middle of the bridge as he dared, with a large three-legged stool in his hand; as the appearance passed, he threw the stool at the horse, but heard nothing except the noise of the stool skipping across the bridge. The toll-gatherer on the next day asserted that the stool went directly through the body of the horse, and he persisted in that belief ever after. Whether Rugg, or whoever the person was, ever passed the bridge again, the toll-gatherer would never tell; and when questioned, seemed anxious to waive the subject. And thus Peter Rugg and his child, horse, and carriage, remain a mystery to this day."

This, sir, is all that I could learn of Peter Rugg in Boston.

Further Account of Peter Rugg By Jonathan Dunwell

In the autumn of 1825 I attended the races at Richmond in Virginia. As two new horses of great promise were run, the race-ground was never better attended, nor was expectation ever more deeply excited. The partisans of Dart and Lightning, the two race-horses, were equally anxious and equally dubious of the result. To an indifferent spectator, it was impossible to perceive any difference. They were equally beautiful to behold, alike in color and height, and as they stood side by side they measured from heel to forefeet within half an inch of each other. The eyes of each were full, prominent, and resolute; and when at time they regarded each other, they assumed a lofty demeanor, seemed to shorten their necks, project their eyes, and rest their bodies equally on their four hoofs. They certainly showed signs of intelligence, and displayed a courtesy to each other unusual even with statesmen.

It was now nearly twelve o'clock, the hour of expectation, doubt, and anxiety. The riders mounted their horses; and so trim, light, and airy they sat on the animals as to seem a part of them. The spectators, many deep in a solid column, had taken their places, and as many thousand breathing statues were there as spectators. All eyes were turned to Dart and

Lightning and their two fairy riders. There was nothing to disturb this calm except a busy woodpecker on a neighboring tree. The signal was given, and Dart and Lightning answered it with ready intelligence. At first they proceed at a slow trot, then they quicken to a canter, and then a gallop; presently they sweep the plain. Both horses lay themselves flat on the ground, their riders bending forward and resting their chins between their horses' ears. Had not the ground been perfectly level, had there been any undulation, the least rise and fall, the spectator would now and then have lost sight of both horses and riders.

While these horses, side by side, thus appeared, flying without wings, flat as a hare, and neither gaining on the other, all eyes were diverted to a new spectacle. Directly in the rear of Dart and Lightning, a majestic black horse of unusual size, drawing an old weather-beaten chair, strode over the plain; and although he appeared to make no effort, for he maintained a steady trot, before Dart and Lightning approached the goal the black horse and chair had overtaken the racers, who, on perceiving this new competitor pass them, threw back their ears, and suddenly stopped in their course. Thus neither Dart nor Lightning carried away the purse.

The spectators now were exceedingly curious to learn whence came the black horse and chair. With many it was the opinion that nobody was in the vehicle. Indeed, this began to be the prevalent opinion; for those at a short distance, so fleet was the black horse, could not easily discern who, if anybody, was in the carriage. But both the riders, very near to whom the black horse passed, agreed in this particular,—that a sad-looking man and a little girl were in the chair. When they stated this I was satisfied that the man was Peter Rugg. But what caused no little surprise, John Spring, one of the riders (he who rode Lightning) asserted that no earthly horse without breaking his trot could, in a carriage, outstrip his race-horse; and he persisted, with some passion, that it was not a horse,—or, he was sure it was not a horse, but a large black ox. "What a great black ox can do," said John, "I cannot pretend to say; but no race-horse, not even flying Childers, could out-trot Lightning in a fair race."

This opinion of John Spring excited no little merriment, for it was obvious to every one that it was a powerful black horse that interrupted the race; but John Spring, jealous of Lightning's reputation as a horse, would rather have it thought that any other beast, even an ox, had been the victor. However, the "horse-laugh" at John Springs expense was soon suppressed; for as soon as Dart and Lightning began to breathe more freely, it was observed that both of them walked deliberately to the track of the race-ground, and putting their heads to the earth, suddenly raised them again and began to snort. They repeated this till John Spring said,—"These horses have discovered something strange; they suspect foul play. Let me go and talk with Lightning."

He went up to Lightning and took hold of his mane; and Lightning put his nose toward the ground and smelt of the earth without touching it, then reared his head very high, and snorted so loudly that the sound echoed from the next hill. Dart did the same. John Spring stooped down to examine the spot where Lightning had smelled. In a moment he raised himself up, and the countenance of the man was changed. His strength failed him, and he sidled against Lightning.

At length John Spring recovered from his stupor and exclaimed, "It was an ox! I told you it was an ox. No real horse ever yet beat Lightning."

And now, on a close inspection of the black horse's tracks in the path, it was evident to every one that the forefeet of the black horse were cloven. Notwithstanding these appearances, to me it was evident that the strange horse was in reality a horse. Yet when the people left the race-ground, I presume one half of all those present would have testified that a large black ox had distanced two of the fleetest coursers that ever trod the Virginia turf. So uncertain are all things called historical facts.

While I was proceeding to my lodgings, pondering on the events of the day, a stranger rode up to me, and accosted me thus,—""I think your name is Dunwell, sir."

"Yes, sir," I replied.

"Did I not see you a year or two since in Boston, at the Marlborough Hotel?"

"Very likely, sir, for I was there."

"And you heard a story about one Peter Rugg."

"I recollect it all," said I.

"The account you heard in Boston must be true, for here he was to-day. The man has found his way to Virginia, and for aught that appears, has been to Cape Horn. I have seen him before to-day, but never saw him travel with such fearful velocity. Pray, sir, where does Peter Rugg spend his winters, for I have seen him only in summer, and always in foul weather, except this time?"

I replied, "No one knows where Peter Rugg spends his winters; where or when he eats, drinks, sleeps, or lodges. He seems to have an indistinct idea of day and night, time and space, storm and sunshine. His only object is Boston. It appears to me that Rugg's horse has some control of the chair; and that Rugg himself is, in some sort, under the control of his horse."

I then inquired of the stranger where he first saw the man and horse.

"Why, sir," said he, "in the summer of 1824, I travelled to the North for my health; and soon after I saw you at the Marlborough Hotel I returned homeward to Virginia, and, if my memory's correct, I saw this man and horse in every State between here and Massachusetts. Sometimes he would meet me, but oftener overtake me. He never spoke but once, and that once was in Delaware. On his approach he checked his horse with some difficulty. A more beautiful horse I never saw; his hide was as fair and rotund and glossy as the skin of a Congo beauty. When Rugg's horse approached mine he reined in his neck, bent his ears forward until they met, and looked my horse full in the face. My horse immediately withered into half a horse, his hide curling up like a piece of burnt leather; spell-bound, he was fixed to the earth as though a nail had been driven through each hoof.

"'Sir,' said Rugg, 'perhaps you are travelling to Boston; and if so, I should be happy to accompany you, for I have lost my way, and I must reach home to-night. See how sleepy this little girl looks; poor thing, she is a picture of patience.'

"'Sir,' said I, 'it is impossible for you to reach home to-night, for you are in Concord, in the county of Sussex, in the State of Delaware.'

"'What do you mean,' said he, 'by State of Delaware? If I were in Concord, that is only twenty miles from Boston, and my horse Lightfoot could carry me to Charlestown ferry in less than two hours. You mistake, sir; you are a stranger here; this town is nothing like Concord. I am well acquainted with Concord. I went to Concord when I left Boston.'

"'But,' said I, 'you are in Concord, in the State of Delaware.'

"'What do you mean by State?' said Rugg.

"'Why, one of the United States.'

"'States!' said he, in a low voice; 'the man is a wag, and would persuade me I am in Holland.' Then, raising his voice, he said, 'You seem, sir, to be a gentleman, and I entreat you to mislead me not: tell me, quickly, for pity's sake, the right road to Boston, for you see my horse will swallow his bits, he has eaten nothing since I left Concord.'

"'Sir, said I, 'this town is Concord,—Concord in Delaware, not Concord in Massachusetts; and you are now five hundred miles from Boston.'

"Rugg looked at me for a moment, more in sorrow than resentment, and then repeated, 'Five hundred miles! Unhappy man, who would have thought him deranged; but nothing in this world is so deceitful as appearances. Five hundred miles! This beats Connecticut River.'

"What he meant by Connecticut River, I know not; his horse broke away, and Rugg disappeared in a moment."

I explained to the stranger the meaning of Rugg's expression, "Connecticut River," and the incident respecting him that occurred at Hartford, as I stood on the door-stone of Mr. Bennett's excellent hotel. We both agreed that the man we had seen that day was the true Peter Rugg.

Soon after, I saw Rugg again, at the toll-gate on the turnpike between Alexandria and Middleburgh. While I was paying the toll, I observed to the toll-gatherer that the drought was more severe in his vicinity than farther south.

"Yes," said he, "the drought is excessive; but if I had not heard yesterday, by a traveller, that the man with the black horse was seen in Kentucky a day or two since, I should be sure of a shower in a few minutes."

I looked all around the horizon, and could not discern a cloud that could hold a pint of water.

"Look, sir," said the toll-gatherer, "you perceive to the east-ward, just above that hill, a small black cloud not bigger than a blackberry, and while I am speaking it is doubling and trebling itself, and rolling up the turnpike steadily, as if its sole design was to deluge some object."

"True," said I, "I do perceive it; but what connection is there between a thunder-cloud and a man and horse?"

"More than you imagine, or I can tell you; but stop a moment, sir, I may need your assistance. I know that cloud; I have seen it several times before, and can testify to its identity. You will soon see a man and black horse under it."

While he was speaking, true enough, we began to hear the distant thunder, and soon the chain-lightning performed all the figures of a country-dance. About a mile distant we saw the man and black horse under the cloud; but before he arrived at the toll-gate, the thunder-cloud had spent itself, and not even a sprinkle fell near us.

As the man, whom I instantly knew to be Rugg, attempted to pass, the toll-gatherer swung the gate across the road, seized Rugg's horse by the reins, and demanded two dollars.

Feeling some little regard for Rugg, I interfered, and began to question the toll-gatherer, and requested him not to be wroth with the man. The toll-gatherer replied that he had just cause, for the man had run his toll ten times, and moreover that the horse had discharged a cannon-ball at him, to the great danger of his life; that the man had always before approached so rapidly that he was too quick for the rusty hinges of the toll-gate; "but now I will have full satisfaction."

Rugg looked wistfully at me, and said, "I entreat you, sir, to delay me not; I have found at length the direct road to Boston, and shall not reach home before night if you detain me. You see I am dripping wet, and ought to change my clothes."

The toll-gatherer then demanded why he had run his toll so many times.

"Toll! Why," said Rugg, "do you demand toll? There is no toll to pay on the king's highway."

"King's highway! Do you not perceive this is a turnpike?"

"Turnpike! there are no turnpikes in Massachusetts."

"That may be, but we have several in Virginia."

"Virginia! Do you pretend I am in Virginia?"

Rugg, then, appealing to me, asked how far it was to Boston.

Said I, "Mr. Rugg, I perceive you are bewildered, and am sorry to see you so far from home; you are, indeed, in Virginia."

"You know me, then, sir, it seems; and you say I am in Virginia. Give me leave to tell you, sir, you are the most impudent man alive; for I was never forty miles from Boston, and I never saw a Virginian in my life. This beats Delaware!"

"Your toll, sir, your toll!"

"I will not pay you a penny," said Rugg; "you are both of you highway robbers. There are no turnpikes in this country. Take toll on the king's highway! Robbers take toll on the king's highway!" Then in a low tone, he said, "Here is evidently a conspiracy against me; alas, I shall never see Boston! The highways refuse me a passage, the rivers change their courses, and there is no faith in the compass."

But Rugg's horse had no idea of stopping more than one minute; for in the midst of this altercation, the horse, whose nose was resting on the upper bar of the turnpike-gate, seized it between his teeth, lifted it gently off its staples, and trotted off with it. The toll-gatherer, confounded, strained his eyes after his gate.

"Let him go," said I, "the horse will soon drop your gate, and you will get it again."

I then questioned the toll-gatherer respecting his knowledge of this man; and he related the following particulars:—

"The first time," said he, "that man ever passed this toll-gate was in the year 1806, at the moment of the great eclipse. I thought the horse was frightened at the sudden darkness, and concluded he had run away with the man. But within a few days after, the same man and horse repassed with equal speed, without the least respect to the toll-gate or to me, except by a vacant stare. Some few years afterward, during the late war, I saw the same man approaching again, and I resolved to check his career. Accordingly I stepped into the middle of the road, and stretched wide both my arms, and cried, 'Stop, sir, on your peril!' At this the man said, 'Now, Lightfoot, confound the robber!' at the same time he gave the whip liberally to the flank of his horse, which bounded off with such force that it appeared to me two such horses, give them a place to stand, would overcome any check man could devise. An ammunition wagon which had just passed on to Baltimore had dropped an eighteen-pounder in the road; this unlucky ball lay in the way of the horse's heels, and the beast, with the sagacity of a demon, clinched it with one of his heels and hurled it behind him. I feel dizzy in relating the fact, but so nearly did the ball pass my head, that the wind thereof blew off my hat; and the ball embedded itself in that gate-post, as you may see if you will cast your eye on the post. I have permitted it to remain there in memory of the occurrence,—as the people of Boston, I am told, preserve the eighteen-pounder which is now to be seen half imbedded in Brattle Street church."

I then took leave of the toll-gatherer, and promised him if I saw or heard of his gate I would send him notice.

A strong inclination had possessed me to arrest Rugg and search his pockets, thinking great discoveries might be made in the examination; but what I saw and heard that day convinced me that no human force could detain Peter Rugg against his consent. I therefore determined if I ever saw Rugg again to treat him in the gentlest manner.

In pursuing my way to New York, I entered on the turnpike in Trenton; and when I arrived at New Brunswick, I perceived the road was newly macadamized. The small stones had just been laid thereon. As I passed this piece of road, I observed that, at regular distances of about eight feet, the stones were entirely displaced from spots as large as the circumference of a half-bushel measure. This singular appearance induced me to inquire the cause of it at the turnpike-gate.

"Sir," said the toll-gatherer, "I wonder not at the question, but I am unable to give you a satisfactory answer. Indeed, sir, I believe I am bewitched, and that the turnpike is under a spell of enchantment; for what appeared to me last night cannot be a real transaction, otherwise a turnpike-gate is a useless thing."

"I do not believe in witchcraft or enchantment," said I; "and if you will relate circumstantially what happened last night, I will endeavour to account for it by natural means."

"You may recollect the night was uncommonly dark. Well, sir, just after I had closed the gate for the night, down the turnpike, as far as my eye could reach, I beheld what at first appeared to be two armies engaged. The report of the musketry, and the flashes of their firelocks, were incessant and continuous. As this strange spectacle approached me with the fury of a tornado, the noise increased; and the appearance rolled on in one compact body over the surface of the ground. The most splendid fireworks rose out of the earth and encircled this moving spectacle. The divers tints of the rainbow, the most brilliant dyes that the sun lays in the lap of spring, added to the whole family of gems, could not display a more beautiful, radiant, and dazzling spectacle than accompanied the black horse. You would have thought all the stars of heaven had met in merriment on the turnpike. In the midst of this luminous configuration sat a man, distinctly to be seen, in a miserable-looking chair, drawn by a black horse. The turnpike-gate ought, by the laws of Nature and the laws of the State, to have made a wreck of the whole, and dissolved the enchantment; but no, the horse without an effort passed over the gate, and drew the man and chair horizontally after him without touching the bar. This is what I call enchantment. What think you, sir?"

"My friend," said I, "you have grossly magnified a natural occurrence. The man was Peter Rugg, on his way to Boston. It is true, his horse travelled with unequalled speed, but as he reared high his forefeet, he could not help displacing the thousand small stones on which he trod, which flying in all directions struck one another, and resounded and scintillated. The top bar of your gate is not more than two feet from the ground, and Rugg's horse at every vault could easily lift the carriage over that gate."

This satisfied Mr. McDoubt, and I was pleased at that occurrence; for otherwise Mr. McDoubt, who is a worthy man, late from the Highlands, might have added to his calendar of superstitions. Having thus disenchanted the macadamized road and the turnpike-gate, and also Mr. McDoubt, I pursued my journey homeward to New York.

Little did I expect to see or hear anything further of Mr. Rugg, for he was now more than twelve hours in advance of me. I could hear nothing of him on my way to Elizabethtown, and therefore concluded that during the past night he had turned off from the turnpike and pursued a westerly direction; but just before I arrived at Powles's Hook, I observed a considerable collection of passengers in the ferry-boat, all standing motionless, and steadily looking at the same object. One of the ferrymen, Mr. Hardy, who knew me well, observing my approach delayed a minute, in order to afford me a passage, and coming up, said, "Mr. Dunwell, we have a curiosity on board that would puzzle Dr. Mitchell."

"Some strange fish, I suppose, has found its way into the Hudson."

"No," said he, "it is a man who looks as if he had lain hidden in the ark, and had just now ventured out. He has a little girl with him, the counterpart of himself, and the finest horse you ever saw, harnessed to the queerest-looking carriage that ever was made."

"Ah, Mr. Hardy," said I, "you have, indeed, hooked a prize; no one before you could ever detain Peter Rugg long enough to examine him."

"Do you know the man?" said Mr. Hardy.

"No, nobody knows him, but everybody has seen him. Detain him as long as possible; delay the boat under any pretence, cut the gear of the horse, do anything to detain him."

As I entered the ferry-boat, I was struck at the spectacle before me. There, indeed, sat Peter Rugg and Jenny Rugg in the chair, and there stood the black horse, all as quiet as lambs, surrounded by more than fifty men and women, who seemed to have lost all their senses but one. Not a motion, not a breath, not a nestle. They were all eye. Rugg appeared to them to be a man not of this world; and they appeared to Rugg a strange generation of men. Rugg spoke not, and they spoke not: nor was I disposed to disturb the calm, satisfied to reconnoitre Rugg in a state of rest. Presently, Rugg observed in a low voice, addressed to nobody, "A new contrivance, horses instead of oars; Boston folks are full of notions."

It was plain that Rugg was of Dutch extraction. He had on three pairs of small-clothes, called in former days of simplicity breeches, not much the worse for wear; but time had proved the fabric, and shrunk one more than another, so that they showed at the knees their different qualities and colours. His several waistcoats, the flaps of which rested on his knees, made him appear rather corpulent. His capacious drab coat would supply the stuff for half a dozen modern ones; the sleeves were like meal bags, in the cuffs of which you might nurse a child to sleep. His hat, probably once black, now of a tan colour, was neither round nor crooked, but in shape much like the one President Monroe wore on his late tour. This dress gave the rotund face of Rugg an antiquated dignity. The man, though deeply sunburned, did not appear to be more than thirty years of age. He had lost his sad and anxious look, was quite composed, and seemed happy. The chair in which Rugg sat was very capacious, evidently made for service, and calculated to last for ages; the timber would supply material for three modern carriages. This chair, like a Nantucket coach, would answer for everything that ever went on wheels. The horse, too, was an object of curiosity; his majestic height, his natural mane and tail, gave him a commanding appearance, and his large open nostrils indicated inexhaustible wind. It was apparent that the hoofs of his forefeet had been split, probably on some newly macadamized road, and were now growing together again; so that John Spring was not altogether in the wrong.

How long this dumb scene would otherwise have continued I cannot tell. Rugg discovered no sign of impatience. But Rugg's horse having been quiet more than five minutes, had no idea of standing idle; he began to whinny, and in a moment after, with his right forefoot he started a plank. Said Rugg, "My horse is impatient, he sees the North End. You must be quick, or he will be ungovernable."

At these words, the horse raised his left forefoot; and when he laid it down every inch of the ferry-boat trembled. Two men immediately seized Rugg's horse by the nostrils. The horse nodded, and both of them were in the Hudson. While we were fishing up the men, the horse was perfectly quiet.

"Fret not the horse," said Rugg, "and he will do no harm. He is only anxious, like myself, to arrive at yonder beautiful shore; he sees the North Church, and smells his own stable."

"Sir," said I to Rugg, practising a little deception, "pray tell me, for I am a stranger here, what river is this, and what city is that opposite, for you seem to be an inhabitant of it?"

"This river, sir, is called Mystic River, and this is Winnisimmet ferry,—we have retained the Indian names,—and that town is Boston. You must, indeed, be a stranger in these parts, not to know that yonder is Boston, the capital of the New England provinces."

"Pray, sir, how long have you been absent from Boston?"

"Why, that I cannot exactly tell. I lately went with this little girl of mine to Concord, to see my friends; and I am ashamed to tell you, in returning lost the way, and have been travelling ever since. No one would direct me right. It is cruel to mislead a traveller. My horse, Lightfoot, has boxed the compass; and it seems to me he has boxed it back again. But, sir, you perceive my horse is uneasy; Lightfoot, as yet, has only given a hint and a nod. I cannot be answerable for his heels."

At these words Lightfoot reared his long tail, and snapped it as you would a whiplash. The Hudson reverberated with the sound. Instantly the six horses began to move the boat. The Hudson was a sea of glass, smooth as oil, not a ripple. The horses, from a smart trot, soon pressed into a gallop; water now ran over the gunwale; the ferry-boat was soon buried in an ocean of foam, and the noise of the spray was like the roaring of many waters. When we arrived at New York, you might see the beautiful white wake of the ferry-boat across the Hudson.

Though Rugg refused to pay toll at turnpikes, when Mr. Hardy reached his hand for the ferriage, Rugg readily put his hand into one of his many pockets, took out a piece of silver, and handed it to Mr. Hardy.

"What is this?" said Mr. Hardy.

"It is thirty shillings," said Rugg.

"It might once have been thirty shillings, old tenor," said Mr. Hardy, "but it is not at present."

"The money is good English coin," said Rugg; "my grandfather brought a bag of them from England, and had them hot from the mint."

Hearing this, I approached near to Rugg, and asked permission to see the coin. It was a half-crown, coined by the English Parliament, dated in the year 1649. On one side, "The Commonwealth of England, "and St. George's cross encircled with a wreath of laurel. On the other, "God with us," and a harp and St. George's cross united. I winked at Mr. Hardy, and pronounced it good current money; and said loudly, "I will not permit the gentleman to be imposed on, for I will exchange the money myself."

On this, Rugg spoke,— "Please to give me your name, sir."

"My name is Dunwell, sir," I replied.

"Mr. Dunwell," said Rugg, "you are the only honest man I have seen since I left Boston. As you are a stranger here, my house is your home; Dame Rugg will be happy to see her husband's friend. Step into my chair, sir, there is room enough; move a little, Jenny, for the gentleman, and we will be in Middle Street in a minute."

Accordingly I took a seat by Peter Rugg.

"Were you never in Boston before?" said Rugg.

"No," said I.

"Well, you will now see the queen of New England, a town second only to Philadelphia, in all North America.

"You forget New York," said I.

"Poh, New York is nothing; though I never was there, I am told you might put all New York in our mill-pond. No, sir. New York, I assure you, is but a sorry affair; no more to be compared with Boston than a wigwam with a palace."

As Rugg's horse turned into Pearl Street, I looked Rugg as fully in the face as good manners would allow, and said, "Sir, if this is Boston, I acknowledge New York is not worthy to be one of its suburbs."

Before we had proceeded far in Pearl Street, Rugg's countenance changed: his nerves began to twitch; his eyes trembled in their sockets; he was evidently bewildered. "What is the matter, Mr. Rugg? you seem disturbed."

"This surpasses all human comprehension; if you know, sir, where we are, I beseech you to tell me."

"If this place," I replied, "is not Boston, it must be New York."

"No, sir, it is not Boston; nor can it be New York. How could I be in New York, which is nearly two hundred miles from Boston?"

By this time we had passed into Broadway, and then Rugg, in truth, discovered a chaotic mind. "There is no such place as this in North America. This is all the effect of enchantment; this is a grand delusion, nothing real. Here is seemingly a great city, magnificent houses, shops and goods, men and women innumerable, and as busy as in real life, all sprung up in one night from the wilderness; or what is more probable, some tremendous convulsion of Nature has thrown London or Amsterdam on the shores of New England. Or, possibly, I may be dreaming, though the night seems rather long; but before now I have sailed in one night to Amsterdam, bought goods of Vandogger, and returned to Boston before morning."

At this moment a hue-and-cry was heard, "Stop the madmen, they will endanger the lives of thousands!" In vain hundreds attempted to stop Rugg's horse. Lightfoot interfered with nothing; his course was straight as a shooting-star. But on my part, fearful that before night I should find myself behind the Alleghanies, I addressed Mr. Rugg in a tone of entreaty, and requested him to restrain the horse and permit me to alight.

"My friend," said he, "we shall be in Boston before dark, and Dame Rugg will be most exceedingly glad to see us."

"Mr. Rugg," said I, "you must excuse me. Pray look to the west; see that thunder-cloud swelling with rage, as if in pursuit of us."

"Ah," said Rugg, "it is in vain to attempt to escape. I know that cloud; it is collecting new wrath to spend on my head." Then checking his horse, he permitted me to descend, saying, "Farewell, Mr. Dunwell, I shall be happy to see you in Boston; I live in Middle Street."

It is uncertain in what direction Mr. Rugg pursued his course, after he disappeared in Broadway; but one thing is sufficiently known to everybody,—that in the course of two months after he was seen in New York, he found his way most opportunely to Boston.

It seems the estate of Peter Rugg had recently fallen to the Commonwealth of Massachusetts for want of heirs; and the Legislature had ordered the solicitor-general to advertise and sell it at public auction. Happening to be in Boston at the time, and observing his advertisement, which described a considerable extent of land, I felt a kindly curiosity to see the spot where Rugg once lived. Taking the advertisement in my hand, I wandered a little way down Middle Street, and without asking a question of any one, when I came to a certain spot I said to myself, "This is Rugg's estate; I will proceed no farther. This must be the spot; it is a counterpart of Peter Rugg." The premises, indeed, looked as if they had fulfilled a sad prophecy. Fronting on Middle Street, they extended in the rear to Ann Street, and embraced about half an acre of land. It was not uncommon in former times to have half an acre for a house-lot; for an acre of land then, in many parts of Boston, was not more valuable than a foot in some places at present. The old mansion-house had become a powder-post, and been blown away. One other building, uninhabited, stood ominous, courting dilapidation. The street had been so much raised that the bed-chamber had descended to the kitchen and was level with the street. The house seemed conscious of its fate; and as though tired of standing there, the front was fast retreating from the rear, and waiting the next south wind to project itself into the street. If the most wary animals had sought a place of refuge, here they would have rendezvoused. Here, under the ridge-pole, the crow would have perched in security; and in the recesses below, you might have caught the fox and the weasel asleep. "The hand of destiny," said I, "has pressed heavy on this spot; still heavier on the former owners. Strange that so large a lot of land as this should want an heir! Yet Peter Rugg, at this day, might pass by his own door-stone, and ask, 'Who once lived here?'"

The auctioneer, appointed by the solicitor to sell this estate, was a man of eloquence, as many of the auctioneers of Boston are. The occasion seemed to warrant, and his duty urged, him to make a display. He addressed his audience as follows,—

"The estate, gentlemen, which we offer you this day, was once the property of a family now extinct. For that reason it has escheated to the

Commonwealth. Lest any one of you should be deterred from bidding on so large an estate as this for fear of a disputed title, I am authorized by the solicitor-general to proclaim that the purchaser shall have the best of all titles,—a warranty-deed from the Commonwealth. I state this, gentlemen, because I know there is an idle rumour in this vicinity, that one Peter Rugg, the original owner of this estate, is still living. This rumour, gentlemen, has no foundation, and can have no foundation in the nature of things. It originated about two years since, from the incredible story of one Jonathan Dunwell, of New York. Mrs. Croft, indeed, whose husband I see present, and whose mouth waters for this estate, has countenanced this fiction. But, gentlemen, was it ever known that any estate, especially an estate of this value, lay unclaimed for nearly half a century, if any heir, ever so remote, were existing? For, gentlemen, all agree that old Peter Rugg, if living, would be at least one hundred years of age. It is said that he and his daughter, with a horse and chaise, were missed more than half a century ago; and because they never returned home, forsooth, they must be now living, and will some day come and claim this great estate. Such logic, gentlemen, never led to a good investment. Let not this idle story cross the noble purpose of consigning these ruins to the genius of architecture. If such a contingency could check the spirit of enterprise, farewell to all mercantile excitement. Your surplus money, instead of refreshing your sleep with the golden dreams of new sources of speculation, would turn to the nightmare. A man's money, if not employed, serves only to disturb his rest. Look, then, to the prospect before you. Here is half an acre of land,—more than twenty thousand square feet,—a corner lot, with wonderful capabilities; none of your contracted lots of forty feet by fifty, where in dog-days, you can breathe only through your scuttles. On the contrary, an architect cannot contemplate this lot of land without rapture, for here is room enough for his genius to shame the temple of Solomon. Then the prospect—how commanding! To the east, so near to the Atlantic that Neptune, freighted with the select treasures of the whole earth, can knock at your door with his trident. From the west, the produce of the river of Paradise—the Connecticut—will soon, by the blessings of steam, railways, and canals pass under your windows; and thus, on this spot, Neptune shall marry Ceres, and Pomona from Roxbury, and Flora from Cambridge, shall dance at the wedding.

"Gentlemen of science, men of taste, ye of the literary emporium,—for I perceive many of you present—to you this holy ground. If the spot on which in times past a hero left only the print of a footstep is now sacred, of what price is the birthplace of one who all the world knows was born in Middle Street, directly opposite to this lot; and who, if his birthplace were not well known, would now be claimed by more than seven cities. To you, then, the value of these premises must be inestimable. For ere long there will arise in full view of the edifice to be erected here, a monument, the wonder and veneration of the world. A column shall spring to the clouds; and on that column will be engraven one word which will convey all that is wise in intellect, useful in science, good in morals, prudent in counsel, and benevolent in principle,—a name of one who, when living, was the patron of the poor, the delight of the cottage, and the admiration of kings; now dead, worth the whole seven wise men of Greece. Need I tell you his name? He fixed the thunder and guided the lightning.

"Men of the North End! Need I appeal to your patriotism, in order to enhance the value of this lot? The earth affords no such scenery as this; there, around that corner, lived James Otis; here, Samuel Adams; there, Joseph Warren; and around that other corner, Josiah Quincy. Here was the birthplace of Freedom; here Liberty was born, and nursed, and grew to manhood. Here man was newly created. Here is the nursery of American Independence—I am too modest—here began the emancipation of the world; a thousand generations hence millions of men will cross the Atlantic just to look at the north end of Boston. Your fathers—what do I say—yourselves,—yes, this moment, I behold several attending this auction who lent a hand to rock the cradle of Independence.

"Men of speculation,—ye who are deaf to everything except the sound of money,—you, I know, will give me both of your ears when I tell you the city of Boston must have a piece of this estate in order to widen Ann Street. Do you hear me,—do you all hear me? I say the city must have a large piece of this land in order to widen Ann Street. What a chance! The city scorns to take a man's land for nothing. If it seizes your property, it is generous beyond the dreams of avarice. The only oppression is, you are in danger of being smothered under a load of wealth. Witness the old lady who lately died of a broken heart when the mayor paid her for a piece of her kitchen-garden. All the faculty agreed that the sight of the treasure, which the mayor incautiously paid her in dazzling dollars, warm from the mint, sped joyfully all the blood of her body into her heart, and rent it with raptures. Therefore, let him who purchases this estate fear his good fortune, and not Peter Rugg. Bid, then, liberally, and do not let the name of Rugg damp your ardor. How much will you give per foot for this estate?"

Thus spoke the auctioneer, and gracefully waved his ivory hammer. From fifty to seventy-five cents per foot were offered in a few moments. The bidding labored from seventy-five to ninety. At length one dollar was offered. The auctioneer seemed satisfied; and looking at his watch, said he would knock off the estate in five minutes, if no one offered more.

There was a deep silence during this short period. While the hammer was suspended, a strange rumbling noise was heard, which arrested the attention of every one. Presently, it was like the sound of many shipwrights driving home the bolts of a seventy-four. As the sound approached nearer, some exclaimed, "The buildings in the new market are falling in promiscuous ruins." Others said, "No, it is an earthquake; we perceive the earth tremble." Others said, "Not so; the sounds proceeds from Hanover Street, and approaches nearer;" and this proved true, for presently Peter Rugg was in the midst of us.

"Alas, Jenny," said Peter, "I am ruined; our house has been burned, and here are all our neighbors around the ruins. Heaven grant your mother, Dame Rugg, is safe."

"They don't look like our neighbors," said Jenny; "but sure enough our house is burned, and nothing left but the door-stone and an old cedar post. Do ask where mother is."

In the mean time more than a thousand men had surrounded Rugg and his horse and chair. Yet neither Rugg personally, nor his horse and carriage, attracted more attention than the auctioneer. The confident look and searching eyes of Rugg carried more conviction to every one present that the estate was his, than could any parchment or paper with signature and seal. The impression which the auctioneer had just made on the company was effaced in a moment; and although the latter words of the auctioneer were, "Fear not Peter Rugg," the moment the auctioneer met the eye of Rugg his occupation was gone; his arm fell down to his hips, his late lively hammer hung heavy in his hand, and the auction was forgotten. The black horse, too, gave his evidence. He knew his journey was ended; for he stretched himself into a horse and a half, rested his head over the cedar post, and whinnied thrice, causing his harness to tremble from headstall to crupper.

Rugg then stood upright in his chair, and asked with some authority, "Who has demolished my house in my absence, for I see no signs of conflagration? I demand by what accident this has happened, and wherefore this collection of strange people has assembled before my doorstep. I thought I knew every man in Boston, but you appear to me a new generation of men. Yet I am familiar with many of the countenances here present, and I can call some of you by name; but in truth I do not recollect that before this moment I ever saw any of you. There, I am certain, is a Winslow, and here a Sargent; there stands a Sewall, and next to him a Dudley. Will none of you speak to me,—or is this all a delusion? I see, indeed, many forms of men, and no want of eyes, but of motion, speech, and hearing, you seem to be destitute. Strange! Will no one inform me who has demolished my house?"

Then spake a voice from the crowd, but whence it came I could not discern: "There is nothing strange here but yourself, Mr. Rugg. Time, which destroys and renews all things, has dilapidated your house, and placed us here. You have suffered many years under an illusion. The tempest which you profanely defied at Menotomy has at length subsided; but you will never see home, for your house and wife and neighbors have all disappeared. Your estate, indeed, remains, but no home. You were cut off from the last age, and you can never be fitted to the present. Your home is gone, and you can never have another home in this world."

NATHANIEL HAWTHORNE
(1804–1864)

Long recognized as our earliest master of the short story and the "romance" (as distinct from the "novel"), Nathaniel Hawthorne endured, in fact, a long, humbling apprenticeship, with numerous false starts, before the publication, in 1837, of Twice-Told Tales. *Prolific out of necessity ("when a man has taken upon himself to beget children, he has no longer any right to a life of his own"), Hawthorne wrote with astonishing swiftness, as the dates of his work suggest:* Mosses from an Old Manse *(1846);* The Scarlet Letter *(1850);* The House of the Seven Gables *(1851);* The Blithedale Romance *(1852);* Tanglewood Tales *(1853);* The Marble Faun *(1860);* Our Old Home *(1863). His work is uniquely his: Gothic in tone and structure, mordantly analytical in narration, infused with a sense of life's profound and ironic mystery, and the tenuous place within it of human conscience. "The Wives of the Dead," the reader will note, is an unusual story for Hawthorne: its dreams entirely plausible, its plot neither fanciful nor strained. The dream as wish-fulfillment! Has anyone ever dramatized this melancholy fact of life with greater poignancy?*

Born on July 4, 1804, in Salem, Massachusetts, Hawthorne was a descendant of Puritan immigrants and the great-grandson of a judge who condemned men and women to death in the notorious Salem witchcraft trials. Through his writing career, Hawthorne considered the weight of history as it presses upon the present; his genius is for the examination of the individual in isolation, in uncertain relationships with other people, and with a Higher Power. A more relaxed Hawthornian voice, unprogrammatic, even, at times, colloquial, is revealed in the marvelous, posthumously published American Notebooks.

The Wives of the Dead

The following story, the simple and domestic incidents of which may be deemed scarcely worth relating, after such a lapse of time, awakened some degree of interest, a hundred years ago, in a principal seaport of the Bay Province. The rainy twilight of an autumn day,—a parlor on the second floor of a small house, plainly furnished, as beseemed the middling circumstances of its inhabitants, yet decorated with little curiosities from beyond the sea, and a few delicate specimens of Indian manufacture,—these are the only particulars to be premised in regard to scene and season. Two young and comely women sat together by the fireside, nursing their mutual and peculiar sorrows. They were the recent brides of two brothers, a sailor and a landsman, and two successive days had brought tidings of the death of each, by the chances of Canadian warfare, and the tempestuous Atlantic. The universal sympathy excited by this bereavement drew numerous condoling guests to the habitation of the widowed sisters. Several, among whom was the minister, had remained till the verge of evening; when, one by one, whispering many comfortable passages of Scripture, that were answered by more abundant tears, they took their leave, and departed to their own happier homes. The mourners, though not insensible to the kindness of their friends, had yearned to be left alone. United, as they had been, by the relationship of the living, and now more closely so by that of the dead, each felt as if whatever consolation her grief admitted were to be found in the bosom of the other. They joined their hearts, and wept together silently. But after an hour of such indulgence, one of the sisters, all of whose emotions were influenced by her mild, quiet, yet not feeble character, began to recollect the precepts of resignation and endurance which piety had taught her, when she did not think to need them. Her misfortune, besides, as earliest known, should earliest cease to interfere with her regular course of duties; accordingly, having placed the table before the fire, and arranged a frugal meal, she took the hand of her companion.

"Come, dearest sister; you have eaten not a morsel to-day," she said. "Arise, I pray you, and let us ask a blessing on that which is provided for us."

Her sister-in-law was of a lively and irritable temperament, and the first pangs of her sorrow had been expressed by shrieks and passionate lamentation. She now shrunk from Mary's words, like a wounded sufferer from a hand that revives the throb.

"There is no blessing left for me, neither will I ask it!" cried Margaret, with a fresh burst of tears. "Would it were His will that I might never taste food more!"

Yet she trembled at these rebellious expressions, almost as soon as they were uttered, and, by degrees, Mary succeeded in bringing her sister's mind nearer to the situation of her own. Time went on, and their usual hour of repose arrived. The brothers and their brides, entering the married state with no more than the slender means which then sanctioned such a step, had confederated themselves in one household, with equal rights to the parlor, and claiming exclusive privileges in two sleeping rooms contiguous to it. Thither the widowed ones retired, after heaping ashes upon the dying embers of their fire, and placing a lighted lamp upon the hearth. The doors of both chambers were left open, so that a part of the interior of each, and the beds with their unclosed curtains, were reciprocally visible. Sleep did not steal upon the sisters at one and the same time. Mary experienced the effect often consequent upon grief quietly borne, and soon sunk into temporary forgetfulness, while Margaret became more disturbed and feverish, in proportion as the night advanced with its deepest and stillest hours. She lay listening to the drops of rain, that came down in monotonous succession, unswayed by a breath of wind; and a nervous impulse continually caused her to lift her head from the pillow, and gaze into Mary's chamber and the intermediate apartment. The cold light of the lamp threw the shadows of the furniture up against the wall, stamping them immovably there, except when they were shaken by a sudden flicker of the flame. Two vacant arm-chairs were in their old positions on opposite sides of the hearth, where the brothers had been wont to sit in young and laughing dignity, as heads of families; two humbler seats were near them, the true thrones of that little empire, where Mary and herself had exercised in love a power that love had won. The cheerful radiance of the fire had shone upon the happy circle, and the dead glimmer of the lamp might have befitted their reunion now. While Margaret groaned in bitterness, she heard a knock at the street-door.

"How would my heart have leapt at that sound but yesterday!" thought she, remembering the anxiety with which she had long awaited tidings from her husband. "I care not for it now; let them begone, for I will not arise."

But even while a sort of childish fretfulness made her thus resolve, she was breathing hurriedly, and straining her ears to catch a repetition of the summons. It is difficult to be convinced of the death of one whom we have deemed another self. The knocking was now renewed in slow and regular strokes, apparently given with the soft end of a doubled fist, and was accompanied by words, faintly heard through several thicknesses of wall. Margaret looked to her sister's chamber, and beheld her still lying in the depths of sleep. She arose, placed her foot upon the floor, and slightly arrayed herself, trembling between fear and eagerness as she did so.

"Heaven help me!" sighed she. "I have nothing left to fear, and me thinks I am ten times more a coward than ever."

Seizing the lamp from the hearth, she hastened to the window that overlooked the street-door. It was a lattice, turning upon hinges; and having thrown it back, she stretched her head a little way into the moist atmosphere. A lantern was reddening the front of the house, and melting its light in the neighboring puddles, while a deluge of darkness overwhelmed every other object. As the window grated on its hinges, a man in a broad-brimmed hat and blanket-coat stepped from under the shelter of the projecting story, and looked upward to discover whom his application had aroused. Margaret knew him as a friendly innkeeper of the town.

"What would you have, Goodman Parker?" cried the widow.

"Lack-a-day, is it you, Mistress Margaret?" replied the innkeeper. "I was afraid it might be your sister Mary; for I hate to see a young woman in trouble, when I have n't a word of comfort to whisper to her."

"For Heaven's sake, what news do you bring?" screamed Margaret.

"Why, there has been an express through the town within this half-hour," said Goodman Parker, "travelling from the eastern jurisdiction with letters from the governor and council. He tarried at my house to refresh himself with a drop and a morsel, and I asked him what tidings on the frontiers. He tells me we had the better in the skirmish you wot of, and that thirteen men reported slain are well and sound, and your husband among them. Besides, he is appointed of the escort to bring the captivated Frenchers and Indians home to the province jail. I judged you wouldn't mind being broke of your rest, and so I stepped over to tell you. Good-night."

So saying, the honest man departed; and his lantern gleamed along the street, bringing to view indistinct shapes of things, and the fragments of a world, like order glimmering through chaos, or memory roaming over the past. But Margaret staid not to watch these picturesque effects. Joy flashed into her heart, and lighted it up at once; and breathless, and with winged steps, she flew to the bedside of her sister. She paused, however, at the door of the chamber, while a thought of pain broke in upon her.

"Poor Mary!" said she to herself. "Shall I waken her, to feel her sorrow sharpened by my happiness? No; I will keep it within my own bosom till the morrow."

She approached the bed, to discover if Mary's sleep were peaceful. Her face was turned partly inward to the pillow, and had been hidden there to weep; but a look of motionless contentment was now visible upon it, as if her heart, like a deep lake, had grown calm because its dead had sunk down so far within. Happy is it, and strange, that the lighter sorrows are those from which dreams are chiefly fabricated. Margaret shrunk from disturbing her sister-in-law, and felt as if her own better fortune had rendered her involuntarily unfaithful, and as if altered and diminished affection must be the consequence of the disclosure she had to make. With a sudden step, she turned away. But joy could not long be repressed, even by circumstances that would have excited heavy grief at another moment. Her mind was thronged with delightful thoughts, till sleep stole on, and transformed them to visions, more delightful and more wild, like the breath of winter (but what a cold comparison!) working fantastic tracery upon a window.

When the night was far advanced, Mary awoke with a sudden start. A vivid dream had latterly involved her in its unreal life, of which, however, she could only remember that it had been broken in upon at the most interesting point. For a little time, slumber hung about her like a morning mist, hindering her from perceiving the distinct outline of her situation.

She listened with imperfect consciousness to two or three volleys of a rapid and eager knocking; and first she deemed the noise a matter of course, like the breath she drew; next, it appeared a thing in which she had no concern; and lastly, she became aware that it was a summons necessary to be obeyed. At the same moment, the pang of recollection darted into her mind; the pall of sleep was thrown back from the face of grief; the dim light of the chamber, and the objects therein revealed, had retained all her suspended ideas, and restored them as soon as she unclosed her eyes. Again there was a quick peal upon the street-door. Fearing that her sister would also be disturbed, Mary wrapped herself in a cloak and hood, took the lamp from the hearth, and hastened to the window. By some accident, it had been left unhasped, and yielded easily to her hand.

"Who's there?" asked Mary, trembling as she looked forth.

The storm was over, and the moon was up; it shone upon broken clouds above, and below upon houses black with moisture, and upon little lakes of the fallen rain, curling into silver beneath the quick enchantment of a breeze. A young man in a sailor's dress, wet as if he had come out of the depths of the sea, stood alone under the window. Mary recognized him as one whose livelihood was gained by short voyages along the coast; nor did she forget that, previous to her marriage, he had been an unsuccessful wooer of her own.

"What do you seek here, Stephen?" said she.

"Cheer up, Mary, for I seek to comfort you," answered the rejected lover. "You must know I got home not ten minutes ago, and the first thing my good mother told me was the news about your husband. So, without saying a word to the old woman, I clapped on my hat, and ran out of the house. I could n't have slept a wink before speaking to you, Mary, for the sake of old times.

"Stephen, I thought better of you!" exclaimed the widow, with gushing tears, and preparing to close the lattice; for she was no whit inclined to imitate the first wife of Zadig.

"But stop, and hear my story out," cried the young sailor. "I tell you we spoke a brig yesterday afternoon, bound in from Old England. And who do you think I saw standing on deck, well and hearty, only a bit thinner than he was five months ago?"

Mary leaned from the window, but could not speak.

"Why, it was your husband himself," continued the generous seaman. "He and three others saved themselves on a spar, when the Blessing turned bottom upwards. The brig will beat into the bay by daylight, with this wind, and you'll see him here to-morrow. There's the comfort I bring you, Mary, and so good-night."

He hurried away, while Mary watched him with a doubt of waking reality, that seemed stronger or weaker as he alternately entered the shade of the houses, or emerged into the broad streaks of moonlight. Gradually, however, a blessed flood of conviction swelled into her heart, in strength enough to overwhelm her, had its increase been more abrupt. Her first impulse was to rouse her sister-in-law, and communicate the new-born gladness. She opened the chamber-door, which had been closed in the course of the night, though not latched, advanced to the bedside, and was about to lay her hand upon the slumberer's shoulder. But then she remembered that Margaret would awake to thoughts of death and woe, rendered not the less bitter by their contrast with her own felicity. She suffered the rays of the lamp to fall upon the unconscious form of the bereaved one. Margaret lay in unquiet sleep, and the drapery was displaced around her; her young cheek was rosy-tinted, and her lips half opened in a vivid smile; an expression of joy, debarred its passage by her sealed eyelids, struggled forth like incense from the whole countenance.

"My poor sister! you will waken too soon from that happy dream," thought Mary.

Before retiring, she set down the lamp, and endeavored to arrange the bed-clothes so that the chill air might not do harm to the feverish slumberer. But her hand trembled against Margaret's neck, a tear also fell upon her cheek, and she suddenly awoke.

EDGAR ALLAN POE
(1809–1849)

Though "The Raven" (1845) brought Edgar Allan Poe international fame, and poems like "Ulalume" and "The Bells" assured that fame, Poe's experience as a professional writer in mid-nineteenth-century America was as bitter and demoralizing as Melville's; and, in personal terms, yet more nightmarish. Orphaned at three, abandoned by the well-to-do Richmond merchant who adopted him, prone to illness, mental instability, and alcoholism through his short life, and, after his death, vilified by his very biographer, Poe has come to typify, in lurid excess, the fate of the imaginative genius who is forced to sell himself in the marketplace and to wear himself out tragically in the effort. Though his work is never autobiographical in any overt way, just as it is never "realistic," Poe's images and melodramatic Gothic plots seem but the reasonable analogues of his experience.

Except for The Raven and Other Poems *(1845), Poe's published works—* Tamerlane and Other Poems *(1827),* The Narrative of A. Gordon Pym *(1838),* Tales of the Grotesque and Arabesque *(1840),* Eureka *(1848)—brought in little income. The "Edgar Allan Poe" celebrated by contemporary critics is in fact a Poe distilled and heightened by foreign men of letters as diverse as Charles Baudelaire and Stéphane Mallarmé on the one hand and August Strindberg and George Bernard Shaw on the other: Poe as genius, not as frenzied hack writer. The value of Poe's best work for other writers lies in his bold use of surreal dream-images, the drama of his various deranged voices, the fluidity of his plots. "The Tell-Tale Heart" is at the very core of Poe: unhampered by the writerly turgidity of certain of his other stories, utterly convincing in its pathology, and in its obvious zest in its pathology. So much, so swiftly; this is genius.*

The Tell-Tale Heart

True!—nervous—very, very dreadfully nervous I had been and am; but why *will* you say that I am mad? The disease had sharpened my senses—not destroyed—not dulled them. Above all was the sense of hearing acute. I heard all things in the heaven and in the earth. I heard many things in hell. How, then, am I mad? Hearken! and observe how healthily—how calmly I can tell you the whole story.

It is impossible to say how first the idea entered my brain; but once conceived, it haunted me day and night. Object there was none. Passion there was none. I loved the old man. He had never wronged me. He had never given me insult. For his gold I had no desire. I think it was his eye! yes, it was this! One of his eyes resembled that of a vulture—a pale blue eye, with a film over it. Whenever it fell upon me, my blood ran cold; and so by degrees—very gradually—I made up my mind to take the life of the old man, and thus rid myself of the eye forever.

Now this is the point. You fancy me mad. Madmen know nothing. But you should have seen *me*. You should have seen how wisely I proceeded—with what caution—with what foresight—with what dissimulation I went to work! I was never kinder to the old man than during the whole week before I killed him. And every night, about midnight, I turned the latch of his door and opened it—oh, so gently! And then, when I had made an opening sufficient for my head, I put in a dark lantern, all closed, closed, so that no light shone out, and then I thrust in my head. Oh, you would have laughed to see how cunningly I thrust it in! I moved it slowly—very, very slowly, so that I might not disturb the old man's sleep. It took me an hour to place my whole head within the opening so far that I could see him as he lay upon his bed. Ha!—would a madman have been so wise as this? And then, when my head was well in the room, I undid the lantern cautiously—oh, so cautiously—cautiously (for the hinges creaked)—I undid it just so much that a single thin ray fell upon the vulture eye. And this I did for seven long nights—every night just at midnight—but I found the eye always closed; and so it was impossible to do the work; for it was not the old man who vexed me, but his Evil Eye. And every morning, when the day broke, I went boldly into the chamber, and spoke courageously to him, calling him by name in a hearty tone, and inquiring how he had passed the night. So you see he would have been a very profound old man, indeed, to suspect that every night, just at twelve, I looked in upon him while he slept.

Upon the eighth night I was more than usually cautious in opening the door. A watch's minute hand moves more quickly than did mine. Never before that night had I *felt* the extent of my own powers—of my sagacity. I could scarcely contain my feelings of triumph. To think that there I was, opening the door, little by little, and he not even to dream of my secret deeds or thoughts. I fairly chuckled at the idea; and perhaps he heard me, for he moved on the bed suddenly, as if startled. Now you may think that I drew back—but no. His room was as black as pitch with the thick darkness (for the shutters were close fastened, through fear of robbers), and so I knew that he could not see the opening of the door, and I kept pushing it on steadily, steadily.

I had my head in, and was about to open the lantern, when my thumb slipped upon the tin fastening, and the old man sprang up in the bed, crying out—"Who's there?"

I kept quite still and said nothing. For a whole hour I did not move a muscle, and in the meantime I did not hear him lie down. He was still sitting up in the bed, listening;—just as I have done, night after night, hearkening to the death watches in the wall.

Presently I heard a slight groan, and I knew it was the groan of mortal terror. It was not a groan of pain or of grief—oh, no!—it was the low stifled sound that arises from the bottom of the soul when overcharged with awe. I knew the sound well. Many a night, just at midnight, when all the world slept, it has welled up from my own bosom, deepening, with its dreadful echo, the terrors that distracted me. I say I knew it well. I knew what the old man felt, and pitied him, although I chuckled at heart. I knew that he had been lying awake ever since the first slight noise, when he had turned in the bed. His fears had been ever since growing upon him. He had been trying to fancy them causeless, but could not. He had been saying to himself—"It is nothing but the wind in the chimney—it is only a mouse crossing the floor," or "it is merely a cricket which has made a single chirp." Yes, he had been trying to comfort himself with these suppositions; but he had found all in vain. *All in vain;* because Death, in approaching him, had stalked with his black shadow before him, and enveloped the victim. And it was the mournful influence of the unperceived shadow that caused him to feel—although he neither saw nor heard—to *feel* the presence of my head within the room.

When I had waited a long time, very patiently, without hearing him lie down, I resolved to open a little—a very, very little crevice in the lantern. So I opened it—you cannot imagine how stealthily, stealthily—until, at length, a single dim ray, like the thread of the spider, shot from out the crevice and fell upon the vulture eye.

It was open—wide, wide open—and I grew furious as I gazed upon it. I saw it with perfect distinctness—all a dull blue, with a hideous veil over it that chilled the very marrow in my bones; but I could see nothing else of the old man's face or person; for I had directed the ray as if by instinct, precisely upon the damned spot.

And now have I not told you that what you mistake for madness is but over-acuteness of the senses?—now, I say, there came to my ears a low, dull, quick sound, such as a watch makes when enveloped in cotton. I knew *that* sound well, too. It was the beating of the old man's heart. It increased my fury, as the beating of a drum stimulates the soldier into courage.

But even yet I refrained and kept still. I scarcely breathed, I held the lantern motionless. I tried how steadily I could maintain the ray upon the eye. Meantime the hellish tattoo of the heart increased. It grew quicker and quicker, and louder and louder every instant. The old man's terror *must* have been extreme! It grew louder, I say, louder every moment!—do you mark me well? I have told you that I am nervous; so I am. And now at the dead hour of the night, amid the dreadful silence of that old house, so strange a noise as this excited me to uncontrollable terror. Yet, for some minutes longer I refrained and stood still. But the beating grew louder, louder! I thought the heart must burst. And now a new anxiety seized me—the sound would be heard by a neighbor! The old man's hour had come! With a loud yell, I threw open the lantern and leaped into the room. He shrieked once—once only. In an instant I dragged him to the floor, and pulled the heavy bed over him. I then smiled gaily, to find the deed so far done. But, for many minutes, the heart beat on with a muffled sound. This, however, did not vex me; it would not be heard through the wall. At length it ceased. The old man was dead. I removed the bed and examined the corpse. Yes, he was stone, stone dead. I placed my hand upon the heart and held it there many minutes. There was no pulsation. He was stone dead. His eye would trouble me no more.

If still you think me mad, you will think so no longer when I describe the wise precautions I took for the concealment of the body. The night waned, and I worked hastily, but in silence. First of all I dismembered the corpse. I cut off the head and the arms and the legs.

I then took up three planks from the flooring of the chamber, and deposited all between the scantlings. I then replaced the boards so cleverly, so cunningly, that no human eye—not even *his*—could have detected anything wrong. There was nothing to wash out—no stain of any kind—no blood-spot whatever. I had been too wary for that. A tub had caught all—ha! ha!

When I had made an end of these labors, it was four o'clock—still dark as midnight. As the bell sounded the hour, there came a knocking at the street door. I went down to open it with a light heart,—for what had I *now* to fear? There entered three men who introduced themselves, with perfect suavity, as officers of the police. A shriek had been heard by a neighbor during the night; suspicion of foul play had been aroused; information had been lodged at the police office, and they (the officers) had been deputed to search the premises.

I smiled—for *what* had I to fear? I bade the gentlemen welcome. The shriek, I said, was my own in a dream. The old man, I mentioned, was absent in the country. I took my visitors all over the house. I bade them search—search *well*. I led them, at length, to *his* chamber. I showed them his treasures, secure, undisturbed. In the enthusiasm of my confidence, I brought chairs into the room, and desired them *here* to rest from their fatigues, while I myself, in the wild audacity of my perfect triumph, placed my own seat upon the very spot beneath which reposed the corpse of the victim.

The officers were satisfied. My *manner* had convinced them. I was singularly at ease. They sat, and while I answered cheerily, they chatted of familiar things. But, ere long, I felt myself getting pale and wished them gone. My head ached, and I fancied a ringing in my ears: but still they sat and still chatted. The ringing became more distinct:—it continued and became more distinct:—I talked more freely to get rid of the feeling: but it continued and gained definitiveness—until, at length, I found that the noise was *not* within my ears.

No doubt I now grew *very* pale;—but I talked more fluently, and with a heightened voice. Yet the sound increased—and what could I do? It was *a low, dull, quick sound—much such a sound as a watch makes when enveloped in cotton*. I gasped for breath—and yet the officers heard it not. I talked more quickly—more vehemently: but the noise steadily increased. I arose and argued about trifles, in a high key and with violent gesticulations; but the noise steadily increased. Why *would* they not be gone? I paced the floor to and fro with heavy strides, as if excited to fury by the observations of the men—but the noise steadily increased. Oh God! what *could* I do? I foamed—I raved—I swore! I swung the chair upon which I had been sitting, and grated it upon the boards, but the noise arose over all and continually increased. It grew louder—louder—*louder!* And still the men chatted pleasantly, and smiled. Was it possible they heard not? Almighty God!—no, no! They heard!—they suspected!—they *knew!*—they were making a mockery of my horror!—this I thought, and this I think. But anything was better than this agony! Anything was more tolerable than this derision! I could bear those hypocritical smiles no longer! I felt that I must scream or die!—and now—again!—hark! louder! louder! louder! *louder!*—

"Villains!" I shrieked, "dissemble no more! I admit the deed!—tear up the planks!—here, here!—it is the beating of his hideous heart!"

HARRIET BEECHER STOWE
(1811–1896)

"Is this the little lady who started such a big war?" Abraham Lincoln was reputed to have said to Harriet Beecher Stowe when they met during the Civil War. The author of Uncle Tom's Cabin *(1852), based upon the slave life she witnessed firsthand, Ms. Stowe was not only the first American woman writer of significance, but one of the most popular and celebrated American writers in our history. Indeed, to consider Melville and Poe as "nineteenth-century American writers," if one considers Harriet Beecher Stowe as a "nineteenth-century American writer," is to have imagined a category broad, deep, and vertiginous as the Grand Canyon. Except in the most self-evident of terms, Melville and Poe do not belong to the same universe as Ms. Stowe.*

Though Ms. Stowe had some initial difficulty publishing Uncle Tom's Cabin *as a book, it was an immediate success when published, and was but the first of the author's numerous popular successes through a career of thirty-five years. Stowe published regularly in* Atlantic Monthly *and other prestigious magazines; among her more important works are the novels* The Pearl of Orr's Island *(1862) and* Oldtown Folks *(1869). "The Ghost in the Mill" is taken from* Sam Lawson's Oldtown Fireside Stories *(1872), which went through fourteen printings. The stories are linked by the children, primarily boys, of Oldtown, Massachusetts, who sit at the knee of Sam Lawson, a storyteller of scary but moral tales. Quaint by contemporary standards, and hardly adult fare, "The Ghost in the Mill" is intriguing for its depiction of the unassimilated Indian woman Ketury with her "scornful ways" and "snaky eyes," who appears elsewhere in the volume, empowered as an outsider of possibly demonic origin.*

The Ghost in the Mill

"Come, Sam, tell us a story," said I, as Harry and I crept to his knees, in the glow of the bright evening firelight; while Aunt Lois was busily rattling the tea-things, and grandmamma, at the other end of the fireplace, was quietly setting the heel of a blue-mixed yarn stocking.

In those days we had no magazines and daily papers, each reeling off a serial story. Once a week, "The Columbian Sentinel" came from Boston with its slender stock of news and editorial; but all the multiform devices—pictorial, narrative, and poetical—which keep the mind of the present generation ablaze with excitement, had not then even an existence. There was no theatre, no opera; there were in Oldtown no parties or balls, except, perhaps, the annual election, or Thanksgiving festival; and when winter came, and the sun went down at half-past four o'clock, and left the long, dark hours of evening to be provided for, the necessity of amusement became urgent. Hence, in those days, chimney-corner storytelling became an art and an accomplishment. Society then was full of traditions and narratives which had all the uncertain glow and shifting mystery of the firelit hearth upon them. They were told to sympathetic audiences, by the rising and falling light of the solemn embers, with the hearth-crickets filling up every pause. Then the aged told their stories to the young,—tales of early life; tales of war and adventure, of forest-days, of Indian captivities and escapes, of bears and wild-cats and panthers, of rattlesnakes, of witches and wizards, and strange and wonderful dreams and appearances and providences.

In those days of early Massachusetts, faith and credence were in the very air. Two-thirds of New England was then dark, unbroken forests, through whose tangled paths the mysterious winter wind groaned and shrieked and howled with weird noises and unaccountable clamors. Along the iron-bound shore, the stormful Atlantic raved and thundered, and dashed its moaning waters, as if to deaden and deafen any voice that might tell of the settled life of the old civilized world, and shut us forever into the wilderness. A good story-teller, in those days, was always sure of a warm seat at the hearth-stone, and the delighted homage of children; and in all Oldtown there was no better story-teller than Sam Lawson.

"Do, do, tell us a story," said Harry, pressing upon him, and opening very wide blue eyes, in which undoubting faith shone as in a mirror; "and let it be something strange, and different from common."

"Wal, I know lots o' strange things," said Sam, looking mysteriously into the fire. "Why, I know things, that ef I should tell,—why, people might say they wa'n't so; but then they *is* so for all that."

"Oh, *do,* do, tell us!"

"Why, I should scare ye to death, mebbe," said Sam doubtingly.

"Oh, pooh! no, you wouldn't," we both burst out at once.

But Sam was possessed by a reticent spirit, and loved dearly to be wooed and importuned; and so he only took up the great kitchen-tongs, and smote on the hickory forestick, when it flew apart in the middle, and scattered a shower of clear bright coals all over the hearth.

"Mercy on us, Sam Lawson!" said Aunt Lois in an indignant voice, spinning round from her dish-washing.

"Don't you worry a grain. Miss Lois," said Sam composedly. "I see that are stick was e'en a'most in two, and I thought I'd jest settle it. I'll sweep up the coals now," he added, vigorously applying a turkey-wing to the purpose, as he knelt on the hearth, his spare, lean figure glowing in the blaze of the firelight, and getting quite flushed with exertion.

"There, now!" he said, when he had brushed over and under and between the fire-irons, and pursued the retreating ashes so far into the red, fiery citadel, that his finger-ends were burning and tingling, "that are's done now as well as Hepsy herself could 'a' done it. I allers sweeps up the haarth: I think it's part o' the man's bisness when he makes the fire. But Hepsy's so used to seein' me a-doin' on't, that she don't see no kind o' merit in't. It's just as Parson Lothrop said in his sermon,—folks allers overlook their common marcies"—

"But come, Sam, that story," said Harry and I coaxingly, pressing upon him, and pulling him down into his seat in the corner.

"Lordy massy, these 'ere young uns!" said Sam. "There's never no contentin' on em: ye tell 'em one story, and they jest swallows it as a dog does a gob o' meat; and they're all ready for another. What do ye want to hear now?"

Now, the fact was, that Sam's stories had been told us so often, that they were all arranged and ticketed in our minds. We knew every word in them, and could set him right if he varied a hair from the usual track; and still the interest in them was unabated. Still we shivered, and clung to his knee, at the mysterious parts, and felt gentle, cold chills run down our spines at appropriate places. We were always in the most receptive and sympathetic condition. To-night, in particular, was one of those thundering stormy ones, when the winds appeared to be holding a perfect mad carnival over my grandfather's house. They yelled and squealed round the corners; they collected in troops, and came tumbling and roaring down chimney; they shook and rattled the buttery-door and the sinkroom-door and the cellar-door and the chamber-door, with a constant undertone of squeak and clatter, as if at every door were a cold, discontented spirit, tired of the chill outside, and longing for the warmth and comfort within.

"Wal, boys," said Sam confidentially, "what'll ye have?"

"Tell us 'Come down, come down!'" we both shouted with one voice. This was, in our mind, an "A No. 1" among Sam's stories.

"Ye mus'n't be frightened now," said Sam paternally.

"Oh, no! we ar'n't frightened *ever,*" said we both in one breath.

"Not when ye go down the cellar arter cider?" said Sam with severe scrutiny. "Ef ye should be down cellar, and the candle should go out, now?"

"I ain't," said I: "I ain't afraid of any thing. I never knew what it was to be afraid in my life."

"Wal, then," said Sam, "I'll tell ye. This 'ere's what Cap'n Eb Sawin told me when I was a boy about your bigness, I reckon.

"Cap'n Eb Sawin was a most respectable man. Your gran'ther knew him very well; and he was a deacon in the church in Dedham afore he died. He was at Lexington when the fust gun was fired agin the British. He was a dreffle smart man, Cap'n Eb was, and driv team a good many years atween here and Boston. He married Lois Peabody, that was cousin to your gran'ther then. Lois was a real sensible woman; and I've heard her tell the story as he told her, and it was jest as he told it to me,—jest exactly; and I shall never forget it if I live to be nine hundred years old, like Mathuselah.

"Ye see, along back in them times, there used to be a fellow come round these 'ere parts, spring and fall, a-peddlin' goods, with his pack on his back; and his name was Jehiel Lommedieu. Nobody rightly knew where he come from. He wasn't much of a talker; but the women rather liked him, and kind o' liked to have him round. Women will like some fellows, when men can't see no sort o' reason why they should; and they liked this 'ere Lommedieu, though he was kind o' mournful and thin and shad-bellied, and hadn't nothin' to say for himself. But it got to be so, that the women would count and calculate so many weeks afore 'twas time for Lommedieu to be along; and they'd make up ginger-snaps and preserves and pies, and make him stay to tea at the houses, and feed him up on the best there was: and the story went round, that he was a-courtin' Phebe Ann Parker, or Phebe Ann was a-courtin' him,—folks didn't rightly know which. Wal, all of a sudden, Lommedieu stopped comin' round; and nobody knew why,—only jest he didn't come. It turned out that Phebe Ann Parker had got a letter from him, sayin' he'd be along afore Thanksgiving; but he didn't come, neither afore nor at Thanksgiving time, nor arter, nor next spring: and finally the women they gin up lookin' for him. Some said he was dead; some said he was gone to Canada; and some said he hed gone over to the Old Country.

"Wal, as to Phebe Ann, she acted like a gal o' sense, and married 'Bijah Moss, and thought no more 'bout it. She took the right view on't, and said she was sartin that all things was ordered out for the best; and it was jest as well folks couldn't always have their own way. And so, in time, Lommedieu was gone out o' folks's minds, much as a last year's apple-blossom.

"It's relly affectin' to think how little these 'ere folks is missed that's so much sot by. There ain't nobody, ef they's ever so important, but what the world gets to goin' on without 'em, pretty much as it did with 'em, though there's some little flurry at fust. Wal, the last thing that was in anybody's mind was, that they ever should hear from Lommedieu agin. But there ain't nothin' but what has its time o' turnin' up; and it seems his turn was to come.

"Wal, ye see, 'twas the 19th o' March, when Cap'n Eb Sawin started with a team for Boston. That day, there come on about the biggest snow-storm that there'd been in them parts sence the oldest man could remember. "Twas this ere fine, siftin' snow, that drives in your face like needles, with a wind to cut your nose off: it made teamin' pretty tedious work. Cap'n Eb was about the toughest man in them parts. He'd spent days in the woods a-loggin', and he'd been up to the deestrict o' Maine a-lumberin', and was about up to any sort o' thing a man gen'ally could be up to; but these 'ere March winds sometimes does set on a fellow so, that neither natur' nor grace can stan' em. The cap'n used to say he could stan' any wind that blew one way 't time for five minutes; but come to winds that blew all four p'ints at the same minit,—why, they flustered him.

"Wal, that was the sort o' weather it was all day: and by sundown Cap'n Eb he got clean bewildered, so that he lost his road; and, when night came on, he didn't know nothin' where he was. Ye see the country was all under drift, and the air so thick with snow, that he couldn't see a foot afore him; and the fact was, he got off the Boston road without knowin' it, and came out at a pair o' bars nigh upon Sherburn, where old Cack Sparrock's mill is.

"Your gran'ther used to know old Cack, boys. He was a dreffuldrinkin' old crittur, that lived there all alone in the woods by himself a-tendin' saw and grist mill. He wa'nt allers jest what he was then. Time was that Cack was a pretty consid'ably likely young man, and his wife was a very respectable woman,—Deacon Amos Petengall's dater from Sherburn.

"But ye see, the year arter his wife died, Cack he gin up goin' to meetin' Sundays, and, all the tithing-men and selectmen could do, they couldn't get him out to meetin'; and, when a man neglects means o' grace and sanctuary privileges, there ain't no sayin' *what* he'll do next. Why, boys, jist think on't!—an immortal crittur lyin' round loose all day Sunday, and not puttin' on so much as a clean shirt, when all 'spectable folks has on their best close, and is to meetin' worshippin' the Lord! What can you spect to come of it, when he lies idlin' round in his old week-day close, fishing, or some sich, but what the Devil should be arter him at last, as he was arter old Cack?"

Here Sam winked impressively to my grandfather in the opposite corner, to call his attention to the moral which he was interweaving with his narrative.

"Wal, ye see, Cap'n Eb he told me, that when he come to them bars and looked up, and saw the dark a-comin' down, and the storm a-thickenin' up, he felt that things was gettin' pretty consid'able serious. There was a dark piece o' woods on ahead of him inside the bars; and he knew, come to get in there, the light would give out clean. So he jest thought he'd take the hoss out o' the team, and go ahead a little, and see where he was. So he driv his oxen up ag'in the fence, and took out the hoss, and got on him, and pushed along through the woods, not rightly knowin' where he was goin'.

"Wal, afore long he see a light through the trees and, sure enough, he come out to Cack Sparrock's old mill.

"It was a pretty consid'able gloomy sort of a place, that are old mill was. There was a great fall of water that come rushin' down the rocks, and fell in a deep pool; and it sounded sort o' wild and lonesome; but Cap'n Eb he knocked on the door with his whip-handle, and got in.

"There, to be sure, sot old Cack beside a great blazin' fire, with his rum-jug at his elbow. He was a dreffful fellow to drink, Cack was! For all that, there was some good in him, for he was pleasant-spoken and 'bliging; and he made the cap'n welcome.

"'Ye see, Cack,' said Cap'n Eb, 'I'm off my road and got snowed up down by your bars,' says he.

"'Want ter know!' says Cack. 'Calculate you'll jest have to camp down here till mornin',' says he.

"Wal, so old Cack he got out his tin lantern, and went with Cap'n Eb back to the bars to help him fetch along his critturs. He told him he could put 'em under the mill-shed. So they got the critturs up to the shed, and got the cart under; and by that time the storm was awful.

"But Cack he made a great roarin' fire, 'cause, ye see, Cack allers had slab-wood a plenty from his mill; and a roarin' fire is jest so much company. It sort o' keeps a fellow's spirits up, a good fire does. So Cack he sot on his old teakettle, and made a swingeing lot o' toddy; and he and Cap'n Eb were havin' a tol'able comfortable time there. Cack was a pretty good hand to tell stories; and Cap'n Eb warn't no way backward in that line, and kep' up his end pretty well: and pretty soon they was a-roarin' and haw-hawin' inside about as loud as the storm outside; when all of a sudden, bout midnight, there come a loud rap on the door.

"'Lordy massy! what's that?' says Cack. Folks is rather startled allers to be checked up sudden when they are a-carryin' on and laughin'; and it was such an awful blowy night, it was a little scary to have a rap on the door.

"Wal, they waited a minit, and didn't hear nothin' but the wind a-screechin' round the chimbley; and old Cack was jest goin' on with his story, when the rap come ag'in, harder'n ever, as if it'd shook the door open.

"'Wal,' says old Cack, 'if 'tis the Devil, we'd jest as good's open, and have it out with him to onst,' says he; and so he got up and opened the door, and, sure enough, there was old Ketury there. Expect you've heard your grandma tell about old Ketury. She used to come to meetin's sometimes, and her husband was one o' the prayin' Indians; but Ketury was one of the real wild sort, and you couldn't no more convert *her* than you could convert a wild-cat or a panth'a. Lordy massy! Ketury used to come to meetin', and sit there on them Indian benches; and when the second bell was a-tollin', and when Parson Lothrop and his wife was comin' up the broad aisle, and everybody in the house ris' up and stood, Ketury would sit there, and look at 'em out o' the corner o' her eyes; and folks used to say she rattled them necklaces o' rattlesnakes' tails and wild-cat teeth, and sich like heathen trumpery, and looked for all the world as if the spirit of the old Sarpent himself was in her. I've seen her sit and look at Lady Lothrop out o' the corner o' her eyes; and her old brown baggy neck would kind o' twist and work; and her eyes they looked so, that 'twas enough to scare a body. For all the world, she looked jest as if she was a-workin' up to spring at her. Lady Lothrop was jest as kind to Ketury as she always was to every poor crittur. She'd bow and smile as gracious to her when meetin was over, and she come down the aisle, passin' out o' meetin'; but Ketury never took no notice. Ye see, Ketury's father was one o' them great powwows down to Martha's Vineyard; and people used to say she was set apart, when she was a child, to the sarvice o' the Devil: any way, she never could be made nothin' of in a Christian way. She come down to Parson Lothrop's study once or twice to be catechised; but he couldn't get a word out o' her, and she kind o' seemed to sit scornful while he was a-talkin'. Folks said, if it was in old times, Ketury wouldn't have been allowed to go on so; but Parson Lothrop's so sort o' mild, he let her take pretty much her own way. Everybody thought that Ketury was a witch: at least, she knew consid'able more'n she ought to know, and so they was kind o' 'fraid on her. Cap'n Eb says he never see a fellow seem scareder than Cack did when he see Ketury a-standin' there.

"Why, ye see, boys, she was as withered and wrinkled and brown as an old frosted punkin-vine; and her little snaky eyes sparkled and snapped, and it made yer head kind o' dizzy to look at 'em; and folks used to say that anybody that Ketury got mad at was sure to get the worst of it fust or last.

And so, no matter what day or hour Ketury had a mind to rap at anybody's door, folks gen'lly thought it was best to let her in; but then, they never thought her coming was for any good, for she was just like the wind,—she came when the fit was on her, she staid jest so long as it pleased her, and went when she got ready, and not before. Ketury understood English, and could talk it well enough, but always seemed to scorn it, and was allers mowin' and mutterin' to herself in Indian, and winkin' and blinkin' as if she saw more folks round than you did, so that she wa'n't no way pleasant company: and yet everybody took good care to be polite to her.

So old Cack asked her to come in, and didn't make no question where she come from, or what she come on; but he knew it was twelve good miles from where she lived to his hut, and the snow was drifted above her middle: and Cap'n Eb declared that there wa'n't no track, nor sign o' a track, of anybody's coming through that snow next morning."

"How did she get there, then?" said I.

"Didn't ye never see brown leaves a-ridin' on the wind? 'Well,' Cap'n Eb he says, 'she came on the wind,' and I'm sure it was strong enough to fetch her. But Cack he got her down into the warm corner, and he poured her out a mug o' hot toddy, and give her: but ye see her bein' there sort o' stopped the conversation; for she sot there a-rockin' back'ards and for'ards, a-sippin her toddy, and a-mutterin', and lookin' up chimbley.

"Cap'n Eb says in all his born days he never hearn such screeches and yells as the wind give over that chimbley; and old Cack got so frightened, you could fairly hear his teeth chatter.

"But Cap'n Eb he was a putty brave man, and he wa'n't goin' to have conversation stopped by no woman, witch or no witch; and so, when he see her mutterin', and lookin' up chimbley, he spoke up, and says he, 'Well, Ketury, what do you see?' says he. 'Come, out with it; don't keep it to yourself.' Ye see Cap'n Eb was a hearty fellow, and then he was a leetle warmed up with the toddy.

"Then he said he see an evil kind o' smile on Ketury's face, and she rattled her necklace o' bones and snakes' tails; and her eyes seemed to snap; and she looked up the chimbley, and called out, 'Come down, come down! let's see who ye be.'

"Then there was a scratchin' and a rumblin' and a groan; and a pair of feet come down the chimbley, and stood right in the middle of the haarth, the toes pi'ntin' out'rds, with shoes and silver buckles a-shinin' in the firelight. Cap'n Eb says he never come so near bein' scared in his life; and, as to old Cack, he jest wilted right down in his chair.

"Then old Ketury got up, and reached her stick up chimbley, and called out louder, 'Come down, come down! Let's see who ye be.' And, sure enough, down came a pair o' legs, and j'ined right on to the feet: good fair legs they was, with ribbed stockings and leather breeches.

"'Wal, we're in for it now,' says Cap'n Eb. 'Go it, Ketury, and let's have the rest on him.'

"Ketury didn't seem to mind him: she stood there as stiff as a stake, and kep' callin' out, 'Come down, come down! Let's see who ye be.' And then come down the body of a man with a brown coat and yellow vest, and j'ined right on to the legs; but there wa'n't no arms to it. Then Ketury shook her stick up chimbley, and called, *'Come down, come down!'* And there came down a pair o' arms, and went on each side o' the body; and there stood a man all finished, only there wa'n't no head on him.

"'Wal, Ketury,' says Cap'n Eb, 'this 'ere's getting serious. I 'spec' you must finish him up, and let's see what he wants of us.'

"Then Ketury called out once more, louder'n ever, 'Come down, come down! let's see who ye be.' And, sure enough, down comes a man's head, and settled on the shoulders straight enough; and Cap'n Eb, the minit he sot eyes on him, knew he was Jehiel Lommedieu.

"Old Cack knew him too; and he fell flat on his face, and prayed the Lord to have mercy on his soul: but Cap'n Eb he was for gettin' to the bottom of matters, and not have his scare for nothin'; so he says to him, 'What do you want, now you hev come?'

"The man he didn't speak; he only sort o' moaned, and p'inted to the chimbley. He seemed to try to speak, but couldn't; for ye see it isn't often that his sort o' folks is permitted to speak: but just then there came a screechin' blast o' wind, and blowed the door open, and blowed the smoke and fire all out into the room, and there seemed to be a whirl-wind and darkness and moans and screeches; and, when it all cleared up, Ketury and the man was both gone, and only old Cack lay on the ground, rolling and moaning as if he'd die.

"Wal, Cap'n Eb he picked him up, and built up the fire, and sort o' comforted him up, 'cause the crittur was in distress o' mind that was drefful. The awful Providence, ye see, had awakened him, and his sin had been set home to his soul; and he was under such conviction, that it all had to come out,—how old Cack's father had murdered poor Lommedieu for his money, and Cack had been privy to it, and helped his father build the body up in that very chimbley; and he said that he hadn't had neither peace nor rest since then, and that was what had driv' him away from ordinances; for ye know sinnin' will always make a man leave prayin'. Wal, Cack didn't live but a day or two. Cap'n Eb he got the minister o' Sherburn and one o' the selectmen down to see him; and they took his deposition. He seemed railly quite penitent; and Parson Carryl he prayed with him, and was faithful in settin' home the providence to his soul: and so, at the eleventh hour, poor old Cack might have got in; at least it looks a leetle like it. He was distressed to think he couldn't live to be hung. He sort o' seemed to think, that if he was fairly tried, and hung, it would make it all square. He made Parson Carryl promise to have the old mill pulled down, and bury the body; and, after he was dead, they did it.

"Cap'n Eb he was one of a party o' eight that pulled down the chimbley; and there, sure enough, was the skeleton of poor Lommedieu.

"So there you see, boys, there can't be no iniquity so hid but what it'll come out. The wild Indians of the forest, and the stormy winds and tempests, j'ined together to bring out this 'ere."

"For my part," said Aunt Lois sharply, "I never believed that story."

"Why, Lois," said my grandmother, "Cap'n Eb Sawin was a regular church-member, and a most respectable man."

"Law, mother! I don't doubt he thought so. I suppose he and Cack got drinking toddy together, till he got asleep, and dreamed it. I wouldn't believe such a thing if it did happen right before my face and eyes. I should only think I was crazy, that's all."

"Come, Lois, if I was you, I wouldn't talk so like a Sadducee," said my grandmother. "What would become of all the accounts in Dr. Cotton Mather's 'Magnilly' if folks were like you?"

"Wal," said Sam Lawson, drooping contemplatively over the coals, and gazing into the fire, "there's a putty consid'able sight o' things in this world that's true; and then ag'in there's a sight o' things that ain't true. Now, my old gran'ther used to say, 'Boys,' says he, 'if ye want to lead a pleasant and prosperous life, ye must contrive allers to keep jest the *happy medium* between truth and falsehood.' Now, that are's my doctrine."

Aunt Lois knit severely.

"Boys," said Sam, "don't you want ter go down with me and get a mug o' cider?"

Of course we did, and took down a basket to bring up some apples to roast.

"Boys," says Sam mysteriously, while he was drawing the cider, "you jest ask your Aunt Lois to tell you what she knows 'bout Ruth Sullivan."

"Why, what is it?"

"Oh! you must ask *her*. These 'ere folks that's so kind o' toppin' about sperits and sich, come sift 'em down, you gen'lly find they knows one story that kind o' puzzles 'em. Now you mind, and jist ask your Aunt Lois about Ruth Sullivan."

HERMAN MELVILLE
(1819–1891)

Of American writers, Herman Melville led, arguably, the most varied life. Born in New York City of English and Dutch colonial ancestry, one of eight children of an impoverished family, he went away to sea as a young man, acquiring experience for his early novels Typee *(1846),* Omoo *(1847),* Mardi *(1849),* Redburn *(1849), and* White-Jacket *(1850). (Note the rapid succession of titles! With* Moby-Dick *to come, in 1851.) Celebrated as the first two novels were, for their South Seas exoticism and the accessibility of their boyish, firsthand narration, they scarcely characterize Melville's later, far more complex and demanding work; and they led readers to expect writing that, for Melville, quickly came to seem the literary equivalent of "sawing wood."*

Astonishing as it seems to contemporary readers, the work of Melville's maturity failed to find any audience. Reviewers almost universally damned Moby-Dick*; the reception of* Pierre *(1852) was yet more virulent.* The Piazza Tales *(1856) and* The Confidence-Man *(1857) are more accessible, yet sold very poorly.* Clarel: A Poem and Pilgrimage in the Holy Land *was privately published in 1876;* Billy Budd, *completed in 1891, was posthumously published. It might be argued that, apart from his masterpiece* Moby-Dick, *Melville's most powerfully realized works of fiction are his idiosyncratic short stories and prose pieces: "Bartleby the Scrivener," "Benito Cereno," "The Encantadas," and the ingeniously paired surreal excursions into "The Paradise of Bachelors and the Tartarus of Maids."*

The Paradise of Bachelors and the Tartarus of Maids

I. The Paradise of Bachelors

It lies not far from Temple-Bar.

Going to it, by the usual way, is like stealing from a heated plain into some cool, deep glen, shady among harboring hills.

Sick with the din and soiled with the mud of Fleet Street—where the Benedick tradesmen are hurrying by, with ledger-lines ruled along their brows, thinking upon rise of bread and fall of babies—you adroitly turn a mystic corner—not a street—glide down a dim, monastic way, flanked by dark, sedate, and solemn piles, and still wending on, give the whole care-worn world the slip, and, disentangled, stand beneath the quiet cloisters of the Paradise of Bachelors.

Sweet are the oases in Sahara; charming the isle-groves of August prairies; delectable pure faith amidst a thousand perfidies: but sweeter, still more charming, most delectable the dreamy Paradise of Bachelors, found in the stony heart of stunning London.

In mild meditation pace the cloisters; take your pleasure, sip your leisure, in the garden waterward; go linger in the ancient library; go worship in the sculptured chapel; but little have you seen, just nothing do you know, not the sweet kernel have you tasted, till you dine among the banded Bachelors, and see their convivial eyes and glasses sparkle. Not dine in bustling commons, during term-time, in the hall; but tranquilly, by private hint, at a private table; some fine Templar's hospitably invited guest.

Templar? That's a romantic name. Let me see. Brian de Bois Gilbert was a Templar, I believe. Do we understand you to insinuate that those famous Templars still survive in modern London? May the ring of their armed heels be heard, and the rattle of their shields, as in mailed prayer the monk-knights kneel before the consecrated Host? Surely a monk-knight were a curious sight picking his way along the Strand, his gleaming corselet and snowy surcoat spattered by an omnibus. Long-bearded, too, according to his order's rule; his face furry as pard's; how would the grim ghost look among the crop-haired, close-shaven citizens? We know indeed—sad history recounts it—that a moral blight tainted at last this sacred Brotherhood. Though no sworded foe might outskill them in the fence, yet the worm of luxury crawled beneath their guard, gnawing the core of knightly troth, nibbling the monastic vow, till at last the monk's austerity relaxed to wassailing, and the sworn knights-bachelors grew to be but hypocrites and rakes.

But for all this, quite unprepared were we to learn that Knights-Templars (if at all in being) were so entirely secularized as to be reduced from carving out immortal fame in glorious battling for the Holy Land, to the carving of roast-mutton at a dinner-board. Like Anacreon, do these degenerate Templars now think it sweeter far to fall in banquet than in war? Or, indeed, how can there be any survival of that famous order? Templars in modern London! Templars in their red-cross mantles smoking cigars at the Divan! Templars crowded in a railway train, till, stacked with steel helmet, spear, and shield, the whole train looks like one elongated locomotive!

No. The genuine Templar is long since departed. Go view the wondrous tombs in the Temple Church; see there the rigidly-haughty forms stretched out, with crossed arms upon their stilly hearts, in everlasting and undreaming rest. Like the years before the flood, the bold Knights-Templars are no more. Nevertheless, the name remains, and the nominal society, and the ancient grounds, and some of the ancient edifices. But the iron heel is changed to a boot of patent-leather; the long two-handed sword to a one-handed quill, the monk-giver of gratuitous ghostly counsel now counsels for a fee; the defender of the sarcophagus (if in good practice with his weapon) now has more than one case to defend; the vowed opener and clearer of all highways leading to the Holy Sepulchre, now has it in particular charge to check, to clog, to hinder, and embarrass all the courts and avenues of Law; the knight-combatant of the Saracen, breasting spear-points at Acre, now fights law-points in Westminster Hall. The helmet is a wig. Struck by Time's enchanter's wand, the Templar is to-day a Lawyer.

But, like many others tumbled from proud glory's height—like the apple, hard on the bough, but mellow on the ground—the Templar's fall has but made him all the finer fellow.

I dare say those old warrior-priests were but gruff and grouty at the best; cased in Birmingham hardware, how could their crimped arms give yours or mine a hearty shake? Their proud, ambitious, monkish souls clasped shut, like horn-hook missals, their very faces clapped in bomb-shells; what sort of genial men were these? But best of comrades, most affable of hosts, capital diner is the modern Templar. His wit and wine are both of sparkling brands.

The church and cloisters, courts and vaults, lanes and passages, banquet-halls, refectories, libraries, terraces, gardens, broad walks, domicils, and dessert-rooms, covering a very large space of ground, and all grouped in central neighborhood, and quite sequestered from the old city's surrounding din; and every thing about the place being kept in most bachelor-like particularity, no part of London offers to a quiet wight so agreeable a refuge.

The Temple is, indeed, a city by itself. A city with all the best appurtenances, as the above enumeration shows. A city with a park to it, and flower-beds, and a river-side—the Thames flowing by as openly, in one part, as by Eden's primal garden flowed the mild Euphrates. In what is now the Temple Garden the old Crusaders used to exercise their steeds and lances; the modern Templars now lounge on the benches beneath the trees, and, switching their patent-leather boots, in gay discourse exercise at repartee.

Long lines of stately portraits in the banquet-halls, show what great men of mark—famous nobles, judges, and Lord Chancellors—have in their time been Templars. But all Templars are not known to universal fame; though, if the having warm hearts and warmer welcomes, full minds and fuller cellars, and giving good advice and glorious dinners, spiced with rare divertisements of fun and fancy, merit immortal mention, set down, ye muses, the names of R. F. C. and his imperial brother.

Though to be a Templar, in the one true sense, you must needs be a lawyer, or a student at the law, and be ceremoniously enrolled as member of the order, yet as many such, though Templars, do not reside within the Temple's precincts, though they may have their offices there, just so, on the other hand, there are many residents of the hoary old domicils who are not admitted Templars. If being, say, a lounging gentleman and bachelor, or a quiet, unmarried, literary man, charmed with the soft seclusion of the spot, you much desire to pitch your shady tent among the rest in this serene encampment, then you must make some special friend among the order, and procure him to rent, in his name but at your charge, whatever vacant chamber you may find to suit.

Thus, I suppose, did Dr. Johnson, that nominal Benedick and widower but virtual bachelor, when for a space he resided here. So, too, did that undoubted bachelor and rare good soul, Charles Lamb. And hundreds more, of sterling spirits. Brethren of the Order of Celibacy, from time to time have dined, and slept, and tabernacled here. Indeed, the place is all a honeycomb of offices and domicils. Like any cheese, it is quite perforated through and through in all directions with the snug cells of bachelors. Dear, delightful spot! Ah! when I bethink me of the sweet hours there passed, enjoying such genial hospitalities beneath those time-honored roofs, my heart only finds due utterance through poetry; and, with a sigh, I softly sing, "Carry me back to old Virginny!"

Such then, at large, is the Paradise of Bachelors. And such I found it one pleasant afternoon in the smiling month of May, when, sallying from my hotel in Trafalgar Square, I went to keep my dinner-appointment with that fine Barrister, Bachelor, and Bencher, R. F. C. (he *is* the first and second, and *should be* the third; I hereby nominate him), whose card I kept fast pinched between my gloved forefinger and thumb, and every now and then snatched still another look at the pleasant address inscribed beneath the name, "No.—, Elm Court, Temple."

At the core he was a right bluff, care-free, right comfortable, and most companionable Englishman. If on a first acquaintance he seemed reserved, quite icy in his air—patience; this Champagne will thaw. And if it never do, better frozen Champagne than liquid vinegar.

There were nine gentlemen, all bachelors, at the dinner. One was from "No.—, King's Bench Walk, Temple;" a second, third, and fourth, and fifth, from various courts or passages christened with some similarly rich resounding syllables. It was indeed a sort of Senate of the Bachelors, sent to this dinner from widely-scattered districts, to represent the general celibacy of the Temple. Nay it was, by representation, a Grand Parliament of the best Bachelors in universal London; several of those present being from distant quarters of the town, noted immemorial seats of lawyers and unmarried men—Lincoln's Inn, Furnival's Inn; and one gentleman, upon whom I looked with a sort of collateral awe, hailed from the spot where Lord Verulam once abode a bachelor—Gray's Inn.

The apartment was well up toward heaven. I know not how many strange old stairs I climbed to get to it. But a good dinner, with famous company, should be well earned. No doubt our host had his dining-room so high with a view to secure the prior exercise necessary to the due relishing and digesting of it.

The furniture was wonderfully unpretending, old, and snug. No new shining mahogany, sticky with undried varnish; no uncomfortably luxurious ottomans, and sofas too fine to use, vexed you in this sedate apartment. It is a thing which every sensible American should learn from every sensible Englishman, that glare and glitter, gimcracks and gewgaws, are not indispensable to domestic solacement. The American Benedick snatches, down-town, a tough chop in a gilded show-box; the English bachelor leisurely dines at home on that incomparable South Down of his, off a plain deal board.

The ceiling of the room was low. Who wants to dine under the dome of St. Peter's? High ceilings! If that is your demand, and the higher the better, and you be so very tall, then go dine out with the topping giraffe in the open air.

In good time the nine gentlemen sat down to nine covers, and soon were fairly under way.

If I remember right, ox-tail soup inaugurated the affair. Of a rich russet hue, its agreeable flavor dissipated my first confounding of its main ingredient with teamster's gads and the rawhides of ushers. (By way of interlude, we here drank a little claret.) Neptune's was the next tribute rendered—turbot coming second; snowwhite, flaky, and just gelatinous enough, not too turtleish in its unctuousness.

(At this point we refreshed ourselves with a glass of sherry.) After these light skirmishers had vanished, the heavy artillery of the feast marched in, led by that well-known English generalissimo, roast beef. For aids-de-camp we had a saddle of mutton, a fat turkey, a chicken-pie, and endless other savory things; while for avant-couriers came nine silver flagons of humming ale. This heavy ordnance having departed on the track of the light skirmishers, a picked brigade of game-fowl encamped upon the board, their camp-fires lit by the ruddiest of decanters.

Tarts and puddings followed, with innumerable niceties; then cheese and crackers. (By way of ceremony, simply, only to keep up good old fashions, we here each drank a glass of good old port.)

The cloth was now removed; and like Blucher's army coming in at the death on the field of Waterloo, in marched a fresh detachment of bottles, dusty with their hurried march.

All these manoeuvrings of the forces were superintended by a surprising old field-marshal (I can not school myself to call him by the inglorious name of waiter), with snowy hair and napkin, and a head like Socrates. Amidst all the hilarity of the feast, intent on important business, he disdained to smile. Venerable man!

I have above endeavored to give some slight schedule of the general plan of operations. But any one knows that a good, genial dinner is a sort of pell-mell, indiscriminate affair, quite baffling to detail in all particulars. Thus, I spoke of taking a glass of claret, and a glass of sherry, and a glass of port, and a mug of ale—all at certain specific periods and times. But those were merely the state bumpers, so to speak. Innumerable impromptu glasses were drained between the periods of those grand imposing ones.

The nine bachelors seemed to have the most tender concern for each other's health. All the time, in flowing wine, they most earnestly expressed their sincerest wishes for the entire well-being and lasting hygiene of the gentlemen on the right and on the left. I noticed that when one of these kind bachelors desired a little more wine (just for his stomach's sake, like Timothy), he would not help himself to it unless some other bachelor would join him. It seemed held something indelicate, selfish, and unfraternal, to be seen taking a lonely, unparticipated glass. Meantime, as the wine ran apace, the spirits of the company grew more and more to perfect genialness and unconstraint. They related all sort of pleasant stories. Choice experiences in their private lives were now brought out, like choice brands of Moselle or Rhenish, only kept for particular company. One told us how mellowly he lived when a student at Oxford; with various spicy anecdotes of most frank-hearted noble lords, his liberal companions. Another bachelor, a gray-headed man, with a sunny face, who, by his own account, embraced every opportunity of leisure to cross over into the Low Countries, on sudden tours of inspection of the fine old Flemish architecture there—this learned, white-haired, sunny-faced old bachelor, excelled in his descriptions of the elaborate splendors of those old guild-halls, town-halls, and stadthold-houses, to be seen in the land of the ancient Flemings. A third was a great frequenter of the British

Museum, and knew all about scores of wonderful antiquities, of Oriental manuscripts, and costly books without a duplicate. A fourth had lately returned from a trip to Old Granada, and, of course, was full of Saracenic scenery. A fifth had a funny case in law to tell. A sixth was erudite in wines. A seventh had a strange characteristic anecdote of the private life of the Iron Duke, never printed, and never before announced in any public or private company. An eighth had lately been amusing his evenings, now and then, with translating a comic poem of Pulci's. He quoted for us the more amusing passages.

And so the evening slipped along, the hours told, not by a water-clock, like King Alfred's, but a wine-chronometer. Meantime the table seemed a sort of Epsom Heath; a regular ring, where the decanters galloped round. For fear one decanter should not with sufficient speed reach his destination, another was sent express after him to hurry him; and then a third to hurry the second; and so on with a fourth and fifth. And throughout all this nothing loud, nothing unmannerly, nothing turbulent. I am quite sure, from the scrupulous gravity and austerity of his air, that had Socrates, the field-marshal, perceived aught of indecorum in the company he served, he would have forthwith departed without giving warning. I afterward learned that, during the repast, an invalid bachelor in an adjoining chamber enjoyed his first sound refreshing slumber in three long, weary weeks.

It was the very perfection of quiet absorption of good living, good drinking, good feeling, and good talk. We were a band of brothers. Comfort—fraternal, household comfort, was the grand trait of the affair. Also, you could plainly see that these easy-hearted men had no wives or children to give an anxious thought. Almost all of them were travelers, too; for bachelors alone can travel freely, and without any twinges of their consciences touching desertion of the fireside.

The thing called pain, the bugbear styled trouble—those two legends seemed preposterous to their bachelor imaginations. How could men of liberal sense, ripe scholarship in the world, and capacious philosophical and convivial understandings—how could they suffer themselves to be imposed upon by such monkish fables? Pain! Trouble! As well talk of Catholic miracles. No such thing.—Pass the sherry. Sir.—Pooh, pooh! Can't be!—The port, Sir, if you please. Nonsense; don't tell me so.—The decanter stops with you, Sir, I believe.

And so it went.

Not long after the cloth was drawn our host glanced significantly upon Socrates, who, solemnly stepping to a stand, returned with an immense convolved horn, a regular Jericho horn, mounted with polished silver, and otherwise chased and curiously enriched; not omitting two life-like goat's heads, with four more horns of solid silver, projecting from opposite sides of the mouth of the noble main horn.

Not having heard that our host was a performer on the bugle, I was surprised to see him lift this horn from the table, as if he were about to blow an inspiring blast. But I was relieved from this and set quite right as touching the purposes of the horn, by his now inserting his thumb and forefinger into its mouth; whereupon a slight aroma was stirred up, and my nostrils were greeted with the smell of some choice Rappee. It was a mull of snuff. It went the rounds. Capital idea this, thought I, of taking snuff about this juncture. This goodly fashion must be introduced among my countrymen at home, further ruminated I.

The remarkable decorum of the nine bachelors—a decorum not to be affected by any quantity of wine—a decorum unassailable by any degree of mirthfulness—this was again set in a forcible light to me, by now observing that, though they took snuff very freely, yet not a man so far violated the proprieties, or so far molested the invalid bachelor in the adjoining room as to indulge himself in a sneeze. The snuff was snuffed silently, as if it had been some fine innoxious powder brushed off the wings of butterflies.

But fine though they be, bachelors' dinners, like bachelors' lives, can not endure forever. The time came for breaking up. One by one the bachelors took their hats, and two by two, and arm-in-arm they descended, still conversing, to the flagging of the court; some going to their neighboring chambers to turn over the Decameron ere retiring for the night; some to smoke a cigar, promenading in the garden on the cool river-side; some to make for the street, call a hack, and be driven snugly to their distant lodgings.

I was the last lingerer.

"Well," said my smiling host, "what do you think of the Temple here, and the sort of life we bachelors make out to live in it?"

"Sir," said I, with a burst of admiring candor—"Sir, this is the very Paradise of Bachelors!"

II. The Tartarus of Maids

It lies not far from Woedolor Mountain in New England. Turning to the east, right out from among bright farms and sunny meadows, nodding in early June with odorous grasses, you enter ascendingly among bleak hills. These gradually close in upon a dusky pass, which, from the violent Gulf Stream of air unceasingly diving between its cloven walls of haggard rock, as well as from the tradition of a crazy spinster's hut having long ago stood somewhere here-abouts, is called the Mad Maid's Bellows'-pipe.

Winding along at the bottom of the gorge is a dangerously narrow wheel-road, occupying the bed of a former torrent. Following this road to its highest point, you stand as within a Dantean gateway. From the steepness of the walls here, their strangely ebon hue, and the sudden contraction of the gorge, this particular point is called the Black Notch. The ravine now expandingly descends into a great, purple, hopper-shaped hollow, far sunk among many Plutonian, shaggy-wooded mountains. By the country people this hollow is called the Devil's Dungeon. Sounds of torrents fall on all sides upon the ear. These rapid waters unite at last in one turbid brick-colored stream, boiling through a flume among enormous boulders. They call this strange-colored torrent Blood River. Gaining a dark precipice it wheels suddenly to the west, and makes one maniac spring of sixty feet into the arms of a stunted wood of gray-haired pines, between which it thence eddies on its further way down to the invisible lowlands.

Conspicuously crowning a rocky bluff high to one side, at the cataract's verge, is the ruin of an old saw-mill, built in those primitive times when vast pines and hemlocks superabounded throughout the neighboring region. The black-mossed bulk of those immense, rough-hewn, and spike-knotted logs, here and there tumbled all together, in long abandonment and decay, or left in solitary, perilous projection over the cataract's gloomy brink, impart to this rude wooden ruin not only much of the aspect of one of rough-quarried stone, but also a sort of feudal, Rhineland, and Thurmberg look, derived from the pinnacled wildness of the neighboring scenery.

Not far from the bottom of the Dungeon stands a large whitewashed building, relieved, like some great whited sepulchre, against the sullen background of mountain-side firs, and other hardy evergreens, inaccessibly rising in grim terraces for some two thousand feet.

The building is a paper-mill.

Having embarked on a large scale in the seedsman's business (so extensively and broadcast, indeed, that at length my seeds were distributed through all the Eastern and Northern States, and even fell into the far soil of Missouri and the Carolinas), the demand for paper at my place became so great, that the expenditure soon amounted to a most important item in the general account. It need hardly be hinted how paper comes into use with seedsmen, as envelopes. These are mostly made of yellowish paper, folded square; and when filled, are all but flat, and being stamped, and superscribed with the nature of the seeds contained, assume not a little the appearance of business-letters ready for the mail. Of these small envelopes I used an incredible quantity—several hundreds of thousands in a year. For a time I had purchased my paper from the whole-sale dealers in a neighboring town. For economy's sake, and partly for the adventure of the trip, I now resolved to cross the mountains, some sixty miles, and order my future paper at the Devil's Dungeon paper-mill.

The sleighing being uncommonly fine toward the end of January, and promising to hold so for no small period, in spite of the bitter cold I started one gray Friday noon in my pung, well fitted with buffalo and wolf robes; and, spending one night on the road, next noon came in sight of Woedolor Mountain.

The far summit fairly smoked with frost; white vapors curled up from its white-wooded top, as from a chimney. The intense congelation made the whole country look like one petrifaction. The steel shoes of my pung craunched and gritted over the vitreous, chippy snow, as if it had been broken glass. The forests here and there skirting the route, feeling the same all-stiffening influence, their inmost fibres penetrated with the cold, strangely groaned—not in the swaying branches merely, but likewise in the vertical trunk—as the fitful gusts remorselessly swept through them. Brittle with excessive frost, many colossal tough-grained maples, snapped in twain like pipe-stems, cumbered the unfeeling earth.

Flaked all over with frozen sweat, white as a milky ram, his nostrils at each breath sending forth two horn-shaped shoots of heated respiration, Black, my good horse, but six years old, started at a sudden turn, where, right across the track—not ten minutes fallen—an old distorted hemlock lay, darkly undulatory as an anaconda.

Gaining the Bellows'-pipe, the violent blast, dead from behind, all but shoved my high-backed pung up-hill. The gust shrieked through the shivered pass, as if laden with lost spirits bound to the unhappy world. Ere gaining the summit, Black, my horse, as if exasperated by the cutting wind, slung out with his strong hind legs, tore the light pung straight up-hill, and sweeping grazingly through the narrow notch, sped downward madly past the ruined saw-mill. Into the Devil's Dungeon horse and cataract rushed together.

With might and main, quitting my seat and robes, and standing backward, with one foot braced against the dash-board, I rasped and churned the bit, and stopped him just in time to avoid collision, at a turn, with the bleak nozzle of a rock, couchant like a lion in the way—a road-side rock.

At first I could not discover the paper-mill.

The whole hollow gleamed with the white, except, here and there, where a pinnacle of granite showed one wind-swept angle bare. The mountains stood pinned in shrouds—a pass of Alpine corpses. Where stands the mill? Suddenly a whirling, humming sound broke upon my ear. I looked, and there, like an arrested avalanche, lay the large white-washed factory. It was subordinately surrounded by a cluster of other and smaller buildings, some of which, from their cheap, blank air, great length, gregarious windows, and comfortless expression, no doubt were boarding-houses of the operatives. A snow-white hamlet amidst the snows. Various rude, irregular squares and courts resulted from the somewhat picturesque clusterings of these buildings, owing to the broken, rocky nature of the ground, which forbade all method in their relative arrangement. Several narrow lanes and alleys, too, partly blocked with snow fallen from the roof, cut up the hamlet in all directions.

When, turning from the traveled highway, jingling with bells of numerous farmers—who, availing themselves of the fine sleighing, were dragging their wood to market—and frequently diversified with swift cutters dashing from inn to inn of the scattered villages—when, I say, turning from that bustling main-road, I by degrees wound into the Mad Maid's Bellows'-pipe, and saw the grim Black Notch beyond, then something latent, as well as something obvious in the time and scene, strangely brought back to my mind my first sight of dark and grimy Temple-Bar. And when Black, my horse, went darting through the Notch, perilously grazing its rocky wall,

I remembered being in a runaway London omnibus, which in much the same sort of style, though by no means at an equal rate, dashed through the ancient arch of Wren. Though the two objects did by no means completely correspond, yet this partial inadequacy but served to tinge the similitude not less with the vividness than the disorder of a dream. So that, when upon reining up at the protruding rock I at last caught sight of the quaint groupings of the factory-buildings, and with the traveled highway and the Notch behind, found myself all alone, silently and privily stealing through deep-cloven passages into this sequestered spot, and saw the long, high-gabled main factory edifice, with a rude tower—for hoisting heavy boxes—at one end, standing among its crowded outbuildings and boarding-houses, as the Temple Church amidst the surrounding offices and dormitories, and when the marvelous retirement of this mysterious mountain nook fastened its whole spell upon me, then, what memory lacked, all tributary imagination furnished, and I said to myself, "This is the very counterpart of the Paradise of Bachelors, but snowed upon, and frost-painted to a sepulchre."

Dismounting, and warily picking my way down the dangerous declivity—horse and man both sliding now and then upon the icy ledges—at length I drove, or the blast drove me, into the largest square, before one side of the main edifice. Piercingly and shrilly the shotted blast blew by the corner; and redly and demoniacally boiled Blood River at one side. A long woodpile, of many scores of cords, all glittering in mail of crusted ice, stood crosswise in the square. A row of horse-posts, their north sides plastered with adhesive snow, flanked the factory wall. The bleak frost packed and paved the square as with some ringing metal.

The inverted similitude recurred—"The sweet, tranquil Temple-garden, with the Thames bordering its green beds," strangely meditated I.

But where are the gay bachelors?

Then, as I and my horse stood shivering in the wind-spray, a girl ran from a neighboring dormitory door, and throwing her thin apron over her bare head, made for the opposite building.

"One moment, my girl; is there no shed here-abouts which I may drive into?"

Pausing, she turned upon me a face pale with work, and blue with cold; an eye supernatural with unrelated misery.

"Nay," faltered I, "I mistook you. Go on; I want nothing."

Leading my horse close to the door from which she had come, I knocked. Another pale, blue girl appeared, shivering in the doorway as, to prevent the blast, she jealously held the door ajar.

"Nay, I mistake again. In God's name shut the door. But hold, is there no man about?"

That moment a dark-complexioned well-wrapped personage passed, making for the factory door, and spying him coming, the girl rapidly closed the other one.

"Is there no horse-shed here, Sir?"

"Yonder, to the wood-shed," he replied, and disappeared inside the factory.

With much ado I managed to wedge in horse and pung between the scattered piles of wood all sawn and split. Then, blanketing my horse, and piling my buffalo on the blanket's top, tucking in its edges well around the breast-hand and breeching, so that the wind might not strip him bare, I tied him fast, and ran lamely for the factory door, stiff with frost, and cumbered with my driver's dread-naught.

Immediately I found myself standing in a spacious place, intolerably lighted by long rows of windows, focusing inward the snowy scene without.

At rows of blank-looking counters sat rows of blank-looking girls, with blank, white folders in the blank hands, all blankly folding blank paper.

In one corner stood some huge frame of ponderous iron, with a vertical thing like a piston periodically rising and falling upon a heavy wooden block. Before it—its tame minister—stood a tall girl, feeding the iron animal with half-quires of rose-hued note paper, which, at every downward dab of the piston-like machine, received in the corner the impress of a wreath of roses. I looked from the rosy paper to the pallid cheek, but said nothing.

Seated before a long apparatus, strung with long, slender strings like any harp, another girl was feeding it with foolscap sheets, which, so soon as they curiously traveled from her on the cords, were withdrawn at the opposite end of the machine by a second girl.

They came to the first girl blank; they went to the second girl ruled. I looked upon the first girl's brow, and saw it was young and fair; I looked upon the second girl's brow, and saw it was ruled and wrinkled. Then, as I still looked, the two—for some small variety to the monotony—changed places; and where had stood the young, fair brow, now stood the ruled and wrinkled one.

Perched high upon a narrow platform, and still higher upon a high stool crowning it, sat another figure serving some other iron animal; while below the platform sat her mate in some sort of reciprocal attendance.

Not a syllable was breathed. Nothing was heard but the low, steady, overruling hum of the iron animals. The human voice was banished from the spot. Machinery—that vaunted slave of humanity—here stood menially served by human beings, who served mutely and cringingly as the slave serves the Sultan. The girls did not so much seem accessory wheels to the general machinery as mere cogs to the wheels.

All this scene around me was instantaneously taken in at one sweeping glance—even before I had proceeded to unwind the heavy fur tippet from around my neck. But as soon as this fell from me the dark-complexioned man, standing close by, raised a sudden cry, and seizing my arm, dragged me out into the open air, and without pausing for a word instantly caught up some congealed snow and began rubbing both my cheeks.

"Two white spots like the whites of your eyes," he said; "man, your cheeks are frozen."

"That may well be," muttered I, "'tis some wonder the frost of the Devil's Dungeon strikes in no deeper. Rub away."

Soon a horrible, tearing pain caught at my reviving cheeks. Two gaunt blood-hounds, one on each side, seemed mumbling them. I seemed Actæon.

Presently, when all was over, I re-entered the factory, made known my business, concluded it satisfactorily, and then begged to be conducted throughout the place to view it.

"Cupid is the boy for that," said the dark-complexioned man. "Cupid!" and by this odd fancy-name calling a dimpled, red-cheeked, spirited-looking, forward little fellow, who was rather impudently, I thought, gliding about among the passive-looking girls—like a gold fish through hueless waves—yet doing nothing in particular that I could see, the man bade him lead the stranger through the edifice.

"Come first and see the water-wheel," said this lively lad, with the air of boyishly-brisk importance.

Quitting the folding-room, we crossed some damp, cold boards, and stood beneath a great wet shed, incessantly showering with foam, like the green barnacled bow of some East India-man in a gale. Round and round here went the enormous revolutions of the dark colossal water-wheel, grim with its one immutable purpose.

"This sets our whole machinery a-going, Sir; in every part of all these buildings; where the girls work and all."

I looked, and saw that the turbid waters of Blood River had not changed their hue by coming under the use of man.

"You make only blank paper; no printing of any sort, I suppose? All blank paper, don't you?"

"Certainly; what else should a paper-factory make?"

The lad here looked at me as if suspicious of my common-sense.

"Oh, to be sure!" said I, confused and stammering; "it only struck me as so strange that red waters should turn out pale chee—paper, I mean."

He took me up a wet and rickety stair to a great light room, furnished with no visible thing but rude, manger-like receptacles running all round its sides; and up to these mangers, like so many mares haltered to the rack, stood rows of girls. Before each was vertically thrust up a long, glittering scythe, immovably fixed at bottom to the manger-edge. The curve of the scythe, and its having no snath to it, made it look exactly like a sword. To and fro, across the sharp edge, the girls forever dragged long strips of rags, washed white, picked from baskets at one side; thus ripping asunder every seam, and converting the tatters almost into lint. The air swam with the fine, poisonous particles, which from all sides darted, subtilely, as motes in sunbeams, into the lungs.

"This is the rag-room," coughed the boy.

"You find it rather stifling here," coughed I, in answer; "but the girls don't cough."

"Oh, they are used to it."

"Where do you get such hosts of rags?" picking up a handful from a basket.

"Some from the country round about; some from far over sea—Leghorn and London."

"'Tis not unlikely, then," murmured I, "that among these heaps of rags there may be some old shirts, gathered from the dormitories of the

Paradise of Bachelors. But the buttons are all dropped off. Pray, my lad, do you ever find any bachelor's buttons hereabouts?"

"None grow in this part of the country. The Devil's Dungeon is no place for flowers."

"Oh! you mean the *flowers* so called—the Bachelor's Buttons?"

"And was not that what you asked about? Or did you mean the gold bosom-buttons of our boss. Old Bach, as our whispering girls all call him?"

"The man, then, I saw below is a bachelor, is he?"

"Oh, yes, he's a Bach."

"The edges of those swords, they are turned outward from the girls, if I see right; but their rags and fingers fly so, I can not distinctly see."

"Turned outward."

Yes, murmured I to myself; I see it now; turned outward; and each erected sword is so borne, edge-outward, before each girl. If my reading fails me not, just so, of old, condemned state-prisoners went from the hall of judgment to their doom: an officer before, bearing a sword, its edge turned outward, in significance of their fatal sentence. So, through consumptive pallors of this blank, raggy life, go these white girls to death.

"Those scythes look very sharp," again turning toward the boy.

"Yes; they have to keep them so. Look!"

That moment two of the girls, dropping their rags, plied each a whet-stone up and down the sword-blade. My unaccustomed blood curdled at the sharp shriek of the tormented steel.

Their own executioners; themselves whetting the very swords that slay them; meditated I.

"What makes those girls so sheet-white, my lad?"

"Why"—with a roguish twinkle, pure ignorant drollery, not knowing heartlessness—"I suppose the handling of such white bits of sheets all the time makes them so sheety."

"Let us leave the rag-room now, my lad."

More tragical and more inscrutably mysterious than any mystic sight, human or machine, throughout the factory, was the strange innocence of cruel-heartedness in this usage-hardened boy.

"And now," said he, cheerily, "I suppose you want to see our great machine, which cost us twelve thousand dollars only last autumn. That's the machine that makes the paper, too. This way, Sir."

Following him, I crossed a large, bespattered place, with two great round vats in it, full of a white, wet, woolly-looking stuff, not unlike the albuminous part of an egg, soft-boiled.

"There," said Cupid, tapping the vats carelessly, "these are the first beginnings of the paper, this white pulp you see. Look how it swims bubbling round and round, moved by the paddle here. From hence it pours from both vats into that one common channel yonder; and so goes, mixed up and leisurely, to the great machine. And now for that."

He led me into a room, stifling with a strange, blood-like, abdominal heat, as if here, true enough, were being finally developed the germinous particles lately seen.

Before me, rolled out like some long Eastern manuscript, lay stretched one continuous length of iron frame-work—multitudinous and mystical, with all sorts of rollers, wheels, and cylinders, in slowly-measured and unceasing motion.

"Here first comes the pulp now," said Cupid, pointing to the nighest end of the machine. "See; first it pours out and spreads itself upon this wide, sloping board; and then—look—slides, thin and quivering, beneath the first roller there. Follow on now, and see it as it slides from under that to the next cylinder. There; see how it has become just a very little less pulpy now. One step more, and it grows still more to some slight consistence. Still another cylinder, and it is so knitted—though as yet mere dragon-fly wing—that it forms an air-bridge here, like a suspended cobweb, between two more separated rollers; and flowing over the last one, and under again, and doubling about there out of sight for a minute among all those mixed cylinders you indistinctly see, it reappears here, looking now at last a little less like pulp and more like paper, but still quite delicate and defective yet awhile. But—a little further onward, Sir, if you please—here now, at this further point, it puts on something of a real look, as if it might turn out to be something you might possibly handle in the end. But it's not yet done, Sir. Good way to travel yet, and plenty more of cylinders must roll it."

"Bless my soul!" said I, amazed at the elongation, interminable convolutions, and deliberate slowness of the machine; "it must take a long time for the pulp to pass from end to end, and come out paper."

"Oh! not so long," smiled the precocious lad, with a superior and patronizing air; "only nine minutes. But look; you may try it for yourself.

Have you a bit of paper? Ah! here's a bit on the floor. Now mark that with any word you please, and let me dab it on here, and we'll see how long before it comes out at the other end."

"Well, let me see," said I, taking out my pencil; "come, I'll mark it with your name."

Bidding me take out my watch, Cupid adroitly dropped the inscribed slip on an exposed part of the incipient mass.

Instantly my eye marked the second-hand on my dial-plate.

Slowly I followed the slip, inch by inch; sometimes pausing for full half a minute as it disappeared beneath inscrutable groups of the lower cylinders, but only gradually to emerge again; and so, on, and on, and on—inch by inch; now in open sight, sliding along like a freckle on the quivering sheet; and then again wholly vanished; and so, on, and on, and on—inch by inch; all the time the main sheet growing more and more to final firmness—when, suddenly, I saw a sort of paper-fall, not wholly unlike a water-fall; a scissory sound smote my ear, as of some cord being snapped; and down dropped an unfolded sheet of perfect foolscap, with my "Cupid" half faded out of it, and still moist and warm.

My travels were at an end, for here was the end of the machine.

"Well, how long was it?" said Cupid.

"Nine minutes to a second," replied I, watch in hand.

"I told you so."

For a moment a curious emotion filled me, not wholly unlike that which one might experience at the fulfillment of some mysterious prophecy. But how absurd, thought I again; the thing is a mere machine, the essence of which is unvarying punctuality and precision.

Previously absorbed by the wheels and cylinders, my attention was now directed to a sad-looking woman standing by.

"That is rather an elderly person so silently tending the machine-end here. She would not seem wholly used to it either."

"Oh," knowingly whispered Cupid, through the din, "she only came last week. She was a nurse formerly. But the business is poor in these parts, and she's left it. But look at the paper she is piling there."

"Ay, foolscap," handling the piles of moist, warm sheets, which continually were being delivered into the woman's waiting hands. "Don't you turn out any thing but foolscap at this machine?"

"Oh, sometimes, but not often, we turn out finer work—cream-laid and royal sheets, we call them. But foolscap being in chief demand, we turn out foolscap most."

It was very curious. Looking at that blank paper continually dropping, dropping, dropping, my mind ran on in wonderings of those strange uses to which those thousand sheets eventually would be put. All sorts of writings would be writ on those now vacant things—sermons, lawyers' briefs, physicians' prescriptions, love-letters, marriage certificates, bills of divorce, registers of births, death-warrants, and so on, without end. Then, recurring back to them as they here lay all blank, I could not but bethink me of that celebrated comparison of John Locke, who, in demonstration of his theory that man had no innate ideas, compared the human mind at birth to a sheet of blank paper; something destined to be scribbled on, but what sort of characters no soul might tell.

Pacing slowly to and fro along the involved machine, still humming with its play, I was struck as well by the inevitability as the evolvement-power in all its motions.

"Does that thin cobweb there," said I, pointing to the sheet in its more imperfect stage, "does that never tear or break? It is marvelous fragile, and yet this machine it passes through is so mighty."

"It never is known to tear a hair's point."

"Does it never stop—get clogged?"

"No. It *must* go. The machinery makes it go just *so;* just that very way, and at that very pace you there plainly *see* it go. The pulp can't help going."

Something of awe now stole over me, as I gazed upon this inflexible iron animal. Always, more or less, machinery of this ponderous, elaborate sort strikes, in some moods, strange dread into the human heart, as some living, panting Behemoth might. But what made the thing I saw so specially terrible to me was the metallic necessity, the unbudging fatality which governed it. Though, here and there, I could not follow the thin, gauzy vail of pulp in the course of its more mysterious or entirely invisible advance, yet it was indubitable that, at those points where it eluded me, it still marched on in unvarying docility to the autocratic cunning of the machine. A fascination fastened on me. I stood spellbound and wandering in my soul. Before my eyes—there, passing in slow procession along the wheeling cylinders, I seemed to see, glued to the pallid incipience of the pulp, the yet more pallid faces of all the pallid girls I had eyed that heavy day. Slowly, mournfully, beseechingly, yet unresistingly, they gleamed along, their agony dimly outlined on the imperfect paper, like the print of the tormented face on the handkerchief of Saint Veronica.

"Halloa! the heat of the room is too much for you," cried Cupid, staring at me.

"No—I am rather chill, if any thing."

"Come out, Sir—out—out," and, with the protecting air of a careful father, the precocious lad hurried me outside.

In a few moments, feeling revived a little, I went into the folding-room—the first room I had entered, and where the desk for transacting business stood, surrounded by the blank counters and blank girls engaged at them.

"Cupid here has led me a strange tour," said I to the dark-complexioned man before mentioned, whom I had ere this discovered not only to be an old bachelor, but also the principal proprietor. "Yours is a most wonderful factory. Your great machine is a miracle of inscrutable intricacy."

"Yes, all our visitors think it so. But we don't have many. We are in a very out-of-the-way corner here. Few inhabitants, too. Most of our girls come from far-off villages."

"The girls," echoed I. glancing round at their silent forms. "Why is it, Sir, that in most factories, female operatives, of whatever age, are indiscriminately called girls, never women?"

"Oh! as to that—why, I suppose, the fact of their being generally unmarried—that's the reason, I should think. But it never struck me before. For our factory here, we will not have married women; they are apt to be off-and-on too much. We want none but steady workers: twelve hours to the day, day after day, through the three hundred and sixty-five days, excepting Sundays, Thanksgiving, and Fastdays. That's our rule. And so, having no married women, what females we have are rightly enough called girls."

"Then these are all maids," said I, while some pained homage to their pale virginity made me involuntarily bow.

"All maids."

Again the strange emotion filled me.

"Your cheeks look whitish yet, Sir," said the man, gazing at me narrowly. "You must be careful going home. Do they pain you at all now? It's a bad sign, if they do."

"No doubt, Sir," answered I, "when once I have got out of the Devil's Dungeon, I shall feel them mending."

"Ah, yes; the winter air in valleys, or gorges, or any sunken place, is far colder and more bitter than elsewhere. You would hardly believe it now, but it is colder here than at the top of Woe-dolor Mountain."

"I dare say it is. Sir. But time presses me; I must depart."

With that, remuffling myself in dread-naught and tippet, thrusting my hands into my huge seal-skin mittens, I sallied out into the nipping air, and found poor Black, my horse, all cringing and doubled up with the cold.

Soon, wrapped in furs and meditations, I ascended from the Devil's Dungeon.

At the Black Notch I paused, and once more bethought me of Temple-Bar. Then, shooting through the pass, all alone with inscrutable nature, I exclaimed—Oh! Paradise of Bachelors! and oh! Tartarus of Maids!

SAMUEL CLEMENS
(1835–1910)

Like Harriet Beecher Stowe, Samuel Clemens, who marketed himself through a career of four decades as "Mark Twain," enjoyed a degree of renown rare to any imaginative artist. Clemens is generally considered America's most beloved humorist, though much of his humor, even in his seemingly artless first-person musings, is laced with a savagely cynical view of mankind. Indeed, part of the satirist's intention seems to be a mockery of the very audience, credulous and eager to be entertained, that made him a distinctly American success: forever looking backward to a mythical "regional" America, a place of childhood and simple homespun virtues, even as the mass-marketing strategies of his time—the proliferation of newspapers, for instance—allowed for a shrewd manufacturing and distribution of such visions.

Samuel Langhorne Clemens was born in Florida, Missouri, grew up in Hannibal, and began his writing career as a newspaperman in various parts of the country, including the Nevada Territory and California. His inspired retelling of a popular tall tale, "The Celebrated Jumping Frog of Calaveras County," published in 1865, brought him instant acclaim and a wide, uncritical readership. Subsequent titles assured the success of "Mark Twain": The Innocents Abroad *(1869),* Old Times on the Mississippi *(1875),* The Adventures of Tom Sawyer *(1876),* The Adventures of Huckleberry Finn *(1884),* The Tragedy of Pudd'nhead Wilson (1894). *The heavy-handed satire of "The Man That Corrupted Hadleyburg" (1900) and "What Is Man?" (1906) did nothing to mitigate Clemens' reputation as a master of a peculiarly American, idiomatic English. "Cannibalism in the Cars," a virtually unknown work, is quintessential Clemens in its comic hyperbole and the angry despair that runs beneath its anecdotal surface.*

Cannibalism in the Cars

I visited St. Louis lately, and on my way West, after changing cars at Terre Haute, Indiana, a mild, benevolent-looking gentleman of about forty-five, or maybe fifty, came in at one of the way stations and sat down beside me. We talked together pleasantly on various subjects for an hour, perhaps, and I found him exceedingly intelligent and entertaining. When he learned that I was from Washington, he immediately began to ask questions about various public men, and about congressional affairs; and I saw very shortly that I was conversing with a man who was perfectly familiar with the ins and outs of political life at the capital, even to the ways and manners, and customs of procedure of senators and representatives in the chambers of the national legislature. Presently two men halted near us for a single moment, and one said to the other: "Harris, if you'll do that for me, I'll never forget you, my boy."

My new comrade's eye lighted pleasantly. The words had touched upon a happy memory, I thought. Then his faced settled into thoughtfulness—almost into gloom. He turned to me and said, "Let me tell you a story, let me give you a secret chapter of my life—a chapter that has never been referred to by me since its events transpired. Listen patiently, and promise that you will not interrupt me."

I said I would not, and he related the following strange adventure, speaking sometimes with animation, sometimes with melancholy, but always with feeling and earnestness.

On the nineteenth of December, 1853, I started from St. Louis on the evening train bound for Chicago. There were only twenty-four passengers, all told. There were no ladies and no children. We were in excellent spirits, and pleasant acquaintanceships were soon formed. The journey bade fair to be a happy one; and no individual in the party, I think, had even the vaguest presentiment of the horrors we were soon to undergo.

At 11:00 P.M. it began to snow hard. Shortly after leaving the small village of Welden, we entered upon that tremendous prairie solitude that stretches its leagues on leagues of houseless dreariness far away toward the Jubilee Settlements. The winds, unobstructed by trees or hills, or even vagrant rocks, whistled fiercely across the level desert, driving the falling snow before it like spray from the crested waves of a stormy sea. The snow was deepening fast; and we knew, by the diminished speed of the train, that the engine was plowing through it with steadily increasing difficulty. Indeed, it almost came to a dead halt sometimes, in the midst of great drifts that piled themselves like colossal graves across the track. Conversation began to flag. Cheerfulness gave place to grave concern. The possibility of being imprisoned in the snow, on the bleak prairie, fifty miles from any house, presented itself to every mind, and extended its depressing influence over every spirit.

At two o'clock in the morning I was aroused out of an uneasy slumber by the ceasing of all motion about me. The appalling truth flashed upon me instantly—we were captives in a snowdrift! "All hands to the rescue!" Every man sprang to obey. Out into the wild night, the pitchy darkness, the billowy snow, the driving storm, every soul leaped, with the consciousness that a moment lost now might bring destruction to us all. Shovels, hands, boards—anything, everything that could displace snow, was brought into instant requisition. It was a weird picture, that small company of frantic men fighting the banking snows, half in the blackest shadow and half in the angry light of the locomotive's reflector.

One short hour sufficed to prove the utter uselessness of our efforts. The storm barricaded the track with a dozen drifts while we dug one away. And worse than this, it was discovered that the last grand charge the engine had made upon the enemy had broken the fore-and-aft shaft of the driving wheel! With a free track before us we should still have been helpless. We entered the car wearied with labor, and very sorrowful. We gathered about the stoves, and gravely canvassed our situation. We had no provisions whatever—in this lay our chief distress. We could not freeze, for there was a good supply of wood in the tender. This was our only comfort. The discussion ended at last in accepting the disheartening decision of the conductor, *viz.*, that it would be death for any man to attempt to travel fifty miles on foot through snow like that. We could not send for help, and even if we could it would not come. We must submit, and await, as patiently as we might, succor or starvation! I think the stoutest heart there felt a momentary chill when those words were uttered.

Within the hour conversation subsided to a low murmur here and there about the car, caught fitfully between the rising and falling of the blast; the lamps grew dim; and the majority of the castaways settled themselves among the flickering shadows to think—to forget the present, if they could—to sleep, if they might.

The eternal night—it surely seemed eternal to us—wore its lagging hours away at last, and the cold gray dawn broke in the east. As the light grew stronger the passengers began to stir and give signs of life, one after another, and each in turn pushed his slouched hat up from his forehead, stretched his stiffened limbs and glanced out of the windows upon the cheerless prospect. It was cheerless, indeed!—not a living thing visible anywhere, not a human habitation; nothing but a vast white desert; uplifted sheets of snow drifting hither and thither before the wind—a world of eddying flakes shutting out the firmament above.

All day we moped about the cars, saying little, thinking much. Another lingering dreary night—and hunger.

Another dawning—another day of silence, sadness, wasting hunger, hopeless watching for succor that could not come. A night of restless slumber, filled with dreams of feasting—wakings distressed with the gnawings of hunger.

The fourth day came and went—and the fifth! Five days of dreadful imprisonment! A savage hunger looked out at every eye. There was in it a sign of awful import—the foreshadowing of a something that was vaguely shaping itself in every heart—a something which no tongue dared yet to frame into words.

The sixth day passed—the seventh dawned upon as gaunt and haggard and hopeless a company of men as ever stood in the shadow of death. It must out now! That thing which had been growing up in every heart was ready to leap from every lip at last! Nature had been taxed to the utmost—she must yield. Richard H. Gaston of Minnesota, tall, cadaverous, and pale, rose up. All knew what was coming. All prepared—every emotion, every semblance of excitement was smothered—only a calm, thoughtful seriousness appeared in the eyes that were lately so wild.

"Gentlemen: It cannot be delayed longer! The time is at hand! We must determine which of us shall die to furnish food for the rest!"

MR. JOHN J. WILLIAMS of Illinois rose and said: "Gentlemen—I nominate the Reverend James Sawyer of Tennessee."

MR. WM. R. ADAMS of Indiana said: "I nominate Mr. Daniel Slote of New York."

MR. CHARLES J. LANGDON: "I nominate Mr. Samuel A. Bowen of St. Louis."

MR. SLOTE: "Gentlemen—I desire to decline in favor of Mr. John A. Van Nostrand, Jr., of New Jersey."

MR. GASTON: "If there be no objection, the gentleman's desire will be acceded to."

Mr. Van Nostrand objecting, the resignation of Mr. Slote was rejected. The resignations of Messrs. Sawyer and Bowen were also offered, and refused upon the same grounds.

MR. A. L. BASCOM of Ohio: "I move that the nominations now close, and that the House proceed to an election by ballot."

MR. SAWYER: "Gentlemen—I protest earnestly against these proceedings. They are, in every way, irregular and unbecoming. I must beg to move that they be dropped at once, and that we elect a chairman of the meeting and proper officers to assist him, and then we can go on with the business before us understandingly."

MR. BELL of Iowa: "Gentlemen—I object. This is no time to stand upon forms and ceremonious observances. For more than seven days we have been without food. Every moment we lose in idle discussion increases our distress. I am satisfied with the nominations that have been made—every gentleman present is, I believe—and I, for one, do not see why we should not proceed at once to elect one or more of them. I wish to offer a resolution—"

MR. GASTON: "It would be objected to, and have to lie over one day under the rules, thus bringing about the very delay you wish to avoid. The gentleman from New Jersey—"

MR. VAN NOSTRAND: "Gentlemen—I am a stranger among you; I have not sought the distinction that has been conferred upon me, and I feel a delicacy—"

MR. MORGAN of Alabama (interrupting): "I move the previous question."

The motion was carried, and further debate shut off, of course. The motion to elect officers was passed, and under it Mr. Gaston was chosen chairman, Mr. Blake, secretary, Messrs. Holcomb, Dyer and Baldwin a committee on nominations, and Mr. R. M. Howland, purveyor, to assist the committee in making selections.

A recess of half an hour was then taken, and some little caucusing followed. At the sound of the gavel the meeting reassembled, and the committee reported in favor of Messrs. George Ferguson of Kentucky, Lucien Herrman of Louisiana and W. Messick of Colorado as candidates. The report was accepted.

Mr. Rogers of Missouri: "Mr. President—The report being properly before the House now, I move to amend it by substituting for the name of Mr. Herrman that of Mr. Lucius Harris of St. Louis, who is well and honorably known to us all. I do not wish to be understood as casting the least reflection upon the high character and standing of the gentleman from Louisiana—far from it. I respect and esteem him as much as any gentleman here present possibly can; but none of us can be blind to the fact that he had lost more flesh during the week that we have lain here than any among us—none of us can be blind to the fact that the committee has been derelict in its duty, either through negligence or a graver fault, in thus offering for our suffrages a gentleman who, however pure his own motives may be, has really less nutriment in him—"

The Chair: "The gentleman from Missouri will take his seat. The Chair cannot allow the integrity of the committee to be questioned save by the regular course, under the rules. What action will the House take upon the gentleman's motion?"

Mr. Halliday of Virginia: "I move to further amend the report by substituting Mr. Harvey Davis of Oregon for Mr. Messick. It may be urged by gentlemen that the hardships and privations of a frontier life have rendered Mr. Davis tough; but, gentlemen, is this a time to cavil at toughness? Is this a time to be fastidious concerning trifles? Is this a time to dispute about matters of paltry significance? No, gentlemen, bulk is what we desire—substance, weight, bulk—these are the supreme requisites now—not talent, not genius, not education. I insist upon my motion."

Mr. Morgan (excitedly): "Mr. Chairman—I do most strenuously object to this amendment. The gentleman from Oregon is old, and furthermore is bulky only in bone—not in flesh. I ask the gentleman from Virginia if it is soup we want instead of solid sustenance? if he would delude us with shadows? if he would mock our suffering with an Oregonian specter? I ask him if he can look upon the anxious faces around him, if he can gaze into our sad eyes, if he can listen to the beating of our expectant hearts, and still thrust this famine-stricken fraud upon us? I ask him if he can think of our desolate state, of our past sorrows, of our dark future, and still unpityingly foist upon us this wreck, this ruin, this tottering swindle, this gnarled and blighted and sapless vagabond from Oregon's inhospitable shores? Never! [Applause.]"

The amendment was put to vote, after a fiery debate, and lost. Mr. Harris was substituted on the first amendment. The balloting then began. Five ballots were held without a choice. On the sixth, Mr. Harris was elected, all voting for him but himself. It was then moved that his election should be ratified by acclamation, which was lost, in consequence of his again voting against himself.

Mr. Radway moved that the House now take up the remaining candidates, and go into an election for breakfast. This was carried.

On the first ballot there was a tie, half the members favoring one candidate on account of his youth, and half favoring the other on account of his superior size. The president gave the casting vote for the latter, Mr. Messick. This decision created considerable dissatisfaction among the friends of Mr. Ferguson, the defeated candidate, and there was some talk of demanding a new ballot; but in the midst of it a motion to adjourn was carried, and the meeting broke up at once.

The preparations for supper diverted the attention of the Ferguson faction from the discussion of their grievance for a long time, and then, when they would have taken it up again, the happy announcement that Mr. Harris was ready drove all thought of it to the winds.

We improvised tables by propping up the backs of car seats, and sat down with hearts full of gratitude to the finest supper that had blessed our vision for seven torturing days. How changed we were from what we had been a few short hours before! Hopeless, sad-eyed misery, hunger, feverish anxiety, desperation, then; thankfulness, serenity, joy too deep for utterance now. That I know was the cheeriest hour of my eventful life. The winds howled, and blew the snow wildly about our prison house, but they were powerless to distress us anymore. I liked Harris. He might have been better done, perhaps, but I am free to say that no man ever agreed with me better than Harris, or afforded me so large a degree of satisfaction. Messick was very well, though rather high-flavored, but for genuine nutritiousness and delicacy of fiber, give me Harris. Messick had his good points—I will not attempt to deny it, nor do I wish to do it—but he was no more fitted for breakfast than a mummy would be, sir—not a bit. Lean?—why, bless me!—and tough? Ah, he was very tough! You could not imagine it—you could never imagine anything like it.

"Do you mean to tell me that—"

"Do not interrupt me, please. After breakfast we elected a man by the name of Walker, from Detroit, for supper. He was very good. I wrote his wife so afterward. He was worthy of all praise. I shall always remember Walker. He was a little rare, but very good. And then the next morning we had Morgan of Alabama for breakfast. He was one of the finest men I ever sat down to—handsome, educated, refined, spoke several languages fluently—a perfect gentleman—he was a perfect gentleman, and singularly juicy. For supper we had that Oregon patriarch, and he *was* a fraud, there is no question about it—old, scraggy, tough, nobody can picture the reality. I finally said, 'Gentlemen, you can do as you like, but I will wait for another election.' And Grimes of Illinois said, 'Gentlemen, *I* will wait also. When you elect a man that has *something* to recommend him, I shall be glad to join you again.' It soon became evident that there was general dissatisfaction with Davis of Oregon, and so, to preserve the good will that had prevailed so pleasantly since we had had Harris, an election was called, and the result of it was that Baker of Georgia was chosen. He was splendid! Well, well—after that we had Doolittle, and Hawkins, and McElroy (there was some complaint about McElroy. because he was uncommonly short and thin), and Penrod, and two Smiths, and Bailey (Bailey had a wooden leg, which was clear loss, but he was otherwise good), and an Indian boy, and an organ-grinder and a gentleman by the name of Buckminster—a poor stick of a vagabond that wasn't any good for company and no account for breakfast. We were glad we got him elected before relief came."

"And so the blessed relief *did* come at last?"

"Yes, it came one bright, sunny morning, just after election. John Murphy was the choice, and there never was a better, I am willing to testify; but John Murphy came home with us, in the train that came to succor us, and lived to marry the widow Harris—"

"Relict of—"

"Relict of our first choice. He married her, and is happy and respected and prosperous yet. Ah, it was like a novel, sir—it was like a romance. This is my stopping-place, sir; I must bid you goodbye. Any time that you can make it convenient to tarry a day or two with me, I shall be glad to have you. I like you, sir; I have conceived an affection for you. I could like you as well as I liked Harris himself, sir. Good day, sir, and a pleasant journey."

He was gone. I never felt so stunned, so distressed, so bewildered in my life. But in my soul I was glad he was gone. With all his gentleness of manner and his soft voice, I shuddered whenever he turned his hungry eye upon me; and when I heard that I had achieved his perilous affection, and that I stood almost with the late Harris in his esteem, my heart fairly stood still!

I was bewildered beyond description. I did not doubt his word; I could not question a single item in a statement so stamped with the earnestness of truth as his; but its dreadful details overpowered me, and threw my thoughts into hopeless confusion. I saw the conductor looking at me. I said, "Who is that man?"

"He was a member of congress once, and a good one. But he got caught in a snowdrift in the cars, and like to have been starved to death. He got so frostbitten and frozen up generally, and used up for want of something to eat, that he was sick and out of his head two or three months afterward. He is all right now, only he is a monomaniac, and when he gets on that old subject he never stops till he has eat up that whole carload of people he talks about. He would have finished the crowd by this time, only he had to get out here. He has got their names as past as *ABC*. When he gets them all eat up but himself, he always says: 'Then the hour for the unusual election for breakfast having arrived, and there being no opposition, I was duly elected, after which, there being no objections offered, I resigned. Thus I am here.'"

I felt inexpressibly relieved to know that I had only been listening to the harmless vagaries of a madman instead of the genuine experiences of a bloodthirsty cannibal.

HENRY JAMES
(1843–1916)

With Henry James, we come to our first American theorist of fictional technique, whose extraordinary career encompassed any number of genres—the novel, the romance, the short story, the essay, the play, as well as countless prefaces, letters, notebooks, and reviews. Of American writers of the first rank, no one is more devoted to his craft than James; no one is more prolific, more fated, for art—like the hapless Dencombe of "The Middle Years" perhaps, for whom the "infinite of life was gone" and all that remained was the "abyss of human illusion that was the real, the tideless deep." (Or is this mere playfulness on the part of James who often sought, for diversity's sake, positions adversarial to his own?)

Henry James was born in New York City on April 15, 1843, to a well-to-do and distinguished family. His elder brother was William James, America's first psychologist and philosopher of significance. James set about consciously, and systematically, to make a career in international terms; he was to be no mere "American" writer, still less a writer bent upon popular success, but a self-determined literary master—one who would attempt to fashion, by way of such closely argued works as "The Art of Fiction," the very standards by which he would be judged. His early successes were The American *(1877),* Daisy Miller *(1878), and* The Portrait of a Lady *(1881); his middle, rather more ambitious works,* The Bostonians *(1886),* The Princess Casamassima *(1886), and* The Tragic Muse *(1890), were less popular. James' most ambitious novels are the later, writerly novels* The Wings of the Dove *(1902),* The Ambassadors *(1903), and* The Golden Bowl *(1904), though it might be argued that his most memorable works of fiction are short stories like "The Beast in the Jungle" and the novella* The Turn of the Screw (1898)*, in which vision, style, and a tightly imagined structure are brilliantly conjoined.*

The Middle Years

The April day was soft and bright, and poor Dencombe, happy in the conceit of reasserted strength, stood in the garden of the hotel, comparing, with a deliberation in which however there was still something of languor, the attractions of easy strolls. He liked the feeling of the south so far as you could have it in the north, he liked the sandy cliffs and the clustered pines, he liked even the colourless sea. "Bournemouth as a health-resort" had sounded like a mere advertisement, but he was thankful now for the commonest conveniences. The sociable country postman, passing through the garden, had just given him a small parcel which he took out with him, leaving the hotel to the right and creeping to a bench he had already haunted, a safe recess in the cliff. It looked to the south, to the tinted walls of the Island, and was protected behind by the sloping shoulder of the down. He was tired enough when he reached it, and for a moment was disappointed; he was better of course, but better, after all, than what? He should never again, as at one or two great moments of the past, be better than himself. The infinite of life was gone, and what remained of the dose a small glass scored like a thermometer by the apothecary. He sat and stared at the sea, which appeared all surface and twinkle, far shallower than the spirit of man. It was the abyss of human illusion that was the real, the tideless deep. He held his packet, which had come by book-post, unopened on his knee, liking, in the lapse of so many joys—his illness had made him feel his age—to know it was there, but taking for granted there could be no complete renewal of the pleasure, dear to young experience, of seeing one's self "just out." Dencombe, who had a reputation, had come out too often and knew too well in advance how he should look.

His postponement associated itself vaguely, after a little, with a group of three persons, two ladies and a young man, whom, beneath him, straggling and seemingly silent, he could see move slowly together along the sands. The gentleman had his head bent over a book and was occasionally brought to a stop by the charm of this volume, which, as Dencombe could perceive even at a distance, had a cover alluringly red. Then his companions, going a little further, waited for him to come up, poking their parasols into the beach, looking around them at the sea and sky and clearly sensible of the beauty of the day. To these things the young man with the book was still more clearly indifferent; lingering, credulous, absorbed, he was an object of envy to an observer from whose connexion with literature all such artlessness had faded. One of the ladies was large and mature; the other had the spareness of comparative youth and of a social situation possibly inferior. The large lady carried back Dencombe's imagination to the age of crinoline; she wore a hat of the shape of a mushroom, decorated with a blue veil, and had the air, in her aggressive amplitude, of clinging to a vanished fashion or even a lost cause. Presently her companion produced from under the folds of a mantle a limp portable chair which she stiffened out and of which the large lady took possession. This act, and something in the movement of either party, at once characterised the performers—they performed for Dencombe's recreation—as opulent matron and humble dependent. Where moreover was the virtue of an approved novelist if one couldn't establish a relation between such figures? the clever theory for instance that the young man was the son of the opulent matron and that the humble dependent, the daughter of a clergyman or an officer, nourished a secret passion for him. Was that not visible from the way she stole behind her protectress to look back at him?—back to where he had let himself come to a full stop when his mother sat down to rest. His book was a novel, it had the catchpenny binding; so that while the romance of life stood neglected at his side he lost himself in that of the circulating library. He moved mechanically to where the sand was softer and ended by plumping down in it to finish his chapter at his ease. The humble dependent, discouraged by his remoteness, wandered with a martyred droop of the head in another direction, and the exorbitant lady, watching the waves, offered a confused resemblance to a dying-machine that had broken down.

When his drama began to fail Dencombe remembered that he had after all another pastime. Though such promptitude on the part of the publisher was rare he was already able to draw from its wrapper his "latest," perhaps his last. The cover of "The Middle Years" was duly meretricious, the smell of the fresh pages the very odour of sanctity; but for the moment he went no further—he had become conscious of a strange alienation. He had forgotten what his book was about. Had the assault of his old ailment, which he had so fallaciously come to Bournemouth to ward off, interposed utter blankness as to what had preceded it? He had finished the revision of proof before quitting London, but his subsequent fortnight in bed had passed the sponge over colour. He couldn't have chanted to himself a single sentence, couldn't have turned with curiosity or confidence to any particular page. His subject had already gone from him, leaving scarce a superstition behind. He uttered a low moan as he breathed the chill of this dark void, so desperately it seemed to represent the completion of a sinister process. The tears filled his mild eyes; something precious had passed away. This was the pang that had been sharpest during the last few years—the sense of ebbing time, of shrinking opportunity; and now he felt not so much that his last chance was going as that it was gone indeed. He had done all he should ever do, and yet hadn't done what he wanted. This was the laceration—that practically his career was over: it was as violent as a grip at his throat. He rose from his seat nervously—a creature hunted by a dread; then he fell back in his weakness and nervously opened his book. It was a single volume; he preferred single volumes and aimed at a rare compression. He began to read and, little by little, in this occupation, was pacified and reassured. Everything came back to him, but came back with a wonder, came back above all with a high and magnificent beauty. He read his own prose, he turned his own leaves, and had as he sat there with the spring sunshine on the page an emotion peculiar and intense. His career was over, no doubt, but it was over, when all was said, with *that.*

He had forgotten during his illness the work of the previous year; but what he had chiefly forgotten was that it was extraordinarily good. He dived once more into his story and was drawn down, as by a siren's hand, to where, in the dim underworld of fiction, the great glazed tank of art, strange silent subjects float. He recognised his motive and surrendered to his talent. Never probably had that talent, such as it was, been so fine. His difficulties were still there, but what was also there, to his perception, though probably, alas! to nobody's else, was the art that in most cases had surmounted them. In his surprised enjoyment of this ability he had a glimpse of a possible reprieve. Surely its force wasn't spent—there was life and service in it yet. It hadn't come to him easily, it had been backward and roundabout. It was the child of time, the nursling of delay; he had struggled and suffered for it, making sacrifices not to be counted, and now that it was really mature was it to cease to yield, to confess itself brutally beaten? There was an infinite charm for Dencombe in feeling as he had never felt before that diligence *vincit omnia*. The result produced in his little book was somehow a result beyond his conscious intention: it was as if he had planted his genius, had trusted his method, and they had grown up and flowered with this sweetness. If the achievement had been real, however, the process had been painful enough. What he saw so intensely today, what he felt as a nail driven in, was that only now, at the very last, had he come into possession. His development had been abnormally slow, almost grotesquely gradual. He had been hindered and retarded by experience, he had for long periods only groped his way. It had taken too much of his life to produce too little of his art. The art had come, but it had come after everything else. At such a rate a first existence was too short—long enough only to collect material; so that to fructify, to use the material, one should have a second age, an extension. This extension was what poor Dencombe sighed for. As he turned the last leaves of his volume he murmured "Ah for another go, ah for a better chance!"

The three persons drawing his attention to the sands had vanished and then reappeared: they had now wandered up a path, an artificial and easy ascent, which led to the top of the cliff. Dencombe's bench was halfway down, on a sheltered ledge, and the large lady, a massive heterogeneous person with bold black eyes and kind red cheeks, now took a few moments to rest. She wore dirty gauntlets and immense diamond ear-rings: at first she looked vulgar, but she contradicted this announcement in an agreeable off-hand tone. While her companions stood waiting for her she spread her skirts on the end of Dencombe's seat. The young man had gold spectacles, through which, with his finger still in his red-covered book, he glanced at the volume, bound in the same shade of the same colour, lying on the lap of the original occupant of the bench. After an instant Dencombe felt him struck with a resemblance: he had recognised the gilt stamp on the crimson cloth, was reading "The Middle Years" and now noted that somebody else had kept pace with him. The stranger was startled, possibly even a little ruffled, to find himself not the only person favoured with an early copy. The eyes of the two proprietors met a moment, and Dencombe borrowed amusement from the expression of those of his competitor, those, it might even be inferred, of his admirer. They confessed to some resentment—they seemed to say: "Hang it, has he got it *already*? Of course he's a brute of a reviewer!" Dencombe shuffled his copy out of sight while the opulent matron, rising from her repose, broke out: "I feel already the good of this air!"

"I can't say I do," said the angular lady- "I find myself quite let down."

"I find myself horribly hungry. At what time did you order luncheon?" her protectress pursued.

The young person put the question by. "Doctor Hugh always orders it."

"I ordered nothing today—I'm going to make you diet," said their comrade.

"Then I shall go home and sleep. *Qui dort dine!*"

"Can I trust you to Miss Vernham?" asked Doctor Hugh of his elder companion.

"Don't I trust *you?*" she archly enquired.

"Not too much!" Miss Vernham, with her eyes on the ground, permitted herself to declare. "You must come with us at least to the house," she went on while the personage on whom they appeared to be in attendance began to mount higher. She had got a little out of ear-shot; nevertheless Miss Vernham became, so far as Dencombe was concerned, less distinctly audible to murmur to the young man: "I don't think you realise all you owe the Countess!"

Absently, a moment. Doctor Hugh caused his gold-rimmed spectacles to shine at her. "Is that the way I strike you? I see—I see!"

"She's awfully good to us," continued Miss Vernham, compelled by the lapse of the other's motion to stand there in spite of his discussion of private matters. Of what use would it have been that Dencombe should be sensitive to shades; hadn't he detected in that arrest a strange influence from the quiet old convalescent in the great tweed cape? Miss Vernham appeared suddenly to become aware of some such connexion, for she added in a moment: "If you want to sun yourself here you can come back after you've seen us home."

Doctor Hugh, at this, hesitated, and Dencombe, in spite of a desire to pass for unconscious, risked a covert glance at him. What his eyes met this time, as happened, was, on the part of the young lady, a queer stare, naturally vitreous, which made her remind him of some figure—he couldn't name it—in a play or a novel, some sinister governess or tragic old maid. She seemed to scan him, to challenge him, to say out of general spite: "What have you got to do with us?" At the same instant the rich humour of the Countess reached them from above: "Come, come, my little lambs; you should follow your old *bergere!*" Miss Vernham turned away for it, pursuing the ascent, and Doctor Hugh, after another mute appeal to Dencombe and a minute's evident demur, deposited his book on the bench as if to keep his place, or even as a gage of earnest return, and bounded without difficulty up the rougher part of the cliff.

Equally innocent and infinite are the pleasures of observation and the resources engendered by the trick of analysing life. It amused poor Dencombe, as he dawdled in his tepid air-bath, to believe himself awaiting a revelation of something at the back of a fine young mind. He looked hard at the book on the end of the bench, but wouldn't have touched it for the world. It served his purpose to have a theory that shouldn't be exposed to refutation. He already felt better of his melancholy; he had, according to his old formula, put his head at the window. A passing Countess could draw off the fancy when, like the elder of the ladies who had just retreated, she was as obvious as the giantess of a caravan. It was indeed general views that were terrible; short ones, contrary to an opinion sometimes expressed, were the refuge, were the remedy. Doctor Hugh couldn't possibly be anything but a reviewer who had understandings for early copies with publishers or with newspapers. He reappeared in a quarter of an hour with visible relief at finding Dencombe on the spot and the gleam of white teeth in an embarrassed but generous smile. He was perceptibly disappointed at the eclipse of the other copy of the book: it made a pretext the less for speaking to the quiet gentleman. But he spoke notwithstanding; he held up his own copy and broke out pleadingly: "*Do* say, if you have occasion to speak of it, that it's the best thing he has done yet!"

Dencombe responded with a laugh: "Done yet" was so amusing to him, made such a grand avenue of the future. Better still, the young man took *him* for a reviewer. He pulled out "The Middle Years" from under his cape, but instinctively concealed any telltale look of fatherhood. This was partly because a person was always a fool for insisting to others on his work. "Is that what you're going to say yourself?" he put to his visitor.

"I'm not quite sure I shall write anything. I don't, as a regular thing—I enjoy in peace. But it's awfully fine."

Dencombe just debated. If the young man had begun to abuse him he would have confessed on the spot to his identity, but there was no harm in drawing out any impulse to praise. He drew it out with such success that in a few moments his new acquaintance, seated by his side, was confessing candidly that the works of the author of the volumes before them were the only ones he could read a second time. He had come the day before from London, where a friend of his, a journalist, had lent him his copy of the last, the copy sent to the office of the journal and already the subject of a "notice" which, as was pretended there—but one had to allow for "swagger"—it had taken a full quarter of an hour to prepare. He intimated that he was ashamed for his friend, and in the case of a work demanding and repaying study, of such inferior manners; and, with his fresh appreciation and his so irregular wish to express it, he speedily became for poor Dencombe a remarkable, a delightful apparition. Chance had brought the weary man of letters face to face with the greatest admirer in the new generation of whom it was supposable he might boast. The admirer in truth was mystifying, so rare a case was it to find a bristling young doctor—he looked like a German physiologist—enamoured of literary form. It was an accident, but happier than most accidents, so that Dencombe, exhilarated as well as confounded, spent half an hour in making his visitor talk while he kept himself quiet. He explained his premature possession of "The Middle Years" by an allusion to the friendship of the publisher, who, knowing he was at Bournemouth for his health, had paid him this graceful attention. He allowed he had been ill, for Doctor Hugh would infallibly have guessed it; he even went so far as to wonder if he mightn't look for some hygienic "tip" from a personage combining so bright an enthusiasm with a presumable knowledge of the remedies now in vogue. It would shake his faith a little perhaps to have to take a doctor seriously who could take *him* so seriously, but he enjoyed this gushing modern youth and felt with an acute pang that there would still be work to do in a world in which such odd combinations were presented. It wasn't true, what he had tried for renunciation's sake to believe, that all the combinations were exhausted. They weren't by any means—they were infinite: the exhaustion was in the miserable artist.

Doctor Hugh, an ardent physiologist, was saturated with the spirit of the age—in other words he had just taken his degree: but he was independent and various, he talked like a man who would have preferred to love literature best. He would fain have made fine phrases, but nature had denied him the trick. Some of the finest in "The Middle Years" had struck him inordinately, and he took the liberty of reading them to Dencombe in support of his plea. He grew vivid, in the balmy air, to his companion, for whose deep refreshment he seemed to have been sent; and was particularly ingenuous in describing how recently he had become acquainted, and how instantly infatuated, with the only man who had put flesh between the ribs of an art that was starving on superstitions. He hadn't yet written to him—he was deterred by a strain of respect. Dencombe at this moment rejoiced more inwardly than ever that he had never answered the photographers. His visitor's attitude promised him a luxury of intercourse, though he was sure a due freedom for Doctor Hugh would depend not a little on the Countess. He learned without delay what type of Countess was involved, mastering as well the nature of the tie that united the curious trio. The large lady, an Englishwoman by birth and the daughter of a celebrated baritone, whose taste *minus* his talent she had inherited, was the widow of a French nobleman and mistress of all that remained of the handsome fortune, the fruit of her father's earnings, that had constituted her dower. Miss Vernham, an odd creature but an accomplished pianist, was attached to her person at a salary. The Countess was generous, independent, eccentric; she travelled with her minstrel and her medical man. Ignorant and passionate she had nevertheless moments in which she was almost irresistible. Dencombe saw her sit for her portrait in Doctor Hugh's free sketch, and felt the picture of his young friend's relation to her frame itself in his mind. This young friend, for a representative of the new psychology, was himself easily hypnotised, and if he became abnormally communicative it was only a sign of his real subjection. Dencombe did accordingly what he wanted with him, even without being known as Dencombe.

Taken ill on a journey in Switzerland the Countess had picked him up at an hotel, and the accident of his happening to please her had made her offer him, with her imperious liberality, terms that couldn't fail to dazzle a practitioner without patients and whose resources had been drained dry by his studies. It wasn't the way he would have proposed to spend his time, but it was time that would pass quickly, and meanwhile she was wonderfully kind. She exacted perpetual attention, but it was impossible not to like her. He gave details about his queer patient, a "type" if there ever was one, who had in connexion with her flushed obesity, and in addition to the morbid strain of a violent and aimless will, a grave organic disorder: but he came back to his loved novelist, whom he was so good as to pronounce more essentially a poet than many of those who went in for verse, with a zeal excited, as all his indiscretion had been excited, by the happy chance of Dencombe's sympathy and the coincidence of their occupation. Dencombe had confessed to a slight personal acquaintance with the author of "The Middle Years," but had not felt himself as ready as he could have wished when his companion, who had never yet encountered a being so privileged, began to be eager for particulars. He even divined in Doctor Hugh's eye at that moment a glimmer of suspicion. But the young man was too inflamed to be shrewd and repeatedly caught up the book to exclaim: "Did you notice this?" or "Weren't you immensely struck with that?" "There's a beautiful passage toward the end," he broke out; and again he laid his hand on the volume. As he turned the pages he came upon something else, while Dencombe saw him suddenly change colour. He had taken up as it lay on the bench Dencombe's copy instead of his own, and his neighbour at once guessed the reason of his start. Doctor Hugh looked grave an instant; then he said: "I see you've been altering the text!" Dencombe was a passionate corrector, a fingerer of style; the last thing he ever arrived at was a form final for himself. His ideal would have been to publish secretly, and then, on the published text, treat himself to the terrified revise, sacrificing always a first edition and beginning for posterity and even for the collectors, poor dears, with a second. This morning, in "The Middle Years," his pencil had pricked a dozen lights. He was amused at the effect of the young man's reproach; for an instant it made him change colour. He stammered at any rate ambiguously, then through a blur of ebbing consciousness saw Doctor Hugh's mystified eyes. He only had time to feel he was about to be ill again—that emotion, excitement, fatigue, the heat of the sun, the solicitation of the air, had combined to play him a trick, before, stretching out a hand to his visitor with a plaintive cry, he lost his senses altogether.

Later he knew he had fainted and that Doctor Hugh had got him home in a Bath-chair, the conductor of which, prowling within hail for custom, had happened to remember seeing him in the garden of the hotel. He had recovered his perception on the way, and had, in bed that afternoon, a vague recollection of Doctor Hugh's young face, as they went together, bent over him in a comforting laugh and expressive of something more than a suspicion of his identity. That identity was ineffaceable now, and all the more that he was rueful and sore. He had been rash, been stupid, had gone out too soon, stayed out too long. He oughtn't to have exposed himself to strangers, he ought to have taken his servant. He felt as if he had fallen into a hole too deep to descry any little patch of heaven. He was confused about the time that had passed—he pieced the fragments together. He had seen his doctor, the real one, the one who had treated him from the first and who had again been very kind. His servant was in and out on tiptoe, looking very wise after the fact. He said more than once something about the sharp young gentleman. The rest was vagueness in so far as it wasn't despair. The vagueness, however, justified itself by dreams, dozing anxieties from which he finally emerged to the consciousness of a dark room and a shaded candle.

"You'll be all right again—I know all about you now," said a voice near him that he felt to be young. Then his meeting with Doctor Hugh came back. He was too discouraged to joke about it yet, but made out after a little that the interest was intense for his visitor. "Of course I can't attend you professionally—you've got your own man, with whom I've talked and who's excellent," Doctor Hugh went on. "But you must let me come to see you as a good friend. I've just looked in before going to bed. You're doing beautifully, but it's a good job I was with you on the cliff. I shall come in early tomorrow. I want to do something for you. I want to do everything. You've done a tremendous lot for me." The young man held his hand, hanging over him, and poor Dencombe, weakly aware of this living pressure, simply lay there and accepted his devotion. He couldn't do anything less—he needed help too much.

The idea of the help he needed was very present to him that night, which he spent in a lucid stillness, an intensity of thought that constituted a reaction from his hours of stupor. He was lost, he was lost—he was lost if he couldn't be saved. He wasn't afraid of suffering, of death, wasn't even in love with life; but he had had a deep demonstration of desire. It came over him in the long quiet hours that only with "The Middle Years" had he taken his flight; only on that day, visited by soundless processions, had he recognised his kingdom. He had had a revelation of his range. What he dreaded was the idea that his reputation should stand on the unfinished. It wasn't with his past but with his future that it should properly be concerned. Illness and age rose before him like spectres with pitiless eyes: how was he to bribe such fates to give him the second chance? He had had the one chance that all men have—he had had the chance of life. He went to sleep again very late, and when he awoke Doctor Hugh was sitting at hand. There was already by this time something beautifully familiar in him.

"Don't think I've turned out your physician," he said; "I'm acting with his consent. He has been here and seen you. Somehow he seems to trust me. I told him how we happened to come together yesterday, and he recognises that I've a peculiar right."

Dencombe felt his own face pressing. "How have you squared the Countess?"

The young man blushed a little, but turned it off. "Oh never mind the Countess!"

"You told me she was very exacting."

Doctor Hugh had a wait. "So she is."

"And Miss Vernham's an *intrigante*."

"How do you know that?"

"I know everything. One *has* to, to write decently!"

"I think she's mad," said limpid Doctor Hugh.

"Well, don't quarrel with the Countess—she's a present help to you."

"I don't quarrel," Doctor Hugh returned. "But I don't get on with silly women." Presently he added: "You seem very much alone."

"That often happens at my age. I've outlived, I've lost by the way."

Doctor Hugh faltered; then surmounting a soft scruple: "Whom have you lost?"

"Every one."

"Ah no," the young man breathed, laying a hand on his arm.

"I once had a wife—I once had a son. My wife died when my child was born, and my boy, at school, was carried off by typhoid."

"I wish I'd been there!" cried Doctor Hugh.

"Well—if you're here!" Dencombe answered with a smile that, in spite of dimness, showed how he valued being sure of his companion's whereabouts.

"You talk strangely of your age. You're not old."

"Hypocrite—so early!"

"I speak physiologically."

"That's the way I've been speaking for the last five years, and it's exactly what I've been saying to myself. It isn't till we *are* old that we begin to tell ourselves we're not."

"Yet I know I myself am young," Doctor Hugh returned.

"Not so well as I!" laughed his patient, whose visitor indeed would have established the truth in question by the honesty with which he changed the point of view, remarking that it must be one of the charms of age—at any rate in the case of high distinction—to feel that one has laboured and achieved. Doctor Hugh employed the common phrase about earning one's rest, and it made poor Dencombe for an instant almost angry. He recovered himself, however, to explain, lucidly enough, that if, ungraciously, he knew nothing of such a balm, it was doubtless because he had wasted inestimable years. He had followed literature from the first, but he had taken a lifetime to get abreast of her. Only today at last had he begun to *see,* so that all he had hitherto shown was a movement without a direction. He had ripened too late and was so clumsily constituted that he had had to teach himself by mistakes.

"I prefer your flowers then to other people's fruit, and your mistakes to other people's successes," said gallant Doctor Hugh. "It's for your mistakes I admire you."

"You're happy—you don't know," Dencombe answered.

Looking at his watch the young man had got up; he named the hour of the afternoon at which he would return. Dencombe warned him against committing himself too deeply, and expressed again all his dread of making him neglect the Countess—perhaps incur her displeasure.

"I want to be like you—I want to learn by mistakes!" Doctor Hugh laughed.

"Take care you don't make too grave a one! But do come back," Dencombe added with the glimmer of a new idea.

"You should have had more vanity!" His friend spoke as if he knew the exact amount required to make a man of letters normal.

"No, no—I only should have had more time. I want another go."

"Another go?"

"I want an extension."

"An extension?" Again Doctor Hugh repeated Dencombe's words, with which he seemed to have been struck.

"Don't you know?—I want to what they call 'live.'"

The young man, for good-bye, had taken his hand, which closed with a certain force. They looked at each other hard. "You *will* live," said Doctor Hugh.

"Don't be superficial. It's too serious!"

"You *shall* live!" Dencombe's visitor declared, turning pale.

"Ah that's better!" And as he retired the invalid, with a troubled laugh, sank gratefully back.

All that day and all the following night he wondered if it mightn't be arranged. His doctor came again, his servant was attentive, but it was to his confident young friend that he felt himself mentally appeal. His collapse on the cliff was plausibly explained and his liberation, on a better basis, promised for the morrow; meanwhile, however, the intensity of his meditations kept him tranquil and made him indifferent. The idea that occupied him was none the less absorbing because it was a morbid fancy. Here was a clever son of the age, ingenious and ardent, who happened to have set him up for connoisseurs to worship. This servant of his altar had all the new learning in science and all the old reverence in faith; wouldn't he therefore put his knowledge at the disposal of his sympathy, his craft at the disposal of his love? Couldn't he be trusted to invent a remedy for a poor artist to whose art he had paid a tribute? If he couldn't the alternative was hard: Dencombe would have to surrender to silence unvindicated and undivined. The rest of the day and all the next he toyed in secret with this sweet futility. Who would work the miracle for him but the young man who could combine such lucidity with such passion?

He thought of the fairy-tales of science and charmed himself into forgetting that he looked for a magic that was not of this world. Doctor Hugh was an apparition, and that placed him above the law. He came and went while his patient, who now sat up, followed him with supplicating eyes. The interest of knowing the great author had made the young man begin "The Middle Years" afresh and would help him to find a richer sense between its covers. Dencombe had told him what he "tried for"; with all his intelligence, on a first perusal, Doctor Hugh had failed to guess it. The baffled celebrity wondered then who in the world *would* guess it: he was amused once more at the diffused massive weight that could be thrown into the missing of an intention. Yet he wouldn't rail at the general mind to-day—consoling as that ever had been: the revelation of his own slowness had seemed to make all stupidity sacred.

Doctor Hugh, after a little, was visibly worried, confessing, on enquiry, to a source of embarrassment at home. "Stick to the Countess—don't mind me," Dencombe said repeatedly; for his companion was frank enough about the large lady's attitude. She was so jealous that she had fallen ill—she resented such a breach of allegiance. She paid so much for his fidelity that she must have it all: she refused him the right to other sympathies, charged him with scheming to make her die alone, for it was needless to point out how little Miss Vernham was a resource in trouble. When Doctor Hugh mentioned that the Countess would already have left Bournemouth if he hadn't kept her in bed, poor Dencombe held his arm tighter and said with decision: "Take her straight away." They had gone out together, walking back to the sheltered nook in which, the other day, they had met. The young man, who had given his companion a personal support, declared with emphasis that his conscience was clear—he could ride two horses at once. Didn't he dream for his future of a time when he should have to ride five hundred? Longing equally for virtue, Dencombe replied that in that golden age no patient would pretend to have contracted with him for his whole attention. On the part of the Countess wasn't such an avidity lawful? Doctor Hugh denied it, said there was no contract, but only a free understanding, and that a sordid servitude was impossible to a generous spirit: he liked moreover to talk about art, and that was the subject on which, this time, as they sat together on the sunny bench, he tried most to engage the author of "The Middle Years."

Dencombe, soaring again a little on the weak wings of convalescence and still haunted by that happy notion of an organised rescue, found another strain of eloquence to plead the cause of a certain splendid "last manner," the very citadel, as it would prove, of his reputation, the stronghold into which his real treasure would be gathered. While his listener gave up the morning and the great still sea ostensibly waited he had a wondrous explanatory hour. Even for himself he was inspired as he told what his treasure would consist of; the precious metals he would dig from the mine, the jewels rare, strings of pearls, he would hang between the columns of his temple. He was wondrous for himself, so thick his convictions crowded, but still more wondrous for Doctor Hugh, who assured him none the less that the very pages he had just published were already encrusted with gems. This admirer, however, panted for the combinations to come and, before the face of the beautiful day, renewed to Dencombe his guarantee that his profession would hold itself responsible for such a life. Then he suddenly clapped his hand upon his watch-pocket and asked leave to absent himself for half an hour. Dencombe waited there for his return, but was at last recalled to the actual by the fall of a shadow across the ground. The shadow darkened into that of Miss Vernham, the young lady in attendance on the Countess; whom Dencombe, recognising her, perceived so clearly to have come to speak to him that he rose from his bench to acknowledge the civility. Miss Vernham indeed proved not particularly civil; she looked strangely agitated, and her type was now unmistakeable.

"Excuse me if I do ask," she said, "whether it's too much to hope that you may be induced to leave Doctor Hugh alone." Then before our poor friend, greatly disconcerted, could protest: "You ought to be informed that you stand in his light—that you may do him a terrible injury."

"Do you mean by causing the Countess to dispense with his services?"

"By causing her to disinherit him." Dencombe stared at this, and Miss Vernham pursued, in the gratification of seeing she could produce an impression: "It has depended on himself to come into something very handsome. He has had a grand prospect, but I think you've succeeded in spoiling it."

"Not intentionally, I assure you. Is there no hope the accident may be repaired?" Dencombe asked.

"She was ready to do anything for him. She takes great fancies, she lets herself go—it's her way. She has no relations, she's free to dispose of her money, and she's very ill," said Miss Vernham for a climax.

"I'm very sorry to hear it," Dencombe stammered.

"Wouldn't it be possible for you to leave Bournemouth? That's what I've come to see about."

He sank to his bench. "I'm very ill myself, but I'll try!"

Miss Vernham still stood there with her colourless eyes and the brutality of her good conscience. "Before it's too late, please!" she said; and with this she turned her back, in order, quickly, as if it had been a business to which she could spare but a precious moment, to pass out of his sight.

Oh yes, after this Dencombe was certainly very ill. Miss Vernham had upset him with her rough fierce news; it was the sharpest shock to him to discover what was at stake for a penniless young man of fine parts. He sat trembling on his bench, staring at the waste of waters, feeling sick with the directness of the blow. He was indeed too weak, too unsteady, too alarmed; but he would make the effort to get away, for he couldn't accept the guilt of interference and his honour was really involved. He would hobble home, at any rate, and then think what was to be done. He made his way back to the hotel and, as he went, had a characteristic vision of Miss Vernham's great motive. The Countess hated women of course—Dencombe was lucid about that; so the hungry pianist had no personal hopes and could only console herself with the bold conception of helping Doctor Hugh in order to marry him after he should get his money or else induce him to recognise her claim for compensation and buy her off. If she had befriended him at a fruitful crisis he would really, as a man of delicacy—and she knew what to think of that point—have to reckon with her.

At the hotel Dencombe's servant insisted on his going back to bed. The invalid had talked about catching a train and had begun with orders to pack; after which his racked nerves had yielded to a sense of sickness. He consented to see his physician, who immediately was sent for, but he wished it to be understood that his door was irrevocably closed to Doctor Hugh. He had his plan, which was so fine that he rejoiced in it after getting back to bed.

Doctor Hugh, suddenly finding himself snubbed without mercy, would, in natural disgust and to the joy of Miss Vernham, renew his allegiance to the Countess. When his physician arrived Dencombe learned that he was feverish and that this was very wrong: he was to cultivate calmness and try, if possible, not to think. For the rest of the day he wooed stupidity; but there was an ache that kept him sentient, the probable sacrifice of his "extension," the limit of his course. His medical adviser was anything but pleased: his successive relapses were ominous. He charged this personage to put out a strong hand and take Doctor Hugh off his mind—it would contribute so much to his being quiet. The agitating name, in his room, was not mentioned again, but his security was a smothered fear, and it was not confirmed by the receipt, at ten o'clock that evening, of a telegram which his servant opened and read him and to which, with an address in London, the signature of Miss Vernham was attached. "Beseech you to use all influence to make our friend join us here in the morning. Countess much the worse for dreadful journey, but everything may still be saved. The two ladies had gathered themselves up and had been capable in the afternoon of a spiteful revolution. They had started for the capital, and if the elder one, as Miss Vernham had announced, was very ill, she had wished to make it clear that she was proportionately reckless. Poor Dencornbe, who was not reckless and who only desired that everything should indeed be "saved," sent this missive straight off to the young man's lodging and had on the morrow the pleasure of knowing that he had quitted Bournemouth by an early train.

Two days later he pressed in with a copy of a literary journal in his hand. He had returned because he was anxious and for the pleasure of flourishing the great review of "The Middle Years." Here at least was something adequate—it rose to the occasion; it was an acclamation, a reparation, a critical attempt to place the author in the niche he had fairly won. Dencombe accepted and submitted; he made neither objection nor enquiry, for old complications had returned and he had had two dismal days. He was convinced not only that he should never again leave his bed, so that his young friend might pardonably remain, but that the demand he should make on the patience of beholders would be of the most moderate. Doctor Hugh had been to town, and he tried to find in his eyes some confession that the Countess was pacified and his legacy clinched; but all he could see there was the light of his juvenile joy in two or three of the phrases of the newspaper. Dencombe couldn't read them, but when his visitor had insisted on repeating them more than once he was able to shake an unintoxicated head. "Ah no—but they would have been true of what I *could* have done!"

"What people 'could have done' is mainly what they've in fact done," Doctor Hugh contended.

"Mainly, yes; but I've been an idiot!" Dencombe said.

Doctor Hugh did remain; the end was coming fast. Two days later his patient observed to him, by way of the feeblest of jokes, that there would now be no question whatever of a second chance. At this the young man stared; then he exclaimed: "Why it has come to pass—it has come to pass! The second chance has been the public's—the chance to find the point of view, to pick up the pearl!"

"Oh the pearl!" poor Dencombe uneasily sighed. A smile as cold as a winter sunset flickered on his drawn lips as he added: "The pearl is the unwritten—the pearl is the unalloyed, the *rest,* the lost!"

From that hour he was less and less present, heedless to all appearance of what went on round him. His disease was definitely mortal, of an action as relentless, after the short arrest that had enabled him to fall in with Doctor Hugh, as a leak in a great ship. Sinking steadily, though this visitor, a man of rare resources, now cordially approved by his physician, showed endless art in guarding him from pain, poor Dencombe kept no reckoning of favour or neglect, betrayed no symptom of regret or speculation. Yet toward the last he gave a sign of having noticed how for two days Doctor Hugh hadn't been in his room, a sign that consisted of his suddenly opening his eyes to put a question. Had he spent those days with the Countess?

"The Countess is dead," said Doctor Hugh. "I knew that in a particular contingency she wouldn't resist. I went to her grave."

Dencombe's eyes opened wider. "She left you 'something handsome'?"

The young man gave a laugh almost too light for a chamber of woe. "Never a penny. She roundly cursed me."

"Cursed you?" Dencombe wailed.

"For giving her up. I gave her up for *you*. I had to choose," his companion explained.

"You chose to let a fortune go?"

"I chose to accept, whatever they might be, the consequences of my infatuation," smiled Doctor Hugh. Then as a larger pleasantry: "The fortune be hanged! It's your own fault if I can't get your things out of my head."

The immediate tribute to his humour was a long bewildered moan; after which, for many hours, many days, Dencombe lay motionless and absent. A response so absolute, such a glimpse of a definite result and such a sense of credit, worked together in his mind and, producing a strange commotion, slowly altered and transfigured his despair. The sense of cold submersion left him—he seemed to float without an effort. The incident was extraordinary as evidence, and it shed an intenser light. At the last he signed to Doctor Hugh to listen and, when he was down on his knees by the pillow, brought him very near. "You've made me think it all a delusion."

"Not your glory, my dear friend," stammered the young man.

"Not my glory—what there is of it! It *is* glory—to have been tested, to have had our little quality and cast our little spell. The thing is to have made somebody care. You happen to be crazy of course, but that doesn't affect the law."

"You're a great success!" said Doctor Hugh, putting into his young voice the ring of a marriage-bell.

Dencombe lay taking this in; then he gathered strength to speak once more. "A second chance—*that's* the delusion. There never was to be but one. We work in the dark—we do what we can—we give what we have. Our doubt is our passion and our passion is our task. The rest is the madness of art."

"If you've doubted, if you've despaired, you've always 'done' it," his visitor subtly argued.

"We've done something or other," Dencombe conceded.

"Something or other is everything. It's the feasible. It's *you!*"

"Comforter!" poor Dencombe ironically sighed.

"But it's true," insisted his friend.

"It's true. It's frustration that doesn't count."

"Frustration's only life," said Doctor Hugh.

"Yes, it's what passes." Poor Dencombe was barely audible, but he had marked with the words the virtual end of his first and only chance.

SARAH ORNE JEWETT
(1849–1909)

Born in South Berwick, Maine, the granddaughter of a prosperous sea captain and the daughter of an obstetrician, Sarah Orne Jewett grew up in a stable, middle-class household nurturing to a girl with literary aspirations. Out of her visits with her father to his rural patients came her novel A Country Doctor *(1884), which features a strong female protagonist.*

Jewett was precocious and industrious, writing both prose and poetry while still in her teens. Her earliest efforts were published by William Dean Howells in Atlantic Monthly, *and were subsequently gathered in her first collection of stories,* Deephaven *(1877). Other acclaimed and popular collections by Jewett are* A White Heron *(1886),* The King of Folly Island *(1888),* A Native of Winby *(1893), and* The Life of Nancy *(1895). Jewett's most famous single work is* The Country of the Pointed Firs *(1896) in which the lives of a small group of men and women are delineated with a quiet, sympathetic lyricism that transcends the merely local and "regional."*

"A White Heron," suspenseful and poetic at once, and, in its dialectics of male and female consciousness, strikingly contemporary, is representative of this fine writer at her best. Even the unabashed sentiment seems, in terms of the child Sylvia's limited experience, an expression of character: "Were the birds better friends than their hunter might have been,—who can tell?"

A White Heron

I

The woods were already filled with shadows one June evening, just before eight o'clock, though a bright sunset still glimmered faintly among the trunks of the trees. A little girl was driving home her cow, a plodding, dilatory, provoking creature in her behavior, but a valued companion for all that. They were going away from whatever light there was, and striking deep into the woods, but their feet were familiar with the path, and it was no matter whether their eyes could see it or not.

There was hardly a night the summer through when the old cow could be found waiting at the pasture bars; on the contrary, it was her greatest pleasure to hide herself away among the huckleberry bushes, and though she wore a loud bell she had made the discovery that if one stood perfectly still it would not ring. So Sylvia had to hunt for her until she found her, and call Co'! Co'! with never an answering Moo, until her childish patience was quite spent. If the creature had not given good milk and plenty of it, the case would have seemed very different to her owners. Besides, Sylvia had all the time there was, and very little use to make of it. Sometimes in pleasant weather it was a consolation to look upon the cow's pranks as an intelligent attempt to play hide and seek, and as the child had no playmates she lent herself to this amusement with a good deal of zest. Though this chase had been so long that the wary animal herself had given an unusual signal of her whereabouts, Sylvia had only laughed when she came upon Mistress Moolly at the swamp-side, and urged her affectionately homeward with a twig of birch leaves. The old cow was not inclined to wander farther, she even turned in the right direction for once as they left the pasture, and stepped along the road at a good pace. She was quite ready to be milked now, and seldom stopped to browse. Sylvia wondered what her grandmother would say because they were so late. It was a great while since she had left home at half-past five o'clock, but everybody knew the difficulty of making this errand a short one. Mrs. Tilley had chased the horned torment too many summer evenings herself to blame any one else for lingering, and was only thankful as she waited that she had Sylvia, nowadays, to give such valuable assistance. The good woman suspected that Sylvia loitered occasionally on her own account; there never was such a child for straying about out-of-doors since the world was made! Everybody said that it was a good change for a little maid who had tried to grow for eight years in a crowded manufacturing town, but, as for Sylvia herself, it seemed as if she never had been alive at all before she came to live at the farm. She thought often with wistful compassion of a wretched geranium that belonged to a town neighbor.

"'Afraid of folks,'" old Mrs. Tilley said to herself, with a smile, after she had made the unlikely choice of Sylvia from her daughter's houseful of children, and was returning to the farm, "'Afraid of folks,' they said! I guess she won't be troubled no great with 'em up to the old place!" When they reached the door of the lonely house and stopped to unlock it, and the cat came to purr loudly, and rub against them, a deserted pussy, indeed, but fat with young robins, Sylvia whispered that this was a beautiful place to live in, and she never should wish to go home.

The companions followed the shady wood-road, the cow taking slow steps and the child very fast ones. The cow stopped long at the brook to drink, as if the pasture were not half a swamp, and Sylvia stood still and waited, letting her bare feet cool themselves in the shoal water, while the great twilight moths struck softly against her. She waded on through the brook as the cow moved away, and listened to the thrushes with a heart that beat fast with pleasure. There was a stirring in the great boughs overhead. They were full of little birds and beasts that seemed to be wide awake, and going about their world, or else saying good-night to each other in sleepy twitters. Sylvia herself felt sleepy as she walked along. However, it was not much farther to the house, and the air was soft and sweet. She was not often in the woods so late as this, and it made her feel as if she were a part of the gray shadows and the moving leaves. She was just thinking how long it seemed since she first came to the farm a year ago, and wondering if everything went on in the noisy town just the same as when she was there; the thought of the great red-faced boy who used to chase and frighten her made her hurry along the path to escape from the shadow of the trees.

Suddenly this little woods-girl is horror-stricken to hear a clear whistle not very far away. Not a bird's-whistle, which would have a sort of friendliness, but a boy's whistle, determined, and somewhat aggressive. Sylvia left the cow to whatever sad fate might await her, and stepped discreetly aside into the brushes, but she was just too late. The enemy had discovered her, and called out in a very cheerful and persuasive tone, "Halloa, little girl, how far is it to the road?" and trembling Sylvia answered almost inaudibly, "A good ways."

She did not dare to look boldly at the tall young man, who carried a gun over his shoulder, but she came out of her bush and again followed the cow, while he walked alongside.

"I have been hunting for some birds," the stranger said kindly, "and I have lost my way, and need a friend very much. Don't be afraid," he added gallantly. "Speak up and tell me what your name is, and whether you think I can spend the night at your house, and go out gunning early in the morning."

Sylvia was more alarmed than before. Would not her grandmother consider her much to blame? But who could have foreseen such an accident as this? It did not seem to be her fault, and she hung her head as if the stem of it were broken, but managed to answer "Sylvy," with much effort when her companion again asked her name.

Mrs. Tilley was standing in the doorway when the trio came into view. The cow gave a loud moo by way of explanation.

"Yes, you'd better speak up for yourself, you old trial! Where'd she tucked herself away this time, Sylvy?" But Sylvia kept an awed silence; she knew by instinct that her grandmother did not comprehend the gravity of the situation. She must be mistaking the stranger for one of the farmer-lads of the region.

The young man stood his gun beside the door, and dropped a lumpy game-bag beside it; then he bade Mrs. Tilley good-evening, and repeated his wayfarer's story, and asked if he could have a night's lodging.

"Put me anywhere you like," he said. "I must be off early in the morning, before day; but I am very hungry, indeed. You can give me some milk at any rate, that's plain."

"Dear sakes, yes," responded the hostess, whose long slumbering hospitality seemed to be easily awakened. "You might fare better if you went out to the main road a mile or so, but you're welcome to what we've got. I'll milk right off, and you make yourself at home. You can sleep on husks or feathers," she proffered graciously. "I raised them all myself. There's good pasturing for geese just below here towards the ma'sh. Now step round and set a plate for the gentleman, Sylvy!" And Sylvia promptly stepped. She was glad to have something to do, and she was hungry herself.

It was a surprise to find so clean and comfortable a little dwelling in this New England wilderness. The young man had known the horrors of its most primitive housekeeping, and the dreary squalor of that level of society which does not rebel at the companionship of hens. This was the best thrift of an old-fashioned farmstead, though on such a small scale that it seemed like a hermitage. He listened eagerly to the old woman's quaint talk, he watched Sylvia's pale face and shining gray eyes with ever growing enthusiasm, and insisted that this was the best supper he had eaten for a month, and afterward the new-made friends sat down in the doorway together while the moon came up.

Soon it would be berry-time, and Sylvia was a great help at picking. The cow was a good milker, though a plaguy thing to keep track of, the hostess gossiped frankly, adding presently that she had buried four children, so Sylvia's mother, and a son (who might be dead) in California were all the children she had left. "Dan, my boy, was a great hand to go gunning," she explained sadly. "I never wanted for pa'tridges or gray squer'ls while he was to home. He's been a great wand'rer, I expect, and he's no hand to write letters. There, I don't blame him, I'd ha' seen the world myself if it had been so I could."

"Sylvy takes after him," the grandmother continued affectionately, after a minute's pause. "There ain't a foot o' ground she don't know her way over, and the wild creaturs counts her one o' themselves. Squer'ls she'll tame to come an' feed right out o' her hands, and all sorts o' birds. Last winter she got the jaybirds to bangeing here, and I believe she'd 'a' scanted herself of her own meals to have plenty to throw out amongst 'em, if I had n't kep' watch. Anything but crows, I tell her, I'm willin' to help support—though Dan he had a tamed one o' them that did seem to have reason same as folks. It was round here a good spell after he went away. Dan an' his father they did n't hitch,—but he never held up his head ag'in after Dan had dared him an' gone off."

The guest did not notice this hint of family sorrows in his eager interest in something else.

"So Sylvy knows all about birds, does she?" he exclaimed, as he looked round at the little girl who sat, very demure but increasingly sleepy, in the moonlight. "I am making a collection of birds myself. I have been at it ever since I was a boy." (Mrs. Tilley smiled.) "There are two or three very rare ones I have been hunting for these five years. I mean to get them on my own ground if they can be found."

"Do you cage 'em up?" asked Mrs. Tilley doubtfully, in response to this enthusiastic announcement.

"Oh no, they 're stuffed and preserved, dozens and dozens of them," said the ornithologist, "and I have shot or snared every one myself. I caught a glimpse of a white heron a few miles from here on Saturday, and I have followed it in this direction. They have never been found in this district at all. The little white heron, it is," and he turned again to look at Sylvia with the hope of discovering that the rare bird was one of her acquaintances.

But Sylvia was watching a hop-toad in the narrow footpath.

"You would know the heron if you saw it," the stranger continued eagerly. "A queer tall white bird with soft feathers and long thin legs. And it would have a nest perhaps in the top of a high tree, made of sticks, something like a hawk's nest."

Sylvia's heart gave a wild beat; she knew that strange white bird, and had once stolen softly near where it stood in some bright green swamp grass, away over at the other side of the woods. There was an open place where the sunshine always seemed strangely yellow and hot, where tall, nodding rushes grew, and her grandmother had warned her that she might sink in the soft black mud underneath and never be heard of more. Not far beyond were the salt marshes just this side the sea itself, which Sylvia wondered and dreamed much about, but never had seen, whose great voice could sometimes be heard above the noise of the woods on stormy nights.

"I can't think of anything I should like so much as to find that heron's nest," the handsome stranger was saying. "I would give ten dollars to anybody who could show it to me," he added desperately, "and I mean to spend my whole vacation hunting for it if need be. Perhaps it was only migrating, or had been chased out of its own region by some bird of prey."

Mrs. Tilley gave amazed attention to all this, but Sylvia still watched the toad, not divining, as she might have done at some calmer time, that the creature wished to get to its hole under the door-step, and was much hindered by the unusual spectators at that hour of the evening. No amount of thought, that night, could decide how many wished-for treasures the ten dollars, so lightly spoken of, would buy.

The next day the young sportsman hovered about the woods, and Sylvia kept him company, having lost her first fear of the friendly lad, who proved to be most kind and sympathetic. He told her many things about the birds and what they knew and where they lived and what they did with themselves. And he gave her a jack-knife, which she thought as great a treasure as if she were a desert-islander. All day long he did not once make her troubled or afraid except when he brought down some unsuspecting singing creature from its bough. Sylvia would have liked him vastly better without his gun; she could not understand why he killed the very birds he seemed to like so much. But as the day waned, Sylvia still watched the young man with loving admiration. She had never seen anybody so charming and delightful; the woman's heart, asleep in the child, was vaguely thrilled by a dream of love. Some premonition of that great power stirred and swayed these young creatures who traversed the solemn woodlands with soft-footed silent care. They stopped to listen to a bird's song; they pressed forward again eagerly, parting the branches—speaking to each other rarely and in whispers; the young man going first and Sylvia following, fascinated, a few steps behind, with her gray eyes dark with excitement.

She grieved because the longed-for white heron was elusive, but she did not lead the guest, she only followed, and there was no such thing as speaking first. The sound of her own unquestioned voice would have terrified her—it was hard enough to answer yes or no when there was need of that. At last evening began to fall, and they drove the cow home together, and Sylvia smiled with pleasure when they came to the place where she heard the whistle and was afraid only the night before.

II

Half a mile from home, at the farther edge of the woods, where the land was highest, a great pine-tree stood, the last of its generation. Whether it was left for a boundary mark, or for what reason, no one could say; the wood-choppers who had felled its mates were dead and gone long ago, and a whole forest of sturdy trees, pines and oaks and maples, had grown again. But the stately head of this old pine toward above them all and made a landmark for sea and shore miles and miles away. Sylvia knew it well. She had always believed that whoever climbed to the top of it could see the ocean; and the little girl had often laid her hand on the great rough trunk and looked up wistfully at those dark boughs that the wind always stirred, no matter how hot and still the air might be below. Now she thought of the tree with a new excitement, for why, if one climbed it at break of day could not one see all the world, and easily discover from whence the white heron flew, and mark the place, and find the hidden nest?

What a spirit of adventure, what wild ambition! What fancied triumph and delight and glory for the later morning when she could make known the secret! It was almost too real and too great for the childish heart to bear.

All night the door of the little house stood open and the whippoorwills came and sang upon the very step. The young sportsman and his old hostess were sound asleep, but Sylvia's great design kept her broad awake and watching. She forgot to think of sleep. The short summer night seemed as long as the winter darkness, and at last when the whippoorwills ceased, and she was afraid the morning would after all come too soon, she stole out of the house and followed the pasture path through the woods, hastening toward the open ground beyond, listening with a sense of comfort and companionship to the drowsy twitter of a half-awakened bird, whose perch she had jarred in passing. Alas, if the great wave of human interest which flooded for the first time this dull little life should sweep away the satisfactions of an existence heart to heart with nature and the dumb life of the forest!

There was the huge tree asleep yet in the paling moonlight, and small and silly Sylvia began with utmost bravery to mount to the top of it, with tingling, eager blood coursing the channels of her whole frame, with her bare feet and fingers, that pinched and held like bird's claws to the monstrous ladder reaching up, up, almost to the sky itself. First she must mount the white oak tree that grew alongside, where she was almost lost among the dark branches and the green leaves heavy and wet with dew; a bird fluttered off its nest, and a red squirrel ran to and fro and scolded pettishly at the harmless housebreaker. Sylvia felt her way easily. She had often climbed there, and knew that higher still one of the oak's upper branches chafed against the pine trunk, just where its lower boughs were set close together. There, when she made the dangerous pass from one tree to the other, the great enterprise would really begin.

She crept out along the swaying oak limb at last, and took the daring step across into the old pine-tree. The way was harder than she thought; she must reach far and hold fast, the sharp dry twigs caught and held her and scratched her like angry talons, the pitch made her thin little fingers clumsy and stiff as she went round and round the tree's great stem, higher and higher upward. The sparrows and robins in the woods below were beginning to wake and twitter to the dawn, yet it seemed much lighter there aloft in the pine-tree, and the child knew she must hurry if her project were to be of any use.

The tree seemed to lengthen itself out as she went up, and to reach farther and farther upward. It was like a great main-mast to the voyaging earth; it must truly have been amazed that morning through all its ponderous frame as it felt this determined spark of human spirit wending its way from higher branch to branch. Who knows how steadily the least twigs held themselves to advantage this light, weak creature on her way! The old pine must have loved his new dependent. More than all the hawks, and bats, and moths, and even the sweet voiced thrushes, was the brave, beating heart of the solitary gray-eyed child. And the tree stood still and frowned away the winds that June morning while the dawn grew bright in the east.

Sylvia's face was like a pale star, if one had seen it from the ground, when the last thorny bough was past, and she stood trembling and tired but wholly triumphant, high in the treetop. Yes, there was the sea with the dawning sun making a golden dazzle over it, and toward that glorious east flew two hawks with slow-moving pinions. How low they looked in the air from that height when one had only seen them before far up, and dark against the blue sky. Their gray feathers were as soft as moths; they seemed only a little way from the tree, and Sylvia felt as if she too could go flying away among the clouds. Westward, the woodlands and farms reached miles and miles into the distance; here and there were church steeples, and white villages, truly it was a vast and awesome world!

The birds sang louder and louder. At last the sun came up bewilderingly bright. Sylvia could see the white sails of ships out at sea, and the clouds that were purple and rose-colored and yellow at first began to fade away. Where was the white heron's nest in the sea of green branches, and was this wonderful sight and pageant of the world the only reward for having climbed to such a giddy height? Now look down again, Sylvia, where the green marsh is set among the shining birches and dark hemlocks; there where you saw the white heron once you will see him again; look, look! a white spot of him like a single floating feather comes up from the dead hemlock and grows larger, and rises, and comes close at last, and goes by the landmark pine with steady sweep of wing and outstretched slender neck and crested head. And wait! wait! do not move a foot or a finger, little girl, do not send an arrow of light and consciousness from your two eager eyes, for the heron has perched on a pine bough not far beyond yours, and cries back to his mate on the nest and plumes his feathers for the new day!

The child gives a long sigh a minute later when a company of shouting cat-birds comes also to the tree, and vexed by their fluttering and lawlessness the solemn heron goes away. She knows his secret now, the wild, light, slender bird that floats and wavers, and goes back like an arrow presently to his home in the green world beneath. Then Sylvia, well satisfied, makes her perilous way down again, not daring to look far below the branch she stands on, ready to cry sometimes because her fingers ache and her lamed feet slip. Wondering over and over again what the stranger would say to her, and what he would think when she told him how to find his way straight to the heron's nest.

"Sylvy, Sylvy!" called the busy old grandmother again and again, but nobody answered, and the small husk bed was empty and Sylvia had disappeared.

The guest waked from a dream, and remembering his day's pleasure hurried to dress himself that might it sooner begin. He was sure from the way the shy little girl looked once or twice yesterday that she had at least seen the white heron, and now she must really be made to tell. Here she comes now, paler than ever, and her worn old frock is torn and tattered, and smeared with pine pitch. The grandmother and the sportsman stand in the door together and question her, and the splendid moment has come to speak of the dead hemlock-tree by the green marsh.

But Sylvia does not speak after all, though the old grandmother fretfully rebukes her, and the young man's kind, appealing eyes are looking straight in her own. He can make them rich with money; he has promised it, and they are poor now. He is so well worth making happy, and he waits to hear the story she can tell.

No, she must keep silence! What is it that suddenly forbids her and makes her dumb? Has she been nine years growing and now, when the great world for the first time puts out a hand to her, must she thrust it aside for a bird's sake? The murmur of the pine's green branches is in her ears, she remembers how the white heron came flying through the golden air and how they watched the sea and the morning together, and Sylvia cannot speak; she cannot tell the heron's secret and give its life away.

Dear loyalty, that suffered a sharp pang as the guest went away disappointed later in the day, that could have served and followed him and loved him as a dog loves! Many a night Sylvia heard the echo of his whistle haunting the pasture path as she came home with the loitering cow. She forgot even her sorrow at the sharp report of his gun and the piteous sight of thrushes and sparrows dropping silent to the ground, their songs hushed and their pretty feathers stained and wet with blood. Were the birds better friends than their hunter might have been,—who can tell? Whatever treasures were lost to her, woodlands and summer time, remember! Bring your gifts and graces and tell your secrets to this lonely country child!

KATE CHOPIN
(1851–1904)

Born to a wealthy Catholic St. Louis family, Kate Chopin (née O'Flaherty) was treated as harshly by critics and the reading public as any writer in this volume, including even Melville and Poe. After a moderately successful early career, Chopin published a second novel, The Awakening *(1899), which was so viciously and universally condemned for its "morbid, poisonous, and vulgar" subject matter that she virtually gave up writing in the few remaining years of her life. Not only did Chopin, a mature artist of forty-eight at this time, have to bear the indignity of such public disapprobation, but she suffered social ostracism by friends and literary acquaintances in St. Louis. And all for having written a slender, carefully composed work of fiction in a Flaubertian vein, about a sensitive and passionate woman's adulterous romance and eventual suicide—a work now recognized as a brilliant tour de force, an American classic.*

Despite her relatively short writing career, Kate Chopin completed an early novel, At Fault *(1890), over one hundred fifty stories and sketches, and a considerable quantity of poetry, reviews, and criticism. A collection of stories of Louisiana rural life,* Bayou Folk *(1894) was well received; a second collection,* A Night in Acadie *(1897), established Chopin's reputation as a local colorist. The story included here, "The Storm," written shortly after* The Awakening, *could certainly never have been published in any magazine of Chopin's time, and was, apparently, never submitted for publication. It did not see print until 1969, in Per Seyersted's edition of* The Complete Works of Kate Chopin.

The Storm

I

The leaves were so still that even Bibi thought it was going to rain. Bobinôt, who was accustomed to converse on terms of perfect equality with his little son, called the child's attention to certain sombre clouds that were rolling with sinister intention from the west, accompanied by a sullen, threatening roar. They were at Friedheimer's store and decided to remain there till the storm had passed. They sat within the door on two empty kegs. Bibi was four years old and looked very wise.

"Mama'll be 'fraid, yes," he suggested with blinking eyes.

"She'll shut the house. Maybe she got Sylvie helpin' her this evenin'," Bobinôt responded reassuringly.

"No; she ent got Sylvie. Sylvie was helpin' her yistiday," piped Bibi.

Bobinôt arose and going across to the counter purchased a can of shrimps, of which Calixta was very fond. Then he returned to his perch on the keg and sat stolidly holding the can of shrimps while the storm burst. It shook the wooden store and seemed to be ripping great furrows in the distant field. Bibi laid his little hand on his father's knee and was not afraid.

II

Calixta, at home, felt no uneasiness for their safety. She sat at a side window sewing furiously on a sewing machine. She was greatly occupied and did not notice the approaching storm. But she felt very warm and often stopped to mop her face on which the perspiration gathered in beads. She unfastened her white sacque at the throat. It began to grow dark, and suddenly realizing the situation she got up hurriedly and went about closing windows and doors.

Out on the small front gallery she had hung Bobinôt's Sunday clothes to air and she hastened out to gather them before the rain fell. As she stepped outside, Alcée Laballière rode in at the gate. She had not seen him very often since her marriage, and never alone. She stood there with Bobinôt's coat in her hands, and the big rain drops began to fall. Alcée rode his horse under the shelter of a side projection where the chickens had huddled and there were plows and a harrow piled up in the corner.

"May I come and wait on your gallery till the storm is over, Calixta?" he asked.

"Come long in, M'sieur Alcée."

His voice and her own startled her as if from a trance, and she seized Bobinôt's vest. Alcée, mounting to the porch, grabbed the trousers and snatched Bibi's braided jacket that was about to be carried away by a sudden gust of wind. He expressed an intention to remain outside, but it was soon apparent that he might as well have been out in the open: the water beat in upon the boards in driving sheets, and he went inside, closing the door after him. It was even necessary to put something beneath the door to keep the water out.

"My! what a rain! It's good two years sence it rain' like that," exclaimed Calixta as she rolled up a piece of bagging and Alcée helped her to thrust it beneath the crack.

She was a little fuller of figure than five years before when she married; but she had lost nothing of her vivacity. Her blue eyes still retained their melting quality; and her yellow hair, dishevelled by the wind and rain, kinked more stubbornly than ever about her ears and temples.

The rain beat upon the low, shingled roof with a force and clatter that threatened to break an entrance and deluge them there. They were in the dining room—the sitting room—the general utility room. Adjoining was her bed room, with Bibi's couch along side her own. The door stood open, and the room with its white, monumental bed, its closed shutters, looked dim and mysterious.

Alcée flung himself into a rocker and Calixta nervously began to gather up from the floor the lengths of a cotton sheet which she had been sewing.

"If this keeps up, *Dieu sait* if the levees goin' to stan' it!" she exclaimed.

"What have you got to do with the levees?"

"I got enough to do! An' there's Bobinot with Bibi out in that storm—if he only didn't left Friedheimer's!"

"Let us hope, Calixta, that Bobinôt's got sense enough to come in out of a cyclone."

She went and stood at the window with a greatly disturbed look on her face. She wiped the frame that was clouded with moisture. It was stiflingly hot. Alcée got up and joined her at the window, looking over her shoulder. The rain was coming down in sheets obscuring the view of far-off cabins and enveloping the distant wood in a gray mist. The playing of the lightning was incessant. A bolt struck a tall chinaberry tree at the edge of the field. It filled all visible space with a blinding glare and the crash seemed to invade the very boards they stood upon.

Calixta put her hands to her eyes, and with a cry, staggered backward. Alcée's arm encircled her, and for an instant he drew her close and spasmodically to him.

"Bonté!" she cried, releasing herself from his encircling arm and retreating from the window, "the house'll go next! If I only knew w'ere Bibi was!" She would not compose herself; she would not be seated. Alcée clasped her shoulders and looked into her face. The contact of her warm, palpitating body when he had unthinkingly drawn her into his arms, had aroused all the old-time infatuation and desire for her flesh.

"Calixta," he said, "don't be frightened. Nothing can happen. The house is too low to be struck, with so many tall trees standing about. There! aren't you going to be quiet? say, aren't you?" He pushed her hair back from her face that was warm and steaming. Her lips were as red and moist as pomegranate seed. Her white neck and a glimpse of her full, firm bosom disturbed him powerfully. As she glanced up at him the fear in her liquid blue eyes had given place to a drowsy gleam that unconsciously betrayed a sensuous desire. He looked down into her eyes and there was nothing for him to do but to gather her lips in a kiss. It reminded him of Assumption.

"Do you remember—in Assumption, Calixta?" he asked in a low voice broken by passion. Oh! she remembered; for in Assumption he had kissed her and kissed and kissed her; until his senses would well nigh fail, and to save her he would resort to a desperate flight. If she was not an immaculate dove in those days, she was still inviolate; a passionate creature whose very defenselessness had made her defense, against which his honor forbade him to prevail. Now—well, now—her lips seemed in a manner free to be tasted, as well as her round, white throat and her whiter breasts.

They did not heed the crashing torrents, and the roar of the elements made her laugh as she lay in his arms. She was a revelation in that dim, mysterious chamber; as white as the couch she lay upon. Her firm, elastic flesh that was knowing for the first time its birthright, was like a creamy lily that the sun invites to contribute its breath and perfume to the undying life of the world.

The generous abundance of her passion, without guile or trickery, was like a white flame which penetrated and found response in depths of his own sensuous nature that had never yet been reached.

When he touched her breasts they gave themselves up in quivering ecstasy, inviting his lips. Her mouth was a fountain of delight. And when he possessed her, they seemed to swoon together at the very borderland of life's mystery.

He stayed cushioned upon her, breathless, dazed, enervated, with his heart beating like a hammer upon her. With one hand she clasped his head, her lips lightly touching his forehead. The other hand stroked with a soothing rhythm his muscular shoulders.

The growl of the thunder was distant and passing away. The rain beat softly upon the shingles, inviting them to drowsiness and sleep. But they dared not yield.

The rain was over; and the sun was turning the glistening green world into a palace of gems. Calixta, on the gallery, watched Alcée ride away. He turned and smiled at her with a beaming face; and she lifted her pretty chin in the air and laughed aloud.

III

Bobinôt and Bibi, trudging home, stopped without at the cistern to make themselves presentable.

"My! Bibi, w'at will yo' mama say! You ought to be ashame'. You oughtn' put on those good pants. Look at 'em! An' that mud on yo' collar!

How you got that mud on yo' collar, Bibi? I never saw such a boy!" Bibi was the picture of pathetic resignation. Bobinôt was the embodiment of serious solicitude as he strove to remove from his own person and his son's the signs of their tramp over heavy roads and through wet fields. He scraped the mud off Bibi's bare legs and feet with a stick and carefully removed all traces from his heavy brogans. Then, prepared for the worst—the meeting with an over-scrupulous housewife, they entered cautiously at the back door.

Calixta was preparing supper. She had set the table and was dripping coffee at the hearth. She sprang up as they came in.

"Oh, Bobinot! You back! My! but I was uneasy. W'ere you been during the rain? An' Bibi? he ain't wet? he ain't hurt?" She had clasped Bibi and was kissing him effusively. Bobinôt's explanations and apologies which he had been composing all along the way, died on his lips as Calixta felt him to see if he were dry, and seemed to express nothing but satisfaction at their safe return.

"I brought you some shrimps, Calixta," offered Bobinôt, hauling the can from his ample side pocket and laying it on the table.

"Shrimps! Oh, Bobinôt! you too good fo' anything!" and she gave him a smacking kiss on the cheek that resounded. "*J'vous réponds,* we'll have a feas' tonight! umph-umph!"

Bobinôt and Bibi began to relax and enjoy themselves, and when the three seated themselves at table they laughed much and so loud that anyone might have heard them as far away as Laballiére's.

IV

Alcée Laballière wrote to his wife, Clarisse, that night. It was a loving letter, full of tender solicitude. He told her not to hurry back, but if she and the babies liked it at Biloxi, to stay a month longer. He was getting on nicely; and though he missed them, he was willing to bear the separation a while longer—realizing that their health and pleasure were the first things to be considered.

V

As for Clarisse, she was charmed upon receiving her husband's letter. She and the babies were doing well. The society was agreeable; many of her old friends and acquaintances were at the bay. And the first free breath since her marriage seemed to restore the pleasant liberty of her maiden days. Devoted as she was to her husband, their intimate conjugal life was something which she was more than willing to forego for a while.

So the storm passed and everyone was happy.

MARY E. WILKINS FREEMAN
(1852–1930)

My first reading of "Old Woman Magoun" gave me one story: my second reading, another. Which is to suggest that there are subtleties of theme beneath the surface of this artfully told "woman's" story that may in fact suggest a critique, from within, of "woman's" sensibility.

Such subtleties, as well as the respectful attentiveness to place, voice, and characters, are typical of the work of this New England writer who, in her time, was a popular success and, along with Edith Wharton, in 1926, elected to membership in the previously all-male National Institute of Arts and Letters. Freeman was also awarded the Howells Medal for Fiction in 1926.

Born in Randolph, Massachusetts, the town in which she would spend most of her life, Mary E. Wilkins Freeman supported herself by writing when her family became destitute. She suffered from nightmares; may have become addicted to sedatives later in her life; had a difficult, late marriage to a doctor who became an alcoholic—yet, when she died at the age of seventy-eight, she had published twenty volumes of adult fiction, both novels and stories, as well as six volumes of children's stories. Her best-known titles are A Humble Romance and Other Stories *(1887) and* A New England Nun and Other Stories *(1891), from which "Old Woman Magoun" is taken. Freemans story "The Revolt of 'Mother" is her most frequently anthologized story, but the theme of female revolt, of various degrees of assertion, fuels such diverse stories as "A New England Nun" and "Old Woman Magoun"—the latter delineating a darker, more secret, and deadly, aspect of revolt.*

Old Woman Magoun

The hamlet of Barry's Ford is situated in a sort of high valley among the mountains. Below it the hills lie in moveless curves like a petrified ocean; above it they rise in green-cresting waves which never break. It is *Barry's* Ford because at one time the Barry family was the most important in the place; and *Ford* because just at the beginning of the hamlet the little turbulent Barry River is fordable. There is, however, now a rude bridge across the river.

Old Woman Magoun was largely instrumental in bringing the bridge to pass. She haunted the miserable little grocery, wherein whiskey and hands of tobacco were the most salient features of the stock in trade, and she talked much. She would elbow herself into the midst of a knot of idlers and talk.

"That bridge ought to be built this very summer," said Old Woman Magoun. She spread her strong arms like wings, and sent the loafers, half laughing, half angry, flying in every direction. "If I were a *man,"* she said, "I'd go out this very minute and lay the fust log. If I were a passel of lazy men layin' round, I'd start up for once in my life, I would." The men cowered visibly—all except Nelson Barry; he swore under his breath and strode over to the counter.

Old Woman Magoun looked after him majestically. "You can cuss all you want to, Nelson Barry," said she; "I ain't afraid of you. I don't expect you to lay ary log of the bridge, but I'm goin' to have it built this very summer." She did. The weakness of the masculine element in Barry's Ford was laid low before such strenuous feminine assertion.

Old Woman Magoun and some other women planned a treat—two sucking pigs, and pies, and sweet cake—for a reward after the bridge should be finished. They even viewed leniently the increased consumption of ardent spirits.

"It seems queer to me," Old Woman Magoun said to Sally Jinks, "that men can't do nothin' without havin' to drink and chew to keep their sperits up. Lord! I've worked all my life and never done nuther."

"Men is different," said Sally Jinks.

"Yes, they be," assented Old Woman Magoun, with open contempt.

The two women sat on a bench in front of Old Woman Magoun's house, and little Lily Barry, her granddaughter, sat holding her doll on a small mossy stone near by. From where they sat they could see the men at work on the new bridge. It was the last day of the work.

Lily clasped her doll—a poor old rag thing—close to her childish bosom, like a little mother, and her face, round which curled her long yellow hair, was fixed upon the men at work. Little Lily had never been allowed to run with the other children of Barry's Ford. Her grandmother had taught her everything she knew—which was not much, but tending at least to a certain measure of spiritual growth—for she, as it were, poured the goodness of her own soul into this little receptive vase of another. Lily was firmly grounded in her knowledge that it was wrong to lie or steal or disobey her grandmother. She had also learned that one should be very industrious. It was seldom that Lily sat idly holding her doll-baby, but this was a holiday because of the bridge. She looked only a child, although she was nearly fourteen; her mother had been married at sixteen. That is, Old Woman Magoun said that her daughter, Lily's mother, had married at sixteen; there had been rumors, but no one had dared openly gainsay the old woman. She said that her daughter had married Nelson Barry, and he had deserted her. She had lived in her mother's house, and Lily had been born there, and she had died when the baby was only a week old. Lily's father, Nelson Barry, was the fairly dangerous degenerate of a good old family. Nelson's father before him had been bad. He was now the last of the family, with the exception of a sister of feeble intellect, with whom he lived in the old Barry house. He was a middle-aged man, still handsome. The shiftless population of Barry's Ford looked up to him as to an evil deity. They wondered how Old Woman Magoun dared brave him as she did. But Old Woman Magoun had within her a mighty sense of reliance upon herself as being on the right track in the midst of a maze of evil, which gave her courage. Nelson Barry had manifested no interest whatever in his daughter. Lily seldom saw her father. She did not often go to the store which was his favorite haunt. Her grandmother took care that she should not do so.

However, that afternoon she departed from her usual custom and sent Lily to the store.

She came in from the kitchen, whither she had been to baste the roasting pig. "There's no use talkin'," said she, "I've got to have some more salt. I've jest used the very last I had to dredge over that pig. I've got to go to the store."

Sally Jinks looked at Lily. "Why don't you send her?" she asked.

Old Woman Magoun gazed irresolutely at the girl. She was herself very tired. It did not seem to her that she could drag herself up the dusty hill to the store. She glanced with covert resentment at Sally Jinks. She thought that she might offer to go. But Sally Jinks said again, "Why don't you let her go?" and looked with a languid eye at Lily holding her doll on the stone.

Lily was watching the men at work on the bridge, with her childish delight in a spectacle of any kind, when her grandmother addressed her.

"Guess I'll let you go down to the store an' git some salt, Lily," said she.

The girl turned uncomprehending eyes upon her grandmother at the sound of her voice. She had been filled with one of the innocent reveries of childhood. Lily had in her the making of an artist or a poet. Her prolonged childhood went to prove it, and also her retrospective eyes, as clear and blue as blue light itself, which seemed to see past all that she looked upon. She had not come of the old Barry family for nothing. The best of the strain was in her, along with the splendid stanchness in humble lines which she had acquired from her grandmother.

"Put on your hat," said Old Woman Magoun; "the sun is hot, and you might git a headache." She called the girl to her, and put back the shower of fair curls under the rubber band which confined the hat. She gave Lily some money, and watched her knot it into a corner of her little cotton handkerchief. "Be careful you don't lose it," said she, "and don't stop to talk to anybody, for I am in a hurry for that salt. Of course, if anybody speaks to you answer them polite, and then come right along."

Lily started, her pocket-handkerchief weighted with the small silver dangling from one hand, and her rag doll carried over her shoulder like a baby. The absurd travesty of a face peeped forth from Lily's yellow curls. Sally Jinks looked after her with a sniff.

"She ain't goin' to carry that rag doll to the store?" said she.

"She likes to," replied Old Woman Magoun, in a half-shamed yet defiantly extenuating voice.

"Some girls at her age is thinkin' about beaux instead of rag dolls," said Sally Jinks.

The grandmother bristled. "Lily ain't big nor old for her age," said she. "I ain't in any hurry to have her git married. She ain't none too strong."

"She's got a good color," said Sally Jinks. She was crocheting white cotton lace, making her thick fingers fly. She really knew how to do scarcely anything except to crochet that coarse lace; somehow her heavy brain or her fingers had mastered that.

"I know she's got a beautiful color," replied Old Woman Magoun, with an odd mixture of pride and anxiety, "but it comes an' goes."

"I've heard that was a bad sign," remarked Sally Jinks, loosening some thread from her spool.

"Yes, it is," said the grandmother. "She's nothin' but a baby, though she's quicker than most to learn."

Lily Barry went on her way to the store. She was clad in a scanty short frock of blue cotton; her hat was tipped back, forming an oval frame for her innocent face. She was very small, and walked like a child, with the clap-clap of little feet of babyhood. She might have been considered, from her looks, under ten.

Presently she heard footsteps behind her; she turned around a little timidly to see who was coming. When she saw a handsome, well-dressed man, she felt reassured. The man came alongside and glanced down carelessly at first, then his look deepened. He smiled, and Lily saw he was very handsome indeed, and that his smile was not only reassuring but wonderfully sweet and compelling.

"Well, little one," said the man, "where are you bound, you and your dolly?"

"I am going to the store to buy some salt for grandma," replied Lily, in her sweet treble. She looked up in the man's face, and he fairly started at the revelation of its innocent beauty. He regulated his pace by hers, and the two went on together. The man did not speak again at once. Lily kept glancing timidly up at him, and every time that she did so the man smiled and her confidence increased. Presently when the man's hand grasped her little childish one hanging by her side, she felt a complete trust in him. Then she smiled up at him. She felt glad that this nice man had come along, for just here the road was lonely.

After a while the man spoke. "What is your name, little one?" he asked, caressingly.

"Lily Barry."

The man started. "What is your father's name?"

"Nelson Barry," replied Lily.

The man whistled. "Is your mother dead?"

"Yes, sir."

"How old are you, my dear?"

"Fourteen," replied Lily.

The man looked at her with surprise. "As old as that?"

Lily suddenly shrank from the man. She could not have told why. She pulled her little hand from his, and he let it go with no remonstrance. She clasped both her arms around her rag doll, in order that her hand should not be free for him to grasp again.

She walked a little farther away from the man, and he looked amused.

"You still play with your doll?" he said, in a soft voice.

"Yes, sir," replied Lily. She quickened her pace and reached the store.

When Lily entered the store, Hiram Gates, the owner, was behind the counter. The only man besides in the store was Nelson Barry. He sat tipping his chair back against the wall; he was half asleep, and his handsome face was bristling with a beard of several days' growth and darkly flushed. He opened his eyes when Lily entered, the strange man following. He brought his chair down on all fours, and he looked at the man—not noticing Lily at all—with a look compounded of defiance and uneasiness.

"Hullo, Jim!" he said.

"Hullo, old man!" returned the stranger.

Lily went over to the counter and asked for the salt, in her pretty little voice. When she had paid for it and was crossing the store, Nelson Barry was on his feet.

"Well, how are you, Lily? It is Lily, isn't it?" he said.

"Yes, sir," replied Lily, faintly.

Her father bent down and, for the first time in her life, kissed her, and the whiskey odor of his breath came into her face.

Lily involuntarily started, and shrank away from him. Then she rubbed her mouth violently with her little cotton handkerchief, which she held gathered up with the rag doll.

"Damn it all! I believe she is afraid of me," said Nelson Barry, in a thick voice.

"Looks a little like it," said the other man, laughing.

"It's that damned old woman," said Nelson Barry. Then he smiled again at Lily. "I didn't know what a pretty little daughter I was blessed with," said he, and he softly stroked Lily's pink cheek under her hat.

Now Lily did not shrink from him. Hereditary instincts and nature itself were asserting themselves in the child's innocent, receptive breast.

Nelson Barry looked curiously at Lily. "How old are you, anyway, child?" he asked.

"I'll be fourteen in September," replied Lily.

"But you still play with your doll?" said Barry, laughing kindly down at her.

Lily hugged her doll more tightly, in spite of her father's kind voice. "Yes, sir," she replied.

Nelson glanced across at some glass jars filled with sticks of candy. "See here, little Lily, do you like candy?" said he.

"Yes, sir."

"Wait a minute."

Lily waited while her father went over to the counter. Soon he returned with a package of the candy.

"I don't see how you are going to carry so much," he said, smiling. "Suppose you throw away your doll?"

Lily gazed at her father and hugged the doll tightly, and there was all at once in the child's expression something mature. It became the reproach of a woman. Nelson's face sobered.

"Oh, it's all right, Lily," he said; "keep your doll. Here, I guess you can carry this candy under your arm."

Lily could not resist the candy. She obeyed Nelson's instructions for carrying it, and left the store laden. The two men also left, and walked in the opposite direction, talking busily.

When Lily reached home, her grandmother, who was watching for her, spied at once the package of candy.

"What's that?" she asked, sharply.

"My father gave it to me," answered Lily, in a faltering voice. Sally regarded her with something like alertness.

"Your father?"

"Yes, ma'am."

"Where did you see him?"

"In the store."

"He gave you this candy?"

"Yes, ma'am."

"What did he say?"

"He asked me how old I was, and—"

"And what?"

"I don't know," replied Lily; and it really seemed to her that she did not know, she was so frightened and bewildered by it all, and, more than anything else, by her grandmother's face as she questioned her.

Old Woman Magoun's face was that of one upon whom a long-anticipated blow had fallen. Sally Jinks gazed at her with a sort of stupid alarm.

Old Woman Magoun continued to gaze at her grandchild with that look of terrible solicitude, as if she saw the girl in the clutch of a tiger. "You can't remember what else he said?" she asked, fiercely, and the child began to whimper softly.

"No, ma'am," she sobbed. "I—don't know, and—"

"And what? Answer me."

"There was another man there. A real handsome man."

"Did he speak to you?" asked Old Woman Magoun.

"Yes, ma'am; he walked along with me a piece," confessed Lily, with a sob of terror and bewilderment.

"What did *he* say to you?" asked Old Woman Magoun, with a sort of despair.

Lily told, in her little, faltering, frightened voice, all of the conversation which she could recall. It sounded harmless enough, but the look of the realization of a long-expected blow never left her grandmother's face.

The sun was getting low, and the bridge was nearing completion. Soon the workmen would be crowding into the cabin for their promised supper. There became visible in the distance, far up the road, the heavily plodding figure of another woman who had agreed to come and help. Old Woman Magoun turned again to Lily.

"You go right up-stairs to your own chamber now," said she.

"Good land! ain't you goin' to let that poor child stay up and see the fun?" said Sally Jinks.

"You jest mind your own business," said Old Woman Magoun, forcibly, and Sally Jinks shrank. "You go right up there now, Lily," said the grandmother, in a softer tone, "and grandma will bring you up a nice plate of supper."

"When be you goin' to let that girl grow up?" asked Sally Jinks, when Lily had disappeared.

"She'll grow up in the Lord's good time," replied Old Woman Magoun, and there was in her voice something both sad and threatening. Sally Jinks again shrank a little.

Soon the workmen came flocking noisily into the house. Old Woman Magoun and her two helpers served the bountiful supper. Most of the men had drunk as much as, and more than, was good for them, and Old Woman Magoun had stipulated that there was to be no drinking of anything except coffee during supper.

"I'll git you as good a meal as I know how," she said, "but if I see ary one of you drinkin' a drop, I'll run you all out. If you want anything to drink, you can go up to the store afterward. That's the place for you to go to, if you've got to make hogs of yourselves. I ain't goin' to have no hogs in my house."

Old Woman Magoun was implicitly obeyed. She had a curious authority over most people when she chose to exercise it. When the supper was in full swing, she quietly stole up-stairs and carried some food to Lily. She found the girl, with the rag doll in her arms, crouching by the window in her little rocking-chair—a relic of her infancy, which she still used.

"What a noise they are makin', grandma!" she said, in a terrified whisper, as her grandmother placed the plate before her on a chair.

"They've 'most all of 'em been drinkin'. They air a passel of hogs," replied the old woman.

"Is the man that was with—with my father down there?" asked Lily, in a timid fashion. Then she fairly cowered before the look in her grandmother's eyes.

"No, he ain't; and what's more, he never will be down there if I can help it," said Old Woman Magoun, in a fierce whisper. "I know who he is. They can't cheat me. He's one of them Willises—that family the Barrys married into. They're worse than the Barrys, ef they *have* got money. Eat your supper, and put him out of your mind, child."

It was after Lily was asleep, when Old Woman Magoun was alone, clearing away her supper dishes, that Lily's father came. The door was closed, and he knocked, and the old woman knew at once who was there. The sound of that knock meant as much to her as the whir of a bomb to the defender of a fortress. She opened the door, and Nelson Barry stood there.

"Good-evening, Mrs. Magoun," he said.

Old Woman Magoun stood before him, filling up the doorway with her firm bulk.

"Good-evening, Mrs. Magoun," said Nelson Barry again.

"I ain't got no time to waste," replied the old woman, harshly. "I've got my supper dishes to clean up after them men."

She stood there and looked at him as she might have looked at a rebellious animal which she was trying to tame. The man laughed.

"It's no use," said he. "You know me of old. No human being can turn me from my way when I am once started in it. You may as well let me come in."

Old Woman Magoun entered the house, and Barry followed her.

Barry began without any preface. "Where is the child?" asked he.

"Up-stairs. She has gone to bed."

"She goes to bed early."

"Children ought to," returned the old woman, polishing a plate.

Barry laughed. "You are keeping her a child a long while," he remarked, in a soft voice which had a sting in it.

"She *is a* child," returned the old woman, defiantly.

"Her mother was only three years older when Lily was born."

The old woman made a sudden motion toward the man which seemed fairly menacing. Then she turned again to her dish-washing.

"I want her," said Barry.

"You can't have her," replied the old woman, in a still stern voice.

"I don't see how you can help yourself. You have always acknowledged that she was my child."

The old woman continued her task, but her strong back heaved. Barry regarded her with an entirely pitiless expression.

"I am going to have the girl, that is the long and short of it," he said, "and it is for her best good, too. You are a fool, or you would see it."

"Her best good?" muttered the old woman.

"Yes, her best good. What are you going to do with her, anyway? The girl is a beauty, and almost a woman grown, although you try to make out that she is a baby. You can't live forever."

"The Lord will take care of her," replied the old woman, and again she turned and faced him, and her expression was that of a prophetess.

"Very well, let Him," said Barry, easily. "All the same I'm going to have her, and I tell you it is for her best good. Jim Willis saw her this afternoon, and—"

Old Woman Magoun looked at him. "Jim Willis!" she fairly shrieked.

"Well, what of it?"

"One of them Willises!" repeated the old woman, and this time her voice was thick. It seemed almost as if she were stricken with paralysis. She did not enunciate clearly.

The man shrank a little. "Now what is the need of your making such a fuss?" he said. "I will take her, and Isabel will look out for her."

"Your half-witted sister?" said Old Woman Magoun.

"Yes, my half-witted sister. She knows more than you think."

"More wickedness."

"Perhaps. Well, a knowledge of evil is a useful thing. How are you going to avoid evil if you don't know what it is like? My sister and I will take care of my daughter."

The old woman continued to look at the man, but his eyes never fell. Suddenly her gaze grew inconceivably keen. It was as if she saw through all externals.

"I know what it is!" she cried. "You have been playing cards and you lost, and this is the way you will pay him."

Then the man's face reddened, and he swore under his breath.

"Oh, my God!" said the old woman; and she really spoke with her eyes aloft as if addressing something outside of them both. Then she turned again to her dish-washing.

The man cast a dogged look at her back. "Well, there is no use talking. I have made up my mind," said he, "and you know me and what that means. I am going to have the girl."

"When?" said the old woman, without turning around.

"Well, I am willing to give you a week. Put her clothes in good order before she comes."

The old woman made no reply. She continued washing dishes. She even handled them so carefully that they did not rattle.

"You understand," said Barry. "Have her ready a week from today."

"Yes," said Old Woman Magoun, "I understand."

Nelson Barry, going up the mountain road, reflected that Old Woman Magoun had a strong character, that she understood much better than her sex in general the futility of withstanding the inevitable.

"Well," he said to Jim Willis when he reached home, "the old woman did not make such a fuss as I expected."

"Are you going to have the girl?"

"Yes; a week from to-day. Look here, Jim; you've got to stick to your promise."

"All right," said Willis. "Go you one better."

The two were playing at cards in the old parlor, once magnificent, now squalid, of the Barry house. Isabel, the half-witted sister, entered, bringing some glasses on a tray. She had learned with her feeble intellect some tricks, like a dog. One of them was the mixing of sundry drinks. She set the tray on a little stand near the two men, and watched them with her silly simper.

"Clear out now and go to bed," her brother said to her, and she obeyed.

Early the next morning Old Woman Magoun went up to Lily's little sleeping-chamber, and watched her a second as she lay asleep, with her yellow locks spread over the pillow. Then she spoke. "Lily," said she—"Lily, wake up. I am going to Greenham across the new bridge, and you can go with me."

Lily immediately sat up in bed and smiled at her grandmother. Her eyes were still misty, but the light of awakening was in them.

"Get right up," said the old woman. "You can wear your new dress if you want to."

Lily gurgled with pleasure like a baby. "And my new hat?" asked she.

"I don't care."

Old Woman Magoun and Lily started for Greenham before Barry Ford, which kept late hours, was fairly awake. It was three miles to Greenham. The old woman said that, since the horse was a little lame, they would walk. It was a beautiful morning, with a diamond radiance of dew over everything. Her grandmother had curled Lily's hair more punctiliously than usual. The little face peeped like a rose out of two rows of golden spirals. Lily wore her new muslin dress with a pink sash, and her best hat of a fine white straw trimmed with a wreath of rosebuds; also the neatest black open-work stockings and pretty shoes. She even had white cotton gloves. When they set out, the old, heavily stepping woman, in her black gown and cape and bonnet, looked down at the little pink fluttering figure. Her face was full of the tenderest love and admiration, and yet there was something terrible about it. They crossed the new bridge—a primitive structure built of logs in a slovenly fashion. Old Woman Magoun pointed to a gap.

"Jest see that," said she. "That's the way men work."

"Men ain't very nice, be they?" said Lily, in her sweet little voice.

"No, they ain't, take them all together," replied her grandmother.

"That man that walked to the store with me was nicer than some, I guess," Lily said, in a wishful fashion. Her grandmother reached down and took the child's hand in its small cotton glove. "You hurt me, holding my hand so tight," Lily said presently, in a deprecatory little voice.

The old woman loosened her grasp. "Grandma didn't know how tight she was holding your hand," said she. "She wouldn't hurt you for nothin', except it was to save your life, or somethin' like that." She spoke with an undertone of tremendous meaning which the girl was too childish to grasp. They walked along the country road. Just before they reached Greenham they passed a stone wall overgrown with blackberry-vines, and, an unusual thing in that vicinity, a lusty spread of deadly nightshade full of berries.

"Those berries look good to eat, grandma," Lily said.

At that instant the old woman's face became something terrible to see. "You can't have any now," she said, and hurried Lily along.

"They look real nice," said Lily.

When they reached Greenham, Old Woman Magoun took her way straight to the most pretentious house there, the residence of the lawyer, whose name was Mason. Old Woman Magoun bade Lily wait in the yard for a few moments, and Lily ventured to seat herself on a bench beneath an oak-tree; then she watched with some wonder her grandmother enter the lawyer's office door at the right of the house. Presently the lawyer's wife came out and spoke to Lily under the tree. She had in her hand a little tray containing a plate of cake, a glass of milk, and an early apple. She spoke very kindly to Lily; she even kissed her, and offered her the tray of refreshments, which Lily accepted gratefully. She sat eating, with Mrs. Mason watching her, when Old Woman Magoun came out of the lawyer's office with a ghastly face.

"What are you eatin'?" she asked Lily, sharply. "Is that a sour apple?"

"I thought she might be hungry," said the lawyer's wife, with loving, melancholy eyes upon the girl.

Lily had almost finished the apple. "It's real sour, but I like it; it's real nice, grandma," she said.

"You ain't been drinkin' milk with a sour apple?"

"It was real nice milk, grandma."

"You ought never to have drunk milk and eat a sour apple," said her grandmother. "Your stomach was all out of order this mornin', an' sour apples and milk is always apt to hurt anybody."

"I don't know but they are," Mrs. Mason said, apologetically, as she stood on the green lawn with her lavender muslin sweeping around her. "I am real sorry, Mrs. Magoun. I ought to have thought. Let me get some soda for her."

"Soda never agrees with her," replied the old woman, in a harsh voice. "Come," she said to Lily, "it's time we were goin' home."

After Lily and her grandmother had disappeared down the road, Lawyer Mason came out of his office and joined his wife, who had seated herself on the bench beneath the tree. She was idle, and her face wore the expression of those who review joys forever past. She had lost a little girl, her only child, years ago, and her husband always knew when she was thinking about her. Lawyer Mason looked older than his wife; he had a dry, shrewd, slightly onesided face.

"What do you think, Maria?" he said. "That old woman came to me with the most pressing entreaty to adopt that little girl."

"She is a beautiful little girl," said Mrs. Mason, in a slightly husky voice.

"Yes, she is a pretty child," assented the lawyer, looking pityingly at his wife; "but it is out of the question, my dear. Adopting a child is a serious measure, and in this case a child who comes from Barry's Ford."

"But the grandmother seems a very good woman," said Mrs. Mason.

"I rather think she is. I never heard a word against her. But the lather! No, Maria, we cannot take a child with Barry blood in her veins. The stock has run out; it is vitiated physically and morally. It won't do, my dear."

"Her grandmother had her dressed up as pretty as a little girl could be," said Mrs. Mason, and this time the tears welled into her faithful, wistful eyes.

"Well, we can't help that," said the lawyer, as he went back to his office.

Old Woman Magoun and Lily returned, going slowly along the road to Barry's Ford. When they came to the stone wall where the blackberry-vines and the deadly nightshade grew, Lily said she was tired, and asked if she could not sit down for a few minutes. The strange look on her grandmother's face had deepened. Now and then Lily glanced at her and had a feeling as if she were looking at a stranger.

"Yes, you can set down if you want to," said Old Woman Magoun, deeply and harshly.

Lily started and looked at her, as if to make sure that it was her grandmother who spoke. Then she sat down on a stone which was comparatively free of the vines.

"Ain't you goin' to set down, grandma?" Lily asked, timidly.

"No; I don't want to get into that mess," replied her grandmother. "I ain't tired. I'll stand here."

Lily sat still; her delicate little face was flushed with heat. She extended her tiny feet in her best shoes and gazed at them. "My shoes are all over dust," said she.

"It will brush off," said her grandmother, still in that strange voice.

Lily looked around. An elm-tree in the field behind her cast a spray of branches over her head; a little cool puff of wind came on her face. She gazed at the low mountains on the horizon, in the midst of which she lived, and she sighed, for no reason that she knew. She began idly picking at the blackberry-vines; there were no berries on them; then she put her little fingers on the berries of the deadly nightshade. "These look like nice berries," she said.

Old Woman Magoun, standing stiff and straight in the road, said nothing.

"They look good to eat," said Lily.

Old Woman Magoun still said nothing, but she looked up into the ineffable blue of the sky, over which spread at intervals great white clouds shaped like wings.

Lily picked some of the deadly nightshade berries and ate them. "Why, they are real sweet," said she. "They are nice." She picked some more and ate them.

Presently her grandmother spoke. "Come," she said, "it is time we were going. I guess you have set long enough."

Lily was still eating the berries when she slipped down from the wall and followed her grandmother obediently up the road.

Before they reached home, Lily complained of being very thirsty. She stopped and made a little cup of a leaf and drank long at a mountain brook. "I am dreadful dry, but it hurts me to swallow," she said to her grandmother when she stopped drinking and joined the old woman waiting for her in the road. Her grandmother's face seemed strangely dim to her. She took hold of Lily's hand as they went on. "My stomach burns," said Lily, presently. "I want some more water."

"There is another brook a little farther on," said Old Woman Magoun, in a dull voice.

When they reached that brook, Lily stopped and drank again, but she whimpered a little over her difficulty in swallowing. "My stomach burns, too," she said, walking on, "and my throat is so dry, grandma." Old Woman Magoun held Lily's hand more tightly. "You hurt me holding my hand so tight, grandma," said Lily, looking up at her grandmother, whose face she seemed to see through a mist, and the old woman loosened her grasp.

When at last they reached home, Lily was very ill. Old Woman Magoun put her on her own bed in the little bedroom out of the kitchen. Lily lay there and moaned, and Sally Jinks came in.

"Why, what ails her?" she asked. "She looks feverish."

Lily unexpectedly answered for herself. "I ate some sour apples and drank some milk," she moaned.

"Sour apples and milk are dreadful apt to hurt anybody," said Sally Jinks. She told several people on her way home that Old Woman Magoun was dreadful careless to let Lily eat such things.

Meanwhile Lily grew worse. She suffered cruelly from the burning in her stomach, the vertigo, and the deadly nausea. "I am so sick, I am so sick, grandma," she kept moaning. She could no longer see her grandmother as she bent over her, but she could hear her talk.

Old Woman Magoun talked as Lily had never heard her talk before, as nobody had ever heard her talk before. She spoke from the depths of her soul; her voice was as tender as the coo of a dove, and it was grand and exalted. "You'll feel better very soon, little Lily," said she.

"I am so sick, grandma."

"You will feel better very soon, and then—"

"I am sick."

"You shall go to a beautiful place."

Lily moaned.

"You shall go to a beautiful place," the old woman went on.

"Where?" asked Lily, groping feebly with her cold little hands. Then she moaned again.

"A beautiful place, where the flowers grow tall."

"What color? Oh, grandma, I am so sick."

"A blue color," replied the old woman. Blue was Lily's favorite color. "A beautiful blue color, and as tall as your knees, and the flowers always stay there, and they never fade."

"Not if you pick them, grandma? Oh!"

"No, not if you pick them; they never fade, and they are so sweet you can smell them a mile off; and there are birds that sing, and all the roads have gold stones in them, and the stone walls are made of gold."

"Like the ring grandpa gave you? I am so sick, grandma."

"Yes, gold like that. And all the houses are built of silver and gold, and the people all have wings, so when they get tired walking they can fly, and—"

"I am so sick, grandma."

"And all the dolls are alive," said Old Woman Magoun. "Dolls like yours can run, and talk, and love you back again."

Lily had her poor old rag doll in bed with her, clasped close to her agonized little heart. She tried very hard with her eyes, whose pupils were so dilated that they looked black, to see her grandmother's face when she said that, but she could not. "It is dark," she moaned, feebly.

"There where you are going it is always light," said the grandmother, "and the commonest things shine like that breastpin Mrs. Lawyer Mason had on to-day."

Lily moaned pitifully, and said something incoherent. Delirium was commencing. Presently she sat straight up in bed and raved; but even then her grandmother's wonderful compelling voice had an influence over her.

"You will come to a gate with all the colors of the rainbow," said her grandmother; "and it will open, and you will go right in and walk up the gold street, and cross the field where the blue flowers come up to your knees, until you find your mother, and she will take you home where you are going to live. She has a little white room all ready for you, white curtains at the windows, and a little white looking-glass, and when you look in it you will see—"

"What will I see? I am so sick, grandma."

"You will see a face like yours, only it's an angel's; and there will be a little white bed, and you can lay down an' rest."

"Won't I be sick, grandma?" asked Lily. Then she moaned and babbled wildly, although she seemed to understand through it all what her grandmother said.

"No, you will never be sick any more. Talkin' about sickness won't mean anything to you."

It continued. Lily talked on wildly, and her grandmother's great voice of soothing never ceased, until the child fell into a deep sleep, or what resembled sleep; but she lay stiffly in that sleep, and a candle flashed before her eyes made no impression on them.

Then it was that Nelson Barry came. Jim Willis waited outside the door. When Nelson entered he found Old Woman Magoun on her knees beside the bed, weeping with dry eyes and a might of agony which fairly shook Nelson Barry, the degenerate of a fine old race.

"Is she sick?" he asked, in a hushed voice.

Old Woman Magoun gave another terrible sob, which sounded like the gasp of one dying.

"Sally Jinks said that Lily was sick from eating milk and sour apples," said Barry, in a tremulous voice. "I remember that her mother was very sick once from eating them."

Lily lay still, and her grandmother on her knees shook with her terrible sobs.

Suddenly Nelson Barry started. "I guess I had better go to Greenham for a doctor if she's as bad as that," he said. He went close to the bed and looked at the sick child. He gave a great start. Then he felt of her hands and reached down under the bedclothes for her little feet. "Her hands and feet are like ice," he cried out. "Good God! why didn't you send for some one—for me—before? Why, she's dying; she's almost gone!"

Barry rushed out and spoke to Jim Willis, who turned pale and came in and stood by the bedside.

"She's almost gone," he said, in a hushed whisper.

"There's no use going for the doctor; she'd be dead before he got here," said Nelson, and he stood regarding the passing child with a strange, sad face—unutterably sad, because of his incapability of the truest sadness.

"Poor little thing, she's past suffering, anyhow," said the other man, and his own face also was sad with a puzzled, mystified sadness.

Lily died that night. There was quite a commotion in Barry's Ford until after the funeral, it was all so sudden, and then everything went on as usual. Old Woman Magoun continued to live as she had done before. She supported herself by the produce of her tiny farm; she was very industrious, but people said that she was a trifle touched, since every time she went over the log bridge with her eggs or her garden vegetables to sell in Greenham, she carried with her, as one might have carried an infant, Lily's old rag doll.

CHARLES CHESNUTT
(1858–1932)

Charles Chesnutt, best known for his dialect stories The Conjure Woman *(1899) and* The Wife of His Youth and Other Stories of the Color Line *(1899), is generally considered the first black writer to find a white readership in America. Born in Cleveland, Ohio, and raised in Fayetteville, North Carolina, Chesnutt was precocious, and ambitious: he published his first story at the age of fourteen, and, like Jack London, subjected himself to a demanding regimen of self-education. He made his living primarily as a lawyer and court stenographer in Cleveland, but published in McClure's syndicated newspapers and in* Atlantic Monthly, *with the encouragement of William Dean Howells, who compared his work favorably with that of James, Turgenev, and Maupassant.*

Though Chesnutt's literary career, by his own decision, was short-lived, he published a number of books in addition to the short story collections, among them the novels The House Behind the Cedars *(1900),* The Marrow of Tradition *(1901), and* The Colonel's Dream *(1905); his* Frederick Douglass *appeared in 1899. Chesnutt was an astute social critic whose great subject was race in America: "The object of my writings would not be so much the elevation of the colored people as the elevation of the whites—for I consider the unjust spirit of caste which is so insidious as to pervade a whole nation... as a barrier to the moral progress of the American people."*

In this exemplary story, from The Wife of His Youth, *Chesnutt probes subtleties of conscience in an atmosphere of racial antagonism and misunderstanding. The expected does not happen; the unexpected, does. Here is a tragic drama powerfully abbreviated and given a vividly rendered local habitation.*

The Sheriff's Children

Branson County, North Carolina, is in a sequestered district of one of the staidest and most conservative States of the Union. Society in Branson County is almost primitive in its simplicity. Most of the white people own the farms they till, and even before the war there were no very wealthy families to force their neighbors, by comparison, into the category of "poor whites."

To Branson County, as to most rural communities in the South, the war is the one historical event that overshadows all others. It is the era from which all local chronicles are dated,—births, deaths, marriages, storms, freshets. No description of the life of any Southern community would be perfect that failed to emphasize the all pervading influence of the great conflict.

Yet the fierce tide of war that had rushed through the cities and along the great highways of the country had comparatively speaking but slightly disturbed the sluggish current of life in this region, remote from railroads and navigable streams. To the north in Virginia, to the west in Tennessee, and all along the seaboard the war had raged; but the thunder of its cannon had not disturbed the echoes of Branson County, where the loudest sounds heard were the crack of some hunter's rifle, the baying of some deep-mouthed hound, or the yodel of some tuneful negro on his way through the pine forest. To the east, Sherman's army had passed on its march to the sea; but no straggling band of "bummers" had penetrated the confines of Branson County. The war, it is true, had robbed the county of the flower of its young manhood; but the burden of taxation, the doubt and uncertainty of the conflict, and the sting of ultimate defeat, had been borne by the people with an apathy that robbed misfortune of half its sharpness.

The nearest approach to town life afforded by Branson County is found in the little village of Troy, the county seat, a hamlet with a population of four or five hundred.

Ten years make little difference in the appearance of these remote Southern towns. If a railroad is built through one of them, it infuses some enterprise; the social corpse is galvanized by the fresh blood of civilization that pulses along the farthest ramifications of our great system of commercial highways. At the period of which I write, no railroad had come to Troy. If a traveler, accustomed to the bustling life of cities, could have ridden through Troy on a summer day, he might easily have fancied himself in a deserted village. Around him he would have seen weather-beaten houses, innocent of paint, the shingled roofs in many instances covered with a rich growth of moss. Here and there he would have met a razor-backed hog lazily rooting his way along the principal thoroughfare; and more than once he would probably have had to disturb the slumbers of some yellow dog, dozing away the hours in the ardent sunshine, and reluctantly yielding up his place in the middle of the dusty road.

On Saturdays the village presented a somewhat livelier appearance, and the shade trees around the court-house square and along Front Street served as hitching-posts for a goodly number of horses and mules and stunted oxen, belonging to the farmer-folk who had come in to trade at the two or three local stores.

A murder was a rare event in Branson County. Every well-informed citizen could tell the number of homicides committed in the county for fifty years back, and whether the slayer, in any given instance, had escaped, either by flight or acquittal, or had suffered the penalty of the law. So, when it became known in Troy early one Friday morning in summer, about ten years after the war, that old Captain Walker, who had served in Mexico under Scott, and had left an arm on the field of Gettysburg, had been foully murdered during the night, there was intense excitement in the village. Business was practically suspended, and the citizens gathered in little groups to discuss the murder, and speculate upon the identity of the murderer. It transpired from testimony at the coroner's inquest, held during the morning, that a strange mulatto had been seen going in the direction of Captain Walker's house the night before, and had been met going away from Troy early Friday morning, by a farmer on his way to town. Other circumstances seemed to connect the stranger with the crime. The sheriff organized a posse to search for him, and early in the evening, when most of the citizens of Troy were at supper, the suspected man was brought in and lodged in the county jail.

By the following morning the news of the capture had spread to the farthest limits of the county. A much larger number of people than usual came to town that Saturday,—bearded men in straw hats and blue homespun shirts, and butternut trousers of great amplitude of material and vagueness of outline: women in homespun frocks and slat-bonnets, with faces as expressionless as the dreary sandhills which gave them a meagre sustenance.

The murder was almost the sole topic of conversation. A steady stream of curious observers visited the house of mourning, and gazed upon the rugged face of the old veteran, now stiff and cold in death; and more than one eye dropped a tear at the remembrance of the cheery smile, and the joke—sometimes superannuated, generally feeble, but always good-natured—with which the captain had been wont to greet his acquaintances. There was a growing sentiment of anger among these stern men, toward the murderer who had thus cut down their friend, and a strong feeling that ordinary justice was too slight a punishment for such a crime.

Toward noon there was an informal gathering of citizens in Dan Tyson's store.

"I hear it 'lowed that Square Kyahtah's too sick ter hol' co'te this evenin'," said one, "an' that the purlim'nary hearin' 'll haf ter go over 'tel nex' week."

A look of disappointment went round the crowd.

"Hit 's the durndes', meanes' murder ever committed in this caounty," said another, with moody emphasis.

"I s'pose the nigger 'lowed the Cap'n had some greenbacks," observed a third speaker.

"The Cap'n," said another, with an air of superior information, "has left two bairls of Confedrit money, which he 'spected 'ud be good some day er nuther."

This statement gave rise to a discussion of the speculative value of Confederate money; but in a little while the conversation returned to the murder.

"Hangin' air too good for the murderer," said one; "he oughter be burnt, stidier bein' hung."

There was an impressive pause at this point, during which a jug of moonlight whiskey went the round of the crowd.

"Well," said a round-shouldered farmer, who, in spite of his peaceable expression and faded gray eye, was known to have been one of the most daring followers of a rebel guerrilla chieftain, "what air yer gwine ter do about it? Ef you fellers air gwine ter set down an' let a wuthless nigger kill the bes' white man in Branson, an' not say nuthin' ner do nuthin', *I'll* move outen the caounty."

This speech gave tone and direction to the rest of the conversation. Whether the fear of losing the round-shouldered farmer operated to bring about the result or not is immaterial to this narrative; but, at all events, the crowd decided to lynch the negro. They agreed that this was the least that could be done to avenge the death of their murdered friend, and that it was a becoming way in which to honor his memory. They had some vague notions of the majesty of the law and the rights of the citizen, but in the passion of the moment these sunk into oblivion; a white man had been killed by a negro.

"The Cap'n was an ole sodger," said one of his friends solemnly. "He'll sleep better when he knows that a co'te-martial has be'n hilt an' jestice done."

By agreement the lynchers were to meet at Tyson's store at five o'clock in the afternoon, and proceed thence to the jail, which was situated down the Lumberton Dirt Road (as the old turnpike antedating the plank-road was called), about half a mile south of the court-house. When the preliminaries of the lynching had been arranged, and a committee appointed to manage the affair, the crowd dispersed, some to go to their dinners, and some to secure recruits for the lynching party.

It was twenty minutes to five o'clock, when an excited negro, panting and perspiring, rushed up to the back door of Sheriff Campbell's dwelling, which stood at a little distance from the jail and somewhat farther than the latter building from the court-house. A turbaned colored woman came to the door in response to the negro's knock.

"Hoddy, Sis' Nance."

"Hoddy, Brer Sam."

"Is de shurff in," inquired the negro.

"Yas, Brer Sam, he's eatin' his dinner," was the answer.

"Will yer ax 'im ter step ter de do' a minute, Sis' Nance?"

The woman went into the dining-room, and a moment later the sheriff came to the door. He was a tall, muscular man, of a ruddier complexion than is usual among Southerners. A pair of keen, deep-set gray eyes looked out from under bushy eyebrows, and about his mouth was a masterful expression, which a full beard, once sandy in color, but now profusely sprinkled with gray, could not entirely conceal. The day was hot; the sheriff had discarded his coat and vest, and had his white shirt open at the throat.

"What do you want, Sam?" he inquired of the negro, who stood hat in hand, wiping the moisture from his face with a ragged shirtsleeve.

"Shurff, dey gwine ter hang de pris'ner w'at's lock' up in de jail. Dey're comin' dis a-way now. I wuz layin' down on a sack er corn down at de sto', behine a pile er flour-bairls, wen I hearn Doc' Cain en Kunnel Wright talkin' erbout it. I slip' outen de back do', en run here as fas' as I could. I hearn you say down ter de sto' once't dat you would n't let nobody take a pris'ner 'way fum you widout walkin' over yo' dead body, en I thought I'd let you know 'fo' dey come, so yer could pertec' de pris'ner."

The sheriff listened calmly, but his face grew firmer, and a determined gleam lit up his gray eyes. His frame grew more erect, and he unconsciously assumed the attitude of a soldier who momentarily expects to meet the enemy face to face.

"Much obliged, Sam," he answered. "I'll protect the prisoner. Who's coming?"

"I dunno who-all *is* comin," replied the negro. "Dere's Mistah McSwayne, en Doc' Cain, en Maje' McDonal', en Kunnel Wright, en a heap er yuthers. I wuz so skeered I done furgot mo' d'n half un em. I spec' dey mus' be mos' here by dis time, so I'll git outen de way, fer I don' want nobody fer ter think I wuz mix' up in dis business." The negro glanced nervously down the road toward the town, and made a movement as if to go away.

"Won't you have some dinner first?" asked the sheriff.

The negro looked longingly in at the open door, and sniffed the appetizing odor of boiled pork and collards.

"I ain't got no time fer ter tarry, Shurff," he said, "but Sis' Nance mought gin me sump'n I could kyar in my han' en eat on de way."

A moment later Nancy brought him a huge sandwich of split cornpone, with a thick slice of fat bacon inserted between the halves, and a couple of baked yams. The negro hastily replaced his ragged hat on his head, dropped the yams in the pocket of his capacious trousers, and, taking the sandwich in his hand, hurried across the road and disappeared in the woods beyond.

The sheriff reentered the house, and put on his coat and hat. He then took down a double-barreled shotgun and loaded it with buckshot. Filling the chambers of a revolver with fresh cartridges, he slipped it into the pocket of the sack-coat which he wore.

A comely young woman in a calico dress watched these proceedings with anxious surprise.

"Where are you going, father?" she asked. She had not heard the conversation with the negro.

"I am goin' over to the jail," responded the sheriff. "There's a mob comin' this way to lynch the nigger we've got locked up. But they won't do it," he added, with emphasis.

"Oh, father! don't go!" pleaded the girl, clinging to his arm; "they'll shoot you if you don't give him up."

"You never mind me, Polly," said her father reassuringly, as he gently unclasped her hands from his arm. "I'll take care of myself and the prisoner, too. There ain't a man in Branson County that would shoot me. Besides, I have faced fire too often to be scared away from my duty. You keep close in the house," he continued, "and if any one disturbs you just use the old horse-pistol in the top bureau drawer. It's a little old-fashioned, but it did good work a few years ago."

The young girl shuddered at this sanguinary allusion, but made no further objection to her father's departure.

The sheriff of Branson was a man far above the average of the community in wealth, education, and social position. His had been one of the few families in the county that before the war had owned large estates and numerous slaves. He had graduated at the State University at Chapel Hill, and had kept up some acquaintance with current literature and advanced thought. He had traveled some in his youth, and was looked up to in the county as an authority on all subjects connected with the outer world. At first an ardent supporter of the Union, he had opposed the secession movement in his native State as long as opposition availed to stem the tide of public opinion. Yielding at last to the force of circumstances, he had entered the Confederate service rather late in the war, and served with distinction through several campaigns, rising in time to the rank of colonel. After the war he had taken the oath of allegiance, and had been chosen by the people as the most available candidate for the office of sheriff, to which he had been elected without opposition. He had filled the office for several terms, and was universally popular with his constituents.

Colonel or Sheriff Campbell, as he was indifferently called, as the military or civil title happened to be most important in the opinion of the person addressing him, had a high sense of the responsibility attaching to his office. He had sworn to do his duty faithfully, and he knew what his duty was, as sheriff, perhaps more clearly than he had apprehended it in other passages of his life. It was, therefore, with no uncertainty in regard to his course that he prepared his weapons and went over to the jail. He had no fears for Polly's safety.

The sheriff had just locked the heavy front door of the jail behind him when a half dozen horsemen, followed by a crowd of men on foot, came round a bend in the road and drew near the jail. They halted in front of the picket fence that surrounded the building, while several of the committee of arrangements rode on a few rods farther to the sheriff's house. One of them dismounted and rapped on the door with his riding-whip.

"Is the sheriff at home?" he inquired.

"No, he has just gone out," replied Polly, who had come to the door.

"We want the jail keys," he continued.

"They are not here," said Polly. "The sheriff has them himself." Then she added, with assumed indifference. "He is at the jail now."

The man turned away, and Polly went into the front room, from which she peered anxiously between the slats of the green blinds of a window that looked toward the jail. Meanwhile the messenger returned to his companions and announced his discovery. It looked as though the sheriff had learned of their design and was preparing to resist it.

One of them stepped forward and rapped on the jail door.

"Well, what is it?" said the sheriff, from within.

"We want to talk to you, Sheriff," replied the spokesman.

There was a little wicket in the door: this the sheriff opened, and answered through it.

"All right, boys, talk away. You are all strangers to me, and I don't know what business you can have." The sheriff did not think it necessary to recognize anybody in particular on such an occasion; the question of identity sometimes comes up in the investigation of these extra-judicial executions.

"We're a committee of citizens and we want to get into the jail."

"What for? It ain't much trouble to get into jail. Most people want to keep out."

The mob was in no humor to appreciate a joke, and the sheriff's witticism fell dead upon an unresponsive audience.

"We want to have a talk with the nigger that killed Cap'n Walker."

"You can talk to that nigger in the courthouse, when he's brought out for trial. Court will be in session here next week. I know what you fellows want, but you can't get my prisoner to-day. Do you want to take the bread out of a poor man's mouth? I get seventy-five cents a day for keeping this prisoner, and he's the only one in jail. I can't have my family suffer just to please you fellows."

One or two young men in the crowd laughed at the idea of Sheriff Campbell's suffering for want of seventy-five cents a day; but they were frowned into silence by those who stood near them.

"Ef yer don't let us in," cried a voice, "we'll bus' the do' open."

"Bust away," answered the sheriff, raising his voice so that all could hear. "But I give you fair warning. The first man that tries it will be filled with buckshot. I'm sheriff of this county; I know my duty, and I mean to do it."

"What's the use of kicking, Sheriff?" argued one of the leaders of the mob. "The nigger is sure to hang anyhow; he richly deserves it; and we've got to do something to teach the niggers their places, or white people won't be able to live in the county."

"There's no use talking, boys," responded the sheriff. "I'm a white man outside, but in this jail I'm sheriff; and if this nigger's to be hung in this county, I propose to do the hanging. So you fellows might as well right-about-face, and march back to Troy. You've had a pleasant trip, and the exercise will be good for you. You know *me*. I've got powder and ball, and I've faced fire before now, with nothing between me and the enemy, and I don't mean to surrender this jail while I'm able to shoot." Having thus announced his determination, the sheriff closed and fastened the wicket, and looked around for the best position from which to defend the building.

The crowd drew off a little, and the leaders conversed together in low tones.

The Branson County jail was a small, two-story brick building, strongly constructed, with no attempt at architectural ornamentation. Each story was divided into two large cells by a passage running from front to rear. A grated iron door gave entrance from the passage to each of the four cells. The jail seldom had many prisoners in it, and the lower windows had been boarded up. When the sheriff had closed the wicket, he ascended the steep wooden stairs to the upper floor. There was no window at the front of the upper passage, and the most available position from which to watch the movements of the crowd below was the front window of the cell occupied by the solitary prisoner.

The sheriff unlocked the door and entered the cell. The prisoner was crouched in a corner, his yellow face, blanched with terror, looking ghastly in the semi-darkness of the room. A cold perspiration had gathered on his forehead, and his teeth were chattering with affright.

"For God's sake. Sheriff," he murmured hoarsely, "don't let em lynch me; I did n't kill the old man."

The sheriff glanced at the cowering wretch with a look of mingled contempt and loathing.

"Get up," he said sharply. "You will probably be hung sooner or later, but it shall not be to-day, if I can help it. I'll unlock your fetters, and if I can't hold the jail, you'll have to make the best fight you can. If I'm shot, I'll consider my responsibility at an end."

There were iron fetters on the prisoner's ankles, and handcuffs on his wrists. These the sheriff unlocked, and they fell clanking to the floor.

"Keep back from the window," said the sheriff. "They might shoot if they saw you."

The sheriff drew toward the window a pine bench which formed a part of the scanty furniture of the cell, and laid his revolver upon it. Then he took his gun in hand, and took his stand at the side of the window where he could with least exposure of himself watch the movements of the crowd below.

The lynchers had not anticipated any determined resistance. Of course they had looked for a formal protest, and perhaps a sufficient show of opposition to excuse the sheriff in the eye of any stickler for legal formalities. They had not however come prepared to fight a battle, and no one of them seemed willing to lead an attack upon the jail. The leaders of the party conferred together with a good deal of animated gesticulation, which was visible to the sheriff from his outlook, though the distance was too great for him to hear what was said. At length one of them broke away from the group, and rode back to the main body of the lynchers, who were restlessly awaiting orders.

"Well, boys," said the messenger, "we'll have to let it go for the present. The sheriff says he'll shoot, and he's got the drop on us this time. There ain't any of us that want to follow Cap'n Walker jest yet. Besides, the sheriff is a good fellow, and we don't want to hurt 'im. But," he added, as if to reassure the crowd, which began to show signs of disappointment, "the nigger might as well say his prayers, for he ain't got long to live."

There was a murmur of dissent from the mob, and several voices insisted that an attack be made on the jail. But pacific counsels finally prevailed, and the mob sullenly withdrew.

The sheriff stood at the window until they had disappeared around the bend in the road. He did not relax his watchfulness when the last one was out of sight. Their withdrawal might be a mere feint, to be followed by a further attempt. So closely, indeed, was his attention drawn to the outside, that he neither saw nor heard the prisoner creep stealthily across the floor, reach out his hand and secure the revolver which lay on the bench behind the sheriff, and creep as noiselessly back to his place in the corner of the room.

A moment after the last of the lynching party had disappeared there was a shot fired from the woods across the road; a bullet whistled by the window and buried itself in the wooden casing a few inches from where the sheriff was standing. Quick as thought, with the instinct born of a semi-guerrilla army experience, he raised his gun and fired twice at the point from which a faint puff of smoke showed the hostile bullet to have been sent. He stood a moment watching, and then rested his gun against the window, and reached behind him mechanically for the other weapon.

It was not on the bench. As the sheriff realized this fact, he turned his head and looked into the muzzle of the revolver.

"Stay where you are. Sheriff," said the prisoner, his eyes glistening, his face almost ruddy with excitement.

The sheriff mentally cursed his own carelessness for allowing him to be caught in such a predicament. He had not expected anything of the kind. He had relied on the negro's cowardice and subordination in the presence of an armed white man as a matter of course. The sheriff was a brave man, but realized that the prisoner had him at an immense disadvantage. The two men stood thus for a moment, fighting a harmless duel with their eyes.

"Well, what do you mean to do?" asked the sheriff with apparent calmness.

"To get away, of course," said the prisoner, in a tone which caused the sheriff to look at him more closely, and with an involuntary feeling of apprehension; if the man was not mad, he was in a state of mind akin to madness, and quite as dangerous. The sheriff felt that he must speak the prisoner fair, and watch for a chance to turn the tables on him. The keen-eyed, desperate man before him was a different being altogether from the groveling wretch who had begged so piteously for life a few minutes before.

At length the sheriff spoke:—

"Is this your gratitude to me for saving your life at the risk of my own? If I had not done so, you would now be swinging from the limb of some neighboring tree."

"True," said the prisoner, "you saved my life, but for how long? When you came in, you said Court would sit next week. When the crowd went away they said I had not long to live. It is merely a choice of two ropes."

"While there's life there's hope," replied the sheriff. He uttered this commonplace mechanically, while his brain was busy in trying to think out some way of escape. "If you are innocent you can prove it."

The mulatto kept his eye upon the sheriff. "I didn't kill the old man," he replied; "but I shall never be able to clear myself. I was at his house at nine o'clock. I stole from it the coat that was on my back when I was taken. I would be convicted, even with a fair trial, unless the real murderer were discovered beforehand."

The sheriff knew this only too well. While he was thinking what argument next to use, the prisoner continued:—

"Throw me the keys—no, unlock the door."

The sheriff stood a moment irresolute. The mulatto's eye glittered ominously. The sheriff crossed the room and unlocked the door leading into the passage.

"Now go down and unlock the outside door."

The heart of the sheriff leaped within him. Perhaps he might make a dash for liberty, and gain the outside. He descended the narrow stairs, the prisoner keeping close behind him.

The sheriff inserted the huge iron key into the lock. The rusty bolt yielded slowly. It still remained for him to pull the door open.

"Stop!" thundered the mulatto, who seemed to divine the sheriff's purpose. "Move a muscle, and I'll blow your brains out."

The sheriff obeyed; he realized that his chance had not yet come.

"Now keep on that side of the passage, and go back upstairs."

Keeping the sheriff under cover of the revolver, the mulatto followed him up the stairs. The sheriff expected the prisoner to lock him into the cell and make his own escape. He had about come to the conclusion that the best thing he could do under the circumstances was to submit quietly, and take his chances of recapturing the prisoner after the alarm had been given. The sheriff had faced death more than once upon the battlefield. A few minutes before, well armed, and with a brick wall between him and them he had dared a hundred men to fight; but he felt instinctively that the desperate man confronting him was not to be trifled with, and he was too prudent a man to risk his life against such heavy odds. He had Polly to look after, and there was a limit beyond which devotion to duty would be quixotic and even foolish.

"I want to get away," said the prisoner, "and I don't want to be captured; for if I am I know I will be hung on the spot. I am afraid," he added somewhat reflectively, "that in order to save myself I shall have to kill you."

"Good God!" exclaimed the sheriff in involuntary terror: "you would not kill the man to whom you owe your own life."

"You speak more truly than you know," replied the mulatto. "I indeed owe my life to you."

The sheriff started. He was capable of surprise, even in that moment of extreme peril. "Who are you?" he asked in amazement.

"Tom, Cicely's son," returned the other. He had closed the door and stood talking to the sheriff through the grated opening. "Don't you remember Cicely—Cicely whom you sold, with her child, to the speculator on his way to Alabama?"

The sheriff did remember. He had been sorry for it many a time since. It had been the old story of debts, mortgages, and bad crops. He had quarreled with the mother. The price offered for her and her child had been unusually large, and he had yielded to the combination of anger and pecuniary stress.

"Good God!" he gasped, "you would not murder your own father?"

"My father?" replied the mulatto. "It were well enough for me to claim the relationship, but it comes with poor grace from you to ask anything by reason of it. What father's duty have you ever performed for me? Did you give me your name, or even your protection? Other white men gave their colored sons freedom and money, and sent them to the free States. *You* sold *me* to the rice swamps."

"I at least gave you the life you cling to," murmured the sheriff.

"Life?" said the prisoner, with a sarcastic laugh. "What kind of a life? You gave me your own blood, your features,—no man need look at us together twice to see that,—and you gave me a black mother. Poor wretch! She died under the lash, because she had enough womanhood to call her soul her own. You gave me a white man's spirit, and you made me a slave, and crushed it out."

"But you are free now," said the sheriff. He had not doubted, could not doubt, the mulatto's word. He knew whose passions coursed beneath that swarthy skin and burned in the black eyes opposite his own. He saw in this mulatto what he himself might have become had not the safeguards of parental restraint and public opinion been thrown around him.

"Free to do what?" replied the mulatto. "Free in name, but despised and scorned and set aside by the people to whose race I belong far more than to my mother's."

"There are schools," said the sheriff. "You have been to school." He had noticed that the mulatto spoke more eloquently and used better language than most Branson County people.

"I have been to school, and dreamed when I went that it would work some marvelous change in my condition. But what did I learn? I learned to feel that no degree of learning or wisdom will change the color of my skin and that I shall always wear what in my own country is a badge of degradation. When I think about it seriously I do not care particularly for such a life. It is the animal in me, not the man, that flees the gallows. I owe you nothing," he went on, "and expect nothing of you; and it would be no more than justice if I should avenge upon you my mother's wrongs and my own. But still I hate to shoot you; I have never yet taken human life—for I did *not* kill the old captain. Will you promise to give no alarm and make no attempt to capture me until morning, if I do not shoot?"

So absorbed were the two men in their colloquy and their own tumultuous thoughts that neither of them had heard the door below move upon its hinges. Neither of them had heard a light step come stealthily up the stairs, nor seen a slender form creep along the darkening passage toward the mulatto.

The sheriff hesitated. The struggle between his love of life and his sense of duty was a terrific one. It may seem strange that a man who could sell his own child into slavery should hesitate at such a moment, when his life was trembling in the balance. But the baleful influence of human slavery poisoned the very fountains of life, and created new standards of right. The sheriff was conscientious: his conscience had merely been warped by his environment. Let no one ask what his answer would have been: he was spared the necessity of a decision.

"Stop," said the mulatto, "you need not promise. I could not trust you if you did. It is your life for mine: there is but one safe way for me; you must die."

He raised his arm to fire, when there was a flash—a report from the passage behind him. His arm fell heavily at his side, and the pistol dropped at his feet.

The sheriff recovered first from his surprise, and throwing open the door secured the fallen weapon. Then seizing the prisoner he thrust him into the cell and locked the door upon him: after which he turned to Polly, who leaned half-fainting against the wall, her hands clasped over her heart.

"Oh, father. I was just in time!" she cried hysterically, and, wildly sobbing, threw herself into her father's arms.

"I watched until they all went away," she said. "I heard the shot from the woods and I saw you shoot. Then when you did not come out I feared something had happened, that perhaps you had been wounded. I got out the other pistol and ran over here. When I found the door open, I knew something was wrong and when I heard voices I crept upstairs, and reached the top just in time to hear him say he would kill you. Oh, it was a narrow escape!"

When she had grown somewhat calmer, the sheriff left her standing there and went back into the cell. The prisoner's arm was bleeding from a flesh wound. His bravado had given place to a stony apathy. There was no sign in his face of fear or disappointment or feeling of any kind. The sheriff sent Polly to the house for cloth, and bound up the prisoner's wound with a rude skill acquired during his army life.

"I'll have a doctor come and dress the wound in the morning," he said to the prisoner. "It will do very well until then, if you will keep quiet. If the doctor asks you how the wound was caused, you can say that you were struck by the bullet fired from the woods. It would do you no good to have it known that you were shot while attempting to escape."

The prisoner uttered no word of thanks or apology, but sat in sullen silence. When the wounded arm had been bandaged, Polly and her father returned to the house.

The sheriff was in an unusually thoughtful mood that evening. He put salt in his coffee at supper, and poured vinegar over his pancakes. To many of Polly's questions he returned random answers. When he had gone to bed he lay awake for several hours.

In the silent watches of the night, when he was alone with God, there came into his mind a flood of unaccustomed thoughts. An hour or two before, standing face to face with death, he had experienced a sensation similar to that which drowning men are said to feel—a kind of clarifying of the moral faculty, in which the veil of the flesh, with its obscuring passions and prejudices, is pushed aside for a moment, and all the acts of one's life stand out, in the clear light of truth, in their correct proportions and relations,—a state of mind in which one sees himself as God may be supposed to see him. In the reaction following his rescue, this feeling had given place for a time to far different emotions. But now, in the silence of midnight, something of this clearness of spirit returned to the sheriff. He saw that he had owed some duty to this son of his,—that neither law nor custom could destroy a responsibility inherent in the nature of mankind. He could not thus, in the eyes of God at least, shake off the consequences of his sin. Had he never sinned, this wayward spirit would never have come back from the vanished past to haunt him. As these thoughts came, his anger against the mulatto died away, and in its place there sprang up a great pity. The hand of parental authority might have restrained the passions he had seen burning in the prisoner's eyes when the desperate man spoke the words which had seemed to doom his father to death. The sheriff felt that he might have saved this fiery spirit from the slough of slavery; that he might have sent him to the free North, and given him there, or in some other land, an opportunity to turn to usefulness and honorable pursuits the talents that had run to crime, perhaps to madness; he might, still less, have given this son of his the poor simulacrum of liberty which men of his caste could possess in a slave-holding community; or least of all, but still something, he might have kept the boy on the plantation, where the burdens of slavery would have fallen lightly upon him.

The sheriff recalled his own youth. He had inherited an honored name to keep untarnished; he had had a future to make; the picture of a fair young bride had beckoned him on to happiness. The poor wretch now stretched upon a pallet of straw between the brick walls of the jail had had none of these things,—no name, no father, no mother—in the true meaning of motherhood,—and until the past few years no possible future, and then one vague and shadowy in its outline, and dependent for form and substance upon the slow solution of a problem in which there were many unknown quantities.

From what he might have done to what he might yet do was an easy transition for the awakened conscience of the sheriff. It occurred to him, purely as a hypothesis, that he might permit his prisoner to escape; but his oath of office, his duty as sheriff, stood in the way of such a course, and the sheriff dismissed the idea from his mind. He could, however, investigate the circumstances of the murder, and move Heaven and earth to discover the real criminal, for he no longer doubted the prisoner's innocence; he could employ counsel for the accused, and perhaps influence public opinion in his favor. An acquittal once secured, some plan could be devised by which the sheriff might in some degree atone for his crime against this son of his—against society—against God.

When the sheriff had reached this conclusion he fell into an unquiet slumber, from which he awoke late the next morning.

He went over to the jail before breakfast and found the prisoner lying on his pallet, his face turned to the wall; he did not move when the sheriff rattled the door.

"Good-morning," said the latter, in a tone intended to waken the prisoner.

There was no response. The sheriff looked more keenly at the recumbent figure; there was an unnatural rigidity about its attitude.

He hastily unlocked the door and, entering the cell, bent over the prostrate form. There was no sound of breathing; he turned the body over—it was cold and stiff. The prisoner had torn the bandage from his wound and bled to death during the night. He had evidently been dead several hours.

CHARLOTTE PERKINS GILMAN
(1860–1935)

There are worse fates than being known for, indeed, exclusively identified with, a single title: in the case of Charlotte Perkins Gilman, author of numerous works of fiction and nonfiction, and, in her time, renowned as a leading feminist-theorist, that title is of course "The Yellow Wallpaper." Had Gilman written nothing else, she would yet be, so far as a general readership is concerned, as famous as she is now. In Gilman's own time, her most popular book was Women and Economics *(1898), called the "Bible" of the women's movement.*

Charlotte Perkins Gilman was born in 1860 in Hartford, Connecticut, where she was raised fatherless. In 1884 she married a Providence artist whom she divorced after four years, convinced that her domestic situation was driving her mad. The "dark fog" of mental illness that precipitated this break is brilliantly suggested by "The Yellow Wallpaper." (For more details of Gilman's self-scrutinized life as it relates to her art, see her autobiography, The Living of Charlotte Perkins Gilman, *published in 1935.)*

It might be noted in passing that Gilman was another important and unconventional talent singled out by William Dean Howells, who included "The Yellow Wallpaper" in his Great Modern American Stories *(1920).*

Gilman was a prominent feminist and woman of letters who lectured widely. Her most important titles include The Man-Made World *(1911),* Herland *(1915),* His Religion and Hers *(1923). Apart from "The Yellow Wallpaper," she wrote a number of engaging short stories, among them the rather more light-hearted, "When I Was a Witch." But "The Yellow Wallpaper," a Poe-like descent into the mind, not of a murderer, but of a victim, a female victim, remains her masterpiece.*

The Yellow Wallpaper

It is very seldom that mere ordinary people like John and myself secure ancestral halls for the summer.

A colonial mansion, a hereditary estate, I would say a haunted house, and reach the height of romantic felicity—but that would be asking too much of fate!

Still I will proudly declare that there is something queer about it.

Else, why should it be let so cheaply? And why have stood so long untenanted?

John laughs at me, of course, but one expects that in man. John is practical in the extreme. He has no patience with faith, an intense horror of superstition, and he scoffs openly at any talk of things not to be felt and seen and put down in figures.

John is a physician, and *perhaps*—(I would not say it to a living soul, of course, but this is dead paper and a great relief to my mind)— *perhaps* that is one reason I do not get well faster.

You see he does not believe I am sick! And what can one do?

If a physician of high standing, and one's own husband, assures friends and relatives that there is really nothing the matter with one but temporary nervous depression—a slight hysterical tendency—what is one to do?

My brother is also a physician, and also of high standing, and he says the same thing.

So I take phosphates or phosphites—whichever it is—and tonics, and journeys, and air, and exercise, and am absolutely forbidden to "work" until I am well again.

Personally, I disagree with their ideas.

Personally, I believe that congenial work, with excitement and change, would do me good.

But what is one to do?

I did write for a while in spite of them; but it *does* exhaust me a good deal—having to be so sly about it, or else meet with heavy opposition.

I sometimes fancy that in my condition if I had less opposition and more society and stimulus—but John says the very worst thing I can do is to think about my condition, and I confess it always makes me feel bad.

So I will let it alone and talk about the house.

The most beautiful place! It is quite alone, standing well back from the road, quite three miles from the village. It makes me think of English places that you read about, for there are hedges and walls and gates that lock, and lots of separate little houses for the gardeners and people.

There is a *delicious* garden! I never saw such a garden—large and shady, full of box-bordered paths, and lined with long grape-covered arbors with seats under them.

There were greenhouses, too, but they are all broken now.

There was some legal trouble, I believe, something about the heirs and co-heirs; anyhow, the place has been empty for years.

That spoils my ghostliness, I am afraid, but I don't care—there is something strange about the house—I can feel it.

I even said so to John one moonlight evening, but he said what I felt was a draught, and shut the window.

I get unreasonably angry with John sometimes. I'm sure I never used to be so sensitive. I think it is due to this nervous condition.

But John says if I feel so I shall neglect proper self-control; so I take pains to control myself-—before him, at least, and that makes me very tired.

I don't like our room a bit. I wanted one downstairs that opened on the piazza and had roses all over the window, and such pretty old-fashioned chintz hangings! But John would not hear of it.

He said there was only one window and not room for two beds, and no near room for him if he took another.

He is very careful and loving, and hardly lets me stir without special direction.

I have a schedule prescription for each hour in the day; he takes all care from me, and so I feel basely ungrateful not to value it more.

He said we came here solely on my account; that I was to have perfect rest and all the air I could get. "Your exercise depends on your strength, my dear," said he, "and your food somewhat on your appetite; but air you can absorb all the time." So we took the nursery at the top of the house.

It is a big, airy room, the whole floor nearly, with windows that look all ways, and air and sunshine galore. It was nursery first and then playroom and gymnasium, I should judge; for the windows are barred for little children, and there are rings and things in the walls.

The paint and paper look as if a boys' school had used it. It is stripped off—the paper—in great patches all around the head of my bed, about as far as I can reach, and in a great place on the other side of the room low down. I never saw a worse paper in my life.

One of those sprawling flamboyant patterns committing every artistic sin.

It is dull enough to confuse the eye in following, pronounced enough constantly to irritate and provoke study, and when you follow the lame uncertain curves for a little distance they suddenly commit suicide—plunge off at outrageous angles, destroy themselves in unheard of contradictions.

The color is repellant, almost revolting; a smouldering unclean yellow, strangely faded by the slow-turning sunlight.

It is a dull yet lurid orange in some places, a sickly sulphur tint in others.

No wonder the children hated it! I should hate it myself if I had to live in this room long.

There comes John, and I must put this away—he hates to have me write a word.

We have been here two weeks, and I haven't felt like writing before, since that first day.

I am sitting by the window now, up in this atrocious nursery, and there is nothing to hinder my writing as much as I please, save lack of strength.

John is away all day, and even some nights when his cases are serious.

I am glad my case is not serious!

But these nervous troubles are dreadfully depressing.

John does not know how much I really suffer. He knows there is no *reason* to suffer, and that satisfies him.

Of course it is only nervousness. It does weigh on me so not to do my duty in any way!

I meant to be such a help to John, such a real rest and comfort, and here I am a comparative burden already!

Nobody would believe what an effort it is to do what little I am able—to dress and entertain, and order things.

It is fortunate Mary is so good with the baby. Such a dear baby!

And yet I *cannot* be with him, it makes me so nervous.

I suppose John never was nervous in his life. He laughs at me so about this wallpaper!

At first he meant to repaper the room, but afterwards he said that I was letting it get the better of me, and that nothing was worse for a nervous patient than to give way to such fancies.

He said that after the wallpaper was changed it would be the heavy bedstead, and then the barred windows, and then that gate at the head of the stairs, and so on.

"You know the place is doing you good," he said, "and really, dear, I don't care to renovate the house just for a three months' rental."

"Then do let us go downstairs," I said, "there are such pretty rooms there."

Then he took me in his arms and called me a blessed little goose, and said he would go down cellar, if I wished, and have it whitewashed into the bargain.

But he is right enough about the beds and windows and things.

It is an airy and comfortable room as any one need wish, and, of course, I would not be so silly as to make him uncomfortable just for a whim.

I'm really getting quite fond of the big room, all but that horrid paper.

Out of one window I can see the garden, those mysterious deep-shaded arbors, the riotous old-fashioned flowers, and bushes and gnarly trees.

Out of another I get a lovely view of the bay and a little private wharf belonging to the estate. There is a beautiful shaded lane that runs down there from the house. I always fancy I see people walking in these numerous paths and arbors, but John has cautioned me not to give way to fancy in the least. He says that with my imaginative power and habit of story-making, a nervous weakness like mine is sure to lead to all manner of excited fancies, and that I ought to use my will and good sense to check the tendency. So I try.

I think sometimes that if I were only well enough to write a little it would relieve the press of ideas and rest me.

But I find I get pretty tired when I try.

It is so discouraging not to have any advice and companionship about my work. When I get really well, John says we will ask Cousin Henry and Julia down for a long visit; but he says he would as soon put fireworks in my pillowcase as to let me have those stimulating people about now.

I wish I could get well faster.

But I must not think about that. This paper looks to me as if it *knew* what a vicious influence it had!

There is a recurrent spot where the pattern lolls like a broken neck and two bulbous eyes stare at you upside down.

I get positively angry with the impertinence of it and the everlastingness. Up and down and sideways they crawl, and those absurd, unblinking eyes are everywhere. There is one place where two breadths didn't match, and the eyes go all up and down the line, one a little higher than the other.

I never saw so much expression in an inanimate thing before, and we all know how much expression they have! I used to lie awake as a child and get more entertainment and terror out of blank walls and plain furniture than most children could find in a toy-store.

I remember what a kindly wink the knobs of our big, old bureau used to have, and there was one chair that always seemed like a strong friend.

I used to feel that if any of the other things looked too fierce I could always hop into that chair and be safe.

The furniture in this room is no worse than inharmonious, however, for we had to bring it all from downstairs. I suppose when this was used as a playroom they had to take the nursery things out, and no wonder! I never saw such ravages as the children have made here.

The wallpaper, as I said before, is torn off in spots, and it sticketh closer than a brother—they must have had perseverance as well as hatred.

Then the floor is scratched and gouged and splintered, the plaster itself is dug out here and there, and this great heavy bed which is all we found in the room, looks as if it had been through the wars.

But I don't mind it a bit—only the paper.

There comes John's sister. Such a dear girl as she is, and so careful of me! I must not let her find me writing.

She is a perfect and enthusiastic housekeeper, and hopes for no better profession. I verily believe she thinks it is the writing which made me sick!

But I can write when she is out, and see her a long way off from these windows.

There is one that commands the road, a lovely shaded winding road, and one that just looks off over the country. A lovely country, too, full of great elms and velvet meadows.

This wallpaper has a kind of sub-pattern in a different shade, a particularly irritating one, for you can only see it in certain lights, and not clearly then.

But in the places where it isn't faded and where the sun is just so—I can see a strange, provoking, formless sort of figure, that seems to skulk about behind that silly and conspicuous front design.

There's sister on the stairs!

Well, the Fourth of July is over! The people are all gone and I am tired out. John thought it might do me good to see a little company, so we just had mother and Nellie and the children down for a week.

Of course I didn't do a thing. Jennie sees to everything now.

But it tired me all the same.

John says if I don't pick up faster he shall send me to Weir Mitchell in the fall.

But I don't want to go there at all. I had a friend who was in his hands once, and she says he is just like John and my brother, only more so!

Besides, it is such an undertaking to go so far.

I don't feel as if it was worth while to turn my hand over for anything, and I'm getting dreadfully fretful and querulous.

I cry at nothing, and cry most of the time.

Of course I don't when John is here, or anybody else, but when I am alone.

And I am alone a good deal just now. John is kept in town very often by serious cases, and Jennie is good and lets me alone when I want her to.

So I walk a little in the garden or down that lovely lane, sit on the porch under the roses, and lie down up here a good deal.

I'm getting really fond of the room in spite of the wallpaper. Perhaps *because* of the wallpaper.

It dwells in my mind so!

I lie here on this great immovable bed—it is nailed down, I believe—and follow that pattern about by the hour. It is as good as gymnastics, I assure you. I start, we'll say, at the bottom, down in the corner over there where it has not been touched, and I determine for the thousandth time that I *will* follow that pointless pattern to some sort of a conclusion.

I know a little of the principle of design, and I know this thing was not arranged on any laws of radiation, or alternation, or repetition, or symmetry, or anything else that I ever heard of.

It is repeated, of course, by the breadths, but not otherwise.

Looked at in one way each breadth stands alone, the bloated curves and flourishes—a kind of "debased Romanesque" with delirium tremens—go waddling up and down in isolated columns of fatuity.

But, on the other hand, they connect diagonally, and the sprawling outlines run off in great slanting waves of optic horror, like a lot of wallowing sea-weeds in full chase.

The whole thing goes horizontally, too, at least it seems so, and I exhaust myself trying to distinguish the order of its going in that direction.

They have used a horizontal breadth for a frieze, and that adds wonderfully to the confusion.

There is one end of the room where it is almost intact, and there, when the crosslights fade and the low sun shines directly upon it, I can almost fancy radiation after all,—the interminable grotesques seem to form around a common centre and rush off in headlong plunges of equal distraction.

It makes me tired to follow it. I will take a nap I guess.

I don't know why I should write this.

I don't want to.

I don't feel able.

And I know John would think it absurd. But I *must* say what I feel and think in some way—it is such a relief!

But the effort is getting to be greater than the relief.

Half the time now I am awfully lazy, and lie down ever so much.

John says I mustn't lose my strength, and has me take cod liver oil and lots of tonics and things, to say nothing of ale and wine and rare meat.

Dear John! He loves me very dearly, and hates to have me sick. I tried to have a real earnest reasonable talk with him the other day, and tell him how I wish he would let me go and make a visit to Cousin Henry and Julia.

But he said I wasn't able to go, nor able to stand it after I got there; and I did not make out a very good case for myself, for I was crying before I had finished.

It is getting to be a great effort for me to think straight. Just this nervous weakness I suppose.

And dear John gathered me up in his arms, and just carried me upstairs and laid me on the bed, and sat by me and read to me till it tired my head.

He said I was his darling and his comfort and all he had, and that I must take care of myself for his sake, and keep well.

He says no one but myself can help me out of it, that I must use my will and self-control and not let any silly fancies run away with me.

There's one comfort, the baby is well and happy, and does not have to occupy this nursery with the horrid wallpaper.

If we had not used it, that blessed child would have! What a fortunate escape! Why, I wouldn't have a child of mine, an impressionable little thing, live in such a room for worlds.

I never thought of it before, but it is lucky that John kept me here after all, I can stand it so much easier than a baby, you see.

Of course I never mention it to them any more—I am too wise—but I keep watch for it all the same.

There arc things in that paper that nobody knows but me, or ever will.

Behind that outside pattern the dim shapes get clearer every day.

It is always the same shape, only very numerous.

And it is like a woman stooping down and creeping about behind that pattern. I don't like it a bit. I wonder—I begin to think—I wish John would take me away from here!

It is so hard to talk with John about my case, because he is so wise, and because he loves me so.

But I tried it last night.

It was moonlight. The moon shines in all around just as the sun does.

I hate to see it sometimes, it creeps so slowly, and always comes in by one window or another.

John was asleep and I hated to waken him, so I kept still and watched the moonlight on that undulating wallpaper till I felt creepy.

The faint figure behind seemed to shake the pattern, just as if she wanted to get out.

I got up softly and went to feel and see if the paper *did* move, and when I came back John was awake.

"What is it, little girl?" he said. "Don't go walking about like that—you'll get cold."

I thought it was a good time to talk so I told him that I really was not gaining here, and that I wished he would take me away.

"Why darling!" said he, "our lease will be up in three weeks, and I can't see how to leave before.

"The repairs are not done at home, and I cannot possibly leave town just now. Of course if you were in any danger, I could and would, but you really are better, dear, whether you can see it or not. I am a doctor, dear, and I know. You are gaining flesh and color, your appetite is better, I feel really much easier about you."

"I don't weigh a bit more," said I, "nor as much; and my appetite may be better in the evening when you are here, but it is worse in the morning when you are away!"

"Bless her little heart!" said he with a big hug, "she shall be as sick as she pleases! But now let's improve the shining hours by going to sleep, and talk about it in the morning!"

"And you won't go away?" I asked gloomily.

"Why, how can I, dear? It is only three weeks more and then we will take a nice little trip of a few days while Jennie is getting the house ready. Really, dear, you are better!"

"Better in body perhaps—" I began, and stopped short, for he sat up straight and looked at me with such a stern, reproachful look that I could not say another word.

"My darling," said he, "I beg of you, for my sake and for our child's sake, as well as for your own, that you will never for one instant let that idea enter your mind! There is nothing so dangerous, so fascinating, to a temperament like yours. It is a false and foolish fancy. Can you not trust me as a physician when I tell you so?"

So of course I said no more on that score, and we went to sleep before long. He thought I was asleep first, but I wasn't, and lay there for hours trying to decide whether that front pattern and the back pattern really did move together or separately.

On a pattern like this, by daylight, there is a lack of sequence, a defiance of law, that is a constant irritant to a normal mind.

The color is hideous enough, and unreliable enough, and infuriating enough, but the pattern is torturing.

You think you have mastered it, but just as you get well underway in following, it turns a back-somersault and there you are. It slaps you in the face, knocks you down, and tramples upon you. It is like a bad dream.

The outside pattern is a florid arabesque, reminding one of a fungus. If you can imagine a toadstool in joints, an interminable string of toadstools, budding and sprouting in endless convolutions—why, that is something like it.

That is, sometimes!

There is one marked peculiarity about this paper, a thing nobody seems to notice but myself, and that is that it changes as the light changes.

When the sun shoots in through the east window—I always watch for that first, long, straight ray—it changes so quickly that I never can quite believe it.

That is why I watch it always.

By moonlight—the moon shines in all night when there is a moon—I wouldn't know it was the same paper.

At night in any kind of light, in twilight, candlelight, lamplight, and worst of all by moonlight, it becomes bars! The outside pattern I mean, and the woman behind it is as plain as can be.

I didn't realize for a long time what the thing was that showed behind, that dim sub-pattern, but now I am quite sure it is a woman.

By daylight she is subdued, quiet. I fancy it is the pattern that keeps her so still. It is so puzzling. It keeps me quiet by the hour.

I lie down ever so much now. John says it is good for me, and to sleep all I can.

Indeed he started the habit by making me lie down for an hour after each meal.

It is a very bad habit I am convinced, for you see I don't sleep.

And that cultivates deceit, for I don't tell them I'm awake—O, no!

The fact is I am getting a little afraid of John.

He seems very queer sometimes, and even Jennie has an inexplicable look.

It strikes me occasionally, just as a scientific hypothesis, that perhaps it is the paper!

I have watched John when he did not know I was looking, and come into the room suddenly on the most innocent excuses, and I've caught him several times *looking at the paper!* And Jennie too. I caught Jennie with her hand on it once.

She didn't know I was in the room, and when I asked her in a quiet, a very quiet voice, with the most restrained manner possible, what she was doing with the paper—she turned around as if she had been caught stealing, and looked quite angry—asked me why I should frighten her so!

Then she said that the paper stained everything it touched, that she had found yellow smooches on all my clothes and John's, and she wished we would be more careful!

Did not that sound innocent? But I know she was studying that pattern, and I am determined that nobody shall find it out but myself!

Life is very much more exciting now than it used to be. You see I have something more to expect, to look forward to, to watch. I really do eat better, and am more quiet than I was.

John is so pleased to see me improve! He laughed a little the other day, and said I seemed to be flourishing in spite of my wallpaper.

I turned it off with a laugh. I had no intention of telling him it was *because* of the wallpaper—he would make fun of me. He might even want to take me away.

I don't want to leave now until I have found it out. There is a week more, and I think that will be enough.

I'm feeling ever so much better! I don't sleep much at night, for it is so interesting to watch developments; but I sleep a good deal in the daytime.

In the daytime it is tiresome and perplexing.

There are always new shoots on the fungus, and new shades of yellow all over it. I cannot keep count of them, though I have tried conscientiously.

It is the strangest yellow, that wallpaper! It makes me think of all the yellow things I ever saw—not beautiful ones like buttercups, but old foul, bad yellow things.

But there is something else about that paper—the smell! I noticed it the moment we came into the room, but with so much air and sun it was not bad. Now we have had a week of fog and rain, and whether the windows are open or not, the smell is here.

It creeps all over the house.

I find it hovering in the dining-room, skulking in the parlor, hiding in the hall, lying in wait for me on the stairs.

It gets into my hair.

Even when I go to ride, if I turn my head suddenly and surprise it—there is that smell!

Such a peculiar odor, too! I have spent hours in trying to analyze it, to find what it smelled like.

It is not bad—at first, and very gentle, but quite the subtlest, most enduring odor I ever met.

In this damp weather it is awful, I wake up in the night and find it hanging over me.

It used to disturb me at first. I thought seriously of burning the house—to reach the smell.

But now I am used to it. The only thing I can think of that it is like is the *color* of the paper! A yellow smell.

There is a very funny mark on this wall, low down, near the mopboard. A streak that runs round the room. It goes behind every piece of furniture, except the bed, a long, straight, even *smooch,* as if it had been rubbed over and over.

I wonder how it was done and who did it, and what they did it for. Round and round and round—round and round and round—it makes me dizzy!

I really have discovered something at last.

Through watching so much at night, when it changes so, I have finally found out.

The front pattern *does* move—and no wonder! The woman behind shakes it!

Sometimes I think there are a great many women behind, and sometimes only one, and she crawls around fast, and her crawling shakes it all over.

Then in the very bright spots she keeps still, and in the very shady spots she just takes hold of the bars and shakes them hard.

And she is all the time trying to climb through. But nobody could climb through that pattern—it strangles so; I think that is why it has so many heads.

They get through, and then the pattern strangles them off and turns them upside down, and makes their eyes white!

If those heads were covered or taken off it would not be half so bad.

I think that woman gets out in the daytime!

And I'll tell you why—privately—I've seen her!

I can see her out of every one of my windows!

It is the same woman, I know, for she is always creeping, and most women do not creep by daylight.

I see her in that long shaded lane, creeping up and down. I see her in those dark grape arbors, creeping all around the garden.

I see her on that long road under the trees, creeping along, and when a carriage comes she hides under the blackberry vines.

I don't blame her a bit. It must be very humiliating to be caught creeping by daylight!

I always lock the door when I creep by daylight. I can't do it at night, for I know John would suspect something at once.

And John is so queer now, that I don't want to irritate him. I wish he would take another room! Besides, I don't want anybody to get that woman out at night but myself.

I often wonder if I could see her out of all the windows at once.

But, turn as fast as I can, I can only see out of one at one time.

And though I always see her, she *may* be able to creep faster than I can turn!

I have watched her sometimes away off in the open country, creeping as fast as a cloud shadow in a high wind.

If only that top pattern could be gotten off from the under one! I mean to try it, little by little.

I have found out another funny thing, but I shan't tell it this time! It does not do to trust people too much.

There are only two more days to get this paper off, and I believe John is beginning to notice. I don't like the look in his eyes.

And I heard him ask Jennie a lot of professional questions about me. She had a very good report to give.

She said I slept a good deal in the daytime.

John knows I don't sleep very well at night, for all I'm so quiet!

He asked me all sorts of questions, too, and pretended to be very loving and kind.

As if I couldn't see through him!

Still, I don't wonder he acts so, sleeping under this paper for three months.

It only interests me, but I feel sure John and Jennie are secretly affected by it.

Hurrah! This is the last day, but it is enough. John is to stay in town over night, and won't be out until this evening.

Jennie wanted to sleep with me—the sly thing! but I told her I should undoubtedly rest better for a night all alone.

That was clever, for really I wasn't alone a bit! As soon as it was moonlight and that poor thing began to crawl and shake the pattern, I got up and ran to help her.

I pulled and she shook, I shook and she pulled, and before morning we had peeled off yards of that paper.

A strip about as high as my head and half around the room.

And then when the sun came and that awful pattern began to laugh at me, I declared I would finish it to-day!

We go away to-morrow, and they are moving all my furniture down again to leave things as they were before.

Jennie looked at the wall in amazement, but I told her merrily that I did it out of pure spite at the vicious thing.

She laughed and said she wouldn't mind doing it herself, but I must not get tired.

How she betrayed herself that time!

But I am here, and no person touches this paper but Me—not *alive!*

She tried to get me out of the room—it was too patent! But I said it was so quiet and empty and clean now that I believed I would lie down again and sleep all I could; and not to wake me even for dinner—I would call when I woke.

So now she is gone, and the servants are gone, and the things are gone, and there is nothing left but that great bedstead nailed down, with the canvas mattress we found on it.

We shall sleep downstairs to-night, and take the boat home tomorrow.

I quite enjoy the room, now it is bare again.

How those children did tear about here!

This bedstead is fairly gnawed!

But I must get to work.

I have locked the door and thrown the key down into the front path.

I don't want to go out, and I don't want to have anybody come in, till John comes.

I want to astonish him.

I've got a rope up here that even Jennie did not find. If that woman does get out, and tries to get away, I can tie her!

But I forgot I could not reach far without anything to stand on!

This bed will nor move!

I tried to lift and push it until I was lame, and then I got so angry I bit off a little piece at one corner—but it hurt my teeth.

Then I peeled off all the paper I could reach standing on the floor. It sticks horribly and the pattern just enjoys it! All those strangled heads and bulbous eyes and waddling fungus growths just shriek with derision!

I am getting angry enough to do something desperate. To jump out of the window would be admirable exercise, but the bars are too strong even to try.

Besides I wouldn't do it. Of course not. I know well enough that a step like that is improper and might be misconstrued.

I don't like to *look* out of the windows even—there are so many of those creeping women, and they creep so fast.

I wonder if they all come out of that wallpaper as I did?

But I am securely fastened now by my well-hidden rope—you don't get *me* out in the road there!

I suppose I shall have to get back behind the pattern when it comes night, and that is hard!

It is so pleasant to be out in this great room and creep around as I please!

I don't want to go outside. I won't, even if Jennie asks me to.

For outside you have to creep on the ground, and everything is green instead of yellow.

But here I can creep smoothly on the floor, and my shoulder just fits in that long smooch around the wall, so I cannot lose my way.

Why there's John at the door!

It is no use, young man, you can't open it!

How he does call and pound!

Now he's crying for an axe.

It would be a shame to break down that beautiful door!

"John dear!" said I in the gentlest voice, "the key is down by the front steps, under a plantain leaf!"

That silenced him for a few moments.

Then he said, very quietly indeed, "Open the door, my darling!"

"I can't," said I. "The key is down by the front door under a plantain leaf!"

And then I said it again, several times, very gently and slowly, and said it so often that he had to go and see, and he got it of course, and came in. He stopped short by the door.

"What is the matter?" he cried. "For God's sake, what are you doing!"

I kept on creeping just the same, but I looked at him over my shoulder.

"I've got out at last," said I, "in spite of you and Jane. And I've pulled off most of the paper, so you can't put me back!"

Now why should that man have fainted? But he did, and right across my path by the wall, so that I had to creep over him every time!

EDITH WHARTON
(1862–1937)

Born into a wealthy and socially prominent old New York City family, Edith Wharton (née Edith Newbold Jones) was to become an enormously successful and critically respected writer—a rarity for a woman of her time, as ours. Despite uncertain health she was tireless in her devotion to writing: she published fifty volumes of work, both fiction and nonfiction, and left a number of unpublished manuscripts at her death. A friend and confidante of Henry James, Wharton was one of the first women to be inducted into the National Institute of Arts and Letters and awarded the Pulitzer Prize.

Her early novel The House of Mirth *(1905) is the sharply observed tragicomedy of an intelligent young woman doomed by a distorted image of herself. It became a bestseller and brought Wharton to immediate literary prominence. Subsequent titles—*Ethan Frome *(1911),* The Reef *(1912),* The Custom of the Country *(1913),* Summer *(1917), and* The Age of Innocence *(1920), for which she was awarded the Pulitzer Prize—established her reputation as a major American writer. Less known as a short story writer, Wharton published a considerable number of excellent stories, including elegantly crafted tales of the supernatural.*

"A Journey," despite its obsessive, dreamlike tone, is not a tale of the supernatural; neither is it one of Wharton's more typical works of short fiction, in which a female protagonist is viewed from without and within, in an ironically rendered social context. Here, the young wife, from a modest social background, is on the brink of acknowledging the fact that her life will diverge from her husband's—at the very hour, it seems, when her husband dies. This is a spare, mysterious story that ends, dramatically, at just the right moment.

A Journey

As she lay in her berth, staring at the shadows overhead, the rush of the wheels was in her brain, driving her deeper and deeper into circles of wakeful lucidity. The sleeping car had sunk into its night silence. Through the wet windowpane she watched the sudden lights, the long stretches of hurrying blackness. Now and then she turned her head and looked through the opening in the hangings at her husband's curtains across the aisle....

She wondered restlessly if he wanted anything and if she could hear him if he called. His voice had grown very weak within the last months and it irritated him when she did not hear. This irritability, this increasing childish petulance seemed to give expression to their imperceptible estrangement. Like two faces looking at one another through a sheet of glass they were close together, almost touching, but they could not hear or feel each other: the conductivity between them was broken. She, at least, had this sense of separation, and she fancied sometimes that she saw it reflected in the look with which he supplemented his failing words. Doubtless the fault was hers. She was too impenetrably healthy to be touched by the irrelevancies of disease. Her self-reproachful tenderness was tinged with the sense of his irrationality: she had a vague feeling that there was a purpose in his helpless tyrannies. The suddenness of the change had found her so unprepared. A year ago their pulses had beat to one robust measure; both had the same prodigal confidence in an exhaustless future. Now their energies no longer kept step: hers still bounded ahead of life, preempting unclaimed regions of hope and activity, while his lagged behind, vainly struggling to overtake her.

When they married, she had such arrears of living to make up: her days had been as bare as the whitewashed schoolroom where she forced innutritious facts upon reluctant children. His coming had broken in on the slumber of circumstance, widening the present till it became the encloser of remotest chances. But imperceptibly the horizon narrowed. Life had a grudge against her: she was never to be allowed to spread her wings.

At first the doctors had said that six weeks of mild air would set him right; but when he came back this assurance was explained as having of course included a winter in a dry climate. They gave up their pretty house, storing the wedding presents and new furniture, and went to Colorado. She had hated it there from the first. Nobody knew her or cared about her; there was no one to wonder at the good match she had made, or to envy her the new dresses and the visiting cards which were still a surprise to her. And he kept growing worse. She felt herself beset with difficulties too evasive to be fought by so direct a temperament. She still loved him, of course; but he was gradually, undefinably ceasing to be himself. The man she had married had been strong, active, gently masterful: the male whose pleasure it is to clear a way through the material obstructions of life; but now it was she who was the protector, he who must be shielded from importunities and given his drops or his beef juice though the skies were falling. The routine of the sickroom bewildered her; this punctual administering of medicine seemed as idle as some uncomprehended religious mummery.

There were moments, indeed, when warm gushes of pity swept away her instinctive resentment of his condition, when she still found his old self in his eyes as they groped for each other through the dense medium of his weakness. But these moments had grown rare. Sometimes he frightened her: his sunken expressionless face seemed that of a stranger; his voice was weak and hoarse; his thin-lipped smile a mere muscular contraction. Her hand avoided his damp soft skin, which had lost the familiar roughness of health: she caught herself furtively watching him as she might have watched a strange animal. It frightened her to feel that this was the man she loved; there were hours when to tell him what she suffered seemed the one escape from her fears. But in general she judged herself more leniently, reflecting that she had perhaps been too long alone with him, and that she would feel differently when they were at home again, surrounded by her robust and buoyant family. How she had rejoiced when the doctors at last gave their consent to his going home! She knew, of course, what the decision meant; they both knew. It meant that he was to die; but they dressed the truth in hopeful euphemisms, and at times, in the joy of preparation, she really forgot the purpose of their journey, and slipped into an eager allusion to next year's plans.

At last the day of leaving came. She had a dreadful fear that they would never get away; that somehow at the last moment he would fail her; that the doctors held one of their accustomed treacheries in reserve; but nothing happened. They drove to the station, he was installed in a seat with a rug over his knees and a cushion at his back, and she hung out of the window waving unregretful farewells to the acquaintances she had really never liked till then.

The first twenty-four hours had passed off well. He revived a little and it amused him to look out of the window and to observe the humors of the car. The second day he began to grow weary and to chafe under the dispassionate stare of the freckled child with the lump of chewing gum. She had to explain to the child's mother that her husband was too ill to be disturbed: a statement received by that lady with a resentment visibly supported by the maternal sentiment of the whole car. . . .

That night he slept badly and the next morning his temperature frightened her: she was sure he was growing worse. The day passed slowly, punctuated by the small irritations of travel. Watching his tired face, she traced in its contractions every rattle and jolt of the train, till her own body vibrated with sympathetic fatigue. She felt the others observing him too, and hovered restlessly between him and the line of interrogative eyes. The freckled child hung about him like a fly; offers of candy and picture books failed to dislodge her: she twisted one leg around the other and watched him imperturbably. The porter, as he passed, lingered with vague proffers of help, probably inspired by philanthropic passengers swelling with the sense that "something ought to be done"; and one nervous man in a skull cap was audibly concerned as to the possible effect on his wife's health.

The hours dragged on in a dreary inoccupation. Towards dusk she sat down beside him and he laid his hand on hers. The touch startled her. He seemed to be calling her from far off. She looked at him helplessly and his smile went through her like a physical pang.

"Are you very tired?" she asked.

"No, not very."

"We'll be there soon now."

"Yes, very soon."

"This time tomorrow—"

He nodded and they sat silent. When she had put him to bed and crawled into her own berth she tried to cheer herself with the thought that in less than twenty-four hours they would be in New York. Her people would all be at the station to meet her—she pictured their round unanxious faces pressing through the crowd. She only hoped they would not tell him too loudly that he was looking splendidly and would be all right in no time: the subtler sympathies developed by long contact with suffering were making her aware of a certain coarseness of texture in the family sensibilities.

Suddenly she thought she heard him call. She parted the curtains and listened. No, it was only a man snoring at the other end of the car. His snores had a greasy sound, as though they passed through tallow. She lay down and tried to sleep.... Had she not heard him move? She started up trembling.... The silence frightened her more than any sound. He might not be able to make her hear—he might be calling her now.... What made her think of such things? It was merely the familiar tendency of an overtired mind to fasten itself on the most intolerable chance within the range of its forebodings.... Putting her head out, she listened: but she could not distinguish his breathing from that of the other pairs of lungs about her. She longed to get up and look at him, but she knew the impulse was a mere vent for her restlessness, and the fear of disturbing him restrained her.... The regular movement of his curtain reassured her, she knew not why; she remembered that he had wished her a cheerful good night; and the sheer inability to endure her fears a moment longer made her put them from her with an effort of her whole sound-tired body. She turned on her side and slept.

She sat up stiffly, staring out at the dawn. The train was rushing through a region of bare hillocks huddled against a lifeless sky. It looked like the first day of creation. The air of the car was close, and she pushed up her window to let in the keen wind. Then she looked at her watch: it was seven o'clock, and soon the people about her would be stirring. She slipped into her clothes, smoothed her disheveled hair and crept to the dressing room. When she had washed her face and adjusted her dress she felt more hopeful. It was always a struggle for her not to be cheerful in the morning. Her cheeks burned deliciously under the coarse towel and the wet hair about her temples broke into strong upward tendrils. Every inch of her was full of life and elasticity. And in ten hours they would be at home!

She stepped to her husband's berth: it was time for him to take his early glass of milk. The window shade was down, and in the dusk of the curtained enclosure she could just see that he lay sideways, with his face away from her. She leaned over him and drew up the shade. As she did so she touched one of his hands. It felt cold....

She bent closer, laying her hand on his arm and calling him by name. He did not move. She spoke again more loudly; she grasped his shoulder and gently shook it. He lay motionless. She caught hold of his hand again: it slipped from her limply, like a dead thing. A dead thing?

Her breath caught. She must see his face. She leaned forward, and hurriedly, shrinkingly, with a sickening reluctance of the flesh, laid her hands on his shoulders and turned him over. His head fell back; his face looked small and smooth; he gazed at her with steady eyes.

She remained motionless for a long time, holding him thus; and they looked at each other. Suddenly she shrank back: the longing to scream, to call out, to fly from him, had almost overpowered her. But a strong hand arrested her. Good God! If it were known that he was dead they would be put off the train at the next station—

In a terrifying flash of remembrance there arose before her a scene she had once witnessed in traveling, when a husband and wife, whose child had died in the train, had been thrust out at some chance station. She saw them standing on the platform with the child's body between them; she had never forgotten the dazed look with which they followed the receding train. And this was what would happen to her. Within the next hour she might find herself on the platform of some strange station, alone with her husband's body.... Anything but that! It was too horrible—She quivered like a creature at bay.

As she cowered there, she felt the train moving more slowly. It was coming then—they were approaching a station! She saw again the husband and wife standing on the lonely platform; and with a violent gesture she drew down the shade to hide her husband's face.

Feeling dizzy, she sank down on the edge of the berth, keeping away from his outstretched body, and pulling the curtains close, so that he and she were shut into a kind of sepulchral twilight. She tried to think. At all costs she must conceal the fact that he was dead. But how? Her mind refused to act: she could not plan, combine. She could think of no way but to sit there, clutching the curtains, all day long....

She heard the porter making up her bed; people were beginning to move about the car; the dressing-room door was being opened and shut. She tried to rouse herself. At length with a supreme effort she rose to her feet, stepping into the aisle of the car and drawing the curtains tight behind her. She noticed that they still parted slightly with the motion of the car, and finding a pin in her dress she fastened them together. Now she was safe. She looked round and saw the porter. She fancied he was watching her.

'Ain't he awake yet?' he inquired.

'No,' she faltered.

'I got his milk all ready when he wants it. You know you told me to have it for him by seven.'

She nodded silently and crept into her seat.

At half-past eight the train reached Buffalo. By this time the other passengers were dressed and the berths had been folded back for the day. The porter, moving to and fro under his burden of sheets and pillows, glanced at her as he passed. At length he said: 'Ain't he going to get up? You know we're ordered to make up the berths as early as we can.'

She turned cold with fear. They were just entering the station.

'Oh, not yet,' she stammered. 'Not till he's had his milk. Won't you get it, please?'

'All right. Soon as we start again.'

When the train moved on he reappeared with the milk. She took it from him and sat vaguely looking at it: her brain moved slowly from one idea to another, as though they were stepping-stones set far apart across a whirling flood. At length she became aware that the porter still hovered expectantly.

'Will I give it to him?' he suggested.

'Oh, no,' she cried, rising. 'He—he's asleep yet, I think—'

She waited till the porter had passed on; then she unpinned the curtains and slipped behind them. In the semiobscurity her husband's face stared up at her like a marble mask with agate eyes. The eyes were dreadful. She put out her hand and drew down the lids. Then she remembered the glass of milk in her other hand: what was she to do with it? She thought of raising the window and throwing it out; but to do so she would have to lean across his body and bring her face close to his. She decided to drink the milk.

She returned to her seat with the empty glass and after a while the porter came back to get it.

"When'll I fold up his bed?' he asked.

'Oh, not now—not yet; he's ill—he's very ill. Can't you let him stay as he is? The doctor wants him to lie down as much as possible.'

He scratched his head. 'Well, if he's *really* sick—'

He took the empty glass and walked away, explaining to the passengers that the party behind the curtains was too sick to get up just yet.

She found herself the center of sympathetic eyes. A motherly woman with an intimate smile sat down beside her.

'I'm really sorry to hear your husband's sick. I've had a remarkable amount of sickness in my family and maybe I could assist you. Can I take a look at him?"

'Oh, no—no please! He mustn't be disturbed.'

The lady accepted the rebuff indulgently.

'Well, it's just as you say, of course, but you don't look to me as if you'd had much experience in sickness and I'd have been glad to assist you. What do you generally do when your husband's taken this way?'

'I—I let him sleep.'

'Too much sleep ain't any too healthful either. Don't you give him any medicine?'

'Y—yes.'

'Don't you wake him to take it?'

'Yes.'

'When does he take the next dose?'

'Not for—two hours—'

The lady looked disappointed. 'Well, if I was you I'd try giving it oftener. That's what I do with my folks.'

After that many faces seemed to press upon her. The passengers were on their way to the dining car, and she was conscious that as they passed down the aisle they glanced curiously at the closed curtains. One lantern-jawed man with prominent eyes stood still and tried to shoot his projecting glance through the division between the folds. The freckled child, returning from breakfast, waylaid the passers with a buttery clutch, saying in a loud whisper, 'He's sick'; and once the conductor came by, asking for tickets. She shrank into her corner and looked out of the window at the flying trees and houses, meaningless hieroglyphs of an endlessly unrolled papyrus.

Now and then the train stopped, and the newcomers on entering the car stared in turn at the closed curtains. More and more people seemed to pass—their faces began to blend fantastically with the images surging in her brain. . . .

Later in the day a fat man detached himself from the mist of faces. He had a creased stomach and soft pale lips. As he pressed himself into the seat facing her she noticed that he was dressed in black broadcloth, with a soiled white tie.

'Husband's pretty bad this morning, is he?'

'Yes.'

'Dear, dear! Now that's terribly distressing, ain't it?' An apostolic smile revealed his gold-filled teeth. 'Of course you know there's no sech thing as sickness. Ain't that a lovely thought? Death itself is but a deloosion of our grosser senses. On'y lay yourself open to the influx of the sperrit, submit yourself passively to the action of the divine force, and disease and dissolution will cease to exist for you. If you could indooce your husband to read this little pamphlet—'

The faces about her again grew indistinct. She had a vague recollection of hearing the motherly lady and the parent of the freckled child ardently disputing the relative advantages of trying several medicines at once, or of taking each in turn; the motherly lady maintaining that the competitive system saved time; the other objecting that you couldn't tell which remedy had effected the cure; their voices went on and on, like bell buoys droning through a fog....The porter came up now and then with questions that she did not understand, but somehow she must have answered since he went away again without repeating them; every two hours the motherly lady reminded her that her husband ought to have his drops; people left the car and others replaced them....

Her head was spinning and she tried to steady herself by clutching at her thoughts as they swept by, but they slipped away from her like bushes on the side of a sheer precipice down which she seemed to be falling. Suddenly her mind grew clear again and she found herself vividly picturing what would happen when the train reached New York. She shuddered as it occurred to her that he would be quite cold and that someone might perceive he had been dead since morning.

She thought hurriedly: 'If they see I am not surprised they will suspect something. They will ask questions, and if I tell them the truth they won't believe me—no one would believe me! It will be terrible'—and she kept repeating to herself—'I must pretend I don't know. I must pretend I don't know. When they open the curtains I must go up to him quite naturally—and then I must scream!' She had an idea that the scream would be very hard to do.

Gradually new thoughts crowded upon her, vivid and urgent: she tried to separate and restrain them, but they beset her clamorously, like her school children at the end of a hot day, when she was too tired to silence them. Her head grew confused, and she felt a sick fear of forgetting her part, of betraying herself by some unguarded word or look.

'I must pretend I don't know,' she went on murmuring. The words had lost their significance, but she repeated them mechanically, as though they had been a magic formula, until suddenly she heard herself saying: 'I can't remember, I can't remember!'

Her voice sounded very loud, and she looked about her in terror; but no one seemed to notice that she had spoken.

As she glanced down the car her eye caught the curtains of her husband's berth, and she began to examine the monotonous arabesques woven through their heavy folds. The pattern was intricate and difficult to trace; she gazed fixedly at the curtains and as she did so the thick stuff grew transparent and through it she saw her husband's face—his dead face. She struggled to avert her look, but her eyes refused to move and her head seemed to be held in vice. At last, with an effort that left her weak and shaking, she turned away; but it was of no use; close in front of her, small and smooth, was her husband's face. It seemed to be suspended in the air between her and the false braids of the woman who sat in front of her. With an uncontrollable gesture she stretched out her hand to push the face away, and suddenly she felt the touch of his smooth skin. She repressed a cry and half started from her seat. The woman with the false braids looked around, and feeling that she must justify her movement in some way she rose and lifted her traveling bag from the opposite seat. She unlocked the bag and looked into it; but the first object her hand met was a small flask of her husband's, thrust there at the last moment, in the haste of departure. She locked the bag and closed her eyes...his face was there again, hanging between her eyeballs and lids like a waxen mask against a red curtain....

She roused herself with a shiver. Had she fainted or slept? Hours seemed to have elapsed; but it was still broad day, and the people about her were sitting in the same attitudes as before.

A sudden sense of hunger made her aware that she had eaten nothing since morning. The thought of food filled her with disgust, but she dreaded a return of faintness, and remembering that she had some biscuits in her bag she took one out and ate it. The dry crumbs choked her, and she hastily swallowed a little brandy from her husband's flask.

The burning sensation in her throat acted as a counterirritant, momentarily relieving the dull ache of her nerves. Then she felt a gently-stealing warmth, as though a soft air fanned her, and the swarming fears relaxed their clutch, receding through the stillness that enclosed her, a stillness soothing as the spacious quietude of a summer day. She slept.

Through her sleep she felt the impetuous rush of the train. It seemed to be life itself that was sweeping her on with headlong inexorable force—sweeping her into darkness and terror, and the awe of unknown days.—Now all at once everything was still—not a sound, not a pulsation.... She was dead in her turn, and lay beside him with smooth upstaring face. How quiet it was!—and yet she heard feet coming, the feet of the men who were to carry them away.... She could feel too—she felt a sudden prolonged vibration, a series of hard shocks, and then another plunge into darkness, the darkness of death this time—a black whirlwind on which they were both spinning like leaves, in wild uncoiling spirals, with millions and millions of the dead....

She sprang up in terror. Her sleep must have lasted a long time, for the winter day had paled and the lights had been lit. The car was in confusion, and as she regained her self-possession she saw that the passengers were gathering up their wraps and bags. The woman with the false braids had brought from the dressing room a sickly ivy plant in a bottle, and the Christian Scientist was reversing his cuffs. The porter passed down the aisle with his impartial brush. An impersonal figure with a gold-banded cap asked for her husband's ticket. A voice shouted 'Baig-gage express!' and she heard the clicking of metal as the passengers handed over their checks.

Presently her window was blocked by an expanse of sooty wall, and the train passed into the Harlem tunnel. The journey was over; in a few minutes she would see her family pushing their joyous way through the throng at the station. Her heart dilated. The worst terror was past....

'We'd better get him up now, hadn't we?' asked the porter, touching her arm.

He had her husband's hat in his hand and was meditatively revolving it under his brush.

She looked at the hat and tried to speak; but suddenly the car grew dark. She flung up her arms, struggling to catch at something, and fell face downward, striking her head against the dead man's berth.

STEPHEN CRANE
(1871–1900)

"Genius" and "prodigious" are the words that come most readily to mind in considering the elusive Stephen Crane, who died at an age (twenty-eight, of tuberculosis, poverty, and overwork) when most of the writers in this volume were just beginning their careers. Yet Crane left behind a remarkable body of work of fiction, nonfiction, and poetry, enough to fill a dozen volumes of a collected edition; his experimental, imagistic poems The Black Riders and Other Lines (1895) alone would guarantee him a permanent place in the American literary canon. Like Jack London, whom he most resembles in terms of the unconventional and frequently dangerous life he led, Crane was clearly a phenomenon of youthful energy, drive, and audacity.

Stephen Crane was born in Newark, New Jersey, the last of fourteen children; his father was a Methodist minister who died when Crane was nine years old. So precocious was Crane, and so determined to be a writer, he published his first novel, Maggie: A Girl of the Streets (1893), at his own expense—at the age of twenty- two. His second novel, which was to make him famous, The Red Badge of Courage (1895), is generally considered the first American "realist" novel to find a reasonably wide audience. A tour de force by a young man who had never witnessed war, let alone participated in combat, The Red Badge of Courage was later described by Crane as a "pot-boiler."

Crane's titles include two volumes of excellent short fiction, The Monster and Other Stories (1899) and Whilomville Stories (1900). Though virtually unknown, "The Little Regiment" is as memorable an accomplishment as any of Crane's most frequently anthologized stories. Note the subtle employment of sentiment, even as the author detaches himself from it. Note the perfection of the story's final line.

The Little Regiment

I

The fog made the clothes of the men of the column in the roadway seem of a luminous quality. It imparted to the heavy infantry overcoats a new colour, a kind of blue which was so pale that a regiment might have been merely a long, low shadow in the mist. However, a muttering, one part grumble, three parts joke, hovered in the air above the thick ranks, and blended in an undertoned roar, which was the voice of the column.

The town on the southern shore of the little river loomed spectrally, a faint etching upon the gray cloud-masses which were shifting with oily languor. A long row of guns upon the northern bank had been pitiless in their hatred, but a little battered belfry could be dimly seen still pointing with invincible resolution toward the heavens.

The enclouded air vibrated with noises made by hidden colossal things. The infantry tramplings, the heavy rumbling of the artillery, made the earth speak of gigantic preparation. Guns on distant heights thundered from time to time with sudden, nervous roar, as if unable to endure in silence a knowledge of hostile troops massing, other guns going to position. These sounds, near and remote, defined an immense battleground, described the tremendous width of the stage of the prospective drama. The voices of the guns, slightly casual, unexcited in their challenges and warnings, could not destroy the unutterable eloquence of the word in the air, a meaning of impending struggle which made the breath halt at the lips.

The column in the roadway was ankle-deep in mud. The men swore piously at the rain which drizzled upon them, compelling them to stand always very erect in fear of the drops that would sweep in under their coat-collars. The fog was as cold as wet cloths. The men stuffed their hands deep in their pockets, and huddled their muskets in their arms. The machinery of orders had rooted these soldiers deeply into the mud precisely as almighty nature roots mullein stalks.

They listened and speculated when a tumult of fighting came from the dim town across the river. When the noise lulled for a time they resumed their descriptions of the mud and graphically exaggerated the number of hours they had been kept waiting. The general commanding their division rode along the ranks, and they cheered admiringly, affectionately, crying out to him gleeful prophecies of the coming battle. Each man scanned him with a peculiarly keen personal interest, and afterward spoke of him with unquestioning devotion and confidence, narrating anecdotes which were mainly untrue.

When the jokers lifted the shrill voices which invariably belonged to them, flinging witticisms at their comrades, a loud laugh would sweep from rank to rank, and soldiers who had not heard would lean forward and demand repetition. When were borne past them some wounded men with gray and blood-smeared faces, and eyes that rolled in that helpless beseeching for assistance from the sky which comes with supreme pain, the soldiers in the mud watched intently, and from time to time asked of the bearers an account of the affair. Frequently they bragged of their corps, their division, their brigade, their regiment. Anon they referred to the mud and the cold drizzle. Upon this threshold of a wild scene of death they, in short, defied the proportion of events with that splendour of heedlessness which belongs only to veterans.

"Like a lot of wooden soldiers," swore Billie Dempster, moving his feet in the thick mass, and casting a vindictive glance indefinitely; "standing in the mud for a hundred years."

"Oh, shut up!" murmured his brother Dan. The manner of his words implied that this fraternal voice near him was an indescribable bore.

"Why should I shut up?" demanded Billie.

"Because you're a fool," cried Dan, taking no time to debate it; "the biggest fool in the regiment."

There was but one man between them, and he was habituated. These insults from brother to brother had swept across his chest, flown past his face, many times during two long campaigns. Upon this occasion he simply grinned first at one, then at the other.

The way of these brothers was not an unknown topic in regimental gossip. They had enlisted simultaneously, with each sneering loudly at the other for doing it. They left their little town, and went forward with the flag, exchanging protestations of undying suspicion. In the camp life they so openly despised each other that, when entertaining quarrels were lacking, their companions often contrived situations calculated to bring forth display of this fraternal dislike.

Both were large-limbed, strong young men, and often fought with friends in camp unless one was near to interfere with the other. This latter happened rather frequently, because Dan, preposterously willing for any manner of combat, had a very great horror of seeing Billie in a fight; and Billie, almost odiously ready himself, simply refused to see Dan stripped to his shirt and with his fists aloft. This sat queerly upon them, and made them the objects of plots.

When Dan jumped through a ring of eager soldiers and dragged forth his raving brother by the arm, a thing often predicted would almost come to pass. When Billie performed the same office for Dan, the prediction would again miss fulfilment by an inch. But indeed they never fought together, although they were perpetually upon the verge.

They expressed longing for such conflict. As a matter of truth, they had at one time made full arrangement for it, but even with the encouragement and interest of half of the regiment they somehow failed to achieve collision.

If Dan became a victim of police duty, no jeering was so destructive to the feelings as Billie's comment. If Billie got a call to appear at the headquarters, none would so genially prophesy his complete undoing as Dan. Small misfortunes to one were, in truth, invariably greeted with hilarity by the other, who seemed to see in them great re-enforcement of his opinion.

As soldiers, they expressed each for each a scorn intense and blasting. After a certain battle, Billie was promoted to corporal. When Dan was told of it, he seemed smitten dumb with astonishment and patriotic indignation. He stared in silence, while the dark blood rushed to Billie's forehead, and he shifted his weight from foot to foot. Dan at last found his tongue, and said: "Well, I'm durned!" If he had heard that an army mule had been appointed to the post of corps commander, his tone could not have had more derision in it. Afterward, he adopted a fervid insubordination, an almost religious reluctance to obey the new corporal's orders, which came near to developing the desired strife.

It is here finally to be recorded also that Dan, most ferociously profane in speech, very rarely swore in the presence of his brother; and that

Billie, whose oaths came from his lips with the grace of falling pebbles, was seldom known to express himself in this manner when near his brother Dan.

At last the afternoon contained a suggestion of evening. Metallic cries rang suddenly from end to end of the column. They inspired at once a quick, business-like adjustment. The long thing stirred in the mud. The men had hushed, and were looking across the river. A moment later the shadowy mass of pale blue figures was moving steadily toward the stream. There could be heard from the town a clash of swift fighting and cheering. The noise of the shooting coming through the heavy air had its sharpness taken from it, and sounded in thuds.

There was a halt upon the bank above the pontoons. When the column went winding down the incline, and streamed out upon the bridge, the fog had faded to a great degree, and in the clearer dusk the guns on a distant ridge were enabled to perceive the crossing. The long whirling outcries of the shells came into the air above the men. An occasional solid shot struck the surface of the river, and dashed into view a sudden vertical jet. The distance was subtly illuminated by the lightning from the deep-booming guns. One by one the batteries on the northern shore aroused, the innumerable guns bellowing in angry oration at the distant ridge. The rolling thunder crashed and reverberated as a wild surf sounds on a still night, and to this music the column marched across the pontoons.

The waters of the grim river curled away in a smile from the ends of the great boats, and slid swiftly beneath the planking. The dark, riddled walls of the town upreared before the troops, and from a region hidden by these hammered and tumbled houses came incessantly the yells and firings of a prolonged and close skirmish.

When Dan had called his brother a fool, his voice had been so decisive, so brightly assured, that many men had laughed, considering it to be great humour under the circumstances. The incident happened to rankle deep in Billie. It was not any strange thing that his brother had called him a fool. In fact, he often called him a fool with exactly the same amount of cheerful and prompt conviction, and before large audiences, too. Billie wondered in his own mind why he took such profound offence in this case; but, at any rate, as he slid down the bank and on to the bridge with his regiment, he was searching his knowledge for something that would pierce Dan's blithesome spirit. But he could contrive nothing at this time, and his impotency made the glance which he was once able to give his brother still more malignant.

The guns far and near were roaring a fearful and grand introduction for this column which was marching upon the stage of death. Billie felt it, but only in a numb way. His heart was cased in that curious dissonant metal which covers a man's emotions at such times. The terrible voices from the hills told him that in this wide conflict his life was an insignificant fact, and that his death would be an insignificant fact. They portended the whirlwind to which he would be as necessary as a butterfly's waved wing. The solemnity, the sadness of it came near enough to make him wonder why he was neither solemn nor sad. When his mind vaguely adjusted events according to their importance to him, it appeared that the uppermost thing was the fact that upon the eve of battle, and before many comrades, his brother had called him a fool.

Dan was in a particularly happy mood. "Hurray! Look at 'em shoot," he said, when the long witches' croon of the shells came into the air. It enraged Billie when he felt the little thorn in him, and saw at the same time that his brother had completely forgotten it.

The column went from the bridge into more mud. At this southern end there was a chaos of hoarse directions and commands. Darkness was coming upon the earth, and regiments were being hurried up the slippery bank. As Billie floundered in the black mud, amid the swearing, sliding crowd, he suddenly resolved that, in the absence of other means of hurting Dan, he would avoid looking at him, refrain from speaking to him, pay absolutely no heed to his existence; and this done skilfully would, he imagined, soon reduce his brother to a poignant sensitiveness.

At the top of the bank the column again halted and rearranged itself, as a man after a climb rearranges his clothing. Presently the great steel-backed brigade, an infinitely graceful thing in the rhythm and ease of its veteran movement, swung up a little narrow, slanting street.

Evening had come so swiftly that the fighting on the remote borders of the town was indicated by thin flashes of flame. Some building was on fire, and its reflection upon the clouds was an oval of delicate pink.

II

All demeanour of rural serenity had been wrenched violently from the little town by the guns and by the waves of men which had surged through it. The hand of war laid upon this village had in an instant changed it to a thing of remnants. It resembled the place of a monstrous shaking of the earth itself. The windows, now mere unsightly holes, made the tumbled and blackened dwellings seem skeletons. Doors lay splintered to fragments. Chimneys had flung their bricks everywhere. The artillery fire had not neglected the rows of gentle shade-trees which had lined the streets. Branches and heavy trunks cluttered the mud in driftwood tangles, while a few shattered forms had contrived to remain dejectedly, mournfully upright. They expressed an innocence, a helplessness, which perforce created a pity for their happening into this cauldron of battle. Furthermore, there was under foot a vast collection of odd things reminiscent of the charge, the fight, the retreat. There were boxes and barrels filled with earth, behind which riflemen had lain snugly, and in these little trenches were the dead in blue with the dead in gray, the poses eloquent of the struggles for possession of the town until the history of the whole conflict was written plainly in the streets.

And yet the spirit of this little city, its quaint individuality, poised in the air above the ruins, defying the guns, the sweeping volleys; holding in contempt those avaricious blazes which had attacked many dwellings. The hard earthen sidewalks proclaimed the games that had been played there during long lazy days, in the careful shadows of the trees. "General Merchandise," in faint letters upon a long board, had to be read with a slanted glance, for the sign dangled by one end; but the porch of the old store was a palpable legend of wide-hatted men, smoking.

This subtle essence, this soul of the life that had been, brushed like invisible wings the thoughts of the men in the swift columns that came up from the river.

In the darkness a loud and endless humming arose from the great blue crowds bivouacked in the streets. From time to time a sharp spatter of firing from far picket lines entered this bass chorus. The smell from the smouldering ruins floated on the cold night breeze.

Dan, seated ruefully upon the doorstep of a shot-pierced house, was proclaiming the campaign badly managed. Orders had been issued forbidding camp-fires.

Suddenly he ceased his oration, and scanning the group of his comrades, said: "Where's Billie? Do you know?"

"Gone on picket."

"Get out! Has he?" said Dan. "No business to go on picket. Why don't some of them other corporals take their turn?"

A bearded private was smoking his pipe of confiscated tobacco, seated comfortably upon a horse-hair trunk which he had dragged from the house. He observed: "*Was* his turn."

"No such thing," cried Dan. He and the man on the horse-hair trunk held discussion in which Dan stoutly maintained that if his brother had been sent on picket it was an injustice. He ceased his argument when another soldier, upon whose arms could faintly be seen the two stripes of a corporal, entered the circle. "Humph," said Dan, "where you been?"

The corporal made no answer. Presently Dan said: "Billie, where you been?"

His brother did not seem to hear these inquiries. He glanced at the house which towered above them, and remarked casually to the man on the horse-hair trunk: "Funny, ain't it? After the pelting this town got, you'd think there wouldn't be one brick left on another."

"Oh," said Dan, glowering at his brother's back. "Getting mighty smart, ain't you?"

The absence of camp-fires allowed the evening to make apparent its quality of faint silver light in which the blue clothes of the throng became black, and the faces became white expanses, void of expression. There was considerable excitement a short distance from the group around the doorstep. A soldier had chanced upon a hoop-skirt, and arrayed in it he was performing a dance amid the applause of his companions. Billie and a greater part of the men immediately poured over there to witness the exhibition.

"What's *the* matter with Billie?" demanded Dan of the man upon the horse-hair trunk.

"How do I know?" rejoined the other in mild resentment. He arose and walked away. When he returned he said briefly, in a weather-wise tone, that it would rain during the night.

Dan took a seat upon one end of the horse-hair trunk. He was facing the crowd around the dancer, which in its hilarity swung this way and that way. At times he imagined that he could recognise his brother's face.

He and the man on the other end of the trunk thoughtfully talked of the army's position. To their minds, infantry and artillery were in a most precarious jumble in the streets of the town; but they did not grow nervous over it, for they were used to having the army appear in a precarious jumble to their minds. They had learned to accept such puzzling situations as a consequence of their position in the ranks, and were now usually in possession of a simple but perfectly immovable faith that somebody understood the jumble. Even if they had been convinced that the army was a headless monster, they would merely have nodded with the veteran's singular cynicism. It was none of their business as soldiers. Their duty was to grab sleep and food when occasion permitted, and cheerfully fight wherever their feet were planted until more orders came. This was a task sufficiently absorbing.

They spoke of other corps, and this talk being confidential, their voices dropped to tones of awe. "The Ninth"—"The First"—"The Fifth"—"The Sixth"—"The Third"—the simple numerals rang with eloquence, each having a meaning which was to float through many years as no intangible arithmetical mist, but as pregnant with individuality as the names of cities.

Of their own corps they spoke with a deep veneration, an idolatry, a supreme confidence which apparently would not blanch to see it match against everything.

It was as if their respect for other corps was due partly to a wonder that organizations not blessed with their own famous numeral could take such an interest in war. They could prove that their division was the best in the corps, and that their brigade was the best in the division. And their regiment—it was plain that no fortune of life was equal to the chance which caused a man to be born, so to speak, into this command, the keystone of the defending arch.

At times Dan covered with insults the character of a vague, unnamed general to whose petulance and busy-body spirit he ascribed the order which made hot coffee impossible.

Dan said that victory was certain in the coming battle. The other man seemed rather dubious. He remarked upon the fortified line of hills, which had impressed him even from the other side of the river. "Shucks," said Dan. "Why, we—" He pictured a splendid overflowing of these hills by the sea of men in blue. During the period of this conversation Dan's glance searched the merry throng about the dancer. Above the babble of voices in the street a faraway thunder could sometimes be heard—evidently from the very edge of the horizon—the boom-boom of restless guns.

III

Ultimately the night deepened to the tone of black velvet. The outlines of the fireless camp were like the faint drawings upon ancient tapestry. The glint of a rifle, the shine of a button, might have been of threads of silver and gold sewn upon the fabric of the night. There was little presented to the vision, but to a sense more subtle there was discernible in the atmosphere something like a pulse; a mystic beating which would have told a stranger of the presence of a giant thing—the slumbering mass of regiments and batteries.

With fires forbidden, the floor of a dry old kitchen was thought to be a good exchange for the cold earth of December, even if a shell had exploded in it and knocked it so out of shape that when a man lay curled in his blanket his last waking thought was likely to be of the wall that bellied out above him as if strongly anxious to topple upon the score of soldiers.

Billie looked at the bricks ever about to descend in a shower upon his face, listened to the industrious pickets plying their rifles on the border of the town, imagined some measure of the din of the coming battle, thought of Dan and Dan's chagrin, and rolling over in his blanket went to sleep with satisfaction.

At an unknown hour he was aroused by the creaking of boards. Lifting himself upon his elbow, he saw a sergeant prowling among the sleeping forms. The sergeant carried a candle in an old brass candle-stick. He would have resembled some old farmer on an unusual midnight tour if it were not for the significance of his gleaming buttons and striped sleeves.

Billie blinked stupidly at the light until his mind returned from the journeys of slumber. The sergeant stooped among the unconscious soldiers, holding the candle close, and peering into each face.

"Hello, Haines," said Billie. "Relief?"

"Hello, Billie," said the sergeant. "Special duty."

"Dan got to go?"

"Jameson, Hunter, McCormack, D. Dempster. Yes. Where is he?"

"Over there by the winder," said Billie, gesturing. "What is it for, Haines?"

"You don't think I know, do you?" demanded the sergeant. He began to pipe sharply but cheerily at men upon the floor. "Come, Mac, get up here. Here's a special for you. Wake up, Jameson. Come along, Dannie, me boy."

Each man at once took this call to duty as a personal affront. They pulled themselves out of their blankets, rubbed their eyes, and swore at whoever was responsible. "Them's orders," cried the sergeant. "Come! Get out of here." An undetailed head with dishevelled hair thrust out from a blanket, and a sleepy voice said: "Shut up, Haines, and go home."

When the detail clanked out of the kitchen, all but one of the remaining men seemed to be again asleep. Billie, leaning on his elbow, was gazing into darkness. When the footsteps died to silence, he curled himself into his blanket.

At the first cool lavender lights of daybreak he aroused again, and scanned his recumbent companions. Seeing a wakeful one he asked: "Is Dan back yet?"

The man said: "Hain't seem 'im."

Billie put both hands behind his head, and scowled into the air. "Can't see the use of these cussed details in the night-time," he muttered in his most unreasonable tones. "Darn nuisances. Why can't they—" He grumbled at length and graphically.

When Dan entered with the squad, however, Billie was convincingly asleep.

IV

The regiment trotted in double time along the street, and the colonel seemed to quarrel over the right of way with many artillery officers. Batteries were waiting in the mud, and the men of them, exasperated by the bustle of this ambitious infantry, shook their fists from saddle and caisson, exchanging all manner of taunts and jests. The slanted guns continued to look reflectively at the ground.

On the outskirts of the crumbled town a fringe of blue figures were firing into the fog. The regiment swung out into skirmish lines, and the fringe of blue figures departed, turning their backs and going joyfully around the flank.

The bullets began a low moan off toward a ridge which loomed faintly in the heavy mist. When the swift crescendo had reached its climax, the missiles zipped just overhead, as if piercing an invisible curtain. A battery on the hill was crashing with such tumult that it was as if the guns had quarrelled and had fallen pell-mell and snarling upon each other. The shells howled on their journey toward the town. From short range distance there came a spatter of musketry, sweeping along an invisible line and making faint sheets of orange light.

Some in the new skirmish lines were beginning to fire at various shadows discerned in the vapour, forms of men suddenly revealed by some humour of the laggard masses of clouds. The crackle of musketry began to dominate the purring of the hostile bullets. Dan, in the front rank, held his rifle poised, and looked into the fog keenly, coldly, with the air of a sportsman. His nerves were so steady that it was as if they had been drawn from his body, leaving him merely a muscular machine; but his numb heart was somehow beating to the pealing march of the fight.

The waving skirmish line went backward and forward, ran this way and that way. Men got lost in the fog, and men were found again. Once they got too close to the formidable ridge, and the thing burst out as if repulsing a general attack. Once another blue regiment was apprehended on the very edge of firing into them. Once a friendly battery began an elaborate and scientific process of extermination. Always as busy as brokers, the men slid here and there over the plain, fighting their foes, escaping from their friends, leaving a history of many movements in the wet yellow turf, cursing the atmosphere, blazing away every time they could identify the enemy.

In one mystic changing of the fog, as if the fingers of spirits were drawing aside these draperies, a small group of the gray skirmishers, silent, statuesque, were suddenly disclosed to Dan and those about him. So vivid and near were they that there was something uncanny in the revelation.

There might have been a second of mutual staring. Then each rifle in each group was at the shoulder. As Dan's glance flashed along the barrel of his weapon, the figure of a man suddenly loomed as if the musket had been a telescope. The short black beard, the slouch hat, the pose of the man as he sighted to shoot, made a quick picture in Dan's mind. The same moment, it would seem, he pulled his own trigger, and the man, smitten, lurched forward, while his exploding rifle made a slanting crimson streak in the air, and the slouch hat fell before the body. The billows of the fog, governed by singular impulses, rolled between.

"You got that feller such enough," said a comrade to Dan. Dan looked at him absent-mindedly.

V

When the next morning calmly displayed another fog, the men of the regiment exchanged eloquent comments; but they did not abuse it at length, because the streets of the town now contained enough galloping aides to make three troops of cavalry, and they knew that they had come to the verge of the great fight.

Dan conversed with the man who had once possessed a horse-hair trunk; but they did not mention the line of hills which had furnished them in more careless moments with an agreeable topic. They avoided it now as condemned men do the subject of death, and yet the thought of it stayed in their eyes as they looked at each other and talked gravely of other things.

The expectant regiment heaved a long sigh of relief when the sharp call: "Fall in," repeated indefinitely, arose in the streets. It was inevitable that a bloody battle was to be fought, and they wanted to get it off their minds. They were, however, doomed again to spend a long period planted firmly in the mud. They craned their necks, and wondered where some of the other regiments were going.

At last the mists rolled carelessly away. Nature made at this time all provisions to enable foes to see each other, and immediately the roar of guns resounded from every hill. The endless cracking of the skirmish had swelled to rolling crashes of musketry. Shells screamed with panther-like noises at the houses. Dan looked at the man of the horse-hair trunk, and the man said: "Well, here she comes!"

The tenor voices of younger officers and the deep and hoarse voices of the older ones rang in the streets. These cries pricked like spurs. The masses of men vibrated from the suddenness with which they were plunged into the situation of troops about to fight. That the orders were long-expected did not concern the emotion.

Simultaneous movement was imparted to all these thick bodies of men and horses that lay in the town. Regiment after regiment swung rapidly into the streets that faced the sinister ridge.

This exodus was theatrical. The little sober-hued village had been like the cloak which disguises the king of drama. It was now put aside, and an army, splendid thing of steel and blue, stood forth in the sunlight.

Even the soldiers in the heavy columns drew deep breaths at the sight, more majestic than they had dreamed. The heights of the enemy's position were crowded with men who resembled people come to witness some mighty pageant. But as the column moved steadily to their positions, the guns, matter-of-fact warriors, doubled their number, and shells burst with red thrilling tumult on the crowded plain. One came into the ranks of the regiment, and after the smoke and the wrath of it had faded, leaving motionless figures, everyone stormed according to the limits of his vocabulary, for veterans detest being killed when they are not busy.

The regiment sometimes looked sideways at its brigade companions composed of men who had never been in battle; but no frozen blood could withstand the heat of the splendour of this army before the eyes on the plain, these lines so long that the flanks were little streaks, this mass of men of one intention. The recruits carried themselves heedlessly. At the rear was an idle battery, and three artillery men in a foolish row on a caisson nudged each other and grinned at the recruits. "You'll catch it pretty soon," they called out. They were impersonally gleeful, as if they themselves were not also likely to catch it pretty soon. But with this picture of an army in their hearts, the new men perhaps felt the devotion which the drops may feel for the wave; they were of its power and glory; they smiled jauntily at the foolish row of gunners, and told them to go to blazes.

The column trotted across some little bridges, and spread quickly into lines of battle. Before them was a bit of plain, and back of the plain was the ridge. There was no time left for considerations. The men were staring at the plain, mightily wondering how it would feel to be out there, when a brigade in advance yelled and charged. The hill was all gray smoke and fire-points.

That fierce elation in the terrors of war, catching a man's heart and making it burn with such ardour that he becomes capable of dying, flashed in the faces of the men like coloured lights, and made them resemble leashed animals, eager, ferocious, daunting at nothing. The line was really in its first leap before the wild, hoarse crying of the orders.

The greed for close quarters which is the emotion of a bayonet charge, came then into the minds of the men and developed until it was a madness. The field, with its faded grass of a Southern winter, seemed to this fury miles in width.

High, slow-moving masses of smoke, with an odour of burning cotton, engulfed the line until the men might have been swimmers. Before them the ridge, the shore of this gray sea, was outlined, crossed, and recrossed by sheets of flame. The howl of the battle arose to the noise of innumerable wind demons.

The line, galloping, scrambling, plunging like a herd of wounded horses, went over a field that was sown with corpses, the records of other charges.

Directly in front of the black-faced, whooping Dan, carousing in this onward sweep like a new kind of fiend, a wounded man appeared, raising his shattered body, and staring at this rush of men down upon him. It seemed to occur to him that he was to be trampled; he made a desperate, piteous effort to escape; then finally huddled in a waiting heap. Dan and the soldier near him widened the interval between them without looking down, without appearing to heed the wounded man. This little clump of blue seemed to reel past them as boulders reel past a train.

Bursting through a smoke-wave, the scampering, unformed bunches came upon the wreck of the brigade that had preceded them, a floudering mass stopped afar from the hill by the swirling volleys.

It was as if a necromancer had suddenly shown them a picture of the fate which awaited them; but the line with muscular spasm hurled itself over this wreckage and onward, until men were stumbling amid the relics of other assaults, the point where the fire from the ridge consumed.

The men, panting, perspiring, with crazed faces, tried to push against it; but it was as if they had come to a wall. The wave halted, shuddered in an agony from the quick struggle of its two desires, then toppled, and broke into a fragmentary thing which has no name.

Veterans could now at last be distinguished from recruits. The new regiments were instantly gone, lost, scattered, as if they never had been. But the sweeping failure of the charge, the battle, could not make the veterans forget their business. With a last throe, the band of maniacs drew itself up and blazed a volley at the hill, insignificant to those iron intrenchments, but nevertheless expressing that singular final despair which enables men coolly to defy the walls of a city of death.

After this episode the men renamed their command. They called it the Little Regiment.

VI

"I seen Dan shoot a feller yesterday. Yes sir. I'm sure it was him that done it. And maybe he thinks about that feller now, and wonders if *he* tumbled down just about the same way. Them things come up in a man's mind."

Bivouac fires upon the sidewalks, in the streets, in the yards, threw high their wavering reflections, which examined, like slim, red fingers, the dingy, scarred walls and the piles of tumbled brick. The droning of voices again arose from great blue crowds.

The odour of frying bacon, the fragrance from countless little coffee-pails floated among the ruins. The rifles, stacked in the shadows, emitted flashes of steely light. Wherever a flag lay horizontally from one stack to another was the bed of an eagle which had led men into the mystic smoke.

The men about a particular fire were engaged in holding in check their jovial spirits. They moved whispering around the blaze, although they looked at it with a certain fine contentment, like labourers after a day's hard work.

There was one who sat apart. They did not address him save in tones suddenly changed. They did not regard him directly, but always in little sidelong glances.

At last a soldier from a distant fire came into this circle of light. He studied for a time the man who sat apart. Then he hesitatingly stepped closer, and said: "Got any news, Dan?"

"No," said Dan.

The new-comer shifted his feet. He looked at the fire, at the sky, at the other men, at Dan. His face expressed a curious despair; his tongue was plainly in rebellion. Finally, however, he contrived to say: "Well, there's some chance yet, Dan. Lots of the wounded are still lying out there, you know. There's some chance yet."

"Yes," said Dan.

The soldier shifted his feet again, and looked miserably into the air. After another struggle he said: "Well, there's some chance yet, Dan." He moved hastily away.

One of the men of the squad, perhaps encouraged by this example, now approached the still figure. "No news yet, hey?" he said, after coughing behind his hand.

"No," said Dan.

"Well," said the man, "I've been thinking of how he was fretting about you the night you went on special duty. You recollect? Well, sir, I was surprised. He couldn't say enough about it. I swan, I don't believe he slep' a wink after you left, but just lay awake cussing special duty and worrying. I was surprised. But there he lay cussing. He__"

Dan made a curious sound, as if a stone had wedged in his throat. He said: "Shut up, will you?"

Afterward the men would not allow this moody contemplation of the fire to be interrupted.

"Oh, let him alone, can't you?"

"Come away from there, Casey!"

"Say, can't you leave him be?"

They moved with reverence about the immovable figure, with its countenance of mask-like invulnerability.

VII

After the red round eye of the sun had stared long at the little plain and its burden, darkness, a sable mercy, came heavily upon it, and the wan hands of the dead were no longer seen in strange frozen gestures.

The heights in front of the plain shone with tiny camp-fires, and from the town in the rear, small shimmerings ascended from the blazes of the bivouac. The plain was a black expanse upon which, from time to time, dots of light, lanterns, floated slowly here and there. These fields were long steeped in grim mystery.

Suddenly, upon one dark spot, there was a resurrection. A strange thing had been groaning there, prostrate. Then it suddenly dragged itself to a sitting posture, and became a man.

The man stared stupidly for a moment at the lights on the hill, then turned and contemplated the faint colouring over the town. For some moments he remained thus, staring with dull eyes, his face unemotional, wooden.

Finally he looked around him at the corpses dimly to be seen. No change flashed into his face upon viewing these men. They seemed to suggest merely that his information concerning himself was not too complete. He ran his fingers over his arms and chest, bearing always the air of an idiot upon a bench at an almshouse door.

Finding no wound in his arms nor in his chest, he raised his hand to his head, and the fingers came away with some dark liquid upon them. Holding these fingers close to his eyes, he scanned them in the same stupid fashion, while his body gently swayed.

The soldier rolled his eyes again toward the town. When he arose, his clothing peeled from the frozen ground like wet paper. Hearing the sound of it, he seemed to see reason for deliberation. He paused and looked at the ground, then at his trousers, then at the ground.

Finally he went slowly off toward the faint reflection, holding his hands palm outward before him, and walking in the manner of a blind man.

VIII

The immovable Dan again sat unaddressed in the midst of comrades, who did not joke aloud. The dampness of the usual morning fog seemed to make the little camp-fires furious.

Suddenly a cry arose in the streets, a shout of amazement and delight. The men making breakfast at the fire looked up quickly. They broke forth in clamorous exclamation: "Well! Of all things! Dan! Dan! Look who's coming! Oh, Dan!"

Dan the silent raised his eyes and saw a man, with a bandage of the size of a helmet about his head, receiving a furious demonstration from the company. He was shaking hands, and explaining, and haranguing to a high degree.

Dan started. His face of bronze flushed to his temples. He seemed about to leap from the ground, but then suddenly he sank back, and resumed his impassive gazing.

The men were in a flurry. They looked from one to the other. "Dan! Look! See who's coming!" some cried again. "Dan! Look!"

He scowled at last, and moved his shoulders sullenly. "Well, don't I know it?"

But they could not be convinced that his eyes were in service. "Dan! Why can't you look? See who's coming!"

He made a gesture then of irritation and rage. "Curse it! Don't I know it?"

The man with a bandage of the size of a helmet moved forward, always shaking hands and explaining. At times his glance wandered to Dan, who saw with his eyes riveted.

After a series of shiftings, it occurred naturally that the man with the bandage was very near to the man who saw the flames. He paused, and there was a little silence. Finally he said: "Hello, Dan."

"Hello, Billie."

WILLA CATHER
(1873–1947)

Born in Virginia, Willa Cather moved with her family to Red Cloud, Nebraska, as a young child. Like Sarah Orne Jewett, whose New England stories first inspired Cather to write, she was a passionate chronicler of her time and place: "When I strike the open plains, something happens. I'm home. I breathe differently. That love of great spaces, of rolling open country like the sea,—it's the grand passion of my life."

Along with Edith Wharton, in many ways her antithesis, Willa Cather is the predominant American woman writer of her era. Her "grand passion" for the Midwest is matched by an equal fascination with the primordial American Southwest; and, as exemplified in this early story "A Death in the Desert," from her collection The Troll Garden *(1905), with the lives and fates of musical artists.*

Cather's literary output was considerable, and its high quality was recognized from the first. Among her outstanding titles are O Pioneers! *(1913),* The Song of the Lark *(1915),* My Ántonia *(1918),* A Lost Lady *(1923),* The Professor's House *(1925), and* Death Comes for the Archbishop *(1927). Her most frequently anthologized short stories are "Paul's Case" and "Neighbor Rosicky"; the story included here makes explicit the author's lifelong fascination with musical artists and with the seemingly impersonal destiny of one fated to serve, like the heroine of* The Song of the Lark, *"the madness of art"—an echo of the powerful concluding lines of Henry James's "The Middle Years."*

A Death in the Desert

Everett Hilgarde was conscious that the man in the seat across the aisle was looking at him intently. He was a large, florid man, wore a conspicuous diamond solitaire upon his third finger, and Everett judged him to be a travelling salesman of some sort. He had the air of an adaptable fellow who had been about the world and who could keep cool and clean under almost any circumstances.

The "High Line Flyer," as this train was derisively called among railroad men, was jerking along through the hot afternoon over the monotonous country between Holdrege and Cheyenne. Besides the blond man and himself the only occupants of the car were two dusty, bedraggled-looking girls who had been to the Exposition at Chicago, and who were earnestly discussing the cost of their first trip out of Colorado. The four uncomfortable passengers were covered with a sediment of fine, yellow dust which clung to their hair and eyebrows like gold powder. It blew up in clouds from the bleak, lifeless country through which they passed, until they were one colour with the sage-brush and sand-hills. The grey and yellow desert was varied only by occasional ruins of deserted towns, and the little red boxes of station-houses, where the spindling trees and sickly vines in the blue-grass yards made little green reserves fenced off in that confusing wilderness of sand.

As the slanting rays of the sun beat in stronger and stronger through the car-windows, the blond gentleman asked the ladies' permission to remove his coat, and sat in his lavender striped shirtsleeves, with a black silk handkerchief tucked carefully about his collar. He had seemed interested in Everett since they had boarded the train at Holdrege, and kept glancing at him curiously and then looking reflectively out of the window, as though he were trying to recall something. But wherever Everett went someone was almost sure to look at him with that curious interest, and it had ceased to embarrass or annoy him. Presently the stranger, seeming satisfied with his observation, leaned back in his seat, half closed his eyes, and began softly to whistle the Spring Song from *Proserpine,* the cantata that a dozen years before had made its young composer famous in a night. Everett had heard that air on guitars in Old Mexico, on mandolins at college glees, on cottage organs in New England hamlets, and only two weeks ago he had heard it played on sleighbells at a variety theatre in Denver. There was literally no way of escaping his brother's precocity. Adriance could live on the other side of the Atlantic, where his youthful indiscretions were forgotten in his mature achievements, but his brother had never been able to outrun *Proserpine,* and here he found it again in the Colorado sand-hills. Not that Everett was exactly ashamed of *Proserpine;* only a man of genius could have written it, but it was the sort of thing that a man of genius outgrows as soon as he can.

Everett unbent a trifle and smiled at his neighbour across the aisle. Immediately the large man rose and coming over dropped into the seat facing Hilgarde, extending his card.

"Dusty ride, isn't it? I don't mind it myself; I'm used to it. Born and bred in de briar patch, like Br'er Rabbit. I've been trying to place you for a long time; I think I must have met you before."

"Thank you," said Everett, taking the card; "my name is Hilgarde. You've probably met my brother, Adriance; people often mistake me for him."

The travelling-man brought his hand down upon his knee with such vehemence that the solitaire blazed.

"So I was right after all, and if you're not Adriance Hilgarde you're his double. I thought I couldn't be mistaken. Seen him? Well, I guess! I never missed one of his recitals at the Auditorium, and he played the piano score of *Proserpine* through to us once at the Chicago Press Club. I used to be on the *Commercial* there before I began to travel for the publishing department of the concern. So you're Hilgarde's brother, and here I've run into you at the jumping-off place. Sounds like a newspaper yarn, doesn't it?"

The travelling-man laughed and offered Everett a cigar and plied him with questions on the only subject that people ever seemed to care to talk to Everett about. At length the salesman and the two girls alighted at a Colorado way station, and Everett went on to Cheyenne alone.

The train pulled into Cheyenne at nine o'clock, late by a matter of four hours or so; but no one seemed particularly concerned at its tardiness except the station agent, who grumbled about being kept in the office overtime on a summer night. When Everett alighted from the train he walked down the platform and stopped at the track crossing, uncertain as to what direction he should take to reach a hotel. A phaeton stood near the crossing and a woman held the reins. She was dressed in white, and her figure was clearly silhouetted against the cushions, though it was too dark to see her face. Everett had scarcely noticed her, when the switch-engine came puffing up from the opposite direction, and the headlight threw a strong glare of light on his face. Suddenly the woman in the phaeton uttered a low cry and dropped the reins. Everett started forward and caught the horse's head, but the animal only lifted its ears and whisked its tail in impatient surprise. The woman sat perfectly still, her head sunk between her shoulders and her handkerchief pressed to her face. Another woman came out of the depot and hurried toward the phaeton, crying, "Katharine, dear, what is the matter?"

Everett hesitated a moment in painful embarrassment, then lifted his hat and passed on. He was accustomed to sudden recognitions in the most impossible places, especially by women, but this cry out of the night had shaken him.

While Everett was breakfasting the next morning, the head waiter leaned over his chair to murmur that there was a gentleman waiting to see him in the parlour. Everett finished his coffee, and went in the direction indicated, where he found his visitor restlessly pacing the floor. His whole manner betrayed a high degree of agitation, though his physique was not that of a man whose nerves lie near the surface. He was something below medium height, square-shouldered and solidly built. His thick, closely cut hair was beginning to show grey about the ears, and his bronzed face was heavily lined. His square brown hands were locked behind him, and he held his shoulders like a man conscious of responsibilities, yet, as he turned to greet Everett, there was an incongruous diffidence in his address.

"Good-morning, Mr. Hilgarde," he said, extending his hand; "I found your name on the hotel register. My name is Gaylord. I'm afraid my sister startled you at the station last night, Mr. Hilgarde, and I've come around to apologize."

"Ah! the young lady in the phaeton? I'm sure I didn't know whether I had anything to do with her alarm or not. If I did, it is I who owe the apology."

The man coloured a little under the dark brown of his face.

"Oh, it's nothing you could help, sir, I fully understand that. You see, my sister used to be a pupil of your brother's, and it seems you favour him; and when the switch-engine threw a light on your face it startled her."

Everett wheeled about in his chair. "Oh! *Katharine* Gaylord! Is it possible! Now it's you who have given me a turn. Why, I used to know her when I was a boy. What on earth—"

"Is she doing here?" said Gaylord, grimly filling out the pause. "You've got at the heart of the matter. You knew my sister had been in bad health for a long time?"

"No, I had never heard a word of that. The last I knew of her she was singing in London. My brother and I correspond infrequently, and seldom get beyond family matters. I am deeply sorry to hear this. There are many reasons why I am [more] concerned than I can tell you."

The lines in Charley Gaylord's brow relaxed a little.

"What I'm trying to say, Mr. Hilgarde, is that she wants to see you. I hate to ask you, but she's so set on it. We live several miles out of town, but my rig's below, and I can take you out any time you can go."

"I can go now, and it will give me real pleasure to do so," said Everett, quickly. "I'll get my hat and be with you in a moment."

When he came downstairs Everett found a cart at the door, and Charley Gaylord drew a long sigh of relief as he gathered up the reins and settled back into his own element.

"You see, I think I'd better tell you something about my sister before you see her, and I don't know just where to begin. She travelled in Europe with your brother and his wife, and sang at a lot of his concerts, but I don't know just how much you know about her."

"Very little, except that my brother always thought her the most gifted of his pupils, and that when I knew her she was very young and very beautiful and turned my head sadly for a while."

Everett saw that Gaylord's mind was quite engrossed by his grief. He was wrought up to the point where his reserve and sense of proportion had quite left him, and his trouble was the one vital thing in the world. "That's the whole thing," he went on, flecking his horses with the whip.

"She was a great woman, as you say, and she didn't come of a great family. She had to fight her own way from the first. She got to Chicago and then to New York, and then to Europe, where she went up like lightning, and got a taste for it all; and now she's dying here like a rat in a hole, out of her own world, and she can't fall back into ours. We've grown apart, some way—miles and miles apart—and I'm afraid she's fearfully unhappy."

"It's a very tragic story that you are telling me, Gaylord," said Everett. They were well out into the country now, spinning along over the dusty plains of red grass, with the ragged blue outline of the mountains before them.

"Tragic!" cried Gaylord, starting up in his seat, "my God, man, nobody will ever know how tragic. It's a tragedy I live with and eat with and sleep with, until I've lost my grip on everything. You see she had made a good bit of money, but she spent it all going to health resorts. It's her lungs, you know. I've got money enough to send her anywhere, but the doctors all say it's no use. She hasn't the ghost of a chance. It's just getting through the days now. I had no notion she was half so bad before she came to me. She just wrote that she was all run down. Now that she's here, I think she'd be happier anywhere under the sun, but she won't leave. She says it's easier to let go of life here, and that to go East would be dying twice. There was a time when I was a brakeman with a run out of Bird City, Iowa, and she was a little thing I could carry on my shoulder, when I could get her everything on earth she wanted, and she hadn't a wish my $80 a month didn't cover; and now, when I've got a little property together, I can't buy her a night's sleep!"

Everett saw that, whatever Charley Gaylord's present status in the world might be, he had brought the brakeman's heart up the ladder with him, and the brakeman's frank avowal of sentiment. Presently Gaylord went on:

"You can understand how she has outgrown her family. We're all a pretty common sort, railroaders from away back. My father was a conductor. He died when we were kids. Maggie, my other sister, who lives with me, was a telegraph operator here while I was getting my grip on things. We had no education to speak of. I have to hire a stenographer because I can't spell straight—the Almighty couldn't teach me to spell. The things that make up life to Kate are all Greek to me, and there's scarcely a point where we touch any more, except in our recollections of the old times when we were all young and happy together, and Kate sang in a church choir in Bird City. But I believe, Mr. Hilgarde, that if she can see just one person like you, who knows about the things and people she's interested in, it will give her about the only comfort she can have now."

The reins slackened in Charley Gaylord's hand as they drew up before a showily painted house with many gables and a round tower. "Here we are," he said, turning to Everett, "and I guess we understand each other."

They were met at the door by a thin, colourless woman, whom Gaylord introduced as "My sister, Maggie." She asked her brother to show Mr. Hilgarde into the music-room, where Katharine wished to see him alone.

When Everett entered the music-room he gave a little start of surprise, feeling that he had stepped from the glaring Wyoming sunlight into some New York studio that he had always known. He wondered which it was of those countless studios, high up under the roofs, over banks and shops and wholesale houses, that this room resembled, and he looked incredulously out of the window at the grey plain that ended in the great upheaval of the Rockies.

The haunting air of familiarity about the room perplexed him. Was it a copy of some particular studio he knew, or was it merely the studio atmosphere that seemed so individual and poignantly reminiscent here in Wyoming? He sat down in a reading-chair and looked keenly about him. Suddenly his eye fell upon a large photograph of his brother above the piano. Then it all became clear to him: this was veritably his brother's room. If it were not an exact copy of one of the many studios that Adriance had fitted up in various parts of the world, wearying of them and leaving almost before the renovator's varnish had dried, it was at least in the same tone. In every detail Adriance's taste was so manifest that the room seemed to exhale his personality.

Among the photographs on the wall there was one of Katharine Gaylord, taken in the days when Everett had known her, and when the flash of her eye or the flutter of her skirt was enough to set his boyish heart in a tumult. Even now, he stood before the portrait with a certain degree of embarrassment. It was the face of a woman already old in her first youth, thoroughly sophisticated and a trifle hard, and it told of what her brother had called her fight. The *camaraderie* of her frank, confident eyes was qualified by the deep lines about her mouth and the curve of the lips, which was both sad and cynical. Certainly she had more good-will than confidence toward the world, and the bravado of her smile could not conceal the shadow of an unrest that was almost discontent. The chief charm of the woman, as Everett had known her, lay in her superb figure and in her eyes, which possessed a warm, life-giving quality like the sunlight; eyes which glowed with a sort of perpetual *salutat* to the world. Her head, Everett remembered as peculiarly well shaped and proudly poised. There had been always a little of the imperatrix about her, and her pose in the photograph revived all his old impressions of her unattachedness, of how absolutely and valiantly she stood alone.

Everett was still standing before the picture, his hands behind him and his head inclined, when he heard the door open. A very tall woman advanced toward him, holding out her hand. As she started to speak she coughed slightly, then, laughing, said, in a low, rich voice, a trifle husky: "You see I make the traditional Camille entrance—with the cough. How good of you to come, Mr. Hilgarde."

Everett was acutely conscious that while addressing him she was not looking at him at all, and, as he assured her of his pleasure in coming, he was glad to have an opportunity to collect himself. He had not reckoned upon the ravages of a long illness. The long, loose folds of her white gown had been especially designed to conceal the sharp outlines of her emaciated body, but the stamp of her disease was there; simple and ugly and obtrusive, a pitiless fact that could not be disguised or evaded. The splendid shoulders were stooped, there was a swaying unevenness in her gait, her arms seemed disproportionately long, and her hands were transparently white, and cold to the touch. The changes in her face were less obvious; the proud carriage of the head, the warm, clear eyes, even the delicate flush of colour in her cheeks, all defiantly remained, though they were all in a lower key—older, sadder, softer.

She sat down upon the divan and began nervously to arrange the pillows. "I know I'm not an inspiring object to look upon, but you must be quite frank and sensible about that and get used to it at once, for we've no time to lose. And if I'm a trifle irritable you won't mind?—for I'm more than usually nervous."

"Don't bother with me this morning, if you are tired," urged Everett. "I can come quite as well tomorrow."

"Gracious, no!" she protested, with a flash of that quick, keen humour that he remembered as a part of her. "It's solitude that I'm tired to death of-—solitude and the wrong kind of people. You see, the minister, not content with reading the prayers for the sick, called on me this morning. He happened to be riding by on his bicycle and felt it his duty to stop. Of course, he disapproves of my profession, and I think he takes it for granted that I have a dark past. The funniest feature of his conversation is that he is always excusing my own vocation to me;—condoning it, you know—and trying to patch up my peace with my conscience by suggesting possible noble uses for what he kindly calls my talent."

Everett laughed. "Oh! I'm afraid I'm not the person to call after such a serious gentleman—I can't sustain the situation. At my best I don't reach higher than low comedy. Have you decided to which one of the noble uses you will devote yourself?"

Katharine lifted her hands in a gesture of renunciation and exclaimed: "I'm not equal to any of them, not even the least noble. I didn't study that method."

She laughed and went on nervously: "The parson's not so bad. His English never offends me, and he has read Gibbon's 'Decline and Fall,' all five volumes, and that's something. Then, he has been to New York, and that's a great deal. But how we are losing time! Do tell me about New York; Charley says you're just on from there. How does it look and taste and smell just now? I think a whiff of the Jersey ferry would be as flagons of cod-liver oil to me. Who conspicuously walks the Rialto now, and what does he or she wear? Are the trees still green in Madison Square, or have they grown brown and dusty? Does the chaste Diana on the Garden Theatre still keep her vestal vows through all the exasperating changes of weather? Who has your brother's old studio now, and what misguided aspirants practise their scales in the rookeries about Carnegie Hall? What do people go to see at the theatres, and what do they eat and drink there in the world nowadays? You see, I'm homesick for it all, from the Battery to Riverside. Oh, let me die in Harlem!" she was interrupted by a violent attack of coughing, and Everett, embarrassed by her discomfort, plunged into gossip about the professional people he had met in town during the summer, and the musical outlook for the winter. He was diagraming with his pencil, on the back of an old envelope he found in his pocket, some new mechanical device to be used at the Metropolitan in the production of the *Rheingold,* when he became conscious that she was looking at him intently, and that he was talking to the four walls.

Katharine was lying back among the pillows, watching him through half-closed eyes, as a painter looks at a picture. He finished his explanation vaguely enough and put the envelope back in his pocket. As he did so, she said, quietly: "How wonderfully like Adriance you are!" and he felt as though a crisis of some sort had been met and tided over.

He laughed, looking up at her with a touch of pride in his eyes that made them seem quite boyish. "Yes, isn't it absurd? It's almost as awkward as looking like Napoleon—But, after all, there are some advantages. It has made some of his friends like me, and I hope it will make you."

Katharine smiled and gave him a quick, meaning glance from under her lashes. "Oh, it did that long ago. What a haughty, reserved youth you were then, and how you used to stare at people, and then blush and look cross if they paid you back in your own coin. Do you remember that night when you took me home from a rehearsal, and scarcely spoke a word to me?"

"It was the silence of admiration," protested Everett, "very crude and boyish, but very sincere and not a little painful. Perhaps you suspected something of the sort? I remember you saw fit to be very grown up and worldly."

"I believe I suspected a pose; the one that college boys usually affect with singers—'an earthen vessel in love with a star,' you know. But it rather surprised me in you, for you must have seen a good deal of your brother's pupils. Or had you an omnivorous capacity, and elasticity that always met the occasion?"

"Don't ask a man to confess the follies of his youth," said Everett, smiling a little sadly; "I am sensitive about some of them even now. But I was not so sophisticated as you imagined. I saw my brother's pupils come and go, but that was about all. Sometimes I was called on to play accompaniments, or to fill out a vacancy at a rehearsal, or to order a carriage for an infuriated soprano who had thrown up her part. But they never spent any time on me, unless it was to notice the resemblance you speak of."

"Yes," observed Katharine, thoughtfully, "I noticed it then, too; but it has grown as you have grown older. That is rather strange, when you have lived such different lives. It's not merely an ordinary family likeness of feature, you know, but a sort of interchangeable individuality; the suggestion of the other man's personality in your face—like an air transposed to another key. But I'm not attempting to define it; it's beyond me; something altogether unusual and a trifle—well, uncanny," she finished, laughing.

"I remember," Everett said, seriously, twirling the pencil between his fingers and looking, as he sat with his head thrown back, out under the red window-blind which was raised just a little, and as it swung back and forth in the wind revealed the glaring panorama of the desert—a blinding stretch of yellow, flat as the sea in dead calm, splotched here and there with deep purple shadows; and, beyond, the ragged blue outline of the mountains and the peaks of snow, white as the white clouds—"I remember, when I was a little fellow I used to be very sensitive about it. I don't think it exactly displeased me, or that I would have had it otherwise if I could, but it seemed to me like a birthmark, or something not to be lightly spoken of. People were naturally always fonder of Ad than of me, and I used to feel the chill of reflected light pretty often. It came into even my relations with my mother. Ad went abroad to study when he was absurdly young, you know, and mother was all broken up over it. She did her whole duty by each of us, but it was sort of generally understood among us that she'd have made burnt-offerings of us all for Ad any day. I was a little fellow then, and when she sat alone on the porch in the summer dusk, she used sometimes to call me to her and turn my face up in the light that streamed out through the shutters and kiss me, and then I always knew she was thinking of Adriance."

"Poor little chap," said Katharine, and her tone was a trifle huskier than usual. "How fond people have always been of Adriance! Now tell me the latest news of him. I haven't heard, except through the press, for a year or more. He was in Algiers then, in the valley of the Chelif, riding horseback night and day in an Arabian costume, and in his usual enthusiastic fashion he had quite made up his mind to adopt the Mahometan faith and become as nearly an Arab as possible. How many countries and faiths has he adopted, I wonder? Probably he was playing Arab to himself all the time. I remember he was a sixteenth-century duke in Florence once for weeks together."

"Oh, that's Adriance," chuckled Everett. "He is himself barely long enough to write checks and be measured for his clothes. I didn't hear from him while he was an Arab; I missed that."

"He was writing an Algerian *suite* for the piano then; it must be in the publisher's hands by this time. I have been too ill to answer his letter, and have lost touch with him."

Everett drew a letter from his pocket. "This came about a month ago. It's chiefly about his new opera, which is to be brought out in London next winter. Read it at your leisure."

"I think I shall keep it as a hostage, so that I may be sure you will come again. Now I want you to play for me. Whatever you like; but if there is anything new in the world, in mercy let me hear it. For nine months I have heard nothing but 'The Baggage Coach Ahead' and 'She is My Baby's Mother.'"

He sat down at the piano, and Katharine sat near him, absorbed in his remarkable physical likeness to his brother, and trying to discover in just what it consisted. She told herself that it was very much as though a sculptor's finished work had been rudely copied in wood. He was of a larger build than Adriance, and his shoulders were broad and heavy, while those of his brother were slender and rather girlish. His face was of the same oval mould, but it was grey, and darkened about the mouth by continual shaving. His eyes were of the same inconstant April colour, but they were reflective and rather dull; while Adriance's were always points of high light, and always meaning another thing than the thing they meant yesterday. But it was hard to see why this earnest young man should so continually suggest that lyric, youthful face that was as gay as his was grave. For Adriance, though he was ten years the elder, and though his hair was streaked with silver, had the face of a boy of twenty, so mobile that it told his thoughts before he could put them into words. A contralto, famous for the extravagance of her vocal methods and of her affections had once said of him that the shepherd-boys who sang in the Vale of Tempe must certainly have looked like young Hilgarde; and the comparison had been appropriated by a hundred shyer women who preferred to quote.

As Everett sat smoking on the veranda of the Inter-Ocean House that night, he was a victim to random recollections. His infatuation for Katharine Gaylord, visionary as it was, had been the most serious of his boyish love-affairs, and had long disturbed his bachelor dreams. He was painfully timid in everything relating to the emotions, and his hurt had withdrawn him from the society of women. The fact that it was all so done and dead and far behind him, and that the woman had lived her life out since then, gave him an oppressive sense of age and loss. He bethought himself of something he had read about "sitting by the hearth and remembering the faces of women without desire," and felt himself an octogenarian.

He remembered how bitter and morose he had grown during his stay at his brother's studio when Katharine Gaylord was working there, and how he had wounded Adriance on the night of his last concert in New York. He had sat there in the box while his brother and Katharine were called back again and again after the last number, watching the roses go up over the footlights until they were stacked half as high as the piano, brooding, in his sullen boy's heart, upon the pride those two felt in each other's work—spurring each other to their best and beautifully contending in song. The footlights had seemed a hard, glittering line drawn sharply between their life and his; a circle of flame set about those splendid children of genius. He walked back to his hotel alone, and sat in his window staring out on Madison Square until long after midnight, resolving to beat no more at doors that he could never enter, and realizing more keenly than ever before how far this glorious world of beautiful creations lay from the paths of men like himself. He told himself that he had in common with this woman only the baser uses of life.

Everett's week in Cheyenne stretched to three, and he saw no prospect of release except through the thing he dreaded. The bright, windy days of the Wyoming autumn passed swiftly. Letters and telegrams came urging him to hasten his trip to the coast, but he resolutely postponed his business engagements. The mornings he spent on one of Charley Gaylord's ponies, or fishing in the mountains, and in the evenings he sat in his room writing letters or reading. In the afternoon he was usually at his post of duty. Destiny, he reflected, seems to have very positive notions about the sort of parts we are fitted to play. The scene changes and the compensation varies, but in the end we usually find that we have played the same class of business from first to last. Everett had been a stop-gap all his life. He remembered going through a looking-glass labyrinth when he was a boy, and trying gallery after gallery, only at every turn to bump his nose against his own face—which, indeed, was not his own, but his brother's. No matter what his mission, east or west, by land or sea, he was sure to find himself employed in his brother's business, one of the tributary lives which helped to swell the shining current of Adriance Hilgarde's. It was not the first time that his duty had been to comfort, as best he could, one of the broken things his brother's imperious speed had cast aside and forgotten. He made no attempt to analyse the situation or to state it in exact terms; but he felt Katharine Gaylord's need for him, and he accepted it as a commission from his brother to help this woman to die. Day by day he felt her demands on him grow more imperious, her need for him grow more acute and positive; and day by day he felt that in his peculiar relation to her, his own individuality played a smaller and smaller part. His power to minister to her comfort, he saw, lay solely in his link with his brother's life. He understood all that his physical resemblance meant to her. He knew that she sat by him always watching for some common trick of gesture, some familiar play of expression, some illusion of light and shadow, in which he should seem wholly Adriance. He knew that she lived upon this and that her disease fed upon it; that it sent shudders of remembrance through her and that in the exhaustion which followed this turmoil of her dying senses, she slept deep and sweet, and dreamed of youth and art and days in a certain old Florentine garden, and not of bitterness and death.

The question which most perplexed him was, "How much shall I know? How much does she wish for me to know?" A few days after his first meeting with Katharine Gaylord, he had cabled his brother to write her. He had merely said that she was mortally ill; he could depend on Adriance to say the right thing—that was a part of his gift. Adriance always said not only the right thing, but the opportune, graceful, exquisite thing. His phrases took the colour of the moment and the then present condition, so that they never savoured of perfunctory compliment or frequent usage. He always caught the lyric essence of the moment, the poetic suggestion of every situation. Moreover, he usually did the right thing, the opportune, graceful, exquisite thing—except, when he did very cruel things—bent upon making people happy when their existence touched his, just as he insisted that his material environment should be beautiful; lavishing upon those near him all the warmth and radiance of his rich nature, all the homage of the poet and troubadour, and, when they were no longer near, forgetting—for that also was a part of Adriance's gift.

Three weeks after Everett had sent his cable, when he made his daily call at the gaily painted ranch-house, he found Katharine laughing like a school-girl. "Have you ever thought," she said, as he entered the music-room, "how much these séances of ours are like Heine's 'Florentine Nights,' except that I don't give you an opportunity to monopolize the conversation as Heine did?" She held his hand longer than usual as she greeted him, and looked searchingly up into his face. "You are the kindest man living, the kindest," she added, softly.

Everett's grey face coloured faintly as he drew his hand away, for he felt that this time she was looking at him and not at a whimsical caricature of his brother. "Why, what have I done now?" he asked, lamely. "I can't remember having sent you any stale candy or champagne since yesterday."

She drew a letter with a foreign postmark from between the leaves of a book and held it out, smiling. "You got him to write it. Don't say you didn't, for it came direct, you see, and the last address I gave him was a place in Florida. This deed shall be remembered of you when I am with the just in Paradise. But one thing you did not ask him to do, for you didn't know about it. He has sent me his latest work, the new sonata, the most ambitious thing he has ever done, and you are to play it for me directly, though it looks horribly intricate. But first for the letter; I think you would better read it aloud to me."

Everett sat down in a low chair facing the window-seat in which she reclined with a barricade of pillows behind her. He opened the letter, his lashes half-veiling his kind eyes, and saw to his satisfaction that it was a long one; wonderfully tactful and tender, even for Adriance, who was tender with his valet and his stable-boy, with his old gondolier and the beggar-women who prayed to the saints for him.

The letter was from Granada, written in the Alhambra, as he sat by the fountain of the Patio di Lindaraxa. The air was heavy with the warm fragrance of the South and full of the sound of splashing, running water, as it had been in a certain old garden in Florence, long ago. The sky was one great turquoise, heated until it glowed. The wonderful Moorish arches threw graceful blue shadows all about him. He had sketched an outline of them on the margin of his notepaper. The subtleties of Arabic decoration had cast an unholy spell over him, and the brutal exaggerations of Gothic art were a bad dream, easily forgotten. The Alhambra itself had, from the first, seemed perfectly familiar to him, and he knew that he must have trod that court, sleek and brown and obsequious, centuries before Ferdinand rode into Andalusia. The letter was full of confidences about his work, and delicate allusions to their old happy days of study and comradeship, and of her own work, still so warmly remembered and appreciatively discussed everywhere he went.

As Everett folded the letter he felt that Adriance had divined the thing needed and had risen to it in his own wonderful way. The letter was consistently egotistical, and seemed to him even a trifle patronizing, yet it was just what she had wanted. A strong realization of his brother's charm and intensity and power came over him; he felt the breath of that whirlwind of flame in which Adriance passed, consuming all in his path, and himself even more resolutely than he consumed others. Then he looked down at this white, burnt-out brand that lay before him. "Like him, isn't it?" she said, quietly.

"I think I can scarcely answer his letter, but when you see him next you can do that for me. I want you to tell him many things for me, yet they can all be summed up in this: I want him to grow wholly into his best and greatest self, even at the cost of the dear boyishness that is half his charm to you and me. Do you understand me?"

"I know perfectly well what you mean," answered Everett, thoughtfully. "I have often felt so about him myself. And yet it's difficult to prescribe for those fellows; so little makes, so little mars."

Katharine raised herself upon her elbow, and her face flushed with feverish earnestness. "Ah, but it is the waste of himself that I mean; his lashing himself out on stupid and uncomprehending people until they take him at their own estimate. He can kindle marble, strike fire from putty, but is it worth what it costs him?"

"Come, come," expostulated Everett, alarmed at her excitement. "Where is the new sonata? Let him speak for himself."

He sat down at the piano and began playing the first movement which was indeed the voice of Adriance, his proper speech. The sonata was the most ambitious work he had done up to that time, and marked the transition from his purely lyric vein to a deeper and nobler style. Everett played intelligently and with that sympathetic comprehension which seems peculiar to a certain lovable class of men who never accomplish anything in particular. When he had finished he turned to Katharine.

"How he has grown!" she cried. "What the three last years have done for him! He used to write only the tragedies of passion; but this is the tragedy of the soul, the shadow coexistent with the soul. This is the tragedy of effort and failure, the thing Keats called hell. This is my tragedy, as I lie here spent by the race-course, listening to the feet of the runners as they pass me—ah, God! the swift feet of the runners!"

She turned her face away and covered it with her straining hands. Everett crossed over to her quickly and knelt beside her. In all the days he had known her she had never before, beyond an occasional ironical jest, given voice to the bitterness of her own defeat. Her courage had become a point of pride with him, and to see it going sickened him.

"Don't do it," he gasped. "I can't stand it, I really can't, I feel it too much. We mustn't speak of that; it's too tragic and too vast."

When she turned her face back to him there was a ghost of the old, brave, cynical smile on it, more bitter than the tears she could not shed. "No, I won't be ungenerous; I will save that for the watches of the night when I have no better company. Now you may mix me another drink of some sort. Formerly, when it was not *if* I should ever sing Brunhilda, but quite simply when I *should* sing Brunhilda, I was always starving myself, and thinking what I might drink and what I might not. But broken music-boxes may drink whatsoever they list, and no one cares whether they lose their figure. Run over that theme at the beginning again. That, at least, is not new. It was running in his head when we were in Venice years ago, and he used to drum it on his glass at the dinner-table. He had just begun to work it out when the late autumn came on, and the paleness of the Adriatic oppressed him, and he decided to go to Florence for the winter, and lost touch with the theme during his illness. Do you remember those frightful days? All the people who have loved him are not strong enough to save him from himself! When I got word from Florence that he had been ill, I was in Nice filling a concert engagement. His wife was hurrying to him from Paris, but I reached him first. I arrived at dusk, in a terrific storm. They had taken an old palace there for the winter, and I found him in the library—a long, dark room full of old Latin books and heavy furniture and bronzes. He was sitting by a wood fire at one end of the room, looking, oh, so worn and pale!—as he always does when he is ill, you know. Ah, it is so good that you *do* know! Even his red smoking-jacket lent no colour to his face. His first words were not to tell me how ill he had been, but that that morning he had been well enough to put the last strokes to the score of his *'Souvenirs d'Automne,'* and he was, as I most like to remember him; so calm and happy and tired; not gay, as he usually is, but just contented and tired with that heavenly tiredness that comes after a good work done at last. Outside, the rain poured down in torrents, and the wind moaned for the pain of all the world and sobbed in the branches of the shivering olives and about the walls of that desolated old palace. How that night comes back to me! There were no lights in the room, only the wood fire which glowed upon the hard features of the bronze Dante like the reflection of purgatorial flames, and threw long black shadows about us; beyond us it scarcely penetrated the gloom at all. Adriance sat staring at the fire with the weariness of all his life in his eyes, and of all the other lives that must aspire and suffer to make up one such life as his. Somehow the wind with all its world-pain had got into the room, and the cold rain was in our eyes, and the wave came up in both of us at once—that awful vague, universal pain, that cold fear of life and death and God and hope—and we were like two clinging together on a spar in mid-ocean after the ship-wreck of everything. Then we heard the front door open with a great gust of wind that shook even the walls, and the servants came running with lights, announcing that Madame had returned, *'and in the book we read no more that night."*

She gave the old line with a certain bitter humour, and with the hard, bright smile in which of old she had wrapped her weakness as in a glittering garment. That ironical smile, worn like a mask through so many years, had gradually changed even the lines of her face completely, and when she looked in the mirror she saw not herself, but the scathing critic, the amused observer and satirist of herself. Everett dropped his head upon his hand and sat looking at the rug. "How much you have cared!" he said.

"Ah, yes, I cared," she replied, closing her eyes with a long-drawn sigh of relief; and lying perfectly still, she went on: "You can't imagine what a comfort it is to have you know how I cared, what a relief it is to be able to tell it to some one. I used to want to shriek it out to the world in the long nights when I could not sleep. It seemed to me that I could not die with it. It demanded some sort of expression. And now that you know, you would scarcely believe how much less sharp the anguish of it is."

Everett continued to look helplessly at the floor. "I was not sure how much you wanted me to know," he said.

"Oh, I intended you should know from the first time I looked into your face, when you came that day with Charley. I flatter myself that I have been able to conceal it when I chose, though I suppose women always think that. The more observing ones may have seen, but discerning people are usually discreet and often kind, for we usually bleed a little before we begin to discern. But I wanted you to know; you are so like him that it is almost like telling him himself. At least, I feel now that he will know some day, and then I will be quite sacred from his compassion, for we none of us dare pity the dead. Since it was what my life has chiefly meant, I should like him to know. On the whole, I am not ashamed of it. I have fought a good fight."

"And has he never known at all?" asked Everett, in a thick voice.

"Oh! never at all in the way that you mean. Of course, he is accustomed to looking into the eyes of women and finding love there; when he doesn't find it there he thinks he must have been guilty of some discourtesy and is miserable about it. He has a genuine fondness for every one who is not stupid or gloomy, or old or preternaturally ugly. Granted youth and cheerfulness, and a moderate amount of wit and some tact, and Adriance will always be glad to see you coming around the corner. I shared with the rest; shared the smiles and the gallantries and the droll little sermons. It was quite like a Sunday-school picnic; we wore our best clothes and a smile and took our turns. It was his kindness that was hardest. I have pretty well used my life up at standing punishment."

"Don't; you'll make me hate him," groaned Everett.

Katharine laughed and began to play nervously with her fan. "It wasn't in the slightest degree his fault; that is the most grotesque part of it. Why, it had really begun before I ever met him. I fought my way to him, and I drank my doom greedily enough."

Everett rose and stood hesitating. "I think I must go. You ought to be quiet, and I don't think I can hear any more just now."

She put out her hand and took his playfully. "You've put in three weeks at this sort of thing, haven't you? Well, it may never be to your glory in this world, perhaps, but it's been the mercy of heaven to me, and it ought to square accounts for a much worse life than yours will ever be."

Everett knelt beside her, saying, brokenly: "I stayed because I wanted to be with you, that's all. I have never cared about other women since I met you in New York when I was a lad. You are a part of my destiny, and I could not leave you if I would."

She put her hands on his shoulders and shook her head. "No, no; don't tell me that. I have seen enough of tragedy, God knows: don't show me any more just as the curtain is going down. No, no, it was only a boy's fancy, and your divine pity and my utter pitiableness have recalled it for a moment. One does not love the dying, dear friend. If some fancy of that sort had been left over from boyhood, this would rid you of it, and that were well. Now go, and you will come again to-morrow, as long as there are to-morrows, will you not?" She took his hand with a smile that lifted the mask from her soul, that was both courage and despair, and full of infinite loyalty and tenderness, as she said softly,

"For ever and for ever, farewell, Cassius;
If we do meet again, why, we shall smile;
If not, why then, this parting was well made."

The courage in her eyes was like the clear light of a star to him as he went out.

On the night of Adriance Hilgarde's opening concert in Paris, Everett sat by the bed in the ranch-house in Wyoming, watching over the last battle that we have with the flesh before we are done with it and free of it forever. At times it seemed that the serene soul of her must have left already and found some refuge from the storm, and only the tenacious animal life were left to do battle with death. She laboured under a delusion at once pitiful and merciful, thinking that she was in the Pullman on her way to New York, going back to her life and her work. When she aroused from her stupor, it was only to ask the porter to waken her half an hour out of Jersey City, or to remonstrate with him about the delays and the roughness of the road. At midnight Everett and the nurse were left alone with her. Poor Charley Gaylord had lain down on a couch outside the door. Everett sat looking at the sputtering night-lamp until it made his eyes ache. His head dropped forward on the foot of the bed, and he sank into a heavy, distressful slumber. He was dreaming of Adriance's concert in Paris, and of Adriance, the troubadour, smiling and debonair, with his boyish face and the touch of silver grey in his hair. He heard the applause and he saw the roses going up over the footlights until they were stacked half as high as the piano, and the petals fell and scattered, making crimson splotches on the floor. Down this crimson pathway came Adriance with his youthful step, leading his prima donna by the hand; a dark woman this time, with Spanish eyes.

The nurse touched him on the shoulder, he started and awoke. She screened the lamp with her hand. Everett saw that Katharine was awake and conscious, and struggling a little. He lifted her gently on his arm and began to fan her. She laid her hands lightly on his hair and looked into his face with eyes that seemed never to have wept or doubted. "Ah, dear Adriance, dear, dear," she whispered.

Everett went to call her brother, but when they came back the madness of art was over for Katharine.

Two days later Everett was pacing the station siding, waiting for the west-bound train. Charley Gaylord walked beside him, but the two men had nothing to say to each other. Everett's bags were piled on the truck, and his step was hurried and his eyes were full of impatience, as he gazed again and again up the track, watching for the train. Gaylord's impatience was not less than his own; these two, who had grown so close, had now become painful and impossible to each other, and longed for the wrench of farewell.

As the train pulled in, Everett wrung Gaylord's hand among the crowd of alighting passengers. The people of a German opera company, *en route* for the coast, rushed by them in frantic haste to snatch their breakfast during the stop. Everett heard an exclamation in a broad German dialect, and a massive woman whose figure persistently escaped from her stays in the most improbable places rushed up to him, her blond hair disordered by the wind, and glowing with joyful surprise she caught his coat-sleeve with her tightly gloved hands.

"Herr Gott, Adriance, *lieber Freund,"* she cried, emotionally.

Everett quickly withdrew his arm, and lifted his hat, blushing. "Pardon me, madame, but I see that you have mistaken me for Adriance Hilgarde. I am his brother," he said, quietly, and turning from the crestfallen singer he hurried into the car.

SHERWOOD ANDERSON
(1876–1941)

Like Samuel Clemens, by whom, in fact, he was influenced, Sherwood Anderson has had an incalculable influence upon generations of American writers. The deceptively artless, unadorned, anecdotal Anderson voice has come to characterize for many readers the distinctive American voice—most recently reconstituted as Minimalism. Simple, often declarative sentences; "realistic" settings, characters, plots; a lack of interest in stylistic experimentation; an absence of philosophical exploration—this is the kind of fiction that many, or most, readers prefer, because it is so readily accessible. Except at its most brilliantly stylized, as in certain short fictions of Ernest Hemingway, the meanings and significance of the Anderson voice lie on the surface of narrative. Which is not to say that they are, or need be, superficial, as in Anderson's exemplary Winesburg, Ohio *(1919), from which "The Strength of God" is taken, and certain of his much-anthologized short stories like "The Egg," "I Want to Know Why," and "Death in the Woods."*

Anderson, born in southern Ohio of a nomadic family, became a writer in early middle age after a business career that seems to have pushed him into a nervous collapse. The author of a number of novels, including Windy McPherson's Son *(1916) and* Poor White *(1920), Anderson most realized his vision as a writer of short stories. These are collected in* The Triumph of the Egg *(1921),* Horses and Men *(1923), and* Death in the Woods and Other Stories *(1933). But his masterpiece remains* Winesburg, Ohio, *that "Book of the Grotesque" sui generis.*

The Strength of God

The Reverend Curtis Hartman was pastor of the Presbyterian Church of Winesburg, and had been in that position ten years. He was forty years old, and by his nature very silent and reticent. To preach, standing in the pulpit before the people, was always a hardship for him and from Wednesday morning until Saturday evening he thought of nothing but the two sermons that must be preached on Sunday. Early on Sunday morning he went into a little room called a study in the bell tower of the church and prayed. In his prayers there was one note that always predominated. "Give me strength and courage for Thy work, O Lord!" he plead, kneeling on the bare floor and bowing his head in the presence of the task that lay before him.

The Reverend Hartman was a tall man with a brown beard. His wife, a stout, nervous woman, was the daughter of a manufacturer of underwear at Cleveland, Ohio. The minister himself was rather a favorite in the town. The elders of the church liked him because he was quiet and unpretentious and Mrs. White, the banker's wife, thought him scholarly and refined.

The Presbyterian Church held itself somewhat aloof from the other churches of Winesburg. It was larger and more imposing and its minister was better paid. He even had a carriage of his own and on summer evenings sometimes drove about town with his wife. Through Main Street and up and down Buckeye Street he went, bowing gravely to the people, while his wife, afire with secret pride, looked at him out of the corners of her eyes and worried lest the horse become frightened and run away.

For a good many years after he came to Winesburg things went well with Curtis Hartman. He was not one to arouse keen enthusiasm among the worshippers in his church but on the other hand he made no enemies. In reality he was much in earnest and sometimes suffered prolonged periods of remorse because he could not go crying the word of God in the highways and byways of the town. He wondered if the flame of the spirit really burned in him and dreamed of a day when a strong sweet new current of power would come like a great wind into his voice and his soul and the people would tremble before the spirit of God made manifest in him. "I am a poor stick and that will never really happen to me," he mused dejectedly and then a patient smile lit up his features. "Oh well, I suppose I'm doing well enough," he added philosophically.

The room in the bell tower of the church, where on Sunday mornings the minister prayed for an increase in him of the power of God, had but one window. It was long and narrow and swung outward on a hinge like a door. On the window, made of little leaded panes, was a design showing the Christ laying his hand upon the head of a child. One Sunday morning in the summer as he sat by his desk in the room with a large Bible opened before him, and the sheets of his sermon scattered about, the minister was shocked to see, in the upper room of the house next door, a woman lying in her bed and smoking a cigarette while she read a book. Curtis Hartman went on tiptoe to the window and closed it softly. He was horror stricken at the thought of a woman smoking and trembled also to think that his eyes, just raised from the pages of the book of God, had looked upon the bare shoulders and white throat of a woman. With his brain in a whirl he went down into the pulpit and preached a long sermon without once thinking of his gestures or his voice. The sermon attracted unusual attention because of its power and clearness. "I wonder if she is listening, if my voice is carrying a message into her soul," he thought and began to hope that on future Sunday mornings he might be able to say words that would touch and awaken the woman apparently far gone in secret sin.

The house next door to the Presbyterian Church, through the windows of which the minister had seen the sight that had so upset him, was occupied by two women. Aunt Elizabeth Swift, a grey competent-looking widow with money in the Winesburg National Bank, lived there with her daughter Kate Swift, a school teacher. The school teacher was thirty years old and had a neat trim-looking figure. She had few friends and bore a reputation of having a sharp tongue. When he began to think about her, Curtis Hartman remembered that she had been to Europe and had lived for two years in New York City. "Perhaps after all her smoking means nothing," he thought. He began to remember that when he was a student in college and occasionally read novels, good, although somewhat worldly women, had smoked through the pages of a book that had once fallen into his hands. With a rush of new determination he worked on his sermons all through the week and forgot, in his zeal to reach the ears and the soul of this new listener, both his embarrassment in the pulpit and the necessity of prayer in the study on Sunday mornings.

Reverend Hartman's experience with women had been somewhat limited. He was the son of a wagon maker from Muncie, Indiana, and had worked his way through college. The daughter of the underwear manufacturer had boarded in a house where he lived during his school days and he had married her after a formal and prolonged courtship, carried on for the most part by the girl herself. On his marriage day the underwear manufacturer had given his daughter five thousand dollars and he promised to leave her at least twice that amount in his will. The minister had thought himself fortunate in marriage and had never permitted himself to think of other women. He did not want to think of other women. What he wanted was to do the work of God quietly and earnestly.

In the soul of the minister a struggle awoke. From wanting to reach the ears of Kate Swift, and through his sermons to delve into her soul, he began to want also to look again at the figure lying white and quiet in the bed. On a Sunday morning when he could not sleep because of his thoughts he arose and went to walk in the streets. When he had gone along Main Street almost to the old Richmond place he stopped and picking up a stone rushed off to the room in the bell tower. With the stone he broke out a corner of the window and then locked the door and sat down at the desk before the open Bible to wait. When the shade of the window to Kate Swift's room was raised he could see, through the hole, directly into her bed, but she was not there. She also had arisen and had gone for a walk and the hand that raised the shade was the hand of Aunt Elizabeth Swift.

The minister almost wept with joy at this deliverance from the carnal desire to "peep" and went back to his own house praising God. In an ill moment he forgot, however, to stop the hole in the window. The piece of glass broken out at the corner of the window just nipped off the bare heel of the boy standing motionless and looking with rapt eyes into the face of the Christ.

Curtis Hartman forgot his sermon on that Sunday morning. He talked to his congregation and in his talk said that it was a mistake for people to think of their minister as a man set aside and intended by nature to lead a blameless life. "Out of my own experience I know that we, who are the ministers of God's word, are beset by the same temptations that assail you," he declared. "I have been tempted and have surrendered to temptation. It is only the hand of God, placed beneath my head, that has raised me up. As he has raised me so also will he raise you. Do not despair. In your hour of sin raise your eyes to the skies and you will be again and again saved."

Resolutely the minister put the thoughts of the woman in the bed out of his mind and began to be something like a lover in the presence of his wife. One evening when they drove out together he turned the horse out of Buckeye Street and in the darkness on Gospel Hill, above Waterworks Pond, put his arm about Sarah Hartman's waist. When he had eaten breakfast in the morning and was ready to retire to his study at the back of his house he went around the table and kissed his wife on the cheek. When thoughts of Kate Swift came into his head, he smiled and raised his eyes to the skies. "Intercede for me, Master," he muttered, "keep me in the narrow path intent on Thy work."

And now began the real struggle in the soul of the brown-bearded minister. By chance he discovered that Kate Swift was in the habit of lying in her bed in the evenings and reading a book. A lamp stood on a table by the side of the bed and the light streamed down upon her white shoulders and bare throat. On the evening when he made the discovery the minister sat at the desk in the study from nine until after eleven and when her light was put out stumbled out of the church to spend two more hours walking and praying in the streets. He did not want to kiss the shoulders and the throat of Kate Swift and had not allowed his mind to dwell on such thoughts. He did not know what he wanted. "I am God's child and he must save me from myself," he cried, in the darkness under the trees as he wandered in the streets. By a tree he stood and looked at the sky that was covered with hurrying clouds. He began to talk to God intimately and closely. "Please, Father, do not forget me. Give me power to go to-morrow and repair the hole in the window. Lift my eyes again to the skies. Stay with me, Thy servant, in his hour of need."

Up and down through the silent streets walked the minister and for days and weeks his soul was troubled. He could not understand the temptation that had come to him nor could he fathom the reason for its coming. In a way he began to blame God, saying to himself that he had tried to keep his feet in the true path and had not run about seeking sin. “Through my days as a young man and all through my life here I have gone quietly about my work,” he declared. “Why now should I be tempted? What have I done that this burden should be laid on me?”

Three times during the early fall and winter of that year Curtis Hartman crept out of his house to the room in the bell tower to sit in the darkness looking at the figure of Kate Swift lying in her bed and later went to walk and pray in the streets. He could not understand himself. For weeks he would go along scarcely thinking of the school teacher and telling himself that he had conquered the carnal desire to look at her body. And then something would happen. As he sat in the study of his own house, hard at work on a sermon, he would become nervous and begin to walk up and down the room. “I will go out into the streets,” he told himself and even as he let himself in at the church door he persistently denied to himself the cause of his being there. “I will not repair the hole in the window and I will train myself to come here at night and sit in the presence of this woman without raising my eyes. I will not be defeated in this thing. The Lord has devised this temptation as a test of my soul and I will grope my way out of darkness into the light of righteousness.”

One night in January when it was bitter cold and snow lay deep on the streets of Winesburg Curtis Hartman paid his last visit to the room in the bell tower of the church. It was past nine o’clock when he left his own house and he set out so hurriedly that he forgot to put on his overshoes. In Main Street no one was abroad but Hop Higgins the night watchman and in the whole town no one was awake but the watchman and young George Willard, who sat in the office of the *Winesburg Eagle* trying to write a story. Along the street to the church went the minister, plowing through the drifts and thinking that this time he would utterly give way to sin. “I want to look at the woman and to think of kissing her shoulders and I am going to let myself think what I choose,” he declared bitterly and tears came into his eyes. He began to think that he would get out of the ministry and try some other way of life. “I shall go to some city and get into business," he declared. "If my nature is such that I cannot resist sin, I shall give myself over to sin. At least I shall not be a hypocrite, preaching the word of God with my mind thinking of the shoulders and neck of a woman who does not belong to me."

It was cold in the room of the bell tower of the church on that January night and almost as soon as he came into the room Curtis Hartman knew that if he stayed he would be ill. His feet were wet from tramping in the snow and there was no fire. In the room in the house next door Kate Swift had not yet appeared. With grim determination the man sat down to wait. Sitting in the chair and gripping the edge of the desk on which lay the Bible he stared into the darkness thinking the blackest thoughts of his life. He thought of his wife and for the moment almost hated her. "She has always been ashamed of passion and has cheated me," he thought. "Man has a right to expect living passion and beauty in a woman. He has no right to forget that he is an animal and in me there is something that is Greek. I will throw off the woman of my bosom and seek other women. I will besiege this school teacher. I will fly in the face of all men and if I am a creature of carnal lusts I will live then for my lusts."

The distracted man trembled from head to foot, partly from cold, partly from the struggle in which he was engaged. Hours passed and a fever assailed his body. His throat began to hurt and his teeth chattered. His feet on the study floor felt like two cakes of ice. Still he would not give up. "I will see this woman and will think the thoughts I have never dared to think," he told himself, gripping the edge of the desk and waiting.

Curtis Hartman came near dying from the effects of that night of waiting in the church, and also he found in the thing that happened what he took to be the way of life for him. On other evenings when he had waited he had not been able to see, through the little hole in the glass, any part of the school teacher's room except that occupied by her bed. In the darkness he had waited until the woman suddenly appeared sitting in the bed in her white night-robe. When the light was turned up she propped herself up among the pillows and read a book. Sometimes she smoked one of the cigarettes. Only her bare shoulders and throat were visible.

On the January night, after he had come near dying with cold and after his mind had two or three times actually slipped away into an odd land of fantasy so that he had by an exercise of will power to force himself back into consciousness, Kate Swift appeared. In the room next door a lamp was lighted and the waiting man stared into an empty bed. Then upon the bed before his eyes a naked woman threw herself. Lying face downward she wept and beat with her fists upon the pillow. With a final outburst of weeping she half arose, and in the presence of the man who had waited to look and to think thoughts the woman of sin began to pray. In the lamplight her figure, slim and strong, looked like the figure of the boy in the presence of the Christ on the leaded window.

Curtis Hartman never remembered how he got out of the church. With a cry he arose, dragging the heavy desk along the floor. The Bible fell, making a great clatter in the silence. When the light in the house next door went out he stumbled down the stairway and into the street. Along the street he went and ran in at the door of the *Winesburg Eagle*. To George Willard, who was tramping up and down in the office undergoing a struggle of his own, he began to talk half incoherently. "The ways of God are beyond human understanding," he cried, running in quickly and closing the door. He began to advance upon the young man, his eyes glowing and his voice ringing with fervor. "I have found the light," he cried. "After ten years in this town, God has manifested himself to me in the body of a woman." His voice dropped and he began to whisper. "I did not understand," he said. "What I took to be a trial of my soul was only a preparation for a new and more beautiful fervor of the spirit. God has appeared to me in the person of Kate Swift, the school teacher, kneeling naked on a bed. Do you know Kate Swift? Although she may not be aware of it, she is an instrument of God, bearing the message of truth."

Reverend Curtis Hartman turned and ran out of the office. At the door he stopped, and after looking up and down the deserted street, turned again to George Willard. "I am delivered. Have no fear." He held up a bleeding fist for the young man to see. "I smashed the glass of the window," he cried. "Now it will have to be wholly replaced. The strength of God was in me and I broke it with my fist."

JACK LONDON
(1876–1916)

Hardly a refined literary theorist like Henry James, Jack London was as determined as James to make himself into a writer of significance, influence, and wealth. The prodigious regimen to which London subjected himself as a young man gave him an autodidact's stubborn faith in his own powers, which seems to have deserted him only at the very end of his foreshortened, feverishly productive career. Boasting that he wrote solely for money, London forced himself to produce a minimum of one thousand publishable words a day, six days a week; he died an alcoholic and a probable suicide, aged forty, by which time he was the highest paid American writer of the era and a world-renowned literary celebrity.

Born in San Francisco to an astrologer and a spiritualist-music teacher, Jack London supported himself, from earliest youth, in a variety of menial jobs. He traveled widely and restlessly, spending the winter of 1897–98 in the Klondike in a futile search for gold; he served time in jail for vagrancy; he became a disciple of Marx on the one hand and of Nietzsche and Darwin on the other. His obsession was the dramatization—in often brutally graphic terms, as in "In a Far Country" and the famous "To Build a Fire"—of man's fate: to be a thinking creature of flesh in a supremely indifferent universe.

When London writes most vividly and powerfully, there is no one quite like him. Perhaps because his most characteristic works do not lend themselves to literary analysis, he tends to be undervalued in this country. Throughout the world, however, his most popular titles remain The Call of the Wild *(1903),* The Sea-Wolf *(1904),* White Fang *(1906), and the autobiographical* Martin Eden *(1909).*

In a Far Country

When a man journeys into a far country, he must be prepared to forget many of the things he has learned, and to acquire such customs as are inherent with existence in the new land; he must abandon the old ideals and the old gods, and oftentimes he must reverse the very codes by which his conduct has hitherto been shaped. To those who have the protean faculty of adaptability, the novelty of such change may even be a source of pleasure; but to those who happen to be hardened to the ruts in which they were created, the pressure of the altered environment is unbearable, and they chafe in body and in spirit under the new restrictions which they do not understand. This chafing is bound to act and react, producing divers evils and leading to various misfortunes. It were better for the man who cannot fit himself to the new groove to return to his own country; if he delay too long, he will surely die.

The man who turns his back upon the comforts of an elder civilization, to face the savage youth, the primordial simplicity of the North, may estimate success at an inverse ratio to the quantity and quality of his hopelessly fixed habits. He will soon discover, if he be a fit candidate, that the material habits are the less important. The exchange of such things as a dainty menu for rough fare, of the stiff leather shoe for the soft, shapeless moccasin, of the feather bed for a couch in the snow, is after all a very easy matter. But his pinch will come in learning properly to shape his mind's attitude toward all things, and especially toward his fellow man. For the courtesies of ordinary life, he must substitute unselfishness, forbearance, and tolerance. Thus, and thus only, can he gain that pearl of great price—true comradeship. He must not say "Thank you"; he must mean it without opening his mouth, and prove it by responding in kind. In short, he must substitute the deed for the word, the spirit for the letter.

When the world rang with the tale of Arctic gold, and the lure of the North gripped the heartstrings of men, Carter Weatherbee threw up his snug clerkship, turned the half of his savings over to his wife, and with the remainder bought an outfit. There was no romance in his nature—the bondage of commerce had crushed all that; he was simply tired ceaseless grind, and wished to risk great hazards in view of corresponding returns. Like many another fool, disdaining the old trails used by the Northland pioneers for a score of years, he hurried to Edmonton in the spring of the year; and there, unluckily for his soul's welfare, he allied himself with a party of men.

There was nothing unusual about this party, except its plans. Even its goal, like that of all the other parties, was the Klondike. But the route it had mapped out to attain that goal took away the breath of the hardiest native, born and bred to the vicissitudes of the Northwest. Even Jacques Baptiste, born of a Chippewa woman and a renegade *voyageur* (having raised his first whimpers in a deerskin lodge north of the sixty-fifth parallel, and had the same hushed by blissful sucks of raw tallow), was surprised. Though he sold his services to them and agreed to travel even to the never-opening ice, he shook his head ominously whenever his advice was asked.

Percy Cuthfert's evil star must have been in the ascendant, for he, too, joined this company of argonauts. He was an ordinary man, with a bank account as deep as his culture, which is saying a good deal. He had no reason to embark on such a venture—no reason in the world, save that he suffered from an abnormal development of sentimentality. He mistook this for the true spirit of romance and adventure. Many another man has done the like, and made as fatal a mistake.

The first break-up of spring found the party following the ice-run of Elk River. It was an imposing fleet, for the outfit was large, and they were accompanied by a disreputable contingent of half-breed *voyageurs* with their women and children. Day in and day out, they labored with the bateaux and canoes, fought mosquitoes and other kindred pests, or sweated and swore at the portages. Severe toil like this lays a man naked to the very roots of his soul, and ere Lake Athabasca was lost in the south, each member of the party had hoisted his true colors.

The two shirks and chronic grumblers were Carter Weatherbee and Percy Cuthfert. The whole party complained less of its aches and pains than did either of them. Not once did they volunteer for the thousand and one petty duties of the camp. A bucket of water to be brought, an extra armful of wood to be chopped, the dishes to be washed and wiped, a search to be made through the outfit for some suddenly indispensable article—and these two effete scions of civilization discovered sprains or blisters requiring instant attention. They were the first to turn in at night, with score of tasks yet undone; the last to turn out in the morning, when the start should be in readiness before the breakfast was begun. They were the first to fall to at meal-time, the last to have a hand in the cooking; the first to dive for a slim delicacy, the last to discover they had added to their own another man's share. If they toiled at the oars, they slyly cut the water at each stroke and allowed the boat's momentum to float up the blade. They thought nobody noticed; but their comrades swore under their breaths and grew to hate them, while Jacques Baptiste sneered openly and damned them from morning till night. But Jacques Baptiste was no gentleman.

At the Great Slave, Hudson Bay dogs were purchased, and the fleet sank to the guards with its added burden of dried fish and pemican. Then canoe and bateau answered to the swift current of the Mackenzie, and they plunged into the Great Barren Ground. Every likely-looking "feeder" was prospected, but the elusive "pay-dirt" danced ever to the north. At the Great Bear, overcome by the common dread of the Unknown Lands, their *voyageurs* began to desert, and Fort of Good Hope saw the last and bravest bending to the tow-lines as they bucked the current down which they had so treacherously glided. Jacques Baptiste alone remained. Had he not sworn to travel even to the never-opening ice?

The lying charts, compiled in main from hearsay, were now constantly consulted. And they felt the need of hurry, for the sun had already passed its northern solstice and was leading the winter south again. Skirting the shores of the bay, where the Mackenzie disembogues into the Arctic Ocean, they entered the mouth of the Little Peel River. Then began the arduous up-stream toil, and the two Incapables fared worse than ever. Tow-line and pole, paddle and tump-line, rapids and portages—such tortures served to give the one a deep disgust for great hazards, and printed for the other a fiery text on the true romance of adventure. One day they waxed mutinous, and being vilely cursed by Jacques Baptiste, turned, as worms sometimes will. But the half-breed thrashed the twain, and sent them, bruised and bleeding, about their work. It was the first time either had been man-handled.

Abandoning their river craft at the headwaters of the Little Peel, they consumed the rest of the summer in the great portage over the Mackenzie watershed to the West Rat. This little stream fed the Porcupine, which in turn joined the Yukon where that mighty highway of the North countermarches on the Arctic Circle. But they had lost in the race with winter, and one day they tied their rafts to the thick eddy-ice and hurried their goods ashore. That night the river jammed and broke several times; the following morning it had fallen asleep for good.

"We can't be more'n four hundred miles from the Yukon," concluded Sloper, multiplying his thumb nails by the scale of the map. The council, in which the two Incapables had whined to excellent disadvantage, was drawing to a close.

"Hudson Bay Post, long time ago. No use um now." Jacques Baptiste's father had made the trip for the Fur Company in the old days, incidentally marking the trail with a couple of frozen toes.

"Sufferin' cracky!" cried another of the party, "No whites?"

"Nary white," Sloper sententiously affirmed; "but it's only five hundred more up the Yukon to Dawson. Call it a rough thousand from here."

Weatherbee and Cuthfert groaned in chorus.

"How long'll that take, Baptiste?"

The half-breed figured for a moment. "Workum like hell, no man play out, ten—twenty—forty—fifty days. Um babies come" (designating the Incapables), "no can tell. Mebbe when hell freeze over; mebbe not then."

The manufacture of snowshoes and moccasins ceased. Somebody called the name of an absent member, who came out of an ancient cabin at the edge of the camp-fire and joined them. The cabin was one of the many mysteries which lurk in the vast recesses of the North. Built when and by whom, no man could tell. Two graves in the open, piled high with stones, perhaps contained the secret of those early wanderers. But whose hand had piled the stones?

The moment had come. Jacques Baptiste paused in the fitting of a harness and pinned the struggling dog in the snow. The cook made mute protest for delay, threw a handful of bacon into a noisy pot of beans, then came to attention. Sloper rose to his feet. His body was a ludicrous contrast to the healthy physiques of the Incapables. Yellow and weak, fleeing from a South American fever-hole, he had not broken his flight across the zones, and was still able to toil with men. His weight was probably ninety pounds, with the heavy hunting-knife thrown in, and his grizzled hair told of a prime which had ceased to be. The fresh young muscles of either Weatherbee or Cuthfert were equal to ten times the endeavor of his; yet he could walk them into the earth in a day's journey. And all this day he had whipped his stronger comrades into venturing a thousand miles of the stiffest hardship man can conceive. He was the incarnation of the unrest of his race, and the old Teutonic stubbornness, dashed with the quick grasp and action of the Yankee, held the flesh in the bondage of the spirit.

"All those in favor of going on with the dogs as soon as the ice sets, say ay."

"Ay!" rang out eight voices—voices destined to string a trail of oaths along many a hundred miles of pain.

"Contrary minded?"

"No!" For the first time the Incapables were united without some compromise of personal interests.

"And what are you going to do about it?" Weatherbee added belligerently.

"Majority rule! Majority rule!" clamored the rest of the party.

"I know the expedition is liable to fall through if you don't come," Sloper replied sweetly; "but I guess, if we try real hard, we can manage to do without you. What do you say, boys?"

The sentiment was cheered to the echo.

"But I say, you know," Cuthfert ventured apprehensively; "what's a chap like me to do?"

"Ain't you coming with us?"

"No-o."

"Then do as you damn well please. We won't have nothing to say."

"Kind o' calkilate yuh might settle it with that canoodlin' pardner of yourn," suggested a heavy-going Westerner from the Dakotas, at the same time pointing out Weatherbee. "He'll be shore to ask yuh what yur a-goin' to do when it comes to cookin' an' gatherin' the wood."

"Then we'll consider it all arranged," concluded Sloper. "We'll pull out to-morrow, if we camp within five miles—just to get everything in running order and remember if we've forgotten anything."

The sleds groaned by on their steel-shod runners, and the dogs strained low in the harnesses in which they were born to die. Jacques Baptiste paused by the side of Sloper to get a last glimpse of the cabin. The smoke curled up pathetically from the Yukon stovepipe. The two Incapables were watching them from the doorway.

Sloper laid his hand on the other's shoulder.

"Jacques Baptiste, did you ever hear of the Kilkenny cats?"

The half-breed shook his head.

"Well, my friend and good comrade, the Kilkenny cats fought till neither hide, nor hair, nor yowl, was left. You understand?—till nothing was left. Very good. Now, these two men don't like work. They'll be all alone in that cabin all winter—a mighty long, dark winter. Kilkenny cats—well?"

The Frenchman in Baptiste shrugged his shoulders, but the Indian in him was silent. Nevertheless, it was an eloquent shrug, pregnant with prophecy.

Things prospered in the little cabin at first. The rough badinage of their comrades had made Weatherbee and Cuthfert conscious of the mutual responsibility which had devolved upon them; besides, there was not so much work after all for two healthy men. And the removal of the cruel whiphand, or in other words the bulldozing half-breed, had brought with it a joyous reaction. At first, each strove to outdo the other, and they performed petty tasks with an unction which would have opened the eyes of their comrades who were now wearing out bodies and souls on the Long Trail.

All care was banished. The forest, which shouldered in upon them from three sides, was an inexhaustible woodyard. A few yards from their door slept the Porcupine, and a hole through its winter robe formed a bubbling spring of water, crystal clear and painfully cold. But they soon grew to find fault with even that. The hole would persist in freezing up, and thus gave them many a miserable hour of ice-chopping. The unknown builders of the cabin had extended the sidelogs so as to support a cache at the rear. In this was stored the bulk of the party's provisions. Food there was, without stint, for three times the men who were fated to live upon it. But the most of it was of the kind which built up brawn and sinew, but did not tickle the palate. True, there was sugar in plenty for two ordinary men; but these two were little else than children. They early discovered the virtues of hot water judiciously saturated with sugar, and they prodigally swam their flapjacks and soaked their crusts in the rich, white syrup. Then coffee and tea, and especially the dried fruits, made disastrous inroads upon it. The first words they had were over the sugar question. And it is a really serious thing when two men, wholly dependent upon each other for company, begin to quarrel.

Weatherbee loved to discourse blatantly on politics, while Cuthfert, who had been prone to clip his coupons and let the commonwealth jog on as best it might, either ignored the subject or delivered himself of startling epigrams. But the clerk was too obtuse to appreciate the clever shaping of thought, and this waste of ammunition irritated Cuthfert. He had been used to blinding people by his brilliancy, and it worked him quite a hardship, this loss of an audience. He felt personally aggrieved and unconsciously held his muttonhead companion responsible for it.

Save existence, they had nothing in common—came in touch on no single point. Weatherbee was a clerk who had known naught but clerking all his life; Cuthfert was a master of arts, a dabbler in oils, and had written not a little. The one was a lower-class man who considered himself a gentleman, and the other was a gentleman who knew himself to be such. From this it may be remarked that a man can be a gentleman without possessing the first instinct of true comradeship. The clerk was as sensuous as the other was aesthetic, and his love adventures, told at great length and chiefly coined from his imagination, affected the supersensitive master of arts in the same way as so many whiffs of sewer gas. He deemed the clerk a filthy, uncultured brute, whose place was in the muck with the swine, and told him so; and he was reciprocally informed that he was a milk-and-water sissy and a cad. Weatherbee could not have defined "cad" for his life; but it satisfied its purpose, which after all seems the main point in life.

Weatherbee flatted every third note and sang such songs as "The Boston Burglar" and "The Handsome Cabin Boy," for hours at a time, while Cuthfert wept with rage, till he could stand it no longer and fled into the outer cold. But there was no escape. The intense frost could not be endured for long at a time, and the little cabin crowded them—beds, stove, table, and all—into a space of ten by twelve. The very presence of either became a personal affront to the other, and they lapsed into sullen silences which increased in length and strength as the days went by. Occasionally, the flash of an eye or the curl of a lip got the better of them, though they strove to wholly ignore each other during these mute periods. And a great wonder sprang up in the breast of each, as to how God had ever come to create the other.

With little to do, time became an intolerable burden to them. This naturally made them still lazier. They sank into a physical lethargy which there was no escaping, and which made them rebel at the performance of the smallest chore. One morning when it was his turn to cook the common breakfast, Weatherbee rolled out of his blankets, and to the snoring of his companion, lighted first the slush-lamp and then the fire. The kettles were frozen hard, and there was no water in the cabin with which to wash. But he did not mind that. Waiting for it to thaw, he sliced the bacon and plunged into the hateful task of bread-making. Cuthfert had been slyly watching through his half-closed lids. Consequently there was a scene, in which they fervently blessed each other, and agreed, thenceforth, that each do his own cooking. A week later, Cuthfert neglected his morning ablutions, but none the less complacently ate the meal which he had cooked. Weatherbee grinned. After that the foolish custom of washing passed out of their lives.

As the sugar-pile and other little luxuries dwindled, they began to be afraid they were not getting their proper shares, and in order that they might not be robbed, they fell to gorging themselves. The luxuries suffered in this gluttonous contest, as did also the men. In the absence of fresh vegetables and exercise, their blood became impoverished, and a loathsome, purplish rash crept over their bodies. Yet they refused to heed the warning. Next, their muscles and joints began to swell, the flesh turning black, while their mouths, gums, and lips took on the color of rich cream. Instead of being drawn together by their misery, each gloated over the other's symptoms as the scurvy took its course.

They lost all regard for personal appearance, and for that matter, common decency. The cabin became a pigpen, and never once were the beds made or fresh pine boughs laid underneath. Yet they could not keep to their blankets, as they would have wished; for the frost was inexorable, and the fire box consumed much fuel. The hair of their heads and faces grew long and shaggy, while their garments would have disgusted a ragpicker. But they did not care. They were sick, and there was no one to see; besides, it was very painful to move about.

To all this was added a new trouble—the Fear of the North. This Fear was the joint child of the Great Cold and the Great Silence, and was born in the darkness of December, when the sun dipped below the horizon for good. It affected them according to their natures. Weatherbee fell prey to the grosser superstitions, and did his best to resurrect the spirits which slept in the forgotten graves. It was a fascinating thing, and in his dreams they came to him from out of the cold, and snuggled into his blankets, and told him of their toils and troubles ere they died. He shrank away from the clammy contact as they drew closer and twined their frozen limbs about him, and when they whispered in his ear of things to come, the cabin rang with his frightened shrieks. Cuthfert did not understand—for they no longer spoke—and when thus awakened he invariably grabbed for his revolver. Then he would sit up in bed, shivering nervously, with the weapon trained on the unconscious dreamer. Cuthfert deemed the man going mad, and so came to fear for his life.

His own malady assumed a less concrete form. The mysterious artisan who had laid the cabin, log by log, had pegged a wind-vane to the ridge-pole. Cuthfert noticed it always pointed south, and one day, irritated by its steadfastness of purpose, he turned it toward the east. He watched eagerly, but never a breath came by to disturb it. Then he turned the vane to the north, swearing never again to touch it till the wind did blow. But the air frightened him with its unearthly calm, and he often rose in the middle of the night to see if the vane had veered—ten degrees would have satisfied him. But no, it poised above him as unchangeable as fate. His imagination ran riot, till it became to him a fetich. Sometimes he followed the path it pointed across the dismal dominions, and allowed his soul to become saturated with the Fear. He dwelt upon the unseen and the unknown till the burden of eternity appeared to be crushing him. Everything in the Northland had that crushing effect—the absence of life and motion; the darkness; the infinite peace of the brooding land; the ghastly silence, which made the echo of each heart-beat a sacrilege; the solemn forest which seemed to guard an awful, inexpressible something, which neither word nor thought could compass.

The world he had so recently left, with its busy nations and great enterprises, seemed very far away. Recollections occasionally obtruded—recollections of marts and galleries and crowded thoroughfares, of evening dress and social functions, of good men and dear women he had known—but they were dim memories of a life he had lived long centuries agone, on some other planet. This phantasm was the Reality. Standing beneath the wind-vane, his eyes fixed on the polar skies, he could not bring himself to realize that the Southland really existed, that at that very moment it was a-roar with life and action. There was no Southland, no men being born of women, no giving and taking in marriage. Beyond his bleak sky-line there stretched vast solitudes, and beyond these still vaster solitudes. There were no lands of sunshine, heavy with the perfume of flowers. Such things were only old dreams of paradise. The sun lands of the West and the spice lands of the East, the smiling Arcadias and blissful Islands of the Blest—ha! ha! His laughter split the void and shocked him with its unwonted sound. There was no sun. This was the Universe, dead and cold and dark, and he its only citizen. Weatherbee? At such moments Weatherbee did not count. He was a Caliban, a monstrous phantom, fettered to him for untold ages, the penalty of some forgotten crime.

He lived with Death among the dead, emasculated by the sense of his own insignificance, crushed by the passive mastery of the slumbering ages. The magnitude of all things appalled him. Everything partook of the superlative save himself—the perfect cessation of wind and motion, the immensity of the snow-covered wildness, the height of the sky and the depth of the silence. That wind-vane—if it would only move. If a thunderbolt would fall, or the forest flare up in flame. The rolling up of the heavens as a scroll, the crash of Doom—anything, anything! But no, nothing moved; the Silence crowded in, and the Fear of the North laid icy fingers on his heart.

Once, like another Crusoe, by the edge of the river he came upon a track—the faint tracery of a snowshoe rabbit on the delicate snow-crust. It was a revelation. There was life in the Northland. He would follow it, look upon it, gloat over it. He forgot his swollen muscles, plunging through the deep snow in an ecstasy of anticipation. The forest swallowed him up, and the brief midday twilight vanished; but he pursued his quest till exhausted nature asserted itself and laid him helpless in the snow. There he groaned and cursed his folly, and knew the track to be the fancy of his brain; and late that night he dragged himself into the cabin on hands and knees, his cheeks frozen and a strange numbness about his feet. Weatherbee grinned malevolently, but made no offer to help him. He thrust needles into his toes and thawed them out by the stove. A week later mortification set in.

But the clerk had his own troubles. The dead men came out of their graves more frequently now, and rarely left him, waking or sleeping. He grew to wait and dread their coming, never passing the twin cairns without a shudder. One night they came to him in his sleep and led him forth to an appointed task. Frightened into inarticulate horror, he awoke between the heaps of stones and fled wildly to the cabin. But he had lain there for some time, for his feet and cheeks were also frozen.

Sometimes he became frantic at their insistent presence, and danced about the cabin, cutting the empty air with an axe, and smashing everything within reach. During these ghostly encounters, Cuthfert huddled into his blankets and followed the madman about with a cocked revolver, ready to shoot him if he came too near. But, recovering from one of these spells, the clerk noticed the weapon trained upon him. His suspicions were aroused, and thenceforth he, too, lived in fear of his life. They watched each other closely after that, and faced about in startled fright whenever either passed behind the other's back. The apprehensiveness became a mania which controlled them even in their sleep. Through mutual fear they tacitly let the slush-lamp burn all night, and saw to a plentiful supply of bacon-grease before retiring. The slightest movement on the part of one was sufficient to arouse the other, and many a still watch their gazes countered as they shook beneath their blankets with fingers on the trigger-guards.

What with the Fear of the North, the mental strain, and the ravages of the disease, they lost all semblance of humanity, taking on the appearance of wild beasts, hunted and desperate. Their cheeks and noses, as an aftermath of the freezing, had turned black. Their frozen toes had begun to drop away at the first and second joints. Every movement brought pain, but the fire box was insatiable, wringing a ransom of torture from their miserable bodies. Day in, day out, it demanded its food—a veritable pound of flesh—and they dragged themselves into the forest to chop wood on their knees. Once, crawling thus in search of dry sticks, unknown to each other they entered a thicket from opposite sides. Suddenly, without warning, two peering death's-heads confronted each other. Suffering had so transformed them that recognition was impossible. They sprang to their feet, shrieking with terror, and dashed away on their mangled stumps; and falling at the cabin's door, they clawed and scratched like demons till they discovered their mistake.

Occasionally they lapsed normal, and during one of these sane intervals, the chief bone of contention, the sugar, had been divided equally between them. They guarded their separate sacks, stored up in the cache, with jealous eyes; for there were but a few cupfuls left, and they were totally devoid of faith in each other. But one day Cuthfert made a mistake. Hardly able to move, sick with pain, with his head swimming and eyes blinded, he crept into the cache, sugar canister in hand, and mistook Weather bee's sack for his own.

January had been born but a few days when this occurred. The sun had some time since passed its lowest southern declination, and at meridian now threw flaunting streaks of yellow light upon the northern sky. On the day following his mistake with the sugar-bag, Cuthfert found himself feeling better, both in body and in spirit. As noontime drew near and the day brightened, he dragged himself outside to feast on the evanescent glow, which was to him an earnest of the sun's future intentions. Weatherbee was also feeling somewhat better, and crawled out beside him. They propped themselves in the snow beneath the moveless windvane, and waited.

The stillness of death was about them. In other climes, when nature falls into such moods, there is a subdued air of expectancy, a waiting for some small voice to take up the broken strain. Not so in the North. The two men had lived seeming eons in this ghostly peace. They could remember no song of the past; they could conjure no song of the future. This unearthly calm had always been—the tranquil silence of eternity.

Their eyes were fixed upon the north. Unseen, behind their backs, behind the towering mountains to the south, the sun swept toward the zenith of another sky than theirs. Sole spectators of the mighty canvas, they watched the false dawn slowly grow. A faint flame began to glow and smoulder. It deepened in intensity, ringing the changes of reddish-yellow, purple, and saffron. So bright did it become that Cuthfert thought the sun must surely be behind it—a miracle, the sun rising in the north! Suddenly, without warning and without fading, the canvas was swept clean. There was no color in the sky. The light had gone out of the day. They caught their breaths in half-sobs. But lo! the air was a-glint with particles of scintillating frost, and there, to the north, the wind-vane lay in vague outline of the snow. A shadow! A shadow! It was exactly midday. They jerked their heads hurriedly to the south. A golden rim peeped over the mountain's snowy shoulder, smiled upon them an instant, then dipped from sight again.

There were tears in their eyes as they sought each other. A strange softening came over them. They felt irresistibly drawn toward each other. The sun was coming back again. It would be with them to-morrow, and the next day, and the next. And it would stay longer every visit, and a time would come when it would ride their heaven day and night, never once dropping below the sky-line. There would be no night. The ice-locked winter would be broken; the winds would blow and the forests answer; the land would bathe in the blessed sunshine, and life renew. Hand in hand, they would quit this horrid dream and journey back to the Southland. They lurched blindly forward, and their hands met—their poor maimed hands, swollen and distorted beneath their mittens.

But the promise was destined to remain unfulfilled. The Northland is the Northland, and men work out their souls by strange rules, which other men, who have not journeyed into far countries, cannot come to understand.

An hour later, Cuthfert put a pan of bread into the oven, and fell to speculating on what the surgeons could do with his feet when he got back. Home did not seem so very far away now. Weatherbee was rummaging in the cache. Of a sudden, he raised a whirlwind of blasphemy, which in turn ceased with startling abruptness. The other man had robbed his sugar-sack. Still, things might have happened differently, had not the two dead men come out from under the stones and hushed the hot words in his throat. They led him quite gently from the cache, which he forgot to close. That consummation was reached; that something they had whispered to him in his dreams was about to happen. They guided him gently, very gently, to the woodpile, where they put the axe in his hands. Then they helped him shove open the cabin door, and he felt sure they shut it after him—at least he heard it slam and the latch fall sharply into place. And he knew they were waiting just without, waiting for him to do his task.

"Carter! I say, Carter!"

Percy Cuthfert was frightened at the look on the clerk's face, and he made haste to put the table between them.

Carter Weatherbee followed, without haste and without enthusiasm. There was neither pity nor passion in his face, but rather the patient, stolid look of one who has certain work to do and goes about it methodically.

"I say, what's the matter?"

The clerk dodged back, cutting off his retreat to the door, but never opening his mouth.

"I say, Carter, I say; let's talk. There's a good chap."

The master of arts was thinking rapidly, now, shaping a skillful flank movement on the bed where his Smith & Wesson lay. Keeping his eyes on the madman, he rolled backward on the bunk, at the same time clutching the pistol.

"Carter!"

The powder flashed full in Weatherbee's face, but he swung his weapon and leaped forward. The axe bit deeply at the base of the spine, and Percy Cuthfert felt all consciousness of his lower limbs leave him. Then the clerk fell heavily upon him, clutching him by the throat with feeble fingers. The sharp bite of the axe had caused Cuthfert to drop the pistol, and as his lungs panted for release, he fumbled aimlessly for it among the blankets. Then he remembered. He slid a hand up the clerk's belt to the sheath-knife; and they drew very close to each other in that last clinch.

Percy Cuthfert felt his strength leave him. The lower portion of his body was useless. The inert weight of Weatherbee crushed him—crushed him and pinned him there like a bear under a trap. The cabin became filled with a familiar odor, and he knew the bread to be burning. Yet what did it matter? He would never need it. And there were all of six cupfuls of sugar in the cache—if he had foreseen this he would not have been so saving the last several days. Would the wind-vane ever move? Why not? Had he not seen the sun to-day? He would go and see. No; it was impossible to move. He had not thought the clerk so heavy a man.

How quickly the cabin cooled! The fire must be out. The cold was forcing in. It must be below zero already, and the ice creeping up the inside of the door. He could not see it, but his past experience enabled him to gauge its progress by the cabin's temperature. The lower hinge must be white ere now. Would the tale of this ever reach the world? How would his friends take it? They would read it over their coffee, most likely, and talk it over at the clubs. He could see them very clearly. "Poor Old Cuthfert," they murmured; "not such a bad sort of a chap, after all." He smiled at their eulogies, and passed on in search of a Turkish bath. It was the same old crowd upon the streets. Strange, they did not notice his moosehide moccasins and tattered German socks! He would take a cab. And after the bath a shave would not be bad. No; he would eat first. Steak, and potatoes, and green things how fresh it all was! And what was that? Squares of honey, streaming liquid amber! But why did they bring so much? Ha! ha! he could never eat it all. Shine! Why certainly. He put his foot on the box. The bootblack looked curiously up at him, and he remembered his moosehide moccasins and went away hastily.

Hark! The wind-vane must be surely spinning. No; a mere singing in his ears. That was all—a mere singing. The ice must have passed the latch by now. More likely the upper hinge was covered. Between the moss-chinked roof-poles, little points of frost began to appear. How slowly they grew! No; not so slowly. There was a new one, and there another. Two—three—four; they were coming too fast to count. There were two growing together. And there, a third had joined them. Why, there were no more spots. They had run together and formed a sheet.

Well, he would have company. If Gabriel ever broke the silence of the North, they would stand together, hand in hand, before the great White Throne. And God would judge them, God would judge them!

Then Percy Cuthfert closed his eyes and dropped off to sleep.

WILLIAM CARLOS WILLIAMS
(1883–1963)

Born in Rutherford, New Jersey, and long associated with the nearby city of Paterson, William Carlos Williams is, along with Langston Hughes, the only writer in this volume to be better known as a poet than a prose fiction writer. He was trained as a physician and set himself in opposition to the more self-consciously literary experiments of Modernism; his attentiveness to the speech that is actually spoken by Americans provided him, by his own account, with the forms and rhythms of his poetry. The spare, even laconic tone of Williams's short fictions, of which "The Girl with a Pimply Face" is exemplary, is in fact a poetic refinement of the Anderson-vernacular style, composed, like music, for the ear.

During the 1930s, William Carlos Williams was active in the establishment of little magazines, as well as in political events. His leftist sympathies would one day cost him the post of consultant in poetry at the Library of Congress. The "politics" of his art, however, is intensely personal, grounded in a celebration of American individualism, as his work amply demonstrates. He was a tireless, prolific writer, and among his major titles are the short story collections The Knife of the Times *(1932) and* Life Along the Passaic River *(1938); the novels* White Mule *(1937) and* In the Money *(1940); the experimental volume of poetry and prose* Spring and All *(1923); and the late works* Paterson *(1946–1958) and* Pictures from Brueghel *(1962). Very possibly underestimated as a writer of prose, Williams has been enormously influential as a poet in America.*

The Girl with a Pimply Face

One of the local druggists sent in the call: 50 Summer St., second floor, the door to the left. It's a baby they've just brought from the hospital. Pretty bad condition I should imagine. Do you want to make it? I think they've had somebody else but don't like him, he added as an afterthought.

It was half past twelve. I was just sitting down to lunch. Can't they wait till after office hours?

Oh I guess so. But they're foreigners and you know how they are. Make it as soon as you can. I guess the baby's pretty bad.

It was two-thirty when I got to the place, over a shop in the business part of town. One of those street doors between plate glass show windows. A narrow entry with smashed mail boxes on one side and a dark stair leading straight up. I'd been to the address a number of times during the past years to see various people who had lived there.

Going up I found no bell so I rapped vigorously on the wavy-glass door-panel to the left. I knew it to be the door to the kitchen, which occupied the rear of that apartment.

Come in, said a loud childish voice.

I opened the door and saw a lank haired girl of about fifteen standing chewing gum and eyeing me curiously from beside the kitchen table. The hair was coal black and one of her eyelids drooped a little as she spoke. Well, what do you want? she said. Boy, she was tough and no kidding but I fell for her immediately. There was that hard, straight thing about her that in itself gives an impression of excellence.

I'm the doctor, I said.

Oh, you're the doctor. The baby's inside. She looked at me. Want to see her?

Sure, that's what I came for. Where's your mother?

She's out. I don't know when she's coming back. But you can take a look at the baby if you want to.

All right. Let's see her.

She led the way into the bedroom, toward the front of the flat, one of the unlit rooms, the only windows being those in the kitchen and along the facade of the building.

There she is.

I looked on the bed and saw a small face, emaciated but quiet, unnaturally quiet, sticking out of the upper end of a tightly rolled bundle made by the rest of the baby encircled in a blue cotton blanket. The whole wasn't much larger than a good sized loaf of rye bread. Hands and everything were rolled up. Just the yellowish face showed, tightly hatted and framed around by a corner of the blanket.

What's the matter with her, I asked.

I dunno, said the girl as fresh as paint and seeming about as indifferent as though it had been no relative of hers instead of her sister. I looked at my informer very much amused and she looked back at me, chewing her gum vigorously, standing there her feet well apart. She cocked her head to one side and gave it to me straight in the eye, as much as to say, Well? I looked back at her. She had one of those small, squeezed up faces, snub nose, overhanging eyebrows, low brow and a terrible complexion, pimply and coarse.

When's your mother coming back do you *think,* I asked again.

Maybe in an hour. But maybe you'd better come some time when my father's here. He talks English. He ought to come in around five I guess.

But can't you tell me something about the baby? I hear it's been sick. Does it have a fever?

I dunno.

But has it diarrhoea, are its movements green?

Sure, she said, I guess so. It's been in the hospital but it got worse so my father brought it home today.

What are they feeding it?

A bottle. You can see that yourself. There it is.

There was a cold bottle of half finished milk lying on the coverlet the nipple end of it fallen behind the baby's head.

How old is she? It's a girl, did you say?

Yeah, it's a girl.

Your sister?

Sure. Want to examine it?

No thanks, I said. For the moment at least I had lost all interest in the baby. This young kid in charge of the house did something to me that I liked. She was just a child but nobody was putting anything over on her if she knew it, yet the real thing about her was the complete lack of the rotten smell of a liar. She wasn't in the least presumptive. Just straight.

But after all she wasn't such a child. She had breasts you knew would be like small stones to the hand, good muscular arms and fine hard legs. Her bare feet were stuck into broken down leather sandals such as you see worn by children at the beach in summer.

She was heavily tanned too, wherever her skin showed. Just one of the kids you'll find loafing around the pools they have outside towns and cities everywhere these days. A tough little nut finding her own way in the world.

What's the matter with your legs? I asked. They were bare and covered with scabby sores.

Poison ivy, she answered, pulling up her skirts to show me.

Gee, but you ought to seen it two days ago. This ain't nothing. You're a doctor. What can I do for it?

Let's see, I said.

She put her leg up on a chair. It had been badly bitten by mosquitoes, as I saw the thing, but she insisted on poison ivy. She had torn at the affected places with her finger nails and that's what made it look worse.

Oh that's not so bad, I said, if you'll only leave it alone and stop scratching it.

Yeah, I know that but I can't. Scratching's the only thing makes it feel better.

What's that on your foot.

Where? looking.

That big brown spot there on the back of your foot.

Dirt I guess. Her gum chewing never stopped and her fixed defensive non-expression never changed.

Why don't you wash it?

I do. Say, what could I do for my face?

I looked at it closely. You have what they call acne, I told her. All those blackheads and pimples you see there, well, let's see, the first thing you ought to do, I suppose is to get some good soap.

What kind of soap? Lifebuoy?

No. I'd suggest one of those cakes of Lux. Not the flakes but the cake.

Yeah, I know, she said. Three for seventeen.

Use it. Use it every morning. Bathe your face in very hot water. You know, until the skin is red from it. That's to bring the blood up to the skin. Then take a piece of ice. You have ice, haven't you?

Sure, we have ice.

Hold it in a face cloth—or whatever you have—and rub that all over your face. Do that right after you've washed it in the very hot water—before it has cooled. Rub the ice all over. And do it every day—for a month. Your skin will improve. If you like, you can take some cold cream once in a while, not much, just a little and rub that in last of all, if your face feels too dry.

Will that help me?

If you stick to it, it'll help you.

All right.

There's a lotion I could give you to use along with that. Remind me of it when I come back later. Why aren't you in school?

Agh, I'm not going any more. They can't make me. Can they?

They can try.

How can they? I know a girl thirteen that don't go and they can't make her either.

Don't you want to learn things?

I know enough already.

Going to get a job?

I got a job. Here. I been helping the Jews across the hall. They give me three fifty a week—all summer.

Good for you, I said. Think your father'll be here around five?

Guess so. He ought to be.

I'll come back then. Make it all the same call.

All right, she said, looking straight at me and chewing her gum as vigorously as ever.

Just then a little blond haired thing of about seven came in through the kitchen and walked to me looking curiously at my satchel and then at the baby.

What are you, a doctor?

See you later, I said to the older girl and went out.

At five-thirty I once more climbed the wooden stairs after passing two women at the street entrance who looked me up and down from where they were leaning on the brick wall of the building talking.

This time a woman's voice said, Come in, when I knocked on the kitchen door.

It was the mother. She was impressive, a bulky woman, growing toward fifty, in a black dress, with lank graying hair and a long seamed face. She stood by the enameled kitchen table. A younger, plumpish woman with blond hair, well cared for and in a neat house dress—as if she had dolled herself up for the occasion—was standing beside her.

The small blank child was there too and the older girl, behind the others, overshadowed by her mother, the two older women at least a head taller than she. No one spoke.

Hello, I said to the girl I had been talking to earlier. She didn't answer me.

Doctor, began the mother, save my baby. She very sick. The woman spoke with a thick, heavy voice and seemed overcome with grief and apprehension. Doctor! Doctor! she all but wept.

All right, I said to cut the woman short, let's take a look at her first.

So everybody headed toward the front of the house, the mother in the lead. As they went I lagged behind to speak to the second woman, the interpreter. What happened?

The baby was not doing so well. So they took it to the hospital to see if the doctors there could help it. But it got worse. So her husband took it out this morning. It looks bad to me.

Yes, said the mother who had overheard us. Me got seven children. One daughter married. This my baby, pointing to the child on the bed. And she wiped her face with the back of her hand. This baby no do good. Me almost crazy. Don't know who can help. What doctor, I don't know. Somebody tell me take to hospital. I think maybe do some good. Five days she there. Cost me two dollar every day. Ten dollar. I no got money. And when I see my baby, she worse. She look dead. I can't leave she there. No. No. I say to everybody, no. I take she home. Doctor, you save my baby. I pay you. I pay you everything—

Wait a minute, wait a minute, I said. Then I turned to the other woman. What happened?

The baby got like a diarrhoea in the hospital. And she was all dirty when they went to see her. They got all excited—

All sore behind, broke in the mother—

The younger woman said a few words to her in some language that sounded like Russian but it didn't stop her—

No. No. I send she to hospital. And when I see my baby like that I can't leave she there. My babies no that way. Never, she emphasized. Never! I take she home.

Take your time, I said. Take off her clothes. Everything off. This is a regular party. It's warm enough in here. Does she vomit?

She no eat. How she can vomit? said the mother.

But the other woman contradicted her. Yes, she was vomiting in the hospital, the nurse said.

It happens that this September we had been having a lot of such cases in my hospital also, an infectious diarrhoea which practically all the children got when they came in from any cause. I supposed that this was what happened to this child. No doubt it had been in a bad way before that, improper feeding, etc., etc. And then when they took it in there, for whatever had been the matter with it, the diarrhoea had developed. These things sometimes don't turn out so well. Lucky, no doubt, that they had brought it home when they did. I told them so, explaining at the same time: One nurse for ten or twenty babies, they do all they can but you can't run and change the whole ward every five minutes. But the infant looked too lifeless for that only to be the matter with it.

You want all clothes off, asked the mother again, hesitating and trying to keep the baby covered with the cotton blanket while undressing it.

Everything off, I said.

There it lay, just skin and bones with a round fleshless head at the top and the usual pot belly you find in such cases.

Look, said the mother, tilting the infant over on its right side with her big hands so that I might see the reddened buttocks. What kind of nurse that. My babies never that way.

Take your time, take your time, I told her. That's not bad. And it wasn't either. Any child with loose movements might have had the same half an hour after being cared for. Come on. Move away, I said and give me a chance. She kept hovering over the baby as if afraid I might expose it.

It had no temperature. There was no rash. The mouth was in reasonably good shape. Eyes, ears negative. The moment I put my stethoscope to the little boney chest, however, the whole thing became clear. The infant had a severe congenital heart defect, a roar when you listened over the heart that meant, to put it crudely, that she was no good, never would be.

The mother was watching me. I straightened up and looking at her told her plainly: She's got a bad heart.

That was the sign for tears. The big woman cried while she spoke. Doctor, she pleaded in blubbering anguish, save my baby.

I'll help her, I said, but she's got a bad heart. That will never be any better. But I knew perfectly well she wouldn't pay the least attention to what I was saying.

I give you anything, she went on. I pay you. I pay you twenty dollar. Doctor, you fix my baby. You good doctor. You fix.

All right, all right, I said. What are you feeding it?

They told me and it was a ridiculous formula, unboiled besides. I regulated it properly for them and told them how to proceed to make it up. Have you got enough bottles, I asked the young girl.

Sure, we got bottles, she told me.

O.K., then go ahead.

You think you cure she? The mother with her long, tearful face was at me again, so different from her tough female fifteen-year-old.

You do what I tell you for three days, I said, and I'll come back and see how you're getting on.

Tank you, doctor, so much. I pay you. I got today no money. I pay ten dollar to hospital. They cheat me. I got no more money. I pay you Friday when my husband get pay. You save my baby.

Boy! what a woman. I couldn't get away.

She my baby, doctor. I no want to lose. Me got seven children—

Yes, you told me.

But this my baby. You understand. She very sick. You good doctor—

Oh my God! To get away from her I turned again to the kid. You better get going after more bottles before the stores close. I'll come back Friday morning.

How about that stuff for my face you were gonna give me.

That's right. Wait a minute. And I sat down on the edge of the bed to write out a prescription for some lotio alba comp, such as we use in acne. The two older women looked at me in astonishment—wondering, I suppose, how I knew the girl. I finished writing the thing and handed it to her. Sop it on your face at bedtime, I said, and let it dry on. Don't get it into your eyes.

No, I won't.

I'll see you in a couple of days, I said to them all.

Doctor! the old woman was still after me. You come back. I pay you. But all a time short. Always tomorrow come milk man. Must pay rent, must pay coal. And no got money. Too much work. Too much wash. Too much cook. Nobody help. I don't know what's a matter. This door, doctor, this door. This house make sick. Make sick.

Do the best I can, I said as I was leaving.

The girl followed on the stairs. How much is this going to cost, she asked shrewdly holding the prescription.

Not much, I said, and then started to think. Tell them you only got half a dollar. Tell them I said that's all it's worth.

Is that right, she said.

Absolutely. Don't pay a cent more for it.

Say, you're all right, she looked at me appreciatively.

Have you got half a dollar.

Sure. Why not.

What's it all about, my wife asked me in the evening. She had heard about the case. Gee! I sure met a wonderful girl, I told her.

What! another?

Some tough baby. I'm crazy about her. Talk about straight stuff... And I recounted to her the sort of case it was and what I had done. The mother's an odd one too. I don't quite make her out.

Did they pay you?

No. I don't suppose they have any cash.

Going back?

Sure. Have to.

Well, I don't see why you have to do all this charity work. Now that's a case you should report to the Emergency Relief. You'll get at least two dollars a call from them.

But the father has a job, I understand. That counts me out.

What sort of a job?

I dunno. Forgot to ask.

What's the baby's name so I can put it in the book?

Damn it. I never thought to ask them that either. I think they must have told me but I can't remember it. Some kind of a Russian name—

You're the limit. Dumbbell, she laughed. Honestly—Who are they anyhow.

You know, I think it must be that family Kate was telling us about. Don't you remember. The time the little kid was playing there one afternoon after school, fell down the front steps and knocked herself senseless.

I don't recall.

Sure you do. That's the family. I get it now. Kate took the brat down there in a taxi and went up with her to see that everything was all right. Yop, that's it. The old woman took the older kid by the hair, because she hadn't watched her sister. And what a beating she gave her. Don't you remember Kate telling us afterward. She thought the old woman was going to murder the child she screamed and threw her around so. Some old gal. You can see they're all afraid of her. What a world. I suppose the damned brat drives her cuckoo. But boy, how she clings to that baby.

The last hope, I suppose, said my wife.

Yeah, and the worst bet in the lot. There's a break for you.

She'll love it just the same.

More, usually.

Three days later I called at the flat again. Come in. This time a resonant male voice. I entered, keenly interested.

By the same kitchen table stood a short, thickset man in baggy working pants and a heavy cotton undershirt. He seemed to have the stability of a cube placed on one of its facets, a smooth, highly colored Slavic face, long black moustaches and widely separated, perfectly candid blue eyes. His black hair, glossy and profuse stood out carelessly all over his large round head. By his look he reminded me at once of his blond haired daughter, absolutely unruffled. The shoulders of an ox. You the doctor, he said. Come in.

The girl and the small child were beside him, the mother was in the bedroom.

The baby no better. Won't eat, said the man in answer to my first question.

How are its bowels?

Not so bad.

Does it vomit?

No.

Then it is better, I objected. But by this time the mother had heard us talking and came in. She seemed worse than the last time. Absolutely inconsolable. Doctor! Doctor! she came up to me.

Somewhat irritated I put her aside and went in to the baby. Of course it was better, much better. So I told them. But the heart, naturally was the same.

How she heart? the mother pressed me eagerly. Today little better?

I started to explain things to the man who was standing back giving his wife precedence but as soon as she got the drift of what I was saying she was all over me again and the tears began to pour. There was no use my talking. Doctor, you good doctor. You do something fix my baby. And before I could move she took my left hand in both hers and kissed it through her tears. As she did so I realized finally that she had been drinking.

I turned toward the man, looking a good bit like the sun at noonday and as indifferent, then back to the woman and I felt deeply sorry for her.

Then, not knowing why I said it nor of whom, precisely I was speaking, I felt myself choking inwardly with the words: Hell! God damn it. The sons of bitches. Why do these things have to be?

The next morning as I came into the coat room at the hospital there were several of the visiting staff standing there with their cigarettes, talking. It was about a hunting dog belonging to one of the doctors. It had come down with distemper and seemed likely to die.

I called up half a dozen vets around here, one of them was saying. I even called up the one in your town, he added turning to me as I came in. And do you know how much they wanted to charge me for giving the serum to that animal?

Nobody answered.

They had the nerve to want to charge me five dollars a shot for it. Can you beat that? Five dollars a shot.

Did you give them the job, someone spoke up facetiously.

Did I? I should say I did not, the first answered. But can you beat that. Why we're nothing but a lot of slop-heels compared to those guys. We deserve to starve.

Get it out of them, someone rasped, kidding. That's the stuff.

Then the original speaker went on, buttonholing me as some of the others faded from the room. Did you ever see practice so rotten. By the way, I was called over to your town about a week ago to see a kid I delivered up here during the summer. Do you know anything about the case?

I probably got them on my list, I said. Russians?

Yeah, I thought as much. Has a job as a road worker or something. Said they couldn't pay me. Well, I took the trouble of going up to your court house and finding out what he was getting. Eighteen dollars a week. Just the type. And they had the nerve to tell me they couldn't pay me.

She told me ten.

She's a liar.

Natural maternal instinct, I guess.

Whisky appetite, if you should ask me.

Same thing.

O.K. buddy. Only I'm telling you. And did I tell *them*. They'll never call me down there again, believe me. I had that much satisfaction out of them anyway. You make 'em pay you. Don't you do anything for them unless they do. He's paid by the county. I tell you if I had taxes to pay down there I'd go and take it out of his salary.

You and how many others?

Say, they're bad actors, that crew. Do you know what they really do with their money? Whisky. Now I'm telling you. That old woman is the slickest customer you ever saw. She's drunk all the time. Didn't you notice it?

Not while I was there.

Don't you let them put any of that sympathy game over on you. Why they tell me she leaves that baby lying on the bed all day long screaming its lungs out until the neighbors complain to the police about it. I'm not lying to you.

Yeah, the old skate's got nerves, you can see that. I can imagine she's a bugger when she gets going.

But what about the young girl, I asked weakly. She seems like a pretty straight kid.

My confrere let out a wild howl. That thing! You mean that pimply faced little bitch. Say, if I had my way I'd run her out of the town tomorrow morning. There's about a dozen wise guys on her trail every night in the week. Ask the cops. Just ask them. They know. Only nobody wants to bring in a complaint. They say you'll stumble over her on the roof, behind the stairs anytime at all. Boy, they sure took you in.

Yes, I suppose they did, I said.

But the old woman's the ringleader. She's got the brains. Take my advice and make them pay.

The last time I went I heard the, Come in! from the front of the house. The fifteen-year-old was in there at the window in a rocking chair with the tightly wrapped baby in her arms. She got up. Her legs were bare to the hips. A powerful little animal.

What are you doing? Going swimming? I asked.

Naw, that's my gym suit. What the kids wear for Physical Training in school.

How's the baby?

She's all right.

Do you mean it?

Sure, she eats fine now.

Tell your mother to bring it to the office some day so I can weigh it. The food'll need increasing in another week or two anyway.

I'll tell her.

How's your face?

Gettin' better.

My God, it *is,* I said. And it was much better. Going back to school now?

Yeah, I had tuh.

H. P. LOVECRAFT
(1890–1937)

The American writer of the twentieth century most frequently compared to Poe, H. P. Lovecraft is a writer of "weird" tales—("weird" is Lovecraft's favored term)—whose posthumous influence has been enormous, from the horrific genre tales of Stephen King to the more restrained and enigmatic genre fictions of Michael Chabon, Peter Straub, Neil Gaiman, and Jeffrey Ford, included in this anthology. A theorist of the gothic genre, Lovecraft is the author of many essays on gothic horror fiction of which the most significant is "Supernatural Horror in Literature" (1927).

Where Edgar Allan Poe is credited with the invention of the mystery-detective story and the perfection of a type of brilliantly mimetic surreal monologue, of which "The Tell-Tale Heart" (included in this volume) is the outstanding example, Lovecraft is credited with the fusion of the gothic tale and what would come to be defined as "science-fiction"—a particular sort of dark-fantasy tale that advances with unnerving psychological precision, a slow gathering of terrific forces that culminate, like the story included here, "The Rats in the Walls," in a revelation that is both personal and cultural. Lovecraft's theme is invariably the psychic reality of Original Sin—humankind's confrontation with an intractable and often incomprehensible evil at the heart of creation. An isolated individual, idealistic but naive, invariably male, bravely seeks forbidden knowledge, with disastrous results.

Like his unhappy predecessor Poe, Lovecraft led a life marked by deep childhood traumas and scars, of which he could not speak directly but could express, indirectly, obsessively and passionately, through the bizarre metaphors of his voluminous fiction and nonfiction. When Lovecraft was two years old, his father died of (untreated, undiagnosed) syphilis; Lovecraft was left with the memory of a relatively young father's increasing dementia, paranoia, mania, and depression, as well as of an emotionally unstable mother who exhibited both extreme possessiveness of her only son, and excessive and debilitating criticism of him. (See S. T. Joshi's excellent biography Lovecraft: A Life, *1996.)*

Though Lovecraft published many fantastic tales during his lifetime, in pulp magazines like Weird Tales, *it was not until after his death, from cancer, malnutrition, and general neglect, that definitive editions of his work began to appear, through the 1950s and beyond, issued from the small press Arkham House (originally established to publish the work of Lovecraft):* At the Mountains of Madness and Other Novels, Dagon and Other Macabre Tales, The Dunwich Horror and Others, *and* The Horror in the Museum and Other Revisions. *Soon, Lovecraft was being published by mainstream commercial publishing houses like Random House and Ecco/ HarperCollins. In 2005 the Library of America issued* H. P. Lovecraft, *a selection of Lovecraft's tales, giving the outcast writer, in effect, the imprimatur of American classic. By this time Lovecraft's weird tales had found a wide and enthusiastic readership of a kind the luckless author could hardly have envisioned during his lifetime. Tellingly, Lovecraft has said:*

> I could not write about "ordinary people" because I am not the slightest interested in them. Without interest there can be no art. Man's relations to man do not captivate my fancy. It is man's relations to the cosmos—to the unknown—which alone arouses in me the spark of creative imagination.

Along with the yet more lurid Lovecraftian tales "The Dunwich Horror," "The Shadow Over Innsmouth," "At the Mountains of Madness," and "The Cats of Ulthar," the story included here, "The Rats in the Walls," is quintessential Lovecraft: an allegory in which humankind's most nightmarish taboo, that of bestiality and cannibalism, is realized in a seemingly civilized American gentleman descended from British nobility.

The Rats in the Walls

On July 16, 1923, I moved into Exham Priory after the last workman had finished his labours. The restoration had been a stupendous task, for little had remained of the deserted pile but a shell-like ruin; yet because it had been the seat of my ancestors I let no expense deter me. The place had not been inhabited since the reign of James the First, when a tragedy of intensely hideous, though largely unexplained, nature had struck down the master, five of his children, and several servants; and driven forth under a cloud of suspicion and terror the third son, my lineal progenitor and the only survivor of the abhorred line. With this sole heir denounced as a murderer, the estate had reverted to the crown, nor had the accused man made any attempt to exculpate himself or regain his property. Shaken by some horror greater that that of conscience or the law, and expressing only a frantic wish to exclude the ancient edifice from his sight and memory, Walter de la Poer, eleventh Baron Exham, fled to Virginia and there founded the family which by the next century had become known as Delapore.

Exham Priory had remained untenanted, though later allotted to the estates of the Norrys family and much studied because of its peculiarly composite architecture; an architecture involving Gothic towers resting on a Saxon or Romanesque substructure, whose foundation in turn was of a still earlier order or blend of orders—Roman, and even Druidic or native Cymric,[5] if legends speak truly. This foundation was a very singular thing, being merged on one side with the solid limestone of the precipice from whose brink the priory overlooked a desolate valley three miles west of the village of Anchester. Architects and antiquarians loved to examine this strange relic of forgotten centuries, but the country folk hated it. They had hated it hundreds of years before, when my ancestors lived there, and they hated it now, with the moss and mould of abandonment on it. I had not been a day in Anchester before I knew I came of an accursed house. And this week workmen have blown up Exham Priory, and are busy obliterating the traces of its foundations.

The bare statistics of my ancestry I had always known, together with the fact that my first American forbear had come to the colonies under a strange cloud. Of details, however, I had been kept wholly ignorant through the policy of reticence always maintained by the Delapores. Unlike our planter neighbors, we seldom boasted of crusading ancestors or other mediaeval and Renaissance heroes; nor was any kind of tradition handed down except what may have been recorded in the sealed envelope left before the Civil War by every squire to his eldest son for posthumous opening. The glories we cherished were those achieved since the migration; the glories of a proud and honourable, if somewhat reserved and unsocial Virginia line.

During the war our fortunes were extinguished and our whole existence changed by the burning of Carfax, our home on the banks of the James. My grandfather, advanced in years, had perished in that incendiary outrage, and with him the envelope that bound us all to the past. I can recall that fire today as I saw it then at the age of seven, with the Federal soldiers shouting, the women screaming, and the negroes howling and praying. My father was in the army, defending Richmond, and after many formalities my mother and I were passed through the line to join him. When the war ended we all moved north, whence my mother had come; and I grew to manhood, middle age, and ultimate wealth as a stolid Yankee. Neither my father nor I ever knew what our hereditary envelope had contained, and as I merged into the greyness of Massachusetts business life I lost all interest in the mysteries which evidently lurked far back in my family tree. Had I suspected their nature, how gladly I would have left Exham Priory to its moss, bats, and cobwebs!

My father died in 1904, but without any message to leave me, or to my only child, Alfred, a motherless boy of ten. It was this boy who reversed the order of family information; for although I could give him only jesting conjectures about the past, he wrote me of some very interesting ancestral legends when the late war took him to England in 1917 as an aviation officer. Apparently the Delapores had a colourful and perhaps sinister history, for a friend of my son's, Capt. Edward Norrys of the Royal Flying Corps, dwelt near the family seat at Anchester and related some peasant superstitions which few novelists could equal for wildness and incredibility. Norrys himself, of course, did not take them seriously; but they amused my son and made good material for his letters to me. It was this legendry which definitely turned my attention to my transatlantic heritage, and made me resolve to purchase and restore the family seat which Norrys shewed to Alfred in its picturesque desertion, and offered to get for him at a surprisingly reasonable figure, since his own uncle was the present owner.

I bought Exham Priory in 1918, but was almost immediately distracted from my plans of restoration by the return of my son as a maimed invalid. During the two years that he lived I thought of nothing but his care, having even placed my business under the direction of partners. In 1921, as I found myself bereaved and aimless, a retired manufacturer no longer young, I resolved to divert my remaining years with my new possession. Visiting Anchester in December, I was entertained by Capt. Norrys, a plump, amiable young man who had thought much of my son, and secured his assistance in gathering plans and anecdotes to guide in the coming restoration. Exham Priory itself I saw without emotion, a jumble of tottering mediaeval ruins covered with lichens and honeycombed with rooks' nests, perched perilously upon a precipice, and denuded of floors or other interior features save the stone walls of the separate towers.

As I gradually recovered the image of the edifice as it had been when my ancestor left it over three centuries before, I began to hire workmen for the reconstruction. In every case I was forced to go outside the immediate locality, for the Anchester villagers had an almost unbelievable fear and hatred of the place. This sentiment was so great that it was sometimes communicated to the outside labourers, causing numerous desertions; whilst its scope appeared to include both the priory and its ancient family.

My son had told me that he was somewhat avoided during his visits because he was a de la Poer, and I now found myself subtly ostracised for a like reason until I convinced the peasants how little I knew of my heritage. Even then they sullenly disliked me, so that I had to collect most of the village traditions through the mediation of Norrys. What the people could not forgive, perhaps, was that I had come to restore a symbol so abhorrent to them; for, rationally or not, they viewed Exham Priory as nothing less than a haunt of fiends and werewolves.

Piecing together the tales which Norrys collected for me, and supplementing them with the accounts of several savants who had studied the ruins, I deduced that Exham Priory stood on the site of a prehistoric temple; a Druidical or ante-Druidical thing which must have been contemporary with Stonehenge. That indescribable rites had been celebrated there, few doubted; and there were unpleasant tales of the transference of these rites into the Cybele-worship which the Romans had introduced. Inscriptions still visible in the sub-cellar bore such unmistakable letters as "DIV... OPS... MAGNA. MAT..." sign of the Magna Mater whose dark worship was once vainly forbidden to Roman citizens. Anchester had been the camp of the third Augustan legion, as many remains attest, and it was said that the temple of Cybele was splendid and thronged with worshippers who performed nameless ceremonies at the bidding of a Phrygian priest. Tales added that the fall of the old religion did not end the orgies at the temple, but that the priests lived on in the new faith without real change. Likewise was it said that the rites did not vanish with the Roman power and that certain among the Saxons added to what remained of the temple, and gave it the essential outline it subsequently preserved, making it the centre of a cult feared through half the heptarchy. About 1000 A.D. the place is mentioned in a chronicle as being a substantial stone priory housing a strange and powerful monastic order and surrounded by extensive gardens which needed no walls to exclude a frightened populace. It was never destroyed by the Danes, though after the Norman Conquest it must have declined tremendously; since there was no impediment when Henry the Third granted the site to my ancestor, Gilbert de la Poer, First Baron Exham, in 1261.

Of my family before this date there is no evil report, but something strange must have happened then. In one chronicle there is a reference to a de la Poer as "cursed of God" in 1307, whilst village legendry had nothing but evil and frantic fear to tell of the castle that went up on the foundations of the old temple and priory. The fireside tales were of the most grisly description, all the ghastlier because of their frightened reticence and cloudly evasiveness. They represented my ancestors as a race of hereditary daemons beside whom Gilles de Retz and the Marquis de Sade would seem the veriest tyros, and hinted whisperingly at their responsibility for the occasional disappearance of villagers through several generations.

The worst characters, apparently, were the barons and their direct heirs; at least, most was whispered about these. If of healthier inclinations, it was said, an heir would early and mysteriously die to make way for another more typical scion. There seemed to be an inner cult in the family, presided over by the head of the house, and sometimes closed except to a few members. Temperament rather than ancestry was evidently the basis of this cult, for it was entered by several who married into the family. Lady Margaret Trevor from Cornwall, wife of Godfrey, the second son of the fifth baron, became a favourite bane of children all over the countryside, and the daemon heroine of a particularly horrible old ballad not yet extinct near the Welsh border. Preserved in balladry, too, though not illustrating the same point, is the hideous tale of Lady Mary de la Poer, who shortly after her marriage to the Earl of Shrewsfield was killed by him and his mother, both of the slayers being absolved and blessed by the priest to whom they confessed what they dared not repeat to the world.

These myths and ballads, typical as they were of crude superstition, repelled me greatly. Their persistence, and their application to so long a line of my ancestors, were especially annoying; whilst the imputations of monstrous habits proved unpleasantly reminiscent of the one known scandal of my immediate forbears—the case of my cousin, young Randolph Delapore of Carfax, who went among the negroes and became a voodoo priest after he returned from the Mexican War.

I was much less disturbed by the vaguer tales of wails and howlings in the barren, windswept valley beneath the limestone cliff; of the graveyard stenches after the spring rains; of the floundering, squealing white thing on which Sir John Clave's horse had trod one night in a lonely field; and of the servant who had gone mad at what he saw in the priory in the full light of day. These things were hackneyed spectral lore, and I was at that time a pronounced sceptic. The accounts of vanished peasants were less to be dismissed, though not especially significant in view of mediaeval custom. Prying curiosity meant death, and more than one severed head had been publicly shewn on the bastions—now effaced—around Exham Priory.

A few of the tales were exceedingly picturesque, and made me wish I had learnt more of comparative mythology in my youth. There was, for instance, the belief that a legion of bat-winged devils kept Witches' Sabbath each night at that priory—a legion whose sustenance might explain the disproportionate abundance of coarse vegetables harvested in the vast gardens. And, most vivid of all, there was the dramatic epic of the rats—the scampering army of obscene vermin which had burst forth from the castle three months after the tragedy that doomed it to desertion—the lean, filthy, ravenous army which had swept all before it and devoured fowl, cats, dogs, hogs, sheep, and even two hapless human beings before its fury was spent. Around that unforgettable rodent army a whole separate cycle of myths revolves, for it scattered among the village homes and brought curses and horrors in its train.

Such was the lore that assailed me as I pushed to completion, with an elderly obstinacy, the work of restoring my ancestral home. It must not be imagined for a moment that these tales formed my principal psychological environment. On the other hand, I was constantly praised and encouraged by Capt. Norrys and the antiquarians who surrounded and aided me. When the task was done, over two years after its commencement, I viewed the great rooms, wainscotted walls, vaulted ceilings, mullioned windows, and broad staircases with a pride which fully compensated for the prodigious expense of the restoration. Every attribute of the Middle Ages was cunningly reproduced, and the new parts blended perfectly with the original walls and foundations. The seat of my fathers was complete, and I looked forward to redeeming at last the local fame of the line which ended in me. I would reside here permanently, and prove that a de la Poer (for I had adopted again the original spelling of the name) need not be a fiend. My comfort was perhaps augmented by the fact that, although Exham Priory was mediaevally fitted, its interior was in truth wholly new and free from old vermin and old ghosts alike.

As I have said, I moved in on July 16, 1923. My household consisted of seven servants and nine cats, of which latter species I am particularly fond. My eldest cat, "Nigger-Man", was seven years old and had come with me from my home in Bolton, Massachusetts; the others I had accumulated whilst living with Capt. Norrys' family during the restoration of the priory. For five days our routine proceeded with the utmost placidity, my time being spent mostly in the codification of old family data. I had now obtained some very circumstantial accounts of the final tragedy and flight of Walter de la Poer, which I conceived to be the probable contents of the hereditary paper lost in the fire at Carfax. It appeared that my ancestor was accused with much reason of having killed all the other members of his household, except four servant confederates, in their sleep, about two weeks after a shocking discovery which changed his whole demeanour, but which, except by implication, he disclosed to no one save perhaps the servants who assisted him and afterward fled beyond reach.

This deliberate slaughter, which included a father, three brothers, and two sisters, was largely condoned by the villagers, and so slackly treated by the law that its perpetrator escaped honoured, unharmed, and undisguised to Virginia; the general whispered sentiment being that he had purged the land of an immemorial curse. What discovery had prompted an act so terrible, I could scarcely even conjecture. Walter de la Poer must have known for years the sinister tales about his family, so that this material could have given him no fresh impulse. Had he, then, witnessed some appalling ancient rite, or stumbled upon some frightful and revealing symbol in the priory or its vicinity? He was reputed to have been a shy, gentle youth in England. In Virginia he seemed not so much hard or bitter as harassed and apprehensive. He was spoken of in the diary of another gentleman-adventurer, Francis Harley of Bellview, as a man of unexampled justice, honour, and delicacy.

On July 22 occurred the first incident which, though lightly dismissed at the time, takes on a preternatural significance in relation to later events. It was so simple as to be almost negligible, and could not possibly have been noticed under the circumstances; for it must be recalled that since I was in a building practically fresh and new except for the walls, and surrounded by a well-balanced staff of servitors, apprehension would have been absurd despite the locality. What I afterward remembered is merely this—that my old black cat, whose moods I know so well, was undoubtedly alert and anxious to an extent wholly out of keeping with his natural character. He roved from room to room, restless and disturbed, and sniffed constantly about the walls which formed part of the old Gothic structure. I realise how trite this sounds—like the inevitable dog in the ghost story, which always growls before his master sees the sheeted figure—yet I cannot consistently suppress it.

The following day a servant complained of restlessness among all the cats in the house. He came to me in my study, a lofty west room on the second story, with groined arches, black oak panelling, and a triple Gothic window overlooking the limestone cliff and desolate valley; and even as he spoke I saw the jetty form of Nigger-Man creeping along the west wall and scratching at the new panels which overlaid the ancient stone. I told the man that there must be some singular odour or emanation from the old stonework, imperceptible to human senses, but affecting the delicate organs of cats even through the new woodwork. This I truly believed, and when the fellow suggested the presence of mice or rats, I mentioned that there had been no rats there for three hundred years, and that even the field mice of the surrounding country could hardly be found in these high walls, where they had never been known to stray. That afternoon I called on Capt. Norrys, and he assured me that it would be quite incredible for field mice to infest the priory in such a sudden and unprecedented fashion.

That night, dispensing as usual with a valet, I retired in the west tower chamber which I had chosen as my own, reached from the study by a stone staircase and short gallery—the former partly ancient, the latter entirely restored This room was circular, very high, and without wainscotting, being hung with arras which I had myself chosen in London. Seeing that Nigger-Man was with me, I shut the heavy Gothic door and retired by the light of the electric bulbs which so cleverly counterfeited candles, finally switching off the light and sinking on the carved and canopied four-poster, with the venerable cat in his accustomed place across my feet. I did not draw the curtains, but gazed out at the narrow north window which I faced. There was a suspicion of aurora in the sky, and the delicate traceries of the window were pleasantly silhouetted.

At some time I must have fallen quietly asleep, for I recall a distinct sense of leaving strange dreams, when the cat started violently from his placid position. I saw him in the faint auroral glow, head strained forward, fore feet on my ankles, and hind feet stretched behind. He was looking intensely at a point on the wall somewhat west of the window, a point which to my eye had nothing to mark it, but toward which all my attention was now directed. And as I watched, I knew that Nigger-Man was not vainly excited. Whether the arras actually moved I cannot say. I think it did, very slightly. But what I can swear to is that behind it, I heard a low, distinct scurrying as of rats or mice. In a moment the cat had jumped bodily on the screening tapestry, bringing the affected section to the floor with his weight, and exposing a damp, ancient wall of stone; patched here and there by the restorers, and devoid of any trace of rodent prowlers. Nigger-Man raced up and down the floor by this part of the wall, clawing the fallen arras and seemingly trying at times to insert a paw between the wall and the oaken floor. He found nothing, and after a time returned wearily to his place across my feet. I had not moved, but I did not sleep again that night.

In the morning I questioned all the servants, and found that none of them had noticed anything unusual, save that the cook remembered that actions of a cat which had rested on her windowsill. This cat had howled at some unknown hour of the night, awaking the cook in time for her to see him dart purposefully out of the open door down the stairs. I drowsed away the noontime, and in the afternoon called again on Capt. Norrys, who became exceedingly interested in what I told him. The odd incidents—so slight yet so curious—appealed to his sense of the picturesque, and elicited from him a number of reminiscences of local ghostly lore. We were genuinely perplexed at the presence of rats, and Norrys lent me some traps and Paris green, which I had the servants place in strategic localities when I returned.

I retired early, being very sleepy, but was harassed by dreams of the most horrible sort. I seemed to be looking down from an immense height upon a twilit grotto, knee-deep with filth, where a white-bearded daemon swineherd drove about with his staff a flock of fungous, flabby beasts whose appearance filled me with unutterable loathing. Then, as the swineherd paused and nodded over his task, a mighty swarm of rats rained down on the stinking abyss and fell to devouring beasts and man alike.

From this terrific vision I was abruptly awaked by the motions of Nigger-Man, who had been sleeping as usual across my feet. This time I did not have to question the source of his snarls and hisses, and of the fear which made him sink his claws into my ankle, unconscious of their effect; for on every side of the chamber the walls were alive with nauseous sound—the verminous slithering of ravenous, gigantic rats. There was now no aurora to shew the state of the arras—the fallen section of which had been replaced—but I was not too frightened to switch on the light.

As the bulbs leapt into radiance I saw the hideous shaking all over the tapestry, causing the somewhat peculiar designs to execute the singular dance of death. This motion disappeared almost at once, and the sound with it. Springing out of bed, I poked at the arras with the long handle of a warming-pan that rested near, and lifted one section to see what lay beneath. There was nothing but the batched stone wall, and even the cat had lost his tense realisation of abnormal presence. When I examined the circular trap that had been placed in the room, I found all of the openings sprung, though no trace remained what had been caught and had escaped.

Further sleep was out of the question, so, lighting a handle, I opened the door and went out in the gallery toward the stairs to my study, Nigger-Man following at my heels. Before we had reached the stone steps, however, the cat darted ahead of me and vanished down the ancient flight. As I descended the stairs myself, I became suddenly aware of sounds in the great room below; sounds of a nature which could not be mistaken. The oak-panelled walls were alive with rats, scampering and milling, whilst Nigger-Man was racing about with the fury of a baffled hunter. Reaching the bottom, I switched on the light, which did not this time cause the noise to subside. The rats continued their riot, stampeding with such force and distinctness that I could finally assign to their motions a definite direction. These creatures, in numbers apparently inexhaustible, were engaged in one stupendous migration from inconceivable heights to some depth conceivably, or inconceivably, below.

I now heard steps in the corridor, and in another moment two servants pushed open the massive door. They were searching the house for some unknown source of disturbance which had thrown all the cats into a snarling panic and caused them to plunge precipitately down several flights of stairs and squat, yowling, before the closed door to the subcellar. I asked them if they had heard the rats, but they replied in the negative. And when I turned to call their attention to the sounds in the panels, I realised that the noise had ceased. With the two men, I went down to the door of the sub-cellar, but found the cats already dispersed. Later I resolved to explore the crypt below, but for the present I merely made a round of the traps. All were sprung, yet all were tenantless. Satisfying myself that no one had heard the rats save the felines and me, I sat in my study till morning; thinking profoundly, and recalling every scrap of legend I had unearthed concerning the building I inhabited.

I slept some in the forenoon, leaning back in the one comfortable library chair which my mediaeval plan of furnishing could not banish. Later I telephoned to Capt. Norrys, who came over and helped me explore the sub-cellar. Absolutely nothing untoward was found, although we could not repress a thrill at the knowledge that this vault was built by Roman hands. Every low arch and massive pillar was Roman—not the debased Romanesque of the bungling Saxons, but the severe and harmonious classicism of the age of the Caesars; indeed, the walls abounded with inscriptions familiar to the antiquarians who had repeatedly explored the place—things like "P. GETAE. PROP... TEMP... DONA ..." and "L. PRAEC... VS... PONTIFI... ATYS..."

The reference to Atys made me shiver, for I had read Catullus and knew something of the hideous rites of the Eastern god, whose worship was so mixed with that of Cybele. Norrys and I, by the light of lanterns, tried to interpret the odd and nearly effaced designs on certain irregularly rectangular blocks of stone generally held to be altars, but could make nothing of them. We remembered that one pattern, a sort of rayed sun, was held by students to imply a non-Roman origin, suggesting that these altars had merely been adopted by the Roman priests from some older and perhaps aboriginal temple on the same site. On one of these blocks were some brown stains which made me wonder. The largest, in the centre of the room, had certain features on the upper surface which indicated its connexion with fire—probably burnt offerings.

Such were the sights in that crypt before whose door the cats had howled, and where Norrys and I now determined to pass the night. Couches were brought down by the servants, who were told not to mind any nocturnal actions of the cats, and Nigger-Man was admitted as much for help as for companionship. We decided to keep the great oak door—a modern replica with slits for ventilation—tightly closed; and, with this attended to, we retired with lanterns still burning to await whatever might occur.

The vault was very deep in the foundations of the priory, and undoubtedly far down on the face of the beetling limestone cliff overlooking the waste valley. That it had been the goal of the scuffling and unexplainable rats I could not doubt, though why, I could not tell. As we lay there expectantly, I found my vigil occasionally mixed with half-formed dreams from which the uneasy motions of the cat across my feet would rouse me. These dreams were not wholesome, but horribly like the one I had had the night before. I saw again the twilit grotto, and the swineherd with his unmentionable fungous beasts wallowing in filth, and as I looked at these things they seemed nearer and more distinct—so distinct that I could almost observe their features. Then I did observe the flabby features of one of them—and awaked with such a scream that Nigger-Man started up, whilst Capt. Norrys, who had not slept, laughed considerably. Norrys might have laughed more—or perhaps less—had he known what it was that made me scream. But I did not remember myself till later. Ultimate horror often paralyses memory in a merciful way.

Norrys waked me when the phenomena began. Out of the same frightful dream I was called by his gentle shaking and his urging to listen to the cats. Indeed, there was much to listen to, for beyond the closed door at the head of the stone steps was a veritable nightmare of feline yelling and clawing, whilst Nigger-Man, unmindful of his kindred outside, was running excitedly around the bare stone walls, in which I heard the same babel of scurrying rats that had troubled me the night before.

An acute terror now rose within me, for here were anomalies which nothing normal could well explain. These rats, if not the creatures of a madness which I shared with the cats alone, must be burrowing and sliding in Roman walls I had thought to be of solid limestone blocks... unless perhaps the action of water through more than seventeen centuries had eaten winding tunnels which rodent bodies had worn clear and ample.... But even so, the spectral horror was no less; for if these were living vermin why did not Norrys hear their disgusting commotion? Why did he urge me to watch Nigger-Man and listen to the cats outside, and why did he guess wildly and vaguely at what could have aroused them?

By the time I had managed to tell him, as rationally as I could, what I thought I was hearing, my ears gave me the last fading impression of the scurrying; which had retreated *still downward,* far underneath this deepest of sub-cellars till it seemed as if the whole cliff below were riddled with questing rats. Norrys was not as sceptical as I had anticipated, but instead seemed profoundly moved. He motioned to me to notice that the cats at the door had ceased their clamour, as if giving up the rats for lost; whilst Nigger-Man had a burst of renewed restlessness, and was clawing frantically around the bottom of the large stone altar in the centre of the room, which was nearer Norrys' couch than mine.

My fear of the unknown was at this point very great. Something astounding had occurred, and I saw that Capt. Norrys, a younger, stouter, and presumably more naturally materialistic man, was affected fully as much as myself—perhaps because of his lifelong and intimate familiarity with local legend. We could for the moment do nothing but watch the old black cat as he pawed with decreasing fevour at the base of the altar, occasionally looking up and mewing to me in that persuasive manner which he used when he wished me to perform some favour for him.

Norrys now took a lantern close to the altar and examined the place where Nigger-Man was pawing; silently kneeling and scraping away the lichens of centuries which joined the massive pre-Roman block to the tessellated floor. He did not find anything, and was about to abandon his effort when I noticed a trivial circumstance which made me shudder, even though it implied nothing more than I had already imagined. I told him of it, and we both looked at its almost imperceptible manifestation with the fixedness of fascinated discovery and acknowledgment. It was only this—that the flame of the lantern set down near the altar was slightly but certainly flickering from a draught of air which it had not before received, and which came indubitably from the crevice between floor and altar where Norrys was scraping away the lichens.

We spent the rest of the night in the brilliantly lighted study, nervously discussing what we should do next. The discovery that some vault deeper than the deepest known masonry of the Romans underlay this accursed pile—some vault unsuspected by the curious antiquarians of three centuries—would have been sufficient to excite us without any background of the sinister. As it was, the fascination became twofold; and we paused in doubt whether to abandon our search and quit the priory forever in superstitious caution, or to gratify our sense of adventure and brave whatever horrors might await us in the unknown depths. By morning we had compromised, and decided to go to London to gather a group of archaeologists and scientific men fit to cope with the mystery. It should be mentioned that before leaving the sub-cellar we had vainly tried to move the central altar which we now recognised as the gate to a new pit of nameless fear. What secret would open the gate, wiser men than we would have to find.

During many days in London Capt. Norrys and I presented our facts, conjectures, and legendary anecdotes to five eminent authorities, all men who could be trusted to respect any family disclosures which future explorations might develop. We found most of them little disposed to scoff, but instead intensely interested and sincerely sympathetic. It is hardly necessary to name them all, but I may say that they included Sir William Brinton, whose excavations in the Troad excited most of the world in their day. As we all took the train for Anchester I felt myself poised on the brink of frightful revelations, a sensation symbolised by the air of mourning among the many Americans at the unexpected death of the President on the other side of the world.

On the evening of August 7th we reached Exham Priory, where the servants assured me that nothing unusual had occurred. The cats, even old Nigger-Man, had been perfectly placid; and not a trap in the house had been sprung. We were to begin exploring on the following day, awaiting which I assigned well-appointed rooms to all my guests. I myself retired in my own tower chamber, with Nigger-Man across my feet. Sleep came quickly, but hideous dreams assailed me. There was a vision of a Roman feast like that of Trimalchio, with a horror in a covered platter. Then came that damnable, recurrent thing about the swineherd and his filthy drove in the twilit grotto. Yet when I awoke it was full daylight, with normal sounds in the house below. The rats, living or spectral, had not troubled me; and Nigger-Man was quietly asleep. On going down, I found that the same tranquillity had prevailed elsewhere; a condition which one of the assembled savants—a fellow named Thornton, devoted to the psychic—rather absurdly laid to the fact that I had now been shewn the thing which certain forces had wished to shew me.

All was now ready, and at 11 a.m. our entire group of seven men, bearing powerful electric searchlights and implements of excavation, went down to the sub-cellar and bolted the door behind us. Nigger-Man was with us, for the investigators found no occasion to despise his excitability, and were indeed anxious that he be present in case of obscure rodent manifestations. We noted the Roman inscriptions and unknown altar designs only briefly, for three of the savants had already seen them, and all knew their characteristics. Prime attention was paid to the momentous central altar, and within an hour Sir William Brinton had caused it to tilt backward, balanced by some unknown species of counterweight.

There now lay revealed such a horror as would have overwhelmed us had we not been prepared. Through a nearly square opening in the tiled floor, sprawling on a flight of stone steps so prodigiously worn that it was little more than an inclined plane at the centre, was a ghastly array of human or semi-human bones. Those which retained their collocation as skeletons shewed attitudes of panic fear, and over all were the marks of rodent gnawing. The skulls denoted nothing short of utter idiocy, cretinism, or primitive semi-apedom. Above the hellishly littered steps arched a descending passage seemingly chiselled from the solid rock, and conducting a current of air. This current was not a sudden and noxious rush as from a closed vault, but a cool breeze with something of freshness in it. We did not pause long, but shiveringly began to clear a passage down the steps. It was then that Sir William, examining the hewn walls, made the odd observation that the passage, according to the direction of the strokes, must have been chiselled *from beneath.*

I must be very deliberate now, and choose my words.

After ploughing down a few steps amidst the gnawed bones we saw that there was light ahead; not any mystic phosphorescence, but a filtered daylight which could not come except from unknown fissures in the cliff that overlooked the waste valley. That such fissures had escaped notice from outside was hardly remarkable, for not only is the valley wholly uninhabited, but the cliff is so high and beetling that only an aeronaut could study its face in detail. A few steps more, and our breaths were literally snatched from us by what we saw, so literally that Thornton, the psychic investigator, actually fainted in the arms of the dazed man who stood behind him. Norrys, his plump face utterly white and flabby, simply cried out inarticulately, whilst I think that what I did was to gasp or hiss, and cover my eyes. The man behind me—the only one of the party older than I—croaked the hackneyed "My God!" in the most cracked voice I ever heard. Of seven cultivated men, only Sir William Brinton retained his composure, a thing more to his credit because he led the party and must have seen the sight first.

It was a twilit grotto of enormous height, stretching away farther than any eye could see, a subterraneous world of limitless mystery and horrible suggestion. There were buildings and other architectural remains—in one terrified glance I saw a weird pattern of tumuli, a savage circle of monoliths, a low-domed Roman ruin, a sprawling Saxon pile, and an early English edifice of wood—but all these were dwarfed by the ghoulish spectacle presented by the general surface of the ground. For yards about the steps extended an insane tangle of human bones, or bones at least as human as those on the steps. Like a foamy sea they stretched, some fallen apart, but others wholly or partly articulated as skeletons, these latter invariably in postures of daemoniac frenzy, either fighting off some menace or clutching other forms with cannibal intent.

When Dr. Trask, the anthropologist, stooped to classify the skulls, he found a degraded mixture which utterly baffled him. They were mostly lower than the Piltdown man in the scale of evolution, but in every case definitely human. Many were of higher grade, and a very few were the skulls of supremely and sensitively developed types. All the bones were gnawed, mostly by rats, but somewhat by others of the half-human drove. Mixed with them were many tiny bones of rats—fallen members of the lethal army which closed the ancient epic.

I wonder that any man among us lived and kept his sanity through that hideous day of discovery. Not Hoffmann or Huysmans could conceive a scene more wildly incredible, more frenetically repellent, or more Gothically grotesque than the twilit grotto through which we seven staggered; each stumbling on revelation after revelation, and trying to keep for the nonce from thinking of the events which must have taken place there three hundred years, or a thousand, or two thousand, or ten thousand years ago. It was the antechamber of hell, and poor Thornton fainted again when Trask told him that some of the skeleton things must have descended as quadrupeds through the last twenty or more generations.

Horror piled on horror as we began to interpret the architectural remains. The quadruped things—with their occasional recruits from the biped class—had been kept in stone pens, out of which they must have broken in their last delirium of hunger or rat-fear. There had been great herds of them, evidently fattened on the coarse vegetables whose remains could be found as a sort of poisonous ensilage at the bottom of huge stone bins older than Rome. I knew now why my ancestors had had such excessive gardens—would to heaven I could forget! The purpose of the herds I did not have to ask.

Sir William, standing with his searchlight in the Roman ruin, translated aloud the most shocking ritual I have ever known; and told of the diet of the antediluvian cult which the priests of Cybele found and mingled with their own. Norrys, used as he was to the trenches, could not walk straight when he came out of the English building. It was a butcher shop and kitchen—he had expected that—but it was too much to see familiar English implements in such a place, and to read familiar English *graffiti* there, some as recent as 1610. I could not go in that building—that building whose daemon activities were stopped only by the dagger of my ancestor Walter de la Poer.

What I did venture to enter was the low Saxon building, whose oaken door had fallen, and there I found a terrible row of ten stone cells with rusty bars. Three had tenants, all skeletons of high grade, and on the bony forefinger of one I found a seal ring with my own coat-of-arms. Sir William found a vault with far older cells below the Roman chapel, but these cells were empty. Below them was a low crypt with cases of formally arranged bones, some of them bearing terrible parallel inscriptions carved in Latin, Greek, and the tongue of Phrygia. Meanwhile, Dr. Trask had opened one of the prehistoric tumuli, and brought to light skulls which were slightly more human than a gorilla's, and which bore indescribable ideographic carvings. Through all this horror my cat stalked unperturbed. Once I saw him monstrously perched atop a mountain of bones, and wondered at the secrets that might lie behind his yellow eyes.

Having grasped to some slight degree the frightful revelations of this twilit area—an area so hideously foreshadowed by my recurrent dream—we turned to that apparently boundless depth of midnight cavern where no ray of light from the cliff could penetrate. We shall never know what sightless Stygian worlds yawn beyond the little distance we went, for it was decided that such secrets are not good for mankind. But there was plenty to engross us close at hand, for we had not gone far before the searchlights shewed that accursed infinity of pits in which the rats had feasted, and whose sudden lack of replenishment had driven the ravenous rodent army first to turn on the living herds of starving things, and then to burst forth from the priory in that historic orgy of devastation which the peasants will never forget.

God! those carrion black pits of sawed, picked bones and opened skulls! Those nightmare chasms choked with the pithecanthropoid, Celtic, Roman, and English bones of countless unhallowed centuries! Some of them were full, and none can say how deep they had once been. Others were still bottomless to our searchlights, and peopled by unnamable fancies. What, I thought, of the hapless rats that stumbled into such traps amidst the blackness of their quests in this grisly Tartarus?

Once my foot slipped near a horribly yawning brink, and I had a moment of ecstatic fear. I must have been musing a long time, for I could not see any of the party but the plump Capt. Norrys. Then there came a sound from that inky, boundless, farther distance that I thought I knew, and I saw my old black cat dart past me like a winged Egyptian god, straight into the illimitable gulf of the unknown. But I was not far behind, for there was no doubt after another second. It was the eldritch scurrying of those fiend-born rats, always questing for new horrors, and determined to lead me on even unto those grinning caverns of earth's centre where Nyarlathotep, the mad faceless god, howls blindly to the piping of two amorphous idiot flute-players.

My searchlight expired, but still I ran. I heard voices, and yowls, and echoes, but above all there gently rose that impious, insidious scurrying; gently rising, rising, as a stiff bloated corpse gently rises above an oily river that flows under endless onyx bridges to a black, putrid sea. Something bumped into me—something soft and plump. It must have been the rats; the viscous, gelatinous, ravenous army that feast on the dead and the living.... Why shouldn't rats eat a de la Poer as a de la Poer eats forbidden things?... The war ate my boy, damn them all... and the Yanks ate Carfax with flames and burnt Grandsire Delapore and the secret...No, no, I tell you, I am *not* that daemon swineherd in the twilit grotto! It was *not* Edward Norrys' fat face on that flabby, fungous thing! Who says I am a de la Poer? He lived, but my boy died!...Shall a Norrys hold the lands of a de la Poer?...It's voodoo, I tell you...that spotted snake...Curse you, Thornton, I'll teach you to faint at what my family do!...'Sblood, thou stinkard, I'll learn ye how to gust...wolde ye swynke me thilke wys?...*Magna Mater! Magna Mater...Atys...Dia ad aghaidh 's ad aodann...agus bas dunach ort! Dhonas 's dholas ort, agus leat-sa!... Ungl...ungl...rrrlh...chchch...*

That is what they say I said I said when they found me in the blackness after three hours; found me crouching in the blackness over the plump, half-eaten body of Capt. Norrys, with my own cat leaping and tearing at my throat. Now they have blown up Exham Priory, taken my Nigger-Man away from me, and shut me into this barred room at Hanwell with fearful whispers about my heredity and experiences. Thornton is in the next room, but they prevent me from talking to him. They are trying, too, to suppress most of the facts concerning the priory. When I speak of poor Norrys they accuse me of a hideous thing, but they must know that I did not do it. They must know it was the rats; the slithering, scurrying rats whose scampering will never let me sleep; the daemon rats that race behind the padding in this room and beckon me down to greater horrors than I have ever known; the rats they can never hear; the rats, the rats in the walls.

JEAN TOOMER
(1894–1967)

Of the writers represented in this gathering, Jean Toomer would seem to be among the most lyrically and imaginatively gifted. Yet, ironically, his fate was to write for decades in obscurity, leaving behind a voluminous quantity of unpublished work—short stories, novels, plays, an autobiography. His Cane *(1923) is a work of literary genius, but never again, perhaps by his own design, did he attempt a work of its type or quality.*

Jean Toomer was born in Washington, D.C., attended a number of colleges without earning a degree, and began writing in his middle twenties. From the first he aligned himself, not with the then-dominant literary mode of Naturalism, but with Modernist experimentation; he published poems in avant-garde magazines like Broom *and the* Little Review, *as well as in black publications. The dazzling* Cane, *though written within a few years of Anderson's* Winesburg, Ohio, *would seem to have sprung from entirely different sources, as from another planet.*

In this brilliant and unclassifiable composition, an isolated, yet deeply sensitive young black man tries to connect himself with his "folk" heritage, without success. Cane *is constructed as a collage, made up of poetry, prose-poetry, fiction, song, drama, and philosophical debate; Negro dialect is used like music, in aria-like interludes of great beauty and intensity. Throughout, and particularly in "Blood-Burning Moon," the selection included here, jazz rhythms underlie prose passages, and give a poetic resonance that, like both music and poetry, must be experienced to be understood. This is the lost, tragic, yet hauntingly beautiful world of the blues singer Robert Johnson, memorialized in prose.*

Blood-Burning Moon

1

Up from the skeleton stone walls, up from the rotting floor boards and the solid hand-hewn beams of oak of the pre-war cotton factory, dusk came. Up from the dusk the full moon came. Glowing like a fired pine-knot, it illumined the great door and soft showered the Negro shanties aligned along the single street of factory town. The full moon in the great door was an omen. Negro women improvised songs against its spell.

Louisa sang as she came over the crest of the hill from the white folks' kitchen. Her skin was the color of oak leaves on young trees in fall. Her breasts, firm and up-pointed like ripe acorns. And her singing had the low murmur of winds in fig trees. Bob Stone, younger son of the people she worked for, loved her. By the way the world reckons things, he had won her. By measure of that warm glow which came into her mind at thought of him, he had won her. Tom Burwell, whom the whole town called Big Boy, also loved her. But working in the fields all day, and far away from her, gave him no chance to show it. Though often enough of evenings he had tried to. Somehow, he never got along. Strong as he was with hands upon the ax or plow, he found it difficult to hold her. Or so he thought. But the fact was that he held her to factory town more firmly than he thought for. His black balanced, and pulled against, the white of Stone, when she thought of them. And her mind was vaguely upon them as she came over the crest of the hill, coming from the white folks' kitchen. As she sang softly at the evil face of the full moon.

A strange stir was in her. Indolently, she tried to fix upon Bob or Tom as the cause of it. To meet Bob in the canebrake, as she was going to do an hour or so later, was nothing new. And Tom's proposal which she felt on its way to her could be indefinitely put off. Separately, there was no unusual significance to either one. But for some reason, they jumbled when her eyes gazed vacantly at the rising moon. And from the jumble came the stir that was strangely within her. Her lips trembled. The slow rhythm of her song grew agitant and restless. Rusty black and tan spotted hounds, lying in the dark corners of porches or prowling around back yards, put their noses in the air and caught its tremor. They began plaintively to yelp and howl. Chickens woke up and cackled. Intermittently, all over the countryside dogs barked and roosters crowed as if heralding a weird dawn or some ungodly awakening. The women sang lustily. Their songs were cotton-wads to stop their ears. Louisa came down into factory town and sank wearily upon the step before her home. The moon was rising towards a thick cloud-bank which soon would hide it.

Red nigger moon. Sinner!
Blood-burning moon. Sinner!
Come out that fact'ry door.

2

Up from the deep dusk of a cleared spot on the edge of the forest a mellow glow arose and spread fan-wise into the low-hanging heavens. And all around the air was heavy with the scent of boiling cane. A large pile of cane-stalks lay like ribboned shadows upon the ground. A mule, harnessed to a pole, trudged lazily round and round the pivot of the grinder. Beneath a swaying oil lamp, a Negro alternately whipped out at the mule, and fed cane-stalks to the grinder. A fat boy waddled pails of fresh ground juice between the grinder and the boiling stove. Steam came from the copper boiling pan. The scent of cane came from the copper pan and drenched the forest and the hill that sloped to factory town, beneath its fragrance. It drenched the men in circle seated around the stove. Some of them chewed at the white pulp of stalks, but there was no need for them to, if all they wanted was to taste the cane. One tasted it in factory town. And from factory town one could see the soft haze thrown by the glowing stove upon the low-hanging heavens.

Old David Georgia stirred the thickening syrup with a long ladle, and ever so often drew it off. Old David Georgia tended his stove and told tales about the white folks, about moonshining and cotton picking, and about sweet nigger gals, to the men who sat there about his stove to listen to him.

Tom Burwell chewed cane-stalk and laughed with the others till some one mentioned Louisa. Till some one said something about Louisa and Bob Stone, about the silk stockings she must have gotten from him. Blood ran up Tom's neck hotter than the glow that flooded from the stove. He sprang up. Glared at the men and said, "She's my gal." Will Manning laughed. Tom strode over to him. Yanked him up and knocked him to the ground. Several of Manning's friends got up to fight for him. Tom whipped out a long knife and would have cut them to shreds if they hadnt ducked into the woods. Tom had had enough. He nodded to Old David Georgia and swung down the path to factory town. Just then, the dogs started barking and the roosters began to crow. Tom felt funny. Away from the fight, away from the stove, chill got to him. He shivered. He shuddered when he saw the full moon rising towards the cloud-bank. He who didnt give a godam for the fears of old women. He forced his mind to fasten on Louisa. Bob Stone. Better not be. He turned into the street and saw Louisa sitting before her home. He went towards her, ambling, touched the brim of a marvelously shaped, spotted, felt hat, said he wanted to say something to her, and then found that he didnt know what he had to say, or if he did, that he couldnt say it. He shoved his big fists in his overalls, grinned, and started to move off.

"Youall want me, Tom?"

"Thats what us wants, sho, Louisa."

"Well, here I am—"

"An here I is, but that aint ahelpin none, all th same."

"You wanted to say something? . . ."

"I did that, sho. But words is like th spots on dice: no matter how y fumbles em, there's times when they jes wont come. I dunno why. Seems like th love I feels fo yo done stole m tongue. I got it now. Whee! Louisa, honey, I oughtnt tell y, I feel I oughtnt cause yo is young an goes t church an I has had other gals, but Louisa I sho do love y. Lil gal, Ise watched y from them first days when youall sat right here befo yo door befo th well an sang some-times in a way that like t broke m heart. Ise carried y with me into th fields, day after day, an after that, an I sho can plow when yo is there, an I can pick cotton. Yassur! Come near beatin Barlo yesterday. I sho did. Yassur! An next year if ole Stone'll trust me, I'll have a farm. My own. My bales will buy yo what y gets from white folks now. Silk stockings an purple dresses—course I dont believe what some folks been whisperin as t how y gets them things now. White folks always did do for niggers what they likes. An they jes cant help alikin yo, Louisa. Bob Stone likes y. Course he does. But not th way folks is awhisperin. Does he, hon?"

"I dont know what you mean, Tom."

"Course y dont. Ise already cut two niggers. Had t hon, t tell em so. Niggers always tryin t make somethin out a nothin. An then besides, white folks aint up t them tricks so much nowadays. Godam better not be. Leastawise not with yo. Cause I wouldnt stand f it. Nassur."

"What would you do, Tom?"

"Cut him jes like I cut a nigger."

"No, Tom—"

"I said I would an there aint no mo to it. But that aint th talk f now. Sing, honey Louisa, an while I'm listenin t y I'll be makin love."

Tom took her hand in his. Against the tough thickness of his own, hers felt soft and small. His huge body slipped down to the step beside her. The full moon sank upward into the deep purple of the cloud-bank. An old woman brought a lighted lamp and hung it on the common well whose bulky shadow squatted in the middle of the road, opposite Tom and Louisa. The old woman lifted the well-lid, took hold the chain, and began drawing up the heavy bucket. As she did so, she sang. Figures shifted, restlesslike, between lamp and window in the front rooms of the shanties. Shadows of the figures fought each other on the gray dust of the road. Figures raised the windows and joined the old woman in song. Louisa and Tom, the whole street, singing:

Red nigger moon. Sinner!
Blood-burning moon. Sinner!
Come out that fact'ry door.

3

Bob Stone sauntered from his veranda out into the gloom of fir trees and magnolias. The clear white of his skin paled, and the flush of his cheeks turned purple. As if to balance this outer change, his mind became consciously a white man's. He passed the house with its huge open hearth which, in the days of slavery, was the plantation cookery. He saw Louisa bent over that hearth. He went in as a master should and took her. Direct, honest, bold. None of this sneaking that he had to go through now. The contrast was repulsive to him. His family had lost ground. Hell no, his family still owned the niggers, practically. Damned if they did, or he wouldnt have to duck around so. What would they think if they knew? His mother? His sister? He shouldnt mention them, shouldnt think of them in this connection. There in the dusk he blushed at doing so. Fellows about town were all right, but how about his friends up North? He could see them incredible, repulsed. They didnt know. The thought first made him laugh. Then, with their eyes still upon him, he began to feel embarrassed. He felt the need of explaining things to them. Explain hell. They wouldnt understand, and moreover, who ever heard of a Southerner getting on his knees to any Yankee, or anyone. No sir. He was going to see Louisa to-night, and love her. She was lovely—in her way. Nigger way. What way was that? Damned if he knew. Must know. He'd known her long enough to know. Was there something about niggers that you couldnt know? Listening to them at church didnt tell you anything. Looking at them didnt tell you anything. Talking to them didnt tell you anything—unless it was gossip, unless they wanted to talk. Of course, about farming, and licker, and craps—but those werent nigger. Nigger was something more. How much more? Something to be afraid of, more? Hell no. Who ever heard of being afraid of a nigger? Tom Burwell. Cartwell had told him that Tom went with Louisa after she reached home. No sir. No nigger had ever been with his girl. He'd like to see one try. Some position for him to be in. Him, Bob Stone, of the old Stone family, in a scrap with a nigger over a nigger girl. In the good old days... Ha! Those were the days. His family had lost ground. Not so much, though. Enough for him to have cut through old Lemon's canefield by way of the woods, that he might meet her. She was worth it. Beautiful nigger gal. Why nigger? Why not, just gal? No, it was because she was nigger that he went to her. Sweet... The scent of boiling cane came to him. Then he saw the rich glow of the stove. He heard the voices of the men circled around it. He was about to skirt the clearing when he heard his own name mentioned. He stopped. Quivering. Leaning against a tree, he listened.

"Bad nigger. Yassur, he sho is one bad nigger when he gets started."

"Tom Burwell's been on th gang three times fo cuttin men."

"What y think he's agwine t do t Bob Stone?"

"Dunno yet. He aint found out. When he does—Baby!"

"Aint no tellin."

"Young Stone aint no quitter an I ken tell y that. Blood of th old uns in his veins."

"Thats right. He'll scrap, sho."

"Be gettin too hot f niggers round this away."

"Shut up, nigger. Y dont know what y talkin bout."

Bob Stone's ears burned as though he had been holding them over the stove. Sizzling heat welled up within him. His feet felt as if they rested on red-hot coals. They stung him to quick movement. He circled the fringe of the glowing. Not a twig cracked beneath his feet. He reached the path that led to factory town. Plunged furiously down it. Halfway along, a blindness within him veered him aside. He crashed into the bordering canebrake. Cane leaves cut his face and lips. He tasted blood. He threw himself down and dug his fingers in the ground. The earth was cool. Cane-roots took the fever from his hands. After a long while, or so it seemed to him, the thought came to him that it must be time to see Louisa. He got to his feet and walked calmly to their meeting place. No Louisa. Tom Burwell had her. Veins in his forehead bulged and distended. Saliva moistened the dried blood on his lips. He bit down on his lips. He tasted blood. Not his own blood; Tom Burwell's blood. Bob drove through the cane and out again upon the road. A hound swung down the path before him towards factory town. Bob couldnt see it. The dog loped aside to let him pass. Bob's blind rushing made him stumble over it. He fell with a thud that dazed him. The hound yelped. Answering yelps came from all over the countryside. Chickens cackled. Roosters crowed, heralding the bloodshot eyes of southern awakening. Singers in the town were silenced. They shut their windows down. Palpitant between the rooster crows, a chill hush settled upon the huddled forms of Tom and Louisa. A figure rushed from the shadow and stood before them. Tom popped to his feet.

"Whats y want?"

"I'm Bob Stone."

"Yassur—an I'm Tom Burwell. Whats y want?"

Bob lunged at him. Tom side-stepped, caught him by the shoulder, and flung him to the ground. Straddled him.

"Let me up."

"Yassur—but watch yo doins. Bob Stone."

A few dark figures, drawn by the sound of scuffle, stood about them. Bob sprang to his feet.

"Fight like a man, Tom Burwell, an I'll lick y."

Again he lunged. Tom side-stepped and flung him to the ground. Straddled him.

"Get off me, you godam nigger you."

"Yo sho has started somethin now. Get up."

Tom yanked him up and began hammering at him. Each blow sounded as if it smashed into a precious, irreplaceable soft something. Beneath them, Bob staggered back. He reached in his pocket and whipped out a knife.

"Thats my game, sho."

Blue flash, a steel blade slashed across Bob Stone's throat. He had a sweetish sick feeling. Blood began to flow. Then he felt a sharp twitch of pain. He let his knife drop. He slapped one hand against his neck. He pressed the other on top of his head as if to hold it down. He groaned. He turned, and staggered towards the crest of the hill in the direction of white town. Negroes who had seen the fight slunk into their homes and blew the lamps out. Louisa, dazed, hysterical, refused to go indoors. She slipped, crumbled, her body loosely propped against the woodwork of the well. Tom Burwell leaned against it. He seemed rooted there.

Bob reached Broad Street. White men rushed up to him. He collapsed in their arms.

"Tom Burwell. . . ."

White men like ants upon a forage rushed about. Except for the taut hum of their moving, all was silent. Shotguns, revolvers, rope, kerosene, torches. Two high-powered cars with glaring search-lights. They came together. The taut hum rose to a low roar. Then nothing could be heard but the flop of their feet in the thick dust of the road. The moving body of their silence preceded them over the crest of the hill into factory town. It flattened the Negroes beneath it. It rolled to the wall of the factory, where it stopped. Tom knew that they were coming. He couldnt move. And then he saw the search-lights of the two cars glaring down on him. A quick shock went through him. He stiffened. He started to run. A yell went up from the mob. Tom wheeled about and faced them. They poured down on him. They swarmed. A large man with dead-white face and flabby cheeks came to him and almost jabbed a gun-barrel through his guts.

"Hands behind y, nigger."

Tom's wrists were bound. The big man shoved him to the well. Burn him over it, and when the woodwork caved in, his body would drop to the bottom. Two deaths for a godam nigger. Louisa was driven back. The mob pushed in. Its pressure, its momentum was too great. Drag him to the factory. Wood and stakes already there. Tom moved in the direction indicated. But they had to drag him. They reached the great door. Too many to get in there. The mob divided and flowed around the walls to either side. The big man shoved him through the door. The mob pressed in from the sides. Taut humming. No words. A stake was sunk into the ground. Rotting floor boards piled around it. Kerosene poured on the rotting floor boards. Tom bound to the stake. His breast was bare. Nails' scratches let little lines of blood trickle down and mat into the hair. His face, his eyes were set and stony. Except for irregular breathing, one would have thought him already dead. Torches were flung onto the pile. A great flare muffled in black smoke shot upward. The mob yelled. The mob was silent. Now Tom could be seen within the flames. Only his head, erect, lean, like a blackened stone. Stench of burning flesh soaked the air. Tom's eyes popped. His head settled downward. The mob yelled. Its yell echoed against the skeleton stone walls and sounded like a hundred yells. Like a hundred mobs yelling. Its yell thudded against the thick front wall and fell back. Ghost of a yell slipped through the flames and out the great door of the factory. It fluttered like a dying thing down the single street of factory town. Louisa, upon the step before her home, did not hear it, but her eyes opened slowly. They saw the full moon glowing in the great door. The full moon, an evil thing, an omen, soft showering the homes of folks she knew. Where were they, these people? She'd sing, and perhaps they'd come out and join her. Perhaps Tom Burwell would come. At any rate, the full moon in the great door was an omen which she must sing to:

> Red nigger moon. Sinner!
> Blood-burning moon. Sinner!
> Come out that fact'ry door.

F. SCOTT FITZGERALD
(1896–1940)

Born in St. Paul, Minnesota, of a middle-class family, F. Scott Fitzgerald enjoyed the most problematic of all good fortunes: early, immediate success and celebrity, for his first novel. This was This Side of Paradise *(1920), published when he was only twenty-four. Titles followed in rapid succession—the stories* Flappers and Philosophers *(1921) and* Tales of the Jazz Age *(1922) and a second novel,* The Beautiful and Damned *(1922)—and then, in effect, the fantasy was over. Fitzgerald was the supreme chronicler of the 1920s because he had shared uncritically in its excesses and delusions. After the Crash, and after Fitzgerald's own breakdown, he was the ideal chronicler of disillusion.*

In addition to a number of excellent, much-anthologized stories—"Babylon Revisited," "Winter Dreams," "The Diamond as Big as the Ritz"—Fitzgerald wrote two outstanding novels, The Great Gatsby *(1925) and* Tender is the Night *(1934);* The Last Tycoon, *uncompleted at the time of his premature death, aged forty-four, was posthumously published in 1941, and a miscellaneous collection of Fitzgerald's prose pieces, titled* The Crack-Up, *was published in 1945. The story included here, "An Alcoholic Case," was published in* Esquire *in early 1937, and, apart from its fluid, gripping narrative, it is fascinating as a document of rueful self-analysis. We see the doomed alcoholic from the point of view of a private nurse to whom he is an "alcoholic case"—the "well-known cartoonist, or artist, whatever. . . ." One of the most spare and least sentimental of Fitzgerald's 178 short stories, "An Alcoholic Case" is not readily forgotten.*

An Alcoholic Case

I

"Let—go—that—oh-h-h! Please, now, will you. *Don't* start drinking again! Come on—give me the bottle. I told you I'd stay awake givin it to you. Come on. If you do like that a-way—then what are you goin to be like when you go home. Come on-—leave it with me—I'll leave half in the bottle. Pul-lease. You know what Dr. Carter says—I'll stay awake and give it to you, or else fix some of it in the bottle—come on—like I told you, I'm too tired to be fightin you all night.... All right, drink your fool self to death."

"Would you like some beer?" he asked.

"No, I don't want any beer. Oh, to think that I have to look at you drunk again. My God!"

"Then I'll drink the Coca-Cola."

The girl sat down panting on the bed.

"Don't you believe in anything?" she demanded.

"Nothing you believe in—please—it'll spill."

She had no business there, she thought, no business trying to help him. Again they struggled, but after this time he sat with his head in his hands awhile, before he turned around once more.

"Once more you try to get it I'll throw it down," she said quickly. "I will—on the tiles in the bathroom."

"Then I'll step on the broken glass—or you'll step on it."

"Then let go—oh you promised—"

Suddenly she dropped it like a torpedo, sliding underneath her hand and slithering with a flash of red and black and the words: SIR GALAHAD, DISTILLED LOUISVILLE GIN.

It was on the floor in pieces and everything was silent for awhile and she read *Gone With the Wind* about things so lovely that had happened long ago. She began to worry that he would have to go into the bathroom and might cut his feet, and looked up from time to time to see if he would go in. She was very sleepy—the last time she looked up he was crying and he looked like an old Jewish man she had nursed once in California; he had had to go to the bathroom many times. On this case she was unhappy all the time but she thought:

"I guess if I hadn't liked him I wouldn't have stayed on the case."

With a sudden resurgence of conscience she go up and put a chair in front of the bathroom door. She had wanted to sleep because he had got her up early that morning to get a paper with the Yale-Harvard game in it and she hadn't been home all day. That afternoon a relative of his had come in to see him and she had waited outside in the hall where there was a draft with no sweater to put over her uniform.

As well as she could she arranged him for sleeping, put a robe over his shoulders as he sat slumped over his chiffonier, and one on his knees. She sat down in the rocker but she was no longer sleepy; there was plenty to enter on the chart and treading lightly about she found a pencil and put it down:

Pulse 120

Respiration 25

Temp 98—98.4—98.2

Remarks—

—She could make so many:

Tried to get bottle of gin. Threw it away and broke it.

She corrected it to read:

In the struggle it dropped and was broken. Patient was generally difficult.

She started to add as part of her report: *I never want to go on an alcoholic case again,* but that wasn't in the picture. She knew she could wake herself at seven and clean up everything before his niece awakened. It was all part of the game. But when she sat down in the chair she looked at his face, white and exhausted, and counted his breathing again, wondering why it had all happened. He had been so nice today, drawn her a whole strip of his cartoon just for the fun and given it to her. She was going to have it framed and hang it in her room. She felt again his thin wrists wrestling against her wrist and remembered the awful things he had said, and she thought too of what the doctor had said to him yesterday:

"You're too good a man to do this to yourself."

She was tired and didn't want to clean up the glass on the bathroom floor, because as soon as he breathed evenly she wanted to get him over to the bed. But she decided finally to clean up the glass first; on her knees, searching a last piece of it, she thought:

—This isn't what I ought to be doing. And this isn't what *he* ought to be doing.

Resentfully she stood up and regarded him. Through the thin delicate profile of his nose came a light snore, sighing, remote, inconsolable. The doctor had shaken his head in a certain way, and she knew that really it was a case that was beyond her. Besides, on her card at the agency was written, on the advice of her elders, "No Alcoholics."

She had done her whole duty, but all she could think of was that when she was struggling about the room with him with that gin bottle there had been a pause when he asked her if she had hurt her elbow against a door and that she had answered: "You don't know how people talk about you, no matter how you think of yourself—" when she knew he had a long time ceased to care about such things.

The glass was all collected—as she got out a broom to make sure, she realized that the glass, in its fragments, was less than a window through which they had seen each other for a moment. He did not know about her sisters, and Bill Markoe whom she had almost married, and she did not know what had brought him to this pitch, when there was a picture on his bureau of his young wife and his two sons and him, all trim and handsome as he must have been five years ago. It was so utterly senseless—as she put a bandage on her finger where she had cut it while picking up the glass she made up her mind she would never take an alcoholic case again.

II

Some Halloween jokester had split the side windows of the bus and she shifted back to the Negro section in the rear for fear the glass might fall out. She had her patient's check but no way to cash it at this time of night; there was a quarter and a penny in her purse.

Two nurses she knew were waiting in the hall of Mrs. Hixson's Agency.

"What kind of case have you been on?"

"Alcoholic," she said.

"Oh yes—Gretta Hawks told me about it—you were on with that cartoonist who lives at the Forest Park Inn."

"Yes, I was."

"I hear he's pretty fresh."

"He's never done anything to bother me," she lied. "You can't treat them as if they were committed—"

"Oh, don't get bothered—I just heard that around town—oh, you know—they want you to play around with them—"

"Oh, be quiet," she said, surprised at her own rising resentment.

In a moment Mrs. Hixson came out and, asking the other two to wait, signaled her into the office.

"I don't like to put young girls on such cases," she began. "I got your call from the hotel."

"Oh, it wasn't bad, Mrs. Hixson. He didn't know what he was doing, and he didn't hurt me in any way. I was thinking much more of my reputation with you. He was really nice all day yesterday. He drew me—"

"I didn't want to send you on that case." Mrs. Hixson thumbed through the registration cards. "You take T.B. cases, don't you? Yes. I see you do. Now here's one—"

The phone rang in a continuous chime. The nurse listened as Mrs. Hixson' s voice said precisely:

"I will do what I can—that is simply up to the doctor.... That is beyond my jurisdiction.... Oh, hello, Hattie, no, I can't now. Look, have you got any nurse that's good with alcoholics? There's someody up at the Forest Park Inn who needs somebody. Call back, will you?"

She put down the receiver. "Suppose you wait outside. What sort of man is this, anyhow? Did he act indecently?"

"He held my hand away," she said, "so I couldn't give him an injection."

"Oh, an invalid he-man," Mrs. Hixson grumbled. "They belong in sanitaria. I've got a case coming along in two minutes that you can get a little rest on. It's an old woman—"

The phone rang again. "Oh, hello, Hattie....Well, how about that big Svensen girl? She ought to be able to take care of any alcoholics.... How about Josephine Markham? Doesn't she live in your apartment house?...Get her to the phone." Then after a moment, "Jo, would you care to take the case of a well-known cartoonist, or artist, whatever they call themselves, at Forest Park Inn?...No. I don't know, but Doctor Carter is in charge and will be around about ten o'clock."

There was a long pause; from time to time Mrs. Hixson spoke:

"I see....Of course, I understand your point of view. Yes, but this isn't supposed to be dangerous—just a little difficult. I never like to send girls to a hotel because I know what riff-raff you're liable to run into....No, I'll find somebody. Even at this hour. Never mind and thanks. Tell Hattie I hope the hat matches the negligee...."

Mrs. Hixson hung up the receiver and made notations on the pad before her. She was a very efficient woman. She had been a nurse and had gone through the worst of it, had been a proud, realistic, overworked probationer, suffered the abuse of smart interns and the insolence of her first patients who thought that she was something to be taken into camp immediately for premature commitment to the service of old age. She swung around suddenly from the desk.

"What kind of cases do you want? I told you I have a nice old woman—"

The nurse's brown eyes were alight with a mixture of thoughts—the movie she had just seen about Pasteur and the book they had all read about Florence Nightingale when they were student nurses. And their pride, swinging across the streets in the cold weather at Philadelphia General, as proud of their new capes as debutantes in their furs going in to balls at the hotels.

"I—I think I would like to try the case again," she said amid a cacophony of telephone bells. "I'd just as soon go back if you can't find anybody else."

"But one minute you say you'll never go on an alcoholic case again and the next minute you say you want to go back to one."

"I think I overestimated how difficult it was. Really, I think I could help him."

"That's up to you. But if he tried to grab your wrists."

"But he couldn't," the nurse said. "Look at my wrists: I played basket ball at Waynesboro High for two years. I'm quite able to take care of him."

Mrs. Hixson looked at her for a long minute. "Well, all right," she said. "But just remember that nothing they say when they're drunk is what they mean when they're sober—I've been all through that: arrange with one of the servants that you can call on him, because you never can tell—some alcoholics are pleasant and some of them are not, but all of them can be rotten."

"I'll remember," the nurse said.

It was an oddly clear night when she went out, with slanting particles of thin sleet making white of a blue-black sky. The bus was the same that had taken her into town but there seemed to be more windows broken now and the bus driver was irritated and talked about what terrible things he would do if he caught any kids. She knew he was just talking about the annoyance in general, just as she had been thinking about the annoyance of an alcoholic. When she came up to the suite and found him all helpless and distraught she would despise him and be sorry for him.

Getting off the bus she went down the long steps to the hotel, feeling a little exalted by the chill in the air. She was going to take care of him because nobody else would, and because the best people of her profession had been interested in taking care of the cases that nobody else wanted.

She knocked at his study door, knowing just what she was going to say.

He answered it himself. He was in dinner clothes even to a derby hat—but minus his studs and tie.

"Oh, hello," he said casually. "Glad you're back. I woke up a while ago and decided I'd go out. Did you get a night nurse?"

"I'm the night nurse too," she said. "I decided to stay on twenty- hour duty."

He broke into a genial, indifferent smile.

"I saw you were gone, but something told me you'd come back. Please find my studs. They ought to be either in a little tortoise shell box or—"

He shook himself a little more into his clothes, and hoisted the cuffs up inside his coat sleeves.

"I thought you had quit me," he said casually.

"I thought I had, too."

"If you look on that table," he said, "you'll find a whole strip of cartoons that I drew you."

"Who are you going to see?" she asked.

"It's the President's secretary," he said. "I had an awful time trying to get ready. I was about to give up when you came in. Will you order me some sherry?"

"One glass," she agreed wearily.

From the bathroom he called presently:

"Oh, nurse, nurse, Light of my Life, where is another stud?"

"I'll put it in."

In the bathroom she saw the pallor and the fever on his face and smelled the mixed peppermint and gin on his breath.

"You'll come up soon?" she asked. "Dr. Carter's coming at ten."

"What nonsense! You're coming down with me."

"Me?" she exclaimed. "In a sweater and skirt? Imagine!"

"Then I won't go."

"All right then, go to bed. That's where you belong anyhow. Can't you see these people tomorrow?"

"No, of course not."

"Of course not!"

She went behind him and reaching over his shoulder tied his tie—his shirt was already thumbed out of press where he had put in the studs, and she suggested:

"Won't you put on another one, if you've got to meet some people you like?"

"All right, but I want to do it myself."

"Why can't you let me help you?" she demanded in exasperation. "Why can't you let me help you with your clothes? What's a nurse for—what good am I doing?"

He sat down suddenly on the toilet seat.

"All right—go on."

"Now don't grab my wrist," she said, and then, "Excuse me."

"Don't worry. It didn't hurt. You'll see in a minute."

She had the coat, vest and stiff shirt off him but before she could pull his undershirt over his head he dragged at his cigarette, delaying her.

"Now watch this," he said. "One—two—three."

She pulled up the undershirt; simultaneously he thrust the crimson-grey point of the cigarette like a dagger against his heart. It crushed out against a copper plate on his left rib about the size of a silver dollar, and he said "ouch!" as a stray spark fluttered down against his stomach.

Now was the time to be hard-boiled, she thought. She knew there were three medals from the war in his jewel box, but she had risked many things herself: tuberculosis among them and one time something worse, though she had not known it and had never quite forgiven the doctor for not telling her.

"You've had a hard time with that, I guess," she said lightly as she sponged him. "Won't it ever heal?"

"Never. That's a copper plate."

"Well, it's no excuse for what you're doing to yourself."

He bent his great brown eyes on her, shrewd—aloof, confused. He signaled to her in one second, his Will to Die, and for all her training and experience she knew she could never do anything constructive with him. He stood up, steadying himself on the wash basin and fixing his eye on some place just ahead.

"Now, if I'm going to stay here you're not going to get at that liquor," she said.

Suddenly she knew he wasn't looking for that. He was looking at the corner where she had thrown the bottle this afternoon. She stared at his handsome face, weak and defiant—afraid to turn even half-way because she knew that death was in that corner where he was looking. She knew death—she had heard it, smelt its unmistakable odor, but she had never seen it before it entered into anyone, and she knew this man saw it in the corner of his bathroom: that it was standing there looking at him while he spit from a feeble cough and rubbed the result into the braid of his trousers. It shone there... crackling for a moment as evidence of the last gesture he ever made.

She tried to express it next day to Mrs. Hixson:

"It's not like anything you can beat—no matter how hard you try. This one could have twisted my wrists until he strained them and that wouldn't matter so much to me. It's just that you can't really help them and it's so discouraging—it's all for nothing."

WILLIAM FAULKNER
(1897–1962)

Faulkner, sui generis. One of the unquestionably great writers of the twentieth century. The extraordinary range and versatility of his work—the brilliance of his formal experimentation—the very ambition of his novels' structural designs: these are but the outward aspects of the man's genius. And that, born in Oxford, Mississippi, Faulkner should have spent virtually all of his writing life in that town, creating an immense body of work out of the soil of an undistinguished rural county in Mississippi, only deepens the wonder of his achievement.

Faulkner's major titles are synonymous with some of the major titles of American literature. Among them are The Sound and the Fury *(1929),* As I Lay Dying *(1930),* Sanctuary *(1931),* Light in August *(1932),* Absalom, Absalom! *(1936),* The Hamlet *(1940). And there are the* Collected Stories *(1950), from which the story included here has been taken.*

Choosing a single story to represent Faulkner, too, is a difficult task. "That Evening Sun" is a masterpiece—but so are "A Rose for Emily," "Spotted Horses," "Barn Burning," among others. The particular appeal of "That Evening Sun" is that, for interested readers who have not yet read The Sound and the Fury, *Nancy's fate is divulged, in a chilling aside, in Quentin Compson's section of the novel. And the story seems to have been, for Faulkner, something of an experiment in dramatic form, rare in his work.*

That Evening Sun

I

Monday is no different from any other weekday in Jefferson now. The streets are paved now, and the telephone and electric companies are cutting down more and more of the shade trees—the water oaks, the maples and locusts and elms—to make room for iron poles bearing clusters of bloated and ghostly and bloodless grapes, and we have a city laundry which makes the rounds on Monday morning, gathering the bundles of clothes into bright-colored, specially-made motor cars: the soiled wearing of a whole week now flees apparitionlike behind alert and irritable electric horns, with a long diminishing noise of rubber and asphalt like tearing silk, and even the Negro women who still take in white people's washing after the old custom, fetch and deliver it in automobiles.

But fifteen years ago, on Monday morning the quiet, dusty, shady streets would be full of Negro women with, balanced on their steady, turbaned heads, bundles of clothes tied up in sheets, almost as large as cotton bales, carried so without touch of hand between the kitchen door of the white house and the blackened washpot beside a cabin door in Negro Hollow.

Nancy would set her bundle on the top of her head, then upon the bundle in turn she would set the black straw sailor hat which she wore winter and summer. She was tall, with a high, sad face sunken a little where her teeth were missing. Sometimes we would go a part of the way down the lane and across the pasture with her, to watch the balanced bundle and the hat that never bobbed nor wavered, even when she walked down into the ditch and up the other side and stooped through the fence. She would go down on her hands and knees and crawl through the gap, her head rigid, uptilted, the bundle steady as a rock or a balloon, and rise to her feet again and go on.

Sometimes the husbands of the washing women would fetch and deliver the clothes, but Jesus never did that for Nancy, even before father told him to stay away from our house, even when Dilsey was sick and Nancy would come to cook for us.

And then about half the time we'd have to go down the lane to Nancy's cabin and tell her to come on and cook breakfast. We would stop at the ditch, because father told us to not have anything to do with Jesus—he was a short black man, with a razor scar down his face—and we would throw rocks at Nancy's house until she came to the door, leaning her head around it without any clothes on.

"What yawl mean, chunking my house?" Nancy said. "What you little devils mean?"

"Father says for you to come on and get breakfast," Caddy said. "Father says it's over a half an hour now, and you've got to come this minute."

"I aint studying no breakfast," Nancy said. "I going to get my sleep out."

"I bet you're drunk," Jason said. "Father says you're drunk. Are you drunk, Nancy?"

"Who says I is?" Nancy said. "I got to get my sleep out. I aint studying no breakfast."

So after a while we quit chunking the cabin and went back home. When she finally came, it was too late for me to go to school. So we thought it was whisky until that day they arrested her again and they were taking her to jail and they passed Mr Stovall. He was the cashier in the bank and a deacon in the Baptist church, and Nancy began to say:

"When you going to pay me, white man? When you going to pay me, white man? It's been three times now since you paid me a cent—" Mr Stovall knocked her down, but she kept on saying, "When you going to pay me, white man? It's been three times now since—" until Mr Stovall kicked her in the mouth with his heel and the marshal caught Mr Stovall back, and Nancy lying in the street, laughing. She turned her head and spat out some blood and teeth and said, "It's been three times now since he paid me a cent."

That was how she lost her teeth, and all that day they told about Nancy and Mr Stovall, and all that night the ones that passed the jail could hear Nancy singing and yelling. They could see her hands holding to the window bars, and a lot of them stopped along the fence, listening to her and to the jailer trying to make her stop. She didn't shut up until almost daylight, when the jailer began to hear a bumping and scraping upstairs and he went up there and found Nancy hanging from the window bar.

He said that it was cocaine and not whisky, because no nigger would try to commit suicide unless he was full of cocaine, because a nigger full of cocaine wasn't a nigger any longer.

The jailer cut her down and revived her; then he beat her, whipped her. She had hung herself with her dress. She had fixed it all right, but when they arrested her she didn't have on anything except a dress and so she didn't have anything to tie her hands with and she couldn't make her hands let go of the window ledge. So the jailer heard the noise and ran up there and found Nancy hanging from the window, stark naked, her belly already swelling out a little, like a little balloon.

When Dilsey was sick in her cabin and Nancy was cooking for us, we could see her apron swelling out; that was before father told Jesus to stay away from the house. Jesus was in the kitchen, sitting behind the stove, with his razor scar on his black face like a piece of dirty string. He said it was a watermelon that Nancy had under her dress.

"It never come off of your vine, though," Nancy said.

"Off of what vine?" Caddy said.

"I can cut down the vine it did come off of," Jesus said.

"What makes you want to talk like that before these chillen?" Nancy said. "Whyn't you go on to work? You done et. You want Mr Jason to catch you hanging around his kitchen, talking that way before these chillen?"

"Talking what way?" Caddy said. "What vine?"

"I cant hang around white man's kitchen," Jesus said. "But white man can hang around mine. White man can come in my house, but I cant stop him. When white man want to come in my house, I aint got no house. I cant stop him, but he cant kick me outen it. He cant do that."

Dilsey was still sick in her cabin. Father told Jesus to stay off our place. Dilsey was still sick. It was a long time. We were in the library after supper.

"Isn't Nancy through in the kitchen yet?" mother said. "It seems to me that she has had plenty of time to have finished the dishes."

"Let Quentin go and see," father said. "Go and see if Nancy is through, Quentin. Tell her she can go on home."

I went to the kitchen. Nancy was through. The dishes were put away and the fire was out. Nancy was sitting in a chair, close to the cold stove. She looked at me.

"Mother wants to know if you are through," I said.

"Yes," Nancy said. She looked at me. "I done finished." She looked at me.

"What is it?" I said. "What is it?"

"I aint nothing but a nigger," Nancy said. "It aint none of my fault."

She looked at me, sitting in the chair before the cold stove, the sailor hat on her head. I went back to the library. It was the cold stove and all, when you think of a kitchen being warm and busy and cheerful. And with a cold stove and the dishes all put away, and nobody wanting to eat at that hour.

"Is she through?" mother said.

"Yessum," I said.

"What is she doing?" mother said.

"She's not doing anything. She's through."

"I'll go and see," father said.

"Maybe she's waiting for Jesus to come and take her home," Caddy said.

"Jesus is gone," I said. Nancy told us how one morning she woke up and Jesus was gone.

"He quit me," Nancy said. "Done gone to Memphis, I reckon. Dodging them city police for a while, I reckon."

"And a good riddance," father said. "I hope he stays there."

"Nancy's scaired of the dark," Jason said.

"So are you," Caddy said.

"I'm not," Jason said.

"Scairy cat," Caddy said.

"I'm not," Jason said.

"You, Candace!" mother said. Father came back.

"I am going to walk down the lane with Nancy," he said. "She says that Jesus is back."

"Has she seen him?" mother said.

"No. Some Negro sent her word that he was back in town. I wont be long."

"You'll leave me alone, to take Nancy home?" mother said. "Is her safety more precious to you than mine?"

"I wont be long," father said.

"You'll leave these children unprotected, with that Negro about?"

"I'm going too," Caddy said. "Let me go, Father."

"What would he do with them, if he were unfortunate enough to have them?" father said.

"I want to go, too," Jason said.

"Jason!" mother said. She was speaking to father. You could tell that by the way she said the name. Like she believed that all day father had been trying to think of doing the thing she wouldn't like the most, and that she knew all the time that after a while he would think of it. I stayed quiet, because father and I both knew that mother would want him to make me stay with her if she just thought of it in time. So father didn't look at me. I was the oldest. I was nine and Caddy was seven and Jason was five.

"Nonsense," father said. "We wont be long."

Nancy had her hat on. We came to the lane. "Jesus always been good to me," Nancy said. "Whenever he had two dollars, one of them was mine." We walked in the lane. "If I can just get through the lane," Nancy said, "I be all right then."

The lane was always dark. "This is where Jason got scared on Hallowe'en," Caddy said.

"I didn't," Jason said.

"Cant Aunt Rachel do anything with him?" father said. Aunt Rachel was old. She lived in a cabin beyond Nancy's, by herself. She had white hair and she smoked a pipe in the door, all day long; she didn't work any more. They said she was Jesus' mother. Sometimes she said she was and sometimes she said she wasn't any kin to Jesus.

"Yes, you did," Caddy said. "You were scairder than Frony. You were scairder than T.P. even. Scairder than niggers."

"Cant nobody do nothing with him," Nancy said. "He say I done woke up the devil in him and aint but one thing going to lay it down again."

"Well, he's gone now," father said. "There's nothing for you to be afraid of now. And if you'd just let white men alone."

"Let what white men alone?" Caddy said. "How let them alone?"

"He aint gone nowhere," Nancy said. "I can feel him. I can feel him now, in this lane. He hearing us talk, every word, hid somewhere, waiting. I aint seen him, and I aint going to see him again but once more, with that razor in his mouth. That razor on that string down his back, inside his shirt. And then I aint going to be even surprised."

"I wasn't scaired," Jason said.

"If you'd behave yourself, you'd have kept out of this," father said. "But it's all right now. He's probably in St. Louis now. Probably got another wife by now and forgot all about you."

"If he has, I better not find out about it," Nancy said. "I'd stand there right over them, and every time he wrapped her, I'd cut that arm off. I'd cut his head off and I'd slit her belly and I'd shove—"

"Hush," father said.

"Slit whose belly, Nancy?" Caddy said.

"I wasn't scaired," Jason said. "I'd walk right down this lane by myself."

"Yah," Caddy said. "You wouldn't dare to put your foot down in it if we were not here too."

II

Dilsey was still sick, so we took Nancy home every night until mother said, "How much longer is this going on? I to be left alone in this big house while you take home a frightened Negro?"

We fixed a pallet in the kitchen for Nancy. One night we waked up, hearing the sound. It was not singing and it was not crying, coming up the dark stairs. There was a light in mother's room and we heard father going down the hall, down the back stairs, and Caddy and I went into the hall. The floor was cold. Our toes curled away from it while we listened to the sound. It was like singing and it wasn't like singing, like the sounds that Negroes make.

Then it stopped and we heard father going down the back stairs, and we went to the head of the stairs. Then the sound began again, in the stairway, not loud, and we could see Nancy's eyes halfway up the stairs, against the wall. They looked like cat's eyes do, like a big cat against the wall, watching us. When we came down the steps to where she was, she quit making the sound again, and we stood there until father came back up from the kitchen, with his pistol in his hand. He went back down with Nancy and they came back with Nancy's pallet.

We spread the pallet in our room. After the light in mother's room went off, we could see Nancy's eyes again. "Nancy," Caddy whispered, "are you asleep, Nancy?"

Nancy whispered something. It was oh or no, I dont know which. Like nobody had made it, like it came from nowhere and went nowhere, until it was like Nancy was not there at all; that I had looked so hard at her eyes on the stairs that they had got printed on my eyeballs, like the sun does when you have closed your eyes and there is no sun. "Jesus," Nancy whispered. "Jesus."

"Was it Jesus?" Caddy said. "Did he try to come into the kitchen?"

"Jesus," Nancy said. Like this: Jeeeeeeeeeeeeeeeesus, until the sound went out, like a match or a candle does.

"It's the other Jesus she means," I said.

"Can you see us, Nancy?" Caddy whispered. "Can you see our eyes too?"

"I aint nothing but a nigger," Nancy said. "God knows. God knows."

"What did you see down there in the kitchen?" Caddy whispered. "What tried to get in?"

"God knows," Nancy said. We could see her eyes. "God knows."

Dilsey got well. She cooked dinner. "You'd better stay in bed a day or two longer," father said.

"What for?" Dilsey said. "If I had been a day later, this place would be to rack and ruin. Get on out of here now, and let me get my kitchen straight again."

Dilsey cooked supper too. And that night, just before dark, Nancy came into the kitchen.

"How do you know he's back?" Dilsey said. "You aint seen him."

"Jesus is a nigger," Jason said.

"I can feel him," Nancy said. "I can feel him laying yonder in the ditch."

"Tonight?" Dilsey said. "Is he there tonight?"

"Dilsey's a nigger too," Jason said.

"You try to eat something," Dilsey said.

"I dont want nothing," Nancy said.

"I aint a nigger," Jason said.

"Drink some coffee," Dilsey said. She poured a cup of coffee for Nancy. "Do you know he's out there tonight? How come you know it's tonight?"

"I know," Nancy said. "He's there, waiting. I know. I done lived with him too long. I know what he is fixing to do fore he know it himself."

"Drink some coffee," Dilsey said. Nancy held the cup to her mouth and blew into the cup. Her mouth pursed out like a spreading adder's, like a rubber mouth, like she had blown all the color out of her lips with blowing the coffee.

"I aint a nigger," Jason said. "Are you a nigger, Nancy?"

"I hellborn, child," Nancy said. "I wont be nothing soon. I going back where I come from soon."

III

She began to drink the coffee. While she was drinking, holding the cup in both hands, she began to make the sound again. She made the sound into the cup and the coffee sploshed out onto her hands and her dress. Her eyes looked at us and she sat there, her elbows on her knees, holding the cup in both hands, looking at us across the wet cup, making the sound. "Look at Nancy," Jason said. "Nancy cant cook for us now. Dilsey's got well now."

"You hush up," Dilsey said. Nancy held the cup in both hands, looking at us, making the sound, like there were two of them: one looking at us and the other making the sound. "Whyn't you let Mr Jason telefoam the marshal?" Dilsey said. Nancy stopped then, holding the cup in her long brown hands. She tried to drink some coffee again, but it sploshed out of the cup, onto her hands and her dress, and she put the cup down. Jason watched her.

"I cant swallow it," Nancy said. "I swallows but it wont go down me."

"You go down to the cabin," Dilsey said. "Frony will fix you a pallet and I'll be there soon."

"Wont no nigger stop him," Nancy said.

"I aint a nigger," Jason said. "Am I, Dilsey?"

"I reckon not," Dilsey said. She looked at Nancy. "I dont reckon so. What you going to do, then?"

Nancy looked at us. Her eyes went fast, like she was afraid there wasn't time to look, without hardly moving at all. She looked at us, at all three of us at one time. "You member that night I stayed in yawls' room?" she said. She told about how we waked up early the next morning, and played. We had to play quiet, on her pallet, until father woke up and it was time to get breakfast. "Go and ask your maw to let me stay here tonight," Nancy said. "I wont need no pallet. We can play some more."

Caddy asked mother. Jason went too. "I cant have Negroes sleeping in the bedrooms," mother said. Jason cried. He cried until mother said he couldn't have any dessert for three days if he didn't stop. Then Jason said he could stop if Dilsey would make a chocolate cake. Father was there.

"Why dont you do something about it?" mother said. "What do we have officers for?"

"Why is Nancy afraid of Jesus?" Caddy said. "Are you afraid of father, mother?"

"What could the officers do?" father said. "If Nancy hasn't seen him, how could the officers find him?"

"Then why is she afraid?" mother said.

"She says he is there. She says she knows he is there tonight."

"Yet we pay taxes," mother said. "I must wait here alone in this big house while you take a Negro woman home."

"You know that I am not lying outside with a razor," father said.

"I'll stop if Dilsey will make a chocolate cake," Jason said. Mother told us to go out and father said he didn't know if Jason would get a chocolate cake or not, but he knew what Jason was going to get in about a minute. We went back to the kitchen and told Nancy.

"Father said for you to go home and lock the door, and you'll be all right," Caddy said. "All right from what, Nancy? Is Jesus mad at you?" Nancy was holding the coffee cup in her hands again, her elbows on her knees and her hands holding the cup between her knees. She was looking into the cup. "What have you done that made Jesus mad?" Caddy said. Nancy let the cup go. It didn't break on the floor, but the coffee spilled out, and Nancy sat there with her hands still making the shape of the cup. She began to make the sound again, not loud. Not singing and not unsinging. We watched her.

"Here," Dilsey said. "You quit that, now. You get aholt of yourself. You wait here. I going to get Versh to walk home with you." Dilsey went out.

We looked at Nancy. Her shoulders kept shaking, but she quit making the sound. We watched her. "What's Jesus going to do to you?" Caddy said. "He went away."

Nancy looked at us. "We had fun that night I stayed in yawls' room, didn't we?"

"I didn't," Jason said. "I didn't have any fun."

"You were asleep in mother's room," Caddy said. "You were not there."

"Let's go down to my house and have some more fun," Nancy said.

"Mother wont let us," I said. "It's too late now."

"Dont bother her," Nancy said. "We can tell her in the morning. She wont mind."

"She wouldn't let us," I said.

"Don't ask her now," Nancy said. "Don't bother her now."

"She didn't say we couldn't go," Caddy said.

"We didn't ask," I said.

"If you go, I'll tell," Jason said.

"Well have fun," Nancy said. "They wont mind, just to my house. I been working for yawl a long time. They wont mind."

"I'm not afraid to go," Caddy said. "Jason is the one that's afraid. He'll tell."

"I'm not," Jason said.

"Yes, you are," Caddy said. "You'll tell."

"I wont tell," Jason said. "I'm not afraid."

"Jason aint afraid to go with me," Nancy said. "Is you, Jason?"

"Jason is going to tell," Caddy said. The lane was dark. We passed the pasture gate. "I bet if something was to jump out from behind that gate, Jason would holler."

"I wouldn't," Jason said. We walked down the lane. Nancy was talking loud.

"What are you talking so loud for, Nancy?" Caddy said.

"Who; me?" Nancy said. "Listen at Quentin and Caddy and Jason saying I'm talking loud."

"You talk like there was five of us here," Caddy said. "You talk like father was here too."

"Who; me talking loud, Mr Jason?" Nancy said.

"Nancy called Jason 'Mister,'" Caddy said.

"Listen how Caddy and Quentin and Jason talk," Nancy said.

"We're not talking loud," Caddy said. "You're the one that's talking like father—"

"Hush," Nancy said; "hush, Mr Jason."

"Nancy called Jason 'Mister' aguh—"

"Hush," Nancy said. She was talking loud when we crossed the ditch and stooped through the fence where she used to stoop through with the clothes on her head. Then we came to her house. We were going fast then. She opened the door. The smell of the house was like the lamp and the smell of Nancy was like the wick, like they were waiting for one another to begin to smell. She lit the lamp and closed the door and put the bar up. Then she quit talking loud, looking at us.

"What're we going to do?" Caddy said.

"What do yawl want to do?" Nancy said.

"You said we would have some fun," Caddy said.

There was something about Nancy's house; something you could smell besides Nancy and the house. Jason smelled it, even. "I dont want to stay here," he said. "I want to go home."

"Go home, then," Caddy said.

"I dont want to go by myself," Jason said.

"We're going to have some fun," Nancy said.

"How?" Caddy said.

Nancy stood by the door. She was looking at us, only it was like she had emptied her eyes, like she had quit using them. "What do you want to do?" she said.

"Tell us a story," Caddy said. "Can you tell a story?"

"Yes," Nancy said.

"Tell it," Caddy said. We looked at Nancy. "You dont know any stories."

"Yes," Nancy said. "Yes, I do."

She came and sat in a chair before the hearth. There was a little fire there. Nancy built it up, when it was already hot inside. She built up a good blaze. She told a story. She talked like her eyes looked, like her eyes watching us and her voice talking to us did not belong to her. Like she was living somewhere else, waiting somewhere else. She was outside the cabin. Her voice was inside and the shape of her, the Nancy that could stoop under a barbed wire fence with a bundle of clothes balanced on her head as though without weight, like a balloon, was there. But that was all. "And so this here queen come walking up to the ditch, where that bad man was hiding. She was walking up to the ditch, and she say, 'If I can just get past this here ditch,' was what she say . . ."

"What ditch?" Caddy said. "A ditch like that one out there? Why did a queen want to go into a ditch?"

"To get to her house," Nancy said. She looked at us. "She had to cross the ditch to get into her house quick and bar the door."

"Why did she want to go home and bar the door?" Caddy said.

IV

Nancy looked at us. She quit talking. She looked at us. Jason's legs stuck straight out of his pants where he sat on Nancy's lap. "I dont think that's a good story," he said. "I want to go home."

"Maybe we had better," Caddy said. She got up from the floor. "I bet they are looking for us right now." She went toward the door.

"No," Nancy said. "Dont open it." She got up quick and passed Caddy. She didn't touch the door, the wooden bar.

"Why not?" Caddy said.

"Come back to the lamp," Nancy said. "We'll have fun. You dont have to go."

"We ought to go," Caddy said. "Unless we have a lot of fun." She and Nancy came back to the fire, the lamp.

"I want to go home," Jason said. "I'm going to tell."

"I know another story," Nancy said. She stood close to the lamp. She looked at Caddy, like when your eyes look up at a stick balanced on your nose. She had to look down to see Caddy, but her eyes looked like that, like when you are balancing a stick.

"I wont listen to it," Jason said. "I'll bang on the floor."

"It's a good one," Nancy said. "It's better than the other one."

"What's it about?" Caddy said. Nancy was standing by the lamp. Her hand was on the lamp, against the light, long and brown.

"Your hand is on that hot globe," Caddy said. "Dont it feel hot to your hand?"

Nancy looked at her hand on the lamp chimney. She took her hand away, slow. She stood there, looking at Caddy, wringing her long hand as though it were tied to her wrist with a string.

"Let's do something else," Caddy said.

"I want to go home," Jason said.

"I got some popcorn," Nancy said. She looked at Caddy and then at Jason and then at me and then at Caddy again. "I got some popcorn."

"I dont like popcorn," Jason said. "I'd rather have candy."

Nancy looked at Jason. "You can hold the popper." She was still wringing her hand; it was long and limp and brown.

"All right," Jason said. "I'll stay a while if I can do that. Caddy cant hold it. I'll want to go home again if Caddy holds the popper."

Nancy built up the fire. "Look at Nancy putting her hands in the fire," Caddy said. "What's the matter with you, Nancy?"

"I got popcorn," Nancy said. "I got some." She took the popper from under the bed. It was broken. Jason began to cry.

"Now we cant have any popcorn," he said.

"We ought to go home, anyway," Caddy said. "Come on, Quentin."

"Wait," Nancy said; "wait. I can fix it. Dont you want to help me fix it?"

"I dont think I want any," Caddy said. "It's too late now."

"You help me, Jason," Nancy said. "Dont you want to help me?"

"No," Jason said. "I want to go home."

"Hush," Nancy said; "hush. Watch. Watch me. I can fix it so Jason can hold it and pop the corn." She got a piece of wire and fixed the popper.

"It wont hold good," Caddy said.

"Yes, it will," Nancy said. "Yawl watch. Yawl help me shell some corn."

The popcorn was under the bed too. We shelled it into the popper and Nancy helped Jason hold the popper over the fire.

"It's not popping," Jason said. "I want to go home."

"You wait," Nancy said. "It'll begin to pop. Well have fun then." She was sitting close to the fire. The lamp was turned up so high it was beginning to smoke.

"Why dont you turn it down some?" I said.

"It's all right," Nancy said. "I'll clean it. Yawl wait. The popcorn will start in a minute."

"I dont believe it's going to start," Caddy said. "We ought to start home, anyway. They'll be worried."

"No," Nancy said. "It's going to pop. Dilsey will tell um yawl with me. I been working for yawl long time. They won't mind if yawl at my house. You wait, now. It'll start popping any minute now."

Then Jason got some smoke in his eyes and he began to cry. He dropped the popper into the fire. Nancy got a wet rag and wiped Jason's face, but he didn't stop crying.

"Hush," she said. "Hush." But he didn't hush. Caddy took the popper out of the fire.

"It's burned up," she said. "You'll have to get some more popcorn, Nancy."

"Did you put all of it in?" Nancy said.

"Yes," Caddy said. Nancy looked at Caddy. Then she took the popper and opened it and poured the cinders into her apron and began to sort the grains, her hands long and brown, and we watching her.

"Haven't you got any more?" Caddy said.

"Yes," Nancy said; "yes. Look. This here ain't burnt. All we need to do is—"

"I want to go home," Jason said. "I'm going to tell."

"Hush," Caddy said. We all listened. Nancy's head was already turned toward the barred door, her eyes filled with red lamplight. "Somebody is coming," Caddy said.

Then Nancy began to make that sound again, not loud, sitting there above the fire, her long hands dangling between her knees; all of a sudden water began to come out on her face in big drops, running down her face, carrying in each one a little turning ball of firelight like a spark until it dropped off her chin. "She's not crying," I said.

"I aint crying," Nancy said. Her eyes were closed. "I aint crying. Who is it?"

"I dont know," Caddy said. She went to the door and looked out. "We've got to go now," she said. "Here comes father."

"I'm going to tell," Jason said. "Yawl made me come."

The water still ran down Nancy's face. She turned in her chair. "Listen. Tell him. Tell him we going to have fun. Tell him I take good care of yawl until in the morning. Tell him to let me come home with yawl and sleep on the floor. Tell him I won't need no pallet. We'll have fun. You member last time how we had so much fun?"

"I didn't have fun," Jason said. "You hurt me. You put smoke in my eyes. I'm going to tell."

V

Father came in. He looked at us. Nancy did not get up.

"Tell him," she said.

"Caddy made us come down here," Jason said. "I didn't want to."

Father came to the fire. Nancy looked up at him. "Cant you go to Aunt Rachel's and stay?" he said. Nancy looked up at father, her hands between her knees. "He's not here," father said. "I would have seen him. There's not a soul in sight."

"He in the ditch," Nancy said. "He waiting in the ditch yonder."

"Nonsense," father said. He looked at Nancy. "Do you know he's there?"

"I got the sign," Nancy said.

"What sign?"

"I got it. It was on the table when I come in. It was a hogbone, with blood meat still on it, laying by the lamp. He's out there. When yawl walk out that door, I gone."

"Gone where, Nancy?" Caddy said.

"I'm not a tattletale," Jason said.

"Nonsense," father said.

"He out there," Nancy said. "He looking through that window this minute, waiting for yawl to go. Then I gone."

"Nonsense," father said. "Lock up your house and we'll take you on to Aunt Rachel's."

"Twont do no good," Nancy said. She didn't look at father now, but he looked down at her, at her long, limp, moving hands. "Putting it off wont do no good."

"Then what do you want to do?" father said.

"I dont know," Nancy said. "I cant do nothing. Just put it off. And that dont do no good. I reckon it belong to me. I reckon what I going to get aint no more than mine."

"Get what?" Caddy said. "What's yours?"

"Nothing," father said. "You all must get to bed."

"Caddy made me come," Jason said.

"Go on to Aunt Rachel's," father said.

"It wont do no good," Nancy said. She sat before the fire, her elbows on her knees, her long hands between her knees. "When even your own kitchen wouldn't do no good. When even if I was sleeping on the floor in the room with your chillen, and the next morning there I am, and blood—"

"Hush," father said. "Lock the door and put out the lamp and go to bed."

"I scared of the dark," Nancy said. "I scared for it to happen in the dark."

"You mean you're going to sit right here with the lamp lighted?' father said. Then Nancy began to make the sound again, sitting before the fire, her long hands between her knees. "Ah, damnation," father said. "Come along, chillen. It's past bedtime."

"When yawl go home, I gone," Nancy said. She talked quieter now, and her face looked quiet, like her hands. "Anyway, I got my coffin money saved up with Mr Lovelady." Mr Lovelady was a short, dirty man who collected the Negro insurance, coming around to the cabins or the kitchens every Saturday morning, to collect fifteen cents. He and his wife lived at the hotel. One morning his wife committed suicide. They had a child, a little girl. He and the child went away. After a week or two he came back alone. We would see him going along the lanes and the back streets on Saturday mornings.

"Nonsense," father said. "You'll be the first thing I'll see in the kitchen tomorrow morning."

"You'll see what you'll see, I reckon," Nancy said. "But it will take the Lord to say what that will be."

VI

We left her sitting before the fire.

"Come and put the bar up," father said. But she didn't move. She didn't look at us again, sitting quietly there between the lamp and the fire. From some distance down the lane we could look back and see her through the open door.

"What, Father?" Caddy said. "What's going to happen?"

"Nothing," father said. Jason was on father's back, so Jason was the tallest of all of us. We went down into the ditch. I looked at it, quiet. I couldn't see much where the moonlight and the shadows tangled.

"If Jesus is hid here, he can see us, cant he?" Caddy said.

"He's not there," father said. "He went away a long time ago."

"You made me come," Jason said, high; against the sky it looked like father had two heads, a little one and a big one. "I didn't want to."

We went up out of the ditch. We could still see Nancy's house and the open door, but we couldn't see Nancy now, sitting before the fire with the door open, because she was tired. "I just done got tired," she said. "I just a nigger. It aint no fault of mine."

But we could hear her, because she began just after we came up out of the ditch, the sound that was not singing and not unsinging. "Who will do our washing now, Father?" I said.

"I'm not a nigger," Jason said, high and close above father's head.

"You're worse," Caddy said, "you are a tattletale. If something was to jump out, you'd be scairder than a nigger."

"I wouldn't," Jason said.

"You'd cry," Caddy said.

"Caddy," father said.

"I wouldn't!" Jason said.

"Scairy cat," Caddy said.

"Candace!" father said.

ERNEST HEMINGWAY
(1899–1961)

So profound has Ernest Hemingway's influence been upon American literature, and upon the short story in particular, any number of his stories might be singled out as "best" or "representative" work. "Hills Like White Elephants" is a model of Minimalist compression and understated pathos; in its highly compressed dialogue-form, as in other succinct masterpieces by Hemingway, "A Very Short Story" and "A Clean Well-Lighted Place," for instance, the author's ironic but highly moral vision is memorably dramatized.

Ernest Hemingway was born in Oak Park, Illinois, but lived most of his adult life—in time, a disconcertingly public life—as an expatriate American. Indeed, Hemingway defined himself in bold opposition to the solidly church-going, middle class Caucasian America that was his heritage. His first published story was "My Old Man," strongly influenced by Sherwood Anderson, and chosen for The Best American Short Stories 1923; *the author was twenty-four years old. His first book to appear in the United States,* In Our Time *(1925), is a gathering of linked short stories and prose sketches, published by way of Sherwood Anderson's intervention. Thereafter, each book by Ernest Hemingway would constitute a literary event, occasionally one of controversy:* The Sun Also Rises *(1926),* Men Without Women *(1927),* A Farewell to Arms *(1929),* Green Hills of Africa *(1935),* To Have and Have Not *(1937),* For Whom the Bell Tolls *(1940),* The Old Man and the Sea *(1952), among others. It is likely that, had Hemingway written only several of his greatest short stories—"The Snows of Kilimanjaro," "The Short Happy Life of Francis Macomber," "Soldier's Home," "Big Two-Hearted River," for instance—he would be as honored as a master of American prose as he is now.*

Hills Like White Elephants

The hills across the valley of the Ebro were long and white. On this side there was no shade and no trees and the station was between two lines of rails in the sun. Close against the side of the station there was the warm shadow of the building and a curtain, made of strings of bamboo beads, hung across the open door into the bar, to keep out flies. The American and the girl with him sat at a table in the shade, outside the building. It was very hot and the express from Barcelona would come in forty minutes. It stopped at this junction for two minutes and went on to Madrid.

"What should we drink?" the girl asked. She had taken off her hat and put it on the table.

"It's pretty hot," the man said.

"Let's drink beer."

"Dos cervezas," the man said into the curtain.

"Big ones?" a woman asked from the doorway.

"Yes. Two big ones."

The woman brought two glasses of beer and two felt pads. She put the felt pads and the beer glasses on the table and looked at the man and the girl. The girl was looking off at the line of hills. They were white in the sun and the country was brown and dry.

"They look like white elephants," she said.

"I've never seen one," the man drank his beer.

"No, you wouldn't have."

"I might have," the man said. "Just because you say I wouldn't have doesn't prove anything."

The girl looked at the bead curtain. "They've painted something on it," she said. "What does it say?"

"Anis del Toro. It's a drink."

"Could we try it?"

The man called "Listen" through the curtain. The woman came out from the bar.

"Four reales."

"We want two Anis del Toro."

"With water?"

"Do you want it with water?"

"I don't know," the girl said. "Is it good with water?"

"It's all right."

"You want them with water?" asked the woman.

"Yes, with water."

"It tastes like licorice," the girl said and put the glass down.

"That's the way with everything."

"Yes," said the girl. "Everything tastes of licorice. Especially all the things you've waited so long for, like absinthe."

"Oh, cut it out."

"You started it," the girl said. "I was being amused. I was having a fine time."

"Well, let's try and have a fine time."

"All right. I was trying. I said the mountains looked like white elephants. Wasn't that bright?"

"That was bright."

"I wanted to try this new drink. That's all we do, isn't it— look at things and try new drinks?"

"I guess so."

The girl looked across at the hills.

"They're lovely hills," she said. "They don't really look like white elephants. I just meant the coloring of their skin through the trees."

"Should we have another drink?"

"All right."

The warm wind blew the bead curtain against the table.

"The beer's nice and cool," the man said.

"It's lovely," the girl said.

"It's really an awfully simple operation, Jig," the man said. "It's not really an operation at all."

The girl looked at the ground the table legs rested on.

"I know you wouldn't mind it, Jig. It's really not anything. It's just to let the air in."

The girl did not say anything.

"I'll go with you and I'll stay with you all the time. They just let the air in and then it's all perfectly natural."

"Then what will we do afterward?"

"We'll be fine afterward. Just like we were before."

"What makes you think so?"

"That's the only thing that bothers us. It's the only thing that's made us unhappy."

The girl looked at the bead curtain, put her hand out and took hold of two of the strings of beads.

"And you think then we'll be all right and be happy?"

"I know we will. You don't have to be afraid. I've known lots of people that have done it."

"So have I," said the girl. "And afterward they were all so happy."

"Well," the man said, "if you don't want to you don't have to. I wouldn't have you do it if you didn't want to. But I know it's perfectly simple."

"And you really want to?"

"I think it's the best thing to do. But I don't want you to do it if you don't really want to."

"And if I do it you'll be happy and things will be like they were and you'll love me?"

"I love you now. You know I love you."

"I know. But if I do it, then it will be nice again if I say things are like white elephants, and you'll like it?"

"I'll love it. I love it now but I just can't think about it. You know how I get when I worry."

"If I do it you won't ever worry?"

"I won't worry about that because it's perfectly simple."

"Then I'll do it. Because I don't care about me."

"What do you mean?"

"I don't care about me."

"Well, I care about you."

"Oh, yes. But I don't care about me. And I'll do it and then everything will be fine."

"I don't want you to do it if you feel that way."

The girl stood up and walked to the end of the station. Across, on the other side, were fields of grain and trees along the banks of the Ebro. Far away, beyond the river, were mountains. The shadow of a cloud moved across the field of grain and she saw the river through the trees.

"And we could have all this," she said. "And we could have everything and every day we make it more impossible."

"What did you say?"

"I said we could have everything."

"We can have everything."

"No, we can't."

"We can have the whole world."

"No, we can't."

"We can go everywhere."

"No, we can't. It isn't ours any more."

"It's ours."

"No, it isn't. And once they take it away, you never get it back."

"But they haven't taken it away."

"We'll wait and see."

"Come on back in the shade," he said. "You mustn't feel that way."

"I don't feel any way," the girl said. "I just know things."

"I don't want you to do anything that you don't want to do—"

"Nor that isn't good for me," she said. "I know. Could we have another beer?"

"All right. But you've got to realize—"

"I realize," the girl said. "Can't we maybe stop talking?"

They sat down at the table and the girl looked across at the hills on the dry side of the valley and the man looked at her and at the table.

"You've got to realize," he said, "that I don't want you to do it if you don't want to. I'm perfectly willing to go through with it if it means anything to you."

"Doesn't it mean anything to you? We could get along."

"Of course it does. But I don't want anybody but you. I don't want any one else. And I know it's perfectly simple."

"Yes, you know it's perfectly simple."

"It's all right for you to say that, but I do know it."

"Would you do something for me now?"

"I'd do anything for you."

"Would you please please please please please please please stop talking?"

He did not say anything but looked at the bags against the wall of the station. There were labels on them from all the hotels where they had spent nights.

"But I don't want you to," he said, "I don't care anything about it."

"I'll scream," the girl said.

The woman came out through the curtains with two glasses of beer and put them down on the damp felt pads.

"The train comes in five minutes," she said.

"What did she say?" asked the girl.

"That the train is coming in five minutes."

The girl smiled brightly at the woman, to thank her.

"I'd better take the bags over to the other side of the station," the man said. She smiled at him.

"All right. Then come back and we'll finish the beer."

He picked up the two heavy bags and carried them around the station to the other tracks. He looked up the tracks but could not see the train. Coming back, he walked through the barroom, where people waiting for the train were drinking. He drank an Anis at the bar and looked at the people. They were all waiting reasonably for the train. He went out through the bead curtain. She was sitting at the table and smiled at him.

"Do you feel better?" he asked.

"I feel fine," she said. "There's nothing wrong with me. I feel fine."

LANGSTON HUGHES
(1902–1967)

Brilliant in narration, powerful in impact, this story from The Ways of White Folks *(1934) cannot suggest the remarkable virtuosity of that volume of short fiction, which portrays, with sympathy, rage, horror, and satiric humor, the manifold relations between American blacks and whites. Any number of stories from the book might have been chosen to represent it, including its most ambitious concluding work, the near-novella "Father and Son."*

Langston Hughes is most celebrated as a poet, but his genius cut across a number of genres including short fiction, novels, and plays; during the 1930s, as the most popular writer connected with the Harlem Renaissance, he became something of a public figure, working as a journalist, lecturing, founding black theatres, and bringing out anthologies of black writing. Born in Joplin, Missouri, Hughes lived variously in Detroit, Cleveland, New York, and Chicago; his identification was "the bard of Harlem." Among African-American writers of our time, no one has been more honored than Hughes.

His output was considerable: more than thirty-five books. Of these, in addition to The Ways of White Folks, *the most significant are the poetry collections* The Weary Blues *(1926),* The Dream Keeper *(1932),* Montage of a Dream Deferred *(1951), and* The Panther and the Lash *(1967); the novel* Not Without Laughter *(1930); the humorous sketches* Simple Speaks His Mind *(1950); and the autobiographical* The Big Sea *(1940) and* I Wonder as I Wander *(1956).*

Red-Headed Baby

"Dead, dead as hell, these little burgs on the Florida coast. Lot of half-built skeleton houses left over from the boom. Never finished. Never will be finished. Mosquitoes, sand, niggers. Christ, I ought to break away from it. Stuck five years on same boat and still nothin' but a third mate puttin' in at dumps like this on a damned coastwise tramp. Not even a good time to be had. Norfolk, Savannah, Jacksonville, ain't bad. Ain't bad. But what the hell kind of port's this? What the hell is there to do except get drunk and go out and sleep with niggers? Hell!"

Feet in the sand. Head under palms, magnolias, stars. Lights and the kid-cries of a sleepy town. Mosquitoes to slap at with hairy freckled hands and a dead hot breeze, when there is any breeze.

"What the hell am I walkin' way out here for? She wasn't nothin' to get excited over—last time I saw her. And that must a been a full three years ago. She acted like she was a virgin then. Name was Betsy. Sure ain't a virgin now, I know that. Not after we'd been anchored here damn near a month, the old man mixed up in some kind of law suit over some rich guy's yacht we rammed in a midnight squall off the bar. Damn good thing I wasn't on the bridge then. And this damn yellow gal, said she never had nothing to do with a seaman before. Lyin' I guess. Three years ago. She's probably on the crib-line now. Hell, how far was that house?"

Crossing the railroad track at the edge of town. Green lights. Sand in the road, seeping into oxfords and the cuffs of dungarees. Surf sounds, mosquito sounds, nigger-cries in the night. No street lights out here. There never is where niggers live. Rickety rundown huts, under palm trees. Flowers and vines all over. Always growing, always climbing. Never finished. Never will be finished climbing, growing. Hell of a lot of stars these Florida nights.

"Say, this ought to be the house. No light in it. Well, I remember this half-fallin'-down gate. Still fallin' down. Hell, why don't it go on and fall? Two or three years, and ain't fell yet. Guess *she's* fell a hell of a lot, though. It don't take them yellow janes long to get old and ugly. Said she was seventeen then. A wonder her old woman let me come in the house that night. They acted like it was the first time a white man had ever come in the house. They acted scared. But she was worth the money that time all right. She played like a kid. Said she liked my red hair. Said she'd never had a white man before.... Holy Jesus, the yellow wenches I've had, though.... Well, it's the same old gate. Be funny if she had another mule in my stall, now wouldn't it?... Say, anybody home there?"

"Yes, suh! Yes, suh! Come right in!"

"Hell, I know they can't recognize my voice.... It's the old woman, sure as a yard arm's long.... Hello! Where's Betsy?"

"Yes, suh, right here, suh. In de kitchen. Wait till I lights de light. Come in. Come in, young gentleman."

"Hell, I can't see to come in."

Little flare of oil light.

"Howdy! Howdy do, suh! Howdy, if 'tain't Mister Clarence, now, 'pon my word! Howdy, Mister Clarence, howdy! Howdy! After sich a long time."

"You must-a knowed my voice."

"No, suh, ain't recollected, suh. No, suh, but I knowed you was some white man comin' up de walk. Yes, indeedy! Set down, set down. Betsy be here directly. Set *right* down. Lemme call her. She's in de kitchen.... You Betsy!"

"Same old woman, wrinkled as hell, and still don't care where the money comes from. Still talkin' loud.... She knew it was some white man comin' up the walk, heh? There must be plenty of 'em, then, comin' here now. She knew it was some white man, heh!... What yuh sayin', Betsy, old gal? Damn if yuh ain't just as plump as ever. Them same damn moles on your cheek! Com'ere, lemme feel 'em."

Young yellow girl in a white house dress. Oiled hair. Skin like an autumn moon. Gold-ripe young yellow girl with a white house dress to her knees. Soft plump bare legs, color of the moon. Barefooted.

"Say, Betsy, here is Mister Clarence come back."

"Sure is! Claren—Mister Clarence! Ma, give him a drink."

"Keepin' licker in the house, now, heh? Yes? I thought you was church members last time I saw yuh? You always had to send out and get licker then."

"Well, we's expectin' company some of the times these days," smiling teeth like bright-white rays of moon, Betsy, nearly twenty, and still pretty.

"You usin' rouge, too, ain't yuh?"

"Sweet rouge."

"Yal?"

"Yeah, man, sweet and red like your hair."

"Yal?"

No such wise cracking three years ago. Too young and dumb for flirtation then: Betsy. Never like the old woman, talkative, "This here rum come right off de boats from Bermudy. Taste it, Mister Clarence. Strong enough to knock a mule down. Have a glass."

"Here's to you. Mister Clarence."

"Drinkin' licker, too, heh? Hell of a baby, ain't yuh? Yuh wouldn't even do that last time I saw yuh."

"Sure wouldn't. Mister Clarence, but three years a long time."

"Don't Mister Clarence *me* so much. Yuh know I christened yuh.... Auntie, yuh right about this bein' good licker."

"Yes, suh, I knowed you'd like it. It's strong."

"Sit on my lap, kid."

"Sure...."

Soft heavy hips. Hot and browner than the moon—good licker. Drinking it down in little nigger house Florida coast palm fronds scratching roof hum mosquitoes night bugs flies ain't loud enough to keep a man named Clarence girl named Betsy old woman named Auntie from talking and drinking in a little nigger house on Florida coast dead warm night with the licker browner and more fiery than the moon. Yeah, man! A blanket of stars in the Florida sky—outside. In oil-lamp house you don't see no stars. Only a white man with red hair—third mate on a lousy tramp, a nigger girl, and Auntie wrinkled as an alligator bringing the fourth bottle of licker and everybody drinking—when the door... slowly...opens.

"Say, what the hell? Who's openin' that room door, peepin' in here? It can't be openin' itself?"

The white man stares intently, looking across the table, past the lamp, the licker bottles, the glasses and the old woman, way past the girl.

Standing in the door from the kitchen—Look! a damn redheaded baby. Standing not saying a damn word, a damn runt of a red-headed baby.

"What the hell?"

"You Clar—...Mister Clarence, 'cuse me!...You hatian, you, get back to you' bed this minute—fo' I tan you in a inch o' yo' life!"

"Ma, let him stay."

Betsy's red-headed child stands in the door looking like one of those goggly-eyed dolls you hit with a ball at the County Fair. The child's face got no change in it. Never changes. Looks like never will change. Just staring—blue-eyed. Hell! God damn! A red-headed blue-eyed yellow-skinned baby!

"You Clarence!...'Cuse me, Mister Clarence. I ain't talkin' to you suh....You, Clarence, go to bed....That chile near 'bout worries de soul-case out o' me. Betsy spiles him, that's why. De po' little thing can't hear, nohow. Just deaf as a post. And over two years old and can't even say, 'Da!' No, suh, can't say, 'Da!'"

"Anyhow, Ma, my child ain't blind."

"Might just as well be blind fo' all de good his eyesight do him. I show him a switch and he don't pay it no mind—'less'n I hit him."

"He's mighty damn white for a nigger child."

"Yes, suh, Mister Clarence, he really ain't got much colored blood in him, a-tall. Betsy's papa, Mister Clarence, now he were a white man, too....Here, lemme pour you some licker. Drink, Mister Clarence, drink."

Damn little red-headed stupid-faced runt of a child, named Clarence. Bow-legged as hell, too. Three shots for a quarter like a loaded doll in a County Fair. Anybody take a chance. For Christ's sake, stop him from walking across the floor! Will yuh?

"Hey! Take your hands off my legs, you lousy little bastard!"

"He can't hear you. Mister Clarence."

"Tell him to stop crawlin' around then under the table before I knock his block off."

"You varmint...."

"Hey! Take him up from there, will you?"

"Yes, suh. Mister Clarence."

"Hey!"

"You little . . ."

"Hurry! Go on! Get him out then! What's he doin' crawlin' round dumb as hell lookin' at me up at me. I said, *me.* Get him the hell out of here! Hey, Betsy, get him out!"

A red-headed baby. Moonlight-gone baby. No kind of yellow-white bow-legged goggled-eyed County Fair baseball baby. Get him the hell out of here pulling at my legs looking like me at me like me at myself like me red-headed as me.

"Christ!"

"Christ!"

Knocking over glasses by the oil lamp on the table where the night flies flutter Florida where skeleton houses left over from boom sand in the road and no lights in the nigger section across the railroad's knocking over glasses at edge of town where a moon-colored girl's got a red-headed baby deaf as a post like the dolls you wham at three shots for a quarter in the County Fair half full of licker and can't hit nothing.

"Lemme pay for those drinks, will yuh? How much is it?"

"Ain't you gonna stay. Mister Clarence?"

"Lemme pay for my licker, I said."

"Ain't you gonna stay all night?"

"Lemme pay for that licker."

"Why, Mister Clarence? You stayed before."

"How much is the licker?"

"Two dollars. Mister Clarence."

"Here."

"Thank you, Mister Clarence."

"Go'bye!"

"Go'bye."

RICHARD WRIGHT
(1908–1960)

"The Man Who Was Almost a Man" contrasts with, and in an oblique way amplifies, Langston Hughes's "Red-Headed Baby": for here we see a further development of certain thematic tensions, the logical, if unarticulated, next step. Its setting would seem to bear a close resemblance to the rural area near Natchez, Mississippi, where Wright was born to extreme poverty, familial disruption, and the violent bigotry of whites.

Like Zora Neale Hurston and Langston Hughes, Richard Wright left the South permanently. He too worked for the Writers' Project and did various freelance journalism; by 1935, he had started to write fiction, strongly influenced by the literary Naturalism of the era. The publication of the original and disturbing Native Son *in 1940 was a turning point in black American literary history, for the novel was unaccommodating in its portrayal of a vengeful black youth named Bigger Thomas, yet it became a bestseller, bought and read by a large audience of white readers. Bigger Thomas as character and symbol entered the American consciousness permanently, as a daemonic counterpart, it might be said, to Samuel Clemens' long-suffering Nigger Jim and Harriet Beecher Stowe's Christly Uncle Tom.*

Long associated with Marxist ideology, Richard Wright is nonetheless an artist of complexity and subtlety, as the story included here demonstrates. Apart from Native Son, *Wright's important titles are the stories* Uncle Tom's Children *(1938), the autobiographical* Black Boy *(1945), and the novel* The Outsider *(1953). An early novel,* Lawd Today, *was published posthumously; and a gathering of stories,* Eight Men, *from which "The Man Who Was Almost a Man" is taken, appeared in 1961.*

The Man Who Was Almost a Man

Dave struck out across the fields, looking homeward through paling light. Whut's the use talkin wid em niggers in the field? Anyhow, his mother was putting supper on the table. Them niggers can't understan nothing. One of these days he was going to get a gun and practice shooting, then they couldn't talk to him as though he were a little boy. He slowed, looking at the ground. Shucks, Ah ain scareda them even ef they are biggern me! Aw, Ah know whut Ahma do. Ahm going by ol Joe's sto n git that Sears Roebuck catlog n look at them guns. Mebbe Ma will lemme buy one when she gits mah pay from ol man Hawkins. Ahma beg her t gimme some money. Ahm ol ernough to hava gun. Ahm seventeen. Almost a man. He strode, feeling his long loose-jointed limbs. Shucks, a man oughta hava little gun aftah he done worked hard all day.

He came in sight of Joe's store. A yellow lantern glowed on the front porch. He mounted steps and went through the screen door, hearing it bang behind him. There was a strong smell of coal oil and mackerel fish. He felt very confident until he saw fat Joe walk in through the rear door, then his courage began to ooze.

"Howdy, Dave! Whutcha want?"

"How yuh, Mistah Joe? Aw, Ah don wanna buy nothing. Ah jus wanted t see ef yuhd lemme look at tha catlog erwhile."

"Sure! You wanna see it here?"

"Nawsuh. Ah wants t take it home wid me. Ah'll bring it back termorrow when Ah come in from the fiels."

"You plannin on buying something?"

"Yessuh."

"Your ma lettin you have your own money now?"

"Shucks. Mistah Joe, Ahm gittin t be a man like anybody else!"

Joe laughed and wiped his greasy white face with a red bandanna.

"What you plannin on buyin?"

Dave looked at the floor, scratched his head, scratched his thigh, and smiled. Then he looked up shyly.

"Ah'll tell yuh, Mistah Joe, ef yuh promise yuh won't tell."

"I promise."

"Waal, Ahma buy a gun."

"A gun? What you want with a gun?"

"Ah wanna keep it."

"You ain't nothing but a boy. You don't need a gun."

"Aw, lemme have the catlog, Mistah Joe. Ah'll bring it back."

Joe walked through the rear door. Dave was elated. He looked around at barrels of sugar and flour. He heard Joe coming back. He craned his neck to see if he were bringing the book. Yeah, he's got it. Gawddog, he's got it!

"Here, but be sure you bring it back. It's the only one I got."

"Sho, Mistah Joe."

"Say, if you wanna buy a gun, why don't you buy one from me? I gotta gun to sell."

"Will it shoot?"

"Sure it'll shoot."

"Whut kind is it?"

"Oh, it's kinda old... a left-hand Wheeler. A pistol. A big one."

"Is it got bullets in it?"

"It's loaded."

"Kin Ah see it?"

"Where's your money?"

"What yuh wan fer it?"

"I'll let you have it for two dollars."

"Just two dollahs? Shucks, Ah could buy tha when Ah git mah pay."

"I'll have it here when you want it."

"Awright, suh. Ah be in fer it."

He went through the door, hearing it slam again behind him. Ahma git some money from Ma n buy me a gun! Only two dollahs! He tucked the thick catalogue under his arm and hurried.

"Where yuh been, boy?" His mother held a steaming dish of black-eyed peas.

"Aw, Ma, Ah just stopped down the road t talk wid the boys."

"Yuh know bettah t keep suppah waiting."

He sat down, resting the catalogue on the edge of the table.

"Yuh git up from there and git to the well n wash yosef! Ah ain feedin no hogs in mah house!"

She grabbed his shoulder and pushed him. He stumbled out of the room, then came back to get the catalogue.

"Whut this?"

"Aw, Ma, it's jusa catlog."

"Who yuh git it from?"

"From Joe, down at the sto."

"Waal, thas good. We kin use it in the outhouse."

"Naw, Ma." He grabbed for it. "Gimme ma catlog. Ma."

She held onto it and glared at him.

"Quit hollerin at me! Whut's wrong wid yuh? Yuh crazy?"

"But Ma, please. It ain mine! It's Joe's! He tol me t bring it back t im termorrow."

She gave up the book. He stumbled down the back steps, hugging the thick book under his arm. When he had splashed water on his face and hands, he groped back to the kitchen and fumbled in a corner for the towel. He bumped into a chair; it clattered to the floor. The catalogue sprawled at his feet. When he had dried his eyes he snatched up the book and held it again under his arms. His mother stood watching him.

"Now, ef yuh gonna act a fool over that ol book, Ah'll take it n burn it up."

"Naw, Ma, please."

"Waal, set down n be still!"

He sat down and drew the oil lamp close. He thumbed page after page, unaware of the food his mother set on the table. His father came in. Then his small brother.

"Whutcha got there, Dave?" his father asked.

"Jusa catlog," he answered, not looking up.

"Yeah, here they is!" His eyes glowed at blue-and-black revolvers. He glanced up, feeling sudden guilt. His father was watching him. He eased the book under the table and rested it on his knees. After the blessing was asked, he ate. He scooped up peas and swallowed fat meat without chewing. Buttermilk helped to wash it down. He did not want to mention money before his father. He would do much better by cornering his mother when she was alone. He looked at his father uneasily out of the edge of his eye.

"Boy, how come yuh don quit foolin wid tha book n eat yo suppah?"

"Yessuh."

"How you n ol man Hawkins gitten erlong?"

"Suh?"

"Can't yuh hear? Why don yuh listen? Ah ast you how wuz yuh n ol man Hawkins gittin erlong?"

"Oh, swell. Pa. Ah plows mo lan than anybody over there."

"Waal, yuh oughta keep you mind on whut yuh doin."

"Yessuh."

He poured his plate full of molasses and sopped it up slowly with a chunk of cornbread. When his father and brother had left the kitchen, he still sat and looked again at the guns in the catalogue, longing to muster courage enough to present his case to his mother. Lawd, ef Ah only had tha pretty one! He could almost feel the slickness of the weapon with his fingers. If he had a gun like that he would polish it and keep it shining so it would never rust. N Ah'd keep it loaded, by Gawd!

"Ma?" His voice was hesitant.

"Hunh?"

"Ol man Hawkins give yuh mah money yit?"

"Yeah, but ain no usa yuh thinking about throwin nona it erway. Ahm keeping tha money sos yuh kin have cloes t go to school this winter."

He rose and went to her side with the open catalogue in his palms. She was washing dishes, her head bent low over a pan. Shyly he raised the book. When he spoke, his voice was husky, faint.

"Ma, Gawd knows Ah wans one of these."

"One of whut?" she asked, not raising her eyes.

"One of these," he said again, not daring even to point. She glanced up at the page, then at him with wide eyes.

"Nigger, is yuh gone plumb crazy?"

"Aw, Ma—"

"Git outta here! Don yuh talk t me bout no gun! Yuh a fool!"

"Ma, Ah kin buy one fer two dollahs."

"Not ef Ah knows it, yuh ain!"

"But yuh promised me one—"

"Ah don care what Ah promised! Yuh ain nothing but a boy yit!"

"Ma ef yuh lemme buy one Ah'll *never* ast yuh fer nothing no mo."

"Ah tol yuh t git outta here! Yuh ain gonna toucha penny of tha money fer no gun! Thas how come Ah has Mistah Hawkins t pay yu wages t me, cause Ah knows yuh ain got no sense."

"But, Ma, we needa gun. Pa ain got no gun. We needa gun in the house. Yuh kin never tell whut might happen."

"Now don yuh try to maka fool outta me, boy! Ef we did hava gun, yuh wouldn't have it!"

He laid the catalogue down and slipped his arm around her waist.

"Aw, Ma, Ah done worked hard alla summer n ain ast yuh fer nothing, is Ah, now?"

"Thas whut yuh spose t do!"

"But Ma, Ah wans a gun. Yuh kin lemme have two dollahs outta mah money. Please, Ma. I kin give it to Pa... Please, Ma! Ah loves yuh, Ma."

When she spoke her voice came soft and low.

"What yu wan wida gun, Dave? Yuh don need no gun. Yuh'll git in trouble. N ef yo pa jus thought Ah let yuh have money t buy a gun he'd hava fit."

"Ah'll hide it. Ma. It ain but two dollahs."

"Lawd, chil, whut's wrong wid yuh?"

"Ain nothin wrong, Ma. Ahm almos a man now. Ah wans a gun."

"Who gonna sell yuh a gun?"

"Ol Joe at the sto."

"N it don cos but two dollahs?"

"Thas all, Ma. Jus two dollahs. Please, Ma."

She was stacking the plates away; her hands moved slowly, reflectively. Dave kept an anxious silence. Finally, she turned to him.

"Ah'll let yuh git tha gun ef yuh promise me one thing."

"Whut's tha. Ma?"

"Yuh bring it straight back t me, yuh hear? It be fer Pa."

"Yessum! Lemme go now. Ma."

She stooped, turned slightly to one side, raised the hem of her dress, rolled down the top of her stocking, and came up with a slender wad of bills.

"Here," she said. "Lawd knows yuh don need no gun. But yer pa does. Yuh bring it right back t me, yuh hear? Ahma put it up. Now ef yuh don, Ahma have yuh pa lick yuh so hard yuh won fergit it."

"Yessum."

He took the money, ran down the steps, and across the yard.

"Dave! Yuuuuu Daaaaave!"

He heard, but he was not going to stop now. "Naw, Lawd!"

The first movement he made the following morning was to reach under his pillow for the gun. In the gray light of dawn he held it loosely, feeling a sense of power. Could kill a man with a gun like this. Kill anybody, black or white. And if he were holding his gun in his hand, nobody could run over him; they would have to respect him. It was a big gun, with a long barrel and a heavy handle. He raised and lowered it in his hand, marveling at its weight.

He had not come straight home with it as his mother had asked; instead he had stayed out in the fields, holding the weapon in his hand, aiming it now and then at some imaginary foe. But he had not fired it; he had been afraid that his father might hear. Also he was not sure he knew how to fire it.

To avoid surrendering the pistol he had not come into the house until he knew that they were all asleep. When his mother had tiptoed to his bedside late that night and demanded the gun, he had first played possum; then he had told her that the gun was hidden outdoors, that he would bring it to her in the morning. Now he lay turning it slowly in his hands. He broke it, took out the cartridges, felt them, and then put them back.

He slid out of bed, got a long strip of old flannel from a trunk, wrapped the gun in it, and tied it to his naked thigh while it was still loaded. He did not go in to breakfast. Even though it was not yet daylight, he started for Jim Hawkins' plantation. Just as the sun was rising he reached the barns where the mules and plows were kept.

"Hey! That you, Dave?"

He turned. Jim Hawkins stood eying him suspiciously.

"What're yuh doing here so early?"

"Ah didn't know Ah wuz gittin up so early, Mistah Hawkins. Ah was fixin t hitch up ol Jenny n take her t the fiels."

"Good. Since you're so early, how about plowing that stretch down by the woods?"

"Suits me, Mistah Hawkins."

"O.K. Go to it!"

He hitched Jenny to a plow and started across the fields. Hot dog! This was just what he wanted. If he could get down by the woods, he could shoot his gun and nobody would hear. He walked behind the plow, hearing the traces creaking, feeling the gun tied tight to his thigh.

When he reached the woods, he plowed two whole rows before he decided to take out the gun. Finally, he stopped, looked in all directions, then untied the gun and held it in his hand. He turned to the mule and smiled.

"Know whut this is, Jenny? Naw, yuh wouldn know! Yuhs jusa ol mule! Anyhow, this is a gun, n it kin shoot, by Gawd!"

He held the gun at arm's length. Whut t hell, Ahma shoot this thing! He looked at Jenny again.

"Lissen here, Jenny! When Ah pull this ol trigger, Ah don wan yuh to run n acka fool now?"

Jenny stood with head down, her short ears pricked straight. Dave walked off about twenty feet, held the gun far out from him at arm's length, and turned his head. Hell, he told himself, Ah ain afraid. The gun felt loose in his fingers; he waved it wildly for a moment. Then he shut his eyes and tightened his forefinger. Bloom! A report half deafened him and he thought his right hand was torn from his arm. He heard Jenny whinnying and galloping over the field, and he found himself on his knees, squeezing his fingers hard between his legs. His hand was numb; he jammed it into his mouth, trying to warm it, trying to stop the pain. The gun lay at his feet. He did not quite know what had happened. He stood up and stared at the gun as though it were a living thing. He gritted his teeth and kicked the gun. Yuh almos broke mah arm! He turned to look for Jenny; she was far over the fields, tossing her head and kicking wildly.

"Hol on there, ol mule!"

When he caught up with her she stood trembling, walling her big white eyes at him. The plow was far away; the traces had broken. Then Dave stopped short, looking, not believing. Jenny was bleeding. Her left side was red and wet with blood. He went closer. Lawd, have mercy! Wondah did Ah shoot this mule? He grabbed for Jenny's mane. She flinched, snorted, whirled, tossing her head.

"Hol on now! Hol on."

Then he saw the hole in Jenny's side, right between the ribs. It was round, wet, red. A crimson stream streaked down the front leg, flowing fast. Good Gawd! Ah wuzn't shootin at tha mule. He felt panic. He knew he had to stop that blood, or Jenny would bleed to death. He had never seen so much blood in all his life. He chased the mule for half a mile, trying to catch her. Finally she stopped, breathing hard, stumpy tail half arched. He caught her mane and led her back to where the plow and gun lay. Then he stooped and grabbed handfuls of damp black earth and tried to plug the bullet hole. Jenny shuddered, whinnied, and broke from him.

"Hol on! Hol on now!"

He tried to plug it again, but blood came anyhow. His fingers were hot and sticky. He rubbed dirt into his palms, trying to dry them. Then again he attempted to plug the bullet hole, but Jenny shied away, kicking her heels high. He stood helpless. He had to do something. He ran at Jenny; she dodged him. He watched a red stream of blood flow down Jenny's leg and form a bright pool at her feet.

"Jenny...Jenny," he called weakly.

His lips trembled. She's bleeding t death! He looked in the direction of home, wanting to go back, wanting to get help. But he saw the pistol lying in the damp black clay. He had a queer feeling that if he only did something, this would not be; Jenny would not be there bleeding to death.

When he went to her this time, she did not move. She stood with sleepy, dreamy eyes; and when he touched her she gave a low-pitched whinny and knelt to the ground, her front knees slopping in blood.

"Jenny...Jenny . . ." he whispered.

For a long time she held her neck erect; then her head sank, slowly. Her ribs swelled with a mighty heave and she went over.

Dave's stomach felt empty, very empty. He picked up the gun and held it gingerly between his thumb and forefinger. He buried it at the foot of a tree. He took a stick and tried to cover the pool of blood with dirt—but what was the use? There was Jenny lying with her mouth open and her eyes walled and glassy. He could not tell Jim Hawkins he had shot his mule. But he had to tell something. Yeah, Ah'll tell em Jenny started gittin ill n fell on the joint of the plow.... But that would hardly happen to a mule. He walked across the field slowly, head down.

It was sunset. Two of Jim Hawkins' men were over near the edge of the woods digging a hole in which to bury Jenny. Dave was surrounded by a knot of people, all of whom were looking down at the dead mule.

"I don't see how in the world it happened," said Jim Hawkins for the tenth time.

The crowd parted and Dave's mother, father, and small brother pushed into the center.

"Where Dave?" his mother called.

"There he is," said Jim Hawkins.

His mother grabbed him.

"Whut happened, Dave? Whut yuh done?"

"Nothin."

"C'mon, boy, talk," his father said.

Dave took a deep breath and told the story he knew nobody believed.

"Waal," he drawled. "Ah brung ol Jenny down here sos Ah could do mah plowin. Ah plowed bout two rows, just like yuh see." He stopped and pointed at the long rows of upturned earth. "Then somethin musta been wrong wid ol Jenny. She wouldn ack right a-tall. She started snortin n kickin her heels. Ah tried t hol her, but she pulled erway, rearin n goin in. Then when the point of the plow was stickin up in the air, she swung erroun n twisted herself back on it... She stuck herself n started t bleed. N fo Ah could do anything, she wuz dead."

"Did you ever hear of anything like that in all your life?" asked Jim Hawkins.

There were white and black standing in the crowd. They murmured. Dave's mother came close to him and looked hard into his face. "Tell the truth, Dave," she said.

"Looks like a bullet hole to me," said one man.

"Dave, whut yuh do wid tha gun?" his mother asked.

The crowd surged in, looking at him. He jammed his hands into his pockets, shook his head slowly from left to right, and backed away. His eyes were wide and painful.

"Did he hava gun?" asked Jim Hawkins.

"By Gawd, Ah tol yuh tha wuz a gun wound," said a man, slapping his thigh.

His father caught his shoulders and shook him till his teeth rattled.

"Tell whut happened, yuh rascal! Tell whut . . ."

Dave looked at Jenny's stiff legs and began to cry.

"Whut yuh do wid tha gun?" his mother asked.

"Whut wuz he doin wida gun?" his father asked.

"Come on and tell the truth," said Hawkins. "Ain't nobody going to hurt you . . ."

His mother crowded close to him.

"Did yuh shoot tha mule, Dave?"

Dave cried, seeing blurred white and black faces.

"Ahh ddinn gggo tt sshooot hher... Ah sswear tt Gawd Ahh ddin.... Ah wuz a-tryin t sssee ef the gggun would sshoot—"

"Where yuh git the gun from?" his father asked.

"Ah got it from Joe, at the sto."

"Where yuh git the money?"

"Ma give it t me."

"He kept worryin me. Bob. Ah had t. Ah tol im t bring the gun right back t me... It was fer yuh, the gun."

"But how yuh happen to shoot that mule?" asked Jim Hawkins.

"Ah wuzn shootin at the mule, Mistah Hawkins! The gun jumped when Ah pulled the trigger... N fo Ah knowed anythin Jenny was there a-bleedin."

Somebody in the crowd laughed. Jim Hawkins walked close to Dave and looked into his face.

"Well, looks like you have bought you a mule, Dave."

"Ah swear fo Gawd. Ah didn go t kill the mule, Mistah Hawkins!"

"But you killed her!"

All the crowd was laughing now. They stood on tiptoe and poked heads over one another's shoulders.

"Well, boy, looks like yuh done bought a dead mule! Hahaha!"

"Ain tha ershame."

"Hohohohoho."

Dave stood, head down, twisting his feet in the dirt.

"Well, you needn't worry about it. Bob," said Jim Hawkins to Dave's father. "Just let the boy keep on working and pay me two dollars a month."

"What yuh wan fer yo mule, Mistah Hawkins?"

Jim Hawkins screwed up his eyes.

"Fifty dollars."

"Whut yuh do wid tha gun?" Dave's father demanded.

Dave said nothing.

"Yuh wan me t take a tree n beat yuh till yuh talk!"

"Nawsuh!"

"Whut yuh do wid it?"

"Ah throwed it erway."

"Where?"

"Ah…Ah throwed it in the creek."

"Waal, c mon home. N firs thing in the mawnin git to tha creek n fin tha gun."

"Yessuh."

"Whut yuh pay fer it?"

"Two dollahs."

"Take tha gun n git yo money back n carry it t Mistah Hawkins, yuh hear? N don fergit Ahma lam you black bottom good fer this! Now march yoself on home, suh!"

Dave turned and walked slowly. He heard people laughing. Dave glared, his eyes welling with tears. Hot anger bubbled in him. Then he swallowed and stumbled on.

That night Dave did not sleep. He was glad that he had gotten out of killing the mule so easily, but he was hurt. Something hot seemed to turn over inside him each time he remembered how they had laughed. He tossed on his bed, feeling his hard pillow. N Pa says he's gonna beat me…He remembered other beatings, and his back quivered. Naw, naw, Ah sho don wan im t beat me tha way no mo. Dam em all! Nobody ever gave him anything. All he did was work. They treat me like a mule, n then they beat me. He gritted his teeth. N Ma had t tell on me.

Well, if he had to, he would take old man Hawkins that two dollars. But that meant selling the gun. And he wanted to keep that gun. Fifty dollars for a dead mule.

He turned over, thinking how he had fired the gun. He had an itch to fire it again. Ef other men kin shoota gun, by Gawd, Ah kin! He was still, listening. Mebbe they all sleepin now. The house was still. He heard the soft breathing of his brother. Yes, now! He would go down and get that gun and see if he could fire it! He eased out of bed and slipped into overalls.

The moon was bright. He ran almost all the way to the edge of the woods. He stumbled over the ground, looking for the spot where he had buried the gun. Yeah, here it is. Like a hungry dog scratching for a bone, he pawed it up. He puffed his black cheeks and blew dirt from the trigger and barrel. He broke it and found four cartridges unshot. He looked around; the fields were filled with silence and moonlight. He clutched the gun stiff and hard in his fingers. But, as soon as he wanted to pull the trigger, he shut his eyes and turned his head. Naw, Ah can't shoot wid mah eyes closed n mah head turned. With effort he held his eyes open; then he squeezed. *Blooooom!* He was stiff, not breathing. The gun was still in his hands. Dammit, he'd done it! He fired again. *Blooooom!* He smiled. *Blooooom! Blooooom! Click, click.* There! It was empty. If anybody could shoot a gun, he could. He put the gun into his hip pocket and started across the fields.

When he reached the top of a ridge he stood straight and proud in the moonlight, looking at Jim Hawkins' big white house, feeling the gun sagging in his pocket. Lawd, ef Ah had just one mo bullet Ah'd taka shot at tha house. Ah'd like t scare ol man Hawkins jusa little...Jusa enough t let im know Dave Saunders is a man.

To his left the road curved, running to the tracks of the Illinois Central. He jerked his head, listening. From far off came a faint *hoooof-hoooof; hoooof-hoooof* . . . He stood rigid. Two dollahs a mont. Les see now...Tha means it'll take bout two years. Shucks! Ah'll be dam!

He started down the road, toward the tracks. Yeah, here she comes! He stood beside the track and held himself stiffly. Here she comes, erroun the ben...C mon, yuh slow poke! C mon! He had his hand on his gun; something quivered in his stomach. Then the train thundered past, the gray and brown box cars rumbling and clinking. He gripped the gun tightly; then he jerked his hand out of his pocket. Ah betcha Bill wouldn't do it! Ah betcha...The cars slid past, steel grinding upon steel. Ahm ridin yuh ternight, so hep me Gawd! He was hot all over. He hesitated just a moment; then he grabbed, pulled atop a car, and lay flat. He felt his pocket; the gun was still there. Ahead the long rails were glinting in the moonlight, stretching away, away to somewhere, somewhere where he could be a man . . .

NELSON ALGREN
(1909–1981)

Born in Detroit, Michigan, Nelson Algren was a longtime resident of Chicago, the west-side slums of which he was a tireless and rhapsodic chronicler. His early novels Somebody in Boots *(1935) and* Never Come Morning *(1942), later denounced by Algren as "primitive," nonetheless brought him immediate recognition as an "urban-realist" contemporary of James T. Farrell and Richard Wright. Algren's more accomplished works of fiction are* The Man With the Golden Arm *(1949), which received the National Book Award and was made into an acclaimed film starring Frank Sinatra, and* A Walk on the Wild Side *(1956), also made into a film, and the powerful stories gathered in* The Neon Wilderness *(1947). Algren is also the author of the corrosively critical essay* Chicago: City on the Make *(1951) which made him enemies in Chicago. (The Chicago Public Library had previously banned* Never Come Morning.) *Other books are* Nelson Algren's Own Book of Lonesome Monsters *(1962), a collection of short stories, and (posthumous)* The Devil's Stocking *(1983).*

Near the end of his life, Algren departed Chicago abruptly to live in Paterson, New Jersey, the hometown of the boxer "Hurricane" Carter, convicted of double homicide following a controversial trial, about which Algren had written for Esquire. *As a young man living in Texas, Algren had been convicted of petty theft and served five months in jail, forging his lifelong sympathy for outsiders, small-time thieves and junkies, and all-round losers. Though Algren was never a member of the Communist Party, his obvious sympathy for left-wing causes brought him to the attention of J. Edgar Hoover and the FBI, which allegedly assembled more than five hundred pages on Algren, without discovering anything criminal or subversive about him.*

Known for his powerful, visceral writing of the most gritty urban subjects rather more than for his writerly style, Nelson Algren yet received a number of literary awards in his career in addition to the National Book Award: several O. Henry Awards and a 1974 Award of Merit from the American Institute of Arts and Letters, which inducted him as a member in 1981. Ironically, in the very city in which some of his books had been banned, and under the auspices of the very newspaper, the Chicago Tribune, *that had pilloried his books in their review pages, the distinguished* Nelson Algren Award for the Short Story *was inaugurated after the author's death.*

Readers unfamiliar with Nelson Algren's evocative prose fiction will find the story included here, "A Bottle of Milk for Mother," the author's most famous and most frequently reprinted work, an ideal entry to his starkly dramatic fictional world that has come to seem as timeless as a ballad, or a fairy tale out of Grimm.

A Bottle of Milk for Mother

I feel I am of them—
I belong to those convicts and prostitutes of myself,
And henceforth I will not deny them—
For how can I deny myself?

—Whitman

Two months after the Polish Warriors S.A.C. had had their heads shaved, Bruno Lefty Bicek got into his final difficulty with the Racine Street police. The arresting officers and a reporter from the *Dziennik Chicagoski* were grouped about the captain's desk when the boy was urged forward into the room by Sergeant Adamovitch, with two fingers wrapped about the boy's broad belt: a full-bodied boy wearing a worn and sleeveless blue work shirt grown too tight across the shoulders; and the shoulders themselves with a loose swing to them. His skull and face were shining from a recent scrubbing, so that the little bridgeless nose glistened between the protective points of the cheekbones. Behind the desk sat Kozak, eleven years on the force and brother to an alderman. The reporter stuck a cigarette behind one ear like a pencil.

"We spotted him followin' the drunk down Chicago—" Sergeant Comiskey began.

Captain Kozak interrupted. "Let the jackroller tell us how he done it hisself."

"I ain't no jackroller."

"What you doin' here, then?"

Bicek folded his naked arms.

"Answer me. If you ain't here for jackrollin' it must be for strong-arm robb'ry—'r you one of them Chicago Av'noo moll-buzzers?"

"I ain't that neither."

"C'mon, c'mon, I seen you in here before—what were you up to, followin' that poor old man?"

"I ain't been in here before."

Neither Sergeant Milano, Comiskey, nor old Adamovitch moved an inch; yet the boy felt the semicircle about him drawing loser. Out of the corner of his eye he watched the reporter undoing the top button of his mangy raccoon coat, as though the barren little query room were already growing too warm for him.

"What were you doin' on Chicago Av'noo in the first place when you live up around Division? Ain't your own ward big enough you have to come down here to get in trouble? What do you *think* you're here for?"

"Well, I was just walkin' down Chicago like I said, to get a bottle of milk for Mother, when the officers jumped me. I didn't even see 'em drive up, they wouldn't let me say a word, I got no idea what I'm here for. I was just doin' a errand for Mother 'n—"

"All right, son, you want us to book you as a pickup 'n hold you overnight, is that it?"

"Yes sir."

"What about this, then?"

Kozak flipped a spring-blade knife with a five-inch blade onto the police blotter; the boy resisted an impulse to lean forward and take it. His own double-edged double-jointed spring-blade cuts-all genuine Filipino twisty-handled all-American gut-ripper.

"Is it yours or ain't it?"

"Never seen it before, Captain."

Kozak pulled a billy out of his belt, spread the blade across the bend of the blotter before him, and with one blow clubbed the blade off two inches from the handle. The boy winced as though he himself had received the blow. Kozak threw the broken blade into a basket and the knife into a drawer.

"Know why I did that, son?"

"Yes sir."

"Tell me."

"'Cause it's three inches to the heart."

"No. 'Cause it's against the law to carry more than three inches of knife. C'mon, Lefty, tell us about it. 'N it better be good."

The boy began slowly, secretly gratified that Kozak appeared to know he was the Warriors' first-string left-hander: maybe he'd been out at that game against the Knothole Wonders the Sunday he'd finished his own game and then had relieved Dropkick Kodadek in the sixth in the second. Why hadn't anyone called him "Iron-Man Bicek" or "Fireball Bruno" for that one?

"Everythin' you say can be used against you," Kozak warned him earnestly. "Don't talk unless you want to." His lips formed each syllable precisely.

Then he added absently, as though talking to someone unseen. "We'll just hold you on an open charge till you do."

And his lips hadn't moved at all.

The boy licked his own lips, feeling a dryness coming into his throat and a tightening in his stomach. "We seen this boo-batch with his collar turned inside out cash'n his check by Konstanty Stachula's Tonsorial Palace of Art on Division. So I followed him a way, that was all. Just break'n the old monotony was all. Just a notion, you might say, that come over me. I'm just a neighborhood kid, Captain."

He stopped as though he had finished the story. Kozak glanced over the boy's shoulder at the arresting officers and Lefty began again hurriedly.

"Ever' once in a while he'd pull a little single-shot of scotch out of his pocket, stop a second t' toss it down, 'n toss the bottle at the car tracks. I picked up a bottle that didn't bust but there wasn't a spider left in 'er, the boobatch'd drunk her dry. 'N do you know, he had his pockets *full* of them little bottles? 'Stead of buyin' hisself a fifth in the first place. Can't understand a man who'll buy liquor that way. Right before the corner of Walton 'n Noble he popped into a hallway. That was Chiney-Eye-the-Princinct-Captain's hallway, so I popped right in after him. Me'n Chiney-Eye 'r just like that." The boy crossed two fingers of his left hand and asked innocently, "Has the alderman been in to straighten this out, Captain?"

"What time was all this, Lefty?"

"Well, some of the street lamps was lit awready 'n I didn't see nobody either way down Noble. It'd just started spitt'n a little snow 'n I couldn't see clear down Walton account of Wojciechowski's Tavern bein' in the way. He was a old guy, a dino you. He couldn't speak a word of English. But he started in cryin' about how every time he gets a little drunk the same old thing happens to him 'n he's gettin' fed up, he lost his last three checks in the very same hallway 'n it's gettin' so his family don't believe him no more . . ."

Lefty paused, realizing that his tongue was going faster than his brain. He unfolded his arms and shoved them down his pants pockets; the pants were turned up at the cuffs and the cuffs were frayed. He drew a colorless cap off his hip pocket and stood clutching it in his left hand.

"I didn't take him them other times, Captain," he anticipated Kozak.

"Who did?"

Silence.

"What's Benkowski doin' for a living these days, Lefty?"

"Just nutsin' around."

"What's Nowogrodski up to?"

"Goes wolfin' on roller skates by Riverview. The rink's open all year round."

"Does he have much luck?"

"Never turns up a hair. They go by too fast."

"What's that evil-eye up to?"

Silence.

"You know who I mean. Idzikowski."

"The Finger?"

"You know who I mean. Don't stall."

"He's hexin' fights, I heard."

"Seen Kodadek lately?"

"I guess. A week 'r two 'r a month ago."

"What was *he* up to?"

"Sir?"

"What was Kodadek doin' the last time you seen him?"

"You mean Dropkick? He was nutsin' around."

"Does he nuts around drunks in hallways?"

Somewhere in the room a small clock or wrist watch began ticking distinctly.

"Nutsin' around ain't jackrollin'."

"You mean Dropkick ain't a jackroller but you are."

The boy's blond lashes shuttered his eyes.

"All right, get ahead with your lyin' a little faster."

Kozak's head came down almost neckless onto his shoulders, and his face was molded like a flatiron, the temples narrow and the jaws rounded. Between the jaws and the open collar, against the graying hair of the chest, hung a tiny crucifix, slender and golden, a shade lighter than his tunic's golden buttons.

"I told him I wasn't gonna take his check, I just needed a little change, I'd pay it back someday. But maybe he didn't understand. He kept hollerin' how he lost his last check, please to let him keep this one. 'Why you drink'n it all up, then,' I put it to him, 'if you're that anxious to hold onto it?' He gimme a foxy grin then 'n pulls out four of them little bottles from four different pockets, 'n each one was a different kind of liquor. I could have one, he tells me in Polish, which do I want, 'n I slapped all four out of his hands. All four. I don't like to see no full-grown man drinkin' that way. A Polak hillbilly he was, 'n certain'y no citizen.

"'Now let me have that change,' I asked him, 'n that wasn't so much t' ask. I don't go around just lookin' fer trouble, Captain. 'N my feet was slop-full of water 'n snow. I'm just a neighborhood fella. But he acted like I was gonna kill him 'r somethin'. I got one hand over his mouth 'n a half nelson behind him 'n talked polite-like in Polish in his ear, 'n he begun sweatin' 'n tryin' t' wrench away on me. 'Take it easy,' I asked him. 'Be reas'nable, we're both in this up to our necks now.' 'N he wasn't drunk no more then, 'n he was plenty t' hold onto. You wouldn't think a old boobatch like that'd have so much stren'th left in him, boozin' down Division night after night, year after year, like he didn't have no home to go to. He pulled my hand off his mouth 'n started hollerin', '*Mlody bandyta! Mlody bandyta!*' 'n I could feel him slippin'. He was just too strong fer a kid like me to hold—"

"Because you were reach'n for his wallet with the other hand?"

"Oh no. The reason I couldn't hold him was my right hand had the nelson 'n I'm not so strong there like in my left 'n even my left ain't what it was before I thrun it out pitchin' that double-header."

"So you kept the rod in your left hand?"

The boy hesitated. Then: "Yes sir." And felt a single drop of sweat slide down his side from under his armpit. Stop and slide again down to the belt.

"What did you get off him?"

"I tell you, I had my hands too full to get *anythin'*—that's just what I been tryin' to tell you. I didn't get so much as one of them little single-shots for all my trouble."

"How many slugs did you fire?"

"Just one, Captain. That was all there was in 'er. I didn't really fire, though. Just at his feet. T' scare him so's he wouldn't jump me. I fired in self-defense. I just wanted to get out of there." He glanced helplessly around at Comiskey and Adamovitch. "You do crazy things sometimes, fellas—well, that's all I was doin."

The boy caught his tongue and stood mute. In the silence of the query room there was only the scraping of the reporter's pencil and the unseen wrist watch. "I'll ask Chiney-Eye if it's legal, a reporter takin' down a confession, that's my out," the boy thought desperately, and added aloud, before he could stop himself: "'N beside I had to show him-"

"Show him what, son?"

Silence.

"Show him what, Left-hander?"

"That I wasn't just another greenhorn sprout like he thought"

"Did he say you were just a sprout?"

"No. But I c'd tell. Lots of people think I'm just a green kid. I show 'em. I guess I showed 'em now all right." He felt he should be apologizing for something and couldn't tell whether it was for strong-arming a man or for failing to strong-arm him.

"I'm just a neighborhood kid. I belonged to the Keep-Our-City-Clean Club at St. John Cant'us. I told him polite-like, like a Polish-American citizen, this was Chiney-Eye-a-Friend-of-Mine's hallway. 'No more after this one,' I told him. 'This is your last time gettin' rolled, old man. After this I'm pertectin' you, I'm seein' to it nobody touches you—but the people who live here don't like this sort of thing goin' on any more'n you 'r I do. There's gotta be a stop to it, old man—'n we all gotta live, don't we?' That's what I told him in Polish."

Kozak exchanged glances with the prim-faced reporter from the *Chicagoski,* who began cleaning his black tortoise-shell spectacles hurriedly yet delicately, with the fringed tip of his cravat. They depended from a black ribbon; he snapped them back onto his beak.

"You shot him in the groin, Lefty. He's dead."

The reporter leaned slightly forward, but perceived no special reaction and so relaxed. A pretty comfy old chair for a dirty old police station, he thought lifelessly. Kozak shaded his eyes with his gloved hand and looked down at his charge sheet. The night lamp on the desk was still lit, as though he had been working all night; as the morning grew lighter behind him lines came out below his eyes, black as though packed with soot, and a curious droop came to the St. Bernard mouth.

"You shot him through the groin—zip." Kozak's voice came, flat and unemphatic, reading from the charge sheet as though without understanding. "Five children. Stella, Mary, Grosha, Wanda, Vincent. Thirteen, ten, six, six, and one two months. Mother invalided since last birth, name of Rose. WPA fifty-five dollars. You told the truth about *that,* at least."

Lefty's voice came in a shout: "You know *what?* That bullet must of bounced, that's what!"

"Who was along?"

"I was singlin'. Lone-wolf stuff." His voice possessed the first faint touch of fear.

"You said, 'We seen the man.' Was he a big man? How big a man was he?"

"I'd judge two hunerd twenty pounds," Comiskey offered, "at least. Fifty pounds heavier 'n this boy, just about. 'N half a head taller."

"Who's 'we,' Left-hander?"

"Captain, I said, 'We seen.' Lots of people, fellas, seen him is all I meant, cashin' his check by Stachula's when the place was crowded. Konstanty cashes checks if he knows you. Say, I even know the project that old man was on, far as that goes, because my old lady wanted we should give up the store so's I c'd get on it. But it was just me done it, Captain."

The raccoon coat readjusted his glasses. He would say something under a by-line like "This correspondent has never seen a colder gray than that in the eye of the wanton killer who arrogantly styles himself the *lone wolf of Potomac Street.*" He shifted uncomfortably, wanting to get farther from the wall radiator but disliking to rise and push the heavy chair.

"Where was that bald-headed pal of yours all this time?"

"Don't know the fella, Captain. Nobody got hair any more around the neighborhood, it seems. The whole damn Triangle went 'n got army haircuts by Stachula's."

"Just you 'n Benkowski, I mean. Don't be afraid, son—we're not tryin' to ring in anythin' you done afore this. Just this one you were out cowboyin' with Benkowski on; were you help'n him 'r was he help'n you? Did you 'r him have the rod?"

Lefty heard a Ford V-8 pull into the rear of the station, and a moment later the splash of the gas as the officers refueled. Behind him he could hear Milano's heavy breathing. He looked down at his shoes, carefully buttoned all the way up and tied with a double bowknot. He'd have to have new laces mighty soon or else start tying them with a single bow.

"That Benkowski's sort of a toothless monkey used to go on at the City Garden at around a hundred an' eighteen pounds, ain't he?"

"Don't know the fella well enough t' say."

"Just from seein' him fight once 'r twice is all. 'N he wore a mouthpiece, I couldn't tell about his teeth. Seems to me he came in about one thirty-three, if he's the same fella you're thinkin' of, Captain."

"I guess you fought at the City Garden once 'r twice yourself, ain't you?"

"Oh, once 'r twice."

"How'd you make out, Left'?"

"Won 'em both on K.O.s. Stopped both fights in the first. One was against that boogie from the Savoy. If he woulda got up I would a killed him fer life. Fer Christ I would. I didn't know I could hit like I can."

"With Benkowski in your corner both times?"

"Oh no, sir."

"That's a bloodsuck'n lie. I seen him in your corner with my own eyes the time you won off Cooney from the G.Y.O. He's your manager, jackroller."

"I didn't say he wasn't"

"You said he wasn't secondin' you."

"He don't."

"Who does?"

"The Finger."

"You told me the Finger was your hex-man. Make up your mind."

"He does both, Captain. He handles the bucket 'n sponge 'n in between he fingers the guy I'm fightin', 'n if it's close he fingers the ref 'n judges. Finger, he never losed a fight. He waited for the boogie outside the dressing room 'n pointed him clear to the ring. He win that one for me awright." The boy spun the frayed greenish cap in his hand in a concentric circle about his index finger, remembering a time when the cap was new and had earlaps. The bright checks were all faded now, to the color of worn pavement, and the earlaps were tatters.

"What possessed your mob to get their heads shaved, Lefty?"

"I strong-armed him myself, I'm rugged as a bull." The boy began to swell his chest imperceptibly; when his lungs were quite full he shut his eyes, like swimming under water at the Oak Street beach, and let his breath out slowly, ounce by ounce.

"I didn't ask you that. I asked you what happened to your hair."

Lefty's capricious mind returned abruptly to the word "possessed" that Kozak had employed. That had a randy ring, sort of: "What possessed you boys?"

"I forgot what you just asked me."

"I asked you why you didn't realize it'd be easier for us to catch up with your mob when all of you had your heads shaved."

"I guess we figured there'd be so many guys with heads shaved it'd be harder to catch a finger than if we all had hair. But that was some accident all the same. A fella was gonna lend Ma a barber chair 'n go fifty-fifty with her shavin' all the Polaks on P'tom'c Street right back of the store, for relief tickets. So she started on me, just to show the fellas, but the hair made her sicker 'n ever 'n back of the store's the only place she got to lie down 'n I hadda finish the job myself.

"The fellas begun giv'n me a Christ-awful razzin' then, ever' day. God oh God, wherever I went around the Triangle, all the neighborhood fellas 'n little niducks 'n old-time hoods by the Broken Knuckle, whenever they seen me they was pointin' 'n laughin' 'n sayin', 'Hi, Baldy Bicek!' So I went home 'n got the clippers 'n the first guy I seen was Bibleback Watrobinski, you wouldn't know him. I jumps him 'n pushes the clip right through the middle of his hair—he ain't had a haircut since the alderman got indicted you—'n then he took one look at what I done in the drugstore window 'n we both bust out laughin' 'n laughin', 'n fin'lly Bible says I better finish what I started. So he set down on the curb 'n I finished him. When I got all I could off that way I took him back to the store 'n heated water 'n shaved him close 'n Ma couldn't see the point at all.

"Me 'n Bible prowled around a couple days 'n here come Catfoot Nowogrodski from Fry Street you, out of Stachula's with a spanty-new sideburner haircut 'n a green tie. I grabbed his arms 'n let Bible run it through the middle just like I done him. Then it was Catfoot's turn, 'n we caught Chester Chekhovka fer *him,* 'n fer Chester we got Cowboy Okulanis from by the Nort'western Viaduct you, 'n fer him we got Mustang, 'n fer Mustang we got John from the Joint, 'n fer John we got Snake Baranowski, 'n we kep' right on goin' that way till we was doin' guys we never seen before even, Wallios 'n Greeks 'n a Flip from Clark Street he musta been, walkin' with a white girl we done it to. 'N fin'lly all the sprouts in the Triangle start comin' around with their heads shaved, they want to join up with the Baldheads A.C., they called it. They thought it was a club you.

"It got so a kid with his head shaved could beat up on a bigger kid because the big one'd be a-scared to fight back hard, he thought the Baldheads'd get him. So that's why we changed our name then, that's why we're not the Warriors any more, we're the Baldhead True American Social 'n Athletic Club.

"I played first for the Warriors when I wasn't on the mound," he added cautiously, "'n I'm enterin' the Gold'n Gloves next year 'less I go to col-litch instead. I went to St. John Cant'us all the way through. Eight' grade, that is. If I keep on gainin' weight I'll be a hunerd ninety-eight this time next year 'n be five-foot-ten—I'm a fair-size light-heavy right this minute. That's what in England they call a cruiser weight you."

He shuffled a step and made as though to unbutton his shirt to show his proportions. But Adamovitch put one hand on his shoulders and slapped the boy's hand down. He didn't like this kid. This was a low-class Polak. He himself was a high-class Polak because his name was Adamovitch and not Adamowski. This sort of kid kept spoiling things for the high-class Polaks by always showing off instead of just being good citizens like the Irish. That was why the Irish ran the City Hall and Police Department and the Board of Education and the Post Office while the Polaks stayed on relief and got drunk and never got anywhere and had everybody down on them. All they could do like the Irish, old Adamovitch reflected bitterly, was to fight under Irish names to get their ears knocked off at the City Garden.

"That's why I want to get out of this jam," this one was saying beside him. "So's it don't ruin my career in the rope' arena. I'm goin' straight. This has sure been one good lesson fer me. Now I'll go to a big-ten collitch 'n make good you."

Now, if the college-coat asked him, "What big-ten college?" he'd answer something screwy like "The Boozological Stoodent-Collitch." That ought to set Kozak back awhile, they might even send him to a bug doc. He'd have to be careful—not *too* screwy. Just screwy enough to get by without involving Benkowski.

He scuffed his shoes and there was no sound in the close little room save his uneasy scuffing; square-toed boy's shoes, laced with a buttonhook. He wanted to look more closely at the reporter but every time he caught the glint of the fellow's glasses he felt awed and would have to drop his eyes; he'd never seen glasses on a string like that before and would have given a great deal to wear them a moment. He took to looking steadily out of the barred window behind Kozak's head, where the January sun was glowing sullenly, like a flame held steadily in a fog. Heard an empty truck clattering east on Chicago, sounding like either a '38 Chevvie or a '37 Ford dragging its safety chain against the car tracks; closed his eyes and imagined sparks flashing from the tracks as the iron struck, bounced, and struck again. The bullet had bounced too. Wow.

"What do you think we ought to do with a man like you, Bicek?"

The boy heard the change from the familiar "Lefty" to "Bicek" with a pang; and the dryness began in his throat again.

"One to fourteen is all I can catch fer manslaughter." He appraised Kozak as coolly as he could.

"You like farm work the next fourteen years? Is that okay with you?"

"I said that's all I could get, at the most. This is a first offense 'n self-defense too. I'll plead the unwritten law."

"Who give you *that* idea?"

"Thought of it myself. Just now. You ain't got a chance to send me over the road 'n you know it."

"We can send you to St. Charles, Bicek. 'N transfer you when you come of age. Unless we can make it first-degree murder."

The boy ignored the latter possibility.

"Why, a few years on a farm'd true me up fine. I planned t' cut out cigarettes 'n whisky anyhow before I turn pro—a farm'd be just the place to do that."

"By the time you're released you'll be thirty-two, Bicek—too late to turn pro then, ain't it?"

"I wouldn't wait that long. Hungry Piontek-from-by-the-Warehouse you, he lammed twice from that St. Charles farm. 'N Hungry don't have all his marbles even. He ain't even a citizen."

"Then let's talk about somethin' you couldn't lam out of so fast 'n easy. Like the chair. Did you know that Bogatski from Noble Street, Bicek? The boy that burned last summer, I mean."

A plain-clothes man stuck his head in the door and called confidently: "That's the man, Captain. That's the man."

Bicek forced himself to grin good-naturedly. He was getting pretty good, these last couple days, at grinning under pressure. When a fellow got sore he couldn't think straight, he reflected anxiously. And so he yawned in Kozak's face with deliberateness, stretching himself as effortlessly as a cat.

"Captain, I ain't been in serious trouble like this before..." he acknowledged, and paused dramatically. He'd let them have it straight from the shoulder now: "So I'm mighty glad to be so close to the alderman. Even if he is indicted."

There. Now they knew. He'd told them.

"You talkin' about my brother, Bicek?"

The boy nodded solemnly. Now they knew who they had hold of at last.

The reporter took the cigarette off his ear and hung it on his lower lip. And Adamovitch guffawed.

The boy jerked toward the officer: Adamovitch was laughing openly at him. Then they were all laughing openly at him. He heard their derision, and a red rain danced one moment before his eyes; when the red rain was past, Kozak was sitting back easily, regarding him with the expression of a man who has just been swung at and missed and plans to use the provocation without undue baste. The captain didn't look like the sort who'd swing back wildly or hurriedly. He didn't look like the sort who missed. His complacency for a moment was as unbearable to the boy as Adamovitch's guffaw had been. He heard his tongue going, trying to regain his lost composure by provoking them all.

"Hey, Stingywhiskers!" He turned on the reporter. "Get your Eversharp goin' there, write down I plugged the old rum-pot, write down Bicek carries a rod night 'n day 'n don't care where he points it. You, I go around slappin' the crap out of whoever I feel like—"

But they all remained mild, calm, and unmoved: for a moment he feared Adamovitch was going to pat him on the head and say something fatherly in Polish.

"Take it easy, lad," Adamovitch suggested. "You're in the query room. We're here to help you, boy. We want to see you through this thing so's you can get back to pugging. You just ain't letting us help you, son."

Kozak blew his nose as though that were an achievement in itself, and spoke with the false friendliness of the insurance man urging a fleeced customer toward the door.

"Want to tell us where you got that rod now, Lefty?"

"I don't want to tell you anything." His mind was setting hard now, against them all. Against them all in here and all like them outside. And the harder it set, the more things seemed to be all right with Kozak: he dropped his eyes to his charge sheet now and everything was all right with everybody. The reporter shoved his notebook into his pocket and buttoned the top button of his coat as though the questioning were over.

It was all too easy. They weren't going to ask him anything more, and he stood wanting them to. He stood wishing them to threaten, to shake their heads ominously, wheedle and cajole and promise him mercy if he'd just talk about the rod.

"I ain't mad, Captain. I don't blame you men either. It's your job, it's your bread 'n butter to talk tough to us neighborhood fellas—ever'body got to have a racket, 'n yours is talkin' tough." He directed this last at the captain, for Comiskey and Milano had left quietly. But Kozak was studying the charge sheet as though Bruno Lefty Bicek were no longer in the room. Nor anywhere at all.

"I'm still here," the boy said wryly, his lip twisting into a dry and bitter grin.

Kozak looked up, his big, wind-beaten, impassive face looking suddenly to the boy like an autographed pitcher's mitt he had once owned. His glance went past the boy and no light of recognition came into his eyes. Lefty Bicek felt a panic rising in him: a desperate fear that they weren't going to press him about the rod, about the old man, about his feelings. "Don't look at me like I ain't nowheres," he asked. And his voice was struck flat by fear.

Something else! The time he and Dropkick had broken into a slot machine! The time he and Casey had played the attention racket and made four dollars! Something! Anything else! The reporter lit his cigarette.

"Your case is well disposed of," Kozak said, and his eyes dropped to the charge sheet forever.

"I'm born in this country, I'm educated here—"

But no one was listening to Bruno Lefty Bicek any more.

He watched the reporter leaving with regret—at least the guy could have offered him a drag—and stood waiting for someone to tell him to go somewhere now, shifting uneasily from one foot to the other. Then he started slowly, backward, toward the door: he'd make Kozak tell Adamovitch to grab him. Halfway to the door he turned his back on Kozak.

There was no voice behind him. Was this what "well disposed of" meant? He turned the knob and stepped confidently into the corridor; at the end of the corridor he saw the door that opened into the courtroom, and his heart began shaking his whole body with the impulse to make a run for it. He glanced back and Adamovitch was five yards behind, coming up catfooted like only an old man who has been a citizen-dress man can come up catfooted, just far enough behind and just casual enough to make it appear unimportant whether the boy made a run for it or not.

The Lone Wolf of Potomac Street waited miserably, in the long unlovely corridor, for the sergeant to thrust two fingers through the back of his belt. Didn't they realize that he might have Dropkick and Catfoot and Benkowski with a sub-machine gun in a streamlined cream-colored roadster right down front, that he'd zigzag through the courtroom onto the courtroom fire escape and—swish—down off the courtroom roof three stories with the chopper still under his arm and through the car's roof and into the driver's seat? Like that George Raft did that time he was innocent at the Chopin, and cops like Adamovitch had better start ducking when Lefty Bicek began making a run for it. He felt the fingers thrust overfamiliarly between his shirt and his belt.

A cold draft came down the corridor when the door at the far end opened; with the opening of the door came the smell of disinfectant from the basement cells. Outside, far overhead, the bells of St. John Cantius were beginning. The boy felt the winding steel of the staircase to the basement beneath his feet and heard the whining screech of a Chicago Avenue streetcar as it paused on Ogden for the traffic fights and then screeched on again, as though a cat were caught beneath its back wheels. Would it be snowing out there still? he wondered, seeing the whitewashed basement walls.

"Feel all right, son?" Adamovitch asked in his most fatherly voice, closing the cell door while thinking to himself: "The kid don't *feel* guilty is the whole trouble. You got to make them *feel* guilty or they'll never go to church at all. A man who goes to church without feeling guilty for *something* is wasting his time, I say." Inside the cell he saw the boy pause and go down on his knees in the cell's gray light. The boy's head turned slowly toward him, a pious oval in the dimness. Old Adamovitch took off his hat.

"This place'll rot down 'n mold over before Lefty Bicek starts prayin', boobatch. Prays, squeals, 'r bawls. So run along 'n I'll see you in hell with yer back broke. I'm lookin' for my cap I dropped is all."

Adamovitch watched him crawling forward on all fours, groping for the pavement-colored cap; when he saw Bicek find it he put his own hat back on and left feeling vaguely dissatisfied.

He did not stay to see the boy, still on his knees, put his hands across his mouth and stare at the shadowed wall.

Shadows were there within shadows.

"I knew I'd never get to be twenty-one anyhow," Lefty told himself softly at last.

EUDORA WELTY
(1909–2001)

Born in Jackson, Mississippi, where she lived most of her life, Eudora Welty, like Flannery O'Connor, is primarily a short story writer. She too takes for her immediate subject the Southern world of her experience, but her range is wider, her narrative voice more varied, and her compassion for her characters greater. Hers is the art of sympathy and of identification. In choosing this so atypical a Welty story, I wanted to suggest the virtuoso quality of that sympathy and identification. (The speaker is the imagined assassin of Medgar Evers.)

Eudora Welty came to immediate prominence with the publication of her first collection of stories, A Curtain of Green *(1941). Other story collections are* The Wide Net *(1943),* The Bride of the Innisfallen *(1955), and, most recently, her* Collected Stories *(1980). Her novels are* The Robber Bridegroom *(1942),* Delta Wedding *(1946),* The Ponder Heart *(1954),* Losing Battles *(1970), and* The Optimist's Daughter *(1972). Her most recent book is the much-acclaimed memoir* One Writer's Beginnings *(1983).*

Like "Why I Live at the P.O." and "Powerhouse," two of Eudora Welty's most frequently anthologized stories, "Where Is the Voice Coming From?" is a masterpiece of voice, rhythm, music. Except, in this case, the music is the music of death.

Where Is the Voice Coming From?

I says to my wife, "You can reach and turn it off. You don't have to set and look at a black nigger face no longer than you want to, or listen to what you don't want to hear. It's still a free country."

I reckon that's how I give myself the idea.

I say, I could find right exactly where in Thermopylae that nigger's living that's asking for equal time. And without a bit of trouble to me.

And I ain't saying it might not be because that's pretty close to where *I* live. The other hand, there could be reasons you might have yourself for knowing how to get there in the dark. It's where you all go for the thing you want when you want it the most. Ain't that right?

The Branch Bank sign tells you in lights, all night long even, what time it is and how hot. When it was quarter to four, and 92, that was me going by in my brother-in-law's truck. He don't deliver nothing at that hour of the morning.

So you leave Four Corners and head west on Nathan B. Forrest Road, past the Surplus & Salvage, not much beyond the Kum Back Drive-In and Trailer Camp, not as far as where the signs starts saying "Live Bait," "Used Parts," "Fireworks," "Peaches," and "Sister Peebles Reader and Adviser." Turn before you hit the city limits and duck back towards the I.C. tracks. And his street's been paved.

And there was his light on, waiting for me. In his garage, if you please. His car's gone. He's out planning still some other ways to do what we tell 'em they can't. I *thought* I'd beat him home. All I had to do was pick my tree and walk in close behind it.

I didn't come expecting not to wait. But it was so hot, all I did was hope and pray one or the other of us wouldn't melt before it was over.

Now, it wasn't no bargain I'd struck.

I've heard what you've heard about Goat Dykeman, in Mississippi. Sure, everybody knows about Goat Dykeman. Goat he got word to the Governor's Mansion he'd go up yonder and shoot that nigger Meredith clean out of school, if he's let out of the pen to do it. Old Ross turned *that* over in his mind before saying him nay, it stands to reason.

I ain't no Goat Dykeman, I ain't in no pen, and I ain't ask no Governor Barnett to give me one thing. Unless he wants to give me a pat on the back for the trouble I took this morning. But he don't have to if he don't want to. I done what I done for my own pure-D satisfaction.

As soon as I heard wheels, I knowed who was coming. That was him and bound to be him. It was the right nigger heading in a new white car up his driveway towards his garage with the light shining, but stopping before he got there, maybe not to wake 'em. That was him. I knowed it when he cut off the car lights and put his foot out and I knowed him standing dark against the light. I knowed him then like I know me now. I knowed him even by his still, listening back.

Never seen him before, never seen him since, never seen anything of his black face but his picture, never seen his face alive, any time at all, or anywheres, and didn't want to, need to, never hope to see that face and never will. As long as there was no question in my mind.

He had to be the one. He stood right still and waited against the light, his back was fixed, fixed on me like a preacher's eyeballs when he's yelling "Are you saved?" He's the one.

I'd already brought up my rifle, I'd already taken my sights. And I'd already got him, because it was too late then for him or me to turn by one hair.

Something darker than him, like the wings of a bird, spread on his back and pulled him down. He climbed up once, like a man under bad claws, and like just blood could weigh a ton he walked with it on his back to better light. Didn't get no further than his door. And fell to stay.

He was down. He was down, and a ton load of bricks on his back wouldn't have laid any heavier. There on his paved driveway, yes sir.

And it wasn't till the minute before, that the mockingbird had quit singing. He'd been singing up my sassafras tree. Either he was up early, or he hadn't never gone to bed, he was like me. And the mocker he'd stayed right with me, filling the air till come the crack, till I turned loose of my load. I was like him. I was on top of the world myself. For once.

I stepped to the edge of his light there, where he's laying flat. I says, "Roland? There was one way left, for me to be ahead of you and stay ahead of you, by Dad, and I just taken it. Now I'm alive and you ain't. We ain't ever now, never going to be equals and you know why? One of us is dead. What about that, Roland?" I said. "Well, you seen to it, didn't you?"

I stood a minute—just to see would somebody inside come out long enough to pick him up. And there she comes, the woman. I doubt she'd been to sleep. Because it seemed to me she'd been in there keeping awake all along.

It was mighty green where I skint over the yard getting back. That nigger wife of his, she wanted nice grass! I bet my wife would hate to pay her water bill. And for burning her electricity. And there's my brother-in-law's truck, still waiting with the door open. "No Riders"—that didn't mean me.

There wasn't a thing I been able to think of since would have made it to go any nicer. Except a chair to my back while I was putting in my waiting. But going home, I seen what little time it takes after all to get a thing done like you really want it. It was 4:34, and while I was looking it moved to 35. And the temperature stuck where it was. All that night I guarantee you it had stood without dropping, a good 92.

My wife says, "What? Didn't the skeeters bite you?" She said, "Well, they been asking that—why somebody didn't trouble to load a rifle and get some of these agitators out of Thermopylae. Didn't the fella keep drumming it in, what a good idea? The one that writes a column ever' day?"

I says to my wife, "Find *some* way I don't get the credit."

"He says do it for Thermopylae," she says. "Don't you ever skim the paper?"

I says, "Thermopylae never done nothing for me. And I don't owe nothing to Thermopylae. Didn't do it for you. Hell, any more'n I'd do something or other for them Kennedys! I done it for my own pure-D satisfaction."

"It's going to get him right back on TV," says my wife. "You watch for the funeral."

I says, "You didn't even leave a light burning when you went to bed. So how was I supposed to even get me home or pull Buddy's truck up safe in our front yard?"

"Well, hear another good joke on you," my wife says next. "Didn't you hear the news? The N. double A.C.P. is fixing to send somebody to

Thermopylae. Why couldn't you waited? You might could have got you somebody better. Listen and hear 'em say so."

I ain't but one. I reckon you have to tell *somebody.*

"Where's the gun, then?" my wife says. "What did you do with our protection?"

I says, "It was scorching! It was scorching!" I told her, "It's laying out on the ground in rank weeds, trying to cool off, that's what it's doing now."

"You dropped it," she says. "Back there."

And I told her, "Because I'm so tired of ever'thing in the world being just that hot to the touch! The keys to the truck, the doorknob, the bedsheet, ever'thing, it's all like a stove lid. There just ain't much going that's worth holding on to it no more," I says, "when it's a hundred and two in the shade by day and by night not too much difference. I wish *you'd* laid *your* finger to that gun."

"Trust you to come off and leave it," my wife says.

"Is that how no-'count I am?" she makes me ask. "You want to go back and get it?"

"You're the one they'll catch. I say it's so hot that even if you get to sleep you wake up feeling like you cried all night!" says my wife. "Cheer up, here's one more joke before time to get up. Heard what *Caroline* said? Caroline said, 'Daddy, I just can't wait to grow up big, so I can marry *James Meredith.'* I heard that where I work. One rich-bitch to another one, to make her cackle."

"At least I kept some dern teen-ager from North Thermopylae getting there and doing it first," I says. "Driving his own car."

On TV and in the paper, they don't know but half of it. They know who Roland Summers was without knowing who I am. His face was in front of the public before I got rid of him, and after I got rid of him there it is again—the same picture. And none of me. I ain't ever had one made. Not ever! The best that newspaper could do for me was offer a five-hundred-dollar reward for finding out who I am. For as long as they don't know who that is, whoever shot Roland is worth a good deal more right now than Roland is.

But by the time I was moving around uptown, it was hotter still. That pavement in the middle of Main Street was so hot to my feet I might've been walking the barrel of my gun. If the whole world could've just felt Main Street this morning through the soles of my shoes, maybe it would've helped some.

Then the first thing I heard 'em say was the N. double A. C. P. done it themselves, killed Roland Summers, and proved it by saying the shooting was done by a expert (I hope to tell you it was!) and at just the right hour and minute to get the whites in trouble.

You can't win.

"They'll never find him," the old man trying to sell roasted peanuts tells me to my face.

And it's so hot.

It looks like the town's on fire already, whichever ways you turn, ever' street you strike, because there's those trees hanging them pones of bloom like split watermelon. And a thousand cops crowding ever'where you go, half of 'em too young to start shaving, but all streaming sweat alike. I'm getting tired of 'em.

I was already tired of seeing a hundred cops getting us white people nowheres. Back at the beginning, I stood on the corner and I watched them new babyface cops loading nothing but nigger children into the paddy wagon and they come marching out of a little parade and into the paddy wagon singing. And they got in and sat down without providing a speck of trouble, and their hands held little new American flags, and all the cops could do was knock them flagsticks a-loose from their hands, and not let 'em pick 'em up, that was all, and give 'em a free ride. And children can just get 'em more flags.

Everybody: It don't get you nowhere to take nothing from nobody unless you make sure it's for keeps, for good and all, for ever and amen.

I won't be sorry to see them brickbats hail down on us for a change. Pop bottles too, they can come flying whenever they want to. Hundreds, all to smash, like Birmingham. I'm waiting on 'em to bring out them switchblade knives, like Harlem and Chicago. Watch TV long enough and you'll see it all to happen on Deacon Street in Thermopylae. What's holding it back, that's all?—Because it's *in* 'em.

I'm ready myself for that funeral.

Oh, they may find me. May catch me one day in spite of 'emselves. (But I grew up in the country.) May try to railroad me into the electric chair, and what that amounts to is something hotter than yesterday and today put together.

But I advise 'em to go careful. Ain't it about time us taxpayers starts to calling the moves? Starts to telling the teachers *and* the preachers *and* the judges of our so-called courts how far they can go?

Even the President so far, he can't walk in my house without being invited, like he's my daddy, just to say whoa. Not yet!

Once, I run away from my home. And there was a ad for me, come to be printed in our county weekly. My mother paid for it. It was from her. It says: "SON: You are not being hunted for anything but to find you." That time, I come on back home.

But people are dead now.

And it's so hot. Without it even being August yet.

Anyways, I seen him fall. I was evermore the one.

So I reach me down my old guitar off the nail in the wall. 'Cause I've got my guitar, what I've held on to from way back when, and I never dropped that, never lost or forgot it, never hocked it but to get it again, never give it away, and I set in my chair, with nobody home but me, and I start to play, and sing a-Down. And sing a-down, down, down, down. Sing a-down, down, down, down. Down.

PAUL BOWLES
(1910–1999)

No one who reads this story ever forgets it, though one might well wish to forget it, like a bad dream that imposes itself, with ominous significance, upon the daylight, civilized world. Though "A Distant Episode" has become the most frequently anthologized of Paul Bowles's fiction, I could not resist including it here. It is both the highest achievement of this intransigent artist's work in fiction and representative of his imagination generally.

Born in New York City, Paul Bowles had two distinct careers: as a composer, and as a writer and translator. During the 1930s and 1940s, he was a music critic for the New York Herald Tribune, *and wrote musical scores for Broadway. From 1945 on, he lived in Tangier, and concentrated upon literature. His first novel,* The Sheltering Sky, *was published in 1949 to considerable acclaim and notoriety; subsequent titles established his reputation as a chronicler of a world almost entirely devoid of the "manners" that constitute most works of fiction in our tradition. These are the story collections* The Delicate Prey *(1950),* The Time of Friendship *(1967), and* Collected Stories *(1979); the novels* Let It Come Down *(1952),* The Spider's House *(1955), and* Up Above the World *(1966). Bowles's nonfiction books include* Their Heads Are Green and Their Hands Are Blue: Scenes from the Non-Christian World *(1963) and* Things Gone and Things Still Here *(1977). His poetry has been collected in* Next to Nothing *(1981) and his autobiography, the enigmatic* Without Stopping, *was published in 1972.*

In 1991, in honor of his contribution to the short story as an art form, Paul Bowles was awarded the $25,000 Rea Award for the Short Story.

A Distant Episode

The September sunsets were at their reddest the week the Professor decided to visit Aïn Tadouirt, which is in the warm country. He came down out of the high, flat region in the evening by bus, with two small overnight bags full of maps, sun lotions and medicines. Ten years ago he had been in the village for three days; long enough, however, to establish a fairly firm friendship with the café-keeper, who had written him several times during the first year after his visit, if never since. "Hassan Ramani," the Professor said over and over, as the bus bumped downward through ever warmer layers of air. Now facing the flaming sky in the west, and now facing the sharp mountains, the car followed the dusty trail down the canyons into air which began to smell of other things besides the endless ozone of the heights: orange blossoms, pepper, sun-baked excrement, burning olive oil, rotten fruit. He closed his eyes happily and lived for an instant in a purely olfactory world. The distant past returned—what part of it, he could not decide.

The chauffeur, whose seat the Professor shared, spoke to him without taking his eyes from the road. *"Vous êtes gêologue?"*

"A geologist? Ah, no! I'm a linguist."

"There are no languages here. Only dialects."

"Exactly. I'm making a survey of variations on Moghrebi."

The chauffeur was scornful. "Keep on going south," he said. "You'll find some languages you never heard of before."

As they drove through the town gate, the usual swarm of urchins rose up out of the dust and ran screaming beside the bus. The Professor folded his dark glasses, put them in his pocket; and as soon as the vehicle had come to a standstill he jumped out, pushing his way through the indignant boys who clutched at his luggage in vain, and walked quickly into the Grand Hotel Saharien. Out of its eight rooms there were two available—one facing the market and the other, a smaller and cheaper one, giving onto a tiny yard full of refuse and barrels, where two gazelles wandered about. He took the smaller room, and pouring the entire pitcher of water into the tin basin, began to wash the grit from his face and ears. The afterglow was nearly gone from the sky, and the pinkness in objects was disappearing, almost as he watched. He lit the carbide lamp and winced at its odor.

After dinner the Professor walked slowly through the streets to Hassan Ramani's café, whose back room hung hazardously out above the river. The entrance was very low, and he had to bend down slightly to get in. A man was tending the fire. There was one guest sipping tea. The *qaouaji* tried to make him take a seat at the other table in the front room, but the Professor walked airily ahead into the back room and sat down. The moon was shining through the reed latticework and there was not a sound outside but the occasional distant bark of a dog. He changed tables so he could see the river. It was dry, but there was a pool here and there that reflected the bright night sky. The *qaouaji* came in and wiped off the table.

"Does this café still belong to Hassan Ramani?" he asked him in the Moghrebi he had taken four years to learn.

The man replied in bad French: "He is deceased."

"Deceased?" repeated the Professor, without noticing the absurdity of the word. "Really? When?"

"I don't know," said the *qaouaji*. "One tea?"

"Yes. But I don't understand . . ."

The man was already out of the room, fanning the fire. The Professor sat still, feeling lonely, and arguing with himself that to do so was ridiculous. Soon the *qaouaji* returned with the tea. He paid him and gave him an enormous tip, for which he received a grave bow.

"Tell me," he said, as the other started away. "Can one still get those little boxes made from camel udders?"

The man looked angry. "Sometimes the Reguibat bring in those things. We do not buy them here." Then insolently, in Arabic: "And why a camel-udder box?"

"Because I like them," retorted the Professor. And then because he was feeling a little exalted, he added, "I like them so much I want to make a collection of them, and I will pay you ten francs for every one you can get me."

"Khamstache," said the *qaouaji*, opening his left hand rapidly three times in succession.

"Never. Ten."

"Not possible. But wait until later and come with me. You can give me what you like. And you will get camel-udder boxes if there are any."

He went out into the front room, leaving the Professor to drink his tea and listen to the growing chorus of dogs that barked and howled as the moon rose higher into the sky. A group of customers came into the front room and sat talking for an hour or so. When they had left, the *qaouaji* put out the fire and stood in the doorway putting on his burnous. "Come," he said.

Outside in the street there was very little movement. The booths were all closed and the only light came from the moon. An occasional pedestrian passed, and grunted a brief greeting to the *qaouaji.*

"Everyone knows you," said the Professor, to cut the silence between them.

"Yes."

"I wish everyone knew me," said the Professor, before he realized how infantile such a remark must sound.

"*No* one knows you," said his companion gruffly.

They had come to the other side of the town, on the promontory above the desert, and through a great rift in the wall the Professor saw the white endlessness, broken in the foreground by dark spots of oasis. They walked through the opening and followed a winding road between rocks, downward toward the nearest small forest of palms. The Professor thought: "He may cut my throat. But his café—he would surely be found out."

"Is it far?" he asked, casually.

"Are you tired?" countered the *qaouaji.*

"They are expecting me back at the Hotel Saharien," he lied.

"You can't be there and here," said the *qaouaji.*

The Professor laughed. He wondered if it sounded uneasy to the other.

"Have you owned Ramani's café long?"

"I work there for a friend." The reply made the Professor more unhappy than he had imagined it would.

"Oh. Will you work tomorrow?"

"That is impossible to say."

The Professor stumbled on a stone, and fell, scraping his hand. The *qaouaji* said: "Be careful."

The sweet black odor of rotten meat hung in the air suddenly.

"Agh!" said the Professor, choking. "What is it?"

The *qaouaji* had covered his face with his burnous and did not answer. Soon the stench had been left behind. They were on flat ground. Ahead the path was bordered on each side by a high mud wall. There was no breeze and the palms were quite still, but behind the walls was the sound of running water. Also, the odor of human excrement was almost constant as they walked between the walls.

The Professor waited until he thought it seemed logical for him to ask with a certain degree of annoyance: "But where are we going?"

"Soon," said the guide, pausing to gather some stones in the ditch.

"Pick up some stones," he advised. "Here are bad dogs."

"Where?" asked the Professor, but he stooped and got three large ones with pointed edges.

They continued very quietly. The walls came to an end and the bright desert lay ahead. Nearby was a ruined marabout, with its tiny dome only half standing, and the front wall entirely destroyed. Behind it were clumps of stunted, useless palms. A dog came running crazily toward them on three legs. Not until it got quite close did the Professor hear its steady low growl. The *qaouaji* let fly a large stone at it, striking it square in the muzzle. There was a strange snapping of jaws and the dog ran sideways in another direction, falling blindly against rocks and scrambling haphazardly about like an injured insect.

Turning off the road, they walked across the earth strewn with sharp stones, past the little ruin, through the trees, until they came to a place where the ground dropped abruptly away in front of them.

"It looks like a quarry," said the Professor, resorting to French for the word "quarry," whose Arabic equivalent he could not call to mind at the moment. The *qaouaji* did not answer. Instead he stood still and turned his head, as if listening. And indeed, from somewhere down below, but very far below, came the faint sound of a low flute. The *qaouaji* nodded his head slowly several times. Then he said: "The path begins here. You can see it well all the way. The rock is white and the moon is strong. So you can see well. I am going back now and sleep. It is late. You can give me what you like."

Standing there at the edge of the abyss which at each moment looked deeper, with the dark face of the *qaouaji* framed in its moonlit burnous close to his own face, the Professor asked himself exactly what he felt. Indignation, curiosity, fear, perhaps, but most of all relief and the hope that this was not a trick, the hope that the *qaouaji* would really leave him alone and turn back without him.

He stepped back a little from the edge, and fumbled in his pocket for a loose note, because he did not want to show his wallet. Fortunately there was a fifty-franc bill there, which he took out and handed to the man. He knew the *qaouaji* was pleased, and so he paid no attention when he heard him saying: "It is not enough. I have to walk a long way home and there are dogs. . . ."

"Thank you and good night," said the Professor, sitting down with his legs drawn up under him, and lighting a cigarette. He felt almost happy.

"Give me only one cigarette," pleaded the man.

"Of course," he said, a bit curtly, and he held up the pack.

The *qaouaji* squatted close beside him. His face was not pleasant to see. "What is it?" thought the Professor, terrified again, as he held out his lighted cigarette toward him.

The man's eyes were almost closed. It was the most obvious registering of concentrated scheming the Professor had ever seen. When the second cigarette was burning, he ventured to say to the still-squatting Arab: "What are you thinking about?"

The other drew on his cigarette deliberately, and seemed about to speak. Then his expression changed to one of satisfaction, but he did not speak. A cool wind had risen in the air, and the Professor shivered. The sound of the flute came up from the depths below at intervals, sometimes mingled with the scraping of nearby palm fronds one against the other. "These people are not primitives," the Professor found himself saying in his mind.

"Good," said the *qaouaji,* rising slowly. "Keep your money. Fifty francs is enough. It is an honor." Then he went back into French: *"Ti n'as qu'à discendre, to' droit."* He spat, chuckled (or was the Professor hysterical?), and strode away quickly.

The Professor was in a state of nerves. He lit another cigarette, and found his lips moving automatically. They were saying: "Is this a situation or a predicament? This is ridiculous." He sat very still for several minutes, waiting for a sense of reality to come to him. He stretched out on the hard, cold ground and looked up at the moon. It was almost like looking straight at the sun. If he shifted his gaze a little at a time, he could make a string of weaker moons across the sky. "Incredible," he whispered. Then he sat up quickly and looked about. There was no guarantee that the *qaouaji* really had gone back to town. He got to his feet and looked over the edge of the precipice. In the moonlight the bottom seemed miles away. And there was nothing to give it scale; not a tree, not a house, not a person.... He listened for the flute, and heard only the wind going by his ears. A sudden violent desire to run back to the road seized him, and he turned and looked in the direction the *qaouaji* had taken. At the same time he felt softly of his wallet in his breast pocket. Then he spat over the edge of the cliff. Then he made water over it, and listened intently, like a child. This gave him the impetus to start down the path into the abyss. Curiously enough, he was not dizzy. But prudently he kept from peering to his right, over the edge. It was a steady and steep downward climb. The monotony of it put him into a frame of mind not unlike that which had been induced by the bus ride. He was murmuring "Hassan Ramani" again, repeatedly and in rhythm. He stopped, furious with himself for the sinister overtones the name now suggested to him. He decided he was exhausted from the trip. "And the walk," he added.

He was now well down the gigantic cliff, but the moon, being directly overhead, gave as much light as ever. Only the wind was left behind, above, to wander among the trees, to blow through the dusty streets of Aïn Tadouirt, into the hall of the Grand Hotel Saharien, and under the door of his little room.

It occurred to him that he ought to ask himself why he was doing this irrational thing, but he was intelligent enough to know that since he was doing it, it was not so important to probe for explanations at that moment.

Suddenly the earth was flat beneath his feet. He had reached the bottom sooner than he expected. He stepped ahead distrustfully still, as if he expected another treacherous drop. It was so hard to know in this uniform, dim brightness. Before he knew what had happened the dog was upon him, a heavy mass of fur trying to push him backwards, a sharp nail rubbing down his chest, a straining of muscles against him to get the teeth into his neck. The Professor thought: "I refuse to die this way." The dog fell back; it looked like an Eskimo dog. As it sprang again, he called out, very loud: "Ay!" It fell against him, there was a confusion of sensations and a pain somewhere. There was also the sound of voices very near to him, and he could not understand what they were saying. Something cold and metallic was pushed brutally against his spine as the dog still hung for a second by his teeth from a mass of clothing and perhaps flesh. The Professor knew it was a gun, and he raised his hands, shouting in Moghrebi: "Take away the dog!" But the gun merely pushed him forward, and since the dog, once it was back on the ground, did not leap again, he took a step ahead. The gun kept pushing; he kept taking steps. Again he heard voices, but the person directly behind him said nothing. People seemed to be running about; it sounded that way, at least. For his eyes, he discovered, were still shut tight against the dog's attack. He opened them. A group of men was advancing toward him. They were dressed in the black clothes of the Reguibat. "The Reguiba is a cloud across the face of the sun." "When the Reguiba appears the righteous man turns away." In how many shops and marketplaces he had heard these maxims uttered banteringly among friends. Never to a Reguiba, to be sure, for these men do not frequent towns. They send a representative in disguise, to arrange with shady elements there for the disposal of captured goods. "An opportunity," he thought quickly, "of testing the accuracy of such statements." He did not doubt for a moment that the adventure would prove to be a kind of warning against such foolishness on his part—a warning which in retrospect would be half sinister, half farcical.

Two snarling dogs came running from behind the oncoming men and threw themselves at his legs. He was scandalized to note that no one paid any attention to this breach of etiquette. The gun pushed him harder as he tried to sidestep the animals' noisy assault. Again he cried: "The dogs! Take them away!" The gun shoved him forward with great force and he fell, almost at the feet of the crowd of men facing him. The dogs were wrenching at his hands and arms. A boot kicked them aside, yelping, and then with increased vigor it kicked the Professor in the hip. Then came a chorus of kicks from different sides, and he was rolled violently about on the earth for a while. During this time he was conscious of hands reaching into his pockets and removing everything from them. He tried to say: "You have all my money; stop kicking me!" But his bruised facial muscles would not work; he felt himself pouting, and that was all. Someone dealt him a terrific blow on the head, and he thought: "Now at least I shall lose consciousness, thank Heaven." Still he went on being aware of the guttural voices he could not understand, and of being bound tightly about the ankles and chest. Then there was black silence that opened like a wound from time to time, to let in the soft, deep notes of the flute playing the same succession of notes again and again. Suddenly he felt excruciating pain everywhere—pain and cold. "So I have been unconscious, after all," he thought. In spite of that, the present seemed only like a direct continuation of what had gone before.

It was growing faintly light. There were camels near where he was lying; he could hear their gurgling and their heavy breathing. He could not bring himself to attempt opening his eyes, just in case it should turn out to be impossible. However, when he heard someone approaching, he found that he had no difficulty in seeing.

The man looked at him dispassionately in the gray morning light. With one hand he pinched together the Professor's nostrils. When the Professor opened his mouth to breathe, the man swiftly seized his tongue and pulled on it with all his might. The Professor was gagging and catching his breath; he did not see what was happening. He could not distinguish the pain of the brutal yanking from that of the sharp knife. Then there was an endless choking and spitting that went on automatically, as though he were scarcely a part of it. The word "operation" kept going through his mind; it calmed his terror somewhat as he sank back into darkness.

The caravan left sometime toward midmorning. The Professor, not unconscious, but in a state of utter stupor, still gagging and drooling blood, was dumped doubled-up into a sack and tied at one side of a camel. The lower end of the enormous amphitheater contained a natural gate in the rocks. The camels, swift *mehara,* were lightly laden on this trip. They passed through single file, and slowly mounted the gentle slope that led up into the beginning of the desert. That night, at a stop behind some low hills, the men took him out, still in a state which permitted no thought, and over the dusty rags that remained of his clothing they fastened a series of curious belts made of the bottoms of tin cans strung together. One after another of these bright girdles was wired about his torso, his arms and legs, even across his face, until he was entirely within a suit of armor that covered him with its circular metal scales. There was a good deal of merriment during this decking-out of the Professor. One man brought out a flute and a younger one did a not ungraceful caricature of an Ouled Naïl executing a cane dance. The Professor was no longer conscious; to be exact, he existed in the middle of the movements made by these other men. When they had finished dressing him the way they wished him to look, they stuffed some food under the tin bangles hanging over his face. Even though he chewed mechanically, most of it eventually fell out onto the ground. They put him back into the sack and left him there.

Two days later they arrived at one of their own encampments. There were women and children here in the tents, and the men had to drive away the snarling dogs they had left there to guard them. When they emptied the Professor out of his sack, there were screams of fright, and it took several hours to convince the last woman that he was harmless, although there had been no doubt from the start that he was a valuable possession. After a few days they began to move on again, taking everything with them, and traveling only at night as the terrain grew warmer.

Even when all his wounds had healed and he felt no more pain, the Professor did not begin to think again; he ate and defecated, and he danced when he was bidden, a senseless hopping up and down that delighted the children, principally because of the wonderful jangling racket it made. And he generally slept through the heat of the day, in among the camels.

Wending its way southeast, the caravan avoided all stationary civilization. In a few weeks they reached a new plateau, wholly wild and with a sparse vegetation. Here they pitched camp and remained, while the *mehara* were turned loose to graze. Everyone was happy here; the weather was cooler and there was a well only a few hours away on a seldom-frequented trail. It was here they conceived the idea of taking the Professor to Fogara and selling him to the Touareg.

It was a full year before they carried out this project. By this time the Professor was much better trained. He could do a handspring, make a series of fearful growling noises which had, nevertheless, a certain element of humor; and when the Reguibat removed the tin from his face they discovered he could grimace admirably while he danced. They also taught him a few basic obscene gestures which never failed to elicit delighted shrieks from the women. He was now brought forth only after especially abundant meals, when there was music and festivity. He easily fell in with their sense of ritual, and evolved an elementary sort of "program" to present when he was called for: dancing, rolling on the ground, imitating certain animals, and finally rushing toward the group in feigned anger, to see the resultant confusion and hilarity.

When three of the men set out for Fogara with him, they took four *mehara* with them, and he rode astride his quite naturally. No precautions were taken to guard him, save that he was kept among them, one man always staying at the rear of the party. They came within sight of the walls at dawn, and they waited among the rocks all day. At dusk the youngest started out, and in three hours he returned with a friend who carried a stout cane. They tried to put the Professor through his routine then and there, but the man from Fogara was in a hurry to get back to town, so they all set out on the *mehara*.

In the town they went directly to the villager's home, where they had coffee in the courtyard sitting among the camels. Here the Professor went into his act again, and this time there was prolonged merriment and much rubbing together of hands. An agreement was reached, a sum of money paid, and the Reguibat withdrew, leaving the Professor in the house of the man with the cane, who did not delay in locking him into a tiny enclosure off the courtyard.

The next day was an important one in the Professor's life, for it was then that pain began to stir again in his being. A group of men came to the house, among whom was a venerable gentleman, better clothed than those others who spent their time flattering him, setting fervent kisses upon his hands and the edges of his garments. This person made a point of going into classical Arabic from time to time, to impress the others, who had not learned a word of the Koran. Thus his conversation would run more or less as follows: "Perhaps at In Salah. The French there are stupid. Celestial vengeance is approaching. Let us not hasten it. Praise the highest and cast thine anathema against idols. With paint on his face. In case the police wish to look close." The others listened and agreed, nodding their heads slowly and solemnly. And the Professor in his stall beside them listened, too. That is, he was *conscious* of the sound of the old man's Arabic. The words penetrated for the first time in many months. Noises, then: "Celestial vengeance is approaching." Then: "It is an honor. Fifty francs is enough. Keep your money. Good." And the *qaouaji* squatting near him at the edge of the precipice. Then "anathema against idols" and more gibberish. He turned over panting on the sand and forgot about it. But the pain had begun. It operated in a kind of delirium, because he had begun to enter into consciousness again. When the man opened the door and prodded him with his cane, he cried out in a rage, and everyone laughed.

They got him onto his feet, but he would not dance. He stood before them, staring at the ground, stubbornly refusing to move. The owner was furious, and so annoyed by the laughter of the others that he felt obliged to send them away, saying that he would await a more propitious time for exhibiting his property, because he dared not show his anger before the elder. However, when they had left he dealt the Professor a violent blow on the shoulder with his cane, called him various obscene things, and went out into the street, slamming the gate behind him. He walked straight to the street of the Ouled Naïl, because he was sure of finding the Reguibat there among the girls, spending the money. And there in a tent he found one of them still abed, while an Ouled Naïl washed the tea glasses. He walked in and almost decapitated the man before the latter had even attempted to sit up. Then he threw his razor on the bed and ran out.

The Ouled Naïl saw the blood, screamed, ran out of her tent into the next, and soon emerged from that with four girls who rushed together into the coffeehouse and told the *qaouaji* who had killed the Reguiba. It was only a matter of an hour before the French military police had caught him at a friend's house, and dragged him off to the barracks. That night the Professor had nothing to eat, and the next afternoon, in the slow sharpening of his consciousness caused by increasing hunger, he walked aimlessly about the courtyard and the rooms that gave onto it. There was no one. In one room a calendar hung on the wall.

The Professor watched nervously, like a dog watching a fly in front of its nose. On the white paper were black objects that made sounds in his head. He heard them: "*Grande Epicerie du Sahel. Juin. Lundi, Mardi, Mercredi. . . .*"

The tiny ink marks of which a symphony consists may have been made long ago, but when they are fulfilled in sound they become imminent and mighty. So a kind of music of feeling began to play in the Professor's head, increasing in volume as he looked at the mud wall, and he had the feeling that he was performing what had been written for him long ago. He felt like weeping; he felt like roaring through the little house, upsetting and smashing the few breakable objects. His emotion got no further than this one overwhelming desire. So, bellowing as loud as he could, he attacked the house and its belongings. Then he attacked the door into the street, which resisted for a while and finally broke. He climbed through the opening made by the boards he had ripped apart, and still bellowing and shaking his arms in the air to make as loud a jangling as possible, he began to gallop along the quiet street toward the gateway of the town. A few people looked at him with great curiosity. As he passed the garage, the last building before the high mud archway that framed the desert beyond, a French soldier saw him. "*Tiens,*" he said to himself, "a holy maniac."

Again it was sunset time. The Professor ran beneath the arched gate, turned his face toward the red sky, and began to trot along the Piste d'In Salah, straight into the setting sun. Behind him, from the garage, the soldier took a potshot at him for good luck. The bullet whistled dangerously near the Professor's head, and his yelling rose into an indignant lament as he waved his arms more wildly, and hopped high into the air at every few steps, in an access of terror.

The soldier watched a while, smiling, as the cavorting figure grew smaller in the oncoming evening darkness, and the rattling of the tin became a part of the great silence out there beyond the gate. The wall of the garage as he leaned against it still gave forth heat, left there by the sun, but even then the lunar chill was growing in the air.

JOHN CHEEVER
(1912–1982)

John Cheever is our fantasist of the close-at-hand; our "realist" touched with his own, and inimitable, species of magic. In such frequently anthologized stories of his as "The Enormous Radio" and "The Swimmer," fantasy elements seep into seemingly normal and ordinary lives, with dramatic effects; yet the fantasizing imagination, the distinctive Cheever tone, is everywhere present in his fiction, like a moon shining just a little too brightly for comfort. Such illuminations are most effective in short works, and Cheever was arguably always a writer of short stories, to whom the form of the novel remained elusive, or willed.

Born in Quincy, Massachusetts, John Cheever was educated at the nearby Thayer Academy. He took for his subject a white, middle- and upper-middle-class suburban world, viewed both sympathetically and cynically. His major titles are the story collections The Way Some People Live *(1943),* The Enormous Radio *(1953),* The Housebreaker of Shady Hill *(1958),* The World of Apples *(1973), and* The Stories of John Cheever *(1978); and the novels* The Wapshot Chronicle *(1957),* The Wapshot Scandal *(1964),* Bullet Park *(1969), and* Falconer *(1977).*

"The Country Husband," one of John Cheever's most frequently reprinted short stories, is a mordantly funny, bittersweet valentine to the romance of lost youth; it ends with a famous flight of prose poetry—one of Cheever's signature gestures toward lyric beauty in the face of ironic (and usually masculine) defeat.

The Country Husband

To begin at the beginning, the airplane from Minneapolis in which Francis Weed was traveling East ran into heavy weather. The sky had been a hazy blue, with the clouds below the plane lying so close together that nothing could be seen of the earth. Then mist began to form outside the windows, and they flew into a white cloud of such density that it reflected the exhaust fires. The color of the cloud darkened to gray, and the plane began to rock. Francis had been in heavy weather before, but he had never been shaken up so much. The man in the seat beside him pulled a flask out of his pocket and took a drink. Francis smiled at his neighbor, but the man looked away; he wasn't sharing his pain killer with anyone. The plane began to drop and flounder wildly. A child was crying. The air in the cabin was overheated and stale, and Francis' left foot went to sleep. He read a little from a paper book that he had bought at the airport, but the violence of the storm divided his attention. It was black outside the ports. The exhaust fires blazed and shed sparks in the dark, and, inside, the shaded lights, the stuffiness, and the window curtains gave the cabin an atmosphere of intense and misplaced domesticity. Then the lights flickered and went out. "You know what I've always wanted to do?" the man beside Francis said suddenly. "I've always wanted to buy a farm in New Hampshire and raise beef cattle." The stewardess announced that they were going to make an emergency landing. All but the children saw in their minds the spreading wings of the Angel of Death. The pilot could be heard singing faintly, "I've got sixpence, jolly, jolly sixpence. I've got sixpence to last me all my life . . ." There was no other sound.

The loud groaning of the hydraulic valves swallowed up the pilot's song, and there was a shrieking high in the air, like automobile brakes, and the plane hit flat on its belly in a cornfield and shook them so violently that an old man up forward howled, "Me kidneys! Me kidneys!" The stewardess flung open the door, and someone opened an emergency door at the back, letting in the sweet noise of their continuing mortality—the idle splash and smell of a heavy rain. Anxious for their lives, they filed out of the doors and scattered over the cornfield in all directions, praying that the thread would hold. It did. Nothing happened. When it was clear that the plane would not burn or explode, the crew and the stewardess gathered the passengers together and led them to the shelter of a barn. They were not far from Philadelphia, and in a little while a string of taxis took them into the city. "It's just like the Marne," someone said, but there was surprisingly little relaxation of that suspiciousness with which many Americans regard their fellow travelers.

In Philadelphia, Francis Weed got a train to New York. At the end of that journey, he crossed the city and caught just as it was about to pull out the commuting train that he took five nights a week to his home in Shady Hill.

He sat with Trace Bearden. "You know, I was in that plane that just crashed outside Philadelphia," he said. "We came down in a field . . ." He had traveled faster than the newspapers or the rain, and the weather in New York was sunny and mild. It was a day in late September, as fragrant and shapely as an apple. Trace listened to the story, but how could he get excited? Francis had no powers that would let him re-create a brush with death—particularly in the atmosphere of a commuting train, journeying through a sunny countryside where already, in the slum gardens, there were signs of harvest. Trace picked up his newspaper, and Francis was left alone with his thoughts. He said good night to Trace on the platform at Shady Hill and drove in his secondhand Volkswagen up to the Blenhollow neighborhood, where he lived.

The Weeds' Dutch Colonial house was larger than it appeared to be from the driveway. The living room was spacious and divided like Gaul into three parts. Around an ell to the left as one entered from the vestibule was the long table, laid for six, with candles and a bowl of fruit in the center. The sounds and smells that came from the open kitchen door were appetizing, for Julia Weed was a good cook. The largest part of the living room centered on a fireplace. On the right were some bookshelves and a piano. The room was polished and tranquil, and from the windows that opened to the west there was some late-summer sunlight, brilliant and as clear as water. Nothing here was neglected; nothing had not been burnished. It was not the kind of household where, after prying open a stuck cigarette box, you would find an old shirt button and a tarnished nickel. The hearth was swept, the roses on the piano were reflected in the polish of the broad top, and there was an album of Schubert waltzes on the rack. Louisa Weed, a pretty girl of nine, was looking out the western windows. Her younger brother Henry was standing beside her. Her still younger brother, Toby, was studying the figures of some tonsured monks drinking beer on the polished brass of the woodbox. Francis, taking off his hat and putting down his paper, was not consciously pleased with the scene; he was not that reflective. It was his element, his creation, and he returned to it with that sense of lightness and strength with which any creature returns to his home. "Hi, everybody," he said. "The plane from Minneapolis..."

Nine times out of ten, Francis would be greeted with affection, but tonight the children are absorbed in their own antagonisms. Francis had not finished his sentence about the plane crash before Henry plants a kick in Louisa's behind. Louisa swings around, saying, "*Damn you*!" Francis makes the mistake of scolding Louisa for bad language before he punishes Henry. Now Louisa turns on her father and accuses him of favoritism. Henry is always right; she is persecuted and lonely; her lot is hopeless. Francis turns to his son, but the boy has justification for the kick—she hit him first; she hit him on the ear, which is dangerous. Louisa agrees with this passionately. She hit him on the ear, and she *meant* to hit him on the ear, because he messed up her china collection. Henry says that this is a lie. Little Toby turns away from the woodbox to throw in some evidence for Louisa. Henry claps his hand over little Toby's mouth. Francis separates the two boys but accidentally pushes Toby into the woodbox. Toby begins to cry. Louisa is already crying. Just then, Julia Weed comes into that part of the room where the table is laid. She is a pretty, intelligent woman, and the white in her hair is premature. She does not seem to notice the fracas. "Hello, darling," she says serenely to Francis. "Wash your hands, everyone. Dinner is ready." She strikes a match and lights the six candles in this vale of tears.

This simple announcement, like the war cries of the Scottish chieftains, only refreshes the ferocity of the combatants. Louisa gives Henry a blow on the shoulder. Henry, although he seldom cries, has pitched nine innings and is tired. He bursts into tears. Little Toby discovers a splinter in his hand and begins to howl. Francis says loudly that he has been in a plane crash and that he is tired. Julia appears again from the kitchen and, still ignoring the chaos, asks Francis to go upstairs and tell Helen that everything is ready. Francis is happy to go; it is like getting back to headquarters company. He is planning to tell his oldest daughter about the airplane crash, but Helen is lying on her bed reading a *True Romance* magazine, and the first thing Francis does is to take the magazine from her hand and remind Helen that he has forbidden her to buy it. She did not buy it, Helen replies. It was given to her by her best friend, Bessie Black. Everybody reads *True Romance.* Bessie Black's father reads *True Romance.* There isn't a girl in Helen's class who doesn't read *True Romance.* Francis expresses his detestation of the magazine and then tells her that dinner is ready—although from the sounds downstairs it doesn't seem so. Helen follows him down the stairs. Julia has seated herself in the candlelight and spread a napkin over her lap. Neither Louisa nor Henry has come to the table. Little Toby is still howling, lying face down on the floor. Francis speaks to him gently: "Daddy was in a plane crash this afternoon, Toby. Don't you want to hear about it?" Toby goes on crying. "If you don't come to the table now, Toby," Francis says, "I'll have to send you to bed without any supper." The little boy rises, gives him a cutting look, flies up the stairs to his bedroom, and slams the door. "Oh dear," Julia says, and starts to go after him. Francis says that she will spoil him. Julia says that Toby is ten pounds underweight and has to be encouraged to eat. Winter is coming, and he will spend the cold months in bed unless he has his dinner. Julia goes upstairs. Francis sits down at the table with Helen. Helen is suffering from the dismal feeling of having read too intently on a fine day, and she gives her father and the room a jaded look. She doesn't understand about the plane crash, because there wasn't a drop of rain in Shady Hill.

Julia returns with Toby, and they all sit down and are served. "Do I have to look at that big, fat slob?" Henry says, of Louisa. Everybody but Toby enters into this skirmish, and it rages up and down the table for five minutes. Toward the end, Henry puts his napkin over his head and, trying to eat that way, spills spinach all over his shirt. Francis asks Julia if the children couldn't have their dinner earlier. Julia's guns are loaded for this. She can't cook two dinners and lay two tables. She paints with lightning strokes that panorama of drudgery in which her youth, her beauty, and her wit have been lost. Francis says that he must be understood; he was nearly killed in an airplane crash, and he doesn't like to come home every night to a battlefield. Now Julia is deeply concerned. Her voice trembles. He doesn't come home every night to a battlefield. The accusation is stupid and mean. Everything was tranquil until he arrived. She stops speaking, puts down her knife and fork, and looks into her plate as if it is a gulf. She begins to cry. "Poor Mummy!" Toby says, and when Julia gets up from the table, drying her tears with a napkin, Toby goes to her side. "Poor Mummy," he says. "Poor Mummy!" And they climb the stairs together. The other children drift away from the battlefield, and Francis goes into the back garden for a cigarette and some air.

IT WAS a pleasant garden, with walks and flower beds and places to sit. The sunset had nearly burned out, but there was still plenty of light. Put into a thoughtful mood by the crash and the battle, Francis listened to the evening sounds of Shady Hill. "Varmints! Rascals!" old Mr. Nixon shouted to the squirrels in his bird-feeding station. "Avaunt and quit my sight!" A door slammed. Someone was cutting grass. Then Donald Goslin, who lived at the corner, began to play the "Moonlight Sonata." He did this nearly every night. He threw the tempo out the window and played it *rubato* from beginning to end, like an outpouring of tearful petulance, lonesomeness, and self-pity—of everything it was Beethoven's greatness not to know. The music rang up and down the street beneath the trees like an appeal for love, for tenderness, aimed at some lovely housemaid—some fresh-faced, homesick girl from Galway, looking at old snapshots in her third-floor room. "Here, Jupiter, here, Jupiter," Francis called to the Mercers' retriever. Jupiter crashed through the tomato vines with the remains of a felt hat in his mouth.

Jupiter was an anomaly. His retrieving instincts and his high spirits were out of place in Shady Hill. He was as black as coal, with a long, alert, intelligent, rakehell face. His eyes gleamed with mischief, and he held his head high. It was the fierce, heavily collared dog's head that appears in heraldry, in tapestry, and that used to appear on umbrella handles and walking sticks. Jupiter went where he pleased, ransacking wastebaskets, clotheslines, garbage pails, and shoe bags. He broke up garden parties and tennis matches, and got mixed up in the processional at Christ Church on Sunday, barking at the men in red dresses. He crashed through old Mr. Nixon's rose garden two or three times a day, cutting a wide swath through the Condesa de Sastagos, and as soon as Donald Goslin lighted his barbecue fire on Thursday nights, Jupiter would get the scent. Nothing the Goslins did could drive him away. Sticks and stones and rude commands only moved him to the edge of the terrace, where he remained, with his gallant and heraldic muzzle, waiting for Donald Goslin to turn his back and reach for the salt. Then he would spring onto the terrace, lift the steak lightly off the fire, and run away with the Goslins' dinner. Jupiter's days were numbered. The Wrightsons' German gardener or the Farquarsons' cook would soon poison him. Even old Mr. Nixon might put some arsenic in the garbage that Jupiter loved. "Here, Jupiter, Jupiter!" Francis called, but the dog pranced off, shaking the hat in his white teeth. Looking at the windows of his house, Francis saw that Julia had come down and was blowing out the candles.

Julia and Francis Weed went out a great deal. Julia was well liked and gregarious, and her love of parties sprang from a most natural dread of chaos and loneliness. She went through her morning mail with real anxiety, looking for invitations, and she usually found some, but she was insatiable, and if she had gone out seven nights a week, it would not have cured her of a reflective look—the look of someone who hears distant music—for she would always suppose that there was a more brilliant party somewhere else. Francis limited her to two week-night parties, putting a flexible interpretation on Friday, and rode through the weekend like a dory in a gale. The day after the airplane crash, the Weeds were to have dinner with the Farquarsons.

Francis got home late from town, and Julia got the sitter while he dressed, and then hurried him out of the house. The party was small and pleasant, and Francis settled down to enjoy himself. A new maid passed the drinks. Her hair was dark, and her face was round and pale and seemed familiar to Francis. He had not developed his memory as a sentimental faculty. Wood smoke, lilac, and other such perfumes did not stir him, and his memory was something like his appendix—a vestigial repository. It was not his limitation at all to be unable to escape the past; it was perhaps his limitation that he had escaped it so successfully.

He might have seen the maid at other parties, he might have seen her taking a walk on Sunday afternoons, but in either case he would not be searching his memory now. Her face was, in a wonderful way, a moon face—Norman or Irish—but it was not beautiful enough to account for his feeling that he had seen her before, in circumstances that he ought to be able to remember. He asked Nellie Farquarson who she was, Nellie said that the maid had come through an agency, and that her home was Trenon, in Normandy—a small place with a church and a restaurant that Nellie had once visited. While Nellie talked on about her travels abroad, Francis realized where he had seen the woman before. It had been at the end of the war. He had left a replacement depot with some other men and taken a three-day pass in Trenon. On their second day, they had walked out to a crossroads to see the public chastisement of a young woman who had lived with the German commandant during the Occupation.

It was a cool morning in the fall. The sky was overcast, and poured down onto the dirt crossroads a very discouraging light. They were on high land and could see how like one another the shapes of the clouds and the hills were as they stretched off toward the sea. The prisoner arrived sitting on a three-legged stool in a farm cart. She stood by the cart while the Mayor read the accusation and the sentence. Her head was bent and her face was set in that empty half smile behind which the whipped soul is suspended. When the Mayor was finished, she undid her hair and let it fall across her back. A little man with a gray mustache cut off her hair with shears and dropped it on the ground. Then, with a bowl of soapy water and a straight razor, he shaved her skull clean. A woman approached and began to undo the fastenings of her clothes, but the prisoner pushed her aside and undressed herself. When she pulled her chemise over her head and threw it on the ground, she was naked. The women jeered; the men were still. There was no change in the falseness or the plaintiveness of the prisoner's smile. The cold wind made her white skin rough and hardened the nipples of her breasts. The jeering ended gradually, put down by the recognition of their common humanity. One woman spat on her, but some inviolable grandeur in her nakedness lasted through the ordeal. When the crowd was quiet, she turned—she had begun to cry—and, with nothing on but a pair of worn black shoes and stockings, walked down the dirt road alone away from the village. The round white face had aged a little, but there was no question but that the maid who passed his cocktails and later served Francis his dinner was the woman who had been punished at the crossroads.

The war seemed now so distant and that world where the cost of partisanship had been death or torture so long ago. Francis had lost track of the men who had been with him in Vesey. He could not count on Julia's discretion. He could not tell anyone. And if he had told the story now, at the dinner table, it would have been a social as well as a human error. The people in the Farquarsons' living room seemed united in their tacit claim that there had been no past, no war—that there was no danger or trouble in the world. In the recorded history of human arrangements, this extraordinary meeting would have fallen into place, but the atmosphere of Shady Hill made the memory unseemly and impolite. The prisoner withdrew after passing the coffee, but the encounter left Francis feeling languid; it had opened his memory and his senses, and left them dilated. Julia went into the house. Francis stayed in the car to take the sitter home.

Expecting to see Mrs. Henlein, the old lady who usually stayed with the children, he was surprised when a young girl opened the door and came out onto the lighted stoop. She stayed in the light to count her textbooks. She was frowning and beautiful. Now, the world is full of beautiful young girls, but Francis saw here the difference between beauty and perfection. All those endearing flaws, moles, birthmarks, and healed wounds were missing, and he experienced in his consciousness that moment when music breaks glass, and felt a pang of recognition as strange, deep, and wonderful as anything in his life. It hung from her frown, from an impalpable darkness in her face—a look that impressed him as a direct appeal for love. When she had counted her books, she came down the steps and opened the car door. In the light, he saw that her cheeks were wet. She got in and shut the door.

"You're new," Francis said.

"Yes. Mrs. Henlein is sick. I'm Anne Murchison."

"Did the children give you any trouble?"

"Oh, no, no." She turned and smiled at him unhappily in the dim dashboard light. Her light hair caught on the collar of her jacket, and she shook her head to set it loose.

"You've been crying."

"Yes."

"I hope it was nothing that happened in our house."

"No, no, it was nothing that happened in your house." Her voice was bleak. "It's no secret. Everybody in the village knows. Daddy's an alcoholic, and he just called me from some saloon and gave me a piece of his mind. He thinks I'm immoral. He called just before Mrs. Weed came back."

"I'm sorry."

"Oh, *Lord!*" She gasped and began to cry. She turned toward Francis, and he took her in his arms and let her cry on his shoulder. She shook in his embrace, and this movement accentuated his sense of the fineness of her flesh and bone. The layers of their clothing felt thin, and when her shuddering began to diminish, it was so much like a paroxysm of love that Francis lost his head and pulled her roughly against him. She drew away. "I live on Belleview Avenue," she said. "You go down Lansing Street to the railroad bridge."

"All right." He started the car.

"You turn left at that traffic light.... Now you turn right here and go straight on toward the tracks."

The road Francis took brought him out of his own neighborhood, across the tracks, and toward the river, to a street where the near-poor lived, in houses whose peaked gables and trimmings of wooden lace conveyed the purest feelings of pride and romance, although the houses themselves could not have offered much privacy or comfort, they were all so small. The street was dark, and, stirred by the grace and beauty of the troubled girl, he seemed, in turning into it, to have come into the deepest part of some submerged memory. In the distance, he saw a porch light burning. It was the only one, and she said that the house with the light was where she lived. When he stopped the car, he could see beyond the porch light into a dimly lighted hallway with an old-fashioned clothes tree. "Well, here we are," he said, conscious that a young man would have said something different.

She did not move her hands from the books, where they were folded, and she turned and faced him. There were tears of lust in his eyes. Determinedly—not sadly—he opened the door on his side and walked around to open hers. He took her free hand, letting his fingers in between hers, climbed at her side the two concrete steps, and went up a narrow walk through a front garden where dahlias, marigolds, and roses—things that had withstood the light frosts—still bloomed, and made a bitter-sweet smell in the night air. At the steps, she freed her hand and then turned and kissed him swiftly. Then she crossed the porch and shut the door. The porch light went out, then the light in the hall. A second later, a light went on upstairs at the side of the house, shining into a tree that was still covered with leaves. It took her only a few minutes to undress and get into bed, and then the house was dark.

Julia was asleep when Francis got home. He opened a second window and got into bed to shut his eyes on that night, but as soon as they were shut—as soon as he had dropped off to sleep—the girl entered his mind, moving with perfect freedom through its shut doors and filling chamber after chamber with her light, her perfume, and the music of her voice. He was crossing the Atlantic with her on the old *Mauretania* and, later, living with her in Paris. When he woke from his dream, he got up and smoked a cigarette at the open window. Getting back into bed, he cast around in his mind for something he desired to do that would injure no one, and he thought of skiing. Up through the dimness in his mind rose the image of a mountain deep in snow. It was late in the day. Wherever his eyes looked, he saw broad and heartening things. Over his shoulder, there was a snow-filled valley, rising into wooded hills where the trees dimmed the whiteness like a sparse coat of hair. The cold deadened all sound but the loud, iron clanking of the lift machinery. The light on the trails was blue; and it was harder than it had been a minute or two earlier to pick the turns, harder to judge—now that the snow was all deep blue—the crust, the ice, the bare spots, and the deep piles of dry powder. Down the mountain he swung, matching his speed against the contours of a slope that had been formed in the first ice age, seeking with ardor some simplicity of feeling and circumstance. Night fell then, and he drank a Martini with some old friend in a dirty country bar.

In the morning, Francis' snow-covered mountain was gone, and he was left with his vivid memories of Paris and the *Mauretania*. He had been bitten gravely. He washed his body, shaved his jaws, drank his coffee, and missed the seven-thirty-one. The train pulled out just as he brought his car to the station, and the longing he felt for the coaches as they drew stubbornly away from him reminded him of the humors of love. He waited for the eight-two, on what was now an empty platform. It was a clear morning; the morning seemed thrown like a gleaming bridge of light over his mixed affairs. His spirits were feverish and high. The image of the girl seemed to put him into a relationship to the world that was mysterious and enthralling. Cars were beginning to fill up the parking lot, and he noticed that those that had driven down from the high land above Shady Hill were white with hoarfrost. This first clear sign of autumn thrilled him. An express train—a night train from Buffalo or Albany—came down the tracks between the platforms, and he saw that the roofs of the foremost cars were covered with a skin of ice. Struck by the miraculous physicalness of everything, he smiled at the passengers in the dining car, who could be seen eating eggs and wiping their mouths with napkins as they traveled. The sleeping-car compartments, with their soiled bed linen, trailed through the fresh morning like a string of rooming-house windows. Then he saw an extraordinary thing; at one of the bedroom windows sat an unclothed woman of exceptional beauty, combing her golden hair. She passed like an apparition through Shady Hill, combing and combing her hair, and Francis followed her with his eyes until she was out of sight. Then old Mrs. Wrightson joined him on the platform and began to talk.

"Well, I guess you must be surprised to see me here the third morning in a row," she said, "but because of my window curtains I'm becoming a regular commuter. The curtains I bought on Monday I returned on Tuesday, and the curtains I bought Tuesday I'm returning today. On Monday, I got exactly what I wanted—it's a wool tapestry with roses and birds—but when I got them home, I found they were the wrong length. Well, I exchanged them yesterday, and when I got them home, I found they were still the wrong length. Now I'm praying to high heaven that the decorator will have them in the right length, because you know my house, you know my living-room windows, and you can imagine what a problem they present. I don't know what to do with them."

"I know what to do with them," Francis said.

"What?"

"Paint them black on the inside, and shut up."

There was a gasp from Mrs. Wrightson, and Francis looked down at her to be sure that she knew he meant to be rude. She turned and walked away from him, so damaged in spirit that she limped. A wonderful feeling enveloped him, as if light were being shaken about him, and he thought again of Venus combing and combing her hair as she drifted through the Bronx. The realization of how many years had passed since he had enjoyed being deliberately impolite sobered him. Among his friends and neighbors, there were brilliant and gifted people—he saw that—but many of them, also, were bores and fools, and he had made the mistake of listening to them all with equal attention. He had confused a lack of discrimination with Christian love, and the confusion seemed general and destructive. He was grateful to the girl for this bracing sensation of independence. Birds were singing—cardinals and the last of the robins. The sky shone like enamel. Even the smell of ink from his morning paper honed his appetite for life, and the world that was spread out around him was plainly a paradise.

If Francis had believed in some hierarchy of love—in spirits armed with hunting bows, in the capriciousness of Venus and Eros—or even in magical potions, philters, and stews, in scapulae and quarters of the moon, it might have explained his susceptibility and his feverish high spirits. The autumnal loves of middle age are well publicized, and he guessed that he was face to face with one of these, but there was not a trace of autumn in what he felt. He wanted to sport in the green woods, scratch where he itched, and drink from the same cup.

His secretary, Miss Rainey, was late that morning—she went to a psychiatrist three mornings a week—and when she came in, Francis wondered what advice a psychiatrist would have for him. But the girl promised to bring back into his life something like the sound of music. The realization that this music might lead him straight to a trial for statutory rape at the county courthouse collapsed his happiness. The photograph of his four children laughing into the camera on the beach at Gay Head reproached him. On the letterhead of his firm there was a drawing of the Laocoon, and the figure of the priest and his sons in the coils of the snake appeared to him to have the deepest meaning.

He had lunch with Pinky Trabert. At a conversational level, the mores of his friends were robust and elastic, but he knew that the moral card house would come down on them all—on Julia and the children as well—if he got caught taking advantage of a baby-sitter. Looking back over the recent history of Shady Hill for some precedent, he found there was none. There was no turpitude; there had not been a divorce since he lived there; there had not even been a breath of scandal. Things seemed arranged with more propriety even than in the Kingdom of Heaven. After leaving Pinky, Francis went to a jeweler's and bought the girl a bracelet. How happy this clandestine purchase made him, how stuffy and comical the jeweler's clerks seemed, how sweet the women who passed at his back smelled! On Fifth Avenue, passing Atlas with his shoulders bent under the weight of the world, Francis thought of the strenuousness of containing his physicalness within the patterns he had chosen.

He did not know when he would see the girl next. He had the bracelet in his inside pocket when he got home. Opening the door of his house; he found her in the hall. Her back was to him, and she turned when she heard the door close. Her smile was open and loving. Her perfection stunned him like a fine day—a day after a thunderstorm. He seized her and covered her lips with his, and she struggled but she did not have to struggle for long, because just then little Gertrude Flannery appeared from somewhere and said, "Oh, Mr. Weed . . ."

Gertrude was a stray. She had been born with a taste for exploration, and she did not have it in her to center her life with her affectionate parents. People who did not know the Flannerys concluded from Gertrude's behavior that she was the child of a bitterly divided family, where drunken quarrels were the rule. This was not true. The fact that little Gertrude's clothing was ragged and thin was her own triumph over her mother's struggle to dress her warmly and neatly. Garrulous, skinny, and unwashed, she drifted from house to house around the Blenhollow neighborhood, forming and breaking alliances based on an attachment to babies, animals, children her own age, adolescents, and sometimes adults. Opening your front door in the morning, you would find Gertrude sitting on your stoop. Going into the bathroom to shave, you would find Gertrude using the toilet. Looking into your son's crib, you would find it empty, and, looking further, you would find that Gertrude had pushed him in his baby carriage into the next village.

She was helpful, pervasive, honest, hungry, and loyal. She never went home of her own choice. When the time to go arrived, she was indifferent to all its signs. "Go home, Gertrude," people could be heard saying in one house or another, night after night. "Go home, Gertrude. It's time for you to go home now, Gertrude." "You had better go home and get your supper, Gertrude." "I told you to go home twenty minutes ago, Gertrude." "Your mother will be worrying about you, Gertrude." "Go home, Gertrude, go home."

There are times when the lines around the human eye seem like shelves of eroded stone and when the staring eye itself strikes us with such a wilderness of animal feeling that we are at a loss. The look Francis gave the little girl was ugly and queer, and it frightened her. He reached into his pockets—his hands were shaking—and took out a quarter. "Go home, Gertrude, go home, and don't tell anyone, Gertrude. Don't—" He choked and ran into the living room as Julia called down to him from upstairs to hurry and dress.

The thought that he would drive Anne Murchison home later that night ran like a golden thread through the events of the party that Francis and Julia went to, and he laughed uproariously at dull jokes, dried a tear when Mabel Mercer told him about the death of her kitten, and stretched, yawned, sighed, and grunted like any other man with a rendezvous at the back of his mind. The bracelet was in his pocket. As he sat talking, the smell of grass was in his nose, and he was wondering where he would park the car. Nobody lived in the old Parker mansion, and the driveway was used as a lovers' lane. Townsend Street was a dead end, and he could park there, beyond the last house. The old lane that used to connect Elm Street to the riverbanks was overgrown, but he had walked there with his children, and he could drive his car deep enough into the brushwoods to be concealed.

The Weeds were the last to leave the party, and their host and hostess spoke of their own married happiness while they all four stood in the hallway saying good night. "She's my girl," their host said, squeezing his wife. "She's my blue sky. After sixteen years, I still bite her shoulders. She makes me feel like Hannibal crossing the Alps."

The Weeds drove home in silence. Francis brought the car up the driveway and sat still, with the motor running. "You can put the car in the garage," Julia said as she got out. "I told the Murchison girl she could leave at eleven. Someone drove her home." She shut the door, and Francis sat in the dark. He would be spared nothing then, it seemed, that a fool was not spared: ravening lewdness, jealousy, this hurt to his feelings that put tears in his eyes, even scorn—for he could see clearly the image he now presented, his arms spread over the steering wheel and his head buried in them for love.

FRANCIS had been a dedicated Boy Scout when he was young, and, remembering the precepts of his youth, he left his office early the next afternoon and played some round-robin squash, but, with his body toned up by exercise and a shower, he realized that he might better have stayed at his desk. It was a frosty night when he got home. The air smelled sharply of change. When he stepped into the house, he sensed an unusual stir. The children were in their best clothes, and when Julia came down, she was wearing a lavender dress and her diamond sunburst. She explained the stir: Mr. Hubber was coming at seven to take their photograph for the Christmas card. She had put out Francis' blue suit and a tie with some color in it, because the picture was going to be in color this year. Julia was lighthearted at the thought of being photographed for Christmas. It was the kind of ceremony she enjoyed.

Francis went upstairs to change his clothes. He was tired from the day's work and tired with longing, and sitting on the edge of the bed had the effect of deepening his weariness. He thought of Anne Murchison, and the physical need to express himself, instead of being restrained by the pink lamps of Julia's dressing table, engulfed him. He went to Julia's desk, took a piece of writing paper, and began to write on it. "Dear Anne, I love you, I love you, I love you . . ." No one would see the letter, and he used no restraint. He used phrases like "heavenly bliss," and "love nest." He salivated, sighed, and trembled. When Julia called him to come down, the abyss between his fantasy and the practical world opened so wide that he felt it affected the muscles of his heart. Julia and the children were on the stoop, and the photographer and his assistant had set up a double battery of floodlights to show the family and the architectural beauty of the entrance to their house. People who had come home on a late train slowed their cars to see the Weeds being photographed for their Christmas card. A few waved and called to the family. It took half an hour of smiling and wetting their lips before Mr. Hubber was satisfied. The heat of the lights made an unfresh smell in the frosty air, and when they were turned off, they lingered on the retina of Francis' eyes.

Later that night, while Francis and Julia were drinking their coffee in the living room, the doorbell rang. Julia answered the door and let in Clayton Thomas. He had come to pay for some theatre tickets that she had given his mother some time ago, and that Helen Thomas had scrupulously insisted on paying for, though Julia had asked her not to. Julia invited him in to have a cup of coffee. "I won't have any coffee," Clayton said, "but I will come in for a minute." He followed her into the living room, said good evening to Francis, and sat awkwardly in a chair.

Clayton's father had been killed in the war, and the young man's fatherlessness surrounded him like an element. This may have been conspicuous in Shady Hill because the Thomases were the only family that lacked a piece; all the other marriages were intact and productive. Clayton was in his second or third year of college, and he and his mother lived alone in a large house, which she hoped to sell. Clayton had once made some trouble. Years ago, he had stolen some money and run away; he had got to California before they caught up with him. He was tall and homely, wore horn-rimmed glasses, and spoke in a deep voice.

"When do you go back to college, Clayton?" Francis asked.

"I'm not going back," Clayton said. "Mother doesn't have the money, and there's no sense in all this pretense. I'm going to get a job, and if we sell the house, we'll take an apartment in New York."

"Won't you miss Shady Hill?" Julia asked.

"No," Clayton said. "I don't like it."

"Why not?" Francis asked.

"Well, there's a lot here I don't approve of," Clayton said gravely. "Things like the club dances. Last Saturday night, I looked in toward the end and saw Mr. Granner trying to put Mrs. Minot into the trophy case. They were both drunk. I disapprove of so much drinking."

"It was Saturday night," Francis said.

"And all the dovecotes are phony," Clayton said. "And the way people clutter up their lives. I've thought about it a lot, and what seems to me to be really wrong with Shady Hill is that it doesn't have any future. So much energy is spent in perpetuating the place—in keeping out undesirables, and so forth—that the only idea of the future anyone has is just more and more commuting trains and more parties. I don't think that's healthy. I think people ought to be able to dream big dreams about the future. I think people ought to be able to dream great dreams."

"It's too bad you couldn't continue with college," Julia said.

"I wanted to go to divinity school," Clayton said.

"What's your church?" Francis asked.

"Unitarian, Theosophist, Transcendentalist Humanist," Clayton said.

"Wasn't Emerson a transcendentalist?" Julia asked.

"I mean the English transcendentalism," Clayton said. "All the American transcendentalists were goops."

"What kind of job do you expect to get?" Francis asked.

"Well, I'd like to work for a publisher," Clayton said, "but everyone tells me there's nothing doing. But it's the kind of thing I'm interested in. I'm writing a long verse play about good and evil. Uncle Charlie might get me into a bank, and that would be good for me. I need the discipline. I have a long way to go in forming my character. I have some terrible habits, I talk too much. I think I ought to take vows of silence. I ought to try not to speak for a week, and discipline myself. I've thought of making a retreat at one of the Episcopalian monasteries, but I don't like Trinitarianism."

"Do you have any girl friends?" Francis asked.

"I'm engaged to be married," Clayton said. "Of course, I'm not old enough or rich enough to have my engagement observed or respected or anything, but I bought a simulated emerald for Anne Murchison with the money I made cutting lawns this summer. We're going to be married as soon as she finishes school."

Francis recoiled at the mention of the girl's name. Then a dingy light seemed to emanate from his spirit, showing everything—Julia, the boy, the chairs—in their true colorlessness. It was like a bitter turn of the weather.

"We're going to have a large family," Clayton said. "Her father's a terrible rummy, and I've had my hard times, and we want to have lots of children. Oh, she's wonderful, Mr. and Mrs. Weed, and we have so much in common. We like all the same things. We sent out the same Christmas card last year without planning it, and we both have an allergy to tomatoes, and our eyebrows grow together in the middle. Well, goodnight."

Julia went to the door with him. When she returned, Francis said that Clayton was lazy, irresponsible, affected, and smelly. Julia said that Francis seemed to be getting intolerant; the Thomas boy was young and should be given a chance. Julia had noticed other cases where Francis had been short-tempered. "Mrs. Wrightson has asked everyone in Shady Hill to her anniversary party but us," she said.

"I'm sorry, Julia."

"Do you know why they didn't ask us?"

"Why?"

"Because you insulted Mrs. Wrightson."

"Then you know about it?"

"June Masterson told me. She was standing behind you."

Julia walked in front of the sofa with a small step that expressed, Francis knew, a feeling of anger.

"I did insult Mrs. Wrightson, Julia, and I meant to. I've never liked her parties, and I'm glad she's dropped us."

"What about Helen?"

"How does Helen come into this?"

"Mrs. Wrightson's the one who decides who goes to the assemblies."

"You mean she can keep Helen from going to the dances?"

"Yes."

"I hadn't thought of that."

"Oh. I knew you hadn't thought of it," Julia cried, thrusting hilt-deep into this chink of his armor. "And it makes me furious to see this kind of stupid thoughtlessness wreck everyone's happiness."

"I don't think I've wrecked anyone's happiness."

"Mrs. Wrightson runs Shady Hill and has run it for the last forty years. I don't know what makes you think that in a community like this you can indulge every impulse you have to be insulting, vulgar, and offensive."

"I have very good manners," Francis said, trying to give the evening a turn toward the light.

"Damn you, Francis Weed!" Julia cried, and the spit of her words struck him in the face. "I've worked hard for the social position we enjoy in this place, and I won't stand by and see you wreck it. You must have understood when you settled here that you couldn't expect to live like a bear in a cave."

"I've got to express my likes and dislikes."

"You can conceal your dislikes. You don't have to meet everything head on, like a child. Unless you're anxious to be a social leper. It's no accident that we get asked out a great deal! It's no accident that Helen has so many friends. How would you like to spend your Saturday nights at the movies? How would you like to spend your Sundays raking up dead leaves? How would you like it if your daughter spent the assembly nights sitting at her window, listening to the music from the club? How would you like it—" He did something then that was, after all, not so unaccountable, since her words seemed to raise up between them a wall so deadening that he gagged. He struck her full in the face. She staggered and then, a moment later, seemed composed. She went up the stairs to their room. She didn't slam the door. When Francis followed, a few minutes later, he found her packing a suitcase.

"Julia, I'm very sorry."

"It doesn't matter," she said. She was crying.

"Where do you think you're going?"

"I don't know. I just looked at a timetable. There's an eleven-sixteen into New York. I'll take that."

"You can't go, Julia."

"I can't stay. I know that."

"I'm sorry about Mrs. Wrightson, Julia, and I'm—"

"It doesn't matter about Mrs. Wrightson. That isn't the trouble."

"What is the trouble?"

"You don't love me."

"I do love you, Julia."

"No, you don't."

"Julia, I do love you, and I would like to be as we were—sweet and bawdy and dark—but now there are so many people."

"You hate me."

"I don't hate you, Julia."

"You have no idea of how much you hate me. I think it's subconscious. You don't realize the cruel things you've done."

"What cruel things, Julia?"

"The cruel acts your subconscious drives you to in order to express your hatred of me."

"What, Julia?"

"I've never complained."

"Tell me."

"You don't know what you're doing."

"Tell me."

"Your clothes."

"What do you mean?"

"I mean the way you leave your dirty clothes around in order to express your subconscious hatred of me."

"I don't understand."

"I mean your dirty socks and your dirty pajamas and your dirty underwear and your dirty shirts!" She rose from kneeling by the suitcase and faced him, her eyes blazing and her voice ringing with emotion. "I'm talking about the fact that you've never learned to hang up anything. You, just leave your clothes all over the floor where they drop, in order to humiliate me. You do it on purpose!" She fell on the bed, sobbing.

"Julia, darling!" he said, but when she felt his hand on her shoulder she got up.

"Leave me alone," she said. "I have to go." She brushed past him to the closet and came back with a dress. "I'm not taking any of the things you've given me," she said. "I'm leaving my pearls and the fur jacket."

"Oh, Julia!" Her figure, so helpless in its self-deceptions, bent over the suitcase made him nearly sick with pity. She did not understand how desolate her life would be without him. She didn't understand the hours that working women have to keep. She didn't understand that most of her friendships existed within the framework of their marriage, and that without this she would find herself alone. She didn't understand about travel, about hotels, about money. "Julia, I can't let you go! What you don't understand, Julia, is that you've come to be dependent on me."

She tossed her head back and covered her face with her hands. "Did you say that *I* was dependent on *you*?" she asked. "Is that what you said? And who is it that tells you what time to get up in the morning and when to go to bed at night? Who is it that prepares your meals and picks up your dirty clothes and invites your friends to dinner? If it weren't for me, your neckties would be greasy and your clothing would be full of moth holes. You were alone when I met you, Francis Weed, and you'll be alone when I leave. When Mother asked you for a list to send out invitations to our wedding, how many names did you have to give her? Fourteen!"

"Cleveland wasn't my home, Julia."

"And how many of your friends came to the church? Two!"

"Cleveland wasn't my home, Julia."

"Since I'm not taking the fur jacket," she said quietly, "you'd better put it back into storage. There's an insurance policy on the pearls that comes due in January. The name of the laundry and the maid's telephone number—all those things are in my desk. I hope you won't drink too much, Francis. I hope that nothing bad will happen to you. If you do get into serious trouble, you can call me."

"Oh, my darling, I can't let you go!" Francis said. "I can't let you go, Julia!" He took her in his arms.

"I guess I'd better stay and take care of you for a little while longer," she said.

Riding to work in the morning, Francis saw the girl walk down the aisle of the coach. He was surprised; he hadn't realized that the school she went to was in the city, but she was carrying books, she seemed to be going to school. His surprise delayed his reaction, but then he got up clumsily and stepped into the aisle. Several people had come between them, but he could see her ahead of him, waiting for someone to open the car door, and then, as the train swerved, putting out her hand to support herself as she crossed the platform into the next car. He followed her through that car and halfway through another before calling her name—"Anne! Anne!"—but she didn't turn. He followed her into still another car, and she sat down in an aisle seat. Coming up to her, all his feelings warm and bent in her direction, he put his hand on the back of her seat—even this touch warmed him—and leaning down to speak to her, he saw that it was not Anne. It was an older woman wearing glasses. He went on deliberately into another car, his face red with embarrassment and the much deeper feeling of having his good sense challenged; for if he couldn't tell one person from another, what evidence was there that his life with Julia and the children had as much reality as his dreams of iniquity in Paris or the litter, the grass smell, and the cave-shaped trees in Lovers' Lane.

Late that afternoon, Julia called to remind Francis that they were going out for dinner. A few minutes later, Trace Bearden called. "Look, fellar," Trace said. "I'm calling for Mrs. Thomas. You know? Clayton, that boy of hers, doesn't seem able to get a job, and I wondered if you could help. If you'd call Charlie Bell—I know he's indebted to you—and say a good word for the kid, I think Charlie would—"

"Trace, I hate to say this," Francis said, "but I don't feel that I can do anything for that boy. The kid's worthless. I know it's a harsh thing to say, but it's a fact. Any kindness done for him would backfire in everybody's face. He's just a worthless kid, Trace, and there's nothing to be done about it. Even if we got him a job, he wouldn't be able to keep it for a week. I know that to be a fact. It's an awful thing, Trace, and I know it is, but instead of recommending that kid, I'd feel obligated to warn people against him—people who knew his father and would naturally want to step in and do something. I'd feel obliged to warn them. He's a thief..."

The moment this conversation was finished, Miss Rainey came in and stood by his desk. "I'm not going to be able to work for you any more, Mr. Weed," she said. "I can stay until the seventeenth if you need me, but I've been offered a whirlwind of a job, and I'd like to leave as soon as possible."

She went out, leaving him to face alone the wickedness of what he had done to the Thomas boy. His children in their photograph laughed and laughed, glazed with all the bright colors of summer, and he remembered that they had met a bagpiper on the beach that day and he had paid the piper a dollar to play them a battle song of the Black Watch. The girl would be at the house when he got home. He would spend another evening among his kind neighbors, picking and choosing dead-end streets, cart tracks, and the driveways of abandoned houses. There was nothing to mitigate his feeling—nothing that laughter or a game of softball with the children would change—and, thinking back over the plane crash, the Farquarsons' new maid, and Anne Murchison's difficulties with her drunken father, he wondered how he could have avoided arriving at just where he was. He was in trouble. He had been lost once in his life, coming back from a trout stream in the north woods, and he had now the same bleak realization that no amount of cheerfulness or hopefulness or valor or perseverance could help him find, in the gathering dark, the path that he'd lost. He smelled the forest. The feeling of bleakness was intolerable, and he saw clearly that he had reached the point where he would have to make a choice.

He could go to a psychiatrist, like Miss Rainey; he could go to church and confess his lusts; he could go to a Danish massage parlor in the West Seventies that had been recommended by a salesman; he could rape the girl or trust that he would somehow be prevented from doing this; or he could get drunk. It was his life, his boat, and, like every other man, he was made to be the father of thousands, and what harm could there be in a tryst that would make them both feel more kindly toward the world? This was the wrong train of thought, and he came back to the first, the psychiatrist. He had the telephone number of Miss Rainey's doctor, and he called and asked for an immediate appointment. He was insistent with the doctor's secretary—it was his manner in business—and when she said that the doctor's schedule was full for the next few weeks, Francis demanded an appointment that day and was told to come at five.

The psychiatrist's office was in a building that was used mostly by doctors and dentists, and the hallways were filled with the candy smell of mouthwash and memories of pain. Francis' character had been formed upon a series of private resolves—resolves about cleanliness, about going off the high diving board or repeating any other feat that challenged his courage, about punctuality, honesty, and virtue. To abdicate the perfect loneliness in which he had made his most vital decisions shattered his concept of character and left him now in a condition that felt like shock. He was stupefied. The scene for his *miserere mei Deus* was, like the waiting room of so many doctor's offices, a crude token gesture toward the sweets of domestic bliss: a place arranged with antiques, coffee tables, potted plants, and etchings of snow-covered bridges and geese in flight, although there were no children, no marriage bed, no stove, even, in this travesty of a house, where no one had ever spent the night and where the curtained windows looked straight onto a dark air shaft. Francis gave his name and address to a secretary and then saw, at the side of the room, a policeman moving toward him. "Hold it, hold it," the policeman said. "Don't move. Keep your hands where they are."

"I think it's all right, Officer," the secretary began. "I think it will be—"

"Let's make sure," the policeman said, and he began to slap Francis' clothes, looking for what—pistols, knives, an icepick? Finding nothing, he went off and the secretary began a nervous apology: "When you called on the telephone, Mr. Weed, you seemed very excited, and one of the doctor's patients has been threatening his life, and we have to be careful. If you want to go in now?" Francis pushed open a door connected to an electrical chime, and in the doctor's lair sat down heavily, blew his nose into a handkerchief, searched in his pockets for cigarettes, for matches, for something, and said hoarsely, with tears in his eyes, "I'm in love, Dr. Herzog."

IT IS a week or ten days later in Shady Hill. The seven-fourteen has come and gone, and here and there dinner is finished and the dishes are in the dish-washing machine. The village hangs, morally and economically, from a thread; but it hangs by its thread in the evening light. Donald Goslin has begun to worry the "Moonlight Sonata" again. *Marcato ma sempre pianissimo!* He seems to be wringing out a wet bath towel, but the housemaid does not heed him. She is writing a letter to Arthur Godfrey. In the cellar of his house, Francis Weed is building a coffee table. Dr. Herzog recommends woodwork as a therapy, and Francis finds some true consolation in the simple arithmetic involved and in the holy smell of new wood. Francis is happy. Upstairs, little Toby is crying, because he is tired. He puts off his cowboy hat, gloves, and fringed jacket, unbuckles the belt studded with gold and rubies, the silver bullets and holsters, slips off his suspenders, his checked shirt, and Levi's, and sits on the edge of his bed to pull off his high boots. Leaving this equipment in a heap, he goes to the closet and takes his space suit off a nail. It is a struggle for him to get into the long tights, but he succeeds. He loops the magic cape over his shoulders and, climbing onto the footboard of his bed, he spreads his arms and flies the short distance to the floor, landing with a thump that is audible to everyone in the house but himself.

"Go home, Gertrude, go home," Mrs. Masterson says. "I told you to go home an hour ago, Gertrude. It's way past your suppertime, and your mother will be worried. Go home!" A door on the Babcocks' terrace flies open, and out comes Mrs. Babcock without any clothes on, pursued by a naked husband. (Their children are away at boarding school, and their terrace is screened by a hedge.) Over the terrace they go and in at the kitchen door, as passionate and handsome a nymph and satyr as you will find on any wall in Venice. Cutting the last of the roses in her garden, Julia hears old Mr. Nixon shouting at the squirrels in his bird-feeding station. "Rapscallions! Varmints! Avaunt and quit my sight!" A miserable cat wanders into the garden, sunk in spiritual and physical discomfort. Tied to its head is a small straw hat—a doll's hat—and it is securely buttoned into a doll's dress, from the skirts of which protrudes its long, hairy tail. As it walks, it shakes its feet, as if it had fallen into water.

"Here, pussy, pussy, pussy!" Julia calls.

"Here, pussy, here, poor pussy!" But the cat gives her a skeptical look and stumbles away in its skirts. The last to come is Jupiter. He prances through the tomato vines, holding in his generous mouth the remains of an evening slipper. Then it is dark; it is a night where kings in golden suits ride elephants over the mountains.

RALPH ELLISON
(1914–1994)

With the publication of his first novel, Invisible Man, *in 1952, Ralph Ellison entered the American literary canon. Deservedly, for* Invisible Man *is a memorable work; yet in a way ironically, for the novel's immediate success and the elevation of the author to the public role of "spokesman-for-his people" would seem to have precluded subsequent work of equal ambition and risk. Of the writers in this volume, only two or three have enjoyed the early success that Ellison had. The rapid movement from "invisibility" to "visibility" is a phenomenon of our consumer culture yet to be fully investigated.*

Ralph Ellison was born in Oklahoma City, studied music at the Tuskegee Institute in Alabama, and moved to New York in 1936, where he began work with the Federal Writers' Project. He was an editor of Negro Quarterly *before serving in the Merchant Marine during World War II. Apart from* Invisible Man, *Ellison published the prose collection* Shadow and Act *(1964) and several short stories, yet uncollected. Of these, "King of the Bingo Game" (1944) is frequently anthologized. "Battle Royal," which, slightly revised, became the opening chapter of* Invisible Man, *was in fact published as a short story in 1948. It is both a work of art complete in itself and a compelling introduction to* Invisible Man, *the chronicle of a black man's search in the United States of the midcentury—"It took me a long time and much painful boomeranging of my expectations to achieve a realization everyone else appears to have been born with: That I am nobody but myself. But first I had to discover that I am an invisible man!"*

Battle Royal

It goes a long way back, some twenty years. All my life I had been looking for something, and everywhere I turned someone tried to tell me what it was. I accepted their answers too, though they were often in contradiction and even self-contradictory. I was naïve. I was looking for myself and asking everyone except myself questions which I, and only I, could answer. It took me a long time and much painful boomeranging of my expectations to achieve a realization everyone else appears to have been born with: That I am nobody but myself. But first I had to discover that I am an invisible man!

And yet I am no freak of nature, nor of history. I was in the cards, other things having been equal (or unequal) eighty-five years ago. I am not ashamed of my grandparents for having been slaves. I am only ashamed of myself for having at one time been ashamed. About eighty-five years ago they were told they were free, united with others of our country in everything pertaining to the common good, and, in everything social, separate like the fingers of the hand. And they believed it. They exulted in it. They stayed in their place, worked hard, and brought up my father to do the same. But my grandfather is the one. He was an odd old guy, my grandfather, and I am told I take after him. It was he who caused the trouble. On his deathbed he called my father to him and said, "Son, after I'm gone I want you to keep up the good fight. I never told you, but our life is a war and I have been a traitor all my born days, a spy in the enemy's country ever since I give up my gun back in the Reconstruction. Live with your head in the lion's mouth. I want you to overcome 'em with yeses, undermine 'em with grins, agree 'em to death and destruction, let 'em swoller you till they vomit or bust wide open." They thought the old man had gone out of his mind. He had been the meekest of men. The younger children were rushed from the room, the shades drawn and the flame of the lamp turned so low that it sputtered on the wick like the old man's breathing. "Learn it to the younguns," he whispered fiercely; then he died.

But my folks were more alarmed over his last words than over his dying. It was as though he had not died at all, his words caused so much anxiety. I was warned emphatically to forget what he had said and, indeed, this is the first time it has been mentioned outside the family circle. It had a tremendous effect upon me, however. I could never be sure of what he meant. Grandfather had been a quiet old man who never made any trouble, yet on his deathbed he had called himself a traitor and a spy, and he had spoken of his meekness as a dangerous activity. It became a constant puzzle which lay unanswered in the back of my mind. And whenever things went well for me I remembered my grandfather and felt guilty and uncomfortable. It was as though I was carrying out his advice in spite of myself. And to make it worse, everyone loved me for it. I was praised by the most lily-white men in town. I was considered an example of desirable conduct—just as my grandfather had been. And what puzzled me was that the old man had defined it as *treachery*. When I was praised for my conduct I felt a guilt that in some way I was doing something that was really against the wishes of the white folks, that if they had understood they would have desired me to act just the opposite, that I should have been sulky and mean, and that that really would have been what they wanted, even though they were fooled and thought they wanted me to act as I did. It made me afraid that some day they would look upon me as a traitor and I would be lost. Still I was more afraid to act any other way because they didn't like that at all. The old man's words were like a curse. On my graduation day I delivered an oration in which I showed that humility was the secret, indeed, the very essence of progress. (Not that I believed this—how could I, remembering my grandfather?—I only believed that it worked.) It was a great success. Everyone praised me and I was invited to give the speech at a gathering of the town's leading white citizens. It was a triumph for the whole community.

It was in the main ballroom of the leading hotel. When I got there I discovered that it was on the occasion of a smoker, and I was told that since I was to be there anyway I might as well take part in the battle royal to be fought by some of my schoolmates as part of the entertainment. The battle royal came first.

All of the town's big shots were there in their tuxedoes, wolfing down the buffet foods, drinking beer and whiskey and smoking black cigars. It was a large room with a high ceiling. Chairs were arranged in neat rows around three sides of a portable boxing ring. The fourth side was clear, revealing a gleaming space of polished floor. I had some misgivings over the battle royal, by the way. Not from a distaste for fighting but because I didn't care too much for the other fellows who were to take part. They were tough guys who seemed to have no grandfather's curse worrying their minds. No one could mistake their toughness. And besides, I suspected that fighting a battle royal might detract from the dignity of my speech. In those pre-invisible days I visualized myself as a potential Booker T. Washington. But the other fellows didn't care too much for me either, and there were nine of them. I felt superior to them in my way, and I didn't like the manner in which we were all crowded together in the servants' elevator. Nor did they like my being there. In fact, as the warmly lighted floors flashed past the elevator we had words over the fact that I, by taking part in the fight, had knocked one of their friends out of a night's work.

We were led out of the elevator through a rococo hall into an anteroom and told to get into our fighting togs. Each of us was issued a pair of boxing gloves and ushered out into the big mirrored hall, which we entered looking cautiously about us and whispering, lest we might accidentally be heard above the noise of the room. It was foggy with cigar smoke. And already the whiskey was taking effect. I was shocked to see some of the most important men of the town quite tipsy. They were all there—bankers, lawyers, judges, doctors, fire chiefs, teachers, merchants. Even one of the more fashionable pastors. Something we could not see was going on up front. A clarinet was vibrating sensuously and the men were standing up and moving eagerly forward. We were a small tight group, clustered together, our bare upper bodies touching and shining with anticipatory sweat: while up front the big shots were becoming increasingly excited over something we still could not see. Suddenly I heard the school superintendent, who had told me to come, yell, "Bring up the shines, gentlemen! Bring up the little shines!"

We were rushed up to the front of the ballroom, where it smelled even more strongly of tobacco and whiskey. Then we were pushed into place. I almost wet my pants. A sea of faces, some hostile, some amused, ringed around us, and in the center, facing us, stood a magnificent blonde—stark naked. There was dead silence. I felt a blast of cold air chill me. I tried to back away, but they were behind me and around me. Some of the boys stood with lowered heads, trembling. I felt a wave of irrational guilt and fear. My teeth chattered, my skin turned to goose flesh, my knees knocked. Yet I was strongly attracted and looked in spite of myself. Had the price of looking been blindness, I would have looked. The hair was yellow like that of a circus kewpie doll, the face heavily powdered and rouged, as though to form an abstract mask, the eyes hollow and smeared a cool blue, the color of a baboon's butt. I felt a desire to spit upon her as my eyes brushed slowly over her body. Her breasts were firm and round as the domes of East Indian temples, and I stood so close as to see the fine skin texture and beads of pearly perspiration glistening like dew around the pink and erected buds of her nipples. I wanted at one and the same time to run from the room, to sink through the floor, or go to her and cover her from my eyes and the eyes of the others with my body; to feel the soft thighs, to caress her and destroy her, to love her and to murder her, to hide from her, and yet to stroke where below the small American flag tattooed upon her belly her thighs formed a capital V. I had a notion that of all in the room she saw only me with her impersonal eyes.

And then she began to dance, a slow sensuous movement; the smoke of a hundred cigars clinging to her like the thinnest of veils. She seemed like a fair bird-girl girdled in veils calling to me from the angry surface of some gray and threatening sea. I was transported. Then I became aware of the clarinet playing and the big shots yelling at us. Some threatened us if we looked and others if we did not. On my right I saw one boy faint. And now a man grabbed a silver pitcher from a table and stepped close as he dashed ice water upon him and stood him up and forced two of us to support him as his head hung and moans issued from his thick bluish lips. Another boy began to plead to go home. He was the largest of the group, wearing dark red fighting trunks much too small to conceal the erection which projected from him as though in answer to the insinuating low-registered moaning of the clarinet. He tried to hide himself with his boxing gloves.

And all the while the blonde continued dancing, smiling faintly at the big shots who watched her with fascination, and faintly smiling at our fear. I noticed a certain merchant who followed her hungrily, his lips loose and drooling. He was a large man who wore diamond studs in a shirtfront which swelled with the ample paunch underneath, and each time the blonde swayed her undulating hips he ran his hand through the thin hair of his bald head and, with his arms upheld, his posture clumsy like that of an intoxicated panda, wound his belly in a slow and obscene grind. This creature was completely hypnotized. The music had quickened. As the dancer flung herself about with a detached expression on her face, the men began reaching out to touch her. I could see their beefy fingers sink into her soft flesh. Some of the others tried to stop them and she began to move around the floor in graceful circles, as they gave chase, slipping and sliding over the polished floor. It was mad. Chairs went crashing, drinks were spilt, as they ran laughing and howling after her. They caught her just as she reached a door, raised her from the floor, and tossed her as college boys are tossed at a hazing, and above her red, fixed-smiling lips I saw the terror and disgust in her eyes, almost like my own terror and that which I saw in some of the other boys. As I watched, they tossed her twice and her soft breasts seemed to flatten against the air and her legs flung wildly as she spun. Some of the more sober ones helped her to escape. And I started off the floor, heading for the anteroom with the rest of the boys.

Some were still crying and in hysteria. But as we tried to leave we were stopped and ordered to get into the ring. There was nothing to do but what we were told. All ten of us climbed under the ropes and allowed ourselves to be blindfolded with broad bands of white cloth. One of the men seemed to feel a bit sympathetic and tried to cheer us up as we stood with our backs against the ropes. Some of us tried to grin. "See that boy over there?" one of the men said. "I want you to run across at the bell and give it to him right in the belly. If you don't get him, I'm going to get you. I don't like his looks." Each of us was told the same. The blindfolds were put on. Yet even then I had been going over my speech. In my mind each word was as bright as a flame. I felt the cloth pressed into place, and frowned so that it would be loosened when I relaxed.

But now I felt a sudden fit of blind terror. I was unused to darkness, it was as though I had suddenly found myself in a dark room filled with poisonous cottonmouths. I could hear the bleary voices yelling insistently for the battle royal to begin.

"Get going in there!"

"Let me at that big nigger!"

I strained to pick up the school superintendent's voice, as though to squeeze some security out of that slightly more familiar sound.

"Let me at those black sonsabitches!" someone yelled.

"No, Jackson, no!" another voice yelled. "Here, somebody, help me hold Jack."

"I want to get at that ginger-colored nigger. Tear him limb from limb," the first voice yelled.

I stood against the ropes trembling. For in those days I was what they called ginger-colored, and he sounded as though he might crunch me between his teeth like a crisp ginger cookie.

Quite a struggle was going on. Chairs were being kicked about and I could hear voices grunting as with terrific effort. I wanted to see, to see more desperately than ever before. But the blindfold was as tight as a thick skin-puckering scab and when I raised my gloved hands to push the layers of white aside a voice yelled, "Oh, no you don't, black bastard! Leave that alone!"

"Ring the bell before Jackson kills him a coon!" someone boomed in the sudden silence. And I heard the bell clang and the sound of the feet scuffling forward.

A glove smacked against my head. I pivoted, striking out stiffly as someone went past, and felt the jar ripple along the length of my arm to my shoulder. Then it seemed as though all nine of the boys had turned upon me at once. Blows pounded me from all sides while I struck out as best I could. So many blows landed upon me that I wondered if I were not the only blindfolded fighter in the ring, or if the man called Jackson hadn't succeeded in getting me after all.

Blindfolded, I could no longer control my motions. I had no dignity. I stumbled about like a baby or a drunken man. The smoke had become thicker and with each new blow it seemed to sear and further restrict my lungs. My saliva became like hot bitter glue. A glove connected with my head, filling my mouth with warm blood. It was everywhere. I could not tell if the moisture I felt upon my body was sweat or blood. A blow landed hard against the nape of my neck. I felt myself going over, my head hitting the floor. Streaks of blue light filled the black world behind the blindfold. I lay prone, pretending that I was knocked out, but felt myself seized by hands and yanked to my feet. "Get going, black boy! Mix it up!" My arms were like lead, my head smarting from blows. I managed to feel my way to the ropes and held on, trying to catch my breath. A glove landed in my midsection and I went over again, feeling as though the smoke had become a knife jabbed into my guts. Pushed this way and that by the legs milling around me, I finally pulled erect and discovered that I could see the black, sweat-washed forms weaving in the smoky-blue atmosphere like drunken dancers weaving to the rapid drum-like thuds of blows.

Everyone fought hysterically. It was complete anarchy. Everybody fought everybody else. No group fought together for long. Two, three, four, fought one, then turned to fight each other, were themselves attacked. Blows landed below the belt and in the kidney, with the gloves open as well as closed, and with my eye partly opened now there was not so much terror. I moved carefully, avoiding blows, although not too many to attract attention, fighting group to group. The boys groped about like blind, cautious crabs crouching to protect their midsections, their heads pulled in short against their shoulders, their arms stretched nervously before them, with their fists testing the smoke-filled air like the knobbed feelers of hypersensitive snails. In one corner I glimpsed a boy violently punching the air and heard him scream in pain as he smashed his hand against a ring post. For a second I saw him bent over holding his hand, then going down as a blow caught his unprotected head. I played one group against the other, slipping in and throwing a punch then stepping out of range while pushing the others into the melee to take the blows blindly aimed at me. The smoke was agonizing and there were no rounds, no bells at three minute intervals to relieve our exhaustion. The room spun round me, a swirl of lights, smoke, sweating bodies surrounded by tense white faces. I bled from both nose and mouth, the blood spattering upon my chest.

The men kept yelling, "Slug him, black boy! Knock his guts out!"

"Uppercut him! Kill him! Kill that big boy!"

Taking a fake fall, I saw a boy going down heavily beside me as though we were felled by a single blow, saw a sneaker-clad foot shoot into his groin as the two who had knocked him down stumbled upon him. I rolled out of range, feeling a twinge of nausea.

The harder we fought the more threatening the men became. And yet, I had begun to worry about my speech again. How would it go? Would they recognize my ability? What would they give me?

I was fighting automatically when suddenly I noticed that one after another of the boys was leaving the ring. I was surprised, filled with panic, as though I had been left alone with an unknown danger. Then I understood. The boys had arranged it among themselves. It was the custom for the two men left in the ring to slug it out for the winner's prize. I discovered this too late. When the bell sounded two men in tuxedoes leaped into the ring and removed the blindfold. I found myself facing Tatlock, the biggest of the gang. I felt sick at my stomach. Hardly had the bell stopped ringing in my ears than it clanged again and I saw him moving swiftly toward me. Thinking of nothing else to do I hit him smash on the nose. He kept coming, bringing the rank sharp violence of stale sweat. His face was a black blank of a face, only his eyes alive—with hate of me and aglow with a feverish terror from what had happened to us all. I became anxious. I wanted to deliver my speech and he came at me as though he meant to beat it out of me. I smashed him again and again, taking his blows as they came. Then on a sudden impulse I struck him lightly and we clinched. I whispered, "Fake like I knocked you out, you can have the prize."

"I'll break your behind," he whispered hoarsely.

"For *them?*"

"For *me,* sonafabitch!"

They were yelling for us to break it up and Tatlock spun me half around with a blow, and as a joggled camera sweeps in a reeling scene, I saw the howling red faces crouching tense beneath the cloud of blue-gray smoke. For a moment the world wavered, unraveled, flowed, then my head cleared and Tatlock bounced before me. That fluttering shadow before my eyes was his jabbing left hand. Then falling forward, my head against his damp shoulder, I whispered.

"I'll make it five dollars more."

"Go to hell!"

But his muscles relaxed a trifle beneath my pressure and I breathed, "Seven?"

"Give it to your ma," he said, ripping me beneath the heart.

And while I still held him I butted him and moved away. I felt myself bombarded with punches. I fought back with hopeless desperation. I wanted to deliver my speech more than anything else in the world, because I felt that only these men could judge truly my ability, and now this stupid clown was ruining my chances. I began fighting carefully now, moving in to punch him and out again with my greater speed. A lucky blow to his chin and I had him going too—until I heard a loud voice yell, "I got my money on the big boy."

Hearing this, I almost dropped my guard. I was confused: Should I try to win against the voice out there? Would not this go against my speech, and was not this a moment for humility, for nonresistance? A blow to my head as I danced about sent my right eye popping like a jack-in-the-box and settled my dilemma. The room went red as I fell. It was a dream fall, my body languid and fastidious as to where to land, until the floor became impatient and smashed up to meet me. A moment later I came to. An hypnotic voice said FIVE emphatically. And I lay there, hazily watching a dark red spot of my own blood shaping itself into a butterfly, glistening and soaking into the soiled gray world of the canvas.

When the voice drawled TEN I was lifted up and dragged to a chair. I sat dazed. My eye pained and swelled with each throb of my pounding heart and I wondered if now I would be allowed to speak. I was wringing wet, my mouth still bleeding. We were grouped along the wall now. The other boys ignored me as they congratulated Tatlock and speculated as to how much they would be paid. One boy whimpered over his smashed hand. Looking up front, I saw attendants in white jackets rolling the portable ring away and placing a small square rug in the vacant space surrounded by chairs. Perhaps, I thought, I will stand on the rug to deliver my speech.

Then the M.C. called to us. "Come on up here boys and get your money."

We ran forward to where the men laughed and talked in their chairs, waiting. Everyone seemed friendly now.

"There it is on the rug," the man said. I saw the rug covered with coins of all dimensions and a few crumpled bills. But what excited me, scattered here and there, were the gold pieces.

"Boys, it's all yours," the man said. "You get all you grab."

"That's right, Sambo," a blond man said, winking at me confidentially.

I trembled with excitement, forgetting my pain. I would get the gold and the bills, I thought. I would use both hands. I would throw my body against the boys nearest me to block them from the gold.

"Get down around the rug now," the man commanded, "and don't anyone touch it until I give the signal."

"This ought to be good," I heard.

As told, we got around the square rug on our knees. Slowly the man raised his freckled hand as we followed it upward with our eyes.

I heard, "These niggers look like they're about to pray!"

Then, "Ready," the man said. "Go!"

I lunged for a yellow coin lying on the blue design of the carpet, touching it and sending a surprised shriek to join those around me. I tried frantically to remove my hand but could not let go. A hot, violent force tore through my body, shaking me like a wet rat. The rug was electrified. The hair bristled up on my head as I shook myself free. My muscles jumped, my nerves jangled, writhed. But I saw that this was not stopping the other boys. Laughing in fear and embarrassment, some were holding back and scooping up the coins knocked off by the painful contortions of others. The men roared above us as we struggled.

"Pick it up, goddamnit, pick it up!" someone called like a bass-voiced parrot. "Go on, get it!"

I crawled rapidly around the floor, picking up the coins, trying to avoid the coppers and to get greenbacks and the gold. Ignoring the shock by laughing, as I brushed the coins off quickly, I discovered that I could contain the electricity—a contradiction but it works. Then the men began to push us onto the rug. Laughing embarrassedly, we struggled out of their hands and kept after the coins. We were all wet and slippery and hard to hold. Suddenly I saw a boy lifted into the air, glistening with sweat like a circus seal, and dropped, his wet back landing flush upon the charged rug, heard him yell and saw him literally dance upon his back, his elbows beating a frenzied tattoo upon the floor, his muscles twitching like the flesh of a horse stung by many flies. When he finally rolled off, his face was gray and no one stopped him when he ran from the floor amid booming laughter.

"Get the money," the M.C. called. "That's good hard American cash!"

And we snatched and grabbed, snatched and grabbed. I was careful not to come too close to the rug now, and when I felt the hot whiskey breath descend upon me like a cloud of foul air I reached out and grabbed the leg of a chair. It was occupied and I held on desperately.

"Leggo, nigger! Leggo!"

The huge face wavered down to mine as he tried to push me free. But my body was slippery and he was too drunk. It was Mr. Colcord, who owned a chain of movie houses and "entertainment palaces." Each time he grabbed me I slipped out of his hands. It became a real struggle. I feared the rug more than I did the drunk, so I held on, surprising myself for a moment by trying to topple *him* upon the rug. It was such an enormous idea that I found myself actually carrying it out. I tried not to be obvious, yet when I grabbed his leg, trying to tumble him out of the chair, he raised up roaring with laughter, and, looking at me with soberness dead in the eye, kicked me viciously in the chest. The chair leg flew out of my hand and I felt myself going and rolled. It was as though I had rolled through a bed of hot coals. It seemed a whole century would pass before I would roll free, a century in which I was seared through the deepest levels of my body to the fearful breath within me and the breath seared and heated to the point of explosion. It'll all be over in a flash, I thought as I rolled clear. It'll all be over in a flash.

But not yet, the men on the other side were waiting, red faces swollen as though from apoplexy as they bent forward in their chairs. Seeing their fingers coming toward me I rolled away as a fumbled football rolls off the receiver's fingertips, back into the coals. That time I luckily sent the rug sliding out of place and heard the coins ringing against the floor and the boys scuffling to pick them up and the M.C. calling, "All right, boys, that's all. Go get dressed and get your money."

I was limp as a dish rag. My back felt as though it had been beaten with wires.

When we had dressed the M.C. came in and gave us each five dollars, except Tatlock, who got ten for being the last in the ring. Then he told us to leave. I was not to get a chance to deliver my speech, I thought. I was going out into the dim alley in despair when I was stopped and told to go back. I returned to the ballroom, where the men were pushing back their chairs and gathering in small groups to talk.

The M.C. knocked on a table for quiet. "Gentlemen," he said, "we almost forgot an important part of the program. A most serious part, gentlemen. This boy was brought here to deliver a speech which he made at his graduation yesterday . . ."

"Bravo!"

"I'm told that he is the smartest boy we've got out there in Greenwood. I'm told that he knows more big words than a pocket-sized dictionary."

Much applause and laughter.

"So now, gentlemen, I want you to give him your attention."

There was still laughter as I faced them, my mouth dry, my eyes throbbing. I began slowly, but evidently my throat was tense, because they began shouting. "Louder! Louder!"

"We of the younger generation extol the wisdom of that great leader and educator," I shouted, "who first spoke these flaming words of wisdom: 'A ship lost at sea for many days suddenly sighted a friendly vessel. From the mast of the unfortunate vessel was seen a signal: "Water, water; we die of thirst!" The answer from the friendly vessel came back: "Cast down your bucket where you are." The captain of the distressed vessel, at last heeding the injunction, cast down his bucket, and it came up full of fresh sparkling water from the mouth of the Amazon River.' And like him I say, and in his words, 'To those of my race who depend upon bettering their condition in a foreign land, or who underestimate the importance of cultivating friendly relations with the Southern white man, who is his next-door neighbor, I would say: "Cast down your bucket where you are"—cast it down in making friends in every manly way of the people of all races by whom we are surrounded . . .'"

I spoke automatically and with such fervor that I did not realize that the men were still talking and laughing until my dry mouth, filling up with blood from the cut, almost strangled me. I coughed, wanting to stop and go to one of the tall brass, sand-filled spittoons to relieve myself, but a few of the men, especially the superintendent, were listening and I was afraid. So I gulped it down, blood, saliva and all, and continued. (What powers of endurance I had during those days! What enthusiasm! What a belief in the rightness of things!) I spoke even louder in spite of the pain. But still they talked and still they laughed, as though deaf with cotton in dirty ears. So I spoke with greater emotional emphasis. I closed my ears and swallowed blood until I was nauseated. The speech seemed a hundred times as long as before, but I could not leave out a single word. All had to be said, each memorized nuance considered, rendered. Nor was that all. Whenever I uttered a word of three or more syllables a group of voices would yell for me to repeat it. I used the phrase "social responsibility" and they yelled:

"What's the word you say, boy?"

"Social responsibility," I said.

"What?"

"Social ..."

"Louder."

"... responsibility."

"More!"

"Respon—"

"Repeat!"

"—sibility."

The room filled with the uproar of laughter until, no doubt, distracted by having to gulp down my blood, I made a mistake and yelled a phrase I had often seen denounced in newspaper editorials, heard debated in private.

"Social ..."

"What?" they yelled.

"...equality—"

The laughter hung smokelike in the sudden stillness. I opened my eyes, puzzled. Sounds of displeasure filled the room. The M.C. rushed forward. They shouted hostile phrases at me. But I did not understand.

A small dry mustached man in the front row blared out, "Say that slowly, son!"

"What, sir?"

"What you just said!"

"Social responsibility, sir," I said.

"You weren't being smart, were you boy?" he said, not unkindly.

"No, sir!"

"You sure that about 'equality' was a mistake?"

"Oh, yes, sir," I said. "I was swallowing blood."

"Well, you had better speak more slowly so we can understand. We mean to do right by you, but you've got to know your place at all times. All right, now, go on with your speech."

I was afraid. I wanted to leave but I wanted also to speak and I was afraid they'd snatch me down.

"Thank you, sir," I said, beginning where I had left off, and having them ignore me as before.

Yet when I finished there was a thunderous applause. I was surprised to see the superintendent come forth with a package wrapped in white tissue paper, and, gesturing for quiet, address the men.

"Gentlemen, you see that I did not overpraise the boy. He makes a good speech and some day he'll lead his people in the proper paths. And I don't have to tell you that this is important in these days and times. This is a good, smart boy, and so to encourage him in the right direction, in the name of the Board of Education I wish to present him a prize in the form of this ..."

He paused, removing the tissue paper and revealing a gleaming calf-skin briefcase.

"... in the form of this first-class article from Shad Whitmore's shop."

"Boy," he said, addressing me, "take this prize and keep it well. Consider it a badge of office. Prize it. Keep developing as you are and some day it will be filled with important papers that will help shape the destiny of your people."

I was so moved that I could hardly express my thanks. A rope of bloody saliva forming a shape like an undiscovered continent drooled upon the leather and I wiped it quickly away. I felt an importance that I had never dreamed.

"Open it and see what's inside," I was told.

My fingers a-tremble, I complied, smelling fresh leather and finding an official-looking document inside. It was a scholarship to the state college for Negroes. My eyes filled with tears and I ran awkwardly off the floor.

I was overjoyed; I did not even mind when I discovered the gold pieces I had scrambled for were brass pocket tokens advertising a certain make of automobile.

When I reached home everyone was excited. Next day the neighbors came to congratulate me. I even felt safe from grandfather, whose deathbed curse usually spoiled my triumphs. I stood beneath his photograph with my briefcase in hand and smiled triumphantly into his stolid black peasant's face. It was a face that fascinated me. The eyes seemed to follow everywhere I went.

That night I dreamed I was at a circus with him and that he refused to laugh at the clowns no matter what they did. Then later he told me to open my briefcase and read what was inside and I did, finding an official envelope stamped with the state seal: and inside the envelope I found another and another, endlessly, and I thought I would fall of weariness. "Them's years," he said. "Now open that one." And I did and in it I found an engraved stamp containing a short message in letters of gold. "Read it," my grandfather said. "Out loud."

"To Whom It May Concern," I intoned. "Keep This Nigger-Boy Running."

I awoke with the old man's laughter ringing in my ears.

BERNARD MALAMUD
(1914–1986)

Bernard Malamud, like a number of the writers in this anthology, was gifted with an unusually sharp, sympathetic, mimetic ear for the cadences of speech; in Malamud's case, for the cadences of Jewish-American speech. (And this surprisingly—at least, for admirers who met with him in person. For, as it happened, Malamud spoke a rather formal, precise, uninflected American English.) Though his fiction is of a near-uniform quality, he was ambitious in its variety: now a chronicler of comic absurdities, now a poet of tragic, thwarted lives, now an Olympian gazing down, with a bemused eye, upon the follies of humankind. "My Son the Murderer" is a tour de force of pathos and betrayal; one of the most memorable, as it is surely one of the most succinct, testimonies to the generational dissonances of the 1960s in an America at war with Vietnam.

Born in Brooklyn, Bernard Malamud taught high school during the 1940s, until, with the publication of his early stories in such influential journals as Partisan Review *and* Commentary, *he began a long and distinguished career as a university teacher. Among his major titles are the novels* The Natural *(1952),* The Assistant *(1957),* The Fixer *(1966), and* Dubin's Lives *(1979), and the short story collections* The Magic Barrel *(1958), which received a National Book Award,* Idiots First *(1963),* Pictures of Fidelman *(1969), and* Rembrandt's Hat *(1973).* The Stories of Bernard Malamud *was published in 1983.*

My Son the Murderer

He wakes feeling his father is in the hallway, listening. He listens to him sleep and dream. Listening to him get up and fumble for his pants. He won't put on his shoes. To him not going to the kitchen to eat. Staring with shut eyes in the mirror. Sitting an hour on the toilet. Flipping the pages of a book he can't read. To his anguish, loneliness. The father stands in the hall. The son hears him listen.

My son the stranger, he won't tell me anything.

I open the door and see my father in the hall. Why are you standing there, why don't you go to work?

On account of I took my vacation in the winter instead of the summer like I usually do.

What the hell for if you spend it in this dark smelly hallway, watching my every move? Guessing what you can't see. Why are you always spying on me?

My father goes to the bedroom and after a while sneaks out in the hallway again, listening.

I hear him sometimes in his room but he don't talk to me and I don't know what's what. It's a terrible feeling for a father. Maybe someday he will write me a letter. My dear father ...

My dear son Harry, open up your door. My son the prisoner.

My wife leaves in the morning to stay with my married daughter, who is expecting her fourth child. The mother cooks and cleans for her and takes care of the three children. My daughter is having a bad pregnancy, with high blood pressure, and lays in bed most of the time. This is what the doctor advised her. My wife is gone all day. She worries something is wrong with Harry. Since he graduated college last summer he is alone, nervous, in his own thoughts. If you talk to him, half the time he yells if he answers you. He reads the papers, smokes, he stays in his room. Or once in a while he goes for a walk in the street.

How was the walk, Harry?

A walk.

My wife advised him to go look for work, and a couple of times he went, but when he got some kind of an offer he didn't take the job.

It's not that I don't want to work. It's that I feel bad.

So why do you feel bad?

I feel what I feel. I feel what is.

Is it your health, sonny? Maybe you ought to go to a doctor?

I asked you not to call me by that name any more. It's not my health. Whatever it is I don't want to talk about it. The work wasn't the kind I want.

So take something temporary in the meantime, my wife said to him.

He starts to yell. Everything's temporary. Why should I add more to what's temporary? My gut feels temporary. The goddamn world is temporary. On top of that I don't want temporary work. I want the opposite of temporary, but where is it? Where do you find it?

My father listens in the kitchen.

My temporary son.

She says I'll feel better if I work. I say I won't. I'm twenty-two since December, a college graduate, and you know where you can stick that. At night I watch the news programs. I watch the war from day to day. It's a big burning war on a small screen. It rains bombs and the flames go higher. Sometimes I lean over and touch the war with the flat of my hand. I wait for my hand to die.

My son with the dead hand.

I expect to be drafted any day but it doesn't bother me the way it used to. I won't go. I'll go to Canada or somewhere I can go.

The way he is frightens my wife and she is glad to go to my daughter's house early in the morning to take care of the three children. I stay with him in the house but he don't talk to me.

You ought to call up Harry and talk to him, my wife says to my daughter.

I will sometime but don't forget there's nine years' difference between our ages. I think he thinks of me as another mother around and one is enough. I used to like him when he was a little boy but now it's hard to deal with a person who won't reciprocate to you.

She's got high blood pressure. I think she's afraid to call.

I took two weeks off from my work. I'm a clerk at the stamps window in the post office. I told the superintendent I wasn't feeling so good, which is no lie, and he said I should take sick leave. I said I wasn't that sick, I only needed a little vacation. But I told my friend Moe Berkman I was staying out because Harry has me worried.

I understand what you mean, Leo. I got my own worries and anxieties about my kids. If you got two girls growing up you got hostages to fortune. Still in all we got to live. Why don't you come to poker on this Friday night? We got a nice game going. Don't deprive yourself of a good form of relaxation.

I'll see how I feel by Friday, how everything is coming along. I can't promise you.

Try to come. These things, if you give them time, all pass away. If it looks better to you, come on over. Even if it don't look so good, come on over anyway because it might relieve your tension and worry that you're under. It's not so good for your heart at your age if you carry that much worry around.

It's the worst kind of worry. If I worry about myself I know what the worry is. What I mean, there's no mystery. I can say to myself, Leo you're a big fool, stop worrying about nothing—over what, a few bucks? Over my health that has always stood up pretty good although I have my ups and downs? Over that I'm now close to sixty and not getting any younger? Everybody that don't die by age fifty-nine gets to be sixty. You can't beat time when it runs along with you. But if the worry is about somebody else, that's the worst kind. That's the real worry because if he won't tell you, you can't get inside of the other person and find out why. You don't know where's the switch to turn off. All you do is worry more.

So I wait out in the hall.

Harry, don't worry so much about the war.

Please don't tell me what to worry about or what not to worry about.

Harry, your father loves you. When you were a little boy, every night when I came home you used to run to me. I picked you up and lifted you up to the ceiling. You liked to touch it with your small hand.

I don't want to hear about that any more. It's the very thing I don't want to hear. I don't want to hear about when I was a child.

Harry, we live like strangers. All I'm saying is I remember better days. I remember when we weren't afraid to show we loved each other.

He says nothing.

Let me cook you an egg.

An egg is the last thing in the world I want.

So what do you want?

He put his coat on. He pulled his hat off the clothes tree and went down into the street.

Harry walked along Ocean Parkway in his long overcoat and creased brown hat. His father was following him and it filled him with rage.

He walked at a fast pace up the broad avenue. In the old days there was a bridle path at the side of the walk where the concrete bicycle path was now. And there were fewer trees, their black branches cutting the sunless sky. At the corner of Avenue X, just about where you can smell Coney Island, he crossed the street and began to walk home. He pretended not to see his father cross over, though he was infuriated. The father crossed over and followed his son home. When he got to the house he figured Harry was upstairs already. He was in his room with the door shut. Whatever he did in his room he was already doing.

Leo took out his small key and opened the mailbox. There were three letters. He looked to see if one of them was, by any chance, from his son to him. My dear father, let me explain myself. The reason I act as I do...There was no such letter. One of the letters was from the Post Office Clerks Benevolent Society, which he slipped into his coat pocket. The other two letters were for Harry. One was from the draft board. He brought it up to his son's room, knocked on the door and waited.

He waited for a while.

To the boy's grunt he said, There is a draft-board letter here for you. He turned the knob and entered the room. His son was lying on his bed with his eyes shut.

Leave it on the table.

Do you want me to open it for you, Harry?

No, I don't want you to open it. Leave it on the table. I know what's in it.

Did you write them another letter?

That's my goddamn business.

The father left it on the table.

The other letter to his son he took into the kitchen, shut the door, and boiled up some water in a pot. He thought he would read it quickly and seal it carefully with a little paste, then go downstairs and put it back in the mailbox. His wife would take it out with her key when she returned from their daughter's house and bring it up to Harry.

The father read the letter. It was a short letter from a girl. The girl said Harry had borrowed two of her books more than six months ago and since she valued them highly she would like him to send them back to her. Could he do that as soon as possible so that she wouldn't have to write again?

As Leo was reading the girl's letter Harry came into the kitchen and when he saw the surprised and guilty look on his father's face, he tore the letter out of his hand.

I ought to murder you the way you spy on me.

Leo turned away, looking out of the small kitchen window into the dark apartment-house courtyard. His face burned, he felt sick.

Harry read the letter at a glance and tore it up. He then tore up the envelope marked personal.

If you do this again don't be surprised if I kill you. I'm sick of you spying on me.

Harry, you are talking to your father.

He left the house.

Leo went into his room and looked around. He looked in the dresser drawers and found nothing unusual. On the desk by the window was a paper Harry had written on. It said: Dear Edith, why don't you go fuck yourself? If you write me another letter I'll murder you.

The father got his hat and coat and left the house. He ran slowly for a while, running then walking, until he saw Harry on the other side of the street. He followed him, half a block behind.

He followed Harry to Coney Island Avenue and was in time to see him board a trolleybus going to the Island. Leo had to wait for the next one. He thought of taking a taxi and following the trolleybus, but no taxi came by. The next bus came by fifteen minutes later and he took it all the way to the Island. It was February and Coney Island was wet, cold, and deserted. There were few cars on Surf Avenue and few people on the streets. It felt like snow. Leo walked on the boardwalk amid snow flurries, looking for his son. The gray sunless beaches were empty. The hot-dog stands, shooting galleries, and bathhouses were shuttered up. The gunmetal ocean, moving like melted lead, looked freezing. A wind blew in off the water and worked its way into his clothes so that he shivered as he walked. The wind white-capped the leaden waves and the slow surf broke on the empty beaches with a quiet roar.

He walked in the blow almost to Sea Gate, searching for his son, and then he walked back again. On his way toward Brighton Beach he saw a man on the shore standing in the foaming surf. Leo hurried down the boardwalk stairs and onto the ribbed-sand beach. The man on the roaring shore was Harry, standing in water to the tops of his shoes.

Leo ran to his son. Harry, it was a mistake, excuse me, I'm sorry I opened your letter.

Harry did not move. He stood in the water, his eyes on the swelling leaden waves.

Harry, I'm frightened. Tell me what's the matter. My son, have mercy on me.

I'm frightened of the world, Harry thought. It fills me with fright.

He said nothing.

A blast of wind lifted his father's hat and carried it away over the beach. It looked as though it were going to be blown into the surf, but then the wind blew it toward the boardwalk, rolling like a wheel along the wet sand. Leo chased after his hat. He chased it one way, then another, then toward the water. The wind blew the hat against his legs and he caught it. By now he was crying. Breathless, he wiped his eyes with icy fingers and returned to his son at the edge of the water.

He is a lonely man. This is the type he is. He will always be lonely.

My son who made himself into a lonely man.

Harry, what can I say to you? All I can say to you is who says life is easy? Since when? It wasn't for me and it isn't for you. It's life, that's the way it is—what more can I say? But if a person don't want to live what can he do if he's dead? Nothing. Nothing is nothing, it's better to live.

Come home, Harry, he said. It's cold here. You'll catch a cold with your feet in the water.

Harry stood motionless in the water and after a while his father left. As he was leaving, the wind plucked his hat off his head and sent it rolling along the shore.

My father listens in the hallway. He follows me in the street. We meet at the edge of the water.

He runs after his hat.

My son stands with his feet in the ocean.

SHIRLEY JACKSON
(1916–1965)

Born in Ashbury Park, a fashionable suburb of San Francisco, Shirley Jackson spent most of her adult years in the East. She graduated from Syracuse University in 1940, lived for a while with her husband Stanley Edgar Hyman in New York City, then moved to Bennington, Vermont, where Hyman would become Professor of English at Bennington College and a distinguished literary critic. Many of Jackson's unnervingly surreal stories, like "The Lottery," as well as her more good-humored accounts of domestic misadventures, are set in a recognizable North Bennington, in which Jackson was said to have felt like an outsider, though she and Hyman, living in a twenty-room house on upper Main Street, were local celebrities. (In the last decade of her life, the agoraphobic Jackson rarely left her house and accused neighbors of harassing her and her family with anonymous hate mail, anti-Semitic remarks, ugly graffiti, and garbage dumped on their property.)

Though Jackson's most famous and most frequently anthologized story is "The Lottery," a masterpiece of stark, minimalist horror that builds to an ending that is both shocking and inevitable, Shirley Jackson's more typical fiction is realistically rendered; one of her predominant models for prose fiction was Henry James, whose precisely calibrated sentences poise subtleties of perception and judgment, and whose vision of moral complexities excludes the relative psychological simplicity of mere "horror" tales. Both of Jackson's acclaimed novels The Haunting of Hill House *(1959; made into an excellent film titled* The Haunting, *1963) and* We Have Always Lived in the Castle *(1962) are Jamesian in their mixture of psychological realism and the seeming "surreal," as in James's great novella* The Turn of the Screw *(1898).*

Though her most compelling work is in the gothic or surreal mode, Jackson achieved a considerable reputation in her lifetime as a writer of domestic sketches that appeared originally in Good Housekeeping *and* The Saturday Evening Post, *collected in the aptly titled* Life Among the Savages *(1953),* Raising Demons *(1957), and* Special Delivery: A Useful Book for Brand-New Mothers *(1960). It's as if the somewhat manic "cute" humor of the domestic sketches has been intensified in Jackson's most characteristic stories, collected in* The Lottery; or, The Adventures of James Harris *(1948) and in the posthumously published* The Magic of Shirley Jackson *(1966),* Come Along With Me *(1968),* Just an Ordinary Day *(1996), and* Shirley Jackson: Novels and Stories *(Library of America, 2010).*

One of those American writers who is continually being rediscovered and reevaluated, Jackson was a best-selling author in her lifetime, frequently anthologized in the yearly best-story collections, a National Book Award nominee, and a winner of an Edgar Award. In addition to the titles above, Jackson also wrote the novels Hangsaman *(1951),* The Bird's Nest *(1954),* The Sundial *(1958), and the posthumously published seriocomic novel-fragment about a female psychic,* Come Along With Me.

Of "The Lottery," which was published in the New Yorker *on June 28, 1948, and elicited torrents of mail from mostly outraged or puzzled readers, Jackson said ruefully: "Millions of people, and my mother, had taken a pronounced dislike to me."*

The Lottery

The morning of June 27th was clear and sunny, with the fresh warmth of a full-summer day; the flowers were blossoming profusely and the grass was richly green. The people of the village began to gather in the square, between the post office and the bank, around ten o'clock; in some towns there were so many people that the lottery took two days and had to be started on June 26th, but in this village, where there were only about three hundred people, the whole lottery took less than two hours, so it could begin at ten o'clock in the morning and still be through in time to allow the villagers to get home for noon dinner.

The children assembled first, of course. School was recently over for the summer, and the feeling of liberty sat uneasily on most of them; they tended to gather together quietly for a while before they broke into boisterous play, and their talk was still of the classroom and the teacher, of books and reprimands. Bobby Martin had already stuffed his pockets full of stones, and the other boys soon followed his example, selecting the smoothest and roundest stones; Bobby and Harry Jones and Dickie Delacroix—the villagers pronounced this name "Dellacroy"—eventually made a great pile of stones in one corner of the square and guarded it against the raids of the other boys. The girls stood aside, talking among themselves, looking over their shoulders at the boys, and the very small children rolled in the dust or clung to the hands of their older brothers or sisters.

Soon the men began to gather, surveying their own children, speaking of planting and rain, tractors and taxes. They stood together, away from the pile of stones in the corner, and their jokes were quiet and they smiled rather than laughed. The women, wearing faded house dresses and sweaters, came shortly after their menfolk. They greeted one another and exchanged bits of gossip as they went to join their husbands. Soon the women, standing by their husbands, began to call to their children, and the children came reluctantly, having to be called four or five times. Bobby Martin ducked under his mother's grasping hand and ran, laughing, back to the pile of stones. His father spoke up sharply, and Bobby came quickly and took his place between his father and his oldest brother.

The lottery was conducted—as were the square dances, the teen-age club, the Halloween program—by Mr. Summers, who had time and energy to devote to civic activities. He was a round-faced, jovial man and he ran the coal business, and people were sorry for him, because he had no children and his wife was a scold. When he arrived in the square, carrying the black wooden box, there was a murmur of conversation among the villagers, and he waved and called, "Little late today, folks." The postmaster, Mr. Graves, followed him, carrying a three-legged stool, and the stool was put in the center of the square and Mr. Summers set the black box down on it. The villagers kept their distance, leaving a space between themselves and the stool, and when Mr. Summers said, "Some of you fellows want to give me a hand?" there was a hesitation before two men, Mr. Martin and his oldest son, Baxter, came forward to hold the box steady on the stool while Mr. Summers stirred up the papers inside it.

The original paraphernalia for the lottery had been lost long ago, and the black box now resting on the stool had been put into use even before Old Man Warner, the oldest man in town, was born. Mr. Summers spoke frequently to the villagers about making a new box, but no one liked to upset even as much tradition as was represented by the black box. There was a story that the present box had been made with some pieces of the box that had preceded it, the one that had been constructed when the first people settled down to make a village here. Every year, after the lottery, Mr. Summers began talking again about a new box, but every year the subject was allowed to fade off without anything's being done. The black box grew shabbier each year; by now it was no longer completely black but splintered badly along one side to show the original wood color, and in some places faded or stained.

Mr. Martin and his oldest son, Baxter, held the black box securely on the stool until Mr. Summers had stirred the papers thoroughly with his hand. Because so much of the ritual had been forgotten or discarded, Mr. Summers had been successful in having slips of paper substituted for the chips of wood that had been used for generations. Chips of wood, Mr. Summers had argued, had been all very well when the village was tiny, but now that the population was more than three hundred and likely to keep on growing, it was necessary to use something that would fit more easily into the black box. The night before the lottery, Mr. Summers and Mr. Graves made up the slips of paper and put them in the box, and it was then taken to the safe of Mr. Summers' coal company and locked up until Mr. Summers was ready to take it to the square next morning. The rest of the year, the box was put away, sometimes one place, sometimes another; it had spent one year in Mr. Graves's barn and another year underfoot in the post office, and sometimes it was set on a shelf in the Martin grocery and left there.

There was a great deal of fussing to be done before Mr. Summers declared the lottery open. There were the lists to make up—of heads of families, heads of households in each family, members of each household in each family. There was the proper swearing-in of Mr. Summers by the postmaster, as the official of the lottery; at one time, some people remembered, there had been a recital of some sort, performed by the official of the lottery, a perfunctory, tuneless chant that had been rattled off duly each year; some people believed that the official of the lottery used to stand just so when he said or sang it, others believed that he was supposed to walk among the people, but years and years ago this part of the ritual had been allowed to lapse. There had been, also, a ritual salute, which the official of the lottery had had to use in addressing each person who came up to draw from the box, but this also had changed with time, until now it was felt necessary only for the official to speak to each person approaching. Mr. Summers was very good at all this; in his clean white shirt and blue jeans, with one hand resting carelessly on the black box, he seemed very proper and important as he talked interminably to Mr. Graves and the Martins.

Just as Mr. Summers finally left off talking and turned to the assembled villagers, Mrs. Hutchinson came hurriedly along the path to the square, her sweater thrown over her shoulders, and slid into place in the back of the crowd. "Clean forgot what day it was," she said to Mrs. Delacroix, who stood next to her, and they both laughed softly. "Thought my old man was out back stacking wood," Mrs. Hutchinson went on, "and then I looked out the window and the kids was gone, and then I remembered it was the twenty-seventh and came a-running." She dried her hands on her apron, and Mrs. Delacroix said, "You're in time, though. They're still talking away up there."

Mrs. Hutchinson craned her neck to see through the crowd and found her husband and children standing near the front. She tapped Mrs. Delacroix on the arm as a farewell and began to make her way through the crowd. The people separated good-humoredly to let her through; two or three people said, in voices just loud enough to be heard across the crowd "Here comes your Missus Hutchinson," and "Bill, she made it after all." Mrs. Hutchinson reached her husband, and Mr. Summers, who had been waiting, said cheerfully, "Thought we were going to have to get on without you, Tessie." Mrs. Hutchinson said, grinning, "Wouldn't have me leave m'dishes in the sink, now, would you, Joe?," and soft laughter ran through the crowd as the people stirred back into position after Mrs. Hutchinson's arrival.

"Well, now," Mr. Summers said soberly, "guess we better get started, get this over with, so's we can go back to work. Anybody ain't here?"

"Dunbar," several people said. "Dunbar, Dunbar."

Mr. Summers consulted his list. "Clyde Dunbar," he said. "That's right. He's broke his leg, hasn't he? Who's drawing for him?"

"Me, I guess," a woman said, and Mr. Summers turned to look at her. "Wife draws for her husband," Mr. Summers said. "Don't you have a grown boy to do it for you, Janey?" Although Mr. Summers and everyone else in the village knew the answer perfectly well, it was the business of the official of the lottery to ask such questions formally. Mr. Summers waited with an expression of polite interest while Mrs. Dunbar answered.

"Horace's not but sixteen yet," Mrs. Dunbar said regretfully. "Guess I gotta fill in for the old man this year."

"Right," Mr. Summers said. He made a note on the list he was holding. Then he asked, "Watson boy drawing this year?"

A tall boy in the crowd raised his hand. "Here," he said. "I'm drawing for m'mother and me." He blinked his eyes nervously and ducked his head as several voices in the crowd said things like "Good fellow, Jack," and "Glad to see your mother's got a man to do it."

"Well," Mr. Summers said, "guess that's everyone. Old Man Warner make it?"

"Here," a voice said, and Mr. Summers nodded.

A sudden hush fell on the crowd as Mr. Summers cleared his throat and looked at the list. "All ready?" he called. "Now, I'll read the names—heads of families first—and the men come up and take a paper out of the box. Keep the paper folded in your hand without looking at it until everyone has had a turn. Everything clear?"

The people had done it so many times that they only half listened to the directions; most of them were quiet, wetting their lips, not looking around. Then Mr. Summers raised one hand high and said, "Adams." A man disengaged himself from the crowd and came forward. "Hi, Steve," Mr. Summers said, and Mr. Adams said, "Hi, Joe." They grinned at one another humorlessly and nervously. Then Mr. Adams reached into the black box and took out a folded paper. He held it firmly by one corner as he turned and went hastily back to his place in the crowd, where he stood a little apart from his family, not looking down at his hand.

"Allen," Mr. Summers said. "Anderson.... Bentham."

"Seems like there's no time at all between lotteries any more," Mrs. Delacroix said to Mrs. Graves in the back row. "Seems like we got through with the last one only last week."

"Time sure goes fast," Mrs. Graves said.

"Clark.... Delacroix."

"There goes my old man," Mrs. Delacroix said. She held her breath while her husband went forward.

"Dunbar," Mr. Summers said, and Mrs. Dunbar went steadily to the box while one of the women said, "Go on, Janey," and another said, "There she goes."

"We're next," Mrs. Graves said. She watched while Mr. Graves came around from the side of the box, greeted Mr. Summers gravely, and selected a slip of paper from the box. By now, all through the crowd there were men holding the small folded papers in their large hands, turning them over and over nervously. Mrs. Dunbar and her two sons stood together, Mrs. Dunbar holding the slip of paper.

"Harburt.... Hutchinson."

"Get up there, Bill," Mrs. Hutchinson said, and the people near her laughed.

"Jones."

"They do say," Mr. Adams said to Old Man Warner, who stood next to him, "that over in the north village they're talking of giving up the lottery."

Old Man Warner snorted. "Pack of crazy fools," he said. "Listening to the young folks, nothing's good enough for *them*. Next thing you know, they'll be wanting to go back to living in caves, nobody work any more, live *that* way for a while. Used to be a saying about 'Lottery in June, corn be heavy soon.' First thing you know, we'd all be eating stewed chickweed and acorns. There's *always* been a lottery," he added petulantly. "Bad enough to see young Joe Summers up there joking with everybody."

"Some places have already quit lotteries," Mrs. Adams said.

"Nothing but trouble in *that,*" Old Man Warner said stoutly. "Pack of young fools."

"Martin." And Bobby Martin watched his father go forward. "Overdyke.... Percy."

"I wish they'd hurry," Mrs. Dunbar said to her older son. "I wish they'd hurry."

"They're almost through," her son said,

"You get ready to run tell Dad," Mrs. Dunbar said.

Mr. Summers called his own name and then stepped forward precisely and selected a slip from the box. Then he called, "Warner."

"Seventy-seventh year I been in the lottery," Old Man Warner said as he went through the crowd. "Seventy-seventh time."

"Watson." The tall boy came awkwardly through the crowd. Someone said, "Don't be nervous, Jack," and Mr. Summers said, "Take your time, son."

"Zanini."

After that, there was a long pause, a breathless pause, until Mr. Summers, holding his slip of paper in the air, said, "All right, fellows." For a minute, no one moved, and then all the slips of paper were opened. Suddenly, all the women began to speak at once, saying, "Who is it?," "Who's got it?,"

"Is it the Dunbars?," "Is it the Watsons?" Then the voices began to say, "It's Hutchinson. It's Bill," "Bill Hutchinson's got it."

"Go tell your father," Mrs. Dunbar said to her older son.

People began to look around to see the Hutchinsons. Bill Hutchinson was standing quiet, staring down at the paper in his hand. Suddenly, Tessie Hutchinson shouted to Mr. Summers, "You didn't give him time enough to take any paper he wanted. I saw you. It wasn't fair!"

"Be a good sport, Tessie," Mrs. Delacroix called, and Mrs. Graves said, "All of us took the same chance."

"Shut up, Tessie," Bill Hutchinson said.

"Well, everyone," Mr. Summers said, "that was done pretty fast, and now we've got to be hurrying a little more to get done in time." He consulted his next list. "Bill," he said, "you draw for the Hutchinson family. You got any other households in the Hutchinsons?"

"There's Don and Eva," Mrs. Hutchinson yelled. "Make *them* take their chance!"

"Daughters draw with their husbands' families, Tessie," Mr. Summers said gently. "You know that as well as anyone else."

"It wasn't *fair*," Tessie said.

"I guess not, Joe," Bill Hutchinson said regretfully. "My daughter draws with her husband's family, that's only fair. And I've got no other family except the kids."

"Then, as far as drawing for families is concerned, it's you," Mr. Summers said in explanation, "and as far as drawing for households is concerned, that's you, too. Right?"

"Right," Bill Hutchinson said.

"How many kids, Bill?" Mr. Summers asked formally.

"Three," Bill Hutchinson said. "There's Bill, Jr., and Nancy, and little Dave. And Tessie and me."

"All right, then," Mr. Summers said. "Harry, you got their tickets back?"

Mr. Graves nodded and held up the slips of paper. "Put them in the box, then," Mr. Summers directed. "Take Bill's and put it in."

"I think we ought to start over," Mrs. Hutchinson said, as quietly as she could. "I tell you it wasn't *fair*. You didn't give him time enough to choose. *Every*body saw that."

Mr. Graves had selected the five slips and put them in the box, and he dropped all the papers but those onto the ground, where the breeze caught them and lifted them off.

"Listen, everybody," Mrs. Hutchinson was saying to the people around her.

"Ready, Bill?" Mr. Summers asked, and Bill Hutchinson, with one quick glance around at his wife and children, nodded.

"Remember," Mr. Summers said, "take the slips and keep them folded until each person has taken one. Harry, you help little Dave." Mr. Graves took the hand of the little boy, who came willingly with him up to the box. "Take a paper out of the box, Davy," Mr. Summers said. Davy put his hand into the box and laughed. "Take just *one* paper," Mr. Summers said. "Harry, you hold it for him." Mr. Graves took the child's hand and removed the folded paper from the tight fist and held it while little Dave stood next to him and looked up at him wonderingly.

"Nancy next," Mr. Summers said. Nancy was twelve, and her school friends breathed heavily as she went forward, switching her skirt, and took a slip daintily from the box. "Bill, Jr.," Mr. Summers said, and Billy, his face red and his feet over-large, nearly knocked the box over as he got a paper out. "Tessie," Mr. Summers said. She hesitated for a minute, looking around defiantly, and then set her lips and went up to the box. She snatched a paper out and held it behind her.

"Bill," Mr. Summers said, and Bill Hutchinson reached into the box and felt around, bringing his hand out at last with the slip of paper in it.

The crowd was quiet. A girl whispered, "I hope it's not Nancy," and the sound of the whisper reached the edges of the crowd.

"It's not the way it used to be," Old Man Warner said clearly. "People ain't the way they used to be."

"All right," Mr. Summers said. "Open the papers. Harry, you open little Dave's."

Mr. Graves opened the slip of paper and there was a general sigh through the crowd as he held it up and everyone could see that it was blank. Nancy and Bill, Jr., opened theirs at the same time, and both beamed and laughed, turning around to the crowd and holding their slip of paper above their heads.

"Tessie," Mr. Summers said. There was a pause, and then Mr. Summers looked at Bill Hutchinson, and Bill unfolded his paper and showed it. It was blank.

"It's Tessie," Mr. Summers said, and his voice was hushed. "Show us her paper, Bill."

Bill Hutchinson went over to his wife and forced the slip of paper out of her hand. It had a black spot on it, the black spot Mr. Summers had made the night before with the heavy pencil in the coal-company office. Bill Hutchinson held it up, and there was a stir in the crowd.

"All right, folks," Mr. Summers said. "Let's finish quickly."

Although the villagers had forgotten the ritual and lost the original black box, they still remembered to use stones. The pile of stones the boys had made earlier was ready; there were stones on the ground with the blowing scraps of paper that had come out of the box. Mrs. Delacroix selected a stone so large she had to pick it up with both hands and turned to Mrs. Dunbar. "Come on," she said. "Hurry up."

Mrs. Dunbar had small stones in both hands, and she said, gasping for breath, "I can't run at all. You'll have to go ahead and I'll catch up with you."

The children had stones already, and someone gave little Davy Hutchinson a few pebbles.

Tessie Hutchinson was in the center of a cleared space by now, and she held her hands out desperately as the villagers moved in on her. "It isn't fair," she said. A stone hit her on the side of the head.

Old Man Warner was saying, "Come on, come on, everyone." Steve Adams was in the front of the crowd of villagers, with Mrs. Graves beside him.

"It isn't fair, it isn't right," Mrs. Hutchinson screamed, and then they were upon her.

RAY BRADBURY
(b. 1920)

Like his fellow American writer of "science fiction," Isaac Asimov, Ray Bradbury is a phenomenon, not easily defined. Since he sold his first story (to a pulp magazine) at the age of twenty-one, he has published hundreds of short stories and has become one of our most widely read American writers here and abroad. Marginalized, at least in part, because of his association with what is perceived to be a nonliterary tradition, Bradbury is, in fact, in such stories as the finely crafted, elegiac work included here, in a vital and ongoing tradition that includes Hawthorne and Poe, and, more generally, such visionaries as H. G. Wells, Karel Čapek, Aldous Huxley, and Stanislaw Lem. At his best, Bradbury is a poet of ominous prophecies—whose vision of a hellish future begins to seem, as the twentieth century has reeled to a close, ever more like realistic fiction and not fantasy.

Born in Waukegan, Illinois, Ray Bradbury has lived most of his adult life in California. His major titles are The Martian Chronicles *(1950), from which this selection has been taken,* The Illustrated Man *(1951),* Fahrenheit 451 *(1953),* Dandelion Wine *(1957),* Something Wicked This Way Comes *(1962) and* The Mummies of Guanajuato *(1978).* The Stories of Ray Bradbury *appeared in 1980.*

The title "There Will Come Soft Rains" is a line from a poem by Sara Teasdale, used to devastating irony here.

There Will Come Soft Rains

In the living room the voice-clock sang, *Tick-tock, seven o'clock, time to get up, time to get up, seven o'clock!* as if it were afraid that nobody would. The morning house lay empty. The clock ticked on, repeating and repeating its sounds into the emptiness. *Seven-nine, breakfast time, seven-nine!*

In the kitchen the breakfast stove gave a hissing sigh and ejected from its warm interior eight pieces of perfectly browned toast, eight eggs sunny-side up, sixteen slices of bacon, two coffees, and two cool glasses of milk.

"Today is August 4, 2026," said a second voice from the kitchen ceiling, "in the city of Allendale, California." It repeated the date three times for memory's sake. "Today is Mr. Featherstone's birthday. Today is the anniversary of Tilita's marriage. Insurance is payable, as are the water, gas, and light bills."

Somewhere in the walls, relays clicked, memory tapes glided under electric eyes.

Eight-one, tick-tock, eight-one o'clock, off to school, off to work, run, run, eight-one! But no doors slammed, no carpets took the soft tread of rubber heels. It was raining outside. The weather box on the front door sang quietly: "Rain, rain, go away; rubbers, raincoats for today ..." And the rain tapped on the empty house, echoing.

Outside, the garage chimed and lifted its door to reveal the waiting car. After a long wait the door swung down again.

At eight-thirty the eggs were shriveled and the toast was like stone. An aluminum wedge scraped them into the sink, where hot water whirled them down a metal throat which digested and flushed them away to the distant sea. The dirty dishes were dropped into a hot washer and emerged twinkling dry.

Nine-fifteen, sang the clock, *time to clean.*

Out of warrens in the wall, tiny robot mice darted. The rooms were acrawl with the small cleaning animals, all rubber and metal. They thudded against chairs, whirling their mustached runners, kneading the rug nap, sucking gently at hidden dust. Then, like mysterious invaders, they popped into their burrows. Their pink electric eyes faded. The house was clean.

Ten o'clock. The sun came out from behind the rain. The house stood alone in a city of rubble and ashes. This was the one house left standing. At night the ruined city gave off a radioactive glow which could be seen for miles.

Ten-fifteen. The garden sprinklers whirled up in golden founts, filling the soft morning air with scatterings of brightness. The water pelted windowpanes running down the charred west side where the house had been burned evenly free of its white paint. The entire west face of the house was black, save for five places. Here the silhouette in paint of a man mowing a lawn. Here, as in a photograph, a woman bent to pick flowers. Still farther over, their images burned on wood in one titanic instant, a small boy, hands flung into the air, higher up, the image of a thrown ball, and opposite him a girl, hands raised to catch a ball which never came down.

The five spots of paint—the man, the woman, the children, the ball—remained. The rest was a thin charcoaled layer.

The gentle sprinkler rain filled the garden with falling light.

Until this day, how well the house had kept its peace. How carefully it had inquired, "Who goes there? What's the password?" and, getting no answer from lonely foxes and whining cats, it had shut up its windows and drawn shades in an old-maidenly preoccupation with self-protection which bordered on a mechanical paranoia.

It quivered at each sound, the house did. If a sparrow brushed a window, the shade snapped up. The bird, startled, flew off! No, not even a bird must touch the house!

The house was an altar with ten thousand attendants, big, small, servicing, attending, in choirs. But the gods had gone away, and the ritual of the religion continued senselessly, uselessly.

Twelve noon.

A dog whined, shivering, on the front porch.

The front door recognized the dog voice and opened. The dog, once huge and fleshy, but now gone to bone and covered with sores, moved in and through the house, tracking mud. Behind it whirred angry mice, angry at having to pick up mud, angry at inconvenience.

For not a leaf fragment blew under the door but what the wall panels flipped open and the copper scrap rats flashed swiftly out. The offending dust, hair, or paper, seized in miniature steel jaws, was raced back to the burrows. There, down tubes which fed into the cellar, it was dropped into the sighing vent of an incinerator which sat like evil Baal in a dark corner.

The dog ran upstairs, hysterically yelping to each door, at last realizing, as the house realized, that only silence was here.

It sniffed the air and scratched the kitchen door. Behind the door, the stove was making pancakes which filled the house with a rich baked odor and the scent of maple syrup.

The dog frothed at the mouth, lying at the door, sniffing, its eyes turned to fire. It ran wildly in circles, biting at its tail, spun in a frenzy, and died. It lay in the parlor for an hour.

Two o'clock, sang a voice.

Delicately sensing decay at last, the regiments of mice hummed out as softly as blown gray leaves in an electrical wind.

Two-fifteen.

The dog was gone.

In the cellar, the incinerator glowed suddenly and a whirl of sparks leaped up the chimney.

Two thirty-five.

Bridge tables sprouted from patio walls. Playing cards fluttered onto pads in a shower of pips. Martinis manifested on an oaken bench with egg-salad sandwiches. Music played.

But the tables were silent and the cards untouched.

At four o'clock the tables folded like great butterflies back through the paneled walls.

Four-thirty.

The nursery walls glowed.

Animals took shape: yellow giraffes, blue lions, pink antelopes, lilac panthers cavorting in crystal substance. The walls were glass. They looked out upon color and fantasy. Hidden films clocked through well-oiled sprockets, and the walls lived. The nursery floor was woven to resemble a crisp, cereal meadow. Over this ran aluminum roaches and iron crickets, and in the hot still air butterflies of delicate red tissue wavered among the sharp aroma of animal spoors! There was the sound like a great matted yellow hive of bees within a dark bellows, the lazy bumble of a purring lion. And there was the patter of okapi feet and the murmur of a fresh jungle rain, like other hoofs, falling upon the summer-starched grass. Now the walls dissolved into distances of parched weed, mile on mile, and warm endless sky. The animals drew away into thorn brakes and water holes.

It was the children's hour.

Five o'clock. The bath filled with clear hot water.

Six, seven, eight o'clock. The dinner dishes manipulated like magic tricks, and in the study a *click*. In the metal stand opposite the hearth where a fire now blazed up warmly, a cigar popped out, half an inch of soft gray ash on it, smoking, waiting.

Nine o'clock. The beds warmed their hidden circuits, for nights were cool here.

Nine-five. A voice spoke from the study ceiling:

"Mrs. McClellan, which poem would you like this evening?"

The house was silent.

The voice said at last, "Since you express no preference, I shall select a poem at random." Quiet music rose to back the voice. "Sara Teasdale. As I recall, your favorite... .

> *"There will come soft rains and the smell of the ground,*
> *And swallows circling with their shimmering sound;*
>
> *And frogs in the pools singing at night,*
> *And wild plum-trees in tremulous white;*
>
> *Robins will wear their feathery fire*
> *Whistling their whims on a low fence-wire;*
>
> *And not one will know of the war, not one*
> *Will care at last when it is done.*
>
> *Not one would mind, either bird nor tree*
> *If mankind perished utterly;*
>
> *And Spring herself, when she woke at dawn,*
> *Would scarcely know that we were gone."*

The fire burned on the stone hearth and the cigar fell away into a mound of quiet ash on its tray. The empty chairs faced each other between the silent walls, and the music played.

At ten o'clock the house began to die.

The wind blew. A falling tree bough crashed through the kitchen window. Cleaning solvent, bottled, shattered over the stove. The room was ablaze in an instant!

"Fire!" screamed a voice. The house lights flashed, water pumps shot water from the ceilings. But the solvent spread on the linoleum, licking, eating under the kitchen door, while the voices took it up in chorus: "Fire, fire, fire!"

The house tried to save itself. Doors sprang tightly shut, but the windows were broken by the heat and the wind blew and sucked upon the fire.

The house gave ground as the fire in ten billion angry sparks moved with flaming ease from room to room and then up the stairs. While scurrying water rats squeaked from the walls, pistoled their water, and ran for more. And the wall sprays let down showers of mechanical rain.

But too late. Somewhere, sighing, a pump shrugged to a stop. The quenching rain ceased. The reserve water supply which had filled baths and washed dishes for many quiet days was gone.

The fire crackled up the stairs. It fed upon Picassos and Matisses in the upper halls, like delicacies, baking off the oily flesh, tenderly crisping the canvases into black shavings.

Now the fire lay in beds, stood in windows, changed the colors of drapes!

And then, reinforcements.

From attic trapdoors, blind robot faces peered down with faucet mouths gushing green chemical.

The fire backed off, as even an elephant must at the sight of a dead snake. Now there were twenty snakes whipping over the floor, killing the fire with a clear cold venom of green froth.

But the fire was clever. It had sent flame outside the house, up through the attic to the pumps there. An explosion! The attic brain which directed the pumps was shattered into bronze shrapnel on the beams.

The fire rushed back into every closet and felt of the clothes hung there.

The house shuddered, oak bone on bone, its bared skeleton cringing from the heat, its wire, its nerves revealed as if a surgeon had torn the skin off to let the red veins and capillaries quiver in the scalded air. Help, help! Fire! Run, run! Heat snapped mirrors like the first brittle winter ice. And the voices wailed Fire, fire, run, run, like a tragic nursery rhyme, a dozen voices, high, low, like children dying in a forest, alone, alone. And the voices fading as the wires popped their sheathings like hot chestnuts. One, two, three, four, five voices died.

In the nursery the jungle burned. Blue lions roared, purple giraffes bounded off. The panthers ran in circles, changing color, and ten million animals, running before the fire, vanished off toward a distant steaming river... .

Ten more voices died. In the last instant under the fire avalanche, other choruses, oblivious, could be heard announcing the time, playing music, cutting the lawn by remote-control mower, or setting an umbrella frantically out and in the slamming and opening front door, a thousand things happening, like a clock shop when each clock strikes the hour insanely before or after the other, a scene of maniac confusion, yet unity; singing, screaming, a few last cleaning mice darting bravely out to carry the horrid ashes away! And one voice, with sublime disregard for the situation, read poetry aloud in the fiery study, until all the film spools burned, until all the wires withered and the circuits cracked.

The fire burst the house and let it slam flat down, puffing out skirts of spark and smoke.

In the kitchen, an instant before the rain of fire and timber, the stove could be seen making breakfasts at a psychopathic rate, ten dozen eggs, six loaves of toast, twenty dozen bacon strips, which, eaten by fire, started the stove working again, hysterically hissing!

The crash. The attic smashing into kitchen and parlor. The parlor into cellar, cellar into sub-cellar. Deep freeze, armchair, film tapes, circuits, beds, and all like skeletons thrown in a cluttered mound deep under.

Smoke and silence. A great quantity of smoke.

Dawn showed faintly in the east. Among the ruins, one wall stood alone. Within the wall, a last voice said, over and over again and again, even as the sun rose to shine upon the heaped rubble and steam:

"Today is August 5, 2026, today is August 5, 2026, today is ..."

JAMES BALDWIN
(1924–1987)

James Baldwin was not naturally a short story writer, though his much-anthologized "Sonny's Blues" is a short story classic. His gift was for longer, denser, more cohesive and combative forms: the novel, the essay, the speech, the memoir. Yet his most passionate nonfiction work, Notes of a Native Son *and* The Fire Next Time *for instance, have the force of fiction, just as the rich, meticulously detailed "Sonny's Blues" has the authenticity of memoir. In speaking of what it means to be black and American and—in such works as* Giovanni's Room*—homosexual, James Baldwin bore witness in a direct, unmediated way; he had no interest in formal or linguistic experimentation, like Ralph Ellison or the contemporary whom he most resembles, Norman Mailer.*

Born in Harlem, the first of nine children, Baldwin began his writing career early. His association with Richard Wright, whom he admired, led to his writing and publishing essays in the influential journal Partisan Review, *which were subsequently gathered into the collection* Notes of a Native Son *(1955). His first novel is the autobiographical* Go Tell It on the Mountain *(1953); his second, the more controversial* Giovanni's Room *(1956), which he had difficulty getting published.* Another Country *(1962) and* Tell Me How Long the Train's Been Gone *(1968) continue earlier themes of racial identity. The son of a Harlem preacher, and an intermittent preacher himself when a young man, Baldwin raised polemics to an art in his more celebrated works* Nobody Knows My Name *(1961),* The Fire Next Time *(1963), and* No Name in the Street *(1972). His collection of short stories is* Going to Meet the Man *(1965).*

Sonny's Blues

I read about it in the paper, in the subway, on my way to work. I read it, and I couldn't believe it, and I read it again. Then perhaps I just stared at it, at the newsprint spelling out his name, spelling out the story. I stared at it in the swinging lights of the subway car, and in the faces and bodies of the people, and in my own face, trapped in the darkness which roared outside.

It was not to be believed and I kept telling myself that as I walked from the subway station to the high school. And at the same time I couldn't doubt it. I was scared, scared for Sonny. He became real to me again. A great block of ice got settled in my belly and kept melting there slowly all day long, while I taught my classes algebra. It was a special kind of ice. It kept melting, sending trickles of ice water all up and down my veins, but it never got less. Sometimes it hardened and seemed to expand until I felt my guts were going to come spilling out or that I was going to choke or scream. This would always be at a moment when I was remembering some specific thing Sonny had once said or done.

When he was about as old as the boys in my classes his face had been bright and open, there was a lot of copper in it; and he'd had wonderfully direct brown eyes, and great gentleness and privacy. I wondered what he looked like now. He had been picked up, the evening before, in a raid on an apartment downtown, for peddling and using heroin.

I couldn't believe it: but what I mean by that is that I couldn't find any room for it anywhere inside me. I had kept it outside me for a long time. I hadn't wanted to know. I had had suspicions, but I didn't name them, I kept putting them away. I told myself that Sonny was wild, but he wasn't crazy. And he'd always been a good boy, he hadn't ever turned hard or evil or disrespectful, the way kids can, so quick, so quick, especially in Harlem. I didn't want to believe that I'd ever see my brother going down, coming to nothing, all that light in his face gone out, in the condition I'd already seen so many others. Yet it had happened and here I was, talking about algebra to a lot of boys who might, every one of them for all I knew, be popping off needles every time they went to the head. Maybe it did more for them than algebra could.

I was sure that the first time Sonny had ever had horse, he couldn't have been much older than these boys were now. These boys, now, were living as we'd been living then, they were growing up with a rush and their heads bumped abruptly against the low ceiling of their actual possibilities. They were filled with rage. All they really knew were two darknesses, the darkness of their lives, which was now closing in on them, and the darkness of the movies, which had blinded them to that other darkness, and in which they now, vindictively, dreamed, at once more together than they were at any other time, and more alone.

When the last bell rang, the last class ended, I let out my breath. It seemed I'd been holding it for all that time. My clothes were wet—I may have looked as though I'd been sitting in a steam bath, all dressed up, all afternoon. I sat alone in the classroom a long time. I listened to the boys outside, downstairs, shouting and cursing and laughing. Their laughter struck me for perhaps the first time. It was not the joyous laughter which—God knows why—one associates with children. It was mocking and insular, its intent was to denigrate. It was disenchanted, and in this, also, lay the authority of their curses. Perhaps I was listening to them because I was thinking about my brother and in them I heard my brother. And myself.

One boy was whistling a tune, at once very complicated and very simple, it seemed to be pouring out of him as though he were a bird, and it sounded very cool and moving through all that harsh, bright air, only just holding its own through all those other sounds.

I stood up and walked over to the window and looked down into the courtyard. It was the beginning of the spring and the sap was rising in the boys. A teacher passed through them every now and again, quickly, as though he or she couldn't wait to get out of that courtyard, to get those boys out of their sight and off their minds. I started collecting my stuff. I thought I'd better get home and talk to Isabel.

The courtyard was almost deserted by the time I got downstairs. I saw this boy standing in the shadow of a doorway, looking just like Sonny. I almost called his name. Then I saw that it wasn't Sonny, but somebody we used to know, a boy from around our block. He'd been Sonny's friend. He'd never been mine, having been too young for me, and, anyway, I'd never liked him. And now, even though he was a grown-up man, he still hung around that block, still spent hours on the street corner, was always high and raggy. I used to run into him from time to time and he'd often work around to asking me for a quarter or fifty cents. He always had some real good excuse, too, and I always gave it to him, I don't know why.

But now, abruptly, I hated him. I couldn't stand the way he looked at me, partly like a dog, partly like a cunning child. I wanted to ask him what the hell he was doing in the school courtyard.

He sort of shuffled over to me, and he said, "I see you got the papers. So you already know about it."

"You mean about Sonny? Yes, I already know about it. How come they didn't get you?"

He grinned. It made him repulsive and it also brought to mind what he'd looked like as a kid. "I wasn't there. I stay away from them people."

"Good for you." I offered him a cigarette and I watched him through the smoke. "You come all the way down here just to tell me about Sonny?"

"That's right." He was sort of shaking his head and his eyes looked strange, as though they were about to cross. The bright sun deadened his damp dark brown skin and it made his eyes look yellow and showed up the dirt in his conked hair. He smelled funky. I moved a little away from him and I said, "Well, thanks. But I already know about it and I got to get home."

"I'll walk you a little ways," he said. We started walking. There were a couple of kids still loitering in the courtyard and one of them said good night to me and looked strangely at the boy beside me.

"What're you going to do?" he asked me. "I mean, about Sonny?"

"Look. I haven't seen Sonny for over a year, I'm not sure I'm going to do anything. Anyway, what the hell *can* I do?"

"That's right," he said quickly, "ain't nothing you can do. Can't much help old Sonny no more, I guess."

It was what I was thinking and so it seemed to me he had no right to say it.

"I'm surprised at Sonny, though," he went on—he had a funny way of talking, he looked straight ahead as though he were talking to himself—"I thought Sonny was a smart boy, I thought he was too smart to get hung."

"I guess he thought so too," I said sharply, "and that's how he got hung. And how about you? You're pretty goddamn smart, I bet."

Then he looked directly at me, just for a minute. "I ain't smart," he said. "If I was smart, I'd have reached for a pistol a long time ago."

"Look. Don't tell *me* your sad story, if it was up to me, I'd give you one." Then I felt guilty—guilty, probably, for never having supposed that the poor bastard *had* a story of his own, much less a sad one, and I asked, quickly, "What's going to happen to him now?"

He didn't answer this. He was off by himself some place. "Funny thing," he said, and from his tone we might have been discussing the quickest way to get to Brooklyn, "when I saw the papers this morning, the first thing I asked myself was if I had anything to do with it. I felt sort of responsible."

I began to listen more carefully. The subway station was on the corner, just before us, and I stopped. He stopped, too. We were in front of a bar and he ducked slightly, peering in, but whoever he was looking for didn't seem to be there. The juke box was blasting away with something black and bouncy and I half watched the barmaid as she danced her way from the juke box to her place behind the bar. And I watched her face as she laughingly responded to something someone said to her, still keeping time to the music. When she smiled one saw the little girl, one sensed the doomed, still-struggling woman beneath the battered face of the semi-whore.

"I never *give* Sonny nothing," the boy said finally, "but a long time ago I come to school high and Sonny asked me how it felt." He paused, I couldn't bear to watch him, I watched the barmaid, and I listened to the music which seemed to be causing the pavement to shake. "I told him it felt great." The music stopped, the barmaid paused and watched the juke box until the music began again. "It did."

All this was carrying me some place I didn't want to go. I certainly didn't want to know how it felt. It filled everything, the people, the houses, the music, the dark, quicksilver barmaid, with menace; and this menace was their reality.

"What's going to happen to him now?" I asked again.

"They'll send him away some place and they'll try to cure him." He shook his head. "Maybe he'll even think he's kicked the habit. Then they'll let him loose"—he gestured, throwing his cigarette into the gutter. "That's all."

"What do you mean, that's *all?*"

But I knew what he meant.

"I *mean,* that's *all.*" He turned his head and looked at me, pulling down the corners of his mouth. "Don't you know what I mean?" he asked softly.

"How the hell *would* I know what you mean?" I almost whispered it, I don't know why.

"That's right," he said to the air, "how would *he* know what I mean?" He turned toward me again, patient and calm, and yet I somehow felt him shaking, shaking as though he were going to fall apart. I felt that ice in my guts again, the dread I'd felt all afternoon; and again I watched the barmaid, moving about the bar, washing glasses, and singing. "Listen. They'll let him out and then it'll just start all over again. That's what I mean."

"You mean—they'll let him out. And then he'll just start working his way back in again. You mean he'll never kick the habit. Is that what you mean?"

"That's right," he said, cheerfully. "*You* see what I mean."

"Tell me," I said at last, "why does he want to die? He must want to die, he's killing himself, why does he want to die?"

He looked at me in surprise. He licked his lips. "He don't want to die. He wants to live. Don't nobody want to die, ever."

Then I wanted to ask him—too many things. He could not have answered, or if he had, I could not have borne the answers. I started walking. "Well, I guess it's none of my business."

"It's going to be rough on old Sonny," he said. We reached the subway station. "This is your station?" he asked. I nodded. I took one step down. "Damn!" he said, suddenly. I looked up at him. He grinned again. "Damn if I didn't leave all my money home. You ain't got a dollar on you, have you? Just for a couple of days, is all."

All at once something inside gave and threatened to come pouring out of me. I didn't hate him any more. I felt that in another moment I'd start crying like a child.

"Sure," I said. "Don't sweat." I looked in my wallet and didn't have a dollar, I only had a five. "Here," I said. "That hold you?"

He didn't look at it—he didn't want to look at it. A terrible, closed look came over his face, as though he were keeping the number on the bill a secret from him and me. "Thanks," he said, and now he was dying to see me go. "Don't worry about Sonny. Maybe I'll write him or something."

"Sure," I said. "You do that. So long."

"Be seeing you," he said. I went on down the steps.

And I didn't write Sonny or send him anything for a long time. When I finally did, it was just after my little girl died, he wrote me back a letter which made me feel like a bastard.

Here's what he said:

DEAR BROTHER,

You don't know how much I needed to hear from you. I wanted to write you many a time but I dug how much I must have hurt you and so I didn't write. But now I feel like a man who's been trying to climb up out of some deep, real deep and funky hole and just saw the sun up there, outside. I got to get outside.

I can't tell you much about how I got here. I mean I don't know how to tell you. I guess I was afraid of something or I was trying to escape from something and you know I have never been very strong in the head (smile). I'm glad Mama and Daddy are dead and can't see what's happened to their son and I swear if I'd known what I was doing I would never have hurt you so, you and a lot of other fine people who were nice to me and who believed in me.

I don't want you to think it had anything to do with me being a musician. It's more than that. Or maybe less than that. I can't get anything straight in my head down here and I try not to think about what's going to happen to me when I get outside again. Sometime I think I'm going to flip and never get outside and sometime I think I'll come straight back. I tell you one thing, though, I'd rather blow my brains out than go through this again. But that's what they all say, so they tell me. If I tell you when I'm coming to New York and if you could meet me, I sure would appreciate it. Give my love to Isabel and the kids and I was sorry to hear about little Gracie. I wish I could be like Mama and say the Lord's will be done, but I don't know it seems to me that trouble is the one thing that never does get stopped and I don't know what good it does to blame it on the Lord. But maybe it does some good if you believe it.

Your brother,
SONNY

Then I kept in constant touch with him and I sent him whatever I could and I went to meet him when he came back to New York. When I saw him many things I thought I had forgotten came flooding back to me. This was because I had begun, finally, to wonder about Sonny, about the life that Sonny lived inside. This life, whatever it was, had made him older and thinner and it had deepened the distant stillness in which he had always moved. He looked very unlike my baby brother. Yet, when he smiled, when we shook hands, the baby brother I'd never known looked out from the depths of his private life, like an animal waiting to be coaxed into the light.

"How you been keeping?" he asked me.

"All right. And you?"

"Just fine." He was smiling all over his face. "It's good to see you again."

"It's good to see you."

The seven years' difference in our ages lay between us like a chasm: I wondered if these years would ever operate between us as a bridge. I was remembering, and it made it hard to catch my breath, that I had been there when he was born; and I had heard the first words he had ever spoken. When he started to walk, he walked from our mother straight to me. I caught him just before he fell when he took the first steps he ever took in this world.

"How's Isabel?"

"Just fine. She's dying to see you."

"And the boys?"

"They're fine, too. They're anxious to see their uncle."

"Oh, come on. You know they don't remember me."

"Are you kidding? Of course they remember you."

He grinned again. We got into a taxi. We had a lot to say to each other, far too much to know how to begin.

As the taxi began to move, I asked, "You still want to go to India?"

He laughed. "You still remember that. Hell, no. This place is Indian enough for me."

"It used to belong to them," I said.

And he laughed again. "They damn sure knew what they were doing when they got rid of it."

Years ago, when he was around fourteen, he'd been all hipped on the idea of going to India. He read books about people sitting on rocks, naked, in all kinds of weather, but mostly bad, naturally, and walking barefoot through hot coals and arriving at wisdom. I used to say that it sounded to me as though they were getting away from wisdom as fast as they could. I think he sort of looked down on me for that.

"Do you mind," he asked, "if we have the driver drive alongside the park? On the west side—I haven't seen the city in so long."

"Of course not," I said. I was afraid that I might sound as though I were humoring him, but I hoped he wouldn't take it that way.

So we drove along, between the green of the park and the stony, lifeless elegance of hotels and apartment buildings, toward the vivid, killing streets of our childhood. These streets hadn't changed, though housing projects jutted up out of them now like rocks in the middle of a boiling sea. Most of the houses in which we had grown up had vanished, as had the stores from which we had stolen, the basements in which we had first tried sex, the rooftops from which we had hurled tin cans and bricks. But houses exactly like the houses of our past yet dominated the landscape, boys exactly like the boys we once had been found themselves smothering in these houses, came down into the streets for light and air and found themselves encircled by disaster. Some escaped the trap, most didn't. Those who got out always left something of themselves behind, as some animals amputate a leg and leave it in the trap. It might be said, perhaps, that I had escaped, after all, I was a school teacher; or that Sonny had, he hadn't lived in Harlem for years. Yet, as the cab moved uptown through streets which seemed, with a rush, to darken with dark people, and as I covertly studied Sonny's face, it came to me that what we both were seeking through our separate cab windows was that part of ourselves which had been left behind. It's always at the hour of trouble and confrontation that the missing member aches.

We hit 110th Street and started rolling up Lenox Avenue. And I'd known this avenue all my life, but it seemed to me again, as it had seemed on the day I'd first heard about Sonny's trouble, filled with a hidden menace which was its very breath of life.

"We almost there," said Sonny.

"Almost." We were both too nervous to say anything more.

We live in a housing project. It hasn't been up long. A few days after it was up it seemed uninhabitably new, now, of course, it's already run-down.

It looks like a parody of the good, clean, faceless life—God knows the people who live in it do their best to make it a parody. The beat-looking grass lying around isn't enough to make their lives green, the hedges will never hold out the streets, and they know it. The big windows fool no one, they aren't big enough to make space out of no space. They don't bother with the windows, they watch the TV screen instead. The playground is most popular with the children who don't play at jacks, or skip rope, or roller skate, or swing, and they can be found in it after dark. We moved in partly because it's not too far from where I teach, and partly for the kids; but it's really just like the houses in which Sonny and I grew up. The same things happen, they'll have the same things to remember. The moment Sonny and I started into the house I had the feeling that I was simply bringing him back into the danger he had almost died trying to escape.

Sonny has never been talkative. So I don't know why I was sure he'd be dying to talk to me when supper was over the first night. Everything went fine, the oldest boy remembered him, and the youngest boy liked him, and Sonny had remembered to bring something for each of them; and Isabel, who is really much nicer than I am, more open and giving, had gone to a lot of trouble about dinner and was genuinely glad to see him. And she's always been able to tease Sonny in a way that I haven't. It was nice to see her face so vivid again and to hear her laugh and watch her make Sonny laugh. She wasn't, or, anyway, she didn't seem to be, at all uneasy or embarrassed. She chatted as though there were no subject which had to be avoided and she got Sonny past his first, faint stiffness. And thank God she was there, for I was filled with that icy dread again. Everything I did seemed awkward to me, and everything I said sounded freighted with hidden meaning. I was trying to remember everything I'd heard about dope addiction and I couldn't help watching Sonny for signs. I wasn't doing it out of malice. I was trying to find out something about my brother. I was dying to hear him tell me he was safe.

"Safe!" my father grunted, whenever Mama suggested trying to move to a neighborhood which might be safer for children. "Safe, hell! Ain't no place safe for kids, nor nobody."

He always went on like this, but he wasn't, ever, really as bad as he sounded, not even on weekends, when he got drunk. As a matter of fact, he was always on the lookout for "something a little better," but he died before he found it. He died suddenly, during a drunken weekend in the middle of the war, when Sonny was fifteen. He and Sonny hadn't ever got on too well. And this was partly because Sonny was the apple of his father's eye. It was because he loved Sonny so much and was frightened for him, that he was always fighting with him. It doesn't do any good to fight with Sonny. Sonny just moves back, inside himself, where he can't be reached. But the principal reason that they never hit it off is that they were so much alike. Daddy was big and rough and loud-talking, just the opposite of Sonny, but they both had—that same privacy.

Mama tried to tell me something about this, just after Daddy died. I was home on leave from the army.

This was the last time I ever saw my mother alive. Just the same, this picture gets all mixed up in my mind with pictures I had of her when she was younger. The way I always see her is the way she used to be on a Sunday afternoon, say, when the old folks were talking after the big Sunday dinner. I always see her wearing pale blue. She'd be sitting on the sofa. And my father would be sitting in the easy chair, not far from her. And the living room would be full of church folks and relatives. There they sit, in chairs all around the living room, and the night is creeping up outside, but nobody knows it yet. You can see the darkness growing against the window-panes and you hear the street noises every now and again, or maybe the jangling beat of a tambourine from one of the churches close by, but it's real quiet in the room. For a moment nobody's talking, but every face looks darkening, like the sky outside. And my mother rocks a little from the waist, and my father's eyes are closed. Everyone is looking at something a child can't see. For a minute they've forgotten the children. Maybe a kid is lying on the rug half asleep. Maybe somebody's got a kid on his lap and is absent-mindedly stroking the kid's head. Maybe there's a kid, quiet and big-eyed, curled up in a big chair in the corner. The silence, the darkness coming, and the darkness in the faces frightens the child obscurely. He hopes that the hand which strokes his forehead will never stop—will never die. He hopes that there will never come a time when the old folks won't be sitting around the living room, talking about where they've come from, and what they've seen, and what's happened to them and their kinfolk.

But something deep and watchful in the child knows that this is bound to end, is already ending. In a moment someone will get up and turn on the light. Then the old folks will remember the children and they won't talk any more that day. And when light fills the room, the child is filled with darkness. He knows that every time this happens he's moved just a little closer to that darkness outside. The darkness outside is what the old folks have been talking about. It's what they've come from. It's what they endure. The child knows that they won't talk any more because if he knows too much about what's happened to *them,* he'll know too much too soon, about what's going to happen to *him.*

The last time I talked to my mother, I remember I was restless. I wanted to get out and see Isabel. We weren't married then and we had a lot to straighten out between us.

There Mama sat, in black, by the window. She was humming an old church song. *Lord, you brought me from a long ways off.* Sonny was out somewhere. Mama kept watching the streets.

"I don't know," she said, "if I'll ever see you again, after you go off from here. But I hope you'll remember the things I tried to teach you."

"Don't talk like that," I said, and smiled. "You'll be here a long time yet."

She smiled, too, but she said nothing. She was quiet for a long time. And I said, "Mama, don't you worry about nothing. I'll be writing all the time, and you be getting the checks… ."

"I want to talk to you about your brother," she said, suddenly. "If anything happens to me he ain't going to have nobody to look out for him."

"Mama," I said, "ain't nothing going to happen to you *or* Sonny. Sonny's all right. He's a good boy and he's got good sense."

"It ain't a question of his being a good boy," Mama said, "nor of his having good sense. It ain't only the bad ones, nor yet the dumb ones that gets sucked under." She stopped, looking at me. "Your Daddy once had a brother," she said, and she smiled in a way that made me feel she was in pain. "Yon didn't never know that, did you?"

"No," I said, "I never knew that," and I watched her face.

"Oh, yes," she said, "your Daddy had a brother." She looked out of the window again. "I know you never saw your Daddy cry. But I did—many a time, through all these years."

I asked her, "What happened to his brother? How come nobody's ever talked about him?"

This was the first time I ever saw my mother look old.

"His brother got killed," she said, "when he was just a little younger than you are now. I knew him. He was a fine boy. He was maybe a little full of the devil, but he didn't mean nobody no harm."

Then she stopped and the room was silent, exactly as it had sometimes been on those Sunday afternoons. Mama kept looking out into the streets.

"He used to have a job in the mill," she said, "and, like all young folks, he just liked to perform on Saturday nights. Saturday nights, him and your father would drift around to different places, go to dances and things like that, or just sit around with people they knew, and your father's brother would sing, he had a fine voice, and play along with himself on his guitar. Well, this particular Saturday night, him and your father was coming home from some place, and they were both a little drunk and there was a moon that night, it was bright like day. Your father's brother was feeling kind of good, and he was whistling to himself, and he had his guitar slung over his shoulder. They was coming down a hill and beneath them was a road that turned off from the highway. Well, your father's brother, being always kind of frisky, decided to run down this hill, and he did, with that guitar banging and clanging behind him, and he ran across the road, and he was making water behind a tree. And your father was sort of amused at him and he was still coming down the hill, kind of slow. Then he heard a car motor and that same minute his brother stepped from behind the tree, into the road, in the moonlight. And he started to cross the road. And your father started to run down the hill, he says he don't know why. This car was full of white men. They was all drunk, and when they seen your father's brother they let out a great whoop and holler and they aimed the car straight at him. They was having fun, they just wanted to scare him, the way they do sometimes, you know. But they was drunk. And I guess the boy, being drunk, too, and scared, kind of lost his head. By the time he jumped it was too late. Your father says he heard his brother scream when the car rolled over him, and he heard the wood of that guitar when it give, and he heard them strings go flying, and he heard them white men shouting, and the car kept on a-going and it ain't stopped till this day. And, time your father got down the hill, his brother weren't nothing but blood and pulp."

Tears were gleaming on my mother's face. There wasn't anything I could say.

"He never mentioned it," she said, "because I never let him mention it before you children. Your Daddy was like a crazy man that night and for many a night thereafter. He says he never in his life seen anything as dark as that road after the lights of that car had gone away. Weren't nothing, weren't nobody on that road, just your Daddy and his brother and that busted guitar. Oh, yes. Your Daddy never did really get right again. Till the day he died he weren't sure but that every white man he saw was the man that killed his brother."

She stopped and took out her handkerchief and dried her eyes and looked at me.

"I ain't telling you all this," she said, "to make you scared or bitter or to make you hate nobody. I'm telling you this because you got a brother. And the world ain't changed."

I guess I didn't want to believe this. I guess she saw this in my face. She turned away from me, toward the window again, searching those streets.

"But I praise my Redeemer," she said at last, "that He called your Daddy home before me. I ain't saying it to throw no flowers at myself, but, I declare, it keeps me from feeling too cast down to know I helped your father get safely through this world. Your father always acted like he was the roughest, strongest man on earth. And everybody took him to be like that. But if he hadn't had *me* there—to see his tears!"

She was crying again. Still, I couldn't move. I said, "Lord, Lord, Mama, I didn't know it was like that."

"Oh, honey," she said, "there's a lot that you don't know. But you are going to find it out." She stood up from the window and came over to me. "You got to hold on to your brother," she said, "and don't let him fall, no matter what it looks like is happening to him and no matter how evil you gets with him. You going to be evil with him many a time. But don't you forget what I told you, you hear?"

"I won't forget," I said. "Don't you worry, I won't forget. I won't let nothing happen to Sonny."

My mother smiled as though she were amused at something she saw in my face. Then, "You may not be able to stop nothing from happening. But you got to let him know you's *there.*"

Two days later I was married, and then I was gone. And I had a lot of things on my mind and I pretty well forgot my promise to Mama until I got shipped home on a special furlough for her funeral.

And, after the funeral, with just Sonny and me alone in the empty kitchen, I tried to find out something about him.

"What do you want to do?" I asked him.

"I'm going to be a musician," he said.

For he had graduated, in the time I had been away, from dancing to the juke box to finding out who was playing what, and what they were doing with it, and he had bought himself a set of drums.

"You mean, you want to be a drummer?" I somehow had the feeling that being a drummer might be all right for other people but not for my brother Sonny.

"I don't think," he said, looking at me very gravely, "that I'll ever be a good drummer. But I think I can play a piano."

I frowned. I'd never played the role of the older brother quite so seriously before, had scarcely ever, in fact, *asked* Sonny a damn thing. I sensed myself in the presence of something I didn't really know how to handle, didn't understand. So I made my frown a little deeper as I asked: "What kind of musician do you want to be?"

He grinned. "How many kinds do you think there are?"

"Be *serious,*" I said.

He laughed, throwing his head back, and then looked at me. "I *am* serious."

"Well, then, for Christ's sake, stop kidding around and answer a serious question. I mean, do you want to be a concert pianist, you want to play classical music and all that, or—or what?" Long before I finished he was laughing again. "For Christ's *sake,* Sonny!"

He sobered, but with difficulty. "I'm sorry. But you sound so *scared!*" and he was off again.

"Well, you may think it's funny now, baby, but it's not going to be so funny when you have to make your living at it, let me tell you *that.*" I was furious because I knew he was laughing at me and I didn't know why.

"No," he said, very sober now, and afraid, perhaps, that he'd hurt me, "I don't want to be a classical pianist. That isn't what interests me. I mean"—he paused, looking hard at me, as though his eyes would help me to understand, and then gestured helplessly, as though perhaps his hand would help—"I mean, I'll have a lot of studying to do, and I'll have to study *everything,* but I mean, I want to play *with*—jazz musicians." He stopped. "I want to play jazz," he said.

Well, the word had never before sounded as heavy, as real, as it sounded that afternoon in Sonny's mouth. I just looked at him and I was probably frowning a real frown by this time. I simply couldn't see why on earth he'd want to spend his time hanging around night clubs, clowning around on bandstands, while people pushed each other around a dance floor. It seemed—beneath him, somehow. I had never thought about it before, had never been forced to, but I suppose I had always put jazz musicians in a class with what Daddy called "good-time people."

"Are you *serious?*"

"Hell, *yes,* I'm serious."

He looked more helpless than ever, and annoyed, and deeply hurt.

I suggested, helpfully: "You mean—like Louis Armstrong?"

His face closed as though I'd struck him. "No. I'm not talking about none of that old-time, down home crap."

"Well, look, Sonny, I'm sorry, don't get mad. I just don't altogether get it, that's all. Name somebody—you know, a jazz musician you admire."

"Bird."

"Who?"

"Bird! Charlie Parker! Don't they teach you nothing in the goddamn army?"

I lit a cigarette. I was surprised and then a little amused to discover that I was trembling. "I've been out of touch," I said. "You'll have to be patient with me. Now. Who's this Parker character?"

"He's just one of the greatest jazz musicians alive," said Sonny, sullenly, his hands in his pockets, his back to me. "Maybe *the* greatest," he added, bitterly, "that's probably why *you* never heard of him."

"All right," I said. "I'm ignorant. I'm sorry. I'll go out and buy all the cat's records right away, all right?"

"It don't," said Sonny, with dignity, "make any difference to me. I don't care what you listen to. Don't do me no favors."

I was beginning to realize that I'd never seen him so upset before. With another part of my mind I was thinking that this would probably turn out to be one of those things kids go through and that I shouldn't make it seem important by pushing it too hard. Still, I didn't think it would do any harm to ask: "Doesn't all this take a lot of time? Can you make a living at it?"

He turned back to me and half leaned, half sat, on the kitchen table. "Everything takes time," he said, "and—well, yes, sure, I can make a living at it. But what I don't seem to be able to make you understand is that it's the only thing I want to do."

"Well Sonny," I said, gently, "you know people can't always do exactly what they *want* to do——"

"No, I don't know that," said Sonny, surprising me. "I think people *ought* to do what they want to do, what else are they alive for?"

"You getting to be a big boy," I said desperately, "it's time you started thinking about your future."

"I'm thinking about my future," said Sonny, grimly. "I think about it all the time."

I gave up. I decided, if he didn't change his mind, that we could always talk about it later. "In the meantime," I said, "you got to finish school." We had already decided that he'd have to move in with Isabel and her folks. I knew this wasn't the ideal arrangement because Isabel's folks are inclined to be dicty and they hadn't especially wanted Isabel to marry me. But I didn't know what else to do. "And we have to get you fixed up at Isabel's."

There was a long silence. He moved from the kitchen table to the window. "That's a terrible idea. You know it yourself."

"Do you have a *better* idea?"

He just walked up and down the kitchen for a minute. He was as tall as I was. He had started to shave. I suddenly had the feeling that I didn't know him at all.

He stopped at the kitchen table and picked up my cigarettes. Looking at me with a kind of mocking, amused defiance, he put one between his lips. "You mind?"

"You smoking already?"

He lit the cigarette and nodded, watching me through the smoke. "I just wanted to see if I'd have the courage to smoke in front of you." He grinned and blew a great cloud of smoke to the ceiling. "It was easy." He looked at my face. "Come on, now. I bet you was smoking at my age, tell the truth."

I didn't say anything but the truth was on my face, and he laughed. But now there was something very strained in his laugh. "Sure. And I bet that ain't all you was doing."

He was frightening me a little. "Cut the crap," I said. "We already decided that you was going to go and live at Isabel's. Now what's got into you all of a sudden?"

"You decided it," he pointed out. "*I* didn't decide nothing." He stopped in front of me, leaning against the stove, arms loosely folded. "Look, brother. I don't want to stay in Harlem no more, I really don't." He was very earnest. He looked at me, then over toward the kitchen window. There was something in his eyes I'd never seen before, some thoughtfulness, some worry all his own. He rubbed the muscle of one arm. "It's time I was getting out of here."

"Where do you want to *go*. Sonny?"

"I want to join the army. Or the navy, I don't care. If I say I'm old enough they'll believe me."

Then I got mad. It was because I was so scared. "You must be crazy. You goddamn fool, what the hell do you want to go and join the *army* for?"

"I just told you. To get out of Harlem."

"Sonny, you haven't even finished *school*. And if you really want to be a musician, how do you expect to study if you're in the *army?*"

He looked at me, trapped, and in anguish. "There's ways. I might be able to work out some kind of deal. Anyway, I'll have the G.I. Bill when I come out."

"*If you* come out." We stared at each other. "Sonny, please. Be reasonable. I know the setup is far from perfect. But we got to do the best we can."

"I ain't learning nothing in school," he said. "Even when I go." He turned away from me and opened the window and threw his cigarette out into the narrow alley. I watched his back. "At least, I ain't learning nothing you'd want me to learn." He slammed the window so hard I thought the glass would fly out, and turned back to me. "And I'm sick of the stink of these garbage cans!"

"Sonny," I said, "I know how you feel. But if you don't finish school now, you're going to be sorry later that you didn't." I grabbed him by the shoulders. "And you only got another year. It ain't so bad. And I'll come back and I swear I'll help you do *whatever* you want to do. Just try to put up with it till I come back. Will you please do that? For me?"

He didn't answer and he wouldn't look at me.

"Sonny. You hear me?"

He pulled away. "I hear you. But you never hear anything I say."

I didn't know what to say to that. He looked out of the window and then back at me. "OK," he said, and sighed. "I'll try."

Then I said, trying to cheer him up a little, "They got a piano at Isabel's. You can practice on it."

And as a matter of fact, it did cheer him up for a minute. "That's right," he said to himself. "I forgot that." His face relaxed a little. But the worry, the thoughtfulness, played on it still, the way shadows play on a face which is staring into the fire.

But I thought I'd never hear the end of that piano. At first, Isabel would write me, saying how nice it was that Sonny was so serious about his music and how, as soon as he came in from school, or wherever he had been when he was supposed to be at school, he went straight to that piano and stayed there until suppertime. And, after supper, he went back to that piano and stayed there until everybody went to bed. He was at the piano all day Saturday and all day Sunday. Then he bought a record player and started playing records. He'd play one record over and over again, all day long sometimes, and he'd improvise along with it on the piano. Or he'd play one section of the record, one chord, one change, one progression, then he'd do it on the piano. Then back to the record. Then back to the piano.

Well, I really don't know how they stood it. Isabel finally confessed that it wasn't like living with a person at all, it was like living with sound. And the sound didn't make any sense to her, didn't make any sense to any of them—naturally. They began, in a way, to be afflicted by this presence that was living in their home. It was as though Sonny were some sort of god, or monster. He moved in an atmosphere which wasn't like theirs at all. They fed him and he ate, he washed himself, he walked in and out of their door; he certainly wasn't nasty or unpleasant or rude, Sonny isn't any of those things; but it was as though he were all wrapped up in some cloud, some fire, some vision all his own; and there wasn't any way to reach him.

At the same time, he wasn't really a man yet, he was still a child, and they had to watch out for him in all kinds of ways. They certainly couldn't throw him out. Neither did they dare to make a great scene about that piano because even they dimly sensed, as I sensed, from so many thousands of miles away, that Sonny was at that piano playing for his life.

But he hadn't been going to school. One day a letter came from the school board and Isabel's mother got it—there had, apparently, been other letters but Sonny had torn them up. This day, when Sonny came in, Isabel's mother showed him the letter and asked where he'd been spending his time. And she finally got it out of him that he'd been down in Greenwich Village, with musicians and other characters, in a white girl's apartment. And this scared her and she started to scream at him and what came up, once she began—though she denies it to this day—was what sacrifices they were making to give Sonny a decent home and how little he appreciated it.

Sonny didn't play the piano that day. By evening, Isabel's mother had calmed down but then there was the old man to deal with, and Isabel herself. Isabel says she did her best to be calm but she broke down and started crying. She says she just watched Sonny's face. She could tell, by watching him, what was happening with him. And what was happening was that they penetrated his cloud, they had reached him. Even if their fingers had been a thousand times more gentle than human fingers ever are, he could hardly help feeling that they had stripped him naked and were spitting on that nakedness. For he also had to see that his presence, that music, which was life or death to him, had been torture for them and that they had endured it, not at all for his sake, but only for mine. And Sonny couldn't take that. He can take it a little better today than he could then but he's still not very good at it and, frankly, I don't know anybody who is.

The silence of the next few days must have been louder than the sound of all the music ever played since time began. One morning, before she went to work, Isabel was in his room for something and she suddenly realized that all of his records were gone. And she knew for certain that he was gone. And he was. He went as far as the navy would carry him. He finally sent me a postcard from some place in Greece and that was the first I knew that Sonny was still alive. I didn't see him any more until we were both back in New York and the war had long been over.

He was a man by then, of course, but I wasn't willing to see it. He came by the house from time to time, but we fought almost every time we met. I didn't like the way he carried himself, loose and dreamlike all the time, and I didn't like his friends, and his music seemed to be merely an excuse for the life he led. It sounded just that weird and disordered.

Then we had a fight, a pretty awful fight, and I didn't see him for months. By and by I looked him up, where he was living, in a furnished room in the Village, and I tried to make it up. But there were lots of other people in the room and Sonny just lay on his bed, and he wouldn't come downstairs with me, and he treated these other people as though they were his family and I weren't. So I got mad and then he got mad, and then I told him that he might just as well be dead as live the way he was living. Then he stood up and he told me not to worry about him any more in life, that he *was* dead as far as I was concerned. Then he pushed me to the door and the other people looked on as though nothing were happening, and he slammed the door behind me. I stood in the hallway, staring at the door. I heard somebody laugh in the room and then the tears came to my eyes. I started down the steps, whistling to keep from crying, I kept whistling to myself, *You going to need me, baby, one of these cold, rainy days.*

I read about Sonny's trouble in the spring. Little Grace died in the fall. She was a beautiful little girl. But she only lived a little over two years. She died of polio and she suffered. She had a slight fever for a couple of days, but it didn't seem like anything and we just kept her in bed. And we would certainly have called the doctor, but the fever dropped, she seemed to be all right. So we thought it had just been a cold. Then, one day, she was up, playing, Isabel was in the kitchen fixing lunch for the two boys when they'd come in from school, and she heard Grace fall down in the living room. When you have a lot of children you don't always start running when one of them falls, unless they start screaming or something. And, this time, Grace was quiet. Yet, Isabel says that when she heard that *thump* and then that silence, something happened in her to make her afraid. And she ran to the living room and there was little Grace on the floor, all twisted up and the reason she hadn't screamed was that she couldn't get her breath. And when she did scream, it was the worst sound, Isabel says, that she'd ever heard in all her life, and she still hears it sometimes in her dreams. Isabel will sometimes wake me up with a low, moaning, strangled sound and I have to be quick to awaken her and hold her to me and where Isabel is weeping against me seems a mortal wound.

I think I may have written Sonny the very day that little Grace was buried. I was sitting in the living room in the dark, by myself, and I suddenly thought of Sonny. My trouble made his real.

One Saturday afternoon, when Sonny had been living with us, or, anyway, been in our house, for nearly two weeks, I found myself wandering aimlessly about the living room, drinking from a can of beer, and trying to work up the courage to search Sonny's room. He was out, he was usually out whenever I was home, and Isabel had taken the children to see their grandparents. Suddenly I was standing still in front of the living room window, watching Seventh Avenue. The idea of searching Sonny's room made me still. I scarcely dared to admit to myself what I'd be searching for. I didn't know what I'd do if I found it. Or if I didn't.

On the sidewalk across from me, near the entrance to a barbecue joint, some people were holding an old-fashioned revival meeting. The barbecue cook, wearing a dirty white apron, his conked hair reddish and metallic in the pale sun, and a cigarette between his lips, stood in the doorway, watching them. Kids and older people paused in their errands and stood there, along with some older men and a couple of very tough-looking women who watched everything that happened on the avenue, as though they owned it, or were maybe owned by it. Well, they were watching this, too. The revival was being carried on by three sisters in black, and a brother. All they had were their voices and their Bibles and a tambourine. The brother was testifying and while he testified two of the sisters stood together, seeming to say, Amen, and the third sister walked around with the tambourine outstretched and a couple of people dropped coins into it. Then the brother's testimony ended and the sister who had been taking up the collection dumped the coins into her palm and transferred them to the pocket of her long black robe. Then she raised both hands, striking the tambourine against the air, and then against one hand, and she started to sing. And the two other sisters and the brother joined in.

It was strange, suddenly, to watch, though I had been seeing these street meetings all my life. So, of course, had everybody else down there. Yet, they paused and watched and listened and I stood still at the window. "*Tis the old ship of Zion*," they sang, and the sister with the tambourine kept a steady, jangling beat, "*It has rescued many a thousand!*" Not a soul under the sound of their voices was hearing this song for the first time, not one of them had been rescued. Nor had they seen much in the way of rescue work being done around them. Neither did they especially believe in the holiness of the three sisters and the brother, they knew too much about them, knew where they lived, and how. The woman with the tambourine, whose voice dominated the air, whose face was bright with joy, was divided by very little from the woman who stood watching her, a cigarette between her heavy, chapped lips, her hair a cuckoo's nest, her face scarred and swollen from many beatings, and her black eyes glittering like coal. Perhaps they both knew this, which was why, when, as rarely, they addressed each other, they addressed each other as Sister. As the singing filled the air the watching, listening faces underwent a change, the eyes focusing on something within; the music seemed to soothe a poison out of them; and time seemed, nearly, to fall away from the sullen, belligerent, battered faces, as though they were fleeing back to their first condition, while dreaming of their last. The barbecue cook half shook his head and smiled, and dropped his cigarette and disappeared into his joint. A man fumbled in his pockets for change and stood holding it in his hand impatiently, as though he had just remembered a pressing appointment further up the avenue. He looked furious. Then I saw Sonny, standing on the edge of the crowd. He was carrying a wide, flat notebook with a green cover, and it made him look, from where I was standing, almost like a schoolboy. The coppery sun brought out the copper in his skin, he was very faintly smiling, standing very still. Then the singing stopped, the tambourine turned into a collection plate again. The furious man dropped in his coins and vanished, so did a couple of the women, and Sonny dropped some change in the plate, looking directly at the woman with a little smile. He started across the avenue, toward the house. He has a slow, loping walk, something like the way Harlem hipsters walk, only he's imposed on this his own halfbeat. I had never really noticed it before.

I stayed at the window, both relieved and apprehensive. As Sonny disappeared from my sight, they began singing again. And they were still singing when his key turned in the lock.

"Hey," he said.

"Hey, yourself. You want some beer?"

"No. Well, maybe." But he came up to the window and stood beside me, looking out. "What a warm voice," he said.

They were singing *If I could only hear my mother pray again!*

"Yes," I said," and she can sure beat that tambourine."

"But what a terrible song," he said, and laughed. He dropped his notebook on the sofa and disappeared into the kitchen. "Where's Isabel and the kids?"

"I think they went to see their grandparents. You hungry?"

"No." He came back into the living room with his can of beer. "You want to come some place with me tonight?"

I sensed, I don't know how, that I couldn't possibly say No. "Sure. Where?"

He sat down on the sofa and picked up his notebook and started leafing through it. "I'm going to sit in with some fellows in a joint in the Village."

"You mean, you're going to play, tonight?"

"That's right." He took a swallow of his beer and moved back to the window. He gave me a sidelong look. "If you can stand it."

"I'll try," I said.

He smiled to himself and we both watched as the meeting across the way broke up. The three sisters and the brother, heads bowed, were singing *God be with you till we meet again.* The faces around them were very quiet. Then the song ended. The small crowd dispersed. We watched the three women and the lone man walk slowly up the avenue.

"When she was singing before," said Sonny, abruptly, "her voice reminded me for a minute of what heroin feels like sometimes—when it's in your veins. It makes you feel sort of warm and cool at the same time. And distant. And—and sure." He sipped his beer, very deliberately not looking at me. I watched his face. "It makes you feel—in control. Sometimes you've got to have that feeling."

"Do you?" I sat down slowly in the easy chair.

"Sometimes." He went to the sofa and picked up his notebook again. "Some people do."

"In order," I asked, "to play?" And my voice was very ugly, full of contempt and anger.

"Well"—he looked at me with great, troubled eyes, as though, in fact, he hoped his eyes would tell me things he could never otherwise say—"they *think* so. And *if* they think so—!"

"And what do *you* think?" I asked.

He sat on the sofa and put his can of beer on the floor. "I don't know," he said, and I couldn't be sure if he were answering my question or pursuing his thoughts. His face didn't tell me. "It's not so much to *play.* It's to *stand* it, to be able to make it at all. On any level." He frowned and smiled: "In order to keep from shaking to pieces."

"But these friends of yours," I said, "they seem to shake themselves to pieces pretty goddamn fast."

"Maybe." He played with the notebook. And something told me that I should curb my tongue, that Sonny was doing his best to talk, that I should listen. "But of course you only know the ones that've gone to pieces. Some don't—or at least they haven't *yet* and that's just about all *any* of us can say." He paused. "And then there are some who just live, really, in hell, and they know it and they see what's happening and they go right on. I don't know." He sighed, dropped the notebook, folded his arms. "Some guys, you can tell from the way they play, they on something *all* the time. And you can see that, well, it makes something real for them. But of course," he picked up his beer from the floor and sipped it and put the can down again, "they *want* to, too, you've got to see that. Even some of them that say they don't—*some,* not all."

"And what about you?" I asked—I couldn't help it. "What about you? Do *you* want to?"

He stood up and walked to the window and remained silent for a long time. Then he sighed. "Me," he said. Then: "While I was downstairs before, on my way here, listening to that woman sing, it struck me all of a sudden how much suffering she must have had to go through—to sing like that. It's *repulsive* to think you have to suffer that much."

I said: "But there's no way not to suffer—is there. Sonny?"

"I believe not," he said, and smiled, "but that's never stopped anyone from trying." He looked at me. "Has it?" I realized, with this mocking look, that there stood between us, forever, beyond the power of time or forgiveness, the fact that I had held silence—so long!—when he had needed human speech to help him. He turned back to the window. "No, there's no way not to suffer. But you try all kinds of ways to keep from drowning in it, to keep on top of it, and to make it seem—well, like *you*. Like you did something, all right, and now you're suffering for it. You know?" I said nothing. "Well you know," he said, impatiently, "why *do* people suffer? Maybe it's better to do something to give it a reason, *any* reason."

"But we just agreed," I said, "that there's no way not to suffer. Isn't it better, then, just to—take it?"

"But nobody just takes it," Sonny cried, "that's what I'm telling you! *Everybody* tries not to. You're just hung up on the *way* some people try—it's not *your* way!"

The hair on my face began to itch, my face felt wet. "That's not true," I said, "that's not true. I don't give a damn what other people do, I don't even care how they suffer. I just care how *you* suffer." And he looked at me. "Please believe me," I said, "I don't want to see you—die—trying not to suffer."

"I won't," he said, flatly, "die trying not to suffer. At least, not any faster than anybody else."

"But there's no need," I said, trying to laugh, "is there? in killing yourself."

I wanted to say more, but I couldn't. I wanted to talk about will power and how life could be—well, beautiful. I wanted to say that it was all within; but was it? or, rather, wasn't that exactly the trouble? And I wanted to promise that I would never fail him again. But it would all have sounded—empty words and lies.

So I made the promise to myself and prayed that I would keep it.

"It's terrible sometimes, inside," he said, "that's what's the trouble. You walk these streets, black and funky and cold, and there's not really a living ass to talk to, and there's nothing shaking, and there's no way of getting it out—that storm inside. You can't talk it and you can't make love with it, and when you finally try to get with it and play it, you realize *nobody's* listening. So *you've* got to listen. You got to find a way to listen."

And then he walked away from the window and sat on the sofa again, as though all the wind had suddenly been knocked out of him. "Sometimes you'll do *anything* to play, even cut your mother's throat." He laughed and looked at me. "Or your brother's." Then he sobered. "Or your own." Then: "Don't worry. I'm all right now and I think I'll *be* all right. But I can't forget—where I've been. I don't mean just the physical place I've been, I mean where I've *been*. And *what* I've been."

"What have you been, Sonny?" I asked.

He smiled—but sat sideways on the sofa, his elbow resting on the back, his fingers playing with his mouth and chin, not looking at me. "I've been something I didn't recognize, didn't know I could be. Didn't know anybody could be." He stopped, looking inward, looking helplessly young, looking old. "I'm not talking about it now because I feel *guilty* or anything like that—maybe it would be better if I did, I don't know. Anyway, I can't really talk about it. Not to you, not to anybody," and now he turned and faced me. "Sometimes, you know, and it was actually when I was most *out* of the world, I felt that I was in it, and that I was *with* it, really, and I could play or I didn't really have to *play*, it just came out of me, it was there. And I don't know how I played, thinking about it now, but I know I did awful things, those times, sometimes, to people. Or it wasn't that I *did* anything to them—it was that they weren't real." He picked up the beer can; it was empty; he rolled it between his palms: "And other times—well, I needed a fix, I needed to find a place to lean, I needed to clear a space to *listen*—and I couldn't find it, and I—went crazy, I did terrible things to *me*, I was terrible *for* me." He began pressing the beer can between his hands, I watched the metal begin to give. It glittered, as he played with it, like a knife, and I was afraid he would cut himself, but I said nothing. "Oh well. I can never tell you. I was all by myself at the bottom of something, stinking and sweating and crying and shaking, and I smelled it, you know? *my* stink, and I thought I'd die if I couldn't get away from it and yet, all the same, I knew that everything I was doing was just locking me in with it. And I didn't know," he paused, still flattening the beer can, "I didn't know, I still *don't* know, something kept telling me that maybe it was good to smell your own stink, but I didn't think that *that* was what I'd been trying to do—and—who can stand it?" and he abruptly dropped the ruined beer can, looking at me with a small, still smile, and then rose, walking to the window as though it were the lodestone rock. I watched his face, he watched the avenue. "I couldn't tell you when Mama died—but the reason I wanted to leave Harlem so bad was to get away from drugs. And then, when I ran away, that's what I was running from—really. When I came back, nothing had changed, I hadn't changed, I was just—older." And he stopped, drumming with his fingers on the windowpane. The sun had vanished, soon darkness would fall. I watched his face. "It can come again," he said, almost as though speaking to himself. Then he turned to me. "It can come again," he repeated. "I just want you to know that."

"All right," I said, at last. "So it can come again. All right."

He smiled, but the smile was sorrowful. "I had to try to tell you," he said.

"Yes," I said. "I understand that."

"You're my brother," he said, looking straight at me, and not smiling at all.

"Yes," I repeated, "yes. I understand that."

He turned back to the window, looking out. "All that hatred down there," he said, "all that hatred and misery and love. It's a wonder it doesn't blow the avenue apart."

We went to the only night club on a short, dark street, downtown. We squeezed through the narrow, chattering, jam-packed bar to the entrance of the big room, where the bandstand was. And we stood there for a moment, for the lights were very dim in this room and we couldn't see. Then, "Hello, boy," said a voice and an enormous black man, much older than Sonny or myself, erupted out of all that atmospheric lighting and put an arm around Sonny's shoulder. "I been sitting right here," he said, "waiting for you."

He had a big voice, too, and heads in the darkness turned toward us.

Sonny grinned and pulled a little away, and said, "Creole, this is my brother. I told you about him."

Creole shook my hand. "I'm glad to meet you, son," he said, and it was clear that he was glad to meet me *there,* for Sonny's sake. And he smiled, "You got a real musician in *your* family," and he took his arm from Sonny's shoulder and slapped him, lightly, affectionately, with the back of his hand.

"Well. Now I've heard it all," said a voice behind us. This was another musician, and a friend of Sonny's, a coal-black, cheerful-looking man, built close to the ground. He immediately began confiding to me, at the top of his lungs, the most terrible things about Sonny, his teeth gleaming like a lighthouse and his laugh coming up out of him like the beginning of an earthquake. And it turned out that everyone at the bar knew Sonny, or almost everyone; some were musicians, working there, or nearby, or not working, some were simply hangers-on, and some were there to hear Sonny play. I was introduced to all of them and they were all very polite to me. Yet, it was clear that, for them, I was only Sonny's brother. Here, I was in Sonny's world. Or, rather: his kingdom. Here, it was not even a question that his veins bore royal blood.

They were going to play soon and Creole installed me, by myself, at a table in a dark corner. Then I watched them, Creole, and the little black man, and Sonny, and the others, while they horsed around, standing just below the bandstand. The light from the bandstand spilled just a little short of them and, watching them laughing and gesturing and moving about, I had the feeling that they, nevertheless, were being most careful not step into that circle of light too suddenly: that if they moved into the light too suddenly, without thinking, they would perish in flame. Then, while I watched, one of them, the small, black man, moved into the light and crossed the bandstand and started fooling around with his drums. Then—being funny and being, also, extremely ceremonious—Creole took Sonny by the arm and led him to the piano. A woman's voice called Sonny's name and a few hands started clapping. And Sonny, also being funny and being ceremonious, and so touched, I think, that he could have cried, but neither hiding it nor showing it, riding it like a man, grinned, and put both hands to his heart and bowed from the waist.

Creole then went to the bass fiddle and a lean, very bright-skinned brown man jumped up on the bandstand and picked up his horn. So there they were, and the atmosphere on the bandstand and in the room began to change and tighten. Someone stepped up to the microphone and announced them. Then there were all kinds of murmurs. Some people at the bar shushed others. The waitress ran around, frantically getting in the last orders, guys and chicks got closer to each other, and the lights on the bandstand, on the quartet, turned to a kind of indigo. Then they all looked different there. Creole looked about him for the last time, as though he were making certain that all his chickens were in the coop, and then he—jumped and struck the fiddle. And there they were.

All I know about music is that not many people ever really hear it. And even then, on the rare occasions when something opens within, and the music enters, what we mainly hear, or hear corroborated, are personal private, vanishing evocations. But the man who creates the music is hearing something else, is dealing with the roar rising from the void and imposing order on it as it hits the air. What is evoked in him, then, is of another order, more terrible because it has no words, and triumphant, too, for that same reason. And his triumph, when he triumphs, is ours. I just watched Sonny's face. His face was troubled, he was working hard, but he wasn't with it. And I had the feeling that, in a way, everyone on the bandstand was waiting for him, both waiting for him and pushing him along. But as I began to watch Creole, I realized that it was Creole who held them all back. He had them on a short rein. Up there, keeping the beat with his whole body, wailing on the fiddle, with his eyes half closed, he was listening to everything, but he was listening to Sonny. He was having a dialogue with Sonny. He wanted Sonny to leave the shore line and strike out for the deep water. He was Sonny's witness that deep water and drowning were not the same thing—he had been there, and he knew. And he wanted Sonny to know. He was waiting for Sonny to do the things on the keys which would let Creole know that Sonny was in the water.

And, while Creole listened, Sonny moved, deep within, exactly like someone in torment. I had never before thought of how awful the relationship must be between the musician and his instrument. He has to fill it, this instrument, with the breath of life, his own. He has to make it do what he wants it to do. And a piano is just a piano. It's made out of so much wood and wires and little hammers and big ones, and ivory. While there's only so much you can do with it, the only way to find this out is to try and make it do everything.

And Sonny hadn't been near a piano for over a year. And he wasn't on much better terms with his life, not the life that stretched before him now. He and the piano stammered, started one way, got scared, stopped; started another way, panicked, marked time, started again; then seemed to have found a direction, panicked again, got stuck. And the face I saw on Sonny I'd never seen before. Everything had been burned out of it, and, at the same time, things usually hidden were being burned in, by the fire and fury of the battle which was occurring in him up there.

Yet, watching Creole's face as they neared the end of the first set, I had the feeling that something had happened, something I hadn't heard. Then they finished, there was scattered applause, and then, without an instant's warning, Creole started into something else, it was almost sardonic, it was *Am I Blue*. And, as though he commanded, Sonny began to play. Something began to happen. And Creole let out the reins. The dry, low, black man said something awful on the drums, Creole answered, and the drums talked back. Then the horn insisted, sweet and high, slightly detached perhaps, and Creole listened, commenting now and then, dry, and driving, beautiful and calm and old. Then they all came together again, and Sonny was part of the family again. I could tell this from his face. He seemed to have found, right there beneath his fingers, a damn brand-new piano. It seemed that he couldn't get over it. Then, for awhile, just being happy with Sonny, they seemed to be agreeing with him that brand-new pianos certainly were a gas.

Then Creole stepped forward to remind them that what they were playing was the blues. He hit something in all of them, he hit something in me, myself, and the music tightened and deepened, apprehension began to beat the air. Creole began to tell us what the blues were all about. They were not about anything very new. He and his boys up there were keeping it new, at the risk of ruin, destruction, madness, and death, in order to find new ways to make us listen. For, while the tale of how we suffer, and how we are delighted, and how we may triumph is never new, it always must be heard. There isn't any other tale to tell, it's the only light we've got in all this darkness.

And this tale, according to that face, that body, those strong hands on those strings, has another aspect in every country, and a new depth in every generation. Listen, Creole seemed to be saying, listen. Now these are Sonny's blues. He made the little black man on the drums know it, and the bright, brown man on the horn. Creole wasn't trying any longer to get Sonny in the water. He was wishing him Godspeed. Then he stepped back, very slowly, filling the air with the immense suggestion that Sonny speak for himself.

Then they all gathered around Sonny and Sonny played. Every now and again one of them seemed to say, Amen. Sonny's fingers filled the air with life, his life. But that life contained so many others. And Sonny went all the way back, he really began with the spare, flat statement of the opening phrase of the song. Then he began to make it his. It was very beautiful because it wasn't hurried and it was no longer a lament. I seemed to hear with what burning he had made it his, with what burning we had yet to make it ours, how we could cease lamenting. Freedom lurked around us and I understood, at last, that he could help us to be free if we would listen, that he would never be free until we did. Yet, there was no battle in his face now. I heard what he had gone through, and would continue to go through until he came to rest in earth. He had made it his: that long line, of which we knew only Mama and Daddy. And he was giving it back, as everything must be given back, so that, passing through death, it can live forever. I saw my mother's face again, and felt, for the first time, how the stones of the road she had walked on must have bruised her feet. I saw the moonlit road where my father's brother died. And it brought something else back to me, and carried me past it, I saw my little girl again and felt Isabel's tears again, and I felt my own tears begin to rise. And I was yet aware that this was only a moment, that the world waited outside, as hungry as a tiger, and that trouble stretched above us, longer than the sky.

Then it was over. Creole and Sonny let out their breath, both soaking wet, and grinning. There was a lot of applause and some of it was real. In the dark, the girl came by and I asked her to take drinks to the bandstand. There was a long pause, while they talked up there in the indigo light and after awhile I saw the girl put a Scotch and milk on top of the piano for Sonny. He didn't seem to notice it, but just before they started playing again, he sipped from it and looked toward me, and nodded. Then he put it back on top of the piano. For me, then, as they began to play again, it glowed and shook above my brother's head like the very cup of trembling.

FLANNERY O'CONNOR
(1925–1964)

Flannery O'Connor is one of the most idiosyncratic and distinctive of American short story writers. Born in Savannah, she lived most of her life on a farm close by Milledgeville, Georgia; she died tragically young, of an inherited disease, lupus. An intensely religious writer, O'Connor took for her subject the provincial Southern world that surrounded her, a world permeated by the "grotesque" (O'Connor's term) that is the consequence of a secular and vulgarized society. Though O'Connor was a Roman Catholic, there is little in her fiction that suggests this faith. Indeed, it is the absence of faith that engages her adamantly unsentimental sympathies.

Flannery O'Connor published two short novels, Wise Blood *(1952) and* The Violent Bear It Away *(1960), but her genius was clearly for the short story. She published two collections of stories during her lifetime—*A Good Man Is Hard To Find *(1955), from which "A Late Encounter with the Enemy" is taken, and* Everything That Rises Must Converge *(1965); her* Complete Stories *(1971) contains these plus others previously uncollected. Her essays were collected in* Mystery and Manners *(1969) and her letters in* The Habit of Being *(1979).*

Flannery O'Connor's stories are widely anthologized, but it is always the same two or three stories that are represented. Her range was narrow, but, within that range, she is capable of subtle distinctions of strategy and tone. This wonderfully comic and unexpectedly moving story, though written early in the author's career, is vintage O'Connor; at the same time its ending, immersed in the hallucinatory consciousness of the dying old "general," gives it a human resonance of a kind missing in O'Connor's flatter and more satirical work.

A Late Encounter with the Enemy

General Sash was a hundred and four years old. He lived with his granddaughter, Sally Poker Sash, who was sixty-two years old and who prayed every night on her knees that he would live until her graduation from college. The General didn't give two slaps for her graduation but he never doubted he would live for it. Living had got to be such a habit with him that he couldn't conceive of any other condition. A graduation exercise was not exactly his idea of a good time, even if, as she said, he would be expected to sit on the stage in his uniform. She said there would be a long procession of teachers and students in their robes but that there wouldn't be anything to equal *him* in his uniform. He knew this well enough without her telling him, and as for the damm procession, it could march to hell and back and not cause him a quiver. He liked parades with floats full of Miss Americas and Miss Daytona Beaches and Miss Queen Cotton Products. He didn't have any use for processions and a procession full of schoolteachers was about as deadly as the River Styx to his way of thinking. However, he was willing to sit on the stage in his uniform so that they could see him.

Sally Poker was not as sure as he was that he would live until her graduation. There had not been any perceptible change in him for the last five years, but she had the sense that she might be cheated out of her triumph because she so often was. She had been going to summer school every year for the past twenty because when she started teaching, there were no such things as degrees. In those times, she said, everything was normal but nothing had been normal since she was sixteen, and for the past twenty summers, when she should have been resting, she had had to take a trunk in the burning heat to the state teacher's college; and though when she returned in the fall, she always taught in the exact way she had been taught not to teach, this was a mild revenge that didn't satisfy her sense of justice. She wanted the General at her graduation because she wanted to show what she stood for, or, as she said, "what all was behind her," and was not behind them. This *them* was not anybody in particular. It was just all the upstarts who had turned the world on its head and unsettled the ways of decent living.

She meant to stand on that platform in August with the General sitting in his wheel chair on the stage behind her and she meant to hold her head very high as if she were saying, "See him! See him! My kin, all you upstarts! Glorious upright old man standing for the old traditions! Dignity! Honor! Courage! See him!" One night in her sleep she screamed, "See him! See him!" and turned her head and found him sitting in his wheel chair behind her with a terrible expression on his face and with all his clothes off except the general's hat and she had waked up and had not dared to go back to sleep again that night.

For his part, the General would not have consented even to attend her graduation if she had not promised to see to it that he sit on the stage. He liked to sit on any stage. He considered that he was still a very handsome man. When he had been able to stand up, he had measured five feet four inches of pure game cock. He had white hair that reached to his shoulders behind and he would not wear teeth because he thought his profile was more striking without them. When he put on his full-dress general's uniform, he knew well enough that there was nothing to match him anywhere.

This was not the same uniform he had worn in the War between the States. He had not actually been a general in that war. He had probably been a foot soldier; he didn't remember what he had been; in fact, he didn't remember that war at all. It was like his feet, which hung down now shriveled at the very end of him, without feeling, covered with a blue-gray afghan that Sally Poker had crocheted when she was a little girl. He didn't remember the Spanish-American War in which he had lost a son; he didn't even remember the son. He didn't have any use for history because he never expected to meet it again. To his mind, history was connected with processions and life with parades and he liked parades. People were always asking him if he remembered this or that—a dreary black procession of questions about the past. There was only one event in the past that had any significance for him and that he cared to talk about; that was twelve years ago when he had received the general's uniform and had been in the premiere.

"I was in that preemy they had in Atlanta," he would tell visitors sitting on his front porch. "Surrounded by beautiful guls. It wasn't a thing local about it. It was nothing local about it. Listen here. It was a nashnul event and they had me in it—up onto the stage. There wa at it. Every person at it had paid ten dollars to get in and had tuxseeder. I was in this uniform. A beautiful gul presented me with it that afternoon in a hotel room."

"It was in a suite in the hotel and I was in it too, Papa," Sally Poker would say, winking at the visitors. "You weren't alone with any young lady in a hotel room."

"Was, I'd a known what to do," the old General would say with a sharp look and the visitors would scream with laughter. "This was a Hollywood, California, gul," he'd continue. "She was from Hollywood, California, and didn't have any part in the pitcher. Out there they have so many beautiful guls that they don't need that they call them a extra and they don't use them for nothing but presenting people with things and having their pitchers taken. They took my pitcher with her. No, it was two of them. One on either side and me in the middle with my arms around each of them's waist and their waist ain't any bigger than a half a dollar."

Sally Poker would interrupt again. "It was Mr. Govisky that gave you the uniform, Papa, and he gave me the most exquisite corsage. Really, I wish you could have seen it. It was made with gladiola petals taken off and painted gold and put back together to look like a rose. It was exquisite. I wish you could have seen it, it was ..."

"It was as big as her head," the General would snarl. "I was tellin it. They gimme this uniform and they gimme this soward and they say, 'Now General, we don't want you to start a war on us. All we want you to do is march right up on that stage when you're innerduced tonight and answer a few questions. Think you can do that?' 'Think I can do it!' I say. 'Listen here. I was doing things before you were born,' and they hollered."

"He was the hit of the show," Sally Poker would say, but she didn't much like to remember the premiere on account of what had happened to her feet at it. She had bought a new dress for the occasion—a long black crepe dinner dress with a rhinestone buckle and a bolero—and a pair of silver slippers to wear with it, because she was supposed to go up on the stage with him to keep him from falling. Everything was arranged for them. A real limousine came at ten minutes to eight and took them to the theater. It drew up under the marquee at exactly the right time, after the big stars and the director and the author and the governor and the mayor and some less important stars. The police kept traffic from jamming and there were ropes to keep the people off who wouldn't go. All the people who couldn't go watched them step out of the limousine into the lights. Then they walked down the red and gold foyer and an usherette in a Confederate cap and little short skirt conducted them to their special seats. The audience was already there and a group of UDC members began to clap when they saw the General in his uniform and that started everybody to clap. A few more celebrities came after them and then the doors closed and the lights went down.

A young man with blond wavy hair who said he represented the motion-picture industry came out and began to introduce everybody and each one who was introduced walked up on the stage and said how really happy he was to be here for this great event. The General and his granddaughter were introduced sixteenth on the program. He was introduced as General Tennessee Flintrock Sash of the Confederacy, though Sally Poker had told Mr. Govisky that his name was George Poker Sash and that he had only been a major. She helped him up from his seat but her heart was beating so fast she didn't know whether she'd make it herself.

The old man walked up the aisle slowly with his fierce white head high and his hat held over his heart. The orchestra began to play the Confederate Battle Hymn very softly and the UDC members rose as a group and did not sit down again until the General was on the stage. When he reached the center of the stage with Sally Poker just behind him guiding his elbow, the orchestra burst out in a loud rendition of the Battle Hymn and the old man, with real stage presence, gave a vigorous trembling salute and stood at attention until the last blast had died away. Two of the usherettes in Confederate caps and short skirts held a Confederate and a Union flag crossed behind them.

The General stood in the exact center of the spotlight and it caught a weird moon-shaped slice of Sally Poker—the corsage, the rhinestone buckle and one hand clenched around a white glove and handkerchief. The young man with the blond wavy hair inserted himself into the circle of light and said he was *really* happy to have here tonight for this great event, one, he said, who had fought and bled in the battles they would soon see daringly re-acted on the screen, and "Tell me, General," he asked, "how old are you?"

"Niiiiiinntty-two!" the General screamed.

The young man looked as if this were just about the most impressive thing that had been said all evening. "Ladies and gentlemen," he said, "let's give the General the biggest hand we've got!" and there was applause immediately and the young man indicated to Sally Poker with a motion of his thumb that she could take the old man back to his seat now so that the next person could be introduced; but the General had not finished. He stood immovable in the exact center of the spotlight, his neck thrust forward, his mouth slightly open, and his voracious gray eyes drinking in the glare and the applause. He elbowed his granddaughter roughly away. "How I keep so young," he screeched, "I kiss all the pretty guls!"

This was met with a great din of spontaneous applause and it was at just that instant that Sally Poker looked down at her feet and discovered that in the excitement of getting ready she had forgotten to change her shoes: two brown Girl Scout oxfords protruded from the bottom of her dress. She gave the General a yank and almost ran with him off the stage. He was very angry that he had not got to say how glad he was to be here for this event and on the way back to his seat, he kept saying as loud as he could, "I'm glad to be here at this preemy with all these beautiful guls!" but there was another celebrity going up the other aisle and nobody paid any attention to him. He slept through the picture, muttering fiercely every now and then in his sleep.

Since then, his life had not been very interesting. His feet were completely dead now, his knees worked like old hinges, his kidneys functioned when they would, but his heart persisted doggedly to beat. The past and the future were the same thing to him, one forgotten and the other not remembered; he had no more notion of dying than a cat. Every year on Confederate Memorial Day, he was bundled up and lent to the Capitol City Museum where he was displayed from one to four in a musty room full of old photographs, old uniforms, old artillery, and historic documents. All these were carefully preserved in glass cases so that children would not put their hands on them. He wore his general's uniform from the premiere and sat, with a fixed scowl, inside a small roped area. There was nothing about him to indicate that he was alive except an occasional movement in his milky gray eyes, but once when a bold child touched his sword, his arm shot forward and slapped the hand off in an instant. In the spring when the old homes were opened for pilgrimages, he was invited to wear his uniform and sit in some conspicuous spot and lend atmosphere to the scene. Some of these times he only snarled at the visitors but sometimes he told about the premiere and the beautiful girls.

If he had died before Sally Poker's graduation, she thought she would have died herself. At the beginning of the summer term, even before she knew if she would pass, she told the Dean that her grandfather, General Tennessee Flintrock Sash of the Confederacy, would attend her graduation and that he was a hundred and four years old and that his mind was still clear as a bell. Distinguished visitors were always welcome and could sit on the stage and be introduced. She made arrangements with her nephew, John Wesley Poker Sash, a Boy Scout, to come wheel the General's chair. She thought how sweet it would be to see the old man in his courageous gray and the young boy in his clean khaki—the old and the new, she thought appropriately—they would be behind her on the stage when she received her degree.

Everything went almost exactly as she had planned. In the summer while she was away at school, the General stayed with other relatives and they brought him and John Wesley, the Boy Scout, down to the graduation. A reporter came to the hotel where they stayed and took the General's picture with Sally Poker on one side of him and John Wesley on the other. The General, who had had his picture taken with beautiful girls, didn't think much of this. He had forgotten precisely what kind of event this was he was going to attend but he remembered that he was to wear his uniform and carry the sword.

On the morning of the graduation, Sally Poker had to line up in the academic procession with the B.S.'s in Elementary Education and she couldn't see to getting him on the stage herself—but John Wesley, a fat blond boy of ten with an executive expression, guaranteed to take care of everything. She came in her academic gown to the hotel and dressed the old man in his uniform. He was as frail as a dried spider. "Aren't you just thrilled, Papa?" she asked. "I'm just thrilled to death!"

"Put the soward acrost my lap, damm you," the old man said, "where it'll shine."

She put it there and then stood back looking at him. "You look just grand," she said.

"God damm it," the old man said in a slow monotonous certain tone as if he were saying it to the beating of his heart. "God damm every goddam thing to hell."

"Now, now," she said and left happily to join the procession.

The graduates were lined up behind the Science building and she found her place just as the line started to move. She had not slept much the night before and when she had, she had dreamed of the exercises, murmuring, "See him, see him?" in her sleep but waking up every time just before she turned her head to look at him behind her. The graduates had to walk three blocks in the hot sun in their black wool robes and as she plodded stolidly along she thought that if anyone considered this academic procession something impressive to behold, they need only wait until they saw that old General in his courageous gray and that clean young Boy Scout stoutly wheeling his chair across the stage with the sunlight catching the sword. She imagined that John Wesley had the old man ready now behind the stage.

The black procession wound its way up the two blocks and started on the main walk leading to the auditorium. The visitors stood on the grass, picking out their graduates. Men were pushing back their hats and wiping their foreheads and women were lifting their dresses slightly from the shoulders to keep them from sticking to their backs. The graduates in their heavy robes looked as if the last beads of ignorance were being sweated out of them. The sun blazed off the fenders of automobiles and beat from the columns of the buildings and pulled the eye from one spot of glare to another. It pulled Sally Poker's toward the big red Coca-Cola machine that had been set up by the side of the auditorium. Here she saw the General parked, scowling and hatless in his chair in the blazing sun while John Wesley, his blouse loose behind, his hip and cheek pressed to the red machine, was drinking a Coca-Cola. She broke from the line and galloped to them and snatched the bottle away. She shook the boy and thrust in his blouse and put the hat on the old man's head. "Now get him in there!" she said, pointing one rigid finger to the side door of the building.

For his part the General felt as if there were a little hole beginning to widen in the top of his head. The boy wheeled him rapidly down a walk and up a ramp and into a building and bumped him over the stage entrance and into position where he had been told and the General glared in front of him at heads that all seemed to flow together and eyes that moved from one face to another. Several figures in black robes came and picked up his hand and shook it. A black procession was flowing up each aisle and forming to stately music in a pool in front of him. The music seemed to be entering his head through the little hole and he thought for a second that the procession would try to enter it too.

He didn't know what procession this was but there was something familiar about it. It must be familiar to him since it had come to meet him, but he didn't like a black procession. Any procession that came to meet him, he thought irritably, ought to have floats with beautiful guls on them like the floats before the preemy. It must be something connected with history like they were always having. He had no use for any of it. What happened then wasn't anything to a man living now and he was living now.

When all the procession had flowed into the black pool, a black figure began orating in front of it. The figure was telling something about history and the General made up his mind he wouldn't listen, but the words kept seeping in through the little hole in his head. He heard his own name mentioned and his chair was shuttled forward roughly and the Boy Scout took a big bow. They called his name and the fat brat bowed. Goddam you, the old man tried to say, get out of my way, I can stand up!—but he was jerked back again before he could get up and take the bow. He supposed the noise they made was for him. If he was over, he didn't intend to listen to any more of it. If it hadn't been for the little hole in the top of his head, none of the words would have got to him. He thought of putting his finger up there into the hole to block them but the hole was a little wider than his finger and it felt as if it were getting deeper.

Another black robe had taken the place of the first one and was talking now and he heard his name mentioned again but they were not talking about him, they were still talking about history. "If we forget our past," the speaker was saying, "we won't remember our future and it will be as well for we won't have one." The General heard some of these words gradually. He had forgotten history and he didn't intend to remember it again. He had forgotten the name and face of his wife and the names and faces of his children or even if he had a wife and children, and he had forgotten the names of places and the places themselves and what had happened at them.

He was considerably irked by the hole in his head. He had not expected to have a hole in his head at this event. It was the slow black music that had put it there and though most of the music had stopped outside, there was still a little of it in the hole, going deeper and moving around in his thoughts, letting the words he heard into the dark places of his brain. He heard the words, Chickamauga, Shiloh, Johnston, Lee, and he knew he was inspiring all these words that meant nothing to him. He wondered if he had been a general at Chickamauga or at Lee. Then he tried to see himself and the horse mounted in the middle of a float full of beautiful girls, being driven slowly through downtown Atlanta. Instead, the old words began to stir in his head as if they were trying to wrench themselves out of place and come to life.

The speaker was through with that war and had gone on to the next one and now he was approaching another and all his words, like the black procession, were vaguely familiar and irritating. There was a long finger of music in the General's head, probing various spots that were words, letting in a little light on the words and helping them to live. The words began to come toward him and he said, Dammit! I ain't going to have it! and he started edging backwards to get out of the way. Then he saw the figure in the black robe sit down and there was a noise and the black pool in front of him began to rumble and to flow toward him from either side to the black slow music, and he said, Stop dammit! I can't do but one thing at a time! He couldn't protect himself from the words and attend to the procession too and the words were coming at him fast. He felt that he was running backwards and the words were coming at him like musket fire, just escaping him but getting nearer and nearer. He turned around and began to run as fast as he could but he found himself running toward the words. He was running into a regular volley of them and meeting them with quick curses. As the music swelled toward him, the entire past opened up on him out of nowhere and he felt his body riddled in a hundred places with sharp stabs of pain and he fell down, returning a curse for every hit. He saw his wife's narrow face looking at him critically through her round gold-rimmed glasses; he saw one of his squinting bald-headed sons; and his mother ran toward him with an anxious look; then a succession of places—Chickamauga, Shiloh, Marthasville—rushed at him as if the past were the only future now and he had to endure it. Then suddenly he saw that the black procession was almost on him. He recognized it, for it had been dogging all his days. He made such a desperate effort to see over it and find out what comes after the past that his hand clenched the sword until the blade touched bone.

The graduates were crossing the stage in a long file to receive their scrolls and shake the president's hand. As Sally Poker, who was near the end, crossed, she glanced at the General and saw him sitting fixed and fierce, his eyes wide open, and she turned her head forward again and held it a perceptible degree higher and received her scroll. Once it was all over and she was out of the auditorium in the sun again, she located her kin and they waited together on a bench in the shade for John Wesley to wheel the old man out. That crafty scout had bumped him out the back way and rolled him at high speed down a flagstone path and was waiting now, with the corpse, in the long line at the Coca-Cola machine.

CYNTHIA OZICK
(b. 1928)

Born, raised, and educated in New York City, Cynthia Ozick has been a longtime resident of New Rochelle, New York. Though most widely known for her short stories (among which "The Shawl" is the most celebrated), she is also the author of essays, poetry, criticism, translations, and novels. Her visionary conviction that the "Hebrew contribution to civilization" is the effort of bearing witness to the Holocaust, thereby making it a part of the human experience, lies at the center of her work in all its diversity.

Cynthia Ozick, by her own testimony, matured relatively late as a writer, after approximately twenty years of writing without significant publication. During these years, however, as the obsessive brilliance of her prose makes clear, she was acquiring an abundance of information and honing her literary skills. Hers is an art that, though cast in prose, employs the strategies of poetry.

Cynthia Ozick is the author of the novels Trust *(1966),* The Cannibal Galaxy *(1983),* The Messiah of Stockholm *(1987),* Heir to the Glimmering World *(2004), and* Foreign Bodies *(2010); the story collections* The Pagan Rabbi *(1971),* Bloodshed *(1976),* Levitation *(1982),* The Shawl *(1989),* Collected Stories *(2007), and* Dictation: A Quartet *(2008). Her collections of essays include* Art & Ardor *(1983),* Metaphor & Memory *(1989),* Quarrel & Quandry *(2000), and* The Din in the Head *(2006). Among her numerous awards are the Rea Award for the Short Story, the National Book Critics Circle Award, the PEN/Malamud Award for the Short Story, and the PEN/Nabokov Award for Lifetime Achievement.*

The Shawl *consists of the title story, included here, and a novella in which the story's heroine, Rosa Lubin, is imagined as a Holocaust survivor living, many years later, in seclusion and near-squalor in Florida.*

The Shawl

Stella, cold, cold, the coldness of hell. How they walked on the roads together, Rosa with Magda curled up between sore breasts, Magda wound up in the shawl. Sometimes Stella carried Magda. But she was jealous of Magda. A thin girl of fourteen, too small, with thin breasts of her own, Stella wanted to be wrapped in a shawl, hidden away, asleep, rocked by the march, a baby, a round infant in arms. Magda took Rosa's nipple, and Rosa never stopped walking, a walking cradle. There was not enough milk; sometimes Magda sucked air; then she screamed. Stella was ravenous. Her knees were tumors on sticks, her elbows chicken bones.

Rosa did not feel hunger; she felt light, not like someone walking but like someone in a faint, in trance, arrested in a fit, someone who is already a floating angel, alert and seeing everything, but in the air, not there, not touching the road. As if teetering on the tips of her fingernails. She looked into Magda's face through a gap in the shawl: a squirrel in a nest, safe, no one could reach her inside the little house of the shawl's windings. The face, very round, a pocket mirror of a face; but it was not Rosa's bleak complexion, dark like cholera, it was another kind of face altogether, eyes blue as air, smooth feathers of hair nearly as yellow as the Star sewn into Rosa's coat. You could think she was one of *their* babies.

Rosa, floating, dreamed of giving Magda away in one of the villages. She could leave the line for a minute and push Magda into the hands of any woman on the side of the road. But if she moved out of line they might shoot. And even if she fled the line for half a second and pushed the shawl-bundle at a stranger, would the woman take it? She might be surprised, or afraid; she might drop the shawl, and Magda would fall out and strike her head and die. The little round head. Such a good child, she gave up screaming, and sucked now only for the taste of the drying nipple itself. The neat grip of the tiny gums. One mite of a tooth tip sticking up in the bottom gum, how shining, an elfin tombstone of white marble, gleaming there. Without complaining, Magda relinquished Rosa's teats, first the left, then the right; both were cracked, not a sniff of milk. The duct crevice extinct, a dead volcano, blind eye, chill hole, so Magda took the corner of the shawl and milked it instead. She sucked and sucked, flooding the threads with wetness. The shawl's good flavor, milk of linen.

It was a magic shawl, it could nourish an infant for three days and three nights. Magda lifted out of her mouth. She held her eyes open every moment, forgetting how to blink or nap, and Rosa and sometimes Stella studied their blueness. On the road they raised one burden of a leg after another and studied Magda's face. "Aryan," Stella said, in a voice grown as thin as a string; and Rosa thought how Stella gazed at Magda like a young cannibal. And the time that Stella said "Aryan," it sounded to Rosa as if Stella had really said "Let us devour her."

But Magda lived to walk. She lived that long, but she did not walk very well, partly because she was only fifteen months old, and partly because the spindles of her legs could not hold up her fat belly. It was fat with air, full and round. Rosa gave almost all her food to Magda. Stella gave nothing; Stella was ravenous, a growing child herself, but not growing much. Stella did not menstruate. Rosa did not menstruate. Rosa was ravenous, but also not; she learned from Magda how to drink the taste of a finger in one's mouth. They were in a place without pity, all pity was annihilated in Rosa, she looked at Stella's bones without pity. She was sure that Stella was waiting for Magda to die so she could put her teeth into the little thighs.

Rosa knew Magda was going to die very soon; she should have been dead already, but she had been buried away deep inside the magic shawl, mistaken there for the shivering mound of Rosa's breasts; Rosa clung to the shawl as if it covered only herself. No one took it away from her. Magda was mute. She never cried. Rosa hid her in the barracks, under the shawl, but she knew that one day someone would inform; or one day someone, not even Stella, would steal Magda to eat her. When Magda began to walk Rosa knew that Magda was going to die very soon, something would happen. She was afraid to fall asleep; she slept with the weight of her thigh on Magda's body; she was afraid she would smother Magda under her thigh. The weight of Rosa was becoming less and less; Rosa and Stella were slowly turning into air.

Magda was quiet, but her eyes were horribly alive, like blue tigers. She watched. Sometimes she laughed—it seemed a laugh, but how could it be? Magda had never seen anyone laugh. Still, Magda laughed at her shawl when the wind blew its corners, the bad wind with pieces of black in it, that made Stella's and Rosa's eyes tear. Magda's eyes were always clear and tearless. She watched like a tiger. She guarded her shawl. No one could touch it; only Rosa could touch it. Stella was not allowed. The shawl was Magda's own baby, her pet, her little sister. She tangled herself up in it and sucked on one of the corners when she wanted to be very still.

Then Stella took the shawl away and made Magda die.

Afterward Stella said: "I was cold."

And afterward she was always cold, always. The cold went into her heart: Rosa saw that Stella's heart was cold. Magda flopped onward with her little pencil legs scribbling this way and that, in search of the shawl; the pencils faltered at the barracks opening, where the light began. Rosa saw and pursued. But already Magda was in the square outside the barracks, in the jolly light. It was the roll-call arena. Every morning Rosa had to conceal Magda under the shawl against a wall of the barracks and go out and stand in the arena with Stella and hundreds of others, sometimes for hours, and Magda, deserted, was quiet under the shawl, sucking on her corner. Every day Magda was silent, and so she did not die. Rosa saw that today Magda was going to die, and at the same time a fearful joy ran in Rosa's two palms, her fingers were on fire, she was astonished, febrile: Magda, in the sunlight, swaying on her pencil legs, was howling. Ever since the drying up of Rosa's nipples, ever since Magda's last scream on the road, Magda had been devoid of any syllable; Magda was a mute. Rosa believed that something had gone wrong with her vocal cords, with her windpipe, with the cave of her larynx; Magda was defective, without a voice; perhaps she was deaf; there might be something amiss with her intelligence; Magda was dumb. Even the laugh that came when the ash-stippled wind made a clown out of Magda's shawl was only the air-blown showing of her teeth. Even when the lice, head lice and body lice, crazed her so that she became as wild as one of the big rats that plundered the barracks at daybreak looking for carrion, she rubbed and scratched and kicked and bit and rolled without a whimper. But now Magda's mouth was spilling a long viscous rope of clamor.

"Maaaa—"

It was the first noise Magda had ever sent out from her throat since the drying up of Rosa's nipples.

"Maaaa...aaa!"

Again! Magda was wavering in the perilous sunlight of the arena, scribbling on such pitiful little bent shins. Rosa saw. She saw that Magda was grieving for the loss of her shawl, she saw that Magda was going to die. A tide of commands hammered in Rosas nipples: Fetch, get, bring! But she did not know which to go after first, Magda or the shawl. If she jumped out into the arena to snatch Magda up, the howling would not stop, because Magda would still not have the shawl; but if she ran back into the barracks to find the shawl, and if she found it, and if she came after Magda holding it and shaking it, then she would get Magda back, Magda would put the shawl in her mouth and turn dumb again.

Rosa entered the dark. It was easy to discover the shawl. Stella was heaped under it, asleep in her thin bones. Rosa tore the shawl free and flew—she could fly, she was only air—into the arena. The sunheat murmured of another life, of butterflies in summer. The light was placid, mellow. On the other side of the steel fence, far away, there were green meadows speckled with dandelions and deep-colored violets; beyond them, even farther, innocent tiger lilies, tall, lifting their orange bonnets. In the barracks they spoke of "flowers," of "rain": excrement, thick turd-braids, and the slow stinking maroon waterfall that slunk down from the upper bunks, the stink mixed with a bitter fatty floating smoke that greased Rosa's skin. She stood for an instant at the margin of the arena. Sometimes the electricity inside the fence would seem to hum; even Stella said it was only an imagining, but Rosa heard real sounds in the wire: grainy sad voices. The farther she was from the fence, the more clearly the voices crowded at her. The lamenting voices strummed so convincingly, so passionately, it was impossible to suspect them of being phantoms. The voices told her to hold up the shawl, high; the voices told her to shake it, to whip with it, to unfurl it like a flag. Rosa lifted, shook, whipped, unfurled. Far off, very far, Magda leaned across her air-fed belly, reaching out with the rods of her arms. She was high up, elevated, riding someone's shoulder. But the shoulder that carried Magda was not coming toward Rosa and the shawl, it was drifting away, the speck of Magda was moving more and more into the smoky distance. Above the shoulder a helmet glinted. The light tapped the helmet and sparkled it into a goblet. Below the helmet a black body like a domino and a pair of black boots hurled themselves in the direction of the electrified fence. The electric voices began to chatter wildly. "Maamaa, maaamaaa," they all hummed together. How far Magda was from Rosa now, across the whole square, past a dozen barracks, all the way on the other side! She was no bigger than a moth.

All at once Magda was swimming through the air. The whole of Magda traveled through loftiness. She looked like a butterfly touching a silver vine. And the moment Magda's feathered round head and her pencil legs and balloonish belly and zigzag arms splashed against the fence, the steel voices went mad in their growling, urging Rosa to run and run to the spot where Magda had fallen from her flight against the electrified fence; but of course Rosa did not obey them. She only stood, because if she ran they would shoot, and if she tried to pick up the sticks of Magda's body they would shoot, and if she let the wolf's screech ascending now through the ladder of her skeleton break out, they would shoot; so she took Magda's shawl and filled her own mouth with it, stuffed it in and stuffed it in, until she was swallowing up the wolfs screech and tasting the cinnamon and almond depth of Magda's saliva; and Rosa drank Magda's shawl until it dried.

DONALD BARTHELME
(1931–1989)

"Fragments are the only forms I trust," Donald Barthelme once said. Yet his brilliantly innovative short fictions have the unity of effect of completely imagined prose-poems; their curve is typically the logic of dreams, selecting only the most significant of images and dropping out all else. Like the Surrealists Max Ernst, Marcel Duchamp, Man Ray, and René Magritte, who exercised a powerful influence upon his work, Barthelme's art is frequently the art of startling juxtapositions and collage. "The School" is atypical Barthelme, risking sentiment, sweetness, sincerity, unmediated yearning.

Donald Barthelme was born in Philadelphia and raised and educated in Houston, where his father worked as an architect. A graduate of the University of Houston, Barthelme worked as a newspaper reporter and museum director, helped edit a journal of art and literature called Location, *and began to publish short fiction in* The New Yorker *in the early 1960s. His major titles are* Come Back, Dr. Caligari *(1964),* Unspeakable Practices, Unnatural Acts *(1968),* City Life *(1970),* Guilty Pleasures *(1974), and* Sixty Stories *(1981)—short story collections; and* Snow White *(1967) and* The Dead Father *(1975)—novels. The posthumous novel* The King *was published in 1990.*

The School

Well, we had all these children out planting trees, see, because we figured that...that was part of their education, to see how you know the root systems...and also the sense of responsibility, taking care of things, being individually responsible. You know what I mean. And the trees all died. They were orange trees. I don't know why they died, they just died. Something wrong with the soil possibly or maybe the stuff we got from the nursery wasn't the best. We complained about it. So we've got thirty kids there, each kid had his or her own little tree to plant, and we've got these thirty dead trees. All these kids looking at these little brown sticks. It was depressing.

It wouldn't have been so bad except that just a couple of weeks before the thing with the trees, the snakes all died. But I think that the snakes—well, the reason that the snakes kicked off was that...you remember, the boiler was shut off for four days because of the strike, and that was explicable. It was something you could explain to the kids because of the strike. I mean, none of their parents would let them cross the picket line and they knew there was a strike going on and what it meant. So when things got started up again and we found the snakes they weren't too disturbed.

With the herb gardens it was probably a case of overwatering, and at least now they know not to overwater. The children were very conscientious with the herb gardens and some of them probably...you know, slipped them a little extra water when we weren't looking. Or maybe... well, I don't like to think about sabotage, although it did occur to us. I mean, it was something that crossed our minds. We were thinking that way probably because before that the gerbils had died, and the white mice had died, and the salamander...well, now they know not to carry them around in plastic bags.

Of course we *expected* the tropical fish to die, that was no surprise. Those numbers, you look at them crooked and they're belly-up on the surface. But the lesson plan called for a tropical-fish input at that point, there was nothing we could do, it happens every year, you just have to hurry past it.

We weren't even supposed to have a puppy.

We weren't even supposed to have one, it was just a puppy the Murdoch girl found under a Gristede's truck one day and she was afraid the truck would run over it when the driver had finished making his delivery, so she stuck it in her knapsack and brought it to school with her. So we had this puppy. As soon as I saw the puppy I thought, Oh Christ, I bet it will live for about two weeks and then...And that's what it did. It wasn't supposed to be in the classroom at all, there's some kind of regulation about it, but you can't tell them they can't have a puppy when the puppy is already there, right in front of them, running around on the floor and yap yap yapping. They named it Edgar—that is, they named it after me. They had a lot of fun running after it and yelling "Here, Edgar! Nice Edgar!" Then they'd laugh like hell. They enjoyed the ambiguity. I enjoyed it myself. I don't mind being kidded. They made a little house for it in the supply closet and all that. I don't know what it died of. Distemper, I guess. It probably hadn't had any shots. I got it out of there before the kids got to school. I checked the supply closet each morning, routinely because I knew what was going to happen. I gave it to the custodian.

And then there was this Korean orphan that the class adopted through the Help the Children program, all the kids brought in a quarter a month, that was the idea. It was an unfortunate thing, the kid's name was Kim and maybe we adopted him too late or something. The cause of death was not stated in the letter we got, they suggested we adopt another child instead and sent us some interesting case histories, but we didn't have the heart. The class took it pretty hard, they began (I think, nobody ever said anything to me directly) to feel that maybe there was something wrong with the school. But I don't think there's anything wrong with the school, particularly, I've seen better and I've seen worse. It was just a run of bad luck. We had an extraordinary number of parents passing away, for instance. There were I think two heart attacks and two suicides, one drowning, and four killed together in a car accident. One stroke. And we had the usual heavy mortality rate among the grandparents, or maybe it was heavier this year, it seemed so. And finally the tragedy.

The tragedy occurred when Matthew Wein and Tony Mavrogordo were playing over where they're excavating for the new federal office building. There were all these big wooden beams stacked, you know, at the edge of the excavation. There's a court case coming out of that, the parents arc claiming that the beams were poorly stacked. I don't know what's true and what's not. It's been a strange year.

I forgot to mention Billy Brandt's father, who was knifed fatally when he grappled with a masked intruder in his home.

One day, we had a discussion in class. They asked me, where did they go? The trees, the salamander, the tropical fish, Edgar, the poppas and mommas, Matthew and Tony, where did they go? And I said, I don't know, I don't know. And they said, who knows? and I said, nobody knows. And they said, is death that which gives meaning to life? And I said, no, life is that which gives meaning to life. Then they said, but isn't death, considered such a fundamental datum, the means by which the taken-for-granted mundanity of the everyday may be transcended in the direction of—

I said, yes, maybe.

They said, we don't like it.

I said, that's sound.

They said, it's a bloody shame!

I said, it is.

They said, will you make love now with Helen (our teaching assistant) so that we can see how it is done? We know you like Helen.

I do like Helen but I said that I would not.

We've heard so much about it, they said, but we've never seen it.

I said I would be fired and that it was never, or almost never, done as a demonstration. Helen looked out of the window.

They said, please, please make love with Helen, we require an assertion of value, we are frightened.

I said that they shouldn't be frightened (although I am often frightened) and that there was value everywhere. Helen came and embraced me. I kissed her a few times on the brow. We held each other. The children were excited. Then there was a knock on the door. I opened the door, and the new gerbil walked in. The children cheered wildly.

JOHN UPDIKE
(1932–2009)

*Though celebrated as the creator of "Rabbit" Angstrom, the hero of the Rabbit quartet (*Rabbit, Run, *1961;* Rabbit Redux, *1971;* Rabbit is Rich, *1981;* Rabbit at Rest, *1990), John Updike is equally admired as one of the finest practitioners of the short story in American literary history. His is an art of vigilance informed by compassion and humor; an art of both dissection and assimilation. This early story, with its oddly Magritte-like title, gives us a young hero already meditating upon mortality, even as he finds himself quickened to a renewal of an old, seemingly lost romance.*

One of our most prodigious and widely acclaimed writers, John Updike was born in Reading, Pennsylvania, and grew up in nearby Shillington. Scarcely out of Harvard, he began publishing stories in the New Yorker *in the mid-1950s.*

Among his titles are the story collections The Same Door *(1959),* Pigeon Feathers *(1962),* The Music School *(1966),* Museums and Women *(1972),* Problems *(1979),* Trust Me *(1987),* The Afterlife and Other Stories *(1994), and the posthumously published* My Father's Tears and Other Stories *(2009); the novels* The Centaur *(1963),* Couples *(1968),* The Coup *(1978),* Roger's Version *(1986),* In the Beauty of the Lilies *(1996),* Toward the End of Time *(1997) and* Terrorist *(2006), in addition to the above named; the poetry collections* Midpoint *(1969),* Facing Nature *(1985), and the posthumously published* Endpoint and Other Poems *(2009); the essay collections* Hugging the Shore *(1983) and* Odd Jobs *(1991); and the memoir* Self-Consciousness *(1989).*

The perfectly realized "The Persistence of Desire" is quintessential Updike; a moment's epiphany firmly grounded in a life, a recognizable world. Here is the very poetry of realism. John Updike is that rarity in our time—the writer's writer who has also achieved popular success.

The Persistence of Desire

Pennypacker's office still smelled of linoleum, a clean, sad scent that seemed to lift from the checkerboard floor in squares of alternating intensity; this pattern had given Clyde as a boy a funny nervous feeling of intersection, and now he stood crisscrossed by a double sense of himself, his present identity extending down from Massachusetts to meet his disconsolate youth in Pennsylvania, projected upward from a distance of years. The enlarged, tinted photograph of a lake in the Canadian wilderness still covered one whole wall, and the walnut-stained chairs and benches continued their vague impersonation of the Shaker manner. The one new thing, set squarely on an orange end table, was a compact black clock constructed like a speedometer; it showed in Arabic numerals the present minute—1:28—and coiled invisibly in its works the two infinites of past and future. Clyde was early; the waiting room was empty. He sat down on a chair opposite the clock. Already it was 1:29, and while he watched, the digits slipped again; another drop into the brimming void. He glanced around for the comfort of a clock with a face and gracious, gradual hands. A stopped grandfather matched the other imitation antiques. He opened a magazine and immediately read, "Science reveals that the cells of the normal human body are replaced *in toto* every seven years."

The top half of a Dutch door at the other end of the room opened, and, framed in the square, Pennypacker's secretary turned the bright disc of her face toward him. "Mr. Behn?" she asked in a chiming voice. "Dr. Pennypacker will be back from lunch in a minute." She vanished backward into the maze of little rooms where Pennypacker, an eye, ear, nose, and throat man, had arranged his fabulous equipment. Through the bay window Clyde could see traffic, gayer in color than he remembered, hustle down Grand Avenue. On the sidewalk, haltered girls identical in all but name with girls he had known strolled past in twos and threes. Small town perennials, they moved rather mournfully under their burdens of bloom. In the opposite direction packs of the opposite sex carried baseball mitts.

Clyde became so lonely watching his old street that when, with a sucking exclamation, the door from the vestibule opened, he looked up gratefully, certain that the person, this being his home town, would be a friend. When he saw who it was, though every cell in his body had been replaced since he had last seen her, his hands jerked in his lap and blood bounded against his skin.

"Clyde Behn," she pronounced, with a matronly and patronizing yet frightened finality, as if he were a child and these words the moral of a story.

"Janet." He awkwardly rose from his chair and crouched, not so much in courtesy as to relieve the pressure on his heart.

"Whatever brings you back to these parts?" She was taking the pose that she was just anyone who once knew him.

He slumped back. "I'm always coming back. It's just you've never been here."

"Well, I've"—she seated herself on an orange bench and crossed her plump legs cockily—"been in Germany with my husband."

"He was in the Air Force."

"Yes." It startled her a little that he knew.

"And he's out now?" Clyde had never met him, but having now seen Janet again, he felt he knew him well—a slight, literal fellow, to judge from the shallowness of the marks he had left on her. He would wear eyebrow-style glasses, be a griper, have some not quite negotiable talent, like playing the clarinet or drawing political cartoons, and now be starting up a drab avenue of business. Selling insurance, most likely. Poor Janet, Clyde felt; except for the interval of himself—his splendid, perishable self—she would never see the light. Yet she had retained her beautiful calm, a sleepless tranquility marked by that pretty little blue puffiness below the eyes. And either she had grown slimmer or he had grown more tolerant of fat. Her thick ankles and the general *obstinacy* of her flesh used to goad him into being cruel.

"Yes." Her voice indicated that she had withdrawn; perhaps some ugliness of their last parting had recurred to her.

"I was 4-F." He was ashamed of this, and his confessing it, though she seemed unaware of the change, turned their talk inward. "A peacetime slacker," he went on, "what could be more ignoble?"

She was quiet a while, then asked, "How many children do you have?"

"Two. Age three and one. A girl and a boy; very symmetrical. Do you"—he blushed lightly, and brushed at his forehead to hide it—"have any?"

"No, we thought it wouldn't be fair, until we were more fixed."

Now the quiet moment was his to hold; she had matched him failing for failing. She recrossed her legs, and in a quaint strained way smiled.

"I'm trying to remember," he admitted, "the last time we saw each other. I can't remember how we broke up."

"I can't either," she said. "It happened so often."

Clyde wondered if with that sarcasm she intended to fetch his eyes to the brink of tears of grief. Probably not; premeditation had never been much of a weapon for her, though she had tried to learn it from him.

He moved across the linoleum to sit on the bench beside her. "I can't tell you," he said, "how much, of all the people in this town, you were the one I wanted to see." It was foolish, but he had prepared it to say, in case he ever saw her again.

"Why?" This was more like her: blunt, pucker-lipped curiosity. He had forgotten it.

"Well, hell. Any number of reasons. I wanted to say something."

"What?"

"Well, that if I hurt you, it was stupidity, because I was young. I've often wondered since if I did, because it seems now that you were the only person outside my family who ever, actually, *liked* me."

"Did I?"

"If you think by doing nothing but asking monosyllabic questions you're making an effect, you're wrong."

She averted her face, leaving, in a sense, only her body—the pale, columnar breadth of arm, the freckled crescent of shoulder muscle under the cotton strap of her summer dress—with him. "You're the one who's making effects." It was such a wan, senseless thing to say to defend herself; Clyde, virtually paralyzed by so heavy an injection of love, touched her arm icily.

With a quickness that suggested she had foreseen this, she got up and went to the table by the bay window, where rows of overlapping magazines were laid. She bowed her head to their titles, the nape of her neck in shadow beneath a half-collapsed bun. She had always had trouble keeping her hair pinned.

Clyde was blushing intensely. "Is your husband working around here?"

"He's looking for work." That she kept her back turned while saying this gave him hope.

"Mr. Behn?" The petite secretary-nurse, switching like a pendulum, led him back through the sanctums and motioned for him to sit in a high hinged chair padded with black leather. Pennypacker's equipment had always made him nervous; tons of it were marshalled through the rooms. A complex tree of tubes and lenses leaned over his left shoulder, and by his right elbow a porcelain basin was cupped expectantly. An eye chart crisply stated gibberish. In time Pennypacker himself appeared: a tall, stooped man with mottled cheekbones and an air of suppressed anger.

"Now what's the trouble, Clyde?"

"It's nothing: I mean it's very little," Clyde began, laughing inappropriately. During his adolescence he had developed a joking familiarity with his dentist and his regular doctor, but he had never become intimate with Pennypacker, who remained, what he had seemed at first, an aloof administrator of expensive humiliations. In the third grade he had made Clyde wear glasses. Later, he annually cleaned, with a shrill push of hot water, wax from Clyde's ears, and once had thrust two copper straws up Clyde's nostrils in a futile attempt to purge his sinuses. Clyde always felt unworthy of Pennypacker, felt himself a dirty conduit balking the smooth onward flow of the doctor's reputation and apparatus. He blushed to mention his latest trivial stoppage. "It's just that for over two months I've had this eyelid that twitters and it makes it difficult to think."

Pennypacker drew little circles with a pencil-sized flashlight in front of Clyde's right eye.

"It's the left lid," Clyde said, without daring to turn his head. "I went to a doctor up where I live, and he said it was like a rattle in the fender and there was nothing to do. He said it would go away, but it didn't and didn't, so I had my mother make an appointment for when I came down here to visit."

Pennypacker moved to the left eye and drew even closer. The distance between the doctor's eyes and the corners of his mouth was very long; the emotional impression of his face close up was like that of those first photographs taken from rockets, in which the earth's curvature was made apparent. "How do you like being in your home territory?" Pennypacker asked.

"Fine."

"Seem a little strange to you?"

The question itself seemed strange. "A little."

"Mm. That's interesting."

"About the eye, there were two things I thought. One was, I got some glasses made in Massachusetts by a man nobody else ever went to, and I thought his prescription might be faulty. His equipment seemed so ancient and kind of full of cobwebs; like a Dürer print." He never could decide how cultured Pennypacker was; the Canadian lake argued against it, but he was county-famous in his trade, in a county where doctors were as high as the intellectual scale went.

The flashlight, a tepid sun girdled by a grid of optical circles behind which Pennypacker's face loomed dim and colorless, came right to the skin of Clyde's eye, and the vague face lurched forward angrily, and Clyde, blind in a world of light, feared that Pennypacker was inspecting the floor of his soul. Paralyzed by panic, he breathed, "The other was that something might be in it. At night it feels as if there's a tiny speck deep in under the lid."

Pennypacker reared back and insolently raked the light back and forth across Clyde's face. "How long have you had this flaky stuff on your lids?"

The insult startled Clyde. "Is there any?"

"How long have you had it?"

"Some mornings I notice little grains like salt that I thought were what I used to call sleepy-dust—"

"This isn't sleepy-dust," the doctor said. He repeated, "This isn't sleepy-dust." Clyde started to smile at what he took to be kidding of his childish vocabulary, but Pennypacker cut him short with "Cases of this can lead to loss of the eyelashes."

"Really?" Clyde was vain of his lashes, which in his boyhood had been exceptionally long, giving his face the alert and tender look of a girl's. "Do you think it's the reason for the tic?" He imagined his face with the lids bald and the lashes lying scattered on his cheeks like insect legs. "What can I do?"

"Are you using your eyes a great deal?"

"Some. No more than I ever did."

Pennypacker's hands, blue after Clyde's dazzlement, lifted an intense brown bottle from a drawer. "It may be bacteria, it may be allergy; when you leave I'll give you something that should knock it out either way. Do you follow me? Now, Clyde"—his voice became murmurous and consolatory as he placed a cupped hand, rigid as an electrode, on the top of Clyde's head—"I'm going to put some drops in your eyes so we can check the prescription of the glasses you bought in Massachusetts."

Clyde didn't remember that the drops stung so; he gasped outright and wept while Pennypacker held the lids apart with his finger and worked them gently open and shut, as if he were playing with snapdragons. Pennypacker set preposterously small, circular dark brown glasses on Clyde's face and in exchange took away the stylish horn-rims Clyde had kept in his pocket. It was Pennypacker's method to fill his little rooms with waiting patients and wander from one to another like a dungeon-keeper.

Clyde heard, far off, the secretary's voice tinkle, and, amplified by the hollow hall, Pennypacker's rumble in welcome and Janet's respond. The one word "headaches," petulantly emphasized, stood up in her answer. Then a door was shut. Silence.

Clyde admired how matter-of-fact she had sounded. He had always admired this competence in her, her authority in the world peripheral to the world of love in which she was so servile. He remembered how she could outface waitresses and how she would bluff her mother when this vicious woman unexpectedly entered the screened porch where they were supposed to be playing cribbage. Potted elephant plants sat in the corners of the porch like faithful dwarfs; robins had built a nest in the lilac outside, inches from the screen. It had been taken as an omen, a blessing, when one evening their being on the glider no longer distressed the birds.

Unlike, say, the effects of Novocain, the dilation of pupils is impalpable. The wallpaper he saw through the open door seemed as distinct as ever. He held his fingernails close to his nose and was unable to distinguish the cuticles. He touched the sides of his nose, where tears had left trails. He looked at his fingers again, and they seemed fuzzier. He couldn't see his fingerprint whorls. The threads of his shirt had melted into an elusive liquid surface.

A door opened and closed, and another patient was ushered into a consulting room and imprisoned by Pennypacker. Janet's footsteps had not mingled with the others. Without ever quite sacrificing his reputation for good behavior, Clyde in high school had become fairly bold in heckling teachers he considered stupid or unjust. He got out of his chair, looked down the hall to where a white splinter of secretary showed, and quickly walked past a closed door to one ajar. His blood told him. This one.

Janet was sitting in a chair as upright as the one he had left, a two-pronged comb in her mouth, her back arched and her arms up, bundling her hair. As he slipped around the door, she plucked the comb from between her teeth and laughed at him. He saw in a little rimless mirror cocked above her head his own head, grimacing with stealth and grotesquely costumed in glasses like two chocolate coins, and appreciated her laughter, though it didn't fit with what he had prepared to say. He said it anyway: "Janet, are you happy?"

She rose with a practical face and walked past him and clicked the door shut. As she stood facing it, listening for a reaction from outside, he gathered her hair in his hand and lilted it from the nape of her neck, which he had expected to find in shadow but which was instead, to his distended eyes, bright as a candle. He clumsily put his lips to it.

"Don't you love your wife?" she asked.

"Incredibly much," he murmured into the fine neck-down.

She moved off, leaving him leaning awkwardly, and in front of the mirror smoothed her hair away from her ears. She sat down again, crossing her wrists in her lap.

"I just got told my eyelashes are going to fall out," Clyde said.

"Your pretty lashes," she said somberly.

"Why do you hate me?"

"Shh. I don't hate you now."

"But you did once."

"No, I did *not* once. Clyde what *is* this bother? What are you after?"

"Son of a bitch, so I'm a bother. I knew it. You've just forgotten, all the time I've been remembering; you're so *damn* dense. I come in here a bundle of pain to tell you I'm sorry and I want you to be happy, and all I get is the back of your neck." Affected by what had happened to his eyes, his tongue had loosened, pouring out impressions; with culminating incoherence he dropped to his knees beside her chair, wondering if the thump would bring Pennypacker. "I must see you again," he blurted.

"Shh."

"I come back here and the only person who was ever pleasant to me I discover I maltreated so much she hates me."

"Clyde," she said, "you didn't maltreat me. You were a good boy to me."

Straightening up on his knees, he fumbled his fingers around the hem of the neck of her dress and pulled it out and looked down into the blurred cavity between her breasts. He had a remembrance of her freckles going down from her shoulders into her bathing suit. His glasses hit her cheek.

She stabbed the back of his hand with the points of her comb and he got to his feet, rearing high into a new, less sorrowful atmosphere. "When?" he asked, short of breath.

"No," she said.

"What's your married name?"

"Clyde, I thought you were successful. I thought you had beautiful children. Aren't you happy?"

"I am, I am; but"—the rest was so purely inspired its utterance only grazed his lips—"happiness isn't everything."

Footsteps ticked down the hall, toward their door, past it. Fear emptied his chest, yet with an excellent imitation of his old high-school flippancy he blew her a kiss, waited, opened the door, and whirled through it. His hand had left the knob when the secretary, emerging from the room where he should have been, confronted him in the linoleum-smelling hall. "Where could I get a drink of water?" he asked plaintively, assuming the hunch and whine of a blind beggar. In truth, he had, without knowing it, become thirsty.

"Once a year I pass through your territory," Pennypacker intoned as he slipped a growing weight of lenses into the tin frame on Clyde's nose. He had returned to Clyde more relaxed and chatty, now that all his little rooms were full. Clyde had tried to figure out from the pattern of noise, if Janet had been dismissed. He believed she had. The thought made his eyelid throb. He didn't even know her married name. "Down the Turnpike," Pennypacker droned on, while his face flickered in and out of focus, "up the New Jersey Pike, over the George Washington Bridge, up the Merritt, then up Route 7 all the way to Lake Champlain. To hunt the big bass. There's an experience for you."

"I notice you have a new clock in your waiting room."

"That's a Christmas present from the Alton Optical Company. Can you read that line?"

"H, L, F, Y, T, something that's either an S or an E—"

"K," Pennypacker said without looking. The poor devil, he had all those letters memorized, all that gibberish—abruptly, Clyde wanted to love him. The oculist altered one lens. "Is it better this way?...Or this way?"

At the end of the examination, Pennypacker said, "Though the man's equipment was dusty, he gave you a good prescription. In your right eye the axis of astigmatism has rotated several degrees, which is corrected in the lenses. If you have been experiencing a sense of strain, part of the reason, Clyde, is that those heavy frames are slipping down on your nose and giving you a prismatic effect. For a firm fit you should have metal frames, with adjustable nose pads."

"They leave such ugly dents on the sides of your nose."

"You should have them. Your bridge, you see"—he tapped his own—"is recessed. It takes a regular face to support unarticulated frames. Do you wear your glasses all the time?"

"For the movies and reading. When I got them in the third grade you told me that was all I needed them for."

"You should wear them all the time."

"Really? Even just for walking around?"

"All the time, yes. You have middle-aged eyes."

Pennypacker gave him a little plastic squeeze bottle of drops. "That is for the fungus on your lids."

"Fungus? There's a brutal thought. Well, will it cure the tic?"

Pennypacker impatiently snapped, "The tic is caused by muscular fatigue."

Thus Clyde was dismissed into a tainted world where things evaded his focus. He went down the hall in his sunglasses and was told by the secretary that he would receive a bill. The waiting room was full now, mostly with downcast old men and myopic children gnawing at their mothers. From out of this crowd a ripe young woman arose and came against his chest, and Clyde, included in the intimacy of the aroma her hair and skin gave off, felt weak and broad and grand, like a declining rose. Janet tucked a folded note into the pocket of his shirt and said conversationally, "He's waiting outside in the car."

The neutral, ominous "he" opened wide a conspiracy Clyde instantly entered. He stayed behind a minute, to give her time to get away. Ringed by the judging eyes of the young and old, he felt like an actor snug behind the blinding protection of the footlights; he squinted prolongedly at the speedometer-clock, which, like a letter delivered on the stage, in fact was blank. Then, smiling ironically toward both sides, he left the waiting room, coming into Pennypacker's entrance hall, a cubicle equipped with a stucco umbrella stand and a red rubber mat saying, in letters so large he could read them, WALK IN.

He had not expected to be unable to read her note. He held it at arm's length and slowly brought it toward his face, wiggling it in the light from outdoors. Though he did this several times, it didn't yield even the simplest word. Just wet blue specks. Under the specks, however, in their intensity and disposition, he believed he could make out the handwriting—slanted, open, unoriginal—familiar to him from other notes received long ago. This glimpse, through the skin of the paper, of Janet's old self quickened and sweetened his desire more than touching her had. He tucked the note back into his shirt pocket and its stiffness there made a shield for his heart. In this armor he stepped into the familiar street. The maples, macadam, shadows, houses, cars were to his violated eyes as brilliant as a scene remembered; he became a child again in this town, where life was a distant adventure, a rumor, an always imminent joy.

PHILIP ROTH
(b. 1933)

Philip Roth grew up in the Weequahic Jewish neighborhood of Newark, New Jersey, the setting for much of his fiction (see particularly The Plot Against America *[2004] and* Nemesis *[2010].) He received a BA degree from Bucknell University in 1954 and a master's degree in English Literature at the University of Chicago in 1955; he taught briefly there and subsequently at the University of Iowa, Princeton University, the University of Pennsylvania, and Hunter College. As a young man Roth spent two years in the U.S. Army. He has been married twice, a subject about which Roth has written with pitiless and tireless candor across the decades, from the early* Letting Go *(1962) and* When She Was Good *(1967) to* My Life as a Man *(1974) and the more recent* I Married a Communist *(1998)—grimly funny examinations of sexual politics and marital strife in the context of a hypocritical pseudo-puritanical American society.*

Among Roth's major titles are Goodbye Columbus *(1959),* Portnoy's Complaint *(1969),* My Life as a Man *(1974),* Zuckerman Unbound *(1981),* The Anatomy Lesson *(1983),* The Counterlife *(1986),* Operation Shylock: A Confession *(1990),* Sabbath's Theater *(1995),* American Pastoral *(1997),* The Human Stain *(2000),* Everyman *(2006),* Exit Ghost *(2007),* Indignation *(2008), and* Nemesis *(2010). Roth is also the author of* The Facts: A Novelist's Autobiography *(1988) and* Patrimony: A True Story *(1991) as well as* Reading Myself and Others *(1975). The Library of America has published a series of Roth's work in several volumes, 2005–2011.*

Roth's work is characterized by an obsessive and provocatively autobiographical focus, a postmodernist confounding of reality and fiction, and inspired rants and diatribes on Jewish and American identity, politics and sexual mores, in the way of a less lofty and less rhetorical Saul Bellow. Overall, a corrosive brilliance irradiates through Roth's fiction making of the vernacular a kind of demotic percussive poetry.

Philip Roth's literary awards are too many to list but include two National Book Awards, three PEN/Faulkner Awards, the PEN/Nabokov Award and the PEN/Bellow Award, the Pulitzer Prize, the Gold Medal for Literature from the American Academy of Arts and Letters, and the Man Booker Award for 2010. Perhaps most significantly, in October 2005 Philip Roth was honored in his old Weequahic neighborhood when the mayor of Newark presided over the unveiling of Philip Roth Plaza and a plaque on the house in which the Roths had once lived.

Defender of the Faith

In May of 1945, only a few weeks after the fighting had ended in Europe, I was rotated back to the States, where I spent the remainder of the war with a training company at Camp Crowder, Missouri. Along with the rest of the Ninth Army, I had been racing across Germany so swiftly during the late winter and spring that when I boarded the plane, I couldn't believe its destination lay to the west. My mind might inform me otherwise, but there was an inertia of the spirit that told me we were flying to a new front, where we would disembark and continue our push eastward—eastward until we'd circled the globe, marching through villages along whose twisting, cobbled streets crowds of the enemy would watch us take possession of what, up till then, they'd considered their own. I had changed enough in two years not to mind the trembling of the old people, the crying of the very young, the uncertainty and fear in the eyes of the once arrogant. I had been fortunate enough to develop an infantryman's heart, which, like his feet, at first aches and swells but finally grows horny enough for him to travel the weirdest paths without feeling a thing.

Captain Paul Barrett was my C.O. in Camp Crowder. The day I reported for duty, he came out of his office to shake my hand. He was short, gruff, and fiery, and—indoors or out—he wore his polished helmet liner pulled down to his little eyes. In Europe, he had received a battlefield commission and a serious chest wound, and he'd been returned to the States only a few months before. He spoke easily to me, and at the evening formation he introduced me to the troops. "Gentlemen," he said, "Sergeant Thurston, as you know, is no longer with this company. Your new first sergeant is Sergeant Nathan Marx, here. He is a veteran of the European theater, and consequently will expect to find a company of soldiers here, and not a company of *boys*."

I sat up late in the orderly room that evening, trying half-heartedly to solve the riddle of duty rosters, personnel forms, and morning reports. The Charge of Quarters slept with his mouth open on a mattress on the floor. A trainee stood reading the next day's duty roster, which was posted on the bulletin board just inside the screen door. It was a warm evening, and I could hear radios playing dance music over in the barracks. The trainee, who had been staring at me whenever he thought I wouldn't notice, finally took a step in my direction.

"Hey, Sarge—we having a G.I. party tomorrow night?" he asked. A G.I. party is a barracks cleaning.

"You usually have them on Friday nights?" I asked him.

"Yes," he said, and then he added, mysteriously, "that's the whole thing."

"Then you'll have a G.I. party."

He turned away, and I heard him mumbling. His shoulders were moving, and I wondered if he was crying.

"What's your name, soldier?" I asked.

He turned, not crying at all. Instead, his green-speckled eyes, long and narrow, flashed like fish in the sun. He walked over to me and sat on the edge of my desk. He reached out a hand. "Sheldon," he said.

"Stand on your feet, Sheldon."

Getting off the desk, he said, "Sheldon Grossbart." He smiled at the familiarity into which he'd led me.

"You against cleaning the barracks Friday night, Grossbart?" I said. "Maybe we shouldn't have G.I. parties. Maybe we should get a maid." My tone startled me. I felt I sounded like every top sergeant I had ever known.

"No, Sergeant." He grew serious, but with a seriousness that seemed to be only the stifling of a smile. "It's just—G.I. parties on Friday night, of all nights."

He slipped up onto the corner of the desk again—not quite sitting, but not quite standing, either. He looked at me with those speckled eyes flashing, and then made a gesture with his hand. It was very slight—no more than a movement back and forth of the wrist—and yet it managed to exclude from our affairs everything else in the orderly room, to make the two of us the center of the world. It seemed, in fact, to exclude everything even about the two of us except our hearts.

"Sergeant Thurston was one thing," he whispered, glancing at the sleeping C.Q., "but we thought that with you here things might be a little different."

"We?"

"The Jewish personnel."

"Why?" I asked, harshly. "What's on your mind?" Whether I was still angry at the "Sheldon" business, or now at something else, I hadn't time to tell, but clearly I was angry.

"We thought you—Marx, you know, like Karl Marx. The Marx Brothers. Those guys are all—M-a-r-x. Isn't that how *you* spell it, Sergeant?"

"M-a-r-x."

"Fishbein said—" He stopped. "What I mean to say, Sergeant—" His face and neck were red, and his mouth moved but no words came out. In a moment, he raised himself to attention, gazing down at me. It was as though he had suddenly decided he could expect no more sympathy from me than from Thurston, the reason being that I was of Thurston's faith, and not his. The young man had managed to confuse himself as to what my faith really was, but I felt no desire to straighten him out. Very simply, I didn't like him.

When I did nothing but return his gaze, he spoke, in an altered tone. "You see, Sergeant," he explained to me, "Friday nights, Jews are supposed to go to services."

"Did Sergeant Thurston tell you you couldn't go to them when there was a G.I. party?"

"No."

"Did he say you had to stay and scrub the floors?"

"No, Sergeant."

"Did the Captain say you had to stay and scrub the floors?"

"That isn't it, Sergeant. It's the other guys in the barracks." He leaned towards me. "They think we're goofing off. But we're not. That's when Jews go to services, Friday night. We have to."

"Then go."

"But the other guys make accusations. They have no right."

"That's not the Army's problem, Grossbart. It's a personal problem you'll have to work out yourself."

"But it's un*fair.*"

I got up to leave. "There's nothing I can do about it," I said.

Grossbart stiffened and stood in front of me. "But this is a matter of *religion*, sir."

"Sergeant," I said.

"I mean 'Sergeant,'" he said, almost snarling.

"Look, go see the chaplain. You want to see Captain Barrett, I'll arrange an appointment."

"No, no. I don't want to make trouble, Sergeant. That's the first thing they throw up to you. I just want my rights!"

"Damn it, Grossbart, stop whining. You have your rights. You can stay and scrub floors or you can go to shul—"

The smile swam in again. Spittle gleamed at the corners of his mouth. "You mean church, Sergeant."

"I mean shul, Grossbart!"

I walked past him and went outside. Near me, I heard the scrunching of a guard's boots on gravel. Beyond the lighted windows of the barracks, young men in T shirts and fatigue pants were sitting on their bunks, polishing their rifles. Suddenly there was a light rustling behind me. I turned and saw Grossbart's dark frame fleeing back to the barracks, racing to tell his Jewish friends that they were right—that, like Karl and Harpo, I was one of them.

The next morning, while chatting with Captain Barrett, I recounted the incident of the previous evening. Somehow, in the telling, it must have seemed to the Captain that I was not so much explaining Grossbart's position as defending it. "Marx, I'd fight side by side with a nigger if the fella proved to me he was a man. I pride myself," he said, looking out the window, "that I've got an open mind. Consequently, Sergeant, nobody gets special treatment here, for the good *or* the bad. All a man's got to do is prove himself. A man fires well on the range, I give him a weekend pass. He scores high in P.T., he gets a weekend pass. He *earns* it." He turned from the window and pointed a finger at me. "You're a Jewish fella, am I right, Marx?"

"Yes, sir."

"And I admire you. I admire you because of the ribbons on your chest. I judge a man by what he shows me on the field of battle, Sergeant. It's what he's got *here*," he said, and then, though I expected he would point to his chest, he jerked a thumb toward the buttons straining to hold his blouse across his belly. "Guts," he said.

"O.K., sir. I only wanted to pass on to you how the men felt."

"Mr. Marx, you're going to be old before your time if you worry about how the men feel. Leave that stuff to the chaplain—that's his business, not yours. Let's us train these fellas to shoot straight. If the Jewish personnel feels the other men are accusing them of goldbricking—well, I just don't know. Seems awful funny that suddenly the Lord is calling so loud in Private Grossman's ear he's just got to run to church."

"Synagogue," I said.

"Synagogue is right, Sergeant. I'll write that down for handy reference. Thank you for stopping by."

That evening, a few minutes before the company gathered outside the orderly room for the chow formation, I called the C.Q., Corporal Robert LaHill, in to see me. LaHill was a dark, burly fellow whose hair curled out of his clothes wherever it could. He had a glaze in his eyes that made one think of caves and dinosaurs. "LaHill," I said, "when you take the formation, remind the men that they're free to attend church services *whenever* they are held, provided they report to the orderly room before they leave the area."

LaHill scratched his wrist, but gave no indication that he'd heard or understood.

"LaHill," I said, "*church*. You remember? Church, priest, Mass, confession."

He curled one lip into a kind of smile; I took it for a signal that for a second he had flickered back up into the human race.

"Jewish personnel who want to attend services this evening are to fall out in front of the orderly room at 1900," I said. Then, as an afterthought, I added, "By order of Captain Barrett."

A little while later, as the day's last light—softer than any I had seen that year—began to drop over Camp Crowder, I head LaHill's thick, inflectionless voice outside my window: "Give me your ears, troopers. Toppie says for me to tell you that at 1900 hours all Jewish personnel is to fall out in front, here, if they want to attend the Jewish mass."

At seven o'clock, I looked out the orderly-room window and saw three soldiers in starched khakis standing on the dusty quadrangle. They looked at their watches and fidgeted while they whispered back and forth. It was getting dimmer, and, alone on the otherwise deserted field, they looked tiny. When I opened the door, I heard the noises of the G.I. party coming from the surrounding barracks—bunks being pushed to the walls, faucets pounding water into buckets, brooms whisking at the wooden floors, cleaning the dirt away for Saturday's inspection. Big puffs of cloth moved round and round on the windowpanes. I walked outside, and the moment my foot hit the ground I thought I heard Grossbart call to the others, "'Ten-*hut!*" Or maybe, when they all three jumped to attention, I imagined I heard the command.

Grossbart stepped forward. "Thank you, sir," he said.

"'Sergeant,' Grossbart," I reminded him. "You call officers 'sir.' I'm not an officer. You've been in the Army three weeks—you know that."

He turned his palms out at his sides to indicate that, in truth, he and I lived beyond convention. "Thank you, anyway," he said.

"Yes," a tall boy behind him said. "Thanks a lot."

And the third boy whispered, "Thank you," but his mouth barely fluttered, so that he did not alter by more than a lip's movement his posture of attention.

"For what?" I asked.

Grossbart snorted happily. "For the announcement. The Corporal's announcement. It helped. It made it—"

"Fancier." The tall boy finished Grossbart's sentence.

Grossbart smiled. "He means formal, sir. Public," he said to me. "Now it won't seem as though we're just taking off—goldbricking because the work has begun."

"It was by order of Captain Barrett," I said.

"Aaah, but you pull a little weight," Grossbart said. "So we thank you." Then he turned to his companions. "Sergeant Marx, I want you to meet Larry Fishbein."

The tall boy stepped forward and extended his hand. I shook it. "You from New York?" he asked.

"Yes."

"Me, too." He had a cadaverous face that collapsed inward from his cheekbone to his jaw, and when he smiled—as he did at the news of our communal attachment—revealed a mouthful of bad teeth. He was blinking his eyes a good deal, as though he were fighting back tears. "What borough?" he asked.

I turned to Grossbart. "It's five after seven. What time are services?"

"Shul," he said, smiling, "is in ten minutes. I want you to meet Mickey Halpern. This is Nathan Marx, our sergeant."

The third boy hopped forward. "Private Michael Halpern." He saluted.

"Salute officers, Halpern," I said. The boy dropped his hand, and, on its way down, in his nervousness, checked to see if his shirt pockets were buttoned.

"Shall I march them over, sir?" Grossbart asked. "Or are you coming along?"

From behind Grossbart, Fishbein piped up. "Afterward, they're having refreshments. A ladies' auxiliary from St. Louis, the rabbi told us last week."

"The chaplain," Halpern whispered.

"You're welcome to come along," Grossbart said.

To avoid his plea, I looked away, and saw, in the windows of the barracks, a cloud of faces staring out at the four of us. "Hurry along, Grossbart," I said.

"O.K., then," he said. He turned to the others. "Double time, *march!*"

They started off, but ten feet away Grossbart spun around and, running backward, called to me, "Good *shabbus,* sir!" And then the three of them were swallowed into the alien Missouri dusk.

Even after they had disappeared over the parade ground, whose green was now a deep blue, I could hear Grossbart singing the double-time cadence, and as it grew dimmer and dimmer, it suddenly touched a deep memory—as did the slant of the light—and I was remembering the shrill sounds of a Bronx playground where, years ago, beside the Grand Concourse, I had played on long spring evenings such as this. It was a pleasant memory for a young man so far from peace and home, and it brought so many recollections with it that I began to grow exceedingly tender about myself. In fact I indulged myself in a reverie so strong that I felt as though a hand were reaching down inside me. It had to reach so very far to touch me! It had to reach past those days in the forests of Belgium, and past the dying I'd refused to weep over; past the nights in German farmhouses whose books we'd burned to warm us;

past endless stretches when I had shut off all softness I might feel for my fellows, and had managed even to deny myself the posture of a conqueror—the swagger that I, as a Jew, might well have worn as my boots whacked against the rubble of Wesel, Münster, and Braunschweig.

But now one night noise, one rumor of home and time past, and memory plunged down through all I had anesthetized, and came to what I suddenly remembered was myself. So it was not altogether curious that, in search of more of me, I found myself following Grossbart's tracks to Chapel No. 3, where the Jewish services were being held.

I took a seat in the last row, which was empty. Two rows in front of me sat Grossbart, Fishbein, and Halpern, holding little white Dixie cups. Each row of seats was raised higher than the one in front of it, and I could see clearly what was going on. Fishbein was pouring the contents of his cup into Grossbart's, and Grossbart looked mirthful as the liquid made a purple arc between Fishbein's hand and his. In the glaring yellow light, I saw the chaplain standing on the platform at the front; he was chanting the first line of the responsive reading. Grossbart's prayer book remained closed on his lap; he was swishing the cup around. Only Halpern responded to the chant by praying. The fingers of his right hand were spread wide across the cover of his open book. His cap was pulled down low onto his brow, which made it round, like a yarmulke. From time to time, Grossbart wet his lips at the cup's edge; Fishbein, his long yellow face a dying light bulb, looked from here to there, craning forward to catch sight of the faces down the row, then of those in front of him, then behind. He saw me, and his eyelids beat a tattoo. His elbow slid into Grossbart's side, his neck inclined toward his friend, he whispered something, and then, when the congregation next responded to the chant, Grossbart's voice was among the others. Fishbein looked into his book now, too; his lips, however, didn't move.

Finally, it was time to drink the wine. The chaplain smiled down at them as Grossbart swigged his in one long gulp, Halpern sipped, meditating, and Fishbein faked devotion with an empty cup. "As I look down amongst the congregation"—the chaplain grinned at the word—"this night, I see many new faces, and I want to welcome you to Friday-night services here at Camp Crowder. I am Major Leo Ben Ezra, your chaplain." Though an American, the chaplain spoke deliberately—syllable by syllable, almost—as though to communicate, above all, with the lip readers in his audience. "I have only a few words to say before we adjourn to the refreshment room, where the kind ladies of the Temple Sinai, St. Louis, Missouri, have a nice setting for you."

Applause and whistling broke out. After another momentary grin, the chaplain raised his hands, palms out, his eyes flicking upward a moment, as if to remind the troops where they were and Who Else might be in attendance. In the sudden silence that followed, I thought I heard Grossbart cackle, "Let the goyim clean the floors!" Were those the words? I wasn't sure, but Fishbein, grinning, nudged Halpern. Halpern looked dumbly at him, then went back to his prayer book, which had been occupying him all through the rabbi's talk. One hand tugged at the black kinky hair that stuck out under his cap. His lips moved.

The rabbi continued. "It is about the food that I want to speak to you for a moment. I know, I know, I know," he intoned, wearily, "how in the mouths of most of you the *trafe* food tastes like ashes. I know how you gag, some of you, and how your parents suffer to think of their children eating foods unclean and offensive to the palate. What can I tell you? I can only say, close your eyes and swallow as best you can. Eat what you must to live, and throw away the rest. I wish I could help more. For those of you who find this impossible, may I ask that you try and try, but then come to see me in private. If your revulsion is so great, we will have to seek aid from those higher up."

A round of chatter rose and subsided. Then everyone sang "Ain Kelohainu"; after all those years, I discovered I still knew the words. Then, suddenly, the service over, Grossbart was upon me. "Higher up? He means the General?"

"Hey, Shelly," Fishbein said, "he means God." He smacked his face and looked at Halpern. "How high can you go!"

"Sh-h-h!" Grossbart said. "What do you think, Sergeant?"

"I don't know," I said. "You better ask the chaplain."

"I'm going to. I'm making an appointment to see him in private. So is Mickey."

Halpern shook his head. "No, no, Sheldon—"

"You have rights, Mickey," Grossbart said. "They can't push us around."

"It's O.K.," said Halpern. "It bothers my mother, not me."

Grossbart looked at me. "Yesterday he threw up. From the hash. It was all ham and God knows what else."

"I have a cold—that was why," Halpern said. He pushed his yarmulke back into a cap.

"What about you, Fishbein?" I asked. "You kosher, too?"

He flushed. "A little. But I'll let it ride. I have a very strong stomach, and I don't eat a lot anyway." I continued to look at him, and he held up his wrist to reinforce what he'd just said; his watch strap was tightened to the last hold, and he pointed that out to me.

"But services are important to you?" I asked him.

He looked at Grossbart. "Sure, sir."

"'Sergeant.'"

"Not so much at home," said Grossbart, stepping between us, "but away from home it gives one a sense of his Jewishness."

"We have to stick together," Fishbein said.

I started to walk toward the door; Halpern stepped back to make way for me.

"That's what happened in Germany," Grossbart was saying, loud enough for me to hear. "They didn't stick together. They let themselves get pushed around."

I turned. "Look, Grossbart. This is the Army, not summer camp."

He smiled. "So?"

Halpern tried to sneak off, but Grossbart held his arm.

"Grossbart, how old are you?" I asked.

"Nineteen."

"And you?" I said to Fishbein.

"The same. The same month, even."

"And what about him?" I pointed to Halpern, who had by now made it safely to the door.

"Eighteen," Grossbart whispered. "But like he can't tie his shoes or brush his teeth himself. I feel sorry for him."

"I feel sorry for all of us, Grossbart," I said, "but just act like a man. Just don't overdo it."

"Overdo what, sir?"

"The 'sir' business, for one thing. Don't overdo that," I said.

I left him standing there. I passed by Halpern, but he did not look at me. Then I was outside, but, behind, I heard Grossbart call, "Hey, Mickey, my *leben*, come on back. Refreshments!"

"*Leben*!" My Grandmother's word for me!

One morning a week later, while I was working at my desk, Captain Barrett shouted for me to come into his office. When I entered, he had his helmet liner squashed down so far on his head that I couldn't even see his eyes. He was on the phone, and when he spoke to me, he cupped one hand over the mouthpiece. "Who the hell is Grossbart?"

"Third platoon, Captain," I said. "A trainee."

"What's all this stink about food? His mother called a goddam congressman about the food." He uncovered the mouthpiece and slid his helmet up until I could see his bottom eyelashes. "Yes, sir," he said into the phone. "Yes, sir. I'm still here, sir. I'm asking Marx, here, right now—"

He covered the mouthpiece again and turned his head back toward me. "Lightfoot Harry's on the phone," he said, between his teeth. "This congressman calls General Lyman, who calls Colonel Sousa, who calls the Major, who calls me. They're just dying to stick this thing on me. Whatsa matter?" He shook the phone at me. "I don't feed the troops? What is this?"

"Sir, Grossbart is strange—" Barrett greeted that with a mockingly indulgent smile. I altered my approach. "Captain, he's a very orthodox Jew, and so he's only allowed to eat certain foods."

"He throws up, the congressman said. Every time he eats something, his mother says, he throws up!"

"He's accustomed to observing the dietary laws, Captain."

"So why's his old lady have to call the White House?"

"Jewish parents, sir—they're apt to be more protective than you expect. I mean, Jews have a very close family life. A boy goes away from home, sometimes the mother is liable to get very upset. Probably the boy mentioned something in a letter, and his mother misinterpreted."

"I'd like to punch him one right in the mouth," the Captain said. "There's a war on, and he wants a silver platter!"

"I don't think the boy's to blame, sir. I'm sure we can straighten it out by just asking him. Jewish parents worry—"

"*All* parents worry, for Christ's sake. But they don't get on their high horse and start pulling strings—"

I interrupted, my voice higher, tighter than before. "The home life, Captain, is very important—but you're right, it may sometimes get out of hand. It's a very wonderful thing, Captain, but because it's so close, this kind of thing ..."

He didn't listen any longer to my attempt to present both myself and Lightfoot Harry with an explanation for the letter. He turned back to the phone. "Sir?" he said. "Sir—Marx, here, tells me Jews have a tendency to be pushy. He says he thinks we can settle it right here in the company.... Yes, sir.... I *will* call back, sir, soon as I can." He hung up. "Where are the men, Sergeant?"

"On the range."

With a whack on the top of his helmet, he crushed it down over his eyes again, and charged out of his chair. "We're going for a ride," he said.

The Captain drove, and I sat beside him. It was a hot spring day, and under my newly starched fatigues I felt as though my armpits were melting down onto my sides and chest. The roads were dry, and by the time we reached the firing range, my teeth felt gritty with dust, though my mouth had been shut the whole trip. The Captain slammed the brakes on and told me to get the hell out and find Grossbart.

I found him on his belly, firing wildly at the five-hundred-feet target. Waiting their turns behind him were Halpern and Fishbein. Fishbein, wearing a pair of rimless G.I. glasses I hadn't seen on him before, had the appearance of an old peddler who would gladly have sold you his rifle and the cartridges that were slung all over him. I stood back by the ammo boxes, waiting for Grossbart to finish spraying the distant targets. Fishbein straggled back to stand near me.

"Hello, Sergeant Marx," he said.

"How are you?" I mumbled.

"Fine, thank you. Sheldon's really a good shot."

"I didn't notice."

"I'm not so good, but I think I'm getting the hang of it now. Sergeant, I don't mean to, you know, ask what I shouldn't—" The boy stopped. He was trying to speak intimately, but the noise of the shooting forced him to shout at me.

"What is it?" I asked. Down the range, I saw Captain Barrett standing up in the jeep, scanning the line for me and Grossbart.

"My parents keep asking and asking where we're going," Fishbein said. "Everybody says the Pacific. I don't care, but my parents—If I could relieve their minds, I think I could concentrate more on my shooting."

"I don't know where, Fishbein. Try to concentrate anyway."

"Sheldon says you might be able to find out."

"I don't know a thing, Fishbein. You just take it easy, and don't let Sheldon—"

"*I'm* taking it easy, Sergeant. It's at home—"

Grossbart had finished on the line, and was dusting his fatigues with one hand. I called to him. "Grossbart, the Captain wants to see you."

He came toward us. His eyes blazed and twinkled. "Hi!"

"Don't point that rifle!" I said.

"I wouldn't shoot you, Sarge." He gave me a smile as wide as a pumpkin, and turned the barrel aside.

"Damn you, Grossbart, this is no joke! Follow me."

I walked ahead of him, and had the awful suspicion that, behind me, Grossbart was *marching*, his rifle on his shoulder, as though he were a one-man detachment. At the jeep, he gave the Captain a rifle salute. "Private Sheldon Grossbart, sir."

"At ease, Grossman." The Captain sat down, slid over into the empty seat, and, crooking a finger, invited Grossbart closer.

"Bart, sir. Sheldon Gross*bart*. It's a common error." Grossbart nodded at me; *I* understood, he indicated. I looked away just as the mess truck pulled up to the range, disgorging a half-dozen K.P.s with rolled-up sleeves. The mess sergeant screamed at them while they set up the chow-line equipment.

"Grossbart, your mama wrote some congressman that we don't feed you right. Do you know that?" the Captain said.

"It was my father, sir. He wrote to Representative Franconi that my religion forbids me to eat certain foods."

"What religion is that, Grossbart?"

"Jewish."

"'Jewish, *sir*,'" I said to Grossbart.

"Excuse me, sir. Jewish, sir."

"What have you been living on?" the Captain asked. "You've been in the Army a month already. You don't look to me like you're falling to pieces."

"I eat because I have to, sir. But Sergeant Marx will testify to the fact that I don't eat one mouthful more than I need to in order to survive."

"Is that so, Marx?" Barrett asked.

"I've never seen Grossbart eat, sir," I said.

"But you heard the rabbi," Grossbart said. "He told us what to do, and I listened."

The Captain looked at me. "Well, Marx?"

"I still don't know what he eats and doesn't eat, sir."

Grossbart raised his arms to plead with me, and it looked for a moment as though he were going to hand me his weapon to hold. "But, Sergeant—"

"Look, Grossbart, just answer the Captain's questions," I said sharply.

Barrett smiled at me, and I resented it. "All right, Grossbart," he said. "What is it you want? The little piece of paper? You want out?"

"No, sir. Only to be allowed to live as a Jew. And for the others, too."

"What others?"

"Fishbein, sir, and Halpern."

"They don't like the way we serve, either?"

"Halpern throws up, sir. I've seen it."

"I thought *you* throw up."

"Just once, sir. I didn't know the sausage was sausage."

"We'll give menus, Grossbart. We'll show training films about the food, so you can identify when we're trying to poison you."

Grossbart did not answer. The men had been organized into two long chow lines. At the tail end of one, I spotted Fishbein—or, rather, his glasses spotted me. They winked sunlight back at me. Halpern stood next to him, patting the inside of his collar with a khaki handkerchief. They moved with the line as it began to edge up toward the food. The mess sergeant was still screaming at the K.P.s. For a moment, I was actually terrified by the thought that somehow the mess sergeant was going to become involved in Grossbart's problem.

"Marx," the Captain said, "you're a Jewish fella—am I right?"

I played straight man. "Yes, sir."

"How long you been in the Army? Tell this boy."

"Three years and two months."

"A year in combat, Grossbart. Twelve goddam months in combat all through Europe. I admire this man." The Captain snapped a wrist against my chest. "Do you hear him peeping about the food? Do you? I want an answer, Grossbart. Yes or no."

"No, sir."

"And why not? He's a Jewish fella."

"Some things are more important to some Jews than other things to other Jews."

Barrett blew up. "Look, Grossbart. Marx, here, is a good man—a goddam hero. When you were in high school, Sergeant Marx was killing Germans. Who does more for the Jews—you, by throwing up over a lousy piece of sausage, a piece of first-cut meat, or Marx, by killing those Nazi bastards? If I was a Jew, Grossbart, I'd kiss this man's feet. He's a goddam hero, and *he* eats what we give him. Why do you have to cause trouble is what I want to know! What is it you're buckin' for—a discharge?"

"No, sir."

"I'm talking to a wall! Sergeant, get him out of my way." Barrett swung himself back into the driver's seat. "I'm going to see the chaplain." The engine roared, the jeep spun around in a whirl of dust, and the Captain was headed back to camp.

For a moment, Grossbart and I stood side by side, watching the jeep. Then he looked at me and said, "I don't want to start trouble. That's the first thing they toss up to us."

When he spoke, I saw that his teeth were white and straight, and the sight of them suddenly made me understand that Grossbart actually did have parents—that once upon a time someone had taken little Sheldon to the dentist. He was their son. Despite all the talk about his parents, it was hard to believe in Grossbart as a child, an heir—as related by blood to anyone, mother, father, or, above all, to me. This realization led me to another.

"What does your father do, Grossbart?" I asked as we started to walk back toward the chow line.

"He's a tailor."

"An American?"

"Now, yes. A son in the Army," he said, jokingly.

"And your mother?" I asked.

He winked. "A *ballabusta*. She practically sleeps with a dustcloth in her hand."

"She's also an immigrant?"

"All she talks is Yiddish, still."

"And your father, too?"

"A little English. 'Clean,' 'Press,' 'Take the pants in.' That's the extent of it. But they're good to me."

"Then, Grossbart—" I reached out and stopped him. He turned toward me, and when our eyes met, his seemed to jump back, to shiver in their sockets. "Grossbart—you were the one who wrote that letter, weren't you?"

It took only a second or two for his eyes to flash happy again. "Yes." He walked on, and I kept pace. "It's what my father *would* have written if he had known how. It was his name, though. *He* signed it. He even mailed it. I sent it home. For the New York postmark."

I was astonished, and he saw it. With complete seriousness, he thrust his right arm in front of me. "Blood is blood, Sergeant," he said, pinching the blue vein in his wrist.

"What the hell *are* you trying to do, Grossbart?" I asked. "I've seen you eat. Do you know that? I told the Captain I don't know what you eat, but I've seen you eat like a hound at chow."

"We work hard, Sergeant. We're in training. For a furnace to work, you've got to feed it coal."

"Why did you say in the letter that you threw up all the time?"

"I was really talking about Mickey there. I was talking *for* him. He would never write, Sergeant, though I pleaded with him. He'll waste away to nothing if I don't help. Sergeant, I used my name—my father's name—but it's Mickey and Fishbein, too, I'm watching out for."

"You're a regular Messiah, aren't you?"

We were at the chow line now.

"That's a good one, Sergeant," he said, smiling. "But who knows? Who can tell? Maybe you're the Messiah—a little bit. What Mickey says is the Messiah is a collective idea. He went to Yeshiva, Mickey, for a while. He says *together* we're the Messiah. Me a little bit, you a little bit. You should hear that kid talk, Sergeant, when he gets going."

"Me a little bit, you a little bit," I said. "You'd like to believe that, wouldn't you, Grossbart? That would make everything so clean for you."

"It doesn't seem too bad a thing to believe, Sergeant. It only means we should all *give* a little, is all."

I walked off to eat my rations with the other noncoms.

Two days later, a letter addressed to Captain Barrett passed over my desk. It had come through the chain of command—from the office of Congressman Franconi, where it had been received, to General Lyman, to Colonel Sousa, to Major Lamont, now to Captain Barrett. I read it over twice. It was dated May 14, the day Barrett had spoken with Grossbart on the rifle range.

Dear Congressman:

First let me thank you for your interest in behalf of my son, Private Sheldon Grossbart. Fortunately, I was able to speak with Sheldon on the phone the other night, and I think I've been able to solve our problem. He is, as I mentioned in my last letter, a very religious boy, and it was only with the greatest difficulty that I could persuade him that the religious thing to do—what God Himself would want Sheldon to do—would be to suffer the pangs of religious remorse for the good of his country and all mankind. It took some doing, Congressman, but finally he saw the light. In fact, what he said (and I wrote down the words on a scratch pad so as never to forget), what he said was "I guess you're right, Dad. So many millions of my fellow-Jews gave up their lives to the enemy, the least I can do is live for a while minus a bit of my heritage so as to help end this struggle and regain for all the children of God dignity and humanity." That, Congressman, would make any father proud.

By the way, Sheldon wanted me to know—and to pass on to you—the name of a soldier who helped him reach this decision: SERGEANT NATHAN MARX. Sergeant Marx is a combat veteran who is Sheldon's first sergeant. This man has helped Sheldon over some of the first hurdles he's had to face in the Army, and is in part responsible for Sheldon's changing his mind about the dietary laws. I know Sheldon would appreciate any recognition Marx could receive.

Thank you and good luck. I look forward to seeing your name on the next election ballot.

Respectfully,
Samuel E. Grossbart

Attached to the Grossbart communiqué was another, addressed to General Marshall Lyman, the post commander, and signed by Representative Charles E. Franconi, of the House of Representatives. The communiqué informed General Lyman that Sergeant Nathan Marx was a credit to the U.S. Army and the Jewish people.

What was Grossbart's motive in recanting? Did he feel he'd gone too far? Was the letter a strategic retreat—a crafty attempt to strengthen what he considered our alliance? Or had he actually changed his mind, via an imaginary dialogue between Grossbart *père* and Grossbart *fils*? I was puzzled, but only for a few days—that is, only until I realized that, whatever his reasons, he had actually decided to disappear from my life; he was going to allow himself to become just another trainee. I saw him at inspection, but he never winked; at chow formations, but he never flashed me a sign. On Sundays, with the other trainees, he would sit around watching the noncoms' softball team, for which I pitched, but not once did he speak an unnecessary word to me. Fishbein and Halpern retreated, too—at Grossbart's command, I was sure. Apparently he had seen that wisdom lay in turning back before he plunged over into the ugliness of privilege undeserved. Our separation allowed me to forgive him our past encounters, and, finally, to admire him for his good sense.

Meanwhile, free of Grossbart, I grew used to my job and my administrative tasks. I stepped on a scale one day, and discovered I had truly become a noncombatant; I had gained seven pounds. I found patience to get past the first three pages of a book. I thought about the future more and more, and wrote letters to girls I'd known before the war. I even got a few answers. I sent away to Columbia for a Law School catalogue. I continued to follow the war in the Pacific, but it was not my war. I thought I could see the end, and sometimes, at night, I dreamed that I was walking on the streets of Manhattan—Broadway, Third Avenue, 116th Street, where I had lived the three years I attended Columbia. I curled myself around these dreams and I began to be happy.

And then, one Sunday, when everybody was away and I was alone in the orderly room reading a month-old copy of the *Sporting News*, Grossbart reappeared.

"You a baseball fan, Sergeant?"

I looked up. "How are you?"

"Fine," Grossbart said. "They're making a soldier out of me."

"How are Fishbein and Halpern?"

"Coming along," he said. "We've got no training this afternoon. They're at the movies."

"How come you're not with them?"

"I wanted to come over and say hello."

He smiled—a shy, regular-guy smile, as though he and I well knew that our friendship drew its sustenance from unexpected visits, remembered birthdays, and borrowed lawnmowers. At first it offended me, and then the feeling was swallowed by the general uneasiness I felt at the thought that everyone on the post was locked away in a dark movie theater and I was here alone with Grossbart. I folded up my paper.

"Sergeant," he said, "I'd like to ask a favor. It is a favor, and I'm making no bones about it."

He stopped, allowing me to refuse him a hearing—which, of course, forced me into a courtesy I did not intend. "Go ahead."

"Well, actually its two favors."

I said nothing.

"The first one's about these rumors. Everybody says we're going to the Pacific."

"As I told your friend Fishbein, I don't know," I said. "You'll just have to wait to find out. Like everybody else."

"You think there's a chance of any of us going East?"

"Germany?" I said. "Maybe."

"I meant New York."

"I don't think so, Grossbart. Offhand."

"Thanks for the information, Sergeant," he said.

"It's not information, Grossbart. Just what I surmise."

"It certainly would be good to be near home. My parents—you know." He took a step toward the door and then turned back. "Oh, the other thing. May I ask the other?"

"What is it?"

"The other thing is—I've got relatives in St. Louis, and they say they'll give me a whole Passover dinner if I can get down there. God, Sergeant, that'd mean an awful lot to me."

I stood up. "No passes during basic, Grossbart."

"But we're off from now till Monday morning, Sergeant. I could leave the post and no one would even know."

"I'd know. You'd know."

"But that's all. Just the two of us. Last night, I called my aunt, and you should have heard her. 'Come—come,' she said. 'I got gefilte fish, *chrain*—the works!' Just a day, Sergeant. I'd take the blame if anything happened."

"The Captain isn't here to sign a pass."

"You could sign."

"Look, Grossbart—"

"Sergeant, for two months, practically, I've been eating *trafe* till I want to die."

"I thought you'd made up your mind to live with it. To be minus a little bit of heritage."

He pointed a finger at me. "You!" he said. "That wasn't for you to read."

"I read it. So what?"

"That letter was addressed to a congressman."

"Grossbart, don't feed me any baloney. You *wanted* me to read it."

"Why are you persecuting me, Sergeant?"

"Are you kidding!"

"I've run into this before," he said, "but never from my own!"

"Get out of here, Grossbart! Get the hell out of my sight!"

He did not move. "Ashamed, that's what you are," he said. "So you take it out on the rest of us. They say Hilter himself was half a Jew. Hearing you, I wouldn't doubt it."

"What are you trying to do with me, Grossbart?" I asked him. "What are you after? You want me to give you special privileges, to change the food, to find out about your orders, to give you weekend passes."

"You even talk like a goy!" Grossbart shook his fist. "Is this just a weekend pass I'm asking for? Is a Seder sacred, or not?"

Seder! It suddenly occurred to me that Passover had been celebrated weeks before. I said so.

"That's right," he replied. "Who says no? A month ago—and I was in the field eating hash! And now all I ask is a simple favor. A Jewish boy I thought would understand. My aunt's willing to go out of her way—to make a Seder a month later...." He turned to go, mumbling.

"Come back here!" I called. He stopped and looked at me. "Grossbart, why can't you be like the rest? Why do you have to stick out like a sore thumb?"

"Because I'm a Jew, Sergeant. I *am* different. Better, maybe not. But different."

"This is a war, Grossbart. For the time being *be* the same."

"I refuse."

"What?"

"I refuse. I can't stop being me, that's all there is to it." Tears came to his eyes. "It's a hard thing to be a Jew. But now I understand what Mickey says—it's a harder thing to stay one." He raised a hand sadly toward me. "Look at *you*."

"Stop crying!"

"Stop this, stop that, stop the other thing! *You* stop, Sergeant. Stop closing your heart to your own!" And, wiping his face with his sleeve, he ran out the door. "The least we can do for one another— the least..."

An hour later, looking out of the window, I saw Grossbart headed across the field. He wore a pair of starched khakis and carried a little leather ditty bag. I went out into the heat of the day. It was quiet; not a soul was in sight except, over by the mess hall, four K.P.s sitting around a pan, sloped forward from their waists, gabbing and peeling potatoes in the sun.

"Grossbart!" I called.

He looked toward me and continue walking.

"Grossbart, get over here!"

He turned and came across the field. Finally, he stood before me.

"Where are you going?" I asked.

"St. Louis. I don't care."

"You'll get caught without a pass."

"So I'll get caught without a pass."

"You'll go to the stockade."

"I'm *in* the stockade." He made an about-face and headed off.

I let him go only a step or two. "Come back here," I said, and he followed me into the office, where I typed out a pass and signed the Captain's name, and my own initials after it.

He took the pass and then, a moment later, reached out and grabbed my hand. "Sergeant, you don't know how much this means to me."

"O.K.," I said. "Don't get in any trouble."

"I wish I could show you how much this means to me."

"Don't do me any favors. Don't write any more congressmen for citations."

He smiled. "You're right. I won't. But let me do something."

"Bring me a piece of that gefilte fish. Just get out of here."

"I will!" he said. "With a slice of carrot and a little horseradish. I won't forget."

"All right. Just show your pass at the gate. And don't tell *anybody.*"

"I won't. It's a month late, but a good Yom Tov to you."

"Good Yom Tov, Grossbart," I said.

"You're a good Jew, Sergeant. You like to think you have a hard heart, but underneath you're a fine, decent man. I mean that."

Those last three words touched me more than any words from Grossbart's mouth had the right to. "All right, Grossbart," I said. "Now call me 'sir,' and get the hell out of here."

He ran out the door and was gone. I felt very pleased with myself; it was a great relief to stop fighting Grossbart, and it had cost me nothing. Barrett would never find out, and if he did, I could manage to invent some excuse. For a while, I sat at my desk, comfortable in my decision. Then the screen door flew back and Grossbart burst in again. "Sergeant!" he said. Behind him I saw Fishbein and Halpern, both in starched khakis, both carrying ditty bags like Grossbart's.

"Sergeant, I caught Mickey and Larry coming out of the movies. I almost missed them."

"Grossbart—did I say tell no one?" I said.

"But my aunt said I could bring friends. That I should, in fact."

"*I'm* the Sergeant, Grossbart—not your aunt!"

Grossbart looked at me in disbelief. He pulled Halpern up by his sleeve. "Mickey, tell the Sergeant what this would mean to you."

Halpern looked at me and, shrugging, said, "A lot."

Fishbein stepped forward without prompting. "This would mean a great deal to me and my parents, Sergeant Marx."

"No!" I shouted.

Grossbart was shaking his head. "Sergeant, I could see you denying me, but how you can deny Mickey, a Yeshiva boy—that's beyond me."

"I'm not denying Mickey anything," I said. "You just pushed a little too hard, Grossbart. *You* denied him."

"I'll give him my pass, then," Grossbart said. "I'll give him my aunt's address and a little note. At least let him go."

In a second he had crammed the pass into Halpern's pants pocket. Halpern looked at me, and so did Fishbein. Grossbart was at the door, pushing it open. "Mickey, bring me a piece of gelfilte fish, at least," he said, and then he was outside again.

The three of us looked at one another, and then I said, "Halpern, hand that pass over."

He took it from his pocket and gave it to me. Fishbein had now moved to the doorway, where he lingered. He stood there for a moment with his mouth slightly open, and then he pointed to himself. "And me?" he asked.

His utter ridiculousness exhausted me. I slumped down in my seat and felt pulses knocking at the back of my eyes. "Fishbein," I said, "you understand I'm not trying to deny you anything, don't you? If it was my Army, I'd serve gefilte fish in the mess hall. I'd sell *kugel* in the PX, honest to God."

Halpern smiled.

"You understand, don't you, Halpern?"

"Yes, Sergeant."

"And you, Fishbein? I don't want enemies. I'm just like you—I want to serve my time and go home. I miss the same things you miss."

"Then, Sergeant," Fishbein said, "why don't you come, too?"

"Where?"

"To St. Louis. To Shelly's aunt. We'll have a regular Seder. Play hide-the-matzoh." He gave me a broad, black-toothed smile.

I saw Grossbart again, on the other side of the screen.

"Pst!" He waved a piece of paper. "Mickey, here's the address. Tell her I couldn't get away."

Halpern did not move. He looked at me, and I saw the shrug moving up his arms into his shoulders again. I took the cover off my typewriter and made out passes for him and Fishbein. "Go," I said. "The three of you."

I thought Halpern was going to kiss my hand.

That afternoon, in a bar in Joplin, I drank beer and listened with half an ear to the Cardinal game. I tried to look squarely at what I'd become involved in, and began to wonder if perhaps the struggle with Grossbart wasn't as much my fault as his. What was I that I had to *muster* generous feelings? Who was I to have been feeling so grudging, so tight-hearted? After all, I wasn't being asked to move the world. Had I a right, then, or a reason, to clamp down on Grossbart, when that meant clamping down on Halpern, too? And Fishbein—that ugly, agreeable soul? Out of the many recollections of my childhood that had tumbled over me these past few days I heard my grandmother's voice: "What are you making a *tsimmes*?" It was what she would ask my mother when, say, I had cut myself while doing something I shouldn't have done, and her daughter was busy bawling me out. I needed a hug and a kiss, and my mother would moralize. But my grandmother knew—mercy overrides justice. I should have known it, too. Who was Nathan Marx to be such a penny pincher with kindness? Surely, I thought, the Messiah himself—if He should ever come—won't niggle over nickels and dimes. God willing, he'll hug and kiss.

The next day, while I was playing softball over on the parade ground, I decided to ask Bob Wright, who was noncom in charge of Classification and Assignment, where he thought our trainees would be sent when their cycle ended, in two weeks. I asked casually, between innings, and he said, "They're pushing them all into the Pacific. Shulman cut the orders on your boys the other day."

The news shocked me, as though I were the father of Halpern, Fishbein, and Grossbart.

That night, I was just sliding into sleep when someone tapped on my door. "Who is it?" I asked.

"Sheldon."

He opened the door and came in. For a moment, I felt his presence without being able to see him. "How was it?" I asked.

He popped into sight in the near-darkness before me. “Great, Sergeant.” Then he was sitting on the edge of the bed. I sat up.

“How about you?” he asked. “Have a nice weekend?”

“Yes.”

“The others went to sleep.” He took a deep, paternal breath. We sat silent for a while, and a homey feeling invaded my ugly little cubicle; the door was locked, the cat was out, the children were safely in bed.

“Sergeant, can I tell you something? Personal?”

I did not answer, and he seemed to know why. “Not about me. About Mickey. Sergeant, I never felt for anybody like I feel for him. Last night I heard Mickey in the bed next to me. He was crying so, it could have broken your heart. Real sobs.”

“I'm sorry to hear that.”

“I had to talk to him to stop him. He held my hand, Sergeant—he wouldn't let it go. He was almost hysterical. He kept saying if he only knew where we were going. Even if he knew it *was* the Pacific, that would be better than nothing. Just to know.

Long ago, someone had taught Grossbart the sad rule that only lies can get the truth. Not that I couldn't believe in the fact of Halpern's crying; his eyes *always* seemed red-rimmed. But, fact or not, it became a lie when Grossbart uttered it. He was entirely strategic. But then—it came with the force of indictment—so was I! There are strategies of aggression, but there are strategies of retreat as well. And so, recognizing that I myself had not been without craft and guile, I told him what I knew. “It is the Pacific.” He let out a small gasp, which was not a lie. “I'll tell him. I wish it was otherwise.”

“So do I.”

He jumped on my words. “You mean you think you could do something? A change, maybe?”

“No, I couldn't do a thing.”

“Don't you know anybody over at C. and A.?”

“Grossbart, there's nothing I can do,” I said. “If your orders are for the Pacific, then it's the Pacific.”

“But Mickey—”

“Mickey, you, me—everybody, Grossbart. There's nothing to be done. Maybe the war'll end before you go. Pray for a miracle.”

“But—”

"Good night, Grossbart." I settled back, and was relieved to feel the springs unbend as Grossbart rose to leave. I could see him clearly now; his jaw had dropped, and he looked like a dazed prizefighter. I noticed for the first time a little paper bag in his hand.

"Grossbart." I smiled. "My gift?"

"Oh, yes, Sergeant. Here—from all of us." He handed me the bag. "It's egg roll."

"Egg roll?" I accepted the bag and felt a damp grease spot on the bottom. I opened it, sure that Grossbart was joking.

"We thought you'd probably like it. You know—Chinese egg roll. We thought you'd probably have a taste for—"

"Your aunt served egg roll?"

"She wasn't home."

"Grossbart, she invited you. You told me she invited you and your friends."

"I know," he said. "I just reread the letter. *Next* week."

I got out of bed and walked to the window. "Grossbart," I said. But I was not calling to him.

"What?"

"What are you, Grossbart? Honest to God, what are you?"

I think it was the first time I'd asked him a question for which he didn't have an immediate answer.

"How can you do this to people?" I went on.

"Sergeant, the day away did us all a world of good. Fishbein, you should see him, he *loves* Chinese food."

"But the Seder," I said.

"We took second best, Sergeant."

Rage came charging at me. I didn't sidestep. "Grossbart, you're a liar!" I said. "You're a schemer and a crook. You've got no respect for anything. Nothing at all. Not for me, for the truth—not even for poor Halpern! You use us all—"

"Sergeant, Sergeant, I feel for Mickey. Honest to God, I do. I *love* Mickey. I try—"

"You try! You feel!" I lurched toward him and grabbed his shirt front. I shook him furiously. "Grossbart, get out! Get out and stay the hell away from me. Because if I see you, I'll make your life miserable. *You understand that?*"

"Yes."

I let him free, and when he walked from the room, I wanted to spit on the floor where he had stood. I couldn't stop the fury. It engulfed me, owned me, till it seemed I could only rid myself of it with tears or an act of violence. I snatched from the bed the bag Grossbart had given me and, with all my strength, threw it out the window. And the next morning, as the men policed the area around the barracks, I heard a great cry go up from one of the trainees, who had been anticipating only his morning handful of cigarette butts and candy wrappers. "Egg roll!" he shouted. "Holy Christ, Chinese goddam egg roll!"

A week later, when I read the orders that had come down from C. and A., I couldn't believe my eyes. Every single trainee was to be shipped to Camp Stoneman, California, and from there to the Pacific—every trainee but one. Private Sheldon Grossbart. He was to be sent to Fort Monmouth, New Jersey. I read the mimeographed sheet several times. Dee, Farrell, Fishbein, Fuselli, Fylypowycz, Glinicki, Gromke, Gucwa, Halpern, Hardy, Helebrandt, right down to Anton Zygadlo—all were to be headed West before the month was out. All except Grossbart. He had pulled a string, and I wasn't it.

I lifted the phone and called C. and A.

The voice on the other end said smartly, "Corporal Shulman, sir."

"Let me speak to Sergeant Wright."

"Who is this calling, sir?"

"Sergeant Marx."

And, to my surprise, the voice said, "*Oh!*" Then, "Just a minute, Sergeant."

Shulman's "*Oh!*" stayed with me while I waited for Wright to come to the phone. Why "*Oh!*"? Who was Shulman? And then, so simply, I knew I'd discovered the string that Grossbart had pulled. In fact, I could hear Grossbart the day he'd discovered Shulman in the PX, or in the bowling alley, or maybe even at services. "Glad to meet you. Where you from? Bronx? Me, too. Do you know So-and-So? And So-and-So? Me, too! You work at C. and A.? Really? Hey, how's chances of getting East? Could you do something? Change something? Swindle, cheat, lie? We gotta help each other, you know. If the Jews in Germany ..."

Bob Wright answered the phone. "How are you, Nate? How's the pitching arm?"

"Good. Bob, I wonder if you could do me a favor." I heard clearly my own words, and they so reminded me of Grossbart that I dropped more easily than I could have imagined into what I had planned. "This may sound crazy, Bob, but I got a kid here on orders to Monmouth who wants them changed. He had a brother killed in Europe, and he's hot to go to the Pacific. Says he'd feel like a coward if he wound up Stateside. I don't know, Bob—can anything be done? Put somebody else in the Monmouth slot?"

"Who?" he asked cagily.

"Anybody. First guy in the alphabet. I don't care. The kid just asked if something could be done."

"What's his name?"

"Grossbart, Sheldon."

Wright didn't answer.

"Yeah," I said. "He's a Jewish kid, so he thought I could help him out. You know."

"I guess I can do something," he finally said. "The Major hasn't been around here for weeks. Temporary duty to the golf course. I'll try, Nate, that's all I can say."

"I'd appreciate it, Bob. See you Sunday." And I hung up, perspiring.

The following day, the corrected orders appeared: Fishbein, Fuselli, Fylypowycz, Glinicki, Gromke, Grossbart, Gucwa, Halpern, Hardy... Lucky Private Harley Alton was to go to Fort Monmouth, New Jersey, where, for some reason or other, they wanted an enlisted man with infantry training.

After chow that night, I stopped back at the orderly room to straighten out the guard-duty roster. Grossbart was waiting for me. He spoke first.

"You son of a bitch!"

I sat down at my desk, and while he glared at me, I began to make the necessary alterations in the duty roster.

"What do you have against me?" he cried. "Against my family? Would it kill you for me to be near my father, God knows how many months he has left to him?"

"Why so?"

"His heart," Grossbart said. "He hasn't had enough troubles in a lifetime, you've got to add to them. I curse the day I ever met you, Marx! Shulman told me what happened over there. There's no limit to your anti-Semitism, is there? The damage you've done here isn't enough. You have to make a special phone call! You really want me dead!"

I made the last few notations in the duty roster and got up to leave. "Good night, Grossbart."

"You owe me an explanation!" He stood in my path.

"Sheldon, you're the one who owes explanations."

He scowled. "To *you?*"

"To me, I think so—yes. Mostly to Fishbein and Halpern."

"That's right, twist things around. I owe nobody nothing, I've done all I could do for them. Now I think I've got the right to watch out for myself."

"For each other we have to learn to watch out, Sheldon. You told me yourself."

"You call this watching out for me—what you did?"

"No. For all of us."

I pushed him aside and started for the door. I heard his furious breathing behind me, and it sounded like steam rushing from an engine of terrible strength.

"*You'll* be all right," I said from the door. And, I thought, so would Fishbein and Halpern be all right, even in the Pacific, if only Grossbart continued to see—in the obsequiousness of the one, the soft spirituality of the other—some profit for himself.

I stood outside the orderly room, and I heard Grossbart weeping behind me. Over in the barracks, in the lighted windows, I could see the boys in their T shirts sitting on their bunks talking about their orders, as they'd been doing for the past two days. With a kind of quiet nervousness, they polished shoes, shined belt buckles, squared away underwear, trying as best they could to accept their fate. Behind me, Grossbart swallowed hard, accepting his. And then, resisting with all my will an impulse to turn and seek pardon for my vindictiveness, I accepted my own.

ANNIE PROULX
(b. 1935)

For me, the story falls out of a place, its geology and climate, the flora, fauna, prevailing winds, the weather. I am not people-centric, and I'm appalled at what human beings have done to the planet.

—Annie Proulx

Through a series of vividly imagined, boldly idiosyncratic, and much acclaimed works of fiction—the collections Heart Songs and Other Stories *(1988),* Close Range: Wyoming Stories *(1999),* Bad Dirt: Wyoming Stories 2 *(2004), and* Fine Just the Way it Is: Wyoming Stories 3 *(2008) and the novels* Postcards *(1992),* The Shipping News *(1993),* Accordion Crimes *(1996) and* That Old Ace in the Hole *(2002)—Annie Proulx has explored rural America with a passion for the exploited and impoverished and patience for research of all kinds, both scholarly and reportorial. Her toughly compassionate story "Brokeback Mountain," from* Close Range, *was made into an award-winning film by Ang Lee in 2005.*

Born in Norwich, Connecticut, Annie Proulx attended Colby College briefly, then graduated from the University of Vermont with a BA in history in 1969. She received an MA at Concordia University in Montreal. Three times married and three times divorced, a longtime resident of small-town New England, Proulx moved to Saratoga, Wyoming in her early sixties, in 1994, to live by herself in a place of great beauty and remoteness, memorialized in Bird Cloud: A Memoir (2011).

All of Proulx's prose is characterized by strong, sinewy American-vernacular speech. The author has little interest in conventional "people-centric" stories and it might be argued that her geographical settings are her most significant "characters"—certainly, the starkly rendered landscape abides in a way that its merely human settlers cannot. Such an intransigent vision has brought Annie Proulx much acclaim and literary honors: among her awards are an NEA grant; a Guggenheim Fellowship; the PEN/Faulkner Award for Postcards; *the Pulitzer and the National Book Award for* The Shipping News; *the Dos Passos Award for Lifetime Achievement; inclusion in* The Best American Short Stories *and the* O. Henry Prize Stories *with citations for "Brokeback Mountain" and "The Mud Below," the unforgettable story included here.*

The Mud Below

Rodeo night in a hot little Okie town and Diamond Felts was inside a metal chute a long way from the scratch on Wyoming dirt he named as home, sitting on the back of bull 82N, a loose-skinned brindle Brahma-cross identified in the program as Little Kisses. There was a sultry feeling of Weather. He kept his butt cocked to one side, his feet up on the chute rails so the bull couldn't grind his leg, brad him up, so that if it thrashed he could get over the top in a hurry. The time came closer and he slapped his face forcefully, bringing the adrenaline roses up on his cheeks, glanced down at his pullers and said, "I guess." Rito, neck gleaming with sweat, caught the free end of the bull-rope with a metal hook, brought it delicately to his hand from under the bull's belly, climbed up the rails and pulled it taut.

"Aw, this's a sumbuck," he said. "Give you the sample card."

Diamond took the end, made his wrap, brought the rope around the back of his hand and over the palm a second time, wove it between his third and fourth fingers, pounded the rosined glove fingers down over it and into his palm. He laid the tail of the rope across the bull's back and looped the excess, but it wasn't right—everything had gone a little slack He undid the wrap and started over, making the loop smaller, waiting while they pulled again and in the arena a clown fired a pink cannon, the fizzing discharge diminished by a deep stir of thunder from the south, Texas T-storm on the roll.

Night perfs had their own hot charge, the glare, the stiff-legged parade of cowboy dolls in sparkle-fringed chaps into the arena, the spotlight that bucked over the squinting contestants and the half-roostered crowd. They were at the end of the night now, into the bullriding, with one in front of him. The bull beneath him breathed, shifted roughly. A hand, fingers outstretched, came across his right shoulder and against his chest, steadying him. He did not know why a bracing hand eased his chronic anxiety. But, in the way these things go, that was when he needed twist, to auger him through the ride.

In the first go-round he'd drawn a bull he knew and got a good scald on him. He'd been in a slump for weeks, wire stretched tight, but things were turning back his way. He'd come off that animal in a flying dismount, sparked a little clapping that quickly died; the watchers knew as well as he that if he burst into flames and sang an operatic aria after the whistle it would make no damn difference.

He drew o.k. bulls and rode them in the next rounds, scores in the high seventies, fixed his eyes on the outside shoulder of the welly bull that tried to drop him, then at the short-go draw he pulled Kisses, rank and salty, big as a boxcar of coal. On that one all you could do was your best and hope for a little sweet luck; if you got the luck he was money.

The announcer's galvanized voice rattled in the speakers above the enclosed arena. "Now folks, it ain't the Constitution or the Bill a Rights that made this a great country. It was *God* who created the mountains and plains and the evenin sunset and put us here and let us look at them. Amen and God bless the Markin flag. And right now we got a bullrider from Redsled, Wyomin, twenty-three-year-old Diamond Felts, who might be wonderin if he'll ever see that beautiful scenery again. Folks, Diamond Felts weighs one hundred and thirty pounds. Little Kisses weighs two thousand ten pounds, he is a big, big bull and he is thirty-eight and one, last year's Dodge City Bullriders' choice. Only one man has stayed on this big bad bull's back for eight seconds and that was Marty Casebolt at Reno, and you better believe that man got all the money. *Will* he be rode tonight? Folks, we're goin a find out in just a minute, soon as our cowboy's ready. And listen at that rain, folks, let's give thanks we're in a enclosed arena or it would be deep mud below."

Diamond glanced back at the flank man, moved up on his rope, nodded, jerking his head up and down rapidly. "Let's go, let's go."

The chute door swung open and the bull squatted, leaped into the waiting silence and a paroxysm of twists, belly-rolls and spins, skipping, bucking and whirling, powerful drop, gave him the whole menu.

Diamond Felts, a constellation of moles on his left cheek, dark hair cropped to the skull, was more than good-looking when cleaned up and combed, in fresh shirt and his neckerchief printed with blue stars, but for most of his life he had not known it. Five-foot three, rapping, tapping, nail-biting, he radiated unease. A virgin at eighteen—not many of either sex in his senior class in that condition—his tries at changing the situation went wrong and as far as his despairing thought carried him, always would go wrong in the forest of tall girls. There were small women out there, but it was the six-footers he mounted in the privacy of his head.

All his life he had heard himself called Half-Pint, Baby Boy, Shorty, Kid, Tiny, Little Guy, Sawed-Off. His mother never let up, always had the needle ready, even the time when she had come into the upstairs hall and caught him stepping naked from the bathroom; she had said, "Well, at least you didn't get shortchanged that way, did you?"

In the spring of his final year of school he drummed his fingers on Wallace Winter's pickup listening to its swan-necked owner pump up a story, trying for the laugh, when a knothead they knew only as Leecil—god save the one who said Lucille—walked up and said, "Either one a you want a work this weekend? The old man's fixin a brand and he's short-handet. Nobody wants to, though." He winked his dime-size eyes. His blunt face was corrugated with plum-colored acne and among the angry swellings grew a few blond whiskers. Diamond couldn't see how he shaved without bleeding to death. The smell of livestock was strong.

"He sure picked the wrong weekend," said Wallace. "Basketball game, parties, fucking, drinking, drugs, car wrecks, cops, food poisoning, fights, hysterical parents. Didn't you tell him?"

"He didn't ast me. Tolt me get some guys. Anyway it's good weather now. Stormt the weekend for a month." Leecil spit.

Wallace pretended serious consideration. "Scratch the weekend I guess we get paid." He winked at Diamond who grimaced to tell him that Leecil was not one to be teased.

"Yeah, six per, you guys. Me and my brothers got a work for nothin, for the ranch. Anyway, we give-or-take quit at suppertime, so you can still do your stuff. Party, whatever." He wasn't going to any town blowout.

"I never did ranch work," Diamond said. "My momma grew up on a ranch and hated it. Only took us up there once and I bet we didn't stay an hour," remembering an expanse of hoof-churned mud, his grandfather turning away, a muscular, sweaty Uncle John in chaps and a filthy hat swatting him on the butt and saying something to his mother that made her mad.

"Don't matter. It's just work. Git the calves into the chute, brand em, fix em, vaccinate em, git em out."

"Fix em," said Diamond.

Leecil made an eloquent gesture at his crotch.

"It could be very weirdly interesting," said Wallace. "I got something that will make it weirdly interesting."

"You don't want a git ironed out too much, have to lay down in the mud," said Leecil severely.

"No," said Wallace. "I fucking don't want to do that. O.k., I'm in. What the hell."

Diamond nodded.

Leecil cracked his mouthful of perfect teeth. "Know where our place is at? There's a bunch a different turnoffs. Here's how you go," and he drew a complicated map on the back of a returned quiz red-marked F. That solved one puzzle; Leecil's last name was Bewd. Wallace looked at Diamond. The Bewd tribe, scattered from Pahaska to Pine Bluffs, filled a double-X space in the local pantheon of troublemakers.

"Seven a.m.," said Leecil.

Diamond turned the map over and looked at the quiz. Cattle brands fine-drawn with a sharp pencil filled the answer spaces; they gave the sheet of paper a kind of narrow-minded authority.

The good weather washed out. The weekend was a windy, overcast cacophony of bawling, manure-caked animals, mud, dirt, lifting, punching the needle, the stink of burning hair that he thought would never get out of his nose. Two crotchscratchers from school showed up; Diamond had seen them around, but he did not know them and thought of them as losers for no reason but that they were inarticulate and lived out on dirt road ranches; friends of Leecil. Como Bewd, a grizzled man wearing a kidney belt, pointed this way and that as Leecil and his brothers worked the calves from pasture to corral to holding pen to branding chute and the yellow-hot electric iron, to cutting table where ranch hand Lovis bent forward with his knife and with the other hand pulled the skin of the scrotum tight over one testicle and made a long, outside cut through skin and membrane, yanked out the hot balls, dropped them into a bucket and waited for the next calf. The dogs sniffed around, the omnipresent flies razzed and turmoiled, three saddled horses shifted from leg to leg under a tree and occasionally nickered.

Diamond glanced again and again at Como Bewd. The man's forehead showed a fence of zigzag scars like white barbwire. He caught the stare and winked.

"Lookin at my decorations? My brother run over me with his truck when I was your age. Took the skin off from ear to here. I was all clawed up. I was scalloped."

They finished late Sunday afternoon and Como Bewd counted out their pay carefully and slowly, added an extra five to each pile, said they'd done a pretty fair job, then, to Leecil, said, "How about it?"

"You want a have some fun?" said Leecil Bewd to Diamond and Wallace. The others were already walking to a small corral some distance away.

"Like what," said Wallace.

Diamond had a flash that there was a woman in the corral.

"Bullridin. Dad's got some good buckin bulls. Our rodeo class come out last month and rode em. Co uldn't hardly stay on one of em."

"I'll watch," said Wallace, in his ironic side-of-the-mouth voice.

Diamond considered rodeo classes the last resort of concrete heads who couldn't figure out how to hold a basketball. He'd taken martial arts and wrestling all the way through until they spiked both courses as frills. "Oh man," he said. "Bulls. I don't guess so."

Leecil Bewd ran ahead to the corral. There was a side pen and in it were three bulls, two of them pawing dirt. At the front of the pen a side-door chute opened into the corral. One of the crotchscratchers was in the arena, jumping around, ready to play bullfighter and toll a bull away from a tossed rider.

To Diamond the bulls looked murderous and wild, but even the ranch hands had a futile go at riding them, Lovis scraped off on the fence; Leecil's father, bounced down in three seconds, hit the ground on his behind, the kidney belt riding up his chest.

"Try it," said Leecil, mouth bloody from a face slam, spitting.

"Aw, not me," said Wallace. "I got a life in front of me."

"Yeah," said Diamond. "Yeah, I guess I'll give it a go."

"Atta boy, atta boy," said Como Bewd, and handed him a rosined left glove. "Ever been on a bull?"

"No sir," said Diamond, no boots, no spurs, no chaps, T-shirted and hatless. Leecil's old man told him to hold his free hand up, not to touch the bull or himself with it, keep his shoulders forward and his chin down, hold on with his feet and legs and left hand, above all not to think, and when he got bucked off, no matter what was broke, get up quick and run like hell for the fence. He helped him make the wrap, ease down on the animal, said, shake your face and git out there, and grinning, blood-speckled Lovis opened the chute door, waiting to see the town kid dumped and dive-bombed.

But he stayed on until someone counting eight hit the rail with the length of pipe to signal time. He flew off, landed on his feet, stumbling headlong but not falling, in a run for the rails. He hauled himself up, panting from the exertion and the intense nervy rush. He'd been shot out of the cannon. The shock of the violent motion, the lightning shifts of balance, the feeling of power as though he were the bull and not the rider, even the fright, fulfilled some greedy physical hunger in him he hadn't known was there. The experience had been exhilarating and unbearably personal.

"You know what," said Como Bewd. "You might make a bullrider."

Redsled, on the west slope of the divide, was fissured with thermal springs which attracted tourists, snowmobilers, skiers, hot and dusty ranch hands, banker bikers dropping fifty-dollar tips. It was the good thing about Redsled, the sulfurous, hellish smell and the wet heat buzzing him until he could not stand it, got out and ran to the river, falling into its dark current with banging heart.

"Let's hit the springs," he said on the way back, still on the adrenaline wave, needing something more.

"No," said Wallace, his first word in an hour. "I got something to do."

"Drop me off and go on home then," he said.

In the violent water, leaning against the slippery rocks, he replayed the ride, the feeling his life had doubled in size. His pale legs wavered under the water, pinprick air beads strung along each hair. Euphoria ran through him like blood, he laughed, remembered he had been on a bull before. He was five years old and they took a trip somewhere, he and his mother and, in those lost days, his father who was still his father, brought him in the afternoons to a county fair with a merry-go-round. He was crazy about the merry-go-round, not for the broad spin which made him throw up, nor for the rear view of the fiberglass horses with their swelled buttocks and the sinister holes where the ends of the nylon tails had been secured before vandals jerked them out, but for the glossy little black bull, the only bull among the ruined horses, tail intact, red saddle and smiling eyes, the eye shine depicted by a painted wedge of white. His father had lifted him on and stood with his hand reaching across Diamond's shoulder, steadying him as the bull went up and down and the galloping music played.

Monday morning on the schoolbus he went for Leecil sitting in the back with one of the crotchscratchers. Leecil touched thumb and forefinger in a circle, winked.

"I need to talk to you. I want to know how to get into it. The bullriding. Rodeo."

"Don't think so," said the crotchscratcher. "First time you git stacked up you'll yip for mama."

"He won't," said Leecil, and to Diamond, "You bet it ain't no picnic. Don't look for a picnic—you are goin a git tore up."

It turned out that it was a picnic and he did get tore up.

His mother, Kaylee Felts, managed a tourist store, one of a chain headquartered in Denver: HIGH WEST—*Vintage Cowboy Gear, Western Antiques, Spurs, Collectibles.* Diamond had helped open boxes, dust showcases, wire-brush crusty spurs since he was twelve and she told him there was probably a place in the business for him after college, one of the other stores if he wanted to see the world. He thought it was his choice but when he told her he was going to bullriding school in California she blew up.

"No. You can't. You're going to college. What is this, some kid thing you kept to yourself all this time? I worked like a fool to bring you boys up in town, get you out of the mud, give you a chance to make something out of yourselves. You're just going to throw everything away to be a rodeo bum? My god, whatever I try to do for you, you kick me right in the face."

"Well, I'm going to rodeo," he answered. "I'm going to ride bulls."

"You little devil," she said. "You're doing this to spite me and I know it. You are just hateful. You're not going to get any cheerleading from me on this one."

"That's all right," he said. "I don't need it."

"Oh, you need it," she said. "You need it, all right. Don't you get it, rodeo's for ranch boys who don't have the good opportunities you do? The stupidest ones are the bullriders. We get them in the shop every week trying to sell us those pot-metal buckles or their dirty chaps."

"Doing it," he said. It could not be explained.

"I can't stop a train," she said. "You're a royal pain, Shorty, and you always were. Grief from day one. You make this bed you'll lie in it. I mean it. You've got the stubbornness in you," she said, "like him. You're just like him, and that's no compliment."

Shut the fuck up, he thought, but didn't say it. He wanted to tell her she could give that set of lies a rest. He was nothing like him, and could not ever be.

"Don't call me Shorty," he said.

At the California bullriding school he rode forty animals in a week, invested in a case of sports tape, watched videos until he fell asleep sitting up. The instructor's tireless nasal voice called, push on it, you can't never think you're goin a lose, don't look into the well, find your balance point, once you're tapped, get right back into the pocket, don't never quit.

Back in Wyoming he found a room in Cheyenne, a junk job, bought his permit and started running the Mountain Circuit. He made his PRCA ticket in a month, thought he was in sweet clover. Somebody told him it was beginner's luck. He ran into Leecil Bewd at almost every rodeo, got drunk with him twice, and, after a time of red-eye solo driving, always broke, too much month and not enough money, they hooked up and traveled together, riding the jumps, covering bulls from one little rodeo to another, eating road dust. He had chosen this rough, bruising life with its confused philosophies of striving to win and apologizing for it when he did, but when he got on there was the dark lightning in his gut, a feeling of blazing real existence.

Leecil drove a thirty-year-old Chevrolet pickup with a bent frame, scabbed and bondo'd, rewired, re-engined, remufflered, a vehicle with a strong head that pulled fiercely to the right. It broke down at mean and crucial times. Once, jamming for Colorado Springs, it quit forty miles short. They leaned under the hood.

"Shoot, I hate pawin around in these goddamn greasy guts, all of a whatness to me. How come you don't know nothin about cars neither?"

"Just lucky."

A truck pulled up behind them, calf roper Sweets Musgrove riding shotgun and his pigtailed wife Neve driving. Sweets got out. He was holding a baby in pink rompers.

"Trouble?"

"Can't tell if it's trouble. Both so ignorant it might be good news and we wouldn't know it."

"I do this for a paycheck," said Musgrove getting under the hood with his baby and pulling at the truck's intestinal wires. "Had to live on rodeo we couldn't make the riffle, could we, baby?" Neve sauntered over, scratched a match on her boot sole and lit a cigarette, leaned on Musgrove.

"You want a knife?" said Leecil. "Cut the sumbuck?"

"You're getting your baby dirty," said Diamond, wishing Neve would take it.

"I rather have a greasy little girl than a lonesome baby, mhhmhh-mhh?" he said into the baby's fat neck. "Try startin it now." It didn't go and there wasn't any time to waste fooling with it.

"You can't both squeeze in with us and my mare don't like sharin her trailer. But that don't mean pig pee because there's a bunch a guys comin on. Somebody'll pick you up. You'll get there." He jammed a mouth-guard—pink, orange and purple—over his teeth and grinned at his charmed baby.

Four bullriders with two buckle bunnies in a convertible gathered them up and one of the girls pressed against Diamond from shoulder to ankle the whole way. He got to the arena in a visible mood to ride but not bulls.

It worked pretty well for a year and then Leecil quit. It had been a scorching, dirty afternoon at a Colorado fairgrounds, the showers dead and dry. Leecil squirted water from a gas station hose over his head and neck, drove with the window cranked down, the dry wind sucking up the moisture immediately. The venomous blue sky threw heat.

"Two big jumps, wrecked in time to git stepped on. Man, he ate me. Out a the money again. I sure wasn't packin enough in my shorts today to ride that trash. Say what, the juice ain't worth the squeeze. Made up my mind while I was rollin in the dirt. I used a think I wanted a rodeo more than anything," said Leecil, "but shoot, I got a say I hate it, the travelin, traffic and stinkin motels, the rest of it. Tired a bein sored up all the time. I don't got that thing you got, the style, the fuck-it-all-I-love-it thing. I miss the ranch bad. The old man's on my mind. He got some medical problem, can't hardly make his water good, told my brother there's blood in his bull stuff. They're doin tests. And there's Renata. What I'm tryin a say is, I'm cuttin out on you. Anyway, guess what, goin a get married." The flaring shadow of the truck sped along a bank cut.

"What do you mean? You knock Renata up?" It was all going at speed.

"Aw, yeah. It's o.k."

"Well shit, Leecil. Won't be much fun now." He was surprised that it was true. He knew he had little talent for friendship or affection, stood armored against love, though when it did come down on him later it came like an axe and he was slaughtered by it. "I never had a girl stick with me more than two hours. I don't know how you get past that two hours," he said.

Leecil looked at him.

He mailed a postcard of a big yellow bull on the charging run, ropes of saliva slung out from his muzzle, to his younger brother Pearl, but did not telephone. After Leecil quit he moved to Texas where there was a rodeo every night for a fast driver red-eyed from staring at pin headlights miles distant alternately dark and burning as the road swelled and fell away.

The second year he was getting some notice and making money until a day or so before the big Fourth of July weekend. He came off a great ride and landed hard on his feet with his right knee sharply flexed, tore the ligaments and damaged cartilage. He was a fast healer but it put him out for the summer. When he was off the crutches, bored and limping around on a cane, he thought about Redsled. The doctor said the hot springs might be a good idea. He picked up a night ride with

Tee Dove, a Texas bullrider, the big car slingshot at the black hump of range, dazzle of morning an hour behind the rim, not a dozen words exchanged.

"It's a bone game," Tee Dove said and Diamond thought he meant injuries, nodded.

For the first time in two years he sat at his mother's table. She said, "Bless this food, amen, oh boy, I knew you'd be back one of these days. And look at you. Just take a look at you. Like you climbed out of a ditch. Look at your hands," she said. "They're a mess. I suppose you're broke." She was dolled up, her hair long and streaked blond, crimped like Chinese noodles, her eyelids iridescent blue.

Diamond extended his fingers, turned his carefully scrubbed hands palm up, palm down, muscular hands with cut knuckles and small scars, two nails purple-black and lifting off at the base.

"They're clean. And I'm not broke. Didn't ask you for money, did I?"

"Oh, eat some salad," she said. They ate in silence, forks clicking among the pieces of cucumber and tomato. He disliked cucumber. She got up, clattered small plates with gold rims onto the table, brought out a supermarket lemon meringue pie, began to cut it with the silver pie server.

"All right," said Diamond, "calf-slobber pie."

Pearl, his ten-year-old brother, let out a bark.

She stopped cutting and fixed him with a stare. "You can talk ugly when you're with your rodeo bums, but when you are home keep your tongue decent."

He looked at her, seeing the cold blame. "I'll pass on that pie."

"I think all of us will after that unforgettable image. You'll want a cup of coffee." She had forbidden it when he lived at home, saying it would stunt his growth. Now it was this powdered stuff in the jar.

"Yeah." There wasn't much point in getting into it his first night home but he wanted a cup of real blackjack, wanted to throw the fucking pie at the ceiling.

She went out then, some kind of western junk meeting at the Redsled Inn, sticking him with the dishes. It was as if he'd never left.

He came down late the next morning. Pearl was sitting at the kitchen table reading a comic book. He was wearing the T-shirt Diamond had sent. It read, *Give Blood, Ride Bulls.* It was too small.

"Momma's gone to the shop. She said you should eat cereal, not eggs. Eggs have cholesterol. I saw you on t.v. once. I saw you get bucked off."

Diamond fried two eggs in butter and ate them out of the pan, fried two more. He looked for coffee but there was only the jar of instant dust.

"I'm going to get a buckle like yours when I'm eighteen," Pearl said. "And I'm not going to get bucked off because I'll hold on with the grip of death. Like this." And he made a white-knuckled fist.

"This ain't a terrific buckle. I hope you get a good one."

"I'm going to tell Momma you said 'ain't.'"

"For Christ sake, that's how everybody talks. Except for one old booger steer roper. I could curl your hair. And I *ain't* foolin. You want an egg?"

"I hate eggs. They aren't good for you. Ain't good for you. How does the old booger talk? Does he say 'calf-slobber pie'?"

"Why do you think she buys eggs if nobody's supposed to eat them? The old booger's religious. Lot of prayers and stuff Always reading pamphlets about Jesus. Actually he's not old. He's no older than me. He's younger than me. He don't never say 'ain't.' He don't say 'shit' or 'fuck' or 'cunt' or 'prick' or 'goddamn.' He says 'good lord' when he's pissed off or gets slammed up the side of his head."

Pearl laughed immoderately, excited by the forbidden words and low-down grammar spoken in their mother's kitchen. He expected to see the floor tiles curl and smoke.

"Rodeo's full of Jesus freaks. And double and triple sets of brothers. All kinds of Texas cousins. There's some fucking strange guys in it. It's like a magic show sometimes, all kinds of prayers and jujus and crosses and amulets and superstitions. Anybody does anything good, makes a good ride, it's not them, it's their mystical power connection helping them out. Guys from all over, Brazil, Canada, Australia dipping and bending, bowing heads, making signs." He yawned, began to rub the bad knee, thinking about the sulfur water deep to his chin and blue sky overhead. "So, you're going to hold on tight and not get bucked off?"

"Yeah. Really tight."

"I'll have to remember to try that," said Diamond.

He called the Bewd ranch to give Leecil a hello but the number had been disconnected. Information gave him a Gillette number. He thought it strange but called throughout the day. There was no answer. He tried again late that night and got Leecil's yawning croak.

"Hey, how come you're not out at the ranch? How come the ranch number's disconnected?" He heard the bad stuff coming before Leecil said anything.

"Aw, I'll tell you what, that didn't work out so good. When Dad died they valued the ranch, said we had a pay two million dollars in estate taxes. Two million dollars? That took the rag off the bush. We never had a pot to piss in, where was we supposed a get that kind a money for our own place that wasn't nothing when Dad took it over? You know what beef is bringin? Fifty-five cents a pound. We went round and round on it. Come down to it we had to sell. Sick about it, hell, I'm red-assed. I'm up here workin in the mines. Tell you, there's somethin wrong with this country."

"That's a dirty ride."

"Yeah. It is. It's been a dirty ride sinct I come back. Fuckin government."

"But you must have got a bunch of money for the place."

"Give my share to my brothers. They went up B.C. lookin for a ranch. It's goin a take all the money buy it, stock it. Guess I'm thinkin about goin up there with em. Wyomin's sure pulled out from under us. Hey, you're doin good with the bulls. Once in a while I think I might git back in it, but I git over that idea quick."

"I was doing o.k. until I messed up my knee. So what about your kid, was it a girl or a boy? I never heard. You didn't pass out cigars."

"You sure do ast the sore questions. That didn't turn out too good neither and I don't want to git into it just now. Done some things I regret. So, anyway, that's what I been doin, goin a funerals, hospitals, divorce court and real estate closins. You make it up here this weekend, get drunk? My birthday. Goin a be twenty-four and I feel like I got mileage on for fifty."

"Man, I can't. My knee's messed up enough I can't drive. I'll call you, I will call you."

It could be the worst kind of luck to go near Leecil.

On Thursday night, sliding the chicken breasts into the microwave, she prodded Pearl to get the silverware. She whipped the dehydrated potatoes with hot water, put the food on the table and sat down, looked at Diamond.

"I smell sulfur," she said. "Didn't you take a shower after the springs?"

"Not this time," he said.

"You reek." She shook open her napkin.

"All rodeo cowboys got a little tang to em."

"Cowboy? You're no more a cowboy than you are a little leather-winged bat. My grandfather was a rancher and he *hired* cowboys or what passed for them. My father gave that up for cattle sales and he hired ranch hands. My brother was never anything but a son-of-a-bee. None of them were cowboys but all of them were more cowboy than a rodeo bullrider ever will be. After supper," she said to Diamond, pushing the dish of pallid chicken breasts at him, "after supper I've got something I want you to see. We'll just take us a little ride."

"Can I come?" said Pearl.

"No. This is something I want your brother to see. Watch t.v. We'll be back in an hour."

"What is it," said Diamond, remembering the dark smear on the street she had brought him to years before. She had pointed, said, he didn't look both ways. He knew it would be something like that. The chicken breast lay on his plate like an inflated water wing. He should not have come back.

She drove through marginal streets, past the scrap-metal pile and the bentonite plant and, at the edge of town, crossed the railroad tracks where the road turned into rough dirt cutting through prairie. To the right, under a yellow sunset, stood several low metal buildings. The windows reflected the bright honey-colored west.

"Nobody here," said Diamond, "wherever we are," a kid again sitting in the passenger seat while his mother drove him around.

"Bar J stables. Don't worry, there's somebody here," said his mother. Gold light poured over her hands on the steering wheel, her arms, splashed the edges of her crimped hair. Her face, in shadow, was private and severe. He saw the withering skin of her throat. She said, "Hondo Gunsch? You know that name?"

"No." But he had heard it somewhere.

"Here," she said, pulling up in front of the largest building. Thousands of insects barely larger than dust motes floated in the luteous air. She walked quickly, he followed, dotting along.

"Hello," she called into the dark hallway. A light snapped on. A man in a white shirt, the pocket stiffened with a piece of plastic to hold his ballpoint pens, came through a door. Under his black hat, brim bent like the wings of a crow, was a face crowded with freckles, spectacles, beard and mustache.

"Hey there, Kaylee." The man looked at her as though she were hot buttered toast.

"This is Shorty, wants to be a rodeo star. Shorty, this is Kerry Moore."

Diamond shook the man's hot hand. It was an exchange of hostilities.

"Hondo's out in the tack room," said the man, looking at her. He laughed. "Always in the tack room. He'd sleep there if we let him. Come on out here."

He opened a door into a large, square room at the end of the stables. The last metaled light fell through high windows, gilding bridles and reins hanging on the wall. Along another wall a row of saddle racks projected, folded blankets resting on the shining saddles. A small refrigerator hummed behind the desk, and on the wall above it Diamond saw a framed magazine cover, *Boots 'N Bronks,* August 1960, showing a saddle bronc rider straight, square and tucked on a high-twisted horse, spurs raked all the way up to the cantle, his outflung arm in front of him. His hat was gone and his mouth open in a crazy smile. A banner read: *Gunsch Takes Cheyenne SB Crown.* The horse's back was humped, his nose pointed down, hind legs straight in a powerful jump and five feet of daylight between the descending front hooves and ground.

In the middle of the room an elderly man worked leather cream into a saddle; he wore a straw hat with the brim rolled high on the sides in a way that emphasized his long head shape. There was something wrong in the set of the shoulders, the forward slope of his torso from the hips. The room smelled of apples and Diamond saw a basket of them on the floor.

"Hondo, we got visitors." The man looked past them at nothing, showing the flat bulb of crushed nose, a dished cheekbone, the great dent above the left eye which seemed sightless. His mouth was still pursed with concentration. There was a pack of cigarettes in his shirt pocket. Emanating from him was a kind of carved-wood quietude common to those who have been a long time without sex, out of the traffic of the world.

"This here's Kaylee Felts and Shorty, stopped by to say howdy. Shorty's into rodeo. Guess *you* know something about rodeo, don't you, Hondo?" He spoke loudly as though the man was deaf.

The bronc rider said nothing, his blue, sweet gaze returning to the saddle, the right hand holding a piece of lambswool beginning again to move back and forth over the leather.

"He don't say much," said Moore. "He has a lot of difficulty but he keeps tryin. He's got plenty of try, haven't you, Hondo?"

The man was silent, working the leather. How many years since he had spurred a horse's shoulders, toes pointed east and west?

"Hondo, looks like you ought a change them sorry old floppy stirrup leathers one day," said Moore in a commanding tone. The bronc rider gave no sign he had heard.

"Well," said Diamond's mother after a long minute of watching the sinewy hands, "it was wonderful to meet you, Hondo. Good luck." She glanced at Moore, and Diamond could see a message fly but did not know their language.

They walked outside, the man and woman together, Diamond following, so deeply angry he staggered.

"Yeah. He's kind a deaf, old Hondo. He was a hot saddle bronc rider on his way to the top. Took the money two years runnin at Cheyenne. Then, some dinky little rodeo up around Meeteetse, his horse threw a fit in the chute, went over backwards, Hondo went down, got his head stepped on. Oh, 1961, and he been cleanin saddles for the Bar J since then. Thirty-seven years. That's a long, long time. He was twenty-six when it happened. Smart as anybody. Well, you rodeo, you're a rooster on Tuesday, feather duster on Wednesday. But like I say, he's still got all the try in the world. We sure think a lot a Hondo."

They stood silently watching Diamond get into the car.

"I'll call you," said the man and she nodded.

Diamond glared out the car window at the plain, the railroad tracks, the pawnshop, the Safeway, the Broken Arrow bar, Custom Cowboy, the vacuum cleaner shop. The topaz light reddened, played out. The sun was down and a velvety dusk coated the street, the bar neons spelling good times.

As she turned onto the river road she said, "I would take you to see a corpse to get you out of rodeo."

"You won't take me to see anything again."

The glassy black river flowed between dim willows. She drove very slowly.

"My god," she shouted suddenly, "what you've cost me!"

"*What!* What have I cost you?" The words shot out like flame from the mouth of a fire-eater.

The low beams of cars coming toward them in the dusk lit the wet run of her tears. There was no answer until she turned into the last street, then, in a guttural, adult woman's voice, raw and deep, as he had never heard it, she said, "You hard little man—*everything*."

He was out of the car before it stopped, limping up the stairs, stuffing clothes in his duffel bag, not answering Pearl.

"Diamond, you can't go yet. You were going to stay for two weeks. You only been here four days. We were going to put up a bucking barrel. We didn't talk about Dad. Not one time."

He had told Pearl many lies beginning "Dad and me and you, when you were a baby"—that was the stuff the kid wanted to hear. He never told him what he knew and if he never found out that was a win.

"I'll come back pretty soon," he lied, "and we'll get her done." He was sorry for the kid but the sooner he learned it was a tough go the better. But maybe there was nothing for Pearl to know. Maybe the bad news was all his.

"Momma likes me better than you," shouted Pearl, saving something from the wreck. He stripped off the T-shirt and threw it at Diamond.

“This I know.” He called a taxi to take him to the crackerbox airport where he sat for five hours until a flight with connections to Calgary left.

In his cocky first year he had adopted a wide-legged walk as though there was swinging weight between his thighs. He felt the bull in himself, hadn’t yet discerned the line of inimical difference between roughstock and rider. He dived headlong into the easy girls, making up for the years of nothing. He wanted the tall ones. In that bullish condition he tangled legs with the wife of Myron Sasser, his second traveling partner. They were in Cheyenne in Myron’s truck and she was with them, sitting in the backseat of the club cab. All of them were hungry. Myron pulled into the Burger Bar. He left the truck running, the radio loud, a dark Texas voice entangled in static.

“How many you want, Diamond, two or three? Londa, you want onions with yours?”

They had picked her up at Myron’s parents’ house in Pueblo the day before. She was five-eleven, long brown curls like Buffalo Bill, had looked at Diamond and said to Myron, “You didn’t say he was hardly fryin size. Hey there, chip,” she said.

“That’s me,” he said, “smaller than the little end of nothing whittled to a point,” smiled through murder.

She showed them an old heart-shaped waffle iron she had bought at a yard sale. It was not electric, a gadget from the days of the wood-burning range. The handles were of twisted wire. She promised Myron a Valentine breakfast.

“I’ll git this,” said Myron and went into the Burger Bar.

Diamond waited with her in the truck, aroused by her orchidaceous female smell. Through the glass window they could see Myron standing near the end of a long line. He thought of what she’d said, moved out of the front seat and into the back with her and pinned her, wrestled her 36-inseam jeans down to her ankles and got it in, like fucking sandpaper, and his stomach growling with hunger the whole time. She was not willing. She bucked and shoved and struggled and cursed him, she was dry, but he wasn’t going to stop then. Something fell off the seat with a hard sound.

“My waffle iron,” she said and nearly derailed him—he finished in five or six crashing strokes and it was done. He was back in the front seat before Myron reached the head of the line.

"I heard it called a lot of things," he said, "but never a waffle iron," and laughed until he choked. He felt fine.

She cried angrily in the seat behind him, pulling at her clothes.

"Hey," he said. "Hush up. It didn't hurt you. I'm too damn small to hurt a big girl like you, right? I'm the one should be crying—could have burred it off." He couldn't believe it when she opened the door and jumped down, ran into the Burger Bar, threw herself at Myron. He saw Myron putting his head over to listen to her, glancing out at the parking lot where he could see nothing, wiping the tears from her face with a paper napkin he took from the counter, and then charging toward the door with squared, snarling mouth. Diamond got out of the truck. Might as well meet it head-on.

"What a you done to Londa."

"Same thing you did to that wormy Texas buckle bunny the other night." He didn't have anything against Myron Sasser except that he was a humorless fascist who picked his nose and left pliant knobs of snot on the steering wheel, but he wanted the big girl to get it clear and loud.

"You little pissant shit," said Myron and came windmilling at him. Diamond had him flat on the macadam, face in a spilled milk shake, but in seconds more lay beside him knocked colder than a wedge by the waffle iron. He heard later that Myron had sloped off to Hawaii without his amazon wife and was doing island rodeo. Let them both break their necks. The girl had too much mustard and she'd find it out if she came his way again.

That old day the bottom dropped had been a Sunday, the day they usually had pancakes and black cherry syrup, but she had not made the pancakes, told him to fix himself a bowl of cereal, feed Pearl his baby pears. He was thirteen, excited about the elk hunt coming up in three weekends. Pearl stank and squirmed in full diapers but by then they were seriously fighting. Diamond, sick of hearing the baby roar, had cleaned him up, dropped the dirty diaper in the stinking plastic pail.

They fought all day, his mother's voice low and vicious, his father shouting questions that were not answered but turned back at him with vindictive silences as powerful as a swinging bat. Diamond watched television, the sound loud enough to damp the accusations and furious abuse cracking back and forth upstairs. There were rushing footsteps overhead as though they were playing basketball, cries and shouts. It had nothing to do with him. He felt sorry for Pearl who bawled every time he heard their mother's anguished sobbing in the room above. One or two long silences held but they could not be mistaken for peace. In the late afternoon Pearl fell asleep on the living room couch with his fist knotted in his blanket. Diamond went out in the yard, kicked around, cleaned the car windshield for something to do. It was cold and windy, a cigar cloud poised over the mountain range forty miles west. He picked up rocks and threw them at the cloud pretending they Were bullets fired at an elk. He could hear them inside, still at it.

The door slammed and his father came across the porch carrying the brown suitcase with a tiny red trademark horse in the corner, strode toward the car as if he were late.

"Dad," said Diamond. "The elk hunt—"

His father stared at him. In that twitching face his pupils were black and huge, eating up the hazel color to the rim.

"Don't never call me that again. Not your father and never was. Now get the fuck out of the way, you little bastard," the words high-pitched and tumbling.

After the breakup with Myron Sasser he bought a third-hand truck, an old Texas hoopy not much better than Leecil's wreck, traveled alone for a few months, needing the solitary distances, blowing past mesas and red buttes piled like meat, humped and horned, and on the highway chunks of mule deer, hair the buckskin color of winter grass, flesh like rough breaks in red country, playas of dried blood. He almost always had a girl in the motel bed with him when he could afford a motel, a half-hour painkiller but without the rush and thrill he got from a bullride. There was no sweet time when it was over. He wanted them to get gone. The in-and-out girls wasped it around that he was quick on the trigger, an arrogant little prick and the hell with his star-spangled bandanna.

"Hit the delete button on you, buddy," flipping the whorish blond hair.

What they said didn't matter because there was an endless supply of them and because he knew he was getting down the page and into the fine print of this way of living. There was nobody in his life to slow him down with love. Sometimes riding the bull was the least part of it, but only the turbulent ride gave him the indescribable rush, shot him mainline with crazyass elation. In the arena everything was real because none of it was real except the chance to get dead. The charged bolt came, he thought, because he wasn't. All around him wild things were falling to the earth.

One night in Cody, running out to the parking lot to beat the traffic, Pake Bitts, a big Jesus-loving steer roper, yelled out to him, "You goin a Roswell?"

"Yeah." Bitts was running parallel with him, the big stout guy with white-blond hair and high color. A sticker, *Praise God,* was peeling loose from his gear bag.

"Can I git a ride? My dee truck quit on me up in Livinston. Had to rent a puny car, thing couldn't hardly haul my trailer. Burned out the transmission. Tee Dove said he thought you was headed for Roswell?"

"You bet. Let's go. If you're ready." They hitched up Bitts's horse trailer, left the rental car standing.

"Fog it, brother, we're short on time," said the roper, jumping in. Diamond had the wheels spattering gravel before he closed the door.

He thought it would be bad, a lot of roadside prayers and upcast eyes, but Pake Bitts was steady, watched the gas gauge, took care of business and didn't preach.

Big and little they went on together to Mollala, to Tuska, to Roswell, Guthrie, Kaycee, to Baker and Bend. After a few weeks Pake said that if Diamond wanted a permanent traveling partner he was up for it. Diamond said yeah, although only a few states still allowed steer roping and Pake had to cover long, empty ground, his main territory in the livestock country of Oklahoma, Wyoming, Oregon and New Mexico. Their schedules did not fit into the same box without patient adjustment. But Pake knew a hundred dirt road shortcuts, steering them through scabland and slope country, in and out of the tiger shits, over the tawny plain still grooved with pilgrim wagon ruts, into early darkness and the first storm laying down black ice, hard orange dawn, the world smoking, snaking dust devils on bare dirt, heat boiling out of the sun until the paint on the truck hood curled, ragged webs of dry rain that never hit the ground, through small-town traffic and stock on the road, band of horses in morning fog, two redheaded cowboys moving a house that filled the roadway and Pake busting around and into the ditch to get past, leaving junkyards and Mexican cafés behind, turning into midnight motel entrances with RING OFFICE BELL signs or steering onto the black prairie for a stunned hour of sleep.

Bitts came from Rawlins and always he wanted to get to the next rodeo and grab at the money, was interested in no woman but his big-leg, pregnant wife Nancy, a heavy Christian girl, studying, said Bitts, for her degree in geology. "You wont a have a good t alk," he said, "have one with Nancy. Good lord, she can tell you all about rock formations."

"How can a geologist believe that the earth was creat ed in seven days?"

"Shoot, she's a Christian geologist. Nothin is impossible for God and he could do it all in seven days, fossils, the whole nine. Life is full a wonders." He laid a chew of long-cut into his cheek for even he had his vices.

"How did you get into it," asked Diamond. "Grow up on a ranch?"

"Big prison."

"Right. My dad's a guard at the pen in Rawlins, but before that he was down at Huntsville. Huntsville had a real good prison rodeo program for years. And my dad took me to all them rodeos. He got me started in the Little Britches program. And here's somethin, my granddad Bitts did most of his ropin at Huntsville. Twist the nose off of a dentist. That bad old cowhand had a tattoo of a rope around his neck and piggin strings around his wrists. He seen the light after a few years and took Jesus into his heart, and that passed on down to my dad and to me. And I try to live a Christian life and help others."

They drove in silence for half an hour, light overcast dulling the basin grass to the shades of dirty pennies, then Pake started in again.

"Bringin me to somethin I wont a say to you. About your bullridin. About rodeo? See, the bull is not supposed a be your role model, he is your opponent and you have to get the best a him, same as the steer is my opponent and I have to pump up and git everthing right to catch and thow em or I *won't* thow em."

"Hey, I know that." He'd known too that there would be a damn sermon sooner or later.

"No, you don't. Because if you did you wouldn't be playin the bull night after night, you wouldn't get in it with your buddies' wives, what I'd call forcible entry what you done, you would be a man lookin for someone to marry and raise up a family with. You'd take Jesus for a role model, not a dee ornery bull. Which you can't deny you done. You got a quit off playin the bull."

"I didn't think Jesus was a married man."

"Maybe not a married man, but he was a cowboy, the original rodeo cowboy. It says it right in the Bible. It's in Matthew, Mark, Luke *and* John." He adopted a sanctimonious tone: "'Go into the village in which, at your enterin, ye shall find a colt tied, on which yet never no man sat; loose him and bring him here. The Lord hath need a him. And they brought him to Jesus, and they cast their garments upon the colt and they set Jesus on it.' Now, if that ain't a description a bareback ridin I don't know what is."

"I ride a bull, the bull's my partner, and if bulls could drive you can bet there'd be one sitting behind the wheel right now. I don't know how you figure all this stuff about me."

"Easy. Myron Sasser's my half-brother." He rolled down the window and spit. "Dad had a little bull in him, too. But he got over it."

Pake started in again a day or two later. Diamond was sick of hearing about Jesus and family values. Pake had said, "You got a kid brother, that right? How come he ain't never at none a these rodeos lookin at his big brother? And your daddy and mama?"

"Pull over a minute."

Bitts eased the truck over on the hard prairie verge, threw it into park, mis-guessing that Diamond wanted to piss, got out himself, unzipping.

"Wait," said Diamond standing where the light fell hard on him. "I want you to take a good look at me. You see me?" He turned sideways and back, faced Bitts. "That's all there is. What you see. Now do your business and let's get down the road."

"Aw, what I mean is," said Bitts, "you don't get how it is for nobody but your own dee self. You don't get it that you can't have a fence with only one post."

Late August and hot as billy hell, getting on out of Miles City Pake's head of maps failed and they ended on rimrock south of the Wyo line, tremendous roll of rough country in front of them, a hundred-mile sightline with bands of antelope and cattle like tiny ink flecks that flew from hard-worked nib pens on old promissory notes. They backtracked and sidetracked and a few miles outside Greybull Diamond pointed at the trucks drawn up in front of a slouched ranch house that had been converted into a bar, the squared logs weathered almost black.

"On the end, that's Sweets Musgrove's horse trailer, right? And Nachtigal's rig. Goddamn calf ropers, talk about their horses like they're women. You hear Nachtigal last night? 'She's honest, she's good, she never cheated on me.' Talking about his horse."

"How I feel about my horse."

"Pull in. I am going to drink a beer without taking a breath."

"Lucky if we git out alive goin where them guys are. Nachtigal's crazy. Rest of em don't talk about nothin but their trailers."

"I don't give a shit, Pake. You have your coffee, but I need a couple beers."

Above the door a slab of pine hung, the name of the place, Saddle Rack, scorched deep. Diamond pushed open the plank door, pocked with bullet holes in a range of calibers. It was one of the good places, dark, the log walls burned with hundreds of cattle brands, dim photographs of long-dead bronc busters high in the clouds and roundup crews in sweaters and woolly chaps. At the back of the room stood the oldest jukebox in the world, a crusty, dented machine with the neon gone dead and a flashlight on a string for patrons fussy enough to want to make a choice. The high gliding 1935 voice of Milton Brown was drifting, *"oh bree-yee-yee-yeeze"* over the zinc bar and four tables.

The bartender was a hardheaded old baldy with a beak and a cleft chin. Bottles, spigots, and a dirty mirror—the bartender's territory was not complex. He looked at them and Pake said ginger ale after gauging the tarry liquid on the hot plate. Diamond recognized he was going to get seriously drunk here. Sweets Musgrove and Nachtigal, Ike Soot, Jim Jack Jett, hats off, receding hairlines in full view, sat at one of the tables, Jim Jack drinking red beer, the others whiskey and they were sliding deep down, cigars in honor of Nachtigal's daughter's first barrel race win, the cigars half-puffed and dead in the ashtray.

"What the hell you doin here?"

"Shit, you don't go past Saddle Rack without you stop and git irrigated."

"Looks like it."

Nachtigal gestured at the jukebox, "Ain't you got no Clint Black? No Dwight Yoakam?"

"Shut up and like what you get," said the bartender. "You're hearin early pedal steel. You're hearin priceless stuff. You rodeo boys don't know nothin about country music."

"Horseshit." Ike Soot took a pair of dice from his pocket.

"Roll the bones, see who's goin a pay."

"You buyin, Nachtigal," said Jim Jack. "I'm cleaned out. What little I won, lost it to that Indan sumbitch, Black Vest, works for one a the stock contractors. All or nothin, not a little bit but the whole damn everthing. One throw. He got a pair a bone dice, only one spot between the two, shakes em, throws em down. It's quick."

"I played that with him. Want some advice?"

"No."

It was come and go with the drinks and in a while Jim Jack said something about babies and wives and the pleasures of home which started Pake off on one of his family-hearth lectures, and with the next round Ike Soot cried a little and said the happiest day of his life was when he put that gold buckle in his daddy's hand and said, I done it for you. Musgrove topped them all by confessing that he had split the $8,200 he picked up at the Finals between his grandmother and a home for blind orphans. With five whiskeys and four beers sloshing, Diamond took a turn, addressing them all, even the two dusty, sweat-runneled ranch hands who'd come in off the baler to press their faces against the cold pitcher of beer Ranny stood between them.

"You all make a big noise about family, what I hear, wife and kids, ma and pa, sis and bub, but none of you spend much time at home and you never wanted to or you wouldn't be in rodeo. Rodeo's the family. Ones back at the ranch don't count for shit."

One of the hands at the bar slapped his palm down and Nachtigal marked him with his eye.

Diamond held up the whiskey glass.

"Here's to it. Nobody sends you out to do chores, treats you like a fool. Take your picture, you're on t.v., ask your wild-hair opinion, get your autograph. You're somebody, right? Here's to it. Rodeo. They say we're dumb but they don't say we're cowards. Here's to big money for short rides, here's to busted spines and pulled groins, empty pockets, damn all-night driving, chance to buck out—if you got good medicine, happens to somebody else. Know what I think? I think—" But he didn't know what he thought except that Ike Soot was swinging at him, but it was only a motion to catch him before he smashed into the cigar butts. That was the night he lost his star-spangled bandanna and went into the slump.

"Last time I seen that wipe somebody was moppin puke off the floor with it," said Bitts. "And it weren't me."

In the sixth second the bull stopped dead, then shifted everything the other way and immediately back again and he was lost, flying to the left into his hand and over the animal's shoulder, his eye catching the wet glare of the bull, but his hand turned upside down and jammed. He was hung up and good. Stay on your feet, he said aloud, jump, amen. The bull was crazy to get rid of him and the clanging bell. Diamond was jerked high off the ground with every lunge, snapped like a towel. The rope was in a half- twist, binding his folded fingers against the bull's back and he could not turn his hand over and open the fingers. Everything in him strained to touch the ground with his feet but the bull was too big and he was too small. The animal spun so rapidly its shape seemed to the watchers like mottled streaks of paint, the rider a paint rag. The bullfighters darted like terriers. The bull whipped him from the Arctic Circle to the Mexico border with every plunge. There was bull hair in his mouth. His arm was being pulled from its socket. It went on and on. This time he was going to die in front of shouting strangers. The bull's drop lifted him high and the bullfighter, waiting for the chance, thrust his hand up under Diamond's arm, rammed the tail of the rope through and jerked. The fingers of his glove opened and he fell cartwheeling away from hooves. The next moment the bull was on him, hooking. He curled, got his good arm over his head.

"Oh man, get up, this's a mean one," someone far away called and he was running on all fours, rump in the air, to the metal rails, a clown there, the bull already gone. The audience suddenly laughed and out of the corner of his eye he saw the other clown mocking his stagger. He pressed against the rails, back to the audience, dazed, unable to move. They were waiting for him to get out of the arena. Beyond the beating rain sirens sounded faint and sad.

A hand patted him twice on the right shoulder, someone said, "Can you walk?" Trembling, he tried to nod his head and could not. His left arm hung limp. He profoundly believed death had marked him out, then had ridden him almost to the buzzer, but had somehow wrecked. The man got in under his right arm, someone else grasped him around the waist, half-carried him to a room where a local sawbones sat swinging one foot and smoking a cigarette. No sports medicine team here. He thought dully that he did not want to be looked at by a doctor who smoked. From the arena the announcer's voice echoed as though in a culvert, "What a ride, folks, far as it went, but all for nothin, a zero for Diamond Felts, but you got a be proud a what this young man stands for, don't let him go away without a big hand, he's goin a be all right, and now here's Dunny Scotus from Whipup, Texas—"

He could smell the doctor's clouded breath, his own rank stench. He was slippery with sweat and the roaring pain.

"Can you move your arm? Are your fingers numb? Can you feel this? O.k., let's get this shirt off." He set the jaws of his scissors at the cuff and began to cut up the sleeve.

"This's a fifty-dollar shirt," whispered Diamond. It was a new one with a design of red feathers and black arrows across the sleeves and breast.

"Believe me, you wouldn't appreciate it if I tried to pull your arm out of the sleeve." The scissors worked across the front yoke and the ruined shirt fell away. The air felt cold on his wet skin. He shook and shook. It was a bad luck shirt now anyway.

"There you go," said the doctor. "Dislocated shoulder. Humerus displaced forward from the shoulder socket. All right, I'm going to try to reposition the humerus." The doctor's chin was against the back of his shoulder, his hands taking the useless arm, powerful smell of tobacco. "This will hurt for a minute. I'm going to manipulate this—"

"Jesus *CHRIST!*" The pain was excruciating and violent. The tears rolled down his hot face and he couldn't help it.

"Cowboy up," said the doctor sardonically.

Pake Bitts walked in, looked at him with interest.

"Got hung up, hah? I didn't see it but they said you got hung up pretty good. Twenty-eight seconds. They'll put you on the videos. Thunderstorm out there." He was damp from the shower, last week's scab still riding his upper lip and a fresh raw scrape on the side of his jaw. He spoke to the doctor. "Thow his shoulder out? Can he drive? It's his turn a drive. We got a be in south Texas two o'clock tomorrow afternoon."

The doctor finished wrapping the cast, lit another cigarette. "I wouldn't want to do it—right hand's all he's got. Dislocated shoulder, it's not just a question of pop it back in and away you go. He could need surgery. There's injured ligaments, internal bleeding, swelling, pain, could be some nerve or blood vessel damage. He's hurting. He's going to be eating aspirin by the handful. He's going to be in the cast for a month. If he's going to drive, one-handed or with his teeth, I can't give him codeine and you'd better not let him take any either. Call your insurance company, make sure you're covered for injury-impaired driving."

"What insurance?" said Pake, then, "You ought a quit off smokin," and to Diamond, "Well, the Good Lord spared you. When can we get out a here? Hey, you see how they spelled my name? Good Lord." He yawned hugely, had driven all the last night coming down from Idaho.

"Give me ten. Let me get in the shower, steady up. You get my rope and war bag. I'll be o.k. to drive. I just need ten."

The doctor said, "On your way, pal."

Someone else was coming in, a deep cut over his left eyebrow, finger pressed below the cut to keep the blood out of his rapidly swelling eyes and he was saying, just tape it up, tape the fuckin eyes open, I'm gettin on one.

He undressed one-handed in the grimy concrete shower room having trouble with the four-buckle chaps and his bootstraps. The pain came in long ocean rollers. He couldn't get on the other side of it. There was someone in one of the shower stalls, leaning his forehead against the concrete, hands flat against the wall and taking hot water on the back of his neck.

Diamond saw himself in the spotted mirror, two black eyes, bloody nostrils, his abraded right cheek, his hair dark with sweat, bull hairs stuck to his dirty, tear-streaked face, a bruise from armpit to buttocks. He was dizzy with the pain and a huge weariness overtook him. The euphoric charge had never kicked in this time. If he were dead this might be hell—smoking doctors and rank bulls, eight hundred miles of night road ahead, hurting all the way.

The cascade of water stopped and Tee Dove came out of the shower, hair plastered flat. He was ancient, Diamond knew, thirty-six, an old man for bullriding but still doing it. His sallow-cheeked face was a map of surgical repair and he carried enough body scars to open a store. A few months earlier Diamond had seen him, broken nose draining dark blood, take two yellow pencils and push one into each nostril, maneuvering them until the smashed cartilage and nasal bones were forced back into position.

Dove rubbed his scarred torso with his ragged but lucky towel, showed his fox teeth to Diamond, said, "Ain't it a bone game, bro."

Outside the rain had stopped, the truck gleamed wet, gutters flooded with runoff. Pake Bitts was in the passenger seat, already asleep and snoring gently. He woke when Diamond, barechested, barefooted, pulled the seat forward, threw in the cut shirt, fumbled one-handed in his duffel bag for an oversize sweatshirt he could get over the cast, jammed into his old athletic shoes, got in and started the engine.

"You o.k. to drive? You hold out two, three hours while I get some sleep I'll take it the rest a the way. You drive the whole road is not a necessity by no means."

"It's o.k. How did they spell your name?"

"C-A-K-E. Cake Bitts. Nance'll laugh her head off over that one. Burn a rag, brother, we're runnin late." And he was asleep again, calloused hand resting on his thigh palm up and a little open as though to receive something in it.

Just over the Texas border he pulled into an all-night truck stop and filled the tank, bought two high-caffeine colas and drank them, washing down his keep-awakes and pain-stoppers. He walked past the cash registers and aisles of junk food to the telephones, fumbled the phone card from his wallet and dialed. It would be two-thirty in Redsled.

She answered on the first ring. Her voice was clear. She was awake.

"It's me," he said. "Diamond."

"Shorty?" she said. "What?"

"Listen, there's no way I can put this that's gentle or polite. Who was my father?"

"What do you mean? Shirley Custer Felts. You know that."

"No," he said. "I don't know that." He told her what Shirley Custer Felts had said getting into his car ten years earlier.

"That dirty man," she said. "He set you up like a time bomb. He knew the kind of kid you were, that you'd brood and sull over it and then blow up."

"I'm not blowing up. I'm asking you; who was he?"

"I told you." As she spoke he heard a deep smothered cough over the wire.

"I don't believe you. Third time, who was my father?"

He waited.

"Who you got there, Momma? The big slob with the black hat?"

"Nobody," she said and hung up. He didn't know which question she'd answered.

He was still standing there when Pake Bitts came in, shuffling and yawning.

"You wont me a drive now?" He pounded the heel of his hand on his forehead.

"No, get you some sleep."

"Aw, yeah. Piss on the fire, boy, and let's go."

He was o.k. to drive. He would drive all the way. He could do it now, this time, many more times to come. Yet it was as though some bearing had seized up inside him and burned out. It had not been the phone call but the flat minute pressed against the rail, when he could not walk out of the arena.

He pulled back onto the empty road. There were a few ranch lights miles away, the black sky against the black terrain drawing them into the hem of the starry curtain. As he drove toward the clangor and flash of the noon arena he considered the old saddle bronc rider rubbing leather for thirty-seven years, Leecil riding off into the mosquito-clouded Canadian sunset, the ranch hand bent over a calf, slitting the scrotal sac. The course of life's events seemed slower than the knife but not less thorough.

There was more to it than that, he supposed, and heard again her hoarse, charged voice saying "*Everything.*" It was all a hard, fast ride that ended in the mud. He passed a coal train in the dark, the dense rectangles that were the cars gliding against indigo night, another, and another, and another. Very slowly, as slowly as light comes on a clouded morning, the euphoric heat flushed through him, or maybe just the memory of it.

RAYMOND CARVER
(1938–1988)

Of the writers in this anthology, Raymond Carver is one of the very few to have devoted himself to the art of the short story and the poem; to have devoted himself, in a sense, to the art of dramatically impacted brevity. In discussing Minimalism as a mode of fiction, Carver spoke of his practice as a form of realism in the Anderson–Hemingway tradition: "the gradual accretion of meaningful detail, the concrete word as opposed to the abstract or arbitrary or slippery word."

Raymond Carver was born in Clatskanie, Oregon, and educated at Humboldt State University and the University of Iowa. He had long been associated with Port Angeles, Washington, where he was living at the time of his death. Though he published relatively few volumes of short fiction, his influence upon younger writers has been considerable. His fiction titles are Will You Please Be Quiet, Please? *(1976),* What We Talk About When We Talk About Love *(1981),* Cathedral *(1983), and* Where I'm Calling From: New and Selected Stories *(1988). His poetry collections include* Winter Insomnia *(1970),* Ultramarine *(1986), and the posthumously published* A New Walk to the River *(1990).*

America is surely not the only culture in which a passion for material things has been elevated to romance, but it is surely one of the few cultures to have so thoroughly examined this romance. "Are These Actual Miles?" is vintage Carver, though written comparatively early in his career. In this wonderfully succinct tale, an entire marriage—an entire way of life—is given an emblematic shape in the lost car remembered "there in the drive, in the sun, gleaming."

Are These Actual Miles?

Fact is the car needs to be sold in a hurry, and Leo sends Toni out to do it. Toni is smart and has personality. She used to sell children's encyclopedias door to door. She signed him up, even though he didn't have kids. Afterward, Leo asked her for a date, and the date led to this. This deal has to be cash, and it has to be done tonight. Tomorrow somebody they owe might slap a lien on the car. Monday they'll be in court, home free—but word on them went out yesterday, when their lawyer mailed the letters of intention. The hearing on Monday is nothing to worry about, the lawyer has said. They'll be asked some questions, and they'll sign some papers, and that's it. But sell the convertible, he said—today, *tonight.* They can hold onto the little car, Leo's car, no problem. But they go into court with that big convertible, the court will take it, and that's that.

Toni dresses up. It's four o'clock in the afternoon. Leo worries the lots will close. But Toni takes her time dressing. She puts on a new white blouse, wide lacy cuffs, the new two-piece suit, new heels. She transfers the stuff from her straw purse into the new patent-leather handbag. She studies the lizard makeup pouch and puts that in too. Toni has been two hours on her hair and face. Leo stands in the bedroom doorway and taps his lips with his knuckles, watching.

"You're making me nervous," she says. "I wish you wouldn't just stand," she says. "So tell me how I look."

"You look fine," he says. "You look great. I'd buy a car from you anytime."

"But you don't have money," she says, peering into the mirror. She pats her hair, frowns. "And your credit's lousy. You're nothing," she says. "Teasing," she says and looks at him in the mirror. "Don't be serious," she says. "It has to be done, so I'll do it. You take it out, you'd be lucky to get three, four hundred and we both know it. Honey, you'd be lucky if you didn't have to pay *them.*" She gives her hair a final pat, gums her lips, blots the lipstick with a tissue. She turns away from the mirror and picks up her purse. "I'll have to have dinner or something, I told you that already, that's the way they work, I know them. But don't worry, I'll get out of it," she says. "I can handle it."

"Jesus," Leo says, "did you have to say that?"

She looks at him steadily. "Wish me luck," she says.

"Luck," he says. "You have the pink slip?" he says.

She nods. He follows her through the house, a tall woman with a small high bust, broad hips and thighs. He scratches a pimple on his neck. "You're sure?" he says. "Make sure. You have to have the pink slip."

"I have the pink slip," she says.

"Make sure."

She starts to say something, instead looks at herself in the front window and then shakes her head.

"At least call," he says. "Let me know what's going on."

"I'll call," she says. "Kiss, kiss. Here," she says and points to the corner of her mouth. "Careful," she says.

He holds the door for her. "Where are you going to try first?" he says. She moves past him and onto the porch.

Ernest Williams looks from across the street. In his Bermuda shorts, stomach hanging, he looks at Leo and Toni as he directs a spray onto his begonias. Once, last winter, during the holidays, when Toni and the kids were visiting his mother's, Leo brought a woman home. Nine o'clock the next morning, a cold foggy Saturday, Leo walked the woman to the car, surprised Ernest Williams on the sidewalk with a newspaper in his hand. Fog drifted, Ernest Williams stared, then slapped the paper against his leg, hard.

Leo recalls that slap, hunches his shoulders, says, "You have someplace in mind first?"

"I'll just go down the line," she says. "The first lot, then I'll just go down the line."

"Open at nine hundred," he says. "Then come down. Nine hundred is low bluebook, even on a cash deal."

"I know where to start," she says.

Ernest Williams turns the hose in their direction. He stares at them through the spray of water. Leo has an urge to cry out a confession.

"Just making sure," he says.

"Okay, okay," she says. "I'm off."

It's her car, they call it her car, and that makes it all the worse. They bought it new that summer three years ago. She wanted something to do after the kids started school, so she went back selling. He was working six days a week in the fiber-glass plant. For a while they didn't know how to spend the money. Then they put a thousand on the convertible and doubled and tripled the payments until in a year they had it paid. Earlier, while she was dressing, he took the jack and spare from the trunk and emptied the glove compartment of pencils, matchbooks, Blue Chip stamps. Then he washed it and vacuumed inside. The red hood and fenders shine.

"Good luck," he says and touches her elbow.

She nods. He sees she is already gone, already negotiating.

"Things are going to be different!" he calls to her as she reaches the driveway. "We start over Monday. I mean it."

Ernest Williams looks at them and turns his head and spits. She gets into the car and lights a cigarette.

"This time next week!" Leo calls again. "Ancient history!"

He waves as she backs into the street. She changes gear and starts ahead. She accelerates and the tires give a little scream.

In the kitchen Leo pours Scotch and carries the drink to the backyard. The kids are at his mother's. There was a letter three days ago, his name penciled on the outside of the dirty envelope, the only letter all summer not demanding payment in full. We are having fun, the letter said. We like Grandma. We have a new dog called Mr. Six. He is nice. We love him. Good-bye.

He goes for another drink. He adds ice and sees that his hand trembles. He holds the hand over the sink. He looks at the hand for a while, sets down the glass, and holds out the other hand. Then he picks up the glass and goes back outside to sit on the steps. He recalls when he was a kid his dad pointing at a fine house, a tall white house surrounded by apple trees and a high white rail fence. "That's Finch," his dad said admiringly. "He's been in bankruptcy at least twice. Look at that house." But bankruptcy is a company collapsing utterly, executives cutting their wrists and throwing themselves from windows, thousands of men on the street.

Leo and Toni still had furniture. Leo and Toni had furniture and Toni and the kids had clothes. Those things were exempt. What else? Bicycles for the kids, but these he had sent to his mother's for safekeeping. The portable air-conditioner and the appliances, new washer and dryer, trucks came for those things weeks ago. What else did they have? This and that, nothing mainly, stuff that wore out or fell to pieces long ago. But there were some big parties back there, some fine travel. To Reno and Tahoe, at eighty with the top down and the radio playing. Food, that was one of the big items. They gorged on food. He figures thousands on luxury items alone. Toni would go to the grocery and put in everything she saw. "I had to do without when I was a kid," she says. "These kids are not going to do without," as if he'd been insisting they should. She joins all the book clubs. "We never had books around when I was a kid," she says as she tears open the heavy packages. They enroll in the record clubs for something to play on the new stereo. They sign up for it all. Even a pedigreed terrier named Ginger. He paid two hundred and found her run over in the street a week later. They buy what they want. If they can't pay, they charge. They sign up.

His undershirt is wet; he can feel the sweat rolling from his underarms. He sits on the step with the empty glass in his hand and watches the shadows fill up the yard. He stretches, wipes his face. He listens to the traffic on the highway and considers whether he should go to the basement, stand on the utility sink, and hang himself with his belt. He understands he is willing to be dead.

Inside he makes a large drink and he turns the TV on and he fixes something to eat. He sits at the table with chili and crackers and watches something about a blind detective. He clears the table. He washes the pan and the bowl, dries these things and puts them away, then allows himself a look at the clock.

It's after nine. She's been gone nearly five hours.

He pours Scotch, adds water, carries the drink to the living room. He sits on the couch but finds his shoulders so stiff they won't let him lean back. He stares at the screen and sips, and soon he goes for another drink. He sits again. A news program begins—it's ten o'clock—and he says, "God, what in God's name has gone wrong?" and goes to the kitchen to return with more Scotch. He sits, he closes his eyes, and opens them when he hears the telephone ringing;

"I wanted to call," she says.

"Where are you?" he says. He hears piano music, and his heart moves.

"I don't know," she says. "Someplace. We're having a drink, then we're going someplace else for dinner. I'm with the sales manager. He's crude, but he's all right. He bought the car. I have to go now. I was on my way to the ladies and saw the phone."

"Did somebody buy the car?" Leo says. He looks out the kitchen window to the place in the drive where she always parks.

"I told you," she says. "I have to go now."

"Wait, wait a minute, for Christ's sake," he says. "Did somebody buy the car or not?"

"He had his checkbook out when I left," she says. "I have to go now. I have to go to the bathroom."

"Wait!" he yells. The line goes dead. He listens to the dial tone. "Jesus Christ," he says as he stands with the receiver in his hand.

He circles the kitchen and goes back to the living room. He sits. He gets up. In the bathroom he brushes his teeth very carefully. Then he uses dental floss. He washes his face and goes back to the kitchen. He looks at the clock and takes a clean glass from a set that has a hand of playing cards painted on each glass. He fills the glass with ice. He stares for a while at the glass he left in the sink.

He sits against one end of the couch and puts his legs up at the other end. He looks at the screen, realizes he can't make out what the people are saying. He turns the empty glass in his hand and considers biting off the rim. He shivers for a time and thinks of going to bed, though he knows he will dream of a large woman with gray hair. In the dream he is always leaning over tying his shoelaces. When he straightens up, she looks at him, and he bends to tie again. He looks at his hand. It makes a fist as he watches. The telephone is ringing.

"Where are you, honey?" he says slowly, gently.

"We're at this restaurant," she says, her voice strong, bright.

"Honey, which restaurant?" he says. He puts the heel of his hand against his eye and pushes.

"Downtown someplace," she says. "I think it's New Jimmy's. Excuse me," she says to someone off the line, "is this place New Jimmy's? This is

New Jimmy's, Leo," she says to him. "Everything is all right, we're almost finished, then he's going to bring me home."

"Honey?" he says. He holds the receiver against his ear and rocks back and forth, eyes closed. "Honey?"

"I have to go," she says. "I wanted to call. Anyway, guess how much?"

"Honey," he says.

"Six and a quarter," she says. "I have it in my purse. He said there's no market for convertibles. I guess we're born lucky," she says and laughs. "I told him everything. I think I had to."

"Honey," Leo says.

"What?" she says.

"Please, honey," Leo says.

"He said he sympathizes," she says. "But he would have said anything." She laughs again. "He said personally he'd rather be classified a robber or a rapist than a bankrupt. He's nice enough, though," she says.

"Come home," Leo says. "Take a cab and come home."

"I can't," she says. "I told you, we're halfway through dinner."

"I'll come for you," he says.

"No," she says. "I said we're just finishing. I told you, it's part of the deal. They're out for all they can get. But don't worry, we're about to leave. I'll be home in a little while." She hangs up.

In a few minutes he calls New Jimmy's. A man answers. "New Jimmy's has closed for the evening," the man says.

"I'd like to talk to my wife," Leo says.

"Does she work here?" the man asks. "Who is she?"

"She's a customer," Leo says. "She's with someone. A business person."

"Would I know her?" the man says. "What is her name?"

"I don't think you know her," Leo says.

"That's all right," Leo says. "That's all right. I see her now."

"Thank you for calling New Jimmy's," the man says.

Leo hurries to the window. A car he doesn't recognize slows in front of the house, then picks up speed. He waits. Two, three hours later, the telephone rings again. There is no one at the other end when he picks up the receiver. There is only a dial tone.

"I'm right here!" Leo screams into the receiver.

Near dawn he hears footsteps on the porch. He gets up from the couch. The set hums, the screen glows. He opens the door. She bumps the wall coming in. She grins. Her face is puffy, as if she's been sleeping under sedation. She works her lips, ducks heavily and sways as he cocks his fist.

"Go ahead," she says thickly. She stands there swaying. Then she makes a noise and lunges, catches his shirt, tears it down the front. "Bankrupt!" she screams. She twists loose, grabs and tears his undershirt at the neck. "You son of a bitch," she says, clawing.

He squeezes her wrists, then lets go, steps back, looking for something heavy. She stumbles as she heads for the bedroom. "Bankrupt," she mutters. He hears her fall on the bed and groan.

He waits awhile, then splashes water on his face and goes to the bedroom. He turns the lights on, looks at her, and begins to take her clothes off. He pulls and pushes her from side to side undressing her. She says something in her sleep and moves her hand. He takes off her underpants, looks at them closely under the light, and throws them into a corner. He turns back the covers and rolls her in, naked. Then he opens her purse. He is reading the check when he hears the car come into the drive.

He looks through the front curtain and sees the convertible in the drive, its motor running smoothly, the headlamps burning, and he closes and opens his eyes. He sees a tall man come around in front of the car and up to the front porch. The man lays something on the porch and starts back to the car. He wears a white linen suit.

Leo turns on the porch light and opens the door cautiously. Her makeup pouch lies on the top step. The man looks at Leo across the front of the car, and then gets back inside and releases the handbrake.

"Wait!" Leo calls and starts down the steps. The man brakes the car as Leo walks in front of the lights. The car creaks against the brake. Leo tries to pull the two pieces of his shirt together, tries to bunch it all into his trousers.

"What is it you want?" the man says. "Look," the man says, "I have to go. No offense. I buy and sell cars, right? The lady left her makeup. She's a fine lady, very refined. What is it?"

Leo leans against the door and looks at the man. The man takes his hands off the wheel and puts them back. He drops the gear into reverse and the car moves backward a little.

"I want to tell you," Leo says and wets his lips.

The light in Ernest Williams' bedroom goes on. The shade rolls up.

Leo shakes his head, tucks in his shirt again. He steps back from the car. "Monday," he says.

"Monday," the man says and watches for sudden movement.

Leo nods slowly.

"Well, goodnight," the man says and coughs. "Take it easy, hear? Monday, that's right. Okay, then." He takes his foot off the brake, puts it on again after he has rolled back two or three feet. "Hey, one question. Between friends, are these actual miles?" The man waits, then clears his throat. "Okay, look, it doesn't matter either way," the man says. "I have to go. Take it easy." He backs into the street, pulls away quickly, and turns the corner without stopping.

Leo tucks at his shirt and goes back in the house. He locks the front door and checks it. Then he goes to the bedroom and locks that door and turns back the covers. He looks at her before he flicks the light. He takes off his clothes, folds them carefully on the floor, and gets in beside her. He lies on his back for a time and pulls the hair on his stomach, considering. He looks at the bedroom door, outlined now in the faint outside light. Presently he reaches out his hand and touches her hip. She does not move. He turns on his side and puts his hand on her hip. He runs his fingers over her hip and feels the stretch marks there. They are like roads, and he traces them in her flesh. He runs his fingers back and forth, first one, then another. They run everywhere in her flesh, dozens, perhaps hundreds of them. He remembers waking up the morning after they bought the car, seeing it, there in the drive, in the sun, gleaming.

JOYCE CAROL OATES
(b. 1938)

Born in Lockport, New York, and educated at Syracuse University and the University of Wisconsin at Madison, Joyce Carol Oates is the author of numerous collections of short stories including By the North Gate *(1963),* The Wheel of Love *(1970),* Marriages & Infidelities *(1972),* Night-Side *(1977),* Raven's Wing *(1986),* Heat and Other Stories *(1991),* Haunted: Tales of the Grotesque *(1994),* Will You Always Love Me? *(1996),* Faithless: Tales of Transgression *(2001),* High Lonesome: New and Selected Stories 1966–2006 *(2006),* Wild Nights! *(2008),* Dear Husband, *(2009),* Sourland *(2010), and* The Corn Maiden *(2011). Her novels include* A Garden of Earthly Delights *(1967; revised and rewritten for the Modern Library edition 2003),* Expensive People *(1968),* them *(1969; revised and rewritten for the Modern Library edition 2006);* Bellefleur *(1980),* You Must Remember This *(1987),* Because It Is Bitter, and Because It Is My Heart *(1990),* Black Water *(1992),* Foxfire *(1993),* What I Lived For *(1994),* We Were the Mulvaneys *(1996),* Blonde *(2000),* I'll Take You There *(2002),* The Falls *(2004),* Missing Mom *(2005),* The Gravedigger's Daughter *(2007),* Little Bird of Heaven *(2009) and* Mudwoman *(2012). She is the author of the memoir* A Widow's Story *(2011).*

Since 1978 Joyce Carol Oates has been on the faculty of Princeton University and a member of the American Academy of Arts and Letters. Among her literary awards are the National Book Award, the Common Wealth Award for Distinguished Service in Literature, the PEN/Malamud Award for the Short Story, the Rea Award for the Short Story, the O. Henry Award, the Ivan Sandrof Award for Lifetime Achievement from the National Book Critics Circle, the Award of the American Festival at Deauville, France, the Prix Femina Award for The Falls, *and the 2011 National Humanities Medal.*

For the author, the formal challenge of "Heat" was to present a coherent and emotionally resonant narrative in a seemingly acausal manner, analogous to the playing of a piano without a pedal, as if each paragraph, or chord, were separated from the rest, as in the memory of trauma. For how else can we speak of the unspeakable, except through the distancing prism of technique?

Heat

It was midsummer, the heat rippling above the macadam roads. Cicadas screaming out of the trees and the sky like pewter, glaring.

The days were the same day, like the shallow mud-brown river moving always in the same direction but so slow you couldn't see it. Except for Sunday: church in the morning, then the fat Sunday newspaper, the color comics and newsprint on your fingers.

Rhea and Rhoda Kunkel went flying on their rusted old bicycles, down the long hill toward the railroad yard, Whipple's Ice, the scrubby pastureland where dairy cows grazed. They'd stolen six dollars from their own grandmother who loved them. They were eleven years old, they were identical twins, they basked in their power.

Rhea and Rhoda Kunkel: it was always Rhea-and-Rhoda, never Rhoda-and-Rhea, I couldn't say why. You just wouldn't say the names that way. Not even the teachers at school would say them that way.

We went to see them in the funeral parlor where they were waked, we were made to. The twins in twin caskets, white, smooth, gleaming, perfect as plastic, with white satin lining puckered like the inside of a fancy candy box. And the waxy white lilies, and the smell of talcum powder and perfume. The room was crowded, there was only one way in and out.

Rhea and Rhoda were the same girl, they'd wanted it that way.

Only looking from one to the other could you see they were two.

The heat was gauzy, you had to push your way through like swimming. On their bicycles Rhea and Rhoda flew through it hardly noticing, from their grandmother's place on Main Street to the end of South Main where the paved road turned to gravel leaving town. That was the summer before seventh grade, when they died. Death was coming for them but they didn't know.

They thought the same thoughts sometimes at the same moment, had the same dream and went all day trying to remember it, bringing it back like something you'd be hauling out of the water on a tangled line. We watched them, we were jealous. None of us had a twin. Sometimes they were serious and sometimes, remembering, they shrieked and laughed like they were being killed. They stole things out of desks and lockers but if you caught them they'd hand them right back, it was like a game.

There were three floor fans in the funeral parlor that I could see, tall whirring fans with propellor blades turning fast to keep the warm air moving. Strange little gusts came from all directions making your eyes water. By this time Roger Whipple was arrested, taken into police custody. No one had hurt him. He would never stand trial, he was ruled mentally unfit, he would never be released from confinement.

He died there, in the state psychiatric hospital, years later, and was brought back home to be buried, the body of him I mean. His earthly remains.

Rhea and Rhoda Kunkel were buried in the same cemetery, the First Methodist. The cemetery is just a field behind the church.

In the caskets the dead girls did not look like anyone we knew really. They were placed on their backs with their eyes closed, and their mouths, the way you don't always in life when you're sleeping. Their faces were too small. Every eyelash showed, too perfect. Like angels everyone was saying and it was strange it was *so.* I stared and stared.

What had been done to them, the lower parts of them, didn't show in the caskets.

Roger Whipple worked for his father at Whipple's Ice. In the newspaper it stated he was nineteen, he'd gone to DeWitt Clinton until he was sixteen; my mother's friend Sadie taught there and remembered him from the special education class. A big slow sweet-faced boy with these big hands and feet, thighs like hams. A shy gentle boy with good manners and a hushed voice.

He wasn't simpleminded exactly, like the others in that class. He was watchful, he held back.

Roger Whipple in overalls squatting in the rear of his father's truck, one of his older brothers drove. There would come the sound of the truck in the driveway, the heavy block of ice smelling of cold, ice tongs over his shoulder. He was strong, round-shouldered like an older man. Never staggered or grunted. Never dropped anything. Pale washed-looking eyes lifting out of a big face, a soft mouth wanting to smile. We giggled and looked away. They said he'd never been the kind to hurt even an animal, all the Whipples swore.

Sucking ice, the cold goes straight into your jaws and deep into the bone.

People spoke of them as the Kunkel twins. Mostly nobody tried to tell them apart. Homely corkscrew-twisty girls you wouldn't know would turn up so quiet and solemn and almost beautiful, perfect little dolls' faces with the freckles powdered over, touches of rouge on the cheeks and mouths. I was tempted to whisper to them, kneeling by the coffins. Hey Rhea! Hey Rhoda! Wake *up!*

They had loud slip-sliding voices that were the same voice. They weren't shy. They were always first in line. One behind you and one in front of you and you'd better be wary of some trick. Flamey-orange hair and the bleached-out skin that goes with it, freckles like dirty raindrops splashed on their faces. Sharp green eyes they'd bug out until you begged them to stop.

Places meant to be serious, Rhea and Rhoda had a hard time sitting still. In church, in school, a sideways glance between them could do it. Jamming their knuckles into their mouths, choking back giggles. Sometimes laughing escaped through their fingers like steam hissing. Sometimes it came out like snorting and then none of us could hold back. The worst time was in assembly, the principal up there telling us that Miss Flagler had died, we would all miss her. Tears shining in the woman's eyes behind her goggle-glasses and one of the twins gave a breathless little snort, you could feel it like flames running down the whole row of girls, none of us could hold back.

Sometimes the word "tickle" was enough to get us going, just that word.

I never dreamt about Rhea and Rhoda so strange in their caskets sleeping out in the middle of a room where people could stare at them, shed tears and pray over them. I never dream about actual things, only things I don't know. Places I've never been, people I've never seen. Sometimes the person I am in the dream isn't me. Who it is, I don't know.

Rhea and Rhoda bounced up the drive behind Whipple's Ice. They were laughing like crazy and didn't mind the potholes jarring their teeth, or the clouds of dust. If they'd had the same dream the night before, the hot sunlight erased it entirely.

When death comes for you you sometimes know and sometimes don't.

Roger Whipple was by himself in the barn, working. Kids went down there to beg him for ice to suck or throw around or they'd tease him, not out of meanness but for something to do. It was slow, the days not changing in the summer, heat sometimes all night long. He was happy with children that age, he was that age himself in his head, sixth grade learning abilities as the newspaper stated though he could add and subtract quickly. Other kinds of arithmetic gave him trouble.

People were saying afterward he'd always been strange. Watchful like he was, those thick soft lips. The Whipples did wrong, to let him run loose.

They said he'd always been a good gentle boy, went to Sunday school and sat still there and never gave anybody any trouble. He collected Bible cards, he hid them away under his mattress for safekeeping. Mr. Whipple started in early, disciplining him the way you might discipline a big dog or a horse. Not letting the creature know he has any power to be himself exactly. Not giving him the opportunity to test his will.

Neighbors said the Whipples worked him like a horse in fact. The older brothers were the most merciless. And why they all wore coveralls, heavy denim and long legs on days so hot, nobody knew. The thermometer above the First Midland Bank read 98° F, on noon of that day, my mother said.

Nights afterward my mother would hug me before I went to bed. Pressing my face hard against her breasts and whispering things I didn't hear, like praying to Jesus to love and protect *her* little girl and keep *her* from harm but I didn't hear; I shut my eyes tight and endured it. Sometimes we prayed together, all of us or just my mother and me kneeling by my bed. Even then I knew she was a good mother, there was this girl she loved as her daughter that was me and loved more than that girl deserved. There was nothing I could do about it.

Mrs. Kunkel would laugh and roll her eyes over the twins. In that house they were "double trouble"—you'd hear it all the time like a joke on the radio that keeps coming back. I wonder did she pray with them too. I wonder would they let her.

In the long night you forget about the day, it's like the other side of the world. Then the sun is there, and the heat. You forget.

We were running through the field behind school, a place where people dumped things sometimes and there was a dead dog there, a collie with beautiful fur but his eyes were gone from the sockets and the maggots had got him where somebody tried to lift him with her foot and when Rhea and Rhoda saw they screamed a single scream and hid their eyes.

They did nice things—gave their friends candy bars, nail polish, some novelty key chains they'd taken from somewhere, movie stars' pictures framed in plastic. In the movies they'd share a box of popcorn not noticing where one or the other of them left off and a girl who wasn't any sister of theirs sat.

Once they made me strip off my clothes where we'd crawled under the Kunkels' veranda. This was a large hollowed-out space where the earth dropped away at one end, you could sit without bumping your head; it was cool and smelled of dirt and stone. Rhea said all of a sudden, Strip! and Rhoda said at once, Strip!—come *on!* So it happened. They wouldn't let me out unless I took off my clothes, my shirt and shorts, yes and my panties too. Come *on* they said whispering and giggling, they were blocking the way out so I had no choice. I was scared but I was laughing too. This is to show our power over you, they said. But they stripped too just like me.

You have power over others you don't realize until you test it.

Under the Kunkels' veranda we stared at each other but we didn't touch each other. My teeth chattered because what if somebody saw us? Some boy, or Mrs. Kunkel herself? I was scared but I was happy too. Except for our faces, their face and mine, we could all be the same girl.

The Kunkel family lived in one side of a big old clapboard house by the river, you could hear the trucks rattling on the bridge, shifting their noisy gears on the hill. Mrs. Kunkel had eight children, Rhea and Rhoda were the youngest. Our mothers wondered why Mrs. Kunkel had let herself go—she had a moon-shaped pretty face but her hair was frizzed ratty, she must have weighed two hundred pounds, sweated and breathed so hard in the warm weather. They'd known her in school. Mr. Kunkel worked construction for the county. Summer evenings after work he'd be sitting on the veranda drinking beer, flicking cigarette butts out into the yard; you'd be fooled almost thinking they were fireflies. He went barechested in the heat, his upper body dark like stained wood. Flat little purplish nipples inside his chest hair the girls giggled to see. Mr. Kunkel teased us all; he'd mix Rhea and Rhoda up the way he'd mix the rest of us up, like it was too much trouble to keep names straight.

Mr. Kunkel was in police custody, he didn't even come to the wake. Mrs. Kunkel was there in rolls of chin fat that glistened with sweat and tears, the makeup on her face so caked and discolored you were embarrassed to look. It scared me, the way she grabbed me as soon as my parents and I came in. Hugging me against her big balloon breasts sobbing and all the strength went out of me, I couldn't push away.

The police had Mr. Kunkel, for his own good they said. He'd gone to the Whipples, though the murderer had been taken away, saying he would kill anybody he could get his hands on, the old man, the brothers. They were all responsible he said, his little girls were dead. Tear them apart with his bare hands he said but he had a tire iron.

Did it mean anything special, or was it just an accident, Rhea and Rhoda had taken six dollars from their grandmother an hour before? Because death was coming for them, it had to happen one way or another.

If you believe in God you believe that. And if you don't believe in God it's obvious.

Their grandmother lived upstairs over a shoe store downtown, an apartment looking out on Main Street. They'd bicycle down there for something to do and she'd give them grape juice or lemonade and try to keep them a while, a lonely old lady but she was nice, she was always nice to me; it was kind of nasty of Rhea and Rhoda to steal from her but they were like that. One was in the kitchen talking with her and without any plan or anything the other went to use the bathroom then slipped into her bedroom, got the money out of her purse like it was something she did every day of the week, that easy. On the stairs going down to the street Rhoda whispered to Rhea what did you *do?* knowing Rhea had done something she hadn't ought to have done but not knowing what it was or anyway how much money it was. They started in poking each other, trying to hold the giggles back until they were safe away.

On their bicycles they stood high on the pedals, coasting, going down the hill but not using their brakes. *What did you do! Oh what did you do!*

Rhea and Rhoda always said they could never be apart. If one didn't know exactly where the other was that one could die. Or the other could die. Or both.

Once they'd gotten some money from somewhere, they wouldn't say where, and paid for us all to go to the movies. And ice cream afterward too.

You could read the newspaper articles twice through and still not know what he did. Adults talked about it for a long time but not so we could hear. I thought probably he'd used an ice pick. Or maybe I heard somebody guess that who didn't know any more than me.

We liked it that Rhea and Rhoda had been killed, and all the stuff in the paper, and everybody talking about it, but we didn't like it that they were dead, we missed them.

Later, in tenth grade, the Kaufmann twins moved into our school district. Doris and Diane. But it wasn't the same thing.

Roger Whipple said he didn't remember any of it. Whatever he did, he didn't remember. At first everybody thought he was lying then they had to accept it as true, or true in some way; doctors from the state hospital examined him. He said over and over he hadn't done anything and he didn't remember the twins there that afternoon but he couldn't explain why their bicycles were where they were at the foot of his stairway and he couldn't explain why he'd taken a bath in the middle of the day. The Whipples admitted that wasn't a practice of Roger's or of any of them, ever, a bath in the middle of the day.

Roger Whipple was a clean boy, though. His hands always scrubbed so you actually noticed, swinging the block of ice off the truck and, inside the kitchen, helping to set it in the ice box. They said he'd go crazy if he got bits of straw under his nails from the ice house or inside his clothes. He'd been taught to shave and he shaved every morning without fail; they said the sight of the beard growing in, the scratchy feel of it, seemed to scare him.

A few years later his sister Linda told us how Roger was built like a horse. She was our age, a lot younger than him; she made a gesture toward her crotch so we'd know what she meant. She'd happened to see him a few times she said, by accident.

There he was squatting in the dust laughing, his head lowered watching Rhea and Rhoda circle him on their bicycles. It was a rough game where the twins saw how close they could come to hitting him, brushing him with the bike fenders and he'd lunge out not seeming to notice if his fingers hit the spokes, it was all happening so fast you maybe wouldn't feel pain. Out back of the ice house the yard blended in with the yard of the old railroad depot next door that wasn't used any more. It was burning hot in the sun, dust rose in clouds behind the girls. Pretty soon they got bored with the game though Roger Whipple even in his heavy overalls wanted to keep going. He was red-faced with all the excitement, he was a boy who loved to laugh and didn't have much chance. Rhea said she was thirsty, she wanted some ice, so Roger Whipple scrambled right up and went to get a big bag of ice cubes!—he hadn't any more sense than that.

They sucked on the ice cubes and fooled around with them. He was panting and lolling his tongue pretending to be a dog and Rhea and Rhoda cried, Here doggie! Here doggie-doggie! tossing ice cubes at Roger Whipple he tried to catch in his mouth. That went on for a while. In the end the twins just dumped the rest of the ice onto the dirt then Roger Whipple was saying he had some secret things that belonged to his brother Eamon he could show them, hidden under his bed mattress, would they like to see what the things were?

He wasn't one who could tell Rhea from Rhoda or Rhoda from Rhea. There was a way some of us knew, the freckles on Rhea's face were a little darker than Rhoda's. Rhea's eyes were just a little darker than Rhoda's. But you'd have to see the two side by side with no clowning around to know.

Rhea said okay, she'd like to see the secret things. She let her bike fall where she was straddling it.

Roger Whipple said he could only take one of them upstairs to his room at a time, he didn't say why.

Okay said Rhea. Of the Kunkel twins Rhea always had to be first.

She'd been born first, she said. Weighed a pound or two more.

Roger Whipple's room was in a strange place—on the second floor of the Whipple house above an unheated storage space that had been added after the main part of the house was built. There was a way of getting to the room from the outside, up a flight of rickety wood stairs. That way Roger could get in and out of his room without going through the rest of the house. People said the Whipples had him live there like some animal, they didn't want him tramping through the house but they denied it. The room had an inside door too.

Roger Whipple weighed about one-hundred ninety pounds that day. In the hospital he swelled up like a balloon, people said, bloated from the drugs, his skin was soft and white as bread dough and his hair fell out. He was an old man when he died aged thirty-one.

Exactly why he died, the Whipples never knew. The hospital just told them his heart had stopped in his sleep.

Rhoda shaded her eyes watching her sister running up the stairs with Roger Whipple behind her and felt the first pinch of fear, that something was wrong, or was going to be wrong. She called after them in a whining voice that she wanted to come along too, she didn't want to wait down there all alone, but Rhea just called back to her to be quiet and wait her turn, so Rhoda waited, kicking at the ice cubes melting in the dirt, and after a while she got restless and shouted up to them—the door was shut, the shade on the window was drawn—saying she was going home, damn them she was sick of waiting she said and she was going home. But nobody came to the door or looked out the window; it was like the place was empty. Wasps had built one of those nests that look like mud in layers under the eaves and the only sound was wasps.

Rhoda bicycled toward the road so anybody who was watching would think she was going home; she was thinking she hated Rhea! hated her damn twin sister! wished she was dead and gone, God damn her! She was going home and the first thing she'd tell their mother was that Rhea had stolen six dollars from Grandma: she had it in her pocket right that moment.

The Whipple house was an old farmhouse they'd tried to modernize by putting on red asphalt siding meant to look like brick. Downstairs the rooms were big and drafty, upstairs they were small, some of them unfinished and with bare floorboards, like Roger Whipple's room which people would afterward say based on what the police said was like an animal's pen, nothing in it but a bed shoved into a corner and some furniture and boxes and things Mrs. Whipple stored there.

Of the Whipples—there were seven in the family still living at home—only Mrs. Whipple and her daughter Iris were home that afternoon. They said they hadn't heard a sound except for kids playing in the back; they swore it.

Rhoda was bent on going home and leaving Rhea behind but at the end of the driveway something made her turn her bicycle wheel back...so if you were watching you'd think she was just cruising around for something to do, a red-haired girl with whitish skin and freckles, skinny little body, pedaling fast, then slow, then coasting, then fast again, turning and dipping and criss-crossing her path, talking to herself as if she was angry. She hated Rhea! She was furious at Rhea! But feeling sort of scared too and sickish in the pit of her belly knowing that she and Rhea shouldn't be in two places, something might happen to one of them or to both. Some things you know.

So she pedaled back to the house. Laid her bike down in the dirt next to Rhea's. The bikes were old hand-me-downs, the kickstands were broken. But their daddy had put on new Goodyear tires for them at the start of the summer and he'd oiled them too.

You never would see just one of the twins' bicycles anywhere, you always saw both of them laid down on the ground and facing in the same direction with the pedals in about the same position.

Rhoda peered up at the second floor of the house, the shade drawn over the window, the door still closed. She called out Rhea? Hey Rhea? starting up the stairs making a lot of noise so they'd hear her, pulling on the railing as if to break it the way a boy would. Still she was scared. But making noise like that and feeling so disgusted and mad helped her get stronger, and there was Roger Whipple with the door open staring down at her flush-faced and sweaty as if he was scared too. He seemed to have forgotten her. He was wiping his hands on his overalls. He just stared, a lemony light coming up in his eyes.

Afterward he would say he didn't remember anything—didn't remember anything. Big as a grown man but round-shouldered so it was hard to judge how tall he was, or how old. His straw-colored hair falling in his eyes and his fingers twined together as if he was praying or trying with all his strength to keep his hands still. He didn't remember anything about the twins or anything in his room or in the ice house afterward but he cried a lot, he acted scared and guilty and sorry, so they decided he shouldn't be put on trial, there was no point to it.

Mrs. Whipple kept to the house afterward, never went out not even to church or grocery shopping. She died of cancer just before Roger died, she'd loved him she said, she always said none of it had been his fault really; he wasn't the kind of boy even to hurt an animal, he'd loved kittens especially and was a good sweet obedient boy and religious too and whatever happened it must have been because those girls were teasing him, he'd had a lifetime of being teased and taunted by children, his heart broken by all the abuse, and something must have snapped that day, that was all.

The Whipples were the ones, though, who called the police. Mr. Whipple found the girls' bodies back in the ice house hidden under some straw and canvas.

He found them around nine that night, with a flashlight. He knew, he said. The way Roger was acting, and the fact the Kunkel girls were missing, word had gotten out. He knew but he didn't know what he knew or what he would find. Roger taking a bath like that in the middle of the day and washing his hair too and shaving for the second time and not answering when his mother spoke to him, just sitting there staring at the floor as if he was listening to something no one else could hear. He knew, Mr. Whipple said. The hardest minute of his life was in the ice house lifting that canvas to see what was under it.

He took it hard too, he never recovered. He hadn't any choice but to think what a lot of people thought—it had been his fault. He was an old-time Methodist, he took all that seriously, but none of it helped him. Believed Jesus Christ was his personal savior and He never stopped loving Roger or turned His face from him and if Roger did truly repent in his heart he would be saved and they would be reunited in Heaven, all the Whipples reunited, he believed, but none of it helped in his life.

The ice house is still there but boarded up and derelict, the Whipples' ice business ended long ago. Strangers live in the house and the yard is littered with rusting hulks of cars and pickup trucks. Some Whipples live scattered around the county but none in town. The old train depot is still there too.

After I'd been married some years I got involved with this man, I won't say his name, his name is not a name I say, but we would meet back there sometimes, back in that old lot that's all weeds and scrub trees. Wild as kids and on the edge of being drunk. I was crazy for this guy, I mean crazy like I could hardly think of anybody but him or anything but the two of us making love the way we did, with him deep inside me I wanted it never to stop just fuck and fuck and fuck I'd whisper to him and this went on for a long time, two or three years then ended the way these things do and looking back on it I'm not able to recognize that woman as if she was someone not even not-me but a crazy woman I would despise, making so much of such a thing, risking her marriage and her kids finding out and her life being ruined for such a thing, my God. The things people do.

It's like living out a story that has to go its own way.

Behind the ice house in his car I'd think of Rhea and Rhoda and what happened that day upstairs in Roger Whipple's room. And the funeral parlor with the twins like dolls laid out and their eyes like dolls' eyes too that shut when you tilt them back. One night when I wasn't asleep but wasn't awake either I saw my parents standing in the doorway of my bedroom watching me and I knew their thoughts, how they were thinking of Rhea and Rhoda and of me their daughter wondering how they could keep me from harm and there was no clear answer.

In his car in his arms I'd feel my mind drift after we'd made love or at least after the first time. And I saw Rhoda Kunkel hesitating on the stairs a few steps down from Roger Whipple. I saw her white-faced and scared but deciding to keep going anyway, pushing by Roger Whipple to get inside the room, to find Rhea, she had to brush against him where he was standing as if he meant to block her but not having the nerve exactly to block her and he was smelling of his body and breathing hard but not in imitation of any dog now, not with his tongue flopping and lolling to make them laugh. Rhoda was asking where was Rhea?—she couldn't see well at first in the dark little cubbyhole of a room because the sunshine had been so bright outside.

Roger Whipple said Rhea had gone home. His voice sounded scratchy as if it hadn't been used in some time. She'd gone home he said and Rhoda said right away that Rhea wouldn't go home without her and Roger Whipple came toward her saying yes she did, yes she *did* as if he was getting angry she wouldn't believe him. Rhoda was calling, Rhea? Where are you? Stumbling against something on the floor tangled with the bedclothes.

Behind her was this big boy saying again and again yes she did, yes she *did,* his voice rising but it would never get loud enough so that anyone would hear and come save her.

I wasn't there, but some things you know.

RUSSELL BANKS
(b. 1940)

Russell Banks is the author of the novels The Book of Jamaica *(1980),* Continental Drift *(1985),* Affliction *(1989),* The Sweet Hereafter *(1991),* Cloudsplitter *(1998),* The Darling *(2004), and* Lost Memory of Skin *(2011), as well as the short story collections* Trailerpark *(1981),* Success Stories *(1986), and* The Angel on the Roof: Collected Stories *(2000). (Both* Affliction *and* The Sweet Hereafter *have been adapted into brilliant award-winning films, and other titles are in film production.) Banks's many literary awards include the Anisfield-Wolf Award, the John Dos Passos Prize, and an award from the American Academy of Arts and Letters, into which the author was subsequently inducted; Banks has been a finalist for the Pulitzer Prize as well as president of the International Parliament of Writers. His short stories have appeared in the* O. Henry Awards: The Best Short Stories of the Year *and* The Best American Short Stories.

*In the tradition of Mark Twain, Theodore Dreiser, John Dos Passos, and Nelson Algren, among others, Russell Banks takes for his subject the breadth and depth of American society, with a particular interest in race. (*Cloudsplitter *is an epic imagined of the life of the Abolitionist John Brown.) Born in Newton, Massachusetts, and raised in a small New Hampshire town, Banks became familiar as a child with the themes of paternal affliction and abandonment and economic anxiety that pervade his work; his often small-town, working-class subjects are examined with a powerful sympathy and compassion.*

Banks attended Colgate University on a scholarship and dropped out with the intention of helping in Castro's Revolution in Cuba. (The young revolutionary got as far as Miami, where he worked in a department store.) Eventually he graduated from the University of North Carolina at Chapel Hill where he helped edit the literary magazine Lillabulero. *Banks has worked at a number of jobs including plumber (his father's occupation), department store window dresser, shoe salesman, and teacher; he has taught at Princeton University and the New York State Summer Writers Institute.*

More or less retired from teaching, he now divides his time between the village of Keene, New York, in the Adirondacks, and Miami, Florida—a "bi-polar" lifestyle that suits his personality, as he has said.

Though his subject matter has always been American society as seen from a working-class perspective, and his sympathies invariably with those individuals whom we might call the "insulted and injured" in our midst, Banks's early fiction was conspicuously experimental. In subsequent decades his style in both his long and short fiction has evolved through the poetic realism of Cloudsplitter, The Darling, *and* The Reserve *to the plainspoken American vernacular of* Lost Memory of Skin. *His ability to give voice to diverse American types and to evoke sympathy for those for whom one might not otherwise feel sympathy is impressive.*

Russell Banks has memorably said of a crucial distinction between long and short forms of fiction: "The novel has a mimetic relationship with time. The novel simulates the flow of time, so once you get very far into a novel, you forget where you began—just as you do in real time. Whereas with a short story the point is not to forget the beginning. The ending only makes sense if you remember the beginning."

The Child Screams and Looks Back at You

When your child shows the first signs of illness—fever, lassitude, aching joints and muscles—you fear that he is dying. You may not admit it to anyone, but the sight of your child lying flushed and feverish in bed becomes for an instant the sight of your child in his coffin. The nature of reality shifts, and it's suddenly not clear to you whether you are beginning to dream or are waking from a dream, for you watch the child's breath stutter and stop, you cry out and then struggle to blow life back into the tiny, inert body lying below you. Or you see the child heave himself into convulsions, thrash wildly in the bed and utter hoarse, incoherent noises, as if he were possessed by a demon, and horrified, helpless, you back to the door, hands to mouth, crying, "Stop, stop, please, oh, God, please stop!" Or, suddenly, the bed is sopped with blood pouring from the child's body, blood seeping into the mattress, over the sheets through the child's tangled pajamas, and the child whitens, stares up pitifully and without understanding, for there is no wound to blame, there is only this blood emptying out of his body, and you cannot stanch its flow, but must stand there and watch your child's miraculous, mysterious life disappear before you. For that is the key that unlocks these awful visions—your child's being simply alive is both miracle and mystery, and therefore it seems both natural and understandable that he should be dead.

Marcelle called her boys from the kitchen to hurry and get dressed for school. One of these mornings she was not going to keep after them like this, and they would all be late for school, and she would not write a note to the teacher to explain anything, she didn't give a damn if the teacher kept them after school, because it would teach them a lesson once and for all, and that lesson was when she woke them in the morning they had to hurry and get dressed and make their beds and get the hell out to the kitchen and eat their breakfasts and brush their teeth and get the hell out the door to school so she could get dressed and eat her breakfast and go to work. There were four of them, the four sons of Marcelle and Richard Chagnon. Joel was the oldest at twelve, and after him, separated by little more than nine months, came Raymond, Maurice, and Charles. The father had moved out, had been thrown out of the apartment by Marcelle's younger brother, Steve, and one of Steve's friends nearly nine years ago, when the youngest, Charles, was still an infant, and though for several years Richard tried to convince Marcelle that she should let him move back in with them and let him be her husband and the father of his four sons again, she had never allowed it, for his way of being a husband and father was to get drunk and beat her and the older boys and then to wake ashamed and beg their forgiveness. For years she had forgiven him, because to her when you forgive someone you make it possible for that person to change, and the boys also forgave him—they were, after all, her sons, too, and she had taught them, in their dealings with each other, to forgive. If you don't forgive someone who has hurt you, he can't change into a new person, she told them. He is stuck in his life with you at the point where he hurt you. But her husband and their father, Richard, after five years of it, had come to seem incapable of using their forgiveness in any way that allowed him to stop hurting them, so finally one night she sent her oldest boy, Joel, down the dark stairs to the street, down the street to the tenements where her brother, Steve, lived with his girlfriend, and Joel found Steve sitting at the kitchen table drinking beer with a friend and said to him, "Come and keep my daddy from hitting my mommy!" That night marked the end of Marcelle's period of forgiveness, for she had permitted outsiders, her brother and his friend, to see how badly her husband, Richard, behaved. By that act she had ceased to protect her husband, and you cannot forgive someone you will not protect. Richard never perceived and understood that shift. If you don't know what you've got when you've got it, you won't know what you've lost when you've lost it. Marcelle was Catholic, and even though she was not a diligent Catholic, she was a loyal one, and she never remarried, which is not to say that over the years she did not now and again fall in love, once even with a married man, only briefly, however, until she became strong enough to reveal her affair to Father Brautigan, after which she broke off with the man, to the relief of her sons, for they had not liked the way he came sneaking around at odd hours to see their mother and talked with her in hushed tones in the kitchen until very late, when the lights went off, and an hour or two later he left. When in the morning the children got up and came out to the kitchen for breakfast, they talked in low voices, as if the married man were still in the apartment and asleep in their mother's bed, and she had deep circles under her eyes and stirred her coffee slowly and looked out the window and now and then quietly reminded them to hurry or they'd be late for school. They were more comfortable when she was hollering at them, standing at the door to their bedroom, her hands on her hips, her dressing gown flapping open as she whirled and stomped back to the kitchen, embarrassing her slightly, for beneath her dressing gown she wore men's long underwear, so that, by the time they got out to the kitchen themselves, her dressing gown had been pulled back tightly around her and tied at the waist, and all they could see of the long underwear beneath it was the top button at her throat, which she tried to cover casually with one hand while she set their breakfasts before them with the other. On this morning, however, only three of her sons appeared at the table, dressed for school, slumping grumpily into their chairs, for it was a gray, wintry day in early December, barely light outside. The oldest, Joel, had not come out with them, and she lost her temper, slammed three plates of scrambled eggs and toast down in front of the others, and fairly jogged back to the bedroom, stalked to the narrow bed by the wall where the boy slept, and yanked the covers away, to expose the boy, curled up on his side, eyes wide open, his face flushed and sweating, his hands clasped together as if in prayer. Horrified, she looked down at the gangly boy, and she saw him dead and quickly lay the covers back over him, gently straightening the blanket and top sheet. Then, slowly, she sat down on the edge of the bed and stroked his hot forehead, brushing his blond hair back, feeling beneath his jawbone as if for a pulse, touching his cheeks with the smooth backside of her cool hand. "Tell me how you feel, honey," she said to the boy. He didn't answer her. His tongue came out and touched his dry lips and went quickly back inside his mouth. "Don't worry, honey," she said, and she got up from the bed. "It's probably the flu, that's all. I'll take your temperature and maybe call Doctor Wickshaw, and he'll tell me what to do. If you're too sick, I'll stay home from the tannery today. All right?" she asked and took a tentative step away from the bed. "Okay," the boy said weakly. The room was dark and cluttered with clothing and toys, model airplanes and boats, weapons, costumes, tools, hockey equipment, portable radios, photographs of athletes and singers, like the prop room of a small theater group. As she left the room, Marcelle stopped in the doorway and looked back. Huddled in his bed, the boy looked like one of the props, a ventriloquist's dummy or a heap of clothes that, in this shadowy half-light, only resembled a human child for a second or two; then, looked at from a second angle, came clearly to be no more than an impatiently discarded costume.

Most people, when they call in a physician, deal with him as they would a priest. They say that what they want is a medical opinion, a professional medical man's professional opinion, when what they really want is his blessing. Information is useful only insofar as it provides peace of mind, release from the horrifying visions of dead children, an end to this dream. Most physicians, like most priests, recognize the need and attempt to satisfy it. This story takes place in the early 1960s, in a small mill town in central New Hampshire, and it was especially true then and there that the physician responded before all other needs to the patient's need for peace of mind, and only when that need had been met would he respond to the patient's need for bodily health. In addition, because he usually knew all the members of the family and frequently treated them for injuries and diseases, he tended to regard an injured or ill person as part of an injured or ill family. Thus it gradually became the physician's practice to minimize the danger or seriousness of a particular injury or illness, so that a broken bone was often called a probable sprain, until X rays proved otherwise, and a concussion was called, with a laugh, a bump on the head, until the symptoms—dizziness, nausea, sleepiness—persisted, and the bump on the head became a possible mild concussion, which eventually may have to be upgraded all the way to fractured skull. It was the same with diseases. A virus, the flu that's going around, a low-grade intestinal infection, and so on, often came to be identified a week or two later as strep throat, bronchial pneumonia, dysentery, without necessarily stopping there. There was an obvious, if limited, use for this practice, because it soothed and calmed both the patient and the family members, which made it easier for the physician to make an accurate diagnosis and to secure the aid of the family members in providing treatment. It was worse than useless, however, when an over-optimistic diagnosis of a disease or injury led to the patient's sudden, crazed descent into sickness, pain, paralysis, and death.

Doctor Wickshaw, a man in his middle forties, portly but in good physical condition, with horn-rimmed glasses and a Vandyke beard, told Marcelle that her son Joel probably had the flu, it was going around, half the school was out with it. "Keep him in bed a few days, and give him lots of liquids," he instructed her after examining the boy. He made house calls, if the cry for help came during morning hours or if it was truly an emergency. Afternoons he was at his office, and evenings he made rounds at the Concord Hospital, twenty-five miles away. Marcelle asked what she should do about the fever, one hundred four degrees, and he told her to give the boy three aspirins now and two more every three or four hours. She saw the man to the door, and as he passed her in the narrow hallway he placed one hand on her rump, and he said to the tall, broad-shouldered woman, "How are things with you, Marcelle? I saw you walking home from the tannery the other day, and I said to myself, 'Now that's a woman who shouldn't be alone in the world.'" He smiled into her bladelike face, the face of a large, powerful bird, and showed her his excellent teeth. His hand was still pressed against her rump, and they stood face-to-face, for she was as tall as he. She was not alone in the world, she reminded him, mentioning her four sons. The doctor's hand slipped to her thigh. She did not move. "But you get lonely," he told her. She had gray eyes, and her face was filled with fatigue, tiny lines that crossed her smooth, pale skin like the cracks in a ceramic jar that had broken long ago and had been glued back together again, as good as new, they say, and even stronger than before, but nevertheless fragile-looking now, and brittle, more likely to break a second time, than when it had not been broken at all "Yes," she said, "I get lonely," and with both hands, she reached up to her temples and pushed her hair back, and holding on to the sides of her own head she leaned it forward and kissed the man for several seconds, pushing at him with her mouth, until he pulled away, red-faced, his hand at his side now, and moved self-consciously sideways toward the door. "I'll come by tomorrow," he said in a low voice. "To see how Joel's doing." She smiled slightly and nodded. "If he's better," she said, "I'll be at work. But the door is always open." From the doorway, he asked if she came home for lunch. "Yes," she said, "when one of the boys is home sick, I do. Otherwise, no." He said that he might be here then, and she said, "Fine," and reached forward and closed the door on him.

Sometimes you dream that you are walking across a meadow beneath sunshine and a cloudless blue sky, hand in hand with your favorite child, and soon you notice that the meadow is sloping, uphill slightly, and walking becomes somewhat more difficult, although it remains a pleasure, for you are with your favorite child, and he is beautiful and happy and confident that you will let nothing terrible happen to him. You cross the crest, a rounded, meandering ridge, and start downhill, walking faster and more easily. The sun is shining, and there are wildflowers all around you, and the grass is golden and drifting in long waves in the breeze. Soon you find that the hill is steeper than before, the slope is falling away beneath your feet, as if the earth were curving in on itself, so you dig in your heels and try to slow your descent. Your child looks up at you, and there is fear in his eyes, as he realizes he is falling away from you. "My hand!" you cry. "Hold tightly to my hand!" And you grasp the hand of the child, who has started to fly away from you, as if over the edge of a crevice, while you dig your heels deeper into the ground and grab with your free hand at the long grasses behind you. The child screams and looks back at you with a pitiful gaze, and suddenly he grows so heavy that his weight is pulling you free of the ground also. You feel your feet leave the ground, and your body falls forward and down, behind your child's body, even though with one hand you still cling to the grasses. You weep, and you let go of your child's hand. The child flies away.

That night the boy's fever went higher. To one hundred five degrees, and Marcelle moved the younger boys into her own room, so that she could sleep in the bed next to the sick boy's. She bathed him in cool water with washcloths, coaxed him into swallowing aspirin with orange juice, and sat on the edge of the bed next to his and watched him sleep, although she knew that he was not truly sleeping, he was merely lying there on his side, his legs out straight now, and breathing rapidly, like an injured dog, stunned and silently healing itself. But the boy was not healing himself, he was hourly growing worse. She could tell that. She tried to move him so that she could straighten the sheets, but when she touched him, he cried out in pain, as if his spine or neck were broken, and, frightened, she drew back from him. She wanted to call Doctor Wickshaw, and several times she got up and walked out to the kitchen where the telephone hung on the wall like a large black insect, and each time she stood for a few seconds before the instrument, remembered the doctor in the hallway and what she had let him promise her with his eyes, remembered then what he had told her about her son's illness, and turned and walked back to the boy and tried again to cool him with damp cloths. Her three other sons slept peace fully through the night and knew nothing of what happened until morning came.

When your child lives, he carries with him all his earlier selves, so that you cannot separate your individual memories of him from your view of him now, at this moment. When you recall a particular event in your and your child's shared past—a day at the beach, a Christmas morning, a sad, weary night of flight from the child's shouting father, a sweet, pathetic supper prepared by the child for your birthday—when you recall these events singly, you cannot see the child as a camera would have photographed him then. You see him simultaneously all the way from infancy to adolescence to adulthood and on, as if he has been moving through your life too rapidly for any camera to catch, and the image is blurred, grayed out, a swatch of your own past pasted across the foreground of a studio photographer's carefully arranged backdrop.

When her son went into convulsions, Marcelle did not at first know it, for his voice was clear and what he said made sense. Suddenly he spoke loudly and in complete sentences. "Ma, I'm not alone. I know that, and it helps me to not be scared. For a while I thought I was alone," he declared. Marcelle sat upright and listened alertly to him in the darkness of the bedroom. "Then I started to see things and think maybe there was someone else in the room here with me, and then I was scared, Ma. Because I didn't know for sure whether I was alone or not. But now I know I'm not alone, and knowing it helps me not be scared." She said that she was glad, because she thought he was talking about her presence in the room, and she took his recognition of her presence as a sign that the fever had broken. But when she reached out in the darkness and touched his neck, it was burning, like an empty, black pot left over a fire, and she almost cried out in pain and might have, had the child not commenced to shout at her, bellowing at her, as if she were a large, ugly animal that he wished to send cowering into the far corner of his room.

Most people, when they do what the physician has told them to do, expect to be cured. When they are not cured, they at first believe it is because they have not done properly what they have been told to do. Sickness is the mystery, the miracle, and the physician understands such things, we say, whereas we, who are not physicians, all we understand is health. This is not the case, of course, for health is the mystery and the miracle. Not sickness. Sickness can be penetrated, understood, predicted. Health cannot. The analogy between the physician and the priest will not hold, for sickness and injury are not at all like divine protection and forgiveness. Sadly, most people and most physicians and most priests do not know this, or if they do, they do not act as if they know it. It's only in dealing with our children that we treat life as if it were indeed the miracle, as if life itself were the mystery of divine protection and forgiveness, and in that way, it is only in dealing with our children that most people are like priests serving God, making it possible for poor sinners to obtain grace.

Doctor Wickshaw hurried into the boy's bedroom and this time knew that the boy had contracted meningitis, probably spinal meningitis, and he also knew that it was too late to save the boy, that if the boy did not die in the next few days, he would suffer irreparable damage to his central nervous system.

Marcelle knew that by her son's death she was now a lost soul. She did not weep. She went grimly about her appointed rounds, she raised her three remaining sons, and each of them, in his turn, forgave her and protected her. The one who died, Joel, the oldest, would never forgive her, never shield her from judgment, never let grace fall on her. Late at night, when she lay in bed alone, she knew this to the very bottom of her mind, and that knowledge was the lamp that illuminated the mystery and the miracle of her remaining days.

EDMUND WHITE
(b. 1940)

Edmund White, born in Cincinnati, Ohio, grew up in the suburban Chicago area and attended prep school at the Cranbrook Academy in Bloomfield Hills, Michigan, the vividly described setting for his acclaimed early novel A Boy's Own Story *(1982). White graduated from the University of Michigan at Ann Arbor in 1962 with a BA degree in Chinese language and literature, and soon moved to New York City to support himself as a journalist, reviewer, and editor at* Saturday Review of Literature, Horizon, *and* Time-Life Books. *In 1981, White helped found the Gay Men's Health Crisis in New York City. In 1983, White moved to Paris where he would write both fiction and journalism until 1998, establishing himself as a writer-in-exile of sorts, one of those American writers, like Paul Auster and Diane Johnson, warmly embraced by a French literary audience while retaining their primary, crucial American identity. (White is a member of the French Order of Arts and Letters.) After his return to the United States, White has been teaching creative writing at Princeton University. He has been a resident of New York City's Chelsea for more than twelve years.*

In addition to White's distinguished list of novels which include Forgetting Elena *(1973),* Nocturnes for the King of Naples *(1978),* The Beautiful Room is Empty *(1988),* The Farewell Symphony *(1997),* The Married Man *(2000),* Fanny: A Fiction *(2003),* Hotel de Dream *(2007), and* Jack Holmes and His Friend *(2012), he is also the author of two story collections,* Skinned Alive *(1995) and* Chaos: A Novella and Stories *(2007) from which the story included here, "Give It Up for Billy," has been taken.*

Unlike most of the writers in this anthology, Edmund White is as admired for his nonfiction—his biographies and memoirs—as he is for his novels and short stories. He is the author of the first biography of Jean Genet, for which he was awarded a National Book Critics Circle Award in 2001, as well as biographies of Rimbaud and Proust; his memoirs, controversial in some quarters for their blend of painful frankness and hilarity, are The Flâneur: A Stroll Through the Paradoxes of Paris *(2001),* My

Lives: An Autobiography *(2005), and* City Boy *(2009). His nonfiction books include* The Joy of Gay Sex *(1977),* States of Desire *(1980),* The Burning Library: Writings on Art, Politics and Sexuality 1969–1993 *(1994),* Arts and Letters *(2004) and* Sacred Monsters *(2011); in 2009 his play* Terre Haute, *an imagined encounter between a young American right-wing terrorist based upon Timothy McVeigh and an older, highly educated and articulate leftist writer based upon Gore Vidal, premiered in New York City.*

Edmund White is celebrated for his candor, openness, and fearlessness in writing of the most painfully intimate of human experiences, that manage to be both intensely personal and representative, as well as for the understated elegance of his prose. Among White's numerous awards are a 1982 Award for Literature from the American Academy of Arts and Letters, into which White was inducted in 1997; Ingram Merrill and Guggenheim Foundation fellowships; and the Literary Prize of the American Festival at Deauville, France, in 2000.

Of the gossipy yet poignant "Give It Up for Billy," a quintessential Edmund White story, the author has said: "I wanted to show how people living in very different political realities can completely fail to understand one another's actions. Sexual politics may play a big role in contemporary America, but in parts of Africa the politics-of-survival have the determining function."

Give It Up for Billy

HAROLD'S LOVER TOM DIDN'T COME WITH him to Key West that winter. Tom thought the heterosexual snowbirds were too old in Key West and the younger gays who worked there year round were too stupid. Since South Beach had become the destination for A-list gays (celebrated decorators, real estate speculators, media moguls and their satellites—muscle builders and models), Key West had turned into a backwater for balding gay couples from Toledo, the sort who owned and operated their own neighborhood dry cleaners and whose foreheads burned easily in the semi-tropical sun. They immediately took up with a similar couple from Lubbock they'd just met. The foursome were happy to go on a glass-bottomed boat out to the reef or to play bridge at night back at their all-male compound where the only men under thirty worked behind the desk.

Harold didn't mind how dowdy Key West had become with its main street lined with Israeli-owned T-shirt shops, its commercialization of Papa Hemingway's bearded face on the coasters at Sloppy Joe's bar on Duval, or its conch train that puttered down shaded streets and informed the tourists in shorts and sun hats about the Hemingway House and his cats with six toes or about Truman's Little White House or the Audubon House. Harold accepted that the world was becoming a product to be consumed by the world's leading industry, mass tourism. He looked at Japanese tourists as models for us all. They didn't seek out private, authentic experiences while traveling, or so at least he imagined. They didn't claim to be the exception, to be solitary and romantic. They weren't a headache for their group leader. No, they were content to buy the best known, most easily recognized luxury brand names at airport shops and to take their photos of the Whaling Museum or the Eiffel Tower or the Oldest House from the exact spot the guide indicated.

Harold had been coming here for a few weeks every winter over the last twenty years and he'd seen Key West go from a rough town of drifters and trailer trash to an elegant stronghold with artistic pretensions, including an annual literary conference on themes such as "Nature Writing" or "Journaling" or "Fact or Fiction?" Property prices had gone up tenfold.

And he was no longer young and wouldn't figure on anybody's A or B list. He was sixty-three, in a few days to be sixty-four, and about to retire from the American History department of Princeton with a handsome teacher's union portfolio. He had an arthritic neck and cataracts he wanted to have removed as soon as they were a bit riper. Tom, his forty-five-year-old lover, worked for Johnson & Johnson in public relations. Tom ran several miles a day and had no wrinkles, possibly because he used Retin-A.

They had an extremely open, easygoing relationship. Their heterosexual friends—and almost all of their friends were heterosexual in Princeton—said they envied them their relaxed attitude toward each other's extramarital adventures. Actually the adventures were embarrassingly rare and the friends in reality found their non-possessiveness confusing since it seemed to mark yet another spot where there wasn't a perfect fit between homosexual and heterosexual couples. People liked homosexuals if they were a sort of fun house reflection of their own image. They didn't want them to be completely different.

What no one knew was that Harold and Tom had long since given up having sex with each other. It was as if their original friendship had flared up into sexuality and jealousy for a few years before subsiding back into mutual esteem. Harold wanted Tom to have fun, even sexual fun, so long as he didn't fall in love with someone else and leave him. He couldn't bear to live alone in Princeton. Recently Tom had begun to date a woman from his office, someone who did community relations, and she represented a more serious threat to their life together. Women played for keeps, Harold believed. He thought female seriousness was biological and had something to do with sperm being cheap and eggs dear, or was it to do with spreading a favorable mutation quickly through the species—but such theories always struck him as kitsch. He knew that straights took their lives more seriously than gays did, and straight women most of all.

Harold relaxed back into his old Key West routines. He rented a bike and went everywhere on it, even on cold nights and rainy days. Literary friends his age thought it absurd that he didn't rent a car and drive around in dignity as they did. They thought it ridiculous that he insisted on teetering around with his big po-po hanging out over the saddle, but Harold loved the boyhood associations of riding a bike, especially at night down the cat-busy lanes and under giant palms churning in the wind. Most of the time he was tired and a bit dazed, as if coming out from under a sedative, but when he was alert, as he was at midnight on his bike, he felt as he always had.

He'd looked forward to going back to Scooter's, the go-go bar, which in the past had been on the edge of town where Truman Avenue shaded into Highway 1. It had been a rowdy but innocent place where skinny, Florida blonds and small compact brunettes from Montreal came out on the tacky runway, one by one, in jeans and layered shirts. Each did two numbers, the first one clothed and the second stripped down to a G-string. The unseen announcer at the end would say, "Okay, fellas. Give it up for Ronnie," a locution Harold never had heard before; apparently it meant "Applaud Ronnie."

He found that there were more and more things he didn't know about. Almost all the guests on late-night talk shows he'd never heard of—pop singers or actors in TV series, which he didn't watch. He didn't follow sports and never knew the names of tennis players and football stars. He could identify most of the current and past names in American studies, of course, as well as many of the principal figures in American history. He was convinced he knew more about his period, Woodrow Wilson's America, than about George W. Bush's.

Scooter's had moved into town. The bar was now smaller and cleaner and better lit. Instead of putting on stage any kid blowing through town, it now had a small permanent cast of dancers, mostly non-English speakers: a big blond Estonian, an intensely black Senegalese with biceps as round as cannonballs, a wispy Czech, a sulky Spaniard, a smiling Macedonian. They would dance for twenty minutes on the two raised daises at the far end of the room, then jump up onto the bar and coax tips out of customers before working the room.

They'd dance standing up on the bar and customers would stick dollar bills in their gym socks, but after a while they'd crouch down, their legs spread wide, and let the older men touch their thighs and crotches. The tips were rarely more than a dollar or two, whereas at Teacher's, the heterosexual strip bar, the men handed out tens and twenties. Were gay men poorer or less competitive—or did they think it a waste to pay out a lot of money to a member of their own sex?

The seedy festive atmosphere of the old Scooter's was gone, with its tables and chairs gathered around the stage and the lights—red or white, strong or soft—which the boys had kicked on with their toes, like Marilyn Monroe in *Bus Stop.* They no longer had an overhead pipe to do pull-ups on. And gone was the cubbyhole separated from the room by glass beads where customers could have extra feels in the dark for twenty bucks: lap dancing, it was called.

Now the proximity of the heavy foot traffic up and down Duval, those herds of tourists grazing along, released from the big cruise ships, acted as an inhibiting presence on the men in the new Scooter's. The whole place was just too visible and few locals dared to drop in.

But it was better than nothing. In Princeton there were no go-go boys and in New York there were too many drag queens for Harold's taste and not much lap dancing. He admired transvestites—their courage, their art, their antic sense of fun—but they didn't turn him on. In Princeton, of course, for so many years the boys had been his students: superb, untouchable. Now that at last he was about to retire, he was the age of their grandfathers and unlikely to attract anyone. He sometimes fancied an older man, but they seldom looked his way. Almost no one looked his way.

Night after night Harold, after a dinner with elderly literary or scholarly friends, would bicycle down the nearly empty streets to Duval, which was always busy, and to Scooter's. Gay bars, straight bars, closing restaurants, a big disco, the Ripley's Believe-It-or-Not, the handsome spotlit facade of the Cuban Cultural Center, the slow passage of cruising cars and pickup trucks up and down the main drag, the clang-clang of bells rung by professional bicyclists conveying one or two passengers in open rickshaws—it was all exciting, an animated little world. Harold chained his bike to a lamppost, visited the outdoor ATM, and ambled into Scooter's. He liked the glow of naked young flesh under the spotlights, the smell of freshly poured beer, the pools of attention as men gathered around a dancer drifting like a big, showy camellia through the crowd. He liked to sit at the bar and look up at these kids with their powerful legs, sweat-drenched torsos, broad shoulders, and unfocused smiles.

Sometimes one of them would drip on him. They were nude and extravagant as hothouse flowers blooming above all these old men. In Italy he'd once seen rose bushes threaded through gnarled olive trees: that was the effect. The boys were more often than not bewitched by their own reflections, which they studied in the mirror with alternating smiles and frowns. As one would turn sideways and suck in his gut you could just hear him asking himself if he was really getting a beer belly as Tommy claimed.

The men, of course, had once been boys, too, but not boys like these, not usually. These men were chemical engineers or hotel managers or accountants: nerds. Two of them whom Harold had met were English and ran a bed-and-breakfast in Brighton. A few, no doubt; had been good-looking, but not in the way these dancers were. Back then very few men worked out—and almost no gays. These dancers had gym-built bodies, legs bowed with muscle, tiny waists giving it up to flaring torsos and wide shoulders, thick necks, cropped heads. "Give it up for Ronnie"—that was the phrase that kept ringing in his head for no good reason. These dancers were shaved, tattooed, bronzed, tinted; even their pubic hair, when they revealed a glimpse of it, was just a shaped, trimmed patch, cut to the quick to make their genitals look still bigger. Everything—sneakers or combat boots, thong or towel, nipple ring or diamond ear-bob—had been thought out, but even so they had a reckless, raucous assertiveness that came through their primping like a trumpet through a thicket of quivering strings. Most of them were straight and spent the dollars they earned on local girls. He'd seen them stumbling out of the Hog's Breath Saloon with girls.

Harold liked them all, all of the boys, and when one of them strolled around the room in a gold G-string and gathered a group of old men (hands liver-spotted, backs twisted, mouths radiant with new teeth), Harold couldn't help but picture *Susannah and the Elders* by—was it Titian? That beautiful naked girl emerging from her bath, her flesh coveted by all the old men peeking through the bushes. Roses threaded through the olive branches.

IT took two or three days for Harold to decide he liked Billy the most. Billy was about five-foot-ten and he had a splash of peroxided hair, though in recent years peroxide no longer signified "cheap." Now it read "punk" or just "young"—nothing clear, in any case. Billy had a knowing smile and a faint scar that traversed his nose. Just a seam, really. A ghost of asymmetry. He had a solemn, level gaze, something serious and noncommittal but friendly about his manner. He had what personal ads on gay Internet called a "six-pack stomach."

He also had an immense uncut penis that once or twice a night he worked up and gave quick glimpses of. Sometimes, when he danced on a dais, he pulled his shorts open and looked down at his penis, which he could see but the audience couldn't. He'd mime the sound, "Wow," and bug his eyes, as if he'd never seen it before. But he went lightly on the comedy. He wasn't a camp. He was a serious, virile man but not forbidding, certainly not unapproachable. A man's man, who treated customers as if they were almost pals, though he definitely maintained a professional distance.

Harold gave him five-dollar tips and never groped him. Sometimes Harold said friendly, noncommittal things, like, "The air conditioner's on the blink tonight?" or, "Where'd they get *this* music?" After four or five days Billy would come over to Harold on his break. If Harold was seated at the bar, Billy would lean against him, throw a hot, heavy arm around his shoulders. "That guy over there," Harold would say, "was sure pawing you."

Billy said, "These guys must think we're really naïve. Man…That guy said he'd just bought a mansion quote-unquote in Key West and had decided he wanted to spend the rest of his life with me. He said he was a multimillionaire quote-unquote and would leave me well provided for. He'd take me away from all this." Billy opened a hand, then let it fall to his side.

"Jesus …" Harold muttered with feigned disgust at the guy's chutzpah. But why not? If the guy were alone, not long for this world, rich enough to feather his last nest with a nice gigolo, why not buy a young man who looked thirty and seemed unusually solid?

"I said to him, Why not tip me a few dollars right now if you're so rich, but the cheap bastard never parted with a penny."

"Hey, Billy," Harold said, wrapping a hand around his tight little waist, "where are you from anyway, Australia?"

"Zimbabwe."

"Oh."

"Do you see—"

"Yes I see. Former Rhodesia."

"You'd be amazed how many Americans think it's next to Tibet."

"Hopeless ..." Harold groaned.

Billy had a polite, deferential manner, an impenetrable but friendly regard, a deep reserve. He might throw his arm over Harold's shoulder but it all felt like a professional engagement; Harold could almost hear the meter ticking.

A very tall blond man in his late thirties wearing a raspberry-colored polo shirt, pleated khakis and gold-bitted loafers signaled Billy, who excused himself. Harold didn't want to stare but he saw the seated man draw Billy down onto one leg and idly stroke his hairless, oiled thigh. There was no lust in it, just intimacy, and the man spoke rapidly, even in a businesslike way, while Billy nodded agreement. They could have been two spies exchanging information while pretending to be dancer and client. In five minutes the conference was over and the man had elbowed his way out of the bar, uninterested in the other dancers, though he did shake hands with the bouncer at the door and even spared him a smile.

The next day Harold watched a porno film his landlord lent him; the eventless subplot was about twins from Hungary, identical down to the tiniest mole on the right forearm or the small, cantilevered buttocks or the overlapping incisors. They seemed happiest when stepping off each other's joined hands and doing a back flip into the pool and the most embarrassed when they had to kiss, and fondle each other's smallish identical erection with an identical hand. They had identical ponytails. The main story was unrelated, all about a superb, dark-haired boy with flawless skin who so enjoyed being penetrated by a blond Dracula that he begged the monster to bite his neck—a declaration so miraculously romantic that Dracula was turned back into an ordinary human being. And saved. From what? Harold wondered. Eternal life? Eternal youth?

Harold worried about dying. He had de-dramatized every moment in his life, giggled at the over-the-top romantic scenes in a movie, accepted his mother's death with equanimity, even indifference, though when he'd won a scholarly prize for his book on Wilson at Versailles, he'd wept, since his mother wasn't alive to enjoy his moment of glory. Egotism, he'd told himself. Egotistical foolishness.

Life at Princeton—the university and the town—was so unchanging that he couldn't remember many key dates in his life there other than his five sabbatical years and the beginnings and ends of his three previous affairs.

He couldn't quite figure it out, but it was as if he'd worked out a strategy that if he didn't bear down too hard on his life it would leave such a faint mark it wouldn't—what? count? be noticed? Go through the carbon onto a master copy? He'd almost never been alone. He'd always had a live-in companion, although in the '60s he had still had to pretend that Jack, the man of the moment, was just rooming in his spare bedroom. By the mid-'70s the mores had so changed that he and Jack had been invited everywhere as a couple.

There had been so few ripples in his life. He'd produced only three books, but two were significant and still in print. He'd inched his way up the ladder to tenure and a full professorship. He'd had three or four star students who were now distinguished Americanists. One was even contemplating early retirement.

He felt he'd somehow slipped through. He'd not had to serve in Vietnam, at first because he'd been in graduate school and then because his asthma had been so crippling. Later, the disease had just gone away, even though central New Jersey was both polluted *and* saturated with pollen, the industrial Garden State. He'd been just a few years too old to become a hippie, and he was never tempted to drop out. He'd supported the student rebels in 1968, but no more so than did most of the other junior faculty. He'd come out when he was in his fifties, back in the 1980s, when gender studies had become trendy and he was able to renew his scholarly image by arguing in an oft-cited essay that World War I had been a forcing shed for modern gay identity. He'd exercised moderately, had never drunk to excess, he'd been afraid to try intravenous drugs, and he'd smoked marijuana just twice, both times with a Puerto Rican trick, and had felt nothing. Just when AIDS had become a real danger he'd met Tom, who was then in his early twenties and virtually a virgin. They'd been faithful for nearly a decade and by then had mastered safe sex techniques.

But he knew he wasn't going to slip past old age, sickness and death. No one did. He wasn't Dracula. He was considered practical and realistic and he'd take all the most rational steps toward the grave—or rather the crematorium. The other day he'd read in a new French novel, "He was accumulating as many experiences as possible so he'd feel less alone when he died," but Harold suspected the author of irony. It didn't work that way.

Harold knew that at best he had just twenty or twenty-five more years to live, which didn't sound very long. The previous twenty years had gone by so fast. Time was speeding up just as it was running out, like the last of the water draining from a sink.

Back in the early eighties Key West had been a good time-thickener because he'd known so few people and had done nothing but lie around and read. But now the island was so busy with elderly activity—luncheons, readings, cocktail parties, art openings—that the days sped by. Key West made Princeton seem tranquil by contrast.

Harold didn't tell Tom every detail about Billy during their daily phone calls but Tom certainly got the highlights. Tom had enough on his plate. Roger, their old wirehaired fox terrier, had become so ill with leukemia and in such pain from arthritis that Dr. Wilkins had put him to sleep.

Harold knew he was being irrational, but he thought they should have waited until he, Harold, could have said good-bye to the dog.

"Closure? Is that it?" Tom asked. "Everybody in America suddenly wants closure. Well, I wasn't worrying about your peace of mind, Harold."

A long silence set in. To change the subject Harold asked Tom about Liz.

"Her name is Beth. She's fine. How's Billy? When are you going to go to bed with him?"

"I'm not sure what my next move should be." Harold was grateful for this fake conversation to replace the real, painful one.

"Ask him over in the afternoon. If that man in the Gucci shoes is keeping him, the late afternoon may be the only time he's free."

"Don't you think it's odd he's from Zimbabwe?"

Tom laughed. "You don't keep up with the news but Zimbabwe is going through hell. The black president, Mugabwe, has encouraged roving bands of black ex-soldiers to kill the white settlers and expropriate their farms, and the soldiers know nothing about farming and the crop yields are diminishing and the World Bank or whatever won't extend them any more loans—it's a nightmare. As for gay life, the gay guide forbids readers to go there at all. The whole country is AYOR, at your own risk. People suspected of homosexuality are pushed off a cliff or is that Yemen? Anyway, it's *dire,* darling. Your little Billy has come to Key West to come out."

Harold said admiringly, "You always can orient yourself to a new person or situation within seconds. Whereas I feel like some sort of moral Mr. Magoo."

"That's right: I'm perfect," Tom said. He didn't take compliments well and was specially immune to Harold's, which were too flowery and heartfelt for someone like Tom, brought up on jokey, shrugging sitcom dialogue.

THAT night Harold invited Billy to drop by his place the following afternoon for a drink.

"I don't drink."

"For a fruit juice."

"But not orange or grapefruit," Billy said. "They're too acidic. Maybe an herbal tea would be best, or mineral water flat."

"What?"

"Non-sparkling. It's better for the digestion."

Although Harold found alimentary pedantry to be tiresome, he welcomed it as a diversion from the real question: Why should they get together at all?

"I can come by after my workout around four forty-five or four-fifty," Billy said.

Despite the precision, he didn't show up until five-fifteen. He came speeding up in a red convertible with the top down and the stereo blaring a Mariah Carey tape (something Tom would have sniffed at). For Harold, who liked no music after early Stravinsky, it was all the same to him. The barbarians had broken through the gate, they were the rulers, there was nothing more to worry about.

They sat outside on a little veranda surrounded by shoulder-height bamboo walls. Harold had brought back from the expensive supermarket cooked shrimp, smoked mackerel bits, blue corn chips, and several kinds of water—as much as he could carry in his bicycle basket without losing control. Billy drank the water but didn't touch the food.

When Harold asked Billy what were his plans in life, the young man said, "You know the tall guy who comes into the club to see me?"

"Yes. Who is he?"

"His name is Ed. He's an agent for models. He arranged for me to be in *Frisk*. Here, I brought you the February issue. It's in the car."

Harold had always imagined most of the readers of the "women's magazine" *Frisk* were gay men, closet cases who needed a heterosexual alibi in order to study other men's bodies. Maybe there were women readers, too. Certainly in this issue, he thought as he thumbed through it, there was a lean man in his fifties, a slightly flabby guy with a small penis and a beautiful face, and there was a photo essay titled "A Romantic Evening by the Fire," which showed a woman being undressed by an entirely depilated man. A hardcore gay magazine wouldn't have had any of these variations—the older man or the flab or the woman, but the guys would have had shaved bodies.

Billy's pictures made up the lead story. He was shown in various stages of undress, though the last spread revealed just how immense his "manhood" was, to use the language of the magazine. The text called him by a different name, Kevin, and said he was a corporate lawyer in Boston.

"So you want to be a model?"

"I'm already thirty and if I watch my diet and work out every day maybe I can stretch it out till I'm forty, but I'm saving every cent. Most of it I'm sending back to my Mum to install an electric fence around her house."

"Shouldn't you get her out of Zimbabwe altogether?"

"The cities aren't dangerous, not yet. She has a very nice house and servants. You can't believe how far the U.S. dollars I send her go. Anyway, she's running the family business."

"What is your family business?"

Billy looked at Harold in a penetrating way—frank, level, unsmiling. "Funeral parlor. My Mum and Dad emigrated from England to Rhodesia in the late sixties. They had a thriving business. When I was eighteen my Dad sent me back to London for a two-year course in embalming techniques, grief counseling, and funeral accountancy. Then he died and I took over the business. My Mum is the business manager. She's the one who has all the contacts in the community."

"Black as well?"

"About a third of our clients are black."

From the very beginning Harold had picked up on something...formal about Billy. When they were just standing around Billy lowered his head, let a noncommittal smile play over his lips. He hooked his hands behind his back and widened his stance like a soldier at ease. Now Harold could easily picture Billy in a white shirt, dark tie and dark suit, producing a white handkerchief for the sobbing widow.

Billy took Harold for a ride in his car out to another island. His cell rang and he laughed and murmured into it, but he wasn't speaking English. When he hung up, Harold asked, "Was that Afrikaans?"

"Zulu. Well, our kind of Zulu."

"Were you speaking to someone in Zimbabwe?"

"Yes, it was my mate Bob. Great guy. We always have a bit of a chinwag once a week."

"Is he black?"

"What? Oh. No. He's white."

"You speak Zulu to another white guy?"

"We go back and forth."

Harold thought it would be hard to maintain that a Zulu-speaking, African-born Zimbabwean was an outsider.

Whenever Harold asked something about politics in Zimbabwe, Billy maintained a low-key tone. *Sixty Minutes* had just done a frightening segment on the deterioration of the country. In one scene a group of armed black men in rags crossed a lush, well-tended field and approached a young white farmer. Their discussion seemed more a dispute over something like a parking ticket, heated but containable, but in another scene the charred, bloated dead bodies of other white settlers were shown.

Someone taped the program for Billy, who seemed shocked, silenced when he saw it. "I knew that young farmer. I *knew* him."

"The president was such an obvious hypocrite," Harold said. But Billy appeared to be way beyond outraged anger.

They had sex every afternoon. Harold paid him two hundred dollars a session. After a few days he suggested they lower the fee to a hundred-fifty dollars, but Billy was firm. "I need all I can get, Harold," he said.

Billy would appear around five in his red convertible outside Harold's gate. They'd sip some herbal tea and then move into the bedroom for a "massage." Harold would apply a thick cocoa butter with an oppressively sweet smell to Billy's back and shoulders, then to his muscular buttocks, finally to his calves and thighs.

Harold didn't really like massaging Billy's body, which felt too hard and unyielding. There was no mystery to it. It was like armor, not responsive flesh. Billy would talk in fits and starts, giving the news of the day, and Harold felt like his trainer. The problem was that Harold didn't really dote on other men, never had. He wasn't an idolater, though Billy was cut out to be an idol.

Decades and decades ago, back in the 1950s, Harold had been famous for his smooth skin; even the three women who had touched and held him had envied him his skin. He'd been lithe, small-sexed, boyish, though he'd dressed in chunky tweeds and worn wire-rims and seldom smiled with his thin lips. But for the handful of men who'd bothered to lift his fragile glasses off and liberate him from his heavy, thickening clothes, he'd been a *bijou*. Once when he'd been in Paris as a tourist he'd been picked up by a couturier who lived in Sartre's old apartment. The man, all sprouting whiskers and smoker's cough, had stood back, slightly amazed at the boyish genie he'd summoned up out of the drab clothes—*"Mais tu es un* bijou, *un petit bijou,"* he'd said as he opened his hands, as if to bear witness.

Harold still felt a bit like that and half expected to amaze other men. On the phone his voice, apparently, sounded like a piping, eager, overeducated kid's, holding a laugh in, and young people who met him first on the phone warmed up to him, called him "Hal" and said funny, sly things to him.

After Harold had massaged Billy's back he tapped his ass, as a trainer might, with an unsuggestive touch, and Billy turned over.

There, suddenly, was the enormous uncircumcised penis, white and marbled and somehow *assembled,* like sausage meat. And Harold applied himself to it, as if this were just a customized kind of massage, given the shape of the body part. Billy kept his eyes closed and made not a sound until the actual moment of explosion, and even then Harold suspected it was less a sensual moan than a warning to back off in the interests of safe sex.

Harold invited Billy to his sixty-fourth birthday party on another island not far away. They all sprayed themselves against the clouds of mosquitoes and Harold's friends, a dozen of them, artists and writers and teachers in their fifties and sixties, were charmed by Billy, who stood about with his hands hooked behind him, his eyes lowered: the perfect mortician.

He was unassertive but friendly and open. He talked about Zimbabwe and his fears for his mother and sister. "I'm trying to raise a bit of money so that my sister can emigrate to Australia."

"We saw the *Sixty Minutes* show," someone murmured sympathetically.

"I knew that farmer. My sister has a beautiful farm, but she can never sell it now. I've got to get her out of there as soon as I can afford it. Every day counts."

Billy played with someone's four-year-old daughter and even laced an arm around the waist of a big-eyed, short-haired woman who'd divorced her husband recently, though the ex-husband was present if subdued. A man who wrote a column on labor problems for *The Nation* kept asking Billy questions about his job as a dancer. Billy smiled mildly; he had no hesitation in responding. Surely, Harold thought, he must be enjoying this freedom. He was never free in Africa.

One of the guests, a sculptor, invited them to his studio to pose for him. "I'm doing terra cotta figurines of lap dancers at Teacher's, women dancers and male customers, so I might as well do some gay pairs, if you're up to it. I don't know what will come of it, if anything."

They went to Sid's studio two days later, in the afternoon, at their usual hour. Sid paid Billy ten dollars for posing. By this time Harold's straight friends had all seen the issue of *Frisk* and they were all astonished by the size of Billy's penis. "But is that trick photography?"

"No," Harold said, lowering his eyes modestly.

Sid's wife said, "And he's a hell of a nice guy, too. He played with Annabelle's daughter for hours. I asked him to dance next month for our guests on Captain Bob's boat—we're giving a big party. Too bad you won't be here."

Harold enjoyed holding Billy's calves and staring up at him. Billy was wearing just a G-string, whereas Harold was in a shirt and slacks. Sid had rigged up a platform that simulated a bar. He kept pushing them closer together, not because he wanted intimacy. No, he just wanted to simplify their forms into a pyramid. Once again Harold thought of roses emerging out of a gnarled, twisted olive tree.

Harold dreaded their sex sessions. The rancid, sweet smell of the cocoa butter that Billy had brought with him that first time and left behind and that now had almost been used up. The lengthy massage of this nearly inert and unfeeling body and the sausage-making, which ended with a single groan. The ruinous expense, which Harold thought he couldn't reduce or eliminate, since it was going to save Billy's mother and sister. Harold couldn't even convince himself he was bringing any special pleasure to Billy, since Billy complained that Harold's teeth were too sharp and hurt him. Of course Harold had never faced such a big challenge before.

Suddenly it was over. The vacation had come to an end. Harold had given his straight friends in Key West something to deplore or admire, in any event to discuss. Did they suspect Harold was paying Billy—and so handsomely? Or did they think all the usual rules didn't apply to gay life and that young Susannahs gave freely, copiously of their charms to their Elders? He suspected his friends thought he was exploiting Billy, but in fact Billy was exploiting him, with his full complicity. Harold sympathized with Billy's family's plight and respected Billy's seriousness.

Billy drove him in the red convertible to the airport. He helped him with his luggage. They shook hands. For a moment Billy stood at ease, with his hands hooked behind him. Then he waved and speeded off.

Harold thought that his own decision to go on having sex at all was either a stubborn sign of the life force or a mere habit, depending on one's interpretation. He smeared Androgel on his body every morning, a clear salve containing androgens, the sex-drive hormone. Without it he'd never feel a twitch of desire. His doctor had prescribed it: "It'll give you some zest for life, improve your energy level. Appetite. Zest," he repeated.

Was he lacking in zest? For sex, yes. But for life?

Yes, he thought. Whereas Billy had a survivor's instincts. He was determined that he and his family would survive.

Harold was so happy to be back with Tom, though he missed the dog. Tom was dating his girlfriend three nights a week now. Beth. Her name was Beth.

A month after Harold came home, Tom said he was moving out.

"I'm going to try to make things work with Beth."

"Really?"

"You know how much I've always wanted children. A child. I only realized that after Roger died."

"What?"

"Roger was our child. But when he died I thought how pathetic it was to heap so much tenderness on a poor, short-lived, dumb animal. I'd like a human child. Beth wants one, too."

Harold didn't like Roger to be called "poor." He was so shaken that he didn't think much about Billy. Once or twice he showed Billy's spread in *Frisk* to his friends in Princeton. They said "Wow" but they were humoring him. They obviously felt sorry for him. Did they think he was to blame for Tom's change of heart, of life?

One day, while researching an article on Woodrow Wilson at Princeton, Harold came across a remark Wilson had made twenty years later, after graduation. "Plenty of people offer me their friendship; but partly because I am reserved and shy, and partly because I am fastidious and have a narrow, uncatholic taste in friends, I reject the offer in almost every case—and then am dismayed to look about and see how few persons in the world stand near me and know me as I am."

Six months later he called Sid just to chat.

"Say, did you know Billy is getting married?" Sid asked.

"No," Harold said. "For immigration reasons?"

"Apparently it's a real romance. She's not even American. She's from South Africa." Sid downshifted. "I don't really get that, do you? Switch-hitting?" He didn't know about Tom and Beth. "You know Billy danced at our annual party. We took everybody on Captain Bob's boat and Billy was the entertainment. If I hadn't talked with him—I mean, he's such a thoughtful guy and then boom! There he was, bumping and grinding."

"Maybe Billy was never gay," Harold said. "Despite all appearances. I assumed he'd come to the States to enjoy sexual freedom, but now I think it was just to earn some quick money to relocate his family."

After he hung up, he threw some pumpkin-stuffed ravioli into boiling water. He was unaccountably hungry, in spite of the clammy summer day. A small, peevish voice somewhere inside of him said, "See? He was just using you and everyone else." But then Harold smiled, pleased at the simplifying form things had taken.

RICHARD FORD
(b. 1944)

Born in Jackson, Mississippi and educated at the University of Michigan in Ann Arbor, Richard Ford has traveled, lived, and taught in numerous regions of the United States and Mexico, which have been rendered into powerfully persuasive settings for his short stories and novels. Ford speaks of "geographical points of reference" for his stories' actions, and indeed it does seem that Ford is among the most geographically precise of writers in this anthology; in a typical work of fiction by Richard Ford, settings function as "characters."

To list Ford's works of fiction is to evoke such settings as Mississippi, in his debut novel A Piece of My Heart *(1976); Oaxaca, Mexico, in* The Ultimate Good Luck *(1981); suburban New Jersey in the acclaimed Frank Bascomb trilogy,* The Sportswriter *(1986),* Independence Day *(1995), and* The Lay of the Land *(2006); Montana in the story collection* Rock Springs *(1987) and the novella* Wildlife *(1990); and the province of Saskatchewan in* Canada *(2012). Ford is the author of two more short story collections,* Women with Men *(1997) and* A Multitude of Sins *(2002). He has edited numerous volumes of short stories including the* Best American Short Stories 1990, *the* Granta Book of the American Short Story *(1992), the* Granta Book of the American Long Story *(1998),* The Essential Chekhov *(1999), and* Blue Collar, White Collar, No Collar: Stories of Work *(2011).*

Richard Ford has described himself as "mildly dyslexic" which may have helped him as a reader since the disability forced him to approach books at a "slow and thoughtful pace." He received a BA degree from the State University of Michigan at East Lansing and attended law school briefly before entering the creative writing program at the University of California-Irvine where he received an MFA in 1970. He has taught creative writing at Princeton University, Trinity College, Dublin, Columbia University, and the University of Mississippi. Among his numerous awards are the Pulitzer Prize and the PEN/Faulkner Award, for Independence Day, *the Rea Award for the Short Story, and the Award of Merit for the Novel from the American Academy of*

Arts and Letters. In his thoughtful interview published in Paris Review *(Fall 1996), Ford speaks of his conception of character as "unfixed, changeable, provisional, unpredictable, decidedly unwhole." In fact, Ford isn't sure that we have "characters" and not rather "histories."*

The provisional and enigmatic nature of such "history" is succinctly dramatized in the story included here, "Under the Radar."

Under the Radar

On the drive over to the Nicholsons' for dinner—their first in some time—Marjorie Reeves told her husband, Steven Reeves, that she had had an affair with George Nicholson (their host) a year ago, but that it was all over with now and she hoped he—Steven—would not be mad about it and could go on with life.

At this point they were driving along Quaker Bridge Road where it leaves the Perkins Great Woods Road and begins to border the Shenipsit Reservoir, dark and shadowy and calmly mirrored in the late spring twilight. On the right were dense young timber, beech and alder saplings in pale leaf, the ground damp and cakey. Peepers were calling out from the watery lows. Their turn onto Apple Orchard Lane was still a mile on.

Steven, on hearing this news, began gradually and very carefully to steer their car—a tan Mercedes wagon with hooded yellow headlights—off of Quaker Bridge Road and onto the damp grassy shoulder so he could organize this information properly before going on.

They were extremely young. Steven Reeves was twenty-eight. Marjorie Reeves a year younger. They weren't rich, but they'd been lucky. Steven's job at Packard-Wells was to stay on top of a small segment of a larger segment of a rather small prefabrication intersection that serviced the automobile industry, and where any sudden alteration, or even the rumor of an alteration in certain polymer-bonding formulas could tip crucial down-the-line demand patterns, and in that way affect the betting lines and comfort zones of a good many meaningful client positions. His job meant poring over dense and esoteric petrochemical-industry journals, attending technical seminars, flying to vendor conventions, then writing up detailed status reports and all the while keeping an eye on the market for the benefit of his higher-ups. He'd been a scholarship boy at Bates, studied chemistry, was the only son of a hard-put but upright lobstering family in Pemaquid, Maine, and had done well. His bosses at Packard-Wells liked him, saw themselves in him, and also in him saw character qualities they'd never quite owned—blond and slender callowness tending to gullibility, but backed by caution, ingenuity and a thoroughgoing, compact toughness. He was sharp. It was his seventh year with the company—his first job. He and Marjorie had been married two years. They had no children. The car had been his bonus two Christmases ago.

When the station wagon eased to a stop, Steven sat for a minute with the motor running, the salmon-colored dash lights illuminating his face. The radio had been playing softly—the last of the news, then an interlude for French horns. Responding to no particular signal, he pressed off the radio and in the same movement switched off the ignition, which left the headlights shining on the empty, countrified road. The windows were down to attract the fresh spring air, and when the engine noise ceased the evening's ambient sounds were waiting. The peepers. A sound of thrush wings fluttering in the brush only a few yards away. The noise of something falling from a small distance and hitting an invisible water surface. Beyond the stand of saplings was the west, and through the darkened trunks, the sky was still pale yellow with the day's light, though here on Quaker Bridge Road it was nearly dark.

When Marjorie said what she had just said, she'd been looking straight ahead to where the headlights made a bright path in the dark. Perhaps she'd looked at Steven once, but having said what she'd said, she kept her hands in her lap and continued looking ahead. She was a pretty, blond, convictionless girl with small demure features—small nose, small ears, small chin, though with a surprisingly full-lipped smile which she practiced on everyone. She was fond of getting a little tipsy at parties and lowering her voice and sitting on a flowered ottoman or a burl table top with a glass of something and showing too much of her legs or inappropriate amounts of her small breasts. She had grown up in Indiana, studied art at Purdue. Steven had met her in New York at a party while she was working for a firm that did child-focused advertising for a large toymaker. He'd liked her bobbed hair, her fragile, wispy features, translucent skin and the slightly husky voice that made her seem more sophisticated than she was, but somehow convinced her she was, too. In their community, east of Hartford, the women who knew Marjorie Reeves thought of her as a bimbo who would not stay married to sweet Steven Reeves for very long. His second wife would be the right wife for him. Marjorie was just a starter.

Marjorie, however, did not think of herself that way, only that she liked men and felt happy and confident around them and assumed Steven thought this was fine and that in the long run it would help his career to have a pretty, spirited wife no one could pigeonhole. To set herself apart and to take an interest in the community she'd gone to work as a volunteer at a grieving-children's center in Hartford, which meant all black. And it was in Hartford that she'd had the chance to encounter George Nicholson and fuck him at a Red Roof Inn until they'd both gotten tired of it. It would never happen again, was her view, since in a year it hadn't happened again.

For the two or possibly five minutes now that they had sat on the side of Quaker Bridge Road in the still airish evening, with the noises of spring floating in and out of the open window, Marjorie had said nothing and Steven had also said nothing, though he realized that he was saying nothing because he was at a loss for words. A loss for words, he realized, meant that nothing that comes to mind seems very interesting to say as a next thing to what has just been said. He knew he was a callow man—a boy in some ways, still—but he was not stupid. At Bates, he had taken Dr. Sudofsky's class on *Ulysses,* and come away with a sense of irony and humor and the assurance that true knowledge was a spiritual process, a quest, not a storage of dry facts—a thing like freedom, which you only fully experienced in practice. He'd also played hockey, and knew that knowledge and aggressiveness were a subtle and surprising and uncommon combination. He had sought to practice both at Packard-Wells.

But for a brief and terrifying instant in the cool padded semi-darkness, just when he began experiencing his loss for words, he entered or at least nearly slipped into a softened fuguelike state in which he began to fear that he perhaps *could* not say another word; that something (work fatigue, shock, disappointment over what Marjorie had admitted) was at that moment causing him to detach from reality and to slide away from the present, and in fact to begin to lose his mind and go crazy to the extent that he was in jeopardy of beginning to gibber like a chimp, or just to slowly slump sideways against the upholstered door and not speak for a long, long time—months—and then only with the aid of drugs be able merely to speak in simple utterances that would seem cryptic, so that eventually he would have to be looked after by his mother's family in Damariscotta. A terrible thought.

And so to avoid that—to save his life and sanity—he abruptly just said a word, any word that he could say into the perfumed twilight inhabiting the car, where his wife was obviously anticipating his reply to her unhappy confession.

And for some reason the word—phrase, really—that he uttered was "ground clutter." Something he'd heard on the TV weather report as they were dressing for dinner.

"Hm?" Marjorie said. "What was it?" She turned her pretty, small-featured face toward him so that her pearl earrings caught light from some unknown source. She was wearing a tiny green cocktail dress and green satin shoes that showed off her incredibly thin ankles and slender, bare brown calves. She had two tiny matching green bows in her hair. She smelled sweet. "I know this wasn't what you wanted to hear, Steven," she said, "but I felt I should tell you before we got to George's. The Nicholsons', I mean. It's all over. It'll never happen again. I promise you. No one will ever mention it. I just lost my bearings last year with the move. I'm sorry." She had made a little steeple of her fingertips, as if she'd been concentrating very hard as she spoke these words. But now she put her hands again calmly in her minty green lap. She had bought her dress especially for this night at the Nicholsons'. She'd thought George would like it and Steven, too. She turned her face away and exhaled a small but detectable sigh in the car. It was then that the headlights went off automatically.

George Nicholson was a big squash-playing, thick-chested, hairy-armed Yale lawyer who sailed his own Hinckley 6 out of Essex and had started backing off from his high-priced Hartford plaintiffs' practice at fifty to devote more time to competitive racket sports and senior skiing. George was a college roommate of one of Steven's firm's senior partners and had "adopted" the Reeveses when they moved into the community following their wedding. Marjorie had volunteered Saturdays with George's wife, Patsy, at the Episcopal Thrift Shop during their first six months in Connecticut. To Steven, George Nicholson had recounted a memorable, seasoning summer spent hauling deep-water lobster traps with some tough old sea dogs out of Matinicus, Maine. Later, he'd been a Marine, and sported a faded anchor, ball and chain tattooed on his forearm. Later yet he'd fucked Steven's wife.

Having said something, even something that made no sense, Steven felt a sense of glum and deflated relief as he sat in the silent car beside Marjorie, who was still facing forward. Two thoughts had begun to compete in his reviving awareness. One was clearly occasioned by his conception of George Nicholson. He thought of George Nicholson as a gasbag, but also a forceful man who'd made his pile by letting very little stand in his way. When he thought about George he always remembered the story about Matinicus, which then put into his mind a mental picture of his own father and himself hauling traps somewhere out toward Monhegan. The reek of the bait, the toss of the ocean in late spring, the consoling monotony of the solid, tree-lined shore barely visible through the mists. Thinking through that circuitry always made him vaguely admire George Nicholson and, oddly, made him think he liked George even now, in spite of everything.

The other competing thought was that part of Marjorie's character had always been to confess upsetting things that turned out, he believed, not to be true: being a hooker for a summer up in Saugatuck; topless dancing while she was an undergraduate; heroin experimentation; taking part in armed robberies with her high-school boyfriend in Goshen, Indiana, where she was from. When she told these far-fetched stories she would grow distracted and shake her head, as though they were true. And now, while he didn't particularly think any of these stories was a bit truer, he did realize that he didn't really know his wife at all; and that in fact the entire conception of knowing another person—of trust, of closeness, of marriage itself—while not exactly a lie since it existed *someplace* if only as an idea (in his parents' life, at least marginally) was still completely out-of-date, defunct, was something typifying another era, now unfortunately gone. Meeting a girl, falling in love, marrying her, moving to Connecticut, buying a fucking house, starting a life with her and thinking you really knew anything about her—the last part was a complete fiction, which made all the rest a joke. Marjorie might as well have *been* a hooker or held up 7-Elevens and shot people, for all he really knew about her. And what was more, if he'd said any of this to her, sitting next to him thinking he would never know what, she either would not have understood a word of it or simply would've said, "Well, okay, that's fine." When people talked about the bottom line, Steven Reeves thought, they weren't talking about money, they were talking about what *this* meant, *this* kind of fatal ignorance. Money—losing it, gaining it, spending it, hoarding it—all that was only an emblem, though a good one, of what was happening here right now.

At this moment a pair of car lights rounded a curve somewhere out ahead of where the two of them sat in their station wagon. The lights found both their white faces staring forward in silence. The lights also found a raccoon just crossing the road from the reservoir shore, headed for the woods that were beside them. The car was going faster than might've been evident. The raccoon paused to peer up into the approaching beams, then continued on into the safe, opposite lane. But only then did it look up and notice Steven and Marjorie's car stopped on the verge of the road, silent in the murky evening. And because of that notice it must've decided that where it had been was much better than where it was going, and so turned to scamper back across Quaker Bridge Road toward the cool waters of the reservoir, which was what caused the car—actually it was a beat-up Ford pickup—to rumble over it, pitching and spinning it off to the side and then motionlessness near the opposite shoulder. "Yaaaa-haaaa-yipeeee!" a man's shrill voice shouted from inside the dark cab of the pickup, followed by another man's laughter.

And then it became very silent again. The raccoon lay on the road twenty yards in front of the Reeveses' car. It didn't struggle. It was merely there.

"Gross," Marjorie said.

Steven said nothing, though he felt less at a loss for words now. His eyes, indeed, felt relieved to fix on the still corpse of the raccoon.

"Do we do something?" Marjorie said. She had leaned forward a few inches as if to study the raccoon through the windshield. Light was dying away behind the slender young beech trees to the west of them.

"No," Steven said. These were his first words—except for the words he took no responsibility for—since Marjorie had said what she'd importantly said and their car was still moving toward dinner.

It was then that he hit her. He hit her before he knew he'd hit her, but not before he knew he wanted to. He hit her with the back of his open hand without even looking at her, hit her straight in the front of her face, straight in the nose. And hard. In a way, it was more a gesture than a blow, though it was, he understood, a blow. He felt the soft tip of her nose, and then the knuckly cartilage against the hard bones of the backs of his fingers. He had never hit a woman before, and he had never even thought of hitting Marjorie, always imagining he *couldn't* hit her when he'd read newspaper accounts of such things happening in the sad lives of others. He'd hit other people, been hit by other people, plenty of times—tough Maine boys on the ice rinks. Girls were out, though. His father always made that clear. His mother, too.

"Oh, my goodness" was all that Marjorie said when she received the blow. She put her hand over her nose immediately, but then sat silently in the car while neither of them said anything. His heart was not beating hard. The back of his hand hurt a little. This was all new ground. Steven had a small rosy birthmark just where his left sideburn ended and his shaved face began. It resembled the shape of the state of West Virginia. He thought he could feel this birthmark now. His skin tingled there.

And the truth was he felt even more relieved, and didn't feel at all sorry for Marjorie, sitting there stoically, making a little tent of her hand to cover her nose and staring ahead as if nothing had happened. He thought she would cry, certainly. She was a girl who cried—when she was unhappy, when he said something insensitive, when she was approaching her period. Crying was natural. Clearly, though, it was a new experience for her to be hit. And so it called upon something new, and if not new then some strength, resilience, self-mastery normally reserved for other experiences.

"I can't go to the Nicholsons' now," Marjorie said almost patiently. She removed her hand and viewed her palm as if her palm had her nose in it. Of course it was blood she was thinking about. He heard her breathe in through what sounded like a congested nose, then the breath was completed out through her mouth. She was not crying yet. And for that moment he felt not even sure he *had* smacked her—if it hadn't just been a thought he'd entertained, a gesture somehow uncommissioned.

What he wanted to do, however, was skip to the most important things now, not get mired down in wrong, extraneous details. Because he didn't give a shit about George Nicholson or the particulars of what they'd done in some shitty motel. Marjorie would never leave him for George Nicholson or anyone like George Nicholson, and George Nicholson and men like him—high rollers with Hinckleys—didn't throw it all away for unimportant little women like Marjorie. He thought of her nose, red, swollen, smeared with sticky blood dripping onto her green dress. He didn't suppose it could be broken. Noses held up. And, of course, there was a phone in the car. He could simply make a call to the party. He pictured the Nicholsons' great rambling white-shingled house brightly lit beyond the curving drive, the original elms exorbitantly preserved, the footlights, the low-lit clay court where they'd all played, the heated pool, the Henry Moore out on the darkened lawn where you just stumbled onto it. He imagined saying to someone—not George Nicholson—that Marjorie was ill, had thrown up on the side of the road.

The *right* details, though. The right details to ascertain from her were: *Are you sorry?* (he'd forgotten Marjorie had already said she was sorry) and *What does this mean for the future?* These were the details that mattered.

Surprisingly, the raccoon that had been cartwheeled by the pickup and then lain motionless, a blob in the near-darkness, had come back to life and was now trying to drag itself and its useless hinder parts off of Quaker Bridge Road and onto the grassy verge and into the underbrush that bordered the reservoir.

"Oh, for God's sake," Marjorie said, and put her hand over her damaged nose again. She could see the raccoon's struggle and turned her head away.

"Aren't you even sorry?" Steven said.

"Yes," Marjorie said, her nose still covered as if she wasn't thinking about the fact that she was covering it. Probably, he thought, the pain had gone away some. It hadn't been so bad. "I mean no," she said.

He wanted to hit her again then—this time in the ear—but he didn't. He wasn't sure why not. No one would ever know. "Well, which is it?" he said, and felt for the first time completely furious. The thing that made him furious—all his life, the very maddest—was to be put into a situation in which everything he did was wrong, when right was no longer an option. Now felt like one of those situations. "Which is it?" he said again angrily. "Really." He should just take her to the Nicholsons', he thought, swollen nose, bloody lips, all stoppered up, and let her deal with it. Or let her sit out in the car, or else start walking the 11.6 miles home. Maybe George could come out and drive her in his Rover. These were only thoughts, of course. "Which is it?" he said for the third time. He was stuck on these words, on this bit of barren curiosity.

"I was sorry when I told you," Marjorie said, very composed. She lowered her hand from her nose to her lap. One of the little green bows that had been in her hair was now resting on her bare shoulder. "Though not very sorry," she said. "Only sorry because I had to tell you. And now that I've told you and you've hit me in my face and probably broken my nose, I'm not sorry about anything—except that. Though I'm sorry about being married to you, which I'll remedy as soon as I can." She was still not crying. "So *now,* will you as a gesture of whatever good there is in you, get out and go over and do something to help that poor injured creature that those motherfucking rednecks maimed with their motherfucking pickup truck and then because they're pieces of shit and low forms of degraded humanity, laughed about? Can you do that, Steven? Is that in your range?" She sniffed back hard through her nose, then expelled a short, deep and defeated moan. Her voice seemed more nasal, more midwestern even, now that her nose was congested.

"I'm sorry I hit you," Steven Reeves said, and opened the car door onto the silent road.

"I know," Marjorie said in an emotionless voice. "And you'll be sorrier." When he had walked down the empty macadam road in his tan suit to where the raccoon had been struck then bounced over onto the road's edge, there was nothing now there. Only a small circle of dark blood he could just make out on the nubby road surface and that might've been an oil smudge. No raccoon. The raccoon with its last reserves of savage, unthinking will had found the strength to pull itself off into the bushes to die. Steven peered down into the dark, stalky confinement of scrubs and bramble that separated the road from the reservoir. It was very still there. He thought he heard a rustling in the low brush where a creature might be, getting itself settled into the soft grass and damp earth to go to sleep forever. Someplace out on the lake he heard a young girl's voice, very distinctly laughing. Then a car door closed farther away. Then another sort of door, a screen door, slapped shut. And then a man's voice saying "Oh no, oh-ho-ho-ho-ho, no." A small white light came on farther back in the trees beyond the reservoir, where he hadn't imagined there was a house. He wondered about how long it would be before his angry feelings stopped mattering to him. He considered briefly why Marjorie would admit this to him now. It seemed so odd.

Then he heard his own car start. The muffled-metal diesel racket of the Mercedes. The headlights came smartly on and disclosed him. Music was instantly loud inside. He turned just in time to see Marjorie's pretty face illuminated, as his own had been, by the salmon dashboard light. He saw the tips of her fingers atop the arc of the steering wheel, heard the surge of the engine. In the woods he noticed a strange glow coming through the trees, something yellow, something out of the low wet earth, a mist, a vapor, something that might be magical. The air smelled sweet now. The peepers stopped peeping. And then that was all.

TOBIAS WOLFF
(b. 1945)

Born in Birmingham, Alabama, Tobias Wolff lived with his divorced mother in Connecticut, Florida, Utah, and Washington State, where he grew up. He attended the Hill School in Pennsylvania (see Wolff's brief, cryptic account in his memoir This Boy's Life, *1989) from which he was expelled; he joined the U.S. Army before finishing high school and spent four years in the paratroops, including a tour in Vietnam. (See the prizewinning memoir* In Pharaoh's Army, *1994.)*

Discharged from the army, Wolff continued his education at Oxford University where he read English and received his BA in 1972. Returning to the United States, he worked variously as a reporter, a teacher, a night watchman, and a waiter before receiving a Wallace Stegner Fellowship at Stanford in 1975. From 1980 to 1997, Wolff taught creative writing at Syracuse University; from 1997 until the present, Wolff has been teaching in the writing program at Stanford.

Tobias Wolff is the author of several highly acclaimed collections of short stories: In the Garden of the North American Martyrs *(1981), from which "Hunters in the Snow" is taken;* Back in the World *(1985);* The Night in Question *(1997), and* Our Story Begins: New and Selected Stories *(2008). Wolff's short novels are* The Barracks Thief *(1984) and* Old School *(2003). In these works of prose fiction, as in Wolff's memoirs, pathos, mordant humor, and an unsparing and unsentimental moral perspective are melded by way of a minimalist prose style elastic enough to accommodate the surreal while suggesting only the "real," as in a trompe l'oeil painting.*

Wolff's many literary honors include the PEN/Faulkner Award, the O. Henry Award, and The Story Prize.

Of the wonderfully grotesque yet entirely convincing "Hunters in the Snow," the author has said: "I began this story as an act of recognition of the violence I grew up with, and that dominated my life for some years. By design it was to be a dark, sober piece, but it got away from me and made me laugh."

(Note: "The Hunters in the Snow" is the title of a celebrated painting by Pieter Brueghel, 1565.)

Hunters in the Snow

Tub had been waiting for an hour in the falling snow. He paced the sidewalk to keep warm and stuck his head out over the curb whenever he saw lights approaching. One driver stopped for him, but before Tub could wave the man on he saw the rifle on Tub's back and hit the gas. The tires spun on the ice.

The fall of snow thickened. Tub stood below the overhang of a building. Across the road the clouds whitened just above the rooftops, and the streetlights went out. He shifted the rifle strap to his other shoulder. The whiteness seeped up the sky.

A truck slid around the corner, horn blaring, rear end sashaying. Tub moved to the sidewalk and held up his hand. The truck jumped the curb and kept coming, half on the street and half on the sidewalk. It wasn't slowing down at all. Tub stood for a moment, still holding up his hand, then jumped back. His rifle slipped off his shoulder and clattered on the ice; a sandwich fell out of his pocket. He ran for the steps of the building. Another sandwich and a package of cookies tumbled onto the new snow. He made the steps and looked back.

The truck had stopped several feet beyond where Tub had been standing. He picked up his sandwiches and his cookies and slung the rifle and went to the driver's window. The driver was bent against the steering wheel, slapping his knees and drumming his feet on the floorboards. He looked like a cartoon of a person laughing, except that his eyes watched the man on the seat beside him.

"You ought to see yourself," said the driver. "He looks just like a beach ball with a hat on, doesn't he? Doesn't he, Frank?"

The man beside him smiled and looked off.

"You almost ran me down," said Tub. "You could've killed me."

"Come on, Tub," said the man beside the driver. "Be mellow, Kenny was just messing around." He opened the door and slid over to the middle of the seat.

Tub took the bolt out of his rifle and climbed in beside him. "I waited an hour," he said. "If you meant ten o'clock, why didn't you say ten o'clock?"

"Tub, you haven't done anything but complain since we got here," said the man in the middle. "If you want to piss and moan all day you might as well go home and bitch at your kids. Take your pick." When Tub didn't say anything, he turned to the driver. "O.K., Kenny, let's hit the road."

Some juvenile delinquents had heaved a brick through the windshield on the driver's side, so the cold and snow tunneled right into the cab. The heater didn't work. They covered themselves with a couple of blankets Kenny had brought along and pulled down the muffs on their caps. Tub tried to keep his hands warm by rubbing them under the blanket, but Frank made him stop.

They left Spokane and drove deep into the country, running along black lines of fences. The snow let up, but still there was no edge to the land where it met the sky. Nothing moved in the chalky fields. The cold bleached their faces and made the stubble stand out on their cheeks and along their upper lips. They had to stop and have coffee several times before they got to the woods where Kenny wanted to hunt.

Tub was for trying some place different; two years in a row they'd been up and down this land and hadn't seen a thing. Frank didn't care one way or the other; he just wanted to get out of the goddamned truck. "Feel that," Frank said. He spread his feet and closed his eyes and leaned his head way back and breathed deeply. "Tune in on that energy."

"Another thing," said Kenny. "This is open land. Most of the land around here is posted."

Frank breathed out. "Stop bitching, Tub. Get centered."

"I wasn't bitching."

"Centered," said Kenny. "Next thing you'll be wearing a nightgown, Frank. Selling flowers out at the airport."

"Kenny," said Frank. "You talk too much."

"O.K.," said Kenny. "I won't say a word. Like I won't say anything about a certain baby-sitter."

"What baby-sitter?" asked Tub.

"That's between us," said Frank, looking at Kenny. "That's confidential. You keep your mouth shut."

Kenny laughed.

"You're asking for it," said Frank.

"Asking for what?"

"You'll see."

"Hey," said Tub. "Are we hunting or what?"

Frank just smiled.

They started off across the field. Tub had trouble getting through the fences. Frank and Kenny could have helped him; they could have lifted up on the top wire and stepped on the bottom wire, but they didn't. They stood and watched him. There were a lot of fences and Tub was puffing when they reached the woods.

They hunted for over two hours and saw no deer, no tracks, no sign. Finally they stopped by the creek to eat. Kenny had several slices of pizza and a couple of candy bars; Frank had a sandwich, an apple, two carrots, and a square of chocolate; Tub put out one hard-boiled egg and a stick of celery.

"You ask me how I want to die today," said Kenny. "I'll tell you, burn me at the stake." He turned to Tub. "You still on that diet?" He winked at Frank.

"What do you think? You think I like hard-boiled eggs?"

"All I can say is, it's the first diet I ever heard of where you gained weight from it."

"Who said I gained weight?"

"Oh, pardon me. I take it back. You're just wasting away before my very eyes. Isn't he, Frank?"

Frank had his fingers fanned out, tips against the bark of the stump where he'd laid his food. His knuckles were hairy. He wore a heavy wedding band, and on his right pinky was another gold ring with a flat face and "F" printed out in what looked like diamonds. He turned it this way and that. "Tub," he said, "you haven't seen your own balls in ten years."

Kenny doubled over laughing. He took off his hat and slapped his leg with it.

"What am I supposed to do?" said Tub. "It's my glands."

They left the woods and hunted along the creek. Frank and Kenny worked one bank and Tub worked the other, moving upstream. The snow was light, but the drifts were deep and hard to move through. Wherever Tub looked, the surface was smooth, undisturbed, and after a time he lost interest. He stopped looking for tracks and just tried to keep up with Frank and Kenny on the other side. A moment came when he realized he hadn't seen them in a long time. The breeze was moving from him to them; when it stilled he could sometimes hear them arguing but that was all. He quickened his pace, breasting hard into the drifts, fighting the snow away with his knees and elbows. He heard his heart and felt the flush on his face, but he never once stopped.

Tub caught up with Frank and Kenny at a bend in the creek. They were standing on a log that stretched from their bank to his. Ice had backed up behind the log. Frozen reeds stuck out, barely nodding when the air moved.

"See anything?" asked Frank.

Tub shook his head.

There wasn't much daylight left, and they decided to head back toward the road. Frank and Kenny crossed the log and started downstream, using the trail Tub had broken. Before they had gone very far, Kenny stopped. "Look at that," he said, and pointed to some tracks going from the creek back into the woods. Tub's footprints crossed right over them. There on the bank, plain as day, were several mounds of deer sign.

"What do you think that is, Tub?" Kenny kicked at it. "Walnuts on vanilla icing?"

"I guess I didn't notice."

Kenny looked at Frank.

"I was lost."

"You were lost. Big deal."

They followed the tracks into the woods. The deer had gone over a fence half buried in drifting snow. A no-hunting sign was nailed to the top of one of the posts. Frank laughed and said the son of a bitch could read. Kenny wanted to go after him, but Frank said no way—the people out here didn't mess around. He thought maybe the farmer who owned the land would let them use it if they asked, though Kenny wasn't so sure. Anyway, he figured that by the time they walked to the truck and drove up the road and doubled back it would be almost dark.

"Relax," said Frank. "You can't hurry nature. If we're meant to get that deer, we'll get it. If we're not, we won't."

They started back toward the truck. This part of the woods was mainly pine. The snow was shaded and had a glaze on it. It held up Kenny and Frank, but Tub kept falling through. As he kicked forward, the edge of the crust bruised his shins. Kenny and Frank pulled ahead of him, to where he couldn't even hear their voices any more. He sat down on a stump and wiped his face. He ate both the sandwiches and half the cookies, taking his own sweet time. It was dead quiet.

When Tub crossed the last fence into the road, the truck started moving. Tub had to run for it and just managed to grab hold of the tailgate and hoist himself into the bed. He lay there panting. Kenny looked out the rear window and grinned. Tub crawled into the lee of the cab to get out of the freezing wind. He pulled his earflaps low and pushed his chin into the collar of his coat. Someone rapped on the window, but Tub would not turn around.

He and Frank waited outside while Kenny went into the farmhouse to ask permission. The house was old, and paint was curling off the sides. The smoke streamed westward off the top of the chimney, fanning away into a thin gray plume. Above the ridge of the hills another ridge of blue clouds was rising.

"You've got a short memory," said Tub.

"What?" said Frank. He had been staring off.

"I used to stick up for you."

"O.K., so you used to stick up for me. What's eating you?"

"You shouldn't have just left me back there like that."

"You're a grown-up, Tub. You can take care of yourself. Anyway, if you think you're the only person with problems, I can tell you that you're not."

"Is something bothering you, Frank?"

Frank kicked at a branch poking out of the snow. "Never mind," he said.

"What did Kenny mean about the baby-sitter?"

"Kenny talks too much," said Frank. "You just mind your own business."

Kenny came out of the farmhouse and gave the thumbs up, and they began walking back toward the woods. As they passed the barn, a large black hound with a grizzled snout ran out and barked at them. Every time he barked he slid backward a bit, like a cannon going off. Kenny got down on all fours and snarled and barked back at him, and the dog slunk away into the barn, looking over his shoulder and peeing a little as he went.

"That's an old-timer," said Frank. "A real graybeard. Fifteen years, if he's a day."

"Too old," said Kenny.

Past the barn they cut off through the fields. The land was unfenced, and the crust was freezing up thick, and they made good time. They kept to the edge of the field until they picked up the tracks again and followed them into the woods, farther and farther back toward the hills. The trees started to blur with the shadows, and the wind rose and needled their faces with the crystals it swept off the glaze. Finally they lost the tracks.

Kenny swore and threw down his hat. "This is the worst day of hunting I ever had, bar none." He picked up his hat and brushed off the snow. "This will be the first season since I was fifteen that I haven't got any deer."

"It isn't the deer," said Frank. "It's the hunting. There are all these forces out here and you just have to go with them."

"You go with them," said Kenny. "I came out here to get me a deer, not listen to a bunch of hippie bullshit. And if it hadn't been for Dimples here, I would have, too.

"That's enough," said Frank.

"And you...you're so busy thinking about that little jailbait of yours, you wouldn't know a deer if you saw one."

"I'm warning you," said Frank.

Kenny laughed. "I think maybe I'll have me a talk with a certain jail-bait's father," he said. "Then you can warn him, too."

"Drop dead," said Frank and turned away.

Kenny and Tub followed him back across the fields. When they were coming up to the barn, Kenny stopped and pointed. "I hate that post," he said. He raised his rifle and fired. It sounded like a dry branch cracking. The post splintered along its right side, up toward the top.

"There," said Kenny. "It's dead."

"Knock it off," said Frank, walking ahead.

Kenny looked at Tub and smiled. "I hate that tree," he said, and fired again. Tub hurried to catch up with Frank. He started to speak, but just then the dog ran out of the barn and barked at them. "Easy, boy," said Frank.

"I hate that dog." Kenny was behind them.

"That's enough," said Frank. "You put that gun down."

Kenny fired. The bullet went in between the dog's eyes. He sank right down into the snow, his legs splayed out on each side, his yellow eyes open and staring. Except for the blood, he looked like a small bearskin rug. The blood ran down the dog's muzzle into the snow.

They all looked at the dog lying there.

"What did he ever do to you?" asked Tub. "He was just barking."

Kenny turned to Tub. "I hate you."

Tub shot from the waist. Kenny jerked backward against the fence and buckled to his knees. He folded his hands across his stomach. "Look," he said. His hands were covered with blood. In the dusk his blood was more blue than red. It seemed to belong to the shadows. It didn't seem out of place. Kenny eased himself onto his back. He sighed several times, deeply. "You shot me," he said.

"I had to," said Tub. He knelt beside Kenny. "Oh, God," he said. "Frank. Frank."

Frank hadn't moved since Kenny killed the dog.

"Frank!" Tub shouted.

"I was just kidding around," said Kenny. "It was a joke. Oh!" he said, and arched his back suddenly. "Oh!" he said again, and dug his heels into the snow and pushed himself along on his head for several feet. Then he stopped and lay there, rocking back and forth on his heels and head like a wrestler doing warm-up exercises.

Frank roused himself. "Kenny," he said. He bent down and put his gloved hand on Kenny's brow. "You shot him," he said to Tub.

"He made me," said Tub.

"No, no, no," said Kenny.

Tub was weeping from the eyes and nostrils. His whole face was wet. Frank closed his eyes, then looked down at Kenny again. "Where does it hurt?"

"Everywhere," said Kenny. "Just everywhere."

"Oh, God," said Tub.

"I mean where did it go in?" said Frank.

"Here." Kenny pointed at the wound in his stomach. It was welling slowly with blood.

"You're lucky," said Frank. "It's on the left side. It missed your appendix. If it had hit your appendix, you'd really be in the soup." He turned and threw up onto the snow, holding his sides as if to keep warm.

"Are you all right?" asked Tub.

"There's some aspirin in the truck," said Kenny.

"I'm all right," said Frank.

"We'd better call an ambulance," said Tub.

"Jesus," said Frank, "what are we going to say?"

"Exactly what happened," said Tub. "He was going to shoot me but I shot him first."

"No, sir!" said Kenny. "I wasn't either!"

Frank patted Kenny on the arm. "Easy does it, partner." He stood. "Let's go."

Tub picked up Kenny's rifle as they walked down toward the farmhouse. "No sense leaving this around," he said. "Kenny might get ideas."

"I can tell you one thing," said Frank. "You've really done it this time. This definitely takes the cake."

They had to knock on the door twice before it was opened by a thin man with lank hair. The room behind him was filled with smoke. He squinted at them. "You get anything?" he asked.

"No," said Frank.

"I knew you wouldn't. That's what I told the other fellow."

"We've had an accident."

The man looked past Frank and Tub into the gloom. "Shoot your friend, did you?"

Frank nodded.

"I did," said Tub.

"I suppose you want to use the phone."

"If it's O.K."

The man in the door looked behind him, then stepped back. Frank and Tub followed him into the house. There was a woman sitting by the stove in the middle of the room. The stove was smoking badly. She looked up and then down again at the child asleep in her lap. Her face was white and damp; strands of hair were pasted across her forehead. Tub warmed his hands over the stove while Frank went into the kitchen to call. The man who had let them in stood at the window, his hands in his pockets.

"My partner shot your dog," said Tub.

The man nodded without turning around. "I should have done it myself. I just couldn't."

"He loved that dog so much," the woman said. The child squirmed and she rocked it.

"You asked him to?" said Tub. "You asked him to shoot your dog?"

"He was old and sick. Couldn't chew his food any more. I would have done it myself but I don't have a gun."

"You couldn't have anyway," said the woman. "Never in a million years."

The man shrugged.

Frank came out of the kitchen. "We'll have to take him ourselves. The nearest hospital is fifty miles from here and all their ambulances are out anyway."

The woman knew a shortcut, but the directions were complicated and Tub had to write them down. The man told where they could find some boards to carry Kenny on. He didn't have a flashlight, but he said he would leave the porch light on.

It was dark outside. The clouds were low and heavy-looking and the wind blew in shrill gusts. There was a screen loose on the house, and it banged slowly and then quickly as the wind rose again. They could hear it all the way to the barn. Frank went for the boards while Tub looked for Kenny, who was not where they had left him. Tub found him farther up the drive, lying on his stomach. "You O.K.?" said Tub.

"It hurts."

"Frank says it missed your appendix."

"I already had my appendix out."

"All right," said Frank, coming up to them. "We'll have you in a nice warm bed before you can say Jack Robinson." He put the two boards on Kenny's right side.

"Just as long as I don't have one of those male nurses," said Kenny.

"Ha ha," said Frank. "That's the spirit. Get ready, set, over you go," and he rolled Kenny onto the boards. Kenny screamed and kicked his legs in the air. When he quieted down, Frank and Tub lifted the boards and carried him down the drive. Tub had the back end, and with the snow blowing into his face he had trouble with his footing. Also he was tired and the man inside had forgotten to turn the porch light on. Just past the house Tub slipped and threw out his hands to catch himself. The boards fell and Kenny tumbled out and rolled to the bottom of the drive, yelling all the way. He came to rest against the right front wheel of the truck.

"You fat moron," said Frank. "You aren't good for diddly."

Tub grabbed Frank by the collar and backed him hard up against the fence. Frank tried to pull his hands away, but Tub shook him and snapped his head back and forth and finally Frank gave up.

"What do you know about fat?" said Tub. "What do you know about glands?" As he spoke, he kept shaking Frank. "What do you know about me?"

"All right," said Frank.

"No more," said Tub.

"All right."

"No more talking to me like that. No more watching. No more laughing."

"O.K., Tub. I promise."

Tub let go of Frank and leaned his forehead against the fence. His arms hung straight at his sides.

"I'm sorry, Tub." Frank touched him on the shoulder. "I'll be down at the truck."

Tub stood by the fence for a while and then got the rifles off the porch. Frank had rolled Kenny back onto the boards and they lifted him into the bed of the truck. Frank spread the seat blankets over him. "Warm enough?" he asked.

Kenny nodded.

"O.K. Now how does reverse work on this thing?"

"All the way to the left and up." Kenny sat up as Frank started forward to the cab. "Frank!"

"What?"

"If it sticks, don't force it."

The truck started right away. "One thing," said Frank, "you've got to hand it to the Japanese. A very ancient, very spiritual culture and they can still make a hell of a truck." He glanced over at Tub. "Look, I'm sorry.

I didn't know you felt that way, honest to God, I didn't. You should have said something."

"I did."

"When? Name one time."

"A couple of hours ago."

"I guess I wasn't paying attention."

"That's true, Frank," said Tub. "You don't pay attention very much."

"Tub," said Frank, "what happened back there—I should have been more sympathetic. I realize that. You were going through a lot. I just want you to know it wasn't your fault. He was asking for it."

"You think so?"

"Absolutely. I would have done the same thing in your shoes, no question."

The wind was blowing into their faces. The snow was a moving white wall in front of their lights; it swirled into the cab through the hole in the windshield and settled on them. Tub clapped his hands and shifted around to stay warm, but it didn't work.

"I'm going to have to stop," said Frank. "I can't feel my fingers."

Up ahead they saw some lights off the road. It was a tavern. Outside in the parking lot were several jeeps and trucks. A couple of them had deer strapped across their hoods. Frank parked and they went back to Kenny. "How you doing, partner?" said Frank.

"I'm cold."

"Well, don't feel like the Lone Ranger. It's worse inside, take my word for it. You should get that windshield fixed."

"Look," said Tub, "he threw the blankets off." They were lying in a heap against the tailgate.

"Now look, Kenny," said Frank, "it's no use whining about being cold if you're not going to try and keep warm. You've got to do your share." He spread the blankets over Kenny and tucked them in at the corners.

"They blew off."

"Hold on to them then."

"Why are we stopping, Frank?"

"Because if me and Tub don't get warmed up we're going to freeze solid and then where will you be?" He punched Kenny lightly in the arm. "So just hold your horses."

The bar was full of men in colored jackets, mostly orange. The waitress brought coffee. "Just what the doctor ordered," said Frank, cradling the steaming cup in his hand. His skin was bone white. "Tub, I've been thinking. What you said about me not paying attention, that's true."

"It's O.K."

"No. I really had that coming. I guess I've just been a little too interested in old number one. I've had a lot on my mind—not that that's any excuse."

"Forget it, Frank. I sort of lost my temper back there. I guess we're all a little on edge."

Frank shook his head. "It isn't just that."

"You want to talk about it?"

"Just between us, Tub?"

"Sure, Frank. Just between us."

"Tub, I think I'm going to be leaving Nancy."

"Oh, Frank. Oh, Frank." Tub sat back. "What's the problem? Has she been seeing someone?"

"No. I wish she was, Tub. I wish to God she was." He reached out and laid his hand on Tub's arm. "Tub, have you ever been really in love?"

"Well ..."

"I mean *really* in love." He squeezed Tub's wrist. "With your whole being."

"I don't know. When you put it like that."

"You haven't, then. Nothing against you, but you'd know it if you had." Frank let go of Tub's arm. "Nancy hasn't been running around, Tub. I have."

"Oh, Frank."

"Running around's not the right word for it. It isn't like that. She's not just some bit of fluff."

"Who is she, Frank?"

Frank paused. He looked into his empty cup. "Roxanne Brewer."

"Cliff Brewer's kid? The baby-sitter?"

"You can't just put people into categories like that, Tub. That's why the whole system is wrong. And that's why this country is going to hell in a rowboat."

"But she can't be more than ..." Tub shook his head.

"Fifteen. She'll be sixteen in May." Frank smiled. "May fourth, three twenty-seven P.M. Hell, Tub, a hundred years ago she'd have been an old maid by that age. Juliet was only thirteen."

"Juliet? Juliet Miller? Jesus, Frank, she doesn't even have breasts. She doesn't even wear a top to her bathing suit. She's still collecting frogs."

"Not Juliet Miller—the real Juliet. Tub, don't you see how you're dividing people up into categories? He's an executive, she's a secretary, he's a truck driver, she's fifteen years old. Tub, this so-called baby-sitter, this so-called fifteen-year-old has more in her little finger than most of us have in our entire bodies. I can tell you this little lady is something special."

Tub nodded. "I know the kids like her."

"She's opened up whole worlds to me that I never knew were there."

"What does Nancy think about all of this?"

"Nothing, Tub. She doesn't know."

"You haven't told her?"

"Not yet. It's not so easy. She's been damned good to me all these years. Then there's the kids to consider." The brightness in Frank's eyes trembled and he wiped quickly at them with the back of his hand. "I guess you think I'm a complete bastard."

"No, Frank. I don't think that."

"Well, you *ought* to."

"Frank, when you've got a friend it means you've always got someone on your side, no matter what. That's how I feel about it anyway."

"You mean that, Tub?"

"Sure I do."

Frank smiled. "You don't know how good it feels to hear you say that."

Kenny had tried to get out of the truck but he hadn't made it. He was jackknifed over the tailgate, his head hanging above the bumper. They lifted him back into the bed and covered him again. He was sweating and his teeth chattered. "It hurts, Frank."

"It wouldn't hurt so much if you just stayed put. Now we're going to the hospital. Got that? Say it: 'I'm going to the hospital.'"

"I'm going to the hospital."

"Again."

"I'm going to the hospital."

"Now just keep saying that to yourself and before you know it we'll be there."

After they had gone a few miles. Tub turned to Frank. "I just pulled a real boner," he said.

"What's that?"

"I left the directions on the table back there."

"That's O.K. I remember them pretty well."

The snowfall lightened and the clouds began to roll back off the fields, but it was no warmer and after a time both Frank and Tub were bitten through and shaking. Frank almost didn't make it around a curve, and they decided to stop at the next roadhouse.

There was an automatic hand dryer in the bathroom and they took turns standing in front of it, opening their jackets and shirts and letting the jet of hot air breathe across their faces and chests.

"You know," said Tub, "what you told me back there, I appreciate it. Trusting me."

Frank opened and closed his fingers in front of the nozzle. "The way I look at it, Tub, no man is an island. You've got to trust someone."

"Frank ..."

Frank waited.

"When I said that about my glands, that wasn't true. The truth is I just shovel it in."

"Well, Tub ..."

"Day and night, Frank. In the shower. On the freeway." He turned and let the air play over his back. "I've even got stuff in the paper towel machine at work."

"There's nothing wrong with your glands at all?" Frank had taken his boots and socks off. He held first his right, then his left foot up to the nozzle.

"No. There never was."

"Does Alice know?" The machine went off and Frank started lacing up his boots.

"Nobody knows. That's the worst of it, Frank, not the being fat—I never got any big kick out of being thin—but the lying. Having to lead a double life like a spy or a hit man. This sounds strange but I feel sorry for those guys, I really do. I know what they go through. Always having to think about what you say and do. Always feeling like people are watching you, trying to catch you at something. Never able to just be yourself. Like when I make a big deal about only having an orange for breakfast and then scarf all the way to work. Oreos, Mars bars, Twinkies, Sugar Babies, Snickers." Tub glanced at Frank and looked quickly away. "Pretty disgusting, isn't it?"

"Tub. Tub." Frank shook his head. "Come on." He took Tub's arm and led him into the restaurant half of the bar. "My friend is hungry," he told the waitress. "Bring four orders of pancakes, plenty of butter and syrup."

"Frank ..."

"Sit down."

When the dishes came, Frank carved out slabs of butter and just laid them on the pancakes. Then he emptied the bottle of syrup, moving it back and forth over the plates. He leaned forward on his elbows and rested his chin on one hand. "Go on. Tub."

Tub ate several mouthfuls, then started to wipe his lips. Frank took the napkin away from him. "No wiping," he said. Tub kept at it. The syrup covered his chin; it dripped to a point like a goatee. "Weigh in, Tub," said Frank, pushing another fork across the table. "Get down to business." Tub took the fork in his left hand and lowered his head and started really chowing down. "Clean your plate," said Frank when the pancakes were gone, and Tub lifted each of the four plates and licked it clean. He sat back, trying to catch his breath.

"Beautiful," said Frank. "Are you full?"

"I'm full," said Tub. "I've never been so full."

Kenny's blankets were bunched up against the tailgate again.

"They must have blown off," said Tub.

"They're not doing him any good," said Frank. "We might as well get some use out of them."

Kenny mumbled. Tub bent over him. "What? Speak up."

"I'm going to the hospital," said Kenny.

"Attaboy," said Frank.

The blankets helped. The wind still got their faces and Frank's hands but it was much better. The fresh snow on the road and the trees sparkled under the beam of the headlight. Squares of light from farmhouse windows fell onto the blue snow in the fields.

"Frank," said Tub after a time, "you know that farmer? He told Kenny to kill the dog."

"You're kidding!" Frank leaned forward, considering. "That Kenny. What a card." He laughed and so did Tub. Tub smiled out the back window. Kenny lay with his arms folded over his stomach, moving his lips at the stars. Right overhead was the Big Dipper, and behind, hanging between Kenny's toes in the direction of the hospital, was the North Star, pole star, help to sailors. As the truck twisted through the gentle hills, the star went back and forth between Kenny's boots, staying always in his sight. "I'm going to the hospital," said Kenny, but he was wrong. They had taken a different turn a long way back.

TIM O'BRIEN
(b. 1946)

William Timothy O'Brien was born in Austin, Minnesota, grew up in Worthington, and educated at Macalester College in St. Paul. Shortly after graduation he was drafted to serve in the Vietnam War where he was a foot soldier from 1969 to 1970; he was wounded near My Lai. In 1970 he began graduate studies in government at Harvard and worked for the national affairs desk of The Washington Post. *The Vietnam War—its history, its politics, its effect upon individual men and women—has provided the dominant theme of Tim O'Brien's work, which, as suggested by his best-known story, "The Things They Carried," is characterized by a distinctive narrative voice and a highly poetic distillation of experience.*

Tim O'Brien is both a short story writer and a novelist—in two of his novels he is both at the same time. Going After Cacciato *(1978), and* The Things They Carried *(1990) are novels constructed out of skillfully linked short stories in which the form (disjointed, with abrupt stops and starts, yet informed by a single unifying vision) most effectively expresses content. Other works of fiction by O'Brien are* Northern Lights *(1974),* The Nuclear Age *(1985),* In the Lake of the Woods *(1994),* Tomcat in Love *(1998), and* July, July *(2002); and his much-acclaimed memoir is* If I Die in a Combat Zone *(1973). A longtime resident of Cambridge, Massachusetts, O'Brien has lived for some time in the Southwest and has acted as director of the MFA program at Texas State University at San Marcos.*

The phenomenon of the Vietnam War—that most divisive of foreign wars in our American history—has resulted in an outpouring of imaginative work (prose fiction, memoirs, poetry, plays, films) of high quality. Among these hundreds, indeed thousands of works, Tim O'Brien's Going After Cacciato *(winner of the National Book Award, 1979) and* The Things They Carried, *like Michael Herr's* Dispatches, *are essential reading.*

O'Brien has said of his boyhood in Minnesota, "It's who I am, and virtually everything I've written is rooted there as much as in Vietnam. It's almost a position between Nam and Main Street, Minnesota."

The Things They Carried

First Lieutenant Jimmy Cross carried letters from a girl named Martha, a junior at Mount Sebastian College in New Jersey. They were not love letters, but Lieutenant Cross was hoping, so he kept them folded in plastic at the bottom of his rucksack. In the late afternoon, after a day's march, he would dig his foxhole, wash his hands under a canteen, unwrap the letters, hold them with the tips of his fingers, and spend the last hour of light pretending. He would imagine romantic camping trips into the White Mountains in New Hampshire. He would sometimes taste the envelope flaps, knowing her tongue had been there. More than anything, he wanted Martha to love him as he loved her, but the letters were mostly chatty, elusive on the matter of love. She was a virgin, he was almost sure. She was an English major at Mount Sebastian, and she wrote beautifully about her professors and roommates and midterm exams, about her respect for Chaucer and her great affection for Virginia Woolf. She often quoted lines of poetry; she never mentioned the war, except to say, Jimmy, take care of yourself. The letters weighed 10 ounces. They were signed Love, Martha, but Lieutenant Cross understood that Love was only a way of signing and did not mean what he sometimes pretended it meant. At dusk, he would carefully return the letters to his rucksack. Slowly, a bit distracted, he would get up and move among his men, checking the perimeter, then at full dark he would return to his hole and watch the night and wonder if Martha was a virgin.

The things they carried were largely determined by necessity. Among the necessities or near-necessities were P-38 can openers, pocket knives, heat tabs, wristwatches, dog tags, mosquito repellent, chewing gum, candy, cigarettes, salt tablets, packets of Kool-Aid, lighters, matches, sewing kits, Military Payment Certificates, C rations, and two or three canteens of water. Together, these items weighed between 15 and 20 pounds, depending upon a man's habits or rate of metabolism. Henry Dobbins, who was a big man, carried extra rations; he was especially fond of canned peaches in heavy syrup over pound cake. Dave Jensen, who practiced field hygiene, carried a toothbrush, dental floss, and several hotel-sized bars of soap he'd stolen on R&R in Sydney, Australia. Ted Lavender, who was scared, carried tranquilizers until he was shot in the head outside the village of Than Khe in mid-April. By necessity, and because it was SOP, they all carried steel helmets that weighed 5 pounds including the liner and camouflage cover. They carried the standard fatigue jackets and trousers. Very few carried underwear. On their feet they carried jungle boots—2.1 pounds—and Dave Jensen carried three pairs of socks and a can of Dr. Scholl's foot powder as a precaution against trench foot. Until he was shot, Ted Lavender carried six or seven ounces of premium dope, which for him was a necessity. Mitchell Sanders, the RTO, carried condoms. Norman Bowker carried a diary. Rat Kiley carried comic books. Kiowa, a devout Baptist, carried an illustrated New Testament that had been presented to him by his father, who taught Sunday school in Oklahoma City, Oklahoma. As a hedge against bad times, however, Kiowa also carried his grandmother's distrust of the white man, his grandfather's old hunting hatchet. Necessity dictated. Because the land was mined and booby-trapped, it was SOP for each man to carry a steel-centered, nylon-covered flak jacket, which weighed 6.7 pounds, but which on hot days seemed much heavier. Because you could die so quickly, each man carried at least one large compress bandage, usually in the helmet band for easy access. Because the nights were cold, and because the monsoons were wet, each carried a green plastic poncho that could be used as a raincoat or groundsheet or makeshift tent. With its quilted liner, the poncho weighed almost two pounds, but it was worth every ounce. In April, for instance, when Ted Lavender was shot, they used his poncho to wrap him up, then to carry him across the paddy, then to lift him into the chopper that took him away.

They were called legs or grunts.

To carry something was to hump it, as when Lieutenant Jimmy Cross humped his love for Martha up the hills and through the swamps. In its intransitive form, to hump meant to walk, or to march, but it implied burdens far beyond the intransitive.

Almost everyone humped photographs. In his wallet. Lieutenant Cross carried two photographs of Martha. The first was a Kodacolor snapshot signed Love, though he knew better. She stood against a brick wall. Her eyes were gray and neutral, her lips slightly open as she stared straight-on at the camera. At night, sometimes, Lieutenant Cross wondered who had taken the picture, because he knew she had boyfriends, because he loved her so much, and because he could see the shadow of the picture-taker spreading out against the brick wall. The second photograph had been clipped from the 1968 Mount Sebastian yearbook. It was an action shot—women's volleyball—and Martha was bent horizontal to the floor, reaching, the palms of her hands in sharp focus, the tongue taut, the expression frank and competitive. There was no visible sweat. She wore white gym shorts. Her legs, he thought, were almost certainly the legs of a virgin, dry and without hair, the left knee cocked and carrying her entire weight, which was just over one hundred pounds. Lieutenant Cross remembered touching that left knee. A dark theater, he remembered, and the movie was *Bonnie and Clyde,* and Martha wore a tweed skirt, and during the final scene, when he touched her knee, she turned and looked at him in a sad, sober way that made him pull his hand back, but he would always remember the feel of the tweed skirt and the knee beneath it and the sound of the gunfire that killed Bonnie and Clyde, how embarrassing it was, how slow and oppressive. He remembered kissing her good night at the dorm door. Right then, he thought, he should've done something brave. He should've carried her up the stairs to her room and tied her to the bed and touched that left knee all night long. He should've risked it. Whenever he looked at the photographs, he thought of new things he should've done.

What they carried was partly a function of rank, partly of field specialty.

As a first lieutenant and platoon leader, Jimmy Cross carried a compass, maps, code books, binoculars, and a .45-caliber pistol that weighed 2.9 pounds fully loaded. He carried a strobe light and the responsibility for the lives of his men.

As an RTO, Mitchell Sanders carried the PRC-25 radio, a killer, 26 pounds with its battery.

As a medic, Rat Kiley carried a canvas satchel filled with morphine and plasma and malaria tablets and surgical tape and comic books and all the things a medic must carry, including M&M's for especially bad wounds, for a total weight of nearly 20 pounds.

As a big man, therefore a machine gunner, Henry Dobbins carried the M-60, which weighed 23 pounds unloaded, but which was almost always loaded. In addition, Dobbins carried between 10 and 15 pounds of ammunition draped in belts across his chest and shoulders.

As PFCs or Spec 4s, most of them were common grunts and carried the standard M-16 gas-operated assault rifle. The weapon weighed 7.5 pounds unloaded, 8.2 pounds with its full 20-round magazine. Depending on numerous factors, such as topography and psychology, the riflemen carried anywhere from 12 to 20 magazines, usually in cloth bandoliers, adding on another 8.4 pounds at minimum, 14 pounds at maximum. When it was available, they also carried M-16 maintenance gear—rods and steel brushes and swabs and tubes of LSA oil—all of which weighed about a pound. Among the grunts, some carried the M-79 grenade launcher, 5.9 pounds unloaded, a reasonably light weapon except for the ammunition, which was heavy. A single round weighed 10 ounces. The typical load was 25 rounds. But Ted Lavender, who was scared, carried 34 rounds when he was shot and killed outside Than Khe, and he went down under an exceptional burden, more than 20 pounds of ammunition, plus the flak jacket and helmet and rations and water and toilet paper and tranquilizers and all the rest, plus the unweighed fear. He was dead weight. There was no twitching or flopping. Kiowa, who saw it happen, said it was like watching a rock fall, or a big sandbag or something—just boom, then down—not like the movies where the dead guy rolls around and does fancy spins and goes ass over teakettle—not like that, Kiowa said, the poor bastard just flat-fuck fell. Boom. Down. Nothing else. It was a bright morning in mid-April. Lieutenant Cross felt the pain. He blamed himself. They stripped off Lavender's canteens and ammo, all the heavy things, and Rat Kiley said the obvious, the guy's dead, and Mitchell Sanders used his radio to report one U.S. KIA and to request a chopper. Then they wrapped Lavender in his poncho. They carried him out to a dry paddy, established security, and sat smoking the dead man's dope until the chopper came. Lieutenant Cross kept to himself. He pictured Martha's smooth young face, thinking he loved her more than anything, more than his men, and now Ted Lavender was dead because he loved her so much and could not stop thinking about her. When the dustoff arrived, they carried Lavender aboard. Afterward they burned Than Khe. They marched until dusk, then dug their holes, and that night Kiowa kept explaining how you had to be there, how fast it was, how the poor guy just dropped like so much concrete. Boom-down, he said. Like cement.

In addition to the three standard weapons—the M-60, M-16, and M-79—they carried whatever presented itself, or whatever seemed appropriate as a means of killing or staying alive. They carried catch-as-catch-can. At various times, in various situations, they carried M-14s and CAR-15s and Swedish Ks and grease guns and captured AK-47s and Chi-Coms and RPGs and Simonov carbines and black market Uzis and .38-caliber Smith & Wesson handguns and 66 mm LAWs and shotguns and silencers and blackjacks and bayonets and C-4 plastic explosives. Lee Strunk carried a slingshot; a weapon of last resort, he called it. Mitchell Sanders carried brass knuckles. Kiowa carried his grandfather's feathered hatchet. Every third or fourth man carried a Claymore antipersonnel mine—3.5 pounds with its firing device. They all carried fragmentation grenades—14 ounces each. They all carried at least one M-18 colored smoke grenade—24 ounces. Some carried CS or tear gas grenades. Some carried white phosphorus grenades. They carried all they could bear, and then some, including a silent awe for the terrible power of the things they carried.

In the first week of April, before Lavender died. Lieutenant Jimmy Cross received a good-luck charm from Martha. It was a simple pebble, an ounce at most. Smooth to the touch, it was a milky white color with flecks of orange and violet, oval-shaped, like a miniature egg. In the accompanying letter, Martha wrote that she had found the pebble on the Jersey shoreline, precisely where the land touched water at high tide, where things came together but also separated. It was this separate-but-together quality, she wrote, that had inspired her to pick up the pebble and to carry it in her breast pocket for several days, where it seemed weightless, and then to send it through the mail, by air, as a token of her truest feelings for him. Lieutenant Cross found this romantic. But he wondered what her truest feelings were, exactly, and what she meant by separate-but-together. He wondered how the tides and waves had come into play on that afternoon along the Jersey shoreline when Martha saw the pebble and bent down to rescue it from geology. He imagined bare feet. Martha was a poet, with the poet's sensibilities, and her feet would be brown and bare, the toenails unpainted, the eyes chilly and somber like the ocean in March, and though it was painful, he wondered who had been with her that afternoon. He imagined a pair of shadows moving along the strip of sand where things came together but also separated. It was phantom jealousy, he knew, but he couldn't help himself. He loved her so much. On the march, through the hot days of early April, he carried the pebble in his mouth, turning it with his tongue, tasting sea salt and moisture. His mind wandered. He had difficulty keeping his attention on the war. On occasion he would yell at his men to spread out the column, to keep their eyes open, but then he would slip away into daydreams, just pretending, walking barefoot along the Jersey shore, with Martha, carrying nothing. He would feel himself rising. Sun and waves and gentle winds, all love and lightness.

What they carried varied by mission.

When a mission took them to the mountains, they carried mosquito netting, machetes, canvas tarps, and extra bug juice.

If a mission seemed especially hazardous, or if it involved a place they knew to be bad, they carried everything they could. In certain heavily mined AOs, where the land was dense with Toe Poppers and Bouncing Betties, they took turns humping a 28-pound mine detector. With its headphones and big sensing plate, the equipment was a stress on the lower back and shoulders, awkward to handle, often useless because of the shrapnel in the earth, but they carried it anyway, partly for safety, partly for the illusion of safety.

On ambush, or other night missions, they carried peculiar little odds and ends. Kiowa always took along his New Testament and a pair of moccasins for silence. Dave Jensen carried night-sight vitamins high in carotene. Lee Strunk carried his slingshot; ammo, he claimed, would never be a problem. Rat Kiley carried brandy and M&M's candy. Until he was shot, Ted Lavender carried the starlight scope, which weighed 6.3 pounds with its aluminum carrying case. Henry Dobbins carried his girlfriend's pantyhose wrapped around his neck as a comforter. They all carried ghosts. When dark came, they would move out single file across the meadows and paddies to their ambush coordinates, where they would quietly set up the Claymores and lie down and spend the night waiting.

Other missions were more complicated and required special equipment. In mid-April, it was their mission to search out and destroy the elaborate tunnel complexes in the Than Khe area south of Chu Lai. To blow the tunnels, they carried one-pound blocks of pentrite high explosives, four blocks to a man, 68 pounds in all. They carried wiring, detonators, and battery-powered clackers. Dave Jensen carried earplugs. Most often, before blowing the tunnels, they were ordered by higher command to search them, which was considered bad news, but by and large they just shrugged and carried out orders. Because he was a big man, Henry Dobbins was excused from tunnel duty. The others would draw numbers. Before Lavender died there were 17 men in the platoon, and whoever drew the number 17 would strip off his gear and crawl in headfirst with a flashlight and Lieutenant Cross's .45-caliber pistol. The rest of them would fan out as security. They would sit down or kneel, not facing the hole, listening to the ground beneath them, imagining cobwebs and ghosts, whatever was down there—the tunnel walls squeezing in—how the flashlight seemed impossibly heavy in the hand and how it was tunnel vision in the very strictest sense, compression in all ways, even time, and how you had to wiggle in—ass and elbows—a swallowed-up feeling—and how you found yourself worrying about odd things: Will your flashlight go dead? Do rats carry rabies? If you screamed, how far would the sound carry? Would your buddies hear it? Would they have the courage to drag you out? In some respects, though not many, the waiting was worse than the tunnel itself. Imagination was a killer.

On April 16, when Lee Strunk drew the number 17, he laughed and muttered something and went down quickly. The morning was hot and very still. Not good, Kiowa said. He looked at the tunnel opening, then out across a dry paddy toward the village of Than Khe. Nothing moved.

No clouds or birds or people. As they waited, the men smoked and drank Kool-Aid, not talking much, feeling sympathy for Lee Strunk but also feeling the luck of the draw. You win some, you lose some, said Mitchell Sanders, and sometimes you settle for a rain check. It was a tired line and no one laughed.

Henry Dobbins ate a tropical chocolate bar. Ted Lavender popped a tranquilizer and went off to pee.

After five minutes. Lieutenant Jimmy Cross moved to the tunnel, leaned down, and examined the darkness. Trouble, he thought—a cave-in maybe. And then suddenly, without willing it, he was thinking about Martha. The stresses and fractures, the quick collapse, the two of them buried alive under all that weight. Dense, crushing love. Kneeling, watching the hole, he tried to concentrate on Lee Strunk and the war, all the dangers, but his love was too much for him, he felt paralyzed, he wanted to sleep inside her lungs and breathe her blood and be smothered. He wanted her to be a virgin and not a virgin, all at once. He wanted to know her. Intimate secrets: Why poetry? Why so sad? Why that grayness in her eyes? Why so alone? Not lonely, just alone—riding her bike across campus or sitting off by herself in the cafeteria—even dancing, she danced alone—and it was the aloneness that filled him with love. He remembered telling her that one evening. How she nodded and looked away. And how, later, when he kissed her, she received the kiss without returning it, her eyes wide open, not afraid, not a virgin's eyes, just flat and uninvolved.

Lieutenant Cross gazed at the tunnel. But he was not there. He was buried with Martha under the white sand at the Jersey shore. They were pressed together, and the pebble in his mouth was her tongue. He was smiling. Vaguely, he was aware of how quiet the day was, the sullen paddies, yet he could not bring himself to worry about matters of security. He was beyond that. He was just a kid at war, in love. He was twenty-four years old. He couldn't help it.

A few moments later Lee Strunk crawled out of the tunnel. He came up grinning, filthy but alive. Lieutenant Cross nodded and closed his eyes while the others clapped Strunk on the back and made jokes about rising from the dead.

Worms, Rat Kiley said. Right out of the grave. Fuckin' zombie.

The men laughed. They all felt great relief.

Spook city, said Mitchell Sanders.

Lee Strunk made a funny ghost sound, a kind of moaning, yet very happy, and right then, when Strunk made that high happy moaning sound, when he went *Ahhooooo,* right then Ted Lavender was shot in the head on his way back from peeing. He lay with his mouth open. The teeth were broken. There was a swollen black bruise under his left eye. The cheekbone was gone. Oh shit, Rat Kiley said, the guy's dead. The guy's dead, he kept saying, which seemed profound—the guy's dead. I mean really.

The things they carried were determined to some extent by superstition. Lieutenant Cross carried his good-luck pebble. Dave Jensen carried a rabbit's foot. Norman Bowker, otherwise a very gentle person, carried a thumb that had been presented to him as a gift by Mitchell Sanders. The thumb was dark brown, rubbery to the touch, and weighed four ounces at most. It had been cut from a VC corpse, a boy of fifteen or sixteen. They'd found him at the bottom of an irrigation ditch, badly burned, flies in his mouth and eyes. The boy wore black shorts and sandals. At the time of his death he had been carrying a pouch of rice, a rifle, and three magazines of ammunition.

You want my opinion, Mitchell Sanders said, there's a definite moral here.

He put his hand on the dead boy's wrist. He was quiet for a time, as if counting a pulse, then he patted the stomach, almost affectionately, and used Kiowa's hunting hatchet to remove the thumb.

Henry Dobbins asked what the moral was.

Moral?

You know. *Moral.*

Sanders wrapped the thumb in toilet paper and handed it across to Norman Bowker. There was no blood. Smiling, he kicked the boy's head, watched the flies scatter, and said, It's like with that old TV show—Paladin. Have gun, will travel.

Henry Dobbins thought about it.

Yeah, well, he finally said. I don't see no moral.

There it *is,* man.

Fuck off.

They carried USO stationery and pencils and pens. They carried Sterno, safety pins, trip flares, signal flares, spools of wire, razor blades, chewing tobacco, liberated joss sticks and statuettes of the smiling Buddha, candles, grease pencils, *The Stars and Stripes,* fingernail clippers, Psy Ops leaflets, bush hats, bolos, and much more. Twice a week, when the resupply choppers came in, they carried hot chow in green mermite cans and large canvas bags filled with iced beer and soda pop. They carried plastic water containers, each with a two-gallon capacity. Mitchell Sanders carried a set of starched tiger fatigues for special occasions. Henry Dobbins carried Black Flag insecticide. Dave Jensen carried empty sandbags that could be filled at night for added protection. Lee Strunk carried tanning lotion. Some things they carried in common. Taking turns, they carried the big PRC-77 scrambler radio, which weighed 30 pounds with its battery. They shared the weight of memory. They took up what others could no longer bear. Often, they carried each other, the wounded or weak. They carried infections. They carried chess sets, basketballs, Vietnamese-English dictionaries, insignia of rank. Bronze Stars and Purple Hearts, plastic cards imprinted with the Code of Conduct. They carried diseases, among them malaria and dysentery. They carried lice and ringworm and leeches and paddy algae and various rots and molds. They carried the land itself—Vietnam, the place, the soil—a powdery orange-red dust that covered their boots and fatigues and faces. They carried the sky. The whole atmosphere, they carried it, the humidity, the monsoons, the stink of fungus and decay, all of it, they carried gravity. They moved like mules. By daylight they took sniper fire, at night they were mortared, but it was not battle, it was just the endless march, village to village, without purpose, nothing won or lost. They marched for the sake of the march. They plodded along slowly, dumbly, leaning forward against the heat, unthinking, all blood and bone, simple grunts, soldiering with their legs, toiling up the hills and down into the paddies and across the rivers and up again and down, just humping, one step and then the next and then another, but no volition, no will, because it was automatic, it was anatomy, and the war was entirely a matter of posture and carriage, the hump was everything, a kind of inertia, a kind of emptiness, a dullness of desire and intellect and conscience and hope and human sensibility. Their principles were in their feet. Their calculations were biological. They had no sense of strategy or mission.

They searched the villages without knowing what to look for, not caring, kicking over jars of rice, frisking children and old men, blowing tunnels, sometimes setting fires and sometimes not, then forming up and moving on to the next village, then other villages, where it would always be the same. They carried their own lives. The pressures were enormous. In the heat of early afternoon, they would remove their helmets and flak jackets, walking bare, which was dangerous but which helped ease the strain. They would often discard things along the route of march. Purely for comfort, they would throw away rations, blow their Claymores and grenades, no matter, because by nightfall the resupply choppers would arrive with more of the same, then a day or two later still more, fresh watermelons and crates of ammunition and sunglasses and woolen sweaters—the resources were stunning—sparklers for the Fourth of July, colored eggs for Easter—it was the great American war chest—the fruits of science, the smokestacks, the canneries, the arsenals at Hartford, the Minnesota forests, the machine shops, the vast fields of corn and wheat—they carried like freight trains; they carried it on their backs and shoulders—and for all the ambiguities of Vietnam, all the mysteries and unknowns, there was at least the single abiding certainty that they would never be at a loss for things to carry.

After the chopper took Lavender away, Lieutenant Jimmy Cross led his men into the village of Than Khe. They burned everything. They shot chickens and dogs, they trashed the village well, they called in artillery and watched the wreckage, then they marched for several hours through the hot afternoon, and then at dusk, while Kiowa explained how Lavender died, Lieutenant Cross found himself trembling.

He tried not to cry. With his entrenching tool, which weighed five pounds, he began digging a hole in the earth.

He felt shame. He hated himself. He had loved Martha more than his men, and as a consequence Lavender was now dead, and this was something he would have to carry like a stone in his stomach for the rest of the war.

All he could do was dig. He used his entrenching tool like an ax, slashing, feeling both love and hate, and then later, when it was full dark, he sat at the bottom of his foxhole and wept. It went on for a long while. In part, he was grieving for Ted Lavender, but mostly it was for Martha, and for himself, because she belonged to another world, which was not quite real, and because she was a junior at Mount Sebastian College in New Jersey, a poet and a virgin and uninvolved, and because he realized she did not love him and never would.

Like cement, Kiowa whispered in the dark. I swear to God—boom, down. Not a word.

I've heard this, said Norman Bowker.

A pisser, you know? Still zipping himself up. Zapped while zipping.

All right, fine. That's enough.

Yeah, but you had to see it, the guy just—

I *heard,* man. Cement. So why not shut the fuck *up?*

Kiowa shook his head sadly and glanced over at the hole where Lieutenant Jimmy Cross sat watching the night. The air was thick and wet. A warm dense fog had settled over the paddies and there was the stillness that precedes rain.

After a time Kiowa sighed.

One thing for sure, he said. The lieutenant's in some deep hurt. I mean that crying jag—the way he was carrying on—it wasn't fake or anything, it was real heavy-duty hurt. The man cares.

Sure, Norman Bowker said.

Say what you want, the man does care.

We all got problems.

Not Lavender.

No, I guess not, Bowker said. Do me a favor, though.

Shut up?

That's a smart Indian. Shut up.

Shrugging, Kiowa pulled off his boots. He wanted to say more, just to lighten up his sleep, but instead he opened his New Testament and arranged it beneath his head as a pillow. The fog made things seem hollow and unattached. He tried not to think about Ted Lavender, but then he was thinking how fast it was, no drama, down and dead, and how it was hard to feel anything except surprise. It seemed unchristian. He wished he could find some great sadness, or even anger, but the emotion wasn't there and he couldn't make it happen. Mostly he felt pleased to be alive. He liked the smell of the New Testament under his cheek, the leather and ink and paper and glue, whatever the chemicals were. He liked hearing the sounds of night. Even his fatigue, it felt fine, the stiff muscles and the prickly awareness of his own body, a floating feeling. He enjoyed not being dead. Lying there, Kiowa admired Lieutenant Jimmy Cross's capacity for grief. He wanted to share the man's pain, he wanted to care as Jimmy Cross cared. And yet when he closed his eyes, all he could think was Boom-down, and all he could feel was the pleasure of having his boots off and the fog curling in around him and the damp soil and the Bible smells and the plush comfort of night.

After a moment Norman Bowker sat up in the dark.

What the hell, he said. You want to talk, *talk*. Tell it to me.

Forget it.

No, man, go on. One thing I hate, it's a silent Indian.

For the most part they carried themselves with poise, a kind of dignity. Now and then, however, there were times of panic, when they squealed or wanted to squeal but couldn't, when they twitched and made moaning sounds and covered their heads and said Dear Jesus and flopped around on the earth and fired their weapons blindly and cringed and sobbed and begged for the noise to stop and went wild and made stupid promises to themselves and to God and to their mothers and fathers, hoping not to die. In different ways, it happened to all of them. Afterward, when the firing ended, they would blink and peek up. They would touch their bodies, feeling shame, then quickly hiding it. They would force themselves to stand. As if in slow motion, frame by frame, the world would take on the old logic—absolute silence, then the wind, then sunlight, then voices. It was the burden of being alive. Awkwardly, the men would reassemble themselves, first in private, then in groups, becoming soldiers again. They would repair the leaks in their eyes. They would check for casualties, call in dustoffs, light cigarettes, try to smile, clear their throats and spit and begin cleaning their weapons. After a time someone would shake his head and say, No lie, I almost shit my pants, and someone else would laugh, which meant it was bad, yes, but the guy had obviously not shit his pants, it wasn't that bad, and in any case nobody would ever do such a thing and then go ahead and talk about it. They would squint into the dense, oppressive sunlight. For a few moments, perhaps, they would fall silent, lighting a joint and tracking its passage from man to man, inhaling, holding in the humiliation. Scary stuff, one of them might say. But then someone else would grin or flick his eyebrows and say, Roger-dodger, almost cut me a new asshole, *almost.*

There were numerous such poses. Some carried themselves with a sort of wistful resignation, others with pride or stiff soldierly discipline or good humor or macho zeal. They were afraid of dying but they were even more afraid to show it.

They found jokes to tell.

They used a hard vocabulary to contain the terrible softness. *Greased* they'd say. *Offed, lit up, zapped while zipping.* It wasn't cruelty, just stage presence. They were actors. When someone died, it wasn't quite dying, because in a curious way it seemed scripted, and because they had their lines mostly memorized, irony mixed with tragedy, and because they called it by other names, as if to encyst and destroy the reality of death itself. They kicked corpses. They cut off thumbs. They talked grunt lingo. They told stories about Ted Lavender's supply of tranquilizers, how the poor guy didn't feel a thing, how incredibly tranquil he was.

There's a moral here, said Mitchell Sanders.

They were waiting for Lavender's chopper, smoking the dead man's dope.

The moral's pretty obvious, Sanders said, and winked. Stay away from drugs. No joke, they'll ruin your day every time.

Cute, said Henry Dobbins.

Mind blower, get it? Talk about wiggy. Nothing left, just blood and brains.

They made themselves laugh.

There it is, they'd say. Over and over—there it is, my friend, there it is—as if the repetition itself were an act of poise, a balance between crazy and almost crazy, knowing without going, there it is, which meant be cool, let it ride, because Oh yeah, man, you can't change what can't be changed, there it is, there it absolutely and positively and fucking well is.

They were tough.

They carried all the emotional baggage of men who might die. Grief, terror, love, longing—these were intangibles, but the intangibles had their own mass and specific gravity, they had tangible weight. They carried shameful memories. They carried the common secret of cowardice barely restrained, the instinct to run or freeze or hide, and in many respects this was the heaviest burden of all, for it could never be put down, it required perfect balance and perfect posture. They carried their reputations. They carried the soldier's greatest fear, which was the fear of blushing. Men killed, and died, because they were embarrassed not to. It was what had brought them to the war in the first place, nothing positive, no dreams of glory or honor, just to avoid the blush of dishonor. They died so as not to die of embarrassment. They crawled into tunnels and walked point and advanced under fire. Each morning, despite the unknowns, they made their legs move. They endured. They kept humping. They did not submit to the obvious alternative, which was simply to close the eyes and fall. So easy, really. Go limp and tumble to the ground and let the muscles unwind and not speak and not budge until your buddies picked you up and lifted you into the chopper that would roar and dip its nose and carry you off to the world. A mere matter of falling, yet no one ever fell. It was not courage, exactly; the object was not valor. Rather, they were too frightened to be cowards.

By and large they carried these things inside, maintaining the masks of composure. They sneered at sick call. They spoke bitterly about guys who had found release by shooting off their own toes or fingers. Pussies, they'd say. Candy-asses. It was fierce, mocking talk, with only a trace of envy or awe, but even so the image played itself out behind their eyes.

They imagined the muzzle against flesh. So easy: squeeze the trigger and blow away a toe. They imagined it. They imagined the quick, sweet pain, then the evacuation to Japan, then a hospital with warm beds and cute geisha nurses.

And they dreamed of freedom birds.

At night, on guard, staring into the dark, they were carried away by jumbo jets. They felt the rush of takeoff. *Gone!* they yelled. And then velocity—wings and engines—a smiling stewardess—but it was more than a plane, it was a real bird, a big sleek silver bird with feathers and talons and high screeching. They were flying. The weights fell off; there was nothing to bear. They laughed and held on tight, feeling the cold slap of wind and altitude, soaring, thinking *It's over, I'm gone!*—they were naked, they were light and free—it was all lightness, bright and fast and buoyant, light as fight, a helium buzz in the brain, a giddy bubbling in the lungs as they were taken up over the clouds and the war, beyond duty, beyond gravity and mortification and global entanglements—*Sin loi!* they yelled. *I'm sorry, motherfuckers, but I'm out of it, I'm goofed, I'm on a space cruise, I'm gone!*—and it was a restful, unencumbered sensation, just riding the light waves, sailing that big silver freedom bird over the mountains and oceans, over America, over the farms and great sleeping cities and cemeteries and highways and the golden arches of McDonald's, it was flight, a kind of fleeing, a kind of falling, falling higher and higher, spinning off the edge of the earth and beyond the sun and through the vast, silent vacuum where there were no burdens and where everything weighed exactly nothing—*Gone!* they screamed. *I'm sorry but I'm gone!*—and so at night, not quite dreaming, they gave themselves over to lightness, they were carried, they were purely borne.

On the morning after Ted Lavender died, First Lieutenant Jimmy Cross crouched at the bottom of his foxhole and burned Martha's letters. Then he burned the two photographs. There was a steady rain falling, which made it difficult, but he used heat tabs and Sterno to build a small fire, screening it with his body, holding the photographs over the tight blue flame with the tips of his fingers.

He realized it was only a gesture. Stupid, he thought. Sentimental, too, but mostly just stupid.

Lavender was dead. You couldn't burn the blame.

Besides, the letters were in his head. And even now, without photographs, Lieutenant Cross could see Martha playing volleyball in her white gym shorts and yellow T-shirt. He could see her moving in the rain.

When the fire died out. Lieutenant Cross pulled his poncho over his shoulders and ate breakfast from a can.

There was no great mystery, he decided.

In those burned letters Martha had never mentioned the war, except to say, Jimmy, take care of yourself. She wasn't involved. She signed the letters Love, but it wasn't love, and all the fine lines and technicalities did not matter. Virginity was no longer an issue. He hated her. Yes, he did. He hated her. Love, too, but it was a hard, hating kind of love.

The morning came up wet and blurry. Everything seemed part of everything else, the fog and Martha and the deepening rain.

He was a soldier, after all.

Half smiling, Lieutenant Jimmy Cross took out his maps. He shook his head hard, as if to clear it, then bent forward and began planning the day's march. In ten minutes, or maybe twenty, he would rouse the men and they would pack up and head west, where the maps showed the country to be green and inviting. They would do what they had always done. The rain might add some weight, but otherwise it would be one more day layered upon all the other days.

He was realistic about it. There was that new hardness in his stomach. He loved her but he hated her.

No more fantasies, he told himself.

Henceforth, when he thought about Martha, it would be only to think that she belonged elsewhere. He would shut down the daydreams. This was not Mount Sebastian, it was another world, where there were no pretty poems or midterm exams, a place where men died because of carelessness and gross stupidity. Kiowa was right. Boom-down, and you were dead, never partly dead.

Briefly, in the rain, Lieutenant Cross saw Martha's gray eyes gazing back at him.

He understood.

It was very sad, he thought. The things men carried inside. The things men did or felt they had to do.

He almost nodded at her, but didn't.

Instead he went back to his maps. He was now determined to perform his duties firmly and without negligence. It wouldn't help Lavender, he knew that, but from this point on he would comport himself as an officer. He would dispose of his good-luck pebble. Swallow it, maybe, or use Lee Strunk's slingshot, or just drop it along the trail. On the march he would impose strict field discipline. He would be careful to send out flank security, to prevent straggling or bunching up, to keep his troops moving at the proper pace and at the proper interval. He would insist on clean weapons. He would confiscate the remainder of Lavender's dope.

Later in the day, perhaps, he would call the men together and speak to them plainly. He would accept the blame for what had happened to Ted Lavender. He would be a man about it. He would look them in the eyes, keeping his chin level, and he would issue the new SOPs in a calm, impersonal tone of voice, a lieutenant's voice, leaving no room for argument or discussion. Commencing immediately, he'd tell them, they would no longer abandon equipment along the route of march. They would police up their acts. They would get their shit together, and keep it together, and maintain it neatly and in good working order.

He would not tolerate laxity. He would show strength, distancing himself.

Among the men there would be grumbling, of course, and maybe worse, because their days would seem longer and their loads heavier, but Lieutenant Jimmy Cross reminded himself that his obligation was not to be loved but to lead. He would dispense with love; it was not now a factor. And if anyone quarreled or complained, he would simply tighten his lips and arrange his shoulders in the correct command posture. He might give a curt little nod. Or he might not. He might just shrug and say, Carry on, then they would saddle up and form into a column and move out toward the villages west of Than Khe.

STEPHEN KING
(b. 1947)

*Born in Portland, Maine, and a long-time resident of Bangor, Maine, Stephen King is the best-selling author of more than one hundred books—novels, short fiction, and nonfiction collections—of which several were published under the pseudonym Richard Bachman (*Rage, *1977;* The Running Man, *1982;* Thinner, *1984) and several were written in collaboration with his novelist-friend Peter Straub (*The Talisman, *1984;* Black House, *2001). King is also a highly successful film director of contemporary horror, suspense, fantasy, and science fiction, very likely the most famous of contemporary American writers with the sort of vast mass-market readership once the province of Jack London and Mark Twain.*

*Fascinated by horror and science-fiction since childhood, King acknowledges his earliest influences to be EC horror comics—*Tales from the Crypt *primarily. His initial literary influence is H. P. Lovecraft, whom he discovered while browsing through an attic among his father's things, years after his father had abandoned the family; a later and more abiding influence has been Richard Matheson, author of* I Am Legend *(1954) and* The Shrinking Man *(1956).*

In 1970, King graduated from the University of Maine with a BA in English; in 1971, King married Tabitha Spruce, a fellow student at the University of Maine who was to become a successful writer herself. (King and Tabitha have three children of whom two are also published writers.) King's first published novel is Carrie *(1974), which was made into a highly successful film, now a familiar staple of movie cable channels; this early success, when the author was in his twenties, inaugurated an extraordinary career that includes the novels* 'Salem's Lot *(1975),* The Shining *(1977),* The Stand *(1978),* Cujo *(1981),* Pet Sematary *(1983),* It *(1986),* Misery *(1987),* Dolores Claiborne *(1992),* The Green Mile *(1996),* Cell *(2006), and* The Dark Tower *series, as well as the story collections* Different Seasons *(1982),* Skeleton Crew *(1985),* Nightmares & Dreamscapes *(1993),* Everything's Eventual *(2002), and* Full Dark, No Stars *(2010). Among King's numerous awards are the British Fantasy Award, the Hugo Award, the Bram Stoker Award, the Grand Master Award from the Mystery Writers of America, the Shirley Jackson Award, and the National Book Foundation 2003 Medal of Distinguished Contribution to American Letters.*

Though best known for his novels, which have sold nearly four hundred million copies in numerous languages, King is also a very effective writer of short fiction, as "The Reach" with its subtlety of presentation and understated denouement suggests.

The Reach

"The Reach was wider in those days," Stella Flanders told her great-grandchildren in the last summer of her life, the summer before she began to see ghosts. The children looked at her with wide, silent eyes, and her son, Alden, turned from his seat on the porch where he was whittling. It was Sunday, and Alden wouldn't take his boat out on Sundays no matter how high the price of lobster was.

"What do you mean, Gram?" Tommy asked, but the old woman did not answer. She only sat in her rocker by the cold stove, her slippers bumping placidly on the floor.

Tommy asked his mother: "What does she mean ?"

Lois only shook her head, smiled, and sent them out with pots to pick berries.

Stella thought: She's forgot. Or did she ever know?

The Reach had been wider in those days. If anyone knew it was so, that person was Stella Flanders. She had been born in 1884, she was the oldest resident of Goat Island, and she had never once in her life been to the mainland.

Do you love? This question had begun to plague her, and she did not even know what it meant.

Fall set in, a cold fall without the necessary rain to bring a really fine color to the trees, either on Goat or on Raccoon Head across the Reach. The wind blew long, cold notes that fall, and Stella felt each note resonate in her heart.

On November 19, when the first flurries came swirling down out of a sky the color of white chrome, Stella celebrated her birthday. Most of the village turned out. Hattie Stoddard came, whose mother had died of pleurisy in 1954 and whose father had been lost with the *Dancer* in 1941. Richard and Mary Dodge came, Richard moving slowly up the path on his cane, his arthritis riding him like an invisible passenger. Sarah Havelock came, of course; Sarah's mother Annabelle had been Stella's best friend. They had gone to the school together, grades one to eight, and Annabelle had married Tommy Frane, who had pulled her hair in the fifth grade and made her cry, just as Stella had married Bill Flanders, who had once knocked all of her schoolbooks out of her arms and into the mud (but she had managed not to cry). Now Both Annabelle and Tommy were gone and Sarah was the only one of their seven children still on the island. *Her* husband, George Havelock, who had been known to everyone as Big George, had died a nasty death over on the mainland in 1967, the year there was no fishing. An ax had slipped in Big George's hand, there had been blood—too much of it! an island funeral three days later. And when Sarah came in to Stella's party and cried, "Happy birthday, Gram!" Stella hugged her tight and closed her eyes.

(*do you do you love?*)

but she did not cry.

There was a tremendous birthday cake. Hattie had made it with her best friend, Vera Spruce. The assembled company bellowed out "Happy Birthday to You" in a combined voice that was loud enough to drown out the wind...for a little while, anyway. Even Alden sang, who in the normal course of events would sing only "Onward, Christian Soldiers" and the doxology in church and would mouth the words of all the rest with his head hunched and his big old jug ears just as red as tomatoes. There were ninety-five candles on Stella's cake, and even over the singing she heard the wind, although her hearing was not what it once had been.

She thought the wind was calling her name.

"It was not the only one," she would have told Lois's Children if she could. "In my day there were many that lived and died on the island. There was no mail boat in those days; Bull Symes used to bring the mail when there was mail. There was no ferry, either. If you had business on the Head, your man took you in the lobster boat. So far as I know, there wasn't a flushing toilet on the island until 1946. 'Twas Bull's boy Harold that put in the first one the year after the heart attack carried Bull off while he was out

dragging traps. I remember seeing them bring Bull home. I remember that they brought him up wrapped in a tarpaulin, and how one of his green boots poked out. I remember ..."

And they would say: "What, Gram? What do you remember?"

How would she answer them? Was there more?

On the first day of winter, a month or so after the birthday party, Stella opened the back door to get stovewood and discovered a dead sparrow on the back stoop. She bent down carefully, picked it up by one foot, and looked at it.

"Frozen," she announced, and something inside her spoke another word. It had been forty years since she had seen a frozen bird—1938. The year the Reach had frozen.

Shuddering, pulling her coat closer, she threw the dead sparrow in the old rusty incinerator as she went by it. The day was cold. The sky was a clear, deep blue. On the night of her birthday four inches of snow had fallen, had melted, and no more had come since then. "Got to come soon," Larry McKeen down at the Goat Island Store said sagely, as if daring winter to stay away.

Stella got to the woodpile, picked herself an armload and carried it back to the house. Her shadow, crisp and clean, followed her.

As she reached the back door, where the sparrow had fallen, Bill spoke to her—but the cancer had taken Bill twelve years before. "Stella," Bill said, and she saw his shadow fall beside her, longer but just as clear-cut, the shadow-bill of his shadow-cap twisted jauntily off to one side just as he had always worn it. Stella felt a scream lodged in her throat. It was too large to touch her lips.

"Stella," he said again, "when you comin cross to the mainland? We'll get Norm Jolley's old Ford and go down to Bean's in Freeport just for a lark. What do you say?"

She wheeled, almost dropping her wood, and there was no one there. Just the dooryard sloping down to the hill, then the wild white grass, and beyond all, at the edge of everything, clear-cut and somehow magnified, the Reach...and the mainland beyond it.

"Gram, what's the Reach?" Lona might have asked... although she never had. And she would have given them the answer any fisherman knew by rote: a Reach is a body of water between two bodies of land, a body of water which is open at either end. The old lobsterman's joke went like this: know how to read y'compass when the fog comes, boys; between Jonesport and London there's a mighty long Reach.

"Reach is the water between the island and the mainland," she might have amplified, giving them molasses cookies and hot tea laced with sugar. "I know that much. I know it as well as my husband's name... and how he used to wear his hat."

"Gram?" Lona would say. "How come you never been across the Reach?"

"Honey," she would say, "I never saw any reason to go."

In January, two months after the birthday party, the Reach froze for the first time since 1938. The radio warned islanders and main-landers alike not to trust the ice, but Stewie McClelland and Russell Bowie took Stewie's Bombardier Skiddoo out anyway after a long afternoon spent drinking Apple Zapple wine, and sure enough, the skiddoo went into the Reach. Stewie managed to crawl out (although he lost one foot to frost-bite). The Reach took Russell Bowie and carried him away.

That January 25 there was a memorial service for Russell. Stella went on her son Alden's arm, and he mouthed the words to the hymns and boomed out the doxology in his great tuneless voice before the bene-diction. Stella sat afterward with Sarah Havelock and Hattie Stoddard and Vera Spruce in the glow of the wood fire in the town-hall basement. A going-away party for Russell was being held, complete with Za-Rex punch and nice little cream-cheese sandwiches cut into triangles. The men, of course, kept wandering out back for a nip of something a bit stronger than Za-Rex. Russell Bowie's new widow sat red-eyed and stunned beside Ewell McCracken, the minister. She was seven months big with child—it would be her fifth—and Stella, half-dozing in the heat of the woodstove, thought: *She'll be crossing the Reach soon enough, I guess. She'll move to Freeport or Lewiston and go for a waitress, I guess.*

She looked around at Vera and Hattie, to see what the discussion was,

"No, I didn't hear," Hattie said. "What *did* Freddy say?"

They were talking about Freddy Dinsmore, the oldest man on the island (two years younger'n me, though, Stella thought with some satisfaction), who had sold out his store to Larry McKeen in 1960 and now lived on his retirement.

"Said he'd never seen such a winter," Vera said, taking out her knitting. "He says it is going to make people sick."

Sarah Havelock looked at Stella, and asked if Stella had ever seen such a winter. There had been no snow since that first little bit; the ground lay crisp and bare and brown. The day before, Stella had walked thirty paces into the back field, holding her right hand level at the height of her thigh, and the grass there had snapped in a neat row with a sound like breaking glass.

"No," Stella said. "The Reach froze in '38, but there was snow that year. Do you remember Bull Symes, Hattie?"

Hattie laughed. "I think I still have the black-and-blue he gave me on my sit-upon at the New Year's party in '53. He pinched me *that* hard. What about him?"

"Bull and my own man walked across to the mainland that year," Stella said. "That February of 1938. Strapped on snowshoes, walked across to Dorrit's Tavern on the Head, had them each a shot of whiskey, and walked back. They asked me to come along. They were like two little boys off to the sliding with a toboggan between them."

They were looking at her, touched by the wonder of it. Even Vera was looking at her wide-eyed, and Vera had surely heard the tale before. If you believed the stories, Bull and Vera had once played some house together, although it was hard, looking at Vera now, to believe she had ever been so young.

"And you didn't go?" Sarah asked, perhaps seeing the reach of the Reach in her mind's eye, so white it was almost blue in the heatless winter sunshine, the sparkle of the snow crystals, the mainland drawing closer, walking across, yes, walking across the ocean just like Jesus-out-of-the-boat, leaving the island for the one and only time in your life on *foot*—

"No," Stella said. Suddenly she wished she had brought her own knitting. "I didn't go with them."

"Why *not?"* Hattie asked, almost indignantly.

"It was washday," Stella almost snapped, and then Missy Bowie, Russell's widow, broke into loud, braying sobs. Stella looked over and there sat Bill Flanders in his red-and-black-checked jacket, hat cocked to one side, smoking a Herbert Tareyton with another tucked behind his ear for later. She felt her heart leap into her chest and choke between beats.

She made a noise, but just then a knot popped like a rifle shot in the stove, and neither of the other ladies heard.

'"Poor *thing*," Sarah nearly cooed.

"Well shut of that good-for-nothing," Hattie grunted. She searched for the grim depth of the truth concerning the-departed Russell Bowie and found it: "Little more than a tramp for pay, that man. She's well out of *that* two-hoss trace."

Stella barely heard these things. There sat Bill, close enough to the Reverend McCracken to have tweaked his nose if he so had a mind; he looked no more than forty, his eyes barely marked by the crow's-feet that had later sunk so deep, wearing his flannel pants and his gum-rubber boots with the gray wool socks folded neatly down over the tops.

"We're waitin on you, Stel," he said. "You come on across and see the mainland. You won't need no snowshoes this year."

There he sat in the town-hall basement, big as Billy-be-damned, and then another knot exploded in the stove and he was gone. And the Reverend McCracken went on comforting Missy Bowie as if nothing had happened.

That night Vera called up Annie Phillips on the phone, and in the course of the conversation mentioned to Annie that Stella Flanders didn't look well, not at all well.

"Alden would have a scratch of a job getting her off-island if she took sick," Annie said. Annie liked Alden because her own son Toby had told her Alden would take nothing stronger than beer. Annie was strictly temperance, herself.

"Wouldn't get her off 'tall unless she was in a coma," Vera said, pronouncing the word in the downcast fashion: *comer.* "When Stella says 'Frog,' Alden jumps. Alden ain't but half-bright, you know. Stella pretty much runs him."

"Oh, ayuh?" Annie said,

Just then there was a metallic crackling sound on the line. Vera hear Annie Phillips for a moment longer not the words, just the sound of her voice going on behind the crackling—and then there was nothing. The wind had gusted up high and the phone lines had gone down, maybe into Godlin's Pond or maybe down by Borrow's Cove, where they went into the Reach sheathed in rubber. It was possible that they had gone down on the other side, on the Head...and some might even have said (only half-joking) that Russell Bowie had reached up a cold hand to snap the cable, just for the hell of it.

Not 700 feet away Stella Flanders lay under her puzzle-quilt and listened to the dubious music of Alden's snores in the other room. She listened to Alden so she wouldn't have to listen to the wind...but she heard the wind anyway, oh yes, coming across the frozen expanse of the Reach, a mile and a half of water that was now overplated with ice, ice with lobsters down below, and groupers, and perhaps the twisting, dancing body of Russell Bowie, who used to come each April with his old Rogers rototiller and turn her garden.

Who'll turn the earth this April? she wondered as she lay cold and curled under her puzzle-quilt. And as a dream in a dream, her voice answered her voice: *Do you love?* The wind gusted, rattling the storm window. It seemed that the storm window was talking to her, but she turned her face away from its words. And did not cry.

"But Gram," Lona would press (she never gave up, not that one, she was like her mom, and her grandmother before her), "you still haven't told why you never went across."

"Why, child, I have always had everything I wanted right here on Goat."

"But it's so small. We live in Portland. There's buses, Gram!"

"I see enough of what goes on in cities on the TV. I guess I'll stay where I am."

Hal was younger, but somehow more intuitive; he would not press her as his sister might, but his question would go closer to the heart of things: "You never wanted to go across, Gram? Never?"

And she would lean toward him, and take his small hands, and tell him how her mother and father had come to the island shortly after they were married, and how Bull Symes's grandfather had taken Stella's father as a 'prentice on his boat. She would tell him how her mother had conceived four times but one of her babies had miscarried and another had died a week after birth—she would have left the island if they could have saved it at the mainland hospital, but of course it was over before that was even thought of.

She would tell them that Bill had delivered Jane, their grandmother, but not that when it was over he had gone into the bathroom and first puked and then wept like a hysterical woman who had her monthlies p'ticularly bad. Jane, of course, had left the island at fourteen to go to high school; girls didn't get married at fourteen anymore, and when Stella saw her go off in the boat with Bradley Maxwell, whose job it had been to ferry the kids back and forth that month, she knew in her heart that Jane was gone for good, although she would come back for a while. She would tell them that Alden had come along ten years later, after they had given up, and as if to make up for his tardiness, here was Alden still, a lifelong bachelor, and in some ways Stella was grateful for that because Alden was not terribly bright and there are plenty of women willing to take advantage of a man with a slow brain and a good heart (although she would not tell the children that last, either).

She would say: "Louis and Margaret Godlin begat Stella Godlin, who became Stella Flanders; Bill and Stella Flanders begat Jane and Alden Flanders and Jane Flanders became Jane Wakefield; Richard and Jane Wakefield begat Lois Wakefield, who became Lois Perrault; David and Lois Perrault begat Lona and Hal. Those are your names, children: you are Godlin-Flanders-Wakefield-Perrault. Your blood is in the stones of this island, and I stay here because the mainland is too far to reach. Yes, I love; I have *loved, anyway, or at least* tried *to love, but memory is so wide and so deep, and I cannot cross, Godlin-Flanders-Wakefield-Perrault ..."*

That was the coldest February since the National Weather Service began keeping records, and by the middle of the month the ice covering the Reach was safe. Snowmobiles buzzed and whined and sometimes turned over when they climbed the ice-heaves wrong. Children tried, to skate, found the ice too bumpy to be any fun, and went back to Godlin's Pond on the far side of the hill, but not before little Justin McCracken, the minister's son, caught his skate in a fissure and broke his ankle. They took him over to the hospital on the mainland where a doctor who owned a Corvette told him, "Son, it's going to be as good as new."

Freddy Dinsmore died very suddenly just three days after Justin McCracken broke his ankle. He caught the flu late in January, would not have the doctor, told everyone it was "Just a cold from goin out to get the mail without m'scarf," took to his bed, and died before anyone could take him across to the mainland and hook him up to all those machines they have waiting for guys like Freddy. His son George, a tosspot of the first water even at the advanced age (for tosspots, anyway) of sixty-eight, found Freddy with a copy of the *Bangor Daily News* in one hand and his Remington, unloaded, near the other. Apparently he had been thinking of cleaning it just before he died. George Dinsmore went on a three-week toot, said toot financed by someone who knew that George would have his old dad's insurance money coming. Hattie Stoddard went around telling anyone who would listen that old George Dinsmore was a sin and a disgrace, no better than a tramp for pay.

There was a lot of flu around. The school closed for two weeks that February instead of the usual one because so many pupils were out sick. "No snow breeds germs," Sarah Havelock said.

Near the end of the month, just as people were beginning to look forward to the false comfort of March, Alden Flanders caught the flu himself. He walked, around with it for nearly a week and then took to his bed with a fever of a hundred and one. Like Freddy, he refused to have the doctor, and Stella stewed and fretted and worried. Alden was not as old as Freddy, but that May he would turn sixty.

The snow came at last. Six inches on Valentine's Day, another six on the twentieth, and a foot in a good old norther on the leap, February 29. The snow lay white and strange between the cove and the mainland, like a sheep's meadow where there had been only gray and surging water at this time of year since time out of mind. Several people walked across to the mainland and back. No snowshoes were necessary this year because the snow had frozen to a firm, glittery crust. They might take a knock of whiskey, too, Stella thought, but they would not take it at Dorrit's. Dorrit's had burned down in 1958.

And she saw Bill all four times. Once he told her- "Y'ought to come soon, Stella We'll go steppin. What do you say?"

She could say nothing. Her fist was crammed deep into her mouth.

"Everything I ever wanted or needed was here," she would tell them "We had the radio and now we have the television and that's all I want of the world beyond the Reach. I had my garden year in and year out. And lobster? Why, we always used to have a pot of lobster stew on the back of the stove and we used to take it off and put it behind the door in the pantry when the minister came calling so he wouldn't see we were eating 'poor man's soup.'

"I have seen good weather and bad, and if there were times when I wondered what it might be like to actually be in the Sears store instead of ordering from the catalogue, or to go into one of those Shaw's markets I see on TV instead of buying at the store here or sending Alden across for something special like a Christmas capon or an Easter ham... or if I ever wanted, just once, to stand on Congress Street in Portland and watch all the people in their cars and on the sidewalks, more people in a single look than there are on the whole island these days... if I ever wanted those things, then I wanted this more. I am not strange, I am not peculiar, or even very eccentric for a woman of my years. My mother sometimes used to say, 'All the difference in the world is between work and want,' and I believe that to my very soul. I believe it is better to plow deep than wide.'

"This is my place, and I love it."

One day in middle March, with the sky as white and lowering as a loss of memory, Stella Flanders sat in her kitchen for the last time, laced up her boots over her skinny calves for the last time, and wrapped her bright red woolen scarf (a Christmas present from Hattie three Christmases past) around her neck for the last time. She wore a suit of Alden's long underwear under her dress. The waist of the drawers came up to just below the limp vestiges of her breasts, the shirt almost down to her knees.

Outside, the wind was picking up again, and the radio said there would be snow by afternoon. She put on her coat and her gloves. After a moment of debate, she put a pair of Alden's gloves on over her own. Alden had recovered from the flu, and this morning he and Harley Blood were over rehanging a storm door for Missy Bowie, who had had a girl. Stella had seen it, and the unfortunate little mite looked just like her father.

She stood at the window for a moment, looking out at the Reach, and Bill was there as she had suspected he might be, standing about halfway between the island and the Head, standing on the Reach just like Jesus-out-of-the-boat, beckoning to her, seeming to tell her by gesture that the time was late if she ever intended to step a foot on the mainland in this life.

"If it's what you want, Bill," she fretted in the silence. "God knows I don't."

But the wind spoke other words. She did want to. She wanted to have this adventure. It had been a painful winter for her—the arthritis which came and went irregularly was back with a vengeance, flaring the joints of her fingers and knees with red fire and blue ice. One of her eyes had gotten dim and blurry (and just the other day Sarah had mentioned—with some unease—that the firespot that had been there since Stella was sixty or so now seemed to be growing by leaps and bounds). Worst of all, the deep, griping pain in her stomach had returned, and two mornings before she had gotten up at five o'clock, worked her way along the exquisitely cold floor into the bathroom, and had spat a great wad of bright red blood into the toilet bowl. This morning there had been some more of it, foul-tasting stuff, coppery and shuddersome.

The stomach pain had come and gone over the last five years, sometimes better, sometimes worse, and she had known almost from the beginning that it must be cancer. It had taken her mother and father and her mother's father as well. None of them had lived past seventy, and so she supposed she had beat the tables those insurance fellows kept by a carpenter's yard.

"You eat like a horse," Alden told her, grinning, not long after the pains had begun and she had first observed the blood in her morning stool. "Don't you know that old fogies like you are supposed to be peckish?"

"Get on or I'll swat ye!" Stella had answered, raising a hand to her gray-haired son, who ducked, mock-cringed, and cried: "Don't, Ma! I take it back!"

Yes, she had eaten hearty, not because she wanted to, but because she believed (as many of her generation did), that if you fed the cancer it would leave you alone. And perhaps it worked, at least for a while; the blood in her stools came and went, and there were long periods when it wasn't there at all. Alden got used to her taking second helpings (and thirds, when the pain was particularly bad), but she never gained a pound.

Now it seemed the cancer had finally gotten around to what the froggies called the *pièce de résistance.*

She started out the door and saw Alden's hat, the one with the fur-lined ear flaps, hanging on one of the pegs in the entry. She put it on—the bill came all the way down to her shaggy salt-and-pepper eyebrows—and then looked around one last time to see if she had forgotten anything. The stove was low, and Alden had left the draw open too much again—she told him and told him, but that was one thing he was just never going to get straight.

"Alden, you'll burn an extra quarter-cord a winter when I'm gone," she muttered, and opened the stove. She looked in and a tight, dismayed gasp escaped her. She slammed the door shut and adjusted the draw with trembling fingers. For a moment—just a moment—she had seen her old friend Annabelle Frane in the coals. It was her face to the life, even down to the mole on her cheek.

And had Annabelle winked at her?

She thought of leaving Alden a note to explain where she had gone, but she thought perhaps Alden would understand, in his own slow way.

Still writing notes in her head—*Since the first day of winter I have been seeing your father and he says dying isn't so bad; at least I think that's it*—Stella stepped out into the white day.

The wind shook her and she had to reset Alden's cap on her head before the wind could steal it for a joke and cartwheel it away. The cold seemed to find every chink in her clothing and twist into her; damp March cold with wet snow on its mind.

She set off down the hill toward the cove, being careful to walk on the cinders and clinkers that George Dinsmore had spread. Once George had gotten a job driving plow for the town of Raccoon Head, but during the big blow of '77 he had gotten smashed on rye whiskey and had driven the plow smack through not one, not two, but three power poles. There had been no lights over the Head for five days. Stella remembered now how strange it had been, looking across the Reach and seeing only blackness. A body got used to seeing that brave little nestle of lights. Now George worked on the island, and since there was no plow, he didn't get into much hurt.

As she passed Russell Bowie's house, she saw Missy, pale as milk, looking out at her. Stella waved. Missy waved back.

She would tell them this:

"On the island we always watched out for our own. When Gerd Henreid broke the blood vessel in his chest that time, we had covered-dish suppers one whole summer to pay for his operation in Boston—and Gerd came back alive, thank God. When George Dinsmore ran down those power poles and the Hydro slapped a lien on his home, it was seen to that the Hydro had their money and George had enough of a job to keep him in cigarettes and booze... why not? He was good for nothing else when his workday was done, although when he was on the clock he would work like a dray-horse. That one time he got into trouble was because it was at night, and night was always George's drinking time. His father kept him fed, at least. Now Missy Bowie's alone with another baby. Maybe she'll stay here and take her welfare and ADC money here, and most likely it won't be enough, but she'll get the help she needs. Probably she'll go, but if she stays she'll not starve... and listen, Lona and Hal: if she stays, she may be able to keep something of this small world with the little Reach on one side and the big Reach on the other, something it would be too easy to lose hustling hash in Lewiston or donuts in Portland or drinks at the Nashville North in Bangor. And I am old enough not to beat around the bush about what that something might be: a way of being and a way of living—a feeling."

They had watched out for their own in other ways as well, but she would not tell them that. The children would not understand, nor would Lois and David, although Jane had known the truth. There was Norman and Ettie Wilson's baby that was born a mongoloid, its poor dear little feet turned in, its bald skull lumpy and cratered, its fingers webbed together as if it had dreamed too long and too deep while swimming that interior Reach; Reverend McCracken had come and baptized the baby, and a day later Mary Dodge came, who even at that time had midwived over a hundred babies, and Norman took Ettie down the hill to see Frank Child's new boat and although she could barely walk, Ettie went with no complaint, although she had stopped in the door to look back at Mary Dodge, who was sitting calmly by the idiot baby's crib and knitting. Mary had looked up at her and when their eyes met, Ettie burst into tears. "Come on," Norman had said, upset. "Come on, Ettie, come on." And when they came back an hour later the baby was dead, one of those crib-deaths, wasn't it merciful he didn't suffer. And many years before that, before the war, during the Depression, three little girls had been molested coming home from school, not badly molested, at least not where you could see the scar of the hurt, and they all told about a man who offered to show them a deck of cards he had with a different kind of dog on each one. He would show them this wonderful deck of cards, the man said, if the little girls would come into the bushes with him, and once in the bushes this man said, "But you have to touch this first." One of the little girls was Gert Symes, who would go on to be voted Maine's Teacher of the Year in 1978, for her work at Brunswick High. And Gert, then only five years old, told her father that the man had some fingers gone on one hand. One of the other little girls agreed that this was so. The third remembered nothing. Stella remembered Alden going out one thundery day that summer without telling her where he was going, although she asked. Watching from the window, she had seen Alden meet Bull Symes at the bottom of the path, and then Freddy Dinsmore had joined them and down at the cove she saw her own husband, whom she had sent out that morning just as usual, with his dinner pail under his arm. More men joined them, and when they finally moved off she counted just one under a dozen. The Reverend McCracken's predecessor had been among them. And that evening a fellow named Daniels was found at the foot of Slyder's Point, where the rocks poke out of the surf like the fangs of a dragon that drowned with its mouth open. This Daniels was a fellow Big George Havelock had hired to help him put new sills under his house and a new engine in his Model A truck. From New Hampshire he was, and he was a sweet-talker who had found other odd jobs to do when the work at the Havelocks' was done... and in church, he could carry a tune! Apparently they said, Daniels had been walking up on top of Slyder's Point and had slipped, tumbling all the way to the bottom. His neck was broken and his head was bashed in. As he had no people that anyone knew of, he was buried on the island, and the Reverend McCracken's predecessor gave the graveyard eulogy, saying as how this Daniels had been a hard worker and a good help even though he was two fingers shy on his right hand.

Then he read the benediction and the graveside group had gone back to the town-hall basement where they drank Za-Rex punch, and ate cream-cheese sandwiches, and Stella never asked her men where they had gone on the day Daniels fell from the top of Slyder's Point.

"Children," she would tell them, "we always watched out for our own. We had to, for the Reach was wider in those days and when the wind roared and the surf pounded and the dark came early, why, we felt very small—no more than dust motes in the mind of God. So it was natural for us to join hands, one with the other.

"We joined hands, children, and if there were times when we wondered what it was all for, or if there was ary such a thing as love at all, it was only because we had heard the wind and the waters on long winter nights, and we were afraid.

"No, I've never felt I needed to leave the island. My life was here. The Reach was wider in those days."

Stella reached the cove. She looked right and left, the wind blowing her dress out behind her like a flag. If anyone had been there she would have walked further down and taken her chance on the tumbled rocks, although they were glazed with ice. But no one was there and she walked out along the pier, past the old Symes boathouse. She reached the end and stood there for a moment, head held up, the wind blowing past the padded flaps of Alden's hat in a muffled flood.

Bill was out there, beckoning. Beyond him, beyond the Reach, she could see the Congo Church over there on the Head, its spire almost invisible against the white sky.

Grunting, she sat down on the end of the pier and then stepped onto the snow crust below. Her boots sank a little; not much. She set Alden's cap again—how the wind wanted to tear it off!—and began to walk toward Bill. She thought once that she would look back, but she did not. She didn't believe her heart could stand that.

She walked, her boots crunching into the crust, and listened to the faint thud and give of the ice. There was Bill, further back now but still beckoning. She coughed, spat blood onto the white snow that covered the ice. Now the Reach spread wide on either side and she could, for the first time in her life, read the "Stanton's Bait and Boat" sign over there without Alden's binoculars. She could see the cars passing to and fro on the Head's main street and thought with real wonder: *They can go as far as they want...Portland...Boston...New York City. Imagine!* And she could almost do it, could almost imagine a road that simply rolled on and on, the boundaries of the world knocked wide.

A snowflake skirled past her eyes. Another. A third. Soon it was snowing lightly and she walked through a pleasant world of shifting bright white; she saw Raccoon Head through a gauzy curtain that sometimes almost cleared. She reached up to set Alden's cap again and snow puffed off the bill into her eyes. The wind twisted fresh snow up in filmy shapes, and in one of them she saw Carl Abersham, who had gone down with Hattie Stoddard's husband on the *Dancer.*

Soon, however, the brightness began to dull as the snow came harder. The Head's main street dimmed, dimmed, and at last was gone. For a time longer she could make out the cross atop the church, and then that faded out too, like a false dream. Last to go was that bright yellow-and-black sign reading "Stanton's Bait and Boat," where you could also get engine oil, flypaper, Italian sandwiches, and Budweiser to go.

Then Stella walked in a world that was totally without color, a gray-white dream of snow. *Just like Jesus-out-of-the-boat,* she thought, and at last she looked back but now the island was gone, too. She could see her tracks going back, losing definition until only the faint half-circles of her heels could be seen...and then nothing. Nothing at all.

She thought: *It's a whiteout. You got to be careful, Stella, or you'll never get to the mainland. You'll just walk around in a big circle until you're worn out and then you'll freeze to death out here.*

She remembered Bill telling her once that when you were lost in the woods, you had to pretend that the leg which was on the same side of your body as your smart hand was lame. Otherwise that smart leg would begin to lead you and you'd walk in a circle and not even realize it until you came around to our backtrail again. Stella didn't believe she could afford to have that happen to her. Snow today, tonight, and tomorrow, the radio had said, and in a whiteout such as this, she would not even know if she came around to her backtrail, for the wind and the fresh snow would erase it long before she could return to it.

Her hands were leaving her in spite of the two pairs of gloves she wore, and her feet had been gone for some time. In a way, this was almost a relief. The numbness at least shut the mouth of her clamoring arthritis .

Stella began to limp now, making her left leg work harder. The arthritis in her knees had not gone to sleep, and soon they were screaming at her. Her white hair flew out behind her. Her lips had drawn back from her teeth (she still had her own, all save four) and she looked straight ahead, waiting for that yellow-and-black sign to materialize out of the flying whiteness.

It did not happen.

Sometime later, she noticed that the day's bright whiteness had begun to dull to a more uniform gray. The snow fell heavier and thicker than ever. Her feet were still planted on the crust but now she was walking through five inches of fresh snow. She looked at her watch, but it had stopped. Stella realized she must have forgotten to wind it that morning for the first time in twenty or thirty years. Or had it just stopped for good? It had been her mother's and she had sent it with Alden twice to the Head, where Mr. Dostie had first marveled over it and then cleaned it. Her watch, at least, had been to the mainland.

She fell down for the first time some fifteen minutes after she began to notice the day's growing grayness. For a moment she remained on her hands and knees, thinking it would be so easy just to stay here, to curl up and listen to the wind, and then the determination that had brought her through so much reasserted itself and she got up, grimacing. She stood in the wind, looking straight ahead, willing her eyes to see...but they saw nothing.

Be dark soon.

Well, she had gone wrong. She had slipped off to one side or the other. Otherwise she would have reached the mainland by now. Yet she didn't believe she had gone so far wrong that she was walking parallel to the mainland or even back in the direction of Goat. An interior navigator in her head whispered that she had overcompensated and slipped off to the left. She believed she was still approaching the mainland but was now on a costly diagonal.

That navigator wanted her to turn right, but she would not do that. Instead, she moved straight on again, but stopped the artificial limp. A spasm of coughing shook her, and she spat bright red into the snow.

Ten minutes later (the gray was now deep indeed, and she found herself in the weird twilight of a heavy snowstorm) she fell again, tried to get up, failed at first, and finally managed to gain her feet. She stood swaying in the snow, barely able to remain upright in the wind, waves of faintness rushing through her head, making her feel alternately heavy and light.

Perhaps not all the roaring she heard in her ears was the wind, but it surely was the wind that finally succeeded in prying Alden's hat from her head. She made a grab for it, but the wind danced it easily out of her reach and she saw it only for a moment, flipping gaily over and over into the darkening gray, a bright spot of orange. It struck the snow, rolled, rose again, was gone. Now her hair flew around her head freely.

"It's all right, Stella," Bill said, "You can wear mine."

She gasped and looked around in the white. Her gloved hands had gone instinctively to her bosom, and she felt sharp fingernails scratch at her heart.

She saw nothing but shifting membranes of snow—and then, moving out of that evening's gray throat, the wind screaming through it like the voice of a devil in a snowy tunnel, came her husband. He was at first only moving colors in the snow: red, black, dark green, lighter green; then these colors resolved themselves into a flannel jacket with a flapping collar, flannel pants, and green boots. He was holding his hat out to her in a gesture that appeared almost absurdly courtly, and his face was Bill's face, unmarked by the cancer that had taken him (had that been all she was afraid of? that a wasted shadow of her husband would come to her, a scrawny concentration-camp figure with the skin pulled taut and shiny over the cheekbones and the eyes sunken deep in the sockets?) and she felt a surge of relief.

"Bill? Is that really you?"

"Course."

"Bill," she said again, and took a glad step toward him. Her legs betrayed her and she thought she would fall, fall right through him—he was, after all, a ghost—but he caught her in arms as strong and as component as those that had carried her over the threshold of the house that she had shared only with Alden in these latter years. He supported her, and a moment later she felt the cap pulled firmly onto her head.

"Is it really you?" she asked again, looking up into his face, at the crow's-feet around his eyes which hadn't sunk deep yet, at the spill of snow on the shoulders of his checked hunting jacket, at his lively brown hair.

"It's me," he said. "It's all of us."

He half-turned with her and she saw the others coming out of the snow that the wind drove across the reach in the gathering darkness. A cry, half cry, half fear, came from her mouth as she saw Madeline Stoddard, Hattie's mother, in a blue dress that swung in the wind like a bell, and holding her hand was Hattie's dad, not a mouldering skeleton somewhere on the bottom with the *Dancer,* but whole and young. And there, behind those two—

"Annabelle!" she cried. "Annabelle France, is it you?"

It *was* Annabelle; even in this snowy gloom Stella recognized the yellow dress Annabelle had worn to Stella's own wedding, and as she struggled toward her dead friend, holding Bill's arm, she thought that she could smell roses.

"Annabelle!"

"We're almost there now, dear," Annabelle said, taking her other arm. The yellow dress, which had been considered Daring in its day (but, to Annabelle's credit and to everyone else's relief, not quite a Scandal), left her shoulders bare, but Annabelle did not seem to feel the cold. Her hair, a soft, dark auburn, blew long in the wind. "only a little further."

She took Stella's other arm and they moved forward again. Other figures came out of the snowy night (for it was night now). Stella recognized many of them, but not all. Tommy Frane had joined Annabelle; Big George Havelock, who had died a dog's death in the woods, walked behind Bill; there was the fellow who had kept the lighthouse on the head for most of twenty years and who used to come over to the island during the cribbage tournament Freddy Dinsmore held every February—Stella could almost but not quite remember his name. And there was Freddy himself! Walking off to one side of Freddy, by himself and looking bewildered, was Russell Bowie.

"Look, Stella," Bill said, and she saw black rising out of the gloom like the splintered prows of many ships. It was not ships, it was split and fissured rock. They had reached the Head. They had crossed the Reach.

She heard voices, but was not sure they actually spoke:

Take my hand, Stella—

(do you)

Take my hand, Bill—

(oh do you do you)

Annabelle... Freddy... Russell... John... Ettie... Fran... take my hand, take my hand... my hand ...

(do you love)

"Will you take my hand, Stella?" a new voice asked.

She looked around and there was Bull Symes. He was smiling kindly at her and yet she felt a kind of terror in her at what was in his eyes and for a moment she drew away, clutching Bill's hand on her other side the tighter.

"Is it—"

"Time?" Bull asked. "Oh, ayuh, Stella, I guess so. But it don't hurt. At least, I never heard so. All that's before."

She burst into tears suddenly—all the tears she had never wept—and put her hand in Bull's hand. "Yes," she said, "yes I will, yes I did, yes I do."

They stood in a circle in the storm, the dead of Goat Island, and the wind screamed around them, driving its packet of snow, and some kind of song burst from her. It went up into the wind and the wind carried it away. They all sang then, as children will sing in their high, sweet voices as a summer evening draws down to summer night. They sang, and Stella felt herself going to them and with them, finally across the Reach. There was a bit of pain, but not much; losing her maidenhead had been worse. They stood in a circle in the night. The snow blew around them and they sang. They sang, and—

—and Alden could not tell David and Lois, but in the summer after Stella died, when the children came out for their annual two weeks, he told Lona and Hal. He told them that during the great storms of winter the wind seems to sing with almost human voices, and that sometimes it seemed to him he could almost make out the words: "Praise God from whom all blessings flow/ Praise Him, ye creatures here below ..."

But he did not tell them (imagine slow, unimaginative Alden Flanders saying such things aloud, even to the children!) that sometimes he would hear that sound and feel cold even by the stove; that he would put his whittling aside, or the trap he had meant to mend, thinking that the wind sang in all the voices of those who were dead and gone... that they stood somewhere out on the Reach and sang as children do. He seemed to hear their voices and on these nights he sometimes slept and dreamed that he was singing the doxology, unseen and unheard, at his own funeral.

There are things that can never be told, and there are things, not exactly secret, that are not discussed. They had found Stella frozen to death on the mainland a day after the storm had blown itself out. She was sitting on a natural chair of rock about one hundred yards south of the Raccoon Head town limits, frozen just as neat as you please. The doctor who owned the Corvette said that he was frankly amazed. It would have been a walk of over four miles, and the autopsy required by law in the case of an unattended, unusual death had shown an advanced cancerous condition—in truth, the old woman had been riddled with it. Was Alden to tell David and Lois that the cap on her head had not been his? Larry McKeen had recognized that cap. So had John Bensohn. He had seen it in their eyes, and he supposed they had seen it in his. He had not lived long enough to forget his dead father's cap, the look of its bill or the places where the visor had been broken.

"These are things made for thinking on slowly," he would have told the children if he had known how. "Things to be thought on at length, while the hands do their work and the coffee sits in a solid china mug nearby. They are questions of Reach, maybe: do the dead sing? And do they love the living?"

On the nights after Lona and Hal had gone back with their parents to the mainland in Al Curry's boat, the children standing astern and waving good bye, Alden considered that question, and others, and the matter of his father's cap.

Do the dead sing? Do they love?

On those long nights alone, with his mother Stella Flanders at long last in her grave, it often seemed to Alden that they did both.

T. C. BOYLE
(b. 1948)

Born in Peekskill, New York, and a long-term resident of Santa Barbara, California, T. C. Boyle is very likely the bravuro performer among contemporary American writers. His work is characterized by jarring anomalies—tall tales narrated in meticulously crafted prose; outrageous satire and domestic realism; a hipster's edgy wit and rebelliousness conjoined with the concern of the informed environmentalist; the perspective of a (reformed) heroin addict and rock musician conjoined with Swiftian moral indignation. Where his older contemporaries—like his friend Raymond Carver—honed their prose to a Minimalist mineral hardness, Boyle has cultivated a lush, head-on, acrobatic and dazzling signature prose style that, when he wishes, he can set temporarily aside, like a racing car driver shifting gears.

Boyle is the author of thirteen novels including Water Music *(1982),* World's End *(1987),* The Road to Wellville *(1993),* Drop City *(2003),* Talk Talk *(2006), and* When the Killing's Done *(2011), and nine story collections including* Descent of Man *(1979),* Greasy Lake & Other Stories *(1985),* T. C. Boyle Stories *(1998),* After the Plague *(2001),* Tooth and Claw *(2005), and* Wild Child & Other Stories *(2010). He has a BA degree from the State University of New York at Potsdam and an MFA and PhD from the Writers Workshop of the University of Iowa where his subject was nineteenth-century British fiction; since 1978, he has been Distinguished Professor of English at the University of Southern California. Among his numerous awards are the PEN/Faulkner Award (for* World's End*), the* Prix Médicis Étranger *(for* The Tortilla Curtain*), and the PEN/Malamud Lifetime Award for the Short Story. His short fiction appears frequently in the* New Yorker, Esquire, Playboy, *and* Atlantic, *as well as the yearly short story anthologies.*

Boyle has said, "To me, a story is an exercise of the imagination, and most of my work comes out of the spirit of game-playing or puzzle-solving."

Boyle has also said, "Life is tragic and absurd and without any purpose whatsoever." Is this a contradiction, or do the two statements complement each other? "Filthy With Things," Boyle's story included here, is quintessential Boyle—high-velocity, brash, rife with headachey detail, and imparting an impact that will linger long in the mind.

Filthy with Things

He dreams, amidst the clutter, of sparseness, purity, the wheeling dark star-haunted reaches beyond the grasp of this constrained little world, where distances are measured in light-years and even the galaxies fall away to nothing. But dreams get you nowhere, and Marsha's latest purchase, the figured-mahogany highboy with carved likenesses of Jefferson, Washington and Adams in place of pulls, will not fit in the garage. The garage, designed to accommodate three big chromium-hung hunks of metal in the two-ton range, will not hold anything at all, not even a Japanese fan folded like a stiletto and sunk to the hilt in a horizontal crevice. There are no horizontal crevices—nor vertical, either. The mass of interlocked things, the great squared-up block of objects, of totems, of purchases made and accreted, of the precious and unattainable, is packed as tightly as the stones at Machu Picchu.

For a long moment Julian stands there in the blistering heat of the driveway, contemplating the abstract sculpture of the garage while the boy from the Antique Warehouse rolls and unrolls the sleeves of his T-shirt and watches a pair of fourteen-year-old girls saunter up the sidewalk. The sun and heat are not salutary for the colonial hardwood of which the highboy is composed, and the problem of where to put it has begun to reach critical proportions. Julian thinks of the storage shed behind the pool, where the newspapers are stacked a hundred deep and Marsha keeps her collection of Brazilian scythes and harrows, but immediately rejects it—the last time he was back there he couldn't even get the door open. Over the course of the next ten seconds or so he develops a fantasy of draining the pool and enclosing it as a sort of step-down warehouse, and it's a rich fantasy, richly rewarding, but he ultimately dismisses it, too. If they were to drain the pool, where would Marsha keep her museum-quality collection of Early American whaling implements, buoys and ship's furniture, not to mention the two hundred twelve antique oarlocks currently mounted on the pool fence?

The boy's eyes are vapid. He's begun to whistle tunelessly and edge back toward the van. "So where'd you decide you want it?" he asks listlessly.

On the moon, Julian wants to say. Saturn. On the bleak blasted ice plains of Pluto. He shrugs. "On the porch, I guess."

The porch. Yes. The only problem is, the screened-in porch is already stacked to the eaves with sideboards, armoires, butter churns and bentwood rockers. The best they can do, after a fifteen-minute struggle, is to wedge the thing two-thirds of the way in the door. "Well," says Julian, and he can feel his heart fluttering round his rib cage like some fist-sized insect, "I guess that'll have to do." The laugh he appends is curt with embarrassment. "Won't have to worry about rain till November, anyway."

The boy isn't even breathing hard. He's long-lipped and thin, strung together with wire, and he's got one of those haircuts that make his head look as if it's been put on backwards. For a long moment he leans over the hand truck, long fingers dangling, giving Julian a look that makes him feel like he's from another planet. "Yeah, that's right," the boy finally murmurs, and he looks at his feet, then jerks himself up as if to drift back to the van, the freeway, the warehouse, before stopping cold again. He looks at Julian as if he's forgotten something, and Julian digs into his pocket and gives the boy three dollars for his efforts.

The sun is there, a living presence, as the boy backs the van out of the driveway, and Julian knows he's going to have to do something about the mahogany highboy—drape a sheet over it or maybe a plastic drop cloth—but somehow he can't really seem to muster the energy. It's getting too much for him—all these things, the addition that was filled before it was finished, the prefab storage sheds on the back lawn, the crammed closets, the unlivable living room—and the butt end of the highboy hanging from the porch door seems a tangible expression of all his deepest fears. Seeing it there, the harsh light glancing off its polished flanks, its clawed feet dangling in the air, he wants to cry out against the injustice of it all, his miserable lot, wants to dig out his binoculars and the thin peeling ground cloth he's had since he was a boy in Iowa and go up to the mountains and let the meteor showers wash him clean, but he can't. That ancient handcrafted butt end represents guilt, Marsha's displeasure, a good and valuable thing left to deteriorate. He's begun to move toward it in a halfhearted shuffle, knowing from experience that he can squeeze it in there somehow, when a horn sounds breathlessly behind him. He turns, condemned like Sisyphus, and watches as Marsha wheels into the drive, the Range Rover packed to the windows and a great dark slab of furniture lashed to the roof like some primitive landing craft. "Julian!" she calls, "Julian! Wait till you see what I found!"

"I've seen worse," the woman says, and Julian can feel the short hairs on the back of his neck begin to stiffen—she's seen worse, but she's seen better, too. They're standing in the living room—or rather on the narrow footpath between the canyons of furniture that obscure the walls, the fireplace, even the ceiling of what was once the living room—and Julian, afraid to look her in the eye, leans back against a curio cabinet crammed with painted porcelain dolls in native costume, nervously turning her card over in his hand. The card is certainly minimalistic—*Susan Certaine,* it reads in a thin black embossed script, *Professional Organizer,* and it gives a telephone number, nothing else—and the woman herself is impressive, brisk, imposing, even; but he's just not sure. Something needs to be done, something radical—and, of course, Marsha, who left to cruise the flea markets an hour ago, will have to agree to it, at least in substance—but for all his misery and sense of oppression, for all the times he's joked about burning the place down or holding the world's biggest yard sale, Julian needs to be reassured, needs to be convinced.

"You've seen worse?" he prompts.

"Sure I have. Of course I have. What do you take me for, an amateur?"

Julian shrugs, turns up his palms, already on the defensive.

"Listen, in my business, Mr. Laxner, you tend to run across the hard cases, the ones anyone else would give up on—the Liberaces, the Warhols, the Nancy Reagans. You remember Imelda Marcos? That was me. I'm the one they called in to straighten out that mess. Twenty-seven hundred pairs of shoes alone, Mr. Laxner. Think about that."

She pauses to let her eyes flicker over the room, the smallest coldest flame burning behind the twin slivers of her contact lenses. She's a tall, pale, hovering presence, a woman stripped to the essentials, the hair torn back from her scalp and strangled in a bun, no cheeks, no lips, no makeup or jewelry, the dress black, the shoes black, the briefcase black as a dead black coal dug out of the bottom of the bag. "There's trouble here," she says finally, holding his eyes. "You're dirty with things, Mr. Laxner, filthy, up to your ears in the muck."

He is, he admits it, but he can't help wincing at the harshness of the indictment.

She leans closer, the briefcase clamped like a breastplate across her chest, her breath hot in his face, soap, Sen-Sen, Listerine. "And do you know who I am, Mr. Laxner?" she asks, a hard combative friction in the back of her throat, a rasp, a growl.

Julian tries to sound casual, tries to work the hint of a smile into the corners of his mouth and ignore the fact that his personal space has suddenly shrunk to nothing. "Susan Certaine?"

"I am the purifying stream, Mr. Laxner, that's who I am. The cleansing torrent, the baptismal font. I'll make a new man of you,"

This is what she's here for, he knows it, this is what he needs, discipline, compulsion, the iron promise, but still he can't help edging away, a little dance of the feet, the condensing of a shoulder. "Well, yes, but"—giving her a sidelong glance, and still she's there, right there, breathing out her Sen-Sen like a dental hygienist—"it's a big job, it's—"

"We inventory everything—*everything*—right down to the paper clips in your drawers and the lint in your pockets. My people are the best, real professionals. There's no one like us in the business, believe me—and believe me when I tell you I'll have this situation under control inside of a week, seven short days. I'll guarantee it, in fact. All I need is your go-ahead."

His go-ahead. A sudden vista opens up before him, unbroken beaches, limitless plains, lunar seas and Venusian deserts, the yawning black interstellar wastes. Would it be too much to ask to see the walls of his own house? Just once? Just for an hour? Yes, okay, sure, he wants to say, but the immensity of it stifles him. "I'll have to ask my wife," he hears himself saying. "I mean, consult with her, think it over."

"Pah! That's what they all say." Her look is incendiary, bitter, the eyes curdling behind the film of the lenses, the lipless mouth clenched round something rotten. "Tell me something, Mr. Laxner, if you don't mind my asking—you're a stargazer, aren't you?"

"Beg pardon?"

"The upstairs room, the one over the kitchen?" Her eyes are jumping, some mad electric impulse shooting through her like a power surge scorching the lines. "Come on now, come clean. All those charts and telescopes, the books—there must be a thousand of them."

Now it's Julian's turn, the ball in his court, the ground solid under his feet. "I'm an astronomer, if you want to know."

She says nothing, just watches him out of those burning messianic eyes, waiting.

"Well, actually, it's more of a hobby really—but I do teach a course Wednesday nights at the community college."

The eyes leap at him. "I knew it. You intellectuals, you're the worst, the very worst."

"But, but"—stammering again despite himself—"it's not me, it's Marsha."

"Yes," she returns, composing herself like some lean effortless snake coiling to strike, "I've heard that one before. It takes two to tango, Mr. Laxner, the pathological aggregator and the enabler. Either way, you're guilty. Don't *ask* your wife, tell her. Take command." Turning her back on him as if the matter's been settled, she props her briefcase up against the near bank of stacked ottomans, produces a note pad and begins jotting down figures in a firm microscopic hand. Without looking up, she swings suddenly round on him. "Family money?" she asks.

And he answers before he can think: "Yes. My late mother."

"All right," she says, "all right, that's fine. But before we go any further, perhaps you'd be interested in hearing a little story one of my clients told me, a journalist, a name you'd recognize in a minute... ." The eyes twitch again, the eyeballs themselves, pulsing with that electric charge. "Well, a few years ago he was in Ethiopia—in the Eritrean province—during the civil war there? He was looking for some refugees to interview and a contact put him onto a young couple with three children, they'd been grain merchants before the war broke out, upper-middle-class, they even had a car. Well, they agreed to be interviewed, because he was giving them a little something and they hadn't eaten in a week, but when the time came they hung back. And do you know why?"

He doesn't know. But the room, the room he passes through twenty times a day like a tourist trapped in a museum, seems to close in on him.

"They were embarrassed, that's why—they didn't have any clothes. And I don't mean as in 'Oh dear, I don't have a thing to wear to the Junior

League Ball,' but literally no clothes. Nothing at all, not even a rag. They finally showed up like Adam and Eve, one hand clamped over their privates." She held his eyes till he had to look away. "And what do you think of that, Mr. Laxner, I'd be interested to know?"

What can he say? He didn't start the war, he didn't take the food from their mouths and strip the clothes from their backs, but he feels guilty all the same, bloated with guilt, fat with it, his pores oozing the golden rancid sheen of excess and waste. "That's terrible," he murmurs, and still he can't quite look her in the eye.

"Terrible?" she cries, her voice homing in, "you're damned right it's terrible. Awful. The saddest thing in the world. And do you know what? Do you?" She's even closer now, so close he could be breathing for her. "That's why I'm charging you a thousand dollars a day."

The figure seizes him, wrings him dry, paralyzes his vocal apparatus. He can feel something jerking savagely at the cords of his throat. "A thousand-*dollars*-a day?" he echoes in disbelief. "I knew it wasn't going to be cheap—"

But she cuts him off, a single insistent finger pressed to his lips. "You're dirty," she whispers, and her voice is different now, thrilling, soft as a lover's, "you're filthy. And I'm the only one to make you clean again."

The following evening, with Julian's collusion, Susan Certaine and her associate, Dr. Doris Hauskopf, appear at the back gate just after supper, It's a clear searing evening, not a trace of moisture in the sky—the kind of evening that would later lure Julian out under the stars if it weren't for the light pollution. He and Marsha are enjoying a cup of decaf after a meal of pita, tabbouleh and dolma from the Armenian deli, sitting out on the patio amidst the impenetrable maze of lawn furniture, when Susan Certaine's crisp penetrating tones break through the muted roar of freeway traffic and sporadic birdsong: "Mr. Laxner? Are you there?"

Marsha, enthroned in wicker and browsing through a collectibles catalogue, gives him a quizzical look, expecting perhaps a delivery boy or a package from the UPS—Marsha, his Marsha, in her pastel shorts and oversized top, the quintessential innocent, so easily pleased. He loves her in that moment, loves her so fiercely he almost wants to call the whole thing off, but Susan Certaine is there, undeniable, and her voice rings out a second time, drilling him with its adamancy: "Mr. Laxner?"

He rises then, ducking ceramic swans and wrought-iron planters, feeling like Judas.

The martial tap of heels on the flagstone walk, the slap of twin briefcases against rigorously conditioned thighs, and there they are, the professional organizer and her colleague the psychologist, hovering over a bewildered Marsha like customs inspectors. There's a moment of silence, Marsha looking from Julian to the intruders and back again, before he realizes that it's up to him to make the introductions. "Marsha," he begins, and he seems to be having trouble finding his voice, "Marsha, this is Ms. Certaine. And her colleague, Dr. Doris Hauskopf—she's a specialist in aggregation disorders. They run a service for people like us...you remember a few weeks ago, when we—" but Marsha's look wraps fingers around his throat and he can't go on.

Blanching, pale to the roots of her hair, Marsha leaps up from the chair and throws a wild hunted look round her. "No," she gasps, "no," and for a moment Julian thinks she's going to bolt, but the psychologist, a compact woman with a hairdo even more severe than Susan Certaine's, steps forward to take charge of the situation. "Poor Marsha," she clucks, spreading her arms to embrace her, "poor, poor Marsha."

The trees bend under the weight of the carved birdhouses from Heidelberg and Zurich, a breeze comes up to play among the Taiwanese wind chimes that fringe the eaves in an unbroken line, and the house—the jam-packed house in which they haven't been able to prepare a meal or even find a frying pan in over two years—seems to rise up off its foundation and settle back again. Suddenly Marsha is sobbing, clutching Dr. Hauskopf's squared-up shoulders and sobbing like a child. "I know I've been wrong," she wails, "I know it, but I just can't, I can't—"

"Hush now, Marsha, hush," the doctor croons, and Susan Certaine gives Julian a fierce, tight-lipped look of triumph, "that's what we're here for. Don't you worry about a thing."

The next morning, at the stroke of seven, Julian is awakened from uneasy dreams by the deep-throated rumble of heavy machinery. In the first startled moment of waking, he thinks it's the noise of the garbage truck and feels a sudden stab of regret for having failed to put out the cans and reduce his load by its weekly fraction, but gradually he becomes aware that the sound is localized, static, stalled at the curb out front of the house. Throwing off the drift of counterpanes, quilts and granny-square afghans beneath which he and his wife lie entombed each night, he struggles through the precious litter of the floor to the bedroom window. Outside, drawn up to the curb in a sleek dark glittering line, their engines snarling, are three eighteen-wheel moving vans painted in metal-flake black and emblazoned with the Certaine logo. And somewhere, deep in the bowels of the house, the doorbell has begun to ring. Insistently.

Marsha isn't there to answer it. Marsha isn't struggling up bewildered from the morass of bedclothes to wonder who could be ringing at this hour. She isn't in the bathroom trying to locate her toothbrush among the mustache cups and fin-de-siécle Viennese soap dishes or in the kitchen wondering which of the coffee drippers/steamers/percolators to use. She isn't in the house at all, and the magnitude of that fact hits him now, hard, like fear or hunger.

No, Marsha is twenty-seven miles away, in the Susan Certaine Residential Treatment Center in Simi Valley, separated from him for the first time in their sixteen years of marriage. It was Dr. Hauskopf's idea. She felt it would be better this way, less traumatic for everyone concerned. After the initial twilit embrace of the preceding evening, the doctor and Susan Certaine had led Marsha out front, away from the house and Julian—her "twin crutches," as the doctor put it—and conducted an impromptu three-hour therapy session on the lawn. Julian preoccupied himself with his lunar maps and some calculations he'd been wanting to make relating to the total area of the Mare Fecunditatis in the Southeast quadrant, but he couldn't help glancing out the window now and again. The three women were camped on the grass, sitting in a circle with their legs folded under them, yoga style, while Marsha's tiki torches blazed over their heads like a forest afire.

Weirdly lit, they dipped their torsos toward one another and their hands flashed white against the shadows while Marsha's menagerie of lawn ornaments clustered round them in silent witness. There was something vaguely disquieting about the scene, and it made Julian feel like an interloper, already bereft in some deep essential way, and he had to turn away from it. He put down his pencil and made himself a drink. He flicked on the TV. Paced. Finally, at quarter to ten, he heard them coming in the front door. Marsha was subdued, her eyes downcast, and it was clear that she'd been crying. They allowed her one suitcase. No cosmetics, two changes of clothing, underwear, a nightgown. Nothing else. Not a thing. Julian embraced his wife on the front steps while Susan Certaine and Dr. Hauskopf looked on impatiently, and then they were gone.

But now the doorbell is ringing and Julian is shrugging into his pants and looking for his shoes even as Susan Certaine's whiplash cry reverberates in the stairwell and stings him to action. "Mr. Laxner! Open up! Open up!"

It takes him sixty seconds. He would have liked to comb his hair, brush his teeth, reacquaint himself with the parameters of human life on the planet, but there it is, sixty seconds, and he's still buttoning his shirt as he throws back the door to admit her. "I thought... I thought you said eight," he gasps.

Susan Certaine stands rigid on the doorstep, flanked by two men in black jumpsuits with the Certaine logo stitched in gold over their left breast pockets. The men are big-headed, bulky, with great slabs of muscle ladled over their shoulders and upper arms. Behind them, massed like a football team coming to the aid of a fallen comrade, are the uncountable others, all in Certaine black. "I did," she breathes, stepping past him without a glance. "We like to keep our clients on their toes. Mike!" she cries, "Fernando!" and the two men spring past Julian and into the ranked gloom of the house. "Clear paths here"—pointing toward the back room—"and here"—and then to the kitchen.

The door stands open. Beyond it, the front lawn is a turmoil of purposefully moving bodies, of ramps, ladders, forklifts, flattened boxes in bundles six feet high. Already, half a dozen workers—they're women, Julian sees now, women cut in the Certaine mold, with their hair shorn or pinned rigidly back—have begun constructing the cardboard containers that will take the measure of his and Marsha's life together. And now others, five, six, seven of them, speaking in low tones and in a language he doesn't recognize, file past him with rolls of bar-code tape, while out on the front walk, just beyond the clutter of the porch, three men in mirror sunglasses set up a gauntlet of tables equipped with computers and electric-eye guns. Barefooted, unshaven, unshowered, his teeth unbrushed and his hair uncombed, Julian can only stand and gape—it's like an invasion. It *is* an invasion.

When he emerges from the shower ten minutes later, wrapped only in a towel, he finds a small hunched Asian woman squatting on her heels in front of the cabinets under the twin sinks, methodically affixing bar-code stickers to jars of petroleum jelly, rolls of toilet paper and cans of cleanser before stacking them neatly in a box at her side. "What do you think you're doing?" Julian demands. This is too much, outrageous, in his own bathroom no less, but the woman just grins out of a toothless mouth, gives him the thumbs-up sign and says, "A-OK, Number One Charlie!"

His heart is going, he can feel it, and he tries to stay calm, tries to remind himself that these people are only doing their job, doing what he could never do, liberating him, cleansing him, but before he can get his pants back on two more women materialize in the bedroom, poking through the drawers with their ubiquitous stickers. "Get out!" he roars, "out!" and he makes a rush at them, but it's as if he doesn't exist, as if he's already become an irrelevance in the face of the terrible weight of his possessions. Unconcerned, they silently hold their ground, heads bowed, hands flicking all the while over his handkerchiefs, underwear, socks, over Marsha's things, her jewelry, brassieres, her ashtray and lacquered-box collections and the glass case that houses her Thimbles of the World set.

"All right," Julian says, "all right. We'll just see about this, we'll just see," and he dresses right there in front of them, boldly, angrily, hands trembling on button and zipper, before slamming out into the hallway in search of Susan Certaine.

The only problem is, he can't find her. The house, almost impossible to navigate in the best of times, is like the hold of a sinking ship. All is chaos. A dark mutter of voices rises up to engulf him; shouts, curses, dust hanging in the air, the floorboards crying out, and things, objects of all shapes and sizes, sailing past him in bizarre array. Susan Certaine is not in the kitchen, not on the lawn, not in the garage or the pool area or the guest wing. Finally, in frustration, he stops a worker with a Chinese vase slung over one shoulder and asks if he's seen her. The man has a hard face, smoldering eyes, a mustache so thick it eliminates his mouth. "And who might you be?" he growls.

"The owner." Julian feels lightheaded. He could swear he's never seen the vase before.

"Owner of what?"

"What do you mean, owner of what? All this"—gesturing at the chaotic tumble of carpets, lamps, furniture and bric-a-brac—"the house. The, the—"

"You want *Ms.* Certaine," the man says, cutting him off, "I'd advise you best look upstairs, in the den," and then he's gone, shouldering his load out the door.

The den. But that's Julian's sanctuary, the only room in the house where you can draw a breath, find a book on the shelves, a chair to sit in—his desk is there, his telescopes, his charts. There's no need for any organizing in his den. What is she thinking? He takes the stairs two at a time, dodging Certaine workers laden with artifacts, and bursts through the door to find Susan Certaine seated at his desk and the room already half-stripped.

"But, but what are you doing?" he cries, snatching at his Velbon tripod as one of the big men in black fends him off with an unconscious elbow. "This room doesn't need anything, this room is off-limits, this is mine—"

"Mine," Susan Certaine mimics, leaping suddenly to her feet. "Did you hear that, Fernando? Mike?" The two men pause, grinning wickedly, and the wizened Asian woman, at work now in here, gives a short sharp laugh of derision. Susan Certaine crosses the room in two strides, thrusting her jaw at Julian, forcing him back a step, "Listen to yourself—'mine, mine, mine:' Don't you see what you're saying? Marsha's only half the problem, as in any codependent relationship. What did you think, that you could solve all your problems by depriving her of *her* things, making *her* suffer, while all your precious little star charts and musty books and whatnot remain untouched? Is that it?"

He can feel the eyes of the big men on him. Across the room, at the bookcase, the Asian woman applies stickers to his first edition of Percival Lowell's *Mars and Its Canals,* the astrolabe that once belonged to Captain Joshua Slocum, the Starview scope his mother gave him when he turned twelve. "No, but, but—"

"Would that be fair, Mr. Laxner? Would that be equitable? Would it?" She doesn't wait for an answer, turning instead to pose the question to her henchmen. "You think it's fair, Mike? Fernando?"

"No gain without pain," Mike says.

"Amen," Fernando chimes in.

"Listen," Julian blurts, and he's upset now, as upset as he's ever been, "I don't care what you say, I'm the boss here and I say the stuff stays, just as it is. You—now put down that tripod."

No one moves. Mike looks to Fernando, Fernando looks to Susan Certaine. After a moment, she lays a hand on Julian's arm. "You're not the boss here, Julian," she says, the voice sunk low in her throat, "not anymore. If you have any doubts, just read the contract." She attempts a smile, though smiles are clearly not her forte. "The question is, do you want to get organized or not? You're paying me a thousand dollars a day, which breaks down to roughly two dollars a minute. You want to stand here and shoot the breeze at two dollars a minute, or do you want action?"

Julian hangs his head. She's right, he knows it. "I'm sorry," he says finally. "It's just that I can't...I mean I want to do something, anything—"

"You want to do something? You really want to help?"

Mike and Fernando are gone, already heading down the stairs with their burdens, and the Asian woman, her hands in constant motion, has turned to his science-fiction collection. He shrugs. "Yes, sure. What can I do?"

She glances at her watch, squares her shoulders, fixes him with her dark unreadable gaze. "You can take me to breakfast."

Susan Certaine orders wheat toast, dry, and coffee, black. Though he's starving, though he feels cored out from the back of his throat to the last constricted loop of his intestines, he follows suit. He's always liked a big breakfast, eggs over easy, three strips of bacon, toast, waffles, coffee, orange juice, yogurt with fruit, and never more so than when he's under stress or feels something coming on, but with Susan Certaine sitting stiffly across from him, her lips pursed in distaste, disapproval, ascetic renunciation of all and everything he stands for, he just doesn't have the heart to order. Besides which, he's on unfamiliar ground here. The corner coffee shop, where he and Marsha have breakfasted nearly every day for the past three years, wasn't good enough for her. She had to drive halfway across the Valley to a place *she* knew, though for the life of him he can't see a whole lot of difference between the two places—same menu, same coffee, even the waitresses look the same. But they're not. And the fact of it throws him off balance.

"You know, I've been thinking, Mr. Laxner," Susan Certaine says, speaking into the void left by the disappearance of the waitress, "you really should come over to us. For the rest of the week, I mean."

Come over? Julian watches her, wondering what in god's name she's talking about, his stomach sinking over the thought of his Heinleins and Asimovs in the hands of strangers, let alone his texts and first editions and all his equipment—if they so much as scratch a lens, he'll, he'll... but his thoughts stop right there. Susan Certaine, locked in the grip of her black rigidity, is giving him a look he hasn't seen before. The liminal smile, the coy arch of the eyebrows. She's a young woman, younger than Marsha, far younger, and the apprehension hits him with a jolt. Here he is, sharing the most intimate meal of the day with a woman he barely knows, a young woman. He feels a wave of surrender wash over him.

"How can I persuade you?"

"I'm sorry," he murmurs, fumbling with his cup, "but I don't think I'm following you. Persuade me of what?"

"The Co-Dependent Hostel. For the spouses. The spoilers. For men like you, Mr. Laxner, who give their wives material things instead of babies, instead of love."

"But I resent that. Marsha's physically incapable of bearing children—and I *do* love her, very much so."

"Whatever." She waves her hand in dismissal. "But don't get the impression that it's a men's club or anything—you'd be surprised how many women are the enablers in these relationships. You're going to need a place to stay until Sunday anyway."

"You mean you want me to, to move out? Of my own house?"

She lays a hand on his. "Don't you think it would be fairer to Marsha? She moved out, didn't she? And by the way, Dr. Hauskopf tells me she passed a very restful night. Very restful." A sigh. A glance out the window. "Well, what do you say?"

Julian pictures a big gray featureless building lost in a vacancy of smog, men in robes and pajamas staring dully at newspapers, the intercom crackling. "But my things—"

"Things are what we're disburdening you of, Mr. Laxner. Things are crushing you, stealing your space, polluting your soul. That's what you hired me for, remember?" She pushes her cup aside and leans forward, and the old look is back, truculent, disdainful. He finds himself gazing into the shimmering nullity of her eyes. "We'll take care of all that," she says, her voice pitched low again, subtle and entrancing, "right on down to your toothbrush, hemorrhoid cream and carpet slippers." As if by legerdemain, a contract has appeared between the creamer and the twin plates of dry unadulterated toast. "Just sign here, Mr. Laxner, right at the bottom."

Julian hesitates, patting down his pockets for his reading glasses. The original contract, the one that spelled out the responsibilities of Certaine Enterprises with respect to his things—and his and Marsha's obligations to Certaine Enterprises—had run to 327 pages, a document he barely had time to skim before signing, and now this. Without his reading glasses he can barely make out the letterhead. "But how much is it, per day, I mean? Marsha's, uh, treatment was four hundred a day, correct? This wouldn't be anywhere in that ballpark, would it?"

"Think of it as a vacation, Mr. Laxner. You're going away on a little trip, that's all. And on Sunday, when you get home, you'll have your space back. Permanently." She looks into his eyes. "Can you put a price on that?"

The Susan Certaine Co-Dependent Hostel is located off a shady street in Sherman Oaks, on the grounds of a defunct private boys' school, and it costs about twice as much as a good hotel in midtown Manhattan. Julian had protested—it was Marsha, Marsha was the problem, she was the one who needed treatment, not him—but Susan Certaine, over two slices of dry wheat toast, had worn him down. He'd given her control over his life, and she was exercising it. That's what he'd paid for, that's what he'd wanted. He asked only to go home and pack a small suitcase, an overnight bag, anything, but she refused him even that—and refused him the use of his own car on top of it. "Withdrawal has got to be total," she says, easing up to the curb out front of the sprawling complex of earth-toned buildings even as a black-clad attendant hustles up to the car to pull open the door, "for *both* partners. I'm sure you'll be very happy here, Mr. Laxner."

"You're not coming in?" he says, a flutter of panic seizing him as he shoots a look from her to the doorman and back again.

The black Mercedes hums beneath them. A bird folds its wings and dips across the lawn. "Oh, no, no, not at all. You're on your own here, Mr. Laxner, I'm afraid—but in the best of hands, I assure you. No, my job is to go back to that black hole of a house and make it livable, to catalogue your things, organize. *Organize,* Mr. Laxner, that's my middle name."

Ten minutes later Julian finds himself sitting on the rock-hard upper bunk in the room he is to share with a lugubrious man named Fred, contemplating the appointments. The place is certainly Essene, but then, he supposes that's the idea. Aside from the bunk bed, the room contains two built-in chests of drawers, two mirrors, two desks and two identical posters revealing an eye-level view of the Bonneville Salt Flats. The communal bathroom/shower is down the checked linoleum hallway to the right. Fred, a big pouchy sack of a man who owns a BMW dealership in Encino, stares gloomily out the window and says only, "Kind of reminds you of college, doesn't it?"

In the evening, there's a meal in the cafeteria—instant mashed potatoes with gravy, some sort of overcooked unidentifiable meatlike substance, Jell-O—and Julian is surprised at the number of his fellow sufferers, slump-shouldered men and women, some of them quite young, who shuffle in and out of the big room like souls in purgatory. After dinner, there's a private get-acquainted chat with Dr. Heiko Hauskopf, Dr. Doris's husband, and then an informational film about acquisitive disorders, followed by a showing of *The Snake Pit* in the auditorium. Fred, as it turns out, is a belcher, tooth grinder and nocturnal mutterer of the first degree, and Julian spends the night awake, staring into the dark corner above him and imagining tiny solar systems there, hanging in the abyss, other worlds radiant with being.

Next morning, after a breakfast of desiccated eggs and corrosive coffee, he goes AWOL. Strides out the door without a glance, calls a taxi from the phone booth on the comer and checks into the nearest motel. From there he attempts to call Marsha, though both Susan Certaine and Dr. Doris had felt it would be better not to "establish contact" during therapy. He can't get through. She's unavailable, indisposed, undergoing counseling, having her nails done, and who is this calling, please?

For two days Julian holes up in his motel room like an escaped convict, feeling dangerous, feeling like a lowlife, a malingerer, a bum, letting the stubble sprout on his face, reveling in the funk of his unwashed clothes. He could walk up the street and buy himself a change of underwear and socks at least—he's still got his credit cards, after all—but something in him resists. Lying there in the sedative glow of the TV, surrounded by the detritus of the local fast-food outlets, belching softly to himself and pulling meditatively at the pint of bourbon balanced on his chest, he begins to see the point of the exercise. He misses Marsha desperately, misses his home, his bed, his things. But this is the Certaine way—to know deprivation, to know the hollowness of the manufactured image and the slow death of the unquenchable tube, to purify oneself through renunciation. These are his thirty days and thirty nights, this is his trial, his penance. He lies there, prostrate, and when the hour of his class at the community college rolls round he gives no account of himself, not even a phone call.

On the third night, the telephone rings. Absorbed in a dramedy about a group of young musician/actor/models struggling to make ends meet in a rented beach house in Malibu, and well into his second pint of bourbon, he stupidly answers it. "Mr. Laxner?" Susan Certaine's hard flat voice drives at him through the wires.

"But, how—?" he gasps, before she cuts him off.

"Don't ask questions, just listen. You understand, of course, that as per the terms of your agreement, you owe Certaine Enterprises for six days' room and board at the Co-Dependent Hostel whether you make use of the facilities or not—"

He understands.

"Good," she snaps. "Fine. Now that that little matter has been resolved, let me tell you that your wife is responding beautifully to treatment and that she, unlike you, Mr. Laxner, is making the most of her stay in a nonacquisitive environment—and by the way, I should caution you against trying to contact her again; it could be terribly detrimental, traumatic, a real setback—"

Whipped, humbled, pried out of his cranny with a sure sharp stick, Julian can only murmur an apology.

There's a pause on the other end of the line—Julian can hear the hiss of gathering breath, the harsh whistle of the air rushing past Susan

Certaine's fleshless lips, down her ascetic throat and into the repository of her disciplined lungs. "The good news," she says finally, drawing it out, "is that you're clean. Clean, Mr. Laxner. As pure as a babe sprung from the womb."

Julian is having difficulty putting it all together. His own breathing is quick and shallow. He rubs at his stubble, sits up and sets the pint of bourbon aside. "You mean—?"

"I mean twelve-o'clock noon, Mr. Laxner, Sunday the twenty-seventh. Your place. You be there."

On Sunday morning, Julian is up at six. Eschewing the religious programming in favor of the newspaper, he pores methodically over each of the twenty-two sections—including the obituaries, the personals and the recondite details of the weather in Rio, Yakutsk and Rangoon—and manages to kill an hour and a half. His things have been washed—twice now, in the bathroom sink, with a bar of Ivory soap standing in for detergent—and before he slips into them he shaves with a disposable razor that gouges his face in half-a-dozen places and makes him yearn for the reliable purr and gentle embrace of his Braun Flex Control. He breakfasts on a stale cruller and coffee that tastes of bile while flicking through the channels. Then he shaves a second time and combs his hair. It is 9:05. The room stinks of stir-fry, pepperoni, garlic, the sad reek of his take-out life. He can wait no longer.

Unfortunately, the cab is forty-five minutes late, and it's nearly ten-thirty by the time they reach the freeway. On top of that, there's a delay—roadwork, they always wait till Sunday for roadwork—and the cab sits inert in an endless field of gleaming metal until finally the cabbie jerks savagely at the wheel and bolts forward, muttering to himself as he rockets along the shoulder and down the nearest off-ramp. Julian hangs on, feeling curiously detached, as they weave in and out of traffic and the streets become increasingly familiar. And then the cab swings into his block and he's there. Home. His heart begins to pound in his chest.

He doesn't know what he's been expecting—banners, brass bands, Marsha embracing him joyously on the front steps of an immaculate house—but as he climbs out of the cab to survey his domain, he can't help feeling a tug of disappointment: the place looks pretty much the same, gray flanks, white trim, a thin sorry plume of bougainvillea clutching at the trellis over the door. But then it hits him: the lawn ornaments are gone. The tiki torches, the plaster pickaninnies and flag holders and all the rest of the outdoor claptrap have vanished as if into the maw of some brooding tropical storm, and for that he's thankful. Deeply thankful. He stands there a moment, amazed at the expanse of the lawn, plain simple grass, each blade a revelation—he never dreamed he had this much grass. The place looks the way it did when they bought it, wondering naively if it would be too big for just the two of them.

He saunters up the walk like a prospective buyer, admiring the house, truly admiring it, for the first time in years. How crisp it looks, how spare and uncluttered! She's a genius, he's thinking, she really is, as he mounts the front steps fingering his keys and humming, actually humming. But then, standing there in the quickening sun, he glances through the window and sees that the porch is empty—swept clean, not a thing left behind—and the tune goes sour in his throat. That's a surprise. A real surprise. He would have thought she'd leave something—the wicker set, the planters, a lamp or two—but even the curtains are gone. In fact, he realizes with a shock, none of the windows seem to have curtains—or blinds, either. What is she thinking? Is she crazy?

Cursing under his breath, he jabs the key in the lock and twists, but nothing happens. He jerks it back out, angry now, impatient, and examines the flat shining indented surface: no, it's the right key, the same key he's been using for sixteen years. Once again. Nothing. It won't even turn. The truth, ugly, frightening, has begun to dawn on him, even as he swings round on his heels and finds himself staring into the black unblinking gaze of Susan Certaine.

"You, you changed the locks," he accuses, and his hands are trembling.

Susan Certaine merely stands there, the briefcase at her feet, two mammoth softbound books clutched under her arms, books the size of unabridged dictionaries. She's in black, as usual, a no-nonsense business suit growing out of sensible heels, her cheeks brushed ever so faintly with blusher. "A little early, aren't we?" she says.

"You changed the locks."

She waits a beat, unhurried, in control. "What did you expect? We really can't have people interfering with our cataloguing, can we? You'd be surprised how desperate some people get, Mr. Laxner. And when you ran out on your therapy...well, we just couldn't take the chance." A thin pinched smile. "Not to worry: I've got your new keys right here—two sets, one for you and one for Marsha."

Her heels click on the pavement, three businesslike strides, and she's standing right beside him on the steps, crowding him. "Here, will you take these, please?" she says, dumping the books in his arms and digging into her briefcase for the keys.

The books are like dumbbells, scrap iron, so heavy he can feel the pull in his shoulders. "God, they're heavy," Julian mutters. "What are they?"

She fits the key in the lock and pauses, her face inches from his. "Your life, Mr. Laxner. The biography of your things. Did you know that you owned five hundred and fifty-two wire hangers, sixty-seven wooden ones and one hundred and sixty-nine plastic? Over two hundred flowerpots? Six hundred doilies? Potholders, Mr. Laxner. You logged in over one hundred twenty—can you imagine that? Can you imagine anyone needing a hundred and twenty potholders? Excess, Mr. Laxner," and he watches her lip curl. "Filthy excess."

The key takes, the tumblers turn, the door swings open. "Here you are, Mr. Laxner, *organization,*" she cries, throwing her arms out. "Welcome to your new life."

Staggering under the burden of his catalogues, Julian moves across the barren porch and into the house, and here he has a second shock: the place is empty. Denuded. There's nothing left, not even a chair to sit in. Bewildered, he turns to her, but she's already moving past him, whirling round the room, her arms spread wide. He's begun to sweat. The scent of Sen-Sen hangs heavy in the air. "But, but there's nothing here," he stammers, bending down to set the catalogues on the stripped floorboards. "I thought...well, I thought you'd pare it down, organize things so we could live here more comfortably, adjust, I mean—"

"Halfway measures, Mr. Laxner?" she says, skating up to him on the newly waxed floors. "Are halfway measures going to save a man—and woman—who own three hundred and nine bookends, forty-seven rocking chairs, over two thousand plates, cups and saucers? This is tabula rasa, Mr. Laxner, square one. Did you know you owned a hundred and thirty-seven dead penlight batteries? Do you really need a hundred and thirty-seven dead penlight batteries, Mr. Laxner? Do you?"

"No, but"—backing off now, distraught, his den, his den—"but we need the basics, at least. Furniture. A TV. My, my textbooks. My scopes."

The light through the unshaded windows is harsh, unforgiving. Every corner is left naked to scrutiny, every board, every nail. "All taken care of, Mr. Laxner, no problem." Susan Certaine stands there in the glare of the window, hands on her hips. "Each couple is allowed to reclaim one item per day from the warehouse—anything you like—for a period of sixty days. Depending on how you exercise your options, that could be as many as sixty items. Most couples request a bed first, and to accommodate them, we consider a bed one item—mattress, box spring, headboard and all."

Julian is stunned. "Sixty items? You're joking."

"I never joke, Mr. Laxner. Never."

"And what about the rest—the furniture, the stereo, our clothes?"

"Read your contract, Mr. Laxner."

He can feel himself slipping. "I don't want to read the contract, damn it. I asked you a question."

"Page two hundred and seventy-eight, paragraph two. I quote: 'After expiration of the sixty-day grace period, all items to be sold at auction, the proceeds going to Certaine Enterprises, Inc., for charitable distribution, charities to be chosen at the sole discretion of the above-named corporation.'" Her eyes are on him, severe, hateful, bright with triumph. This is what it's all about, this—cutting people down to size, squashing them. "You'd be surprised how many couples never recall a thing, not a single item."

"No," Julian says, stalking across the room, "no, I won't stand for it. I won't. I'll sue."

She shrugs. "I won't even bother to remind you to listen to yourself. You're like the brat on the playground—you don't like the way the game goes, you take your bat and ball and go home, right? Go ahead, sue. You'll find it won't be so easy. You signed the contract, Mr. Laxner. Both of you."

There's a movement in the open doorway. Shadow and light. Marsha. Marsha and Dr. Hauskopf, frozen there on the doorstep, watching. "Julian," Marsha cries, and then she's in his arms, clinging to him as if he were the last thing in the world, the only thing left her.

Dr. Doris and Susan Certaine exchange a look. "Be happy," Susan Certaine says after a moment. "Think of that couple in Ethiopia." And then they're gone.

Julian doesn't know how long he stands there, in the middle of that barren room in the silence of that big empty house, holding Marsha, holding his wife, but when he shuts his eyes he sees only the sterile deeps of space, the remotest regions beyond even the reach of light. And he knows this: it is cold out there, inhospitable, alien. There's nothing there, nothing contained in nothing. Nothing at all.

AMY HEMPEL
(b. 1951)

Born in Chicago and a longtime resident of New York City, Amy Hempel is the author of several collections of short stories including Reasons to Live (1985), At the Gates of the Animal Kingdom (1990), The Dog of the Marriage (2005), *and the novella* Tumble Home (1997). *Her celebrated* Collected Stories *(2006) was one of the* New York Times *Ten Best Books of the Year and a finalist for the PEN/Faulkner award. Hempel has received a number of distinguished awards including a literature award from the American Academy of Arts and Letters, a Guggenheim Fellowship, a United States Artists Fellowship, and an Ambassador Book Award.*

Known for her dedication to the training of service dogs, Hempel is the editor of Unleashed: Poems by Writers' Dogs *(1999). Uncanny relationships between human beings and dogs irradiate Hempel's work as brilliantly as her depictions of the drama of human relationships. Her work, as Hempel has described it, is akin to poetry: her stories are built around final lines, and are as tautly constructed as poems. Her contemporary Chuck Palahniuck has said of Amy Hempel that one of the lessons to be learned from her prose is: "You will never write so well."*

A devoted teacher, currently teaching at Harvard, Amy Hempel encourages young writers to seek out volunteer work, to put them into direct contact with experience. In her work she is fascinated by "moments when power shifts between two people, or moments when something small but encompassing happens." Both motives are stunningly realized in the ironically titled "Today Will Be a Quiet Day."

Today Will Be a Quiet Day

"I think it's the other way around," the boy said. "I think if the quake hit now the *bridge* would collapse and the *ramps* would be left."

He looked at his sister with satisfaction.

"You are just trying to scare your sister," the father said. "You know that is not true."

"No, really," the boy insisted, "and I heard birds in the middle of the night. Isn't that a warning?"

The girl gave her brother a toxic look and ate a handful of Raisinets. The three of them were stalled in traffic on the Golden Gate Bridge.

That morning, before waking his children, the father had canceled their music lessons and decided to make a day of it. He wanted to know how they were, is all. Just—how were they. He thought his kids were as self-contained as one of those dogs you sometimes see carrying home its own leash. But you could read things wrong.

Could you ever.

The boy had a friend who jumped from a floor of Langley Porter. The friend had been there for two weeks, mostly playing Ping-Pong. All the friend said the day the boy visited and lost every game was never play Ping-Pong with a mental patient because it's all we do and we'll kill you. That night the friend had cut the red belt he wore in two and left the other half on his bed.

That was this time last year when the boy was twelve years old.

You think you're safe, the father thought, but it's thinking you're invisible because you closed your eyes.

This day they were headed for Peta.luma—the chicken, egg, and arm-wrestling capital of the nation—for lunch. The father had offered to take them to the men's arm-wrestling semifinals. But it was said that arm-wrestling wasn't so interesting since the new safety precautions, that hardly anyone broke an arm or a wrist anymore. The best anyone could hope to see would be dislocation, so they said they would rather go to Pete's. Pete's was a gas station turned into a place to eat. The hamburgers there were named after cars, and the gas pumps in front still pumped gas.

"Can I have one?" the boy asked, meaning the Raisinets.

"No," his sister said.

"Can I have two?"

"Neither of you should be eating candy before lunch," the father said. He said it with the good sport of a father who enjoys his kids and gets a kick out of saying Dad things.

"You mean dinner," said the girl. "It will be dinner before we get to Pete's."

Only the northbound lanes were stopped. Southbound traffic flashed past at the normal speed.

"Check it out," the boy said from the back seat. "Did you see the bumper sticker on that Porsche? 'If you don't like the way I drive, stay off the sidewalk.'"

He spoke directly to his sister. "I've just solved my Christmas shopping."

"I got the highest score in my class in Driver's Ed," she said.

"I thought I would let your sister drive home today," the father said.

From the back seat came sirens, screams for help, and then a dirge.

The girl spoke to her father in a voice rich with complicity. "Don't people make you want to give up?"

"Don't the two of you know any jokes? I haven't laughed all day," the father said.

"Did I tell you the guillotine joke?" the girl said.

"He hasn't laughed all day, so you must've," her brother said.

The girl gave her brother a look you could iron clothes with. Then her gaze dropped down. "Oh-oh," she said, "Johnny's out of jail."

Her brother zipped his pants back up. He said, "Tell the joke."

"Two Frenchmen and a Belgian were about to be beheaded," the girl began. "The first Frenchman was led to the block and blindfolded. The executioner let the blade go. But it stopped a quarter inch above the Frenchman's neck. So he was allowed to go free, and ran off shouting, *'C'est un miracle! C'est un miracle!'*"

"What does that mean?" her brother asked.

"It's a miracle," the father said.

"Then the second Frenchman was led to the block, and same thing—the blade stopped just before cutting off his head. So *he* got to go free, and ran off shouting *'C'est un miracle!'*

"Finally the Belgian was led to the block. But before they could blindfold him, he looked up, pointed to the guillotine, and cried, *'Voilà la difficulté!'*"

She doubled over.

"Maybe *I* would be wetting *my* pants if I knew what that meant," the boy said.

"You can't explain after the punchline," the girl said, "and have it still be funny."

"There's the problem," said the father.

The waitress handed out menus to the party of three seated in the corner booth of what used to be the lube bay. She told them the specialty of the day was Moroccan chicken.

"That's what I want," the boy said, "Morerotten chicken."

But he changed his order to a Studeburger and fries after his father and sister had ordered.

"So," the father said, "who misses music lessons?"

"I'm serious about what I asked you last week," the girl said. "About switching to piano? My teacher says a real flutist only breathes with the stomach, and I can't."

"The real reason she wants to change," said the boy, "is her waist will get two inches bigger when she learns to stomach-breathe. That's what *else* her teacher said."

The boy buttered a piece of sourdough bread and flipped a chunk of cold butter onto his sister's sleeve.

"Jeezo-beezo," the girl said, "why don't they skip the knife and fork and just set his place with a slingshot!"

"Who will ever adopt you if you don't mind your manners?" the father said. "Maybe we could try a little quiet today."

"You sound like your tombstone," the girl said. "Remember what you wanted it to say?"

Her brother joined in with his mouth full: "Today will be a quiet day."

"Because it never is with us around," the boy said.

"You guys," said the father.

The waitress brought plates. The father passed sugar to the boy and salt to the girl without being asked. He watched the girl shake out salt onto the fries.

"If I had a sore throat, I would gargle with those," he said.

"Looks like she's trying to melt a driveway," the boy offered.

The father watched his children eat. They ate fast. They called it Hoovering. He finished while they sucked at straws in empty drinks.

"Funny," he said thoughtfully, "I'm not hungry anymore."

Every meal ended this way. It was his benediction, one of the Dad things they expected him to say.

"That reminds me," the girl said. "Did you feed Rocky before we left?"

"Uh-uh," her brother said. "I fed him yesterday."

"*I* fed him yesterday!" the girl said.

"Okay, we'll compromise," the boy said. "We won't feed the cat today."

"I'd say you are out of bounds on that one," the father said.

He meant you could not tease her about animals. Once, during dinner, that cat ran into the dining room shot from guns. He ran around the table at top speed, then spun out on the parquet floor into a leg of the table. He fell onto his side and made short coughing sounds. "Isn't he smart?" the girl had crooned, kneeling beside him. "He knows he's hurt."

For years, her father had to say that the animals seen on shoulders of roads were napping.

"He never would have not fed Homer," she said to her father.

"Homer was a dog," the boy said. "If I forgot to feed him, he could just go into the hills and bite a deer."

"Or a Campfire Girl selling candy at the front door," their father reminded them.

"Homer," the girl sighed. "I hope he likes chasing sheep on that ranch in the mountains."

The boy looked at her, incredulous.

"You *believed* that? You actually *believed* that?"

In her head, a clumsy magician yanked the cloth and the dishes all crashed to the floor. She took air into her lungs until they filled, and then she filled her stomach, too.

"I thought she knew," the boy said.

The dog was five years ago.

"The girl's parents insisted," the father said. "It's the law in California."

"Then I hate California," she said. "I hate its guts."

The boy said he would wait for them in the car, and left the table.

"What would help?" the father asked.

"For Homer to be alive," she said.

"What would help?"

"Nothing."

"Help."

She pinched a trail of salt on her plate.

"A ride," she said. "I'll drive."

"The girl started the car and screamed. "Goddammit!"

With the power off, the boy had tuned in the Spanish station. Mariachis exploded on ignition.

"Dammit isn't God's last name," the boy said, quoting another bumper sticker.

"Don't people make you want to give up?" the father said.

"No talking," the girl said to the rearview mirror, and put the car in gear.

She drove for hours. Through groves of eucalyptus with their damp peeling bark, past acacia bushes with yellow flowers pulsing off their stems. She cut over to the coast route and the stony gray-green tones of Inverness.

"What you'd call scenic," the boy tried.

Otherwise, they were quiet.

No one said anything else until the sky started to close, and then it was the boy again, asking shouldn't they be going home.

"No, no," the father said, and made a show of looking out the window, up at the sky and back at his watch. "No," he said, "keep driving—it's getting earlier."

But the sky spilled rain, and the girl headed south towards the bridge. She turned on the headlights and the dashboard lit up green. She read off the odometer on the way home: "Twenty-six thousand, three hundred eighty-three and eight-tenths miles."

"Today?" the boy said.

The boy got to Rocky first. "Let's play the cat," he said, and carried the Siamese to the upright piano. He sat on the bench holding the cat in his lap and pressed its paws to the keys. Rocky played "Born Free." He tried to twist away.

"Come on, Rocky, ten more minutes and we'll break."

"Give him to me," the girl said.

She puckered up and gave the cat a five-lipper.

"Bring the Rock upstairs," the father called. "Bring sleeping bags, too."

Pretty soon three sleeping bags formed a triangle in the master bedroom. The father was the hypotenuse. The girl asked him to brush out her hair, which he did while the boy ate a tangerine, peeling it up close to his face, inhaling the mist. Then he held each segment to the light to find seeds. In his lap, cat paws fluttered like dreaming eyes.

"What are you thinking?" the father asked.

"Me?" the girl said. "Fifty-seven T-bird, white with red interior, convertible. I drive it to Texas and wear skirts with rick-rack. I'm changing my name to Ruby," she said, "or else Easy."

The father considered her dream of a checkered future.

"Early ripe, early rot," he warned.

A wet wind slammed the window in its warped sash, and the boy jumped.

"I hate rain," he said. "I hate its guts."

The father got up and closed the window tighter against the storm. "It's a real frog-choker," he said.

In darkness, lying still, it was no less camplike than if they had been under the stars singing to a stone-ringed fire burned down to embers.

They had already said good-night some minutes earlier when the boy and girl heard their father's voice in the dark.

"Kids, I just remembered—I have some good news and some bad news. Which do you want first?"

It was his daughter who spoke. "Let's get it over with," she said. "Let's get the bad news over with."

The father smiled. They are all right, he decided. My kids are as right as this rain. He smiled at the exact spots he knew their heads were turned to his, and doubted he would ever feel—not better, but *more* than he did now.

"I lied," he said. "There is no bad news."

LOUISE ERDRICH
(b. 1954)

Louise Erdrich was born in Little Falls, Minnesota, of German-American and Native American parents. She grew up in North Dakota, the mythopoetic setting for much of her fiction, received her bachelor's degree from Dartmouth, and returned to teach in the Poetry in the Schools program in North Dakota. She then studied in the writing program at Johns Hopkins University. In 1981 she was married to the writer Michael Dorris, also of Native American descent; they lived in New Hampshire where both she and Dorris were associated with Dartmouth University. Though Erdrich and Dorris allegedly collaborated on many fiction projects, the sole collaborative novel attributed to both is The Crown of Columbus *(1991).*

Like a number of other writers in this volume, Louise Erdrich is a stylist whose language, while certainly prose, possesses the bold metaphors and musical cadences of poetry. "Fleur," included here, is a magical tale overlaid with a vision of history that is unsentimental and unsparing; it begins the author's account of the legendary Fleur Pillager, a figure of power and destructiveness, who is a presence, as an ancestor, in other, linked work by the author. Fleur and other members of two families of the Turtle Mountain Chippewas are the protagonists of a projected tetralogy set between 1912–1984, consisting so far of Love Medicine *(1984),* The Beet Queen *(1986), and* Tracks *(1988), in which "Fleur" appears. The version of "Fleur" presented here appeared originally in* Esquire, *in 1986.*

Louise Erdrich is the author of a number of acclaimed novels in addition to those cited: The Bingo Palace *(1994),* The Antelope Wife *(1998),* The Painted Drum *(2005), and* Shadow Tag *(2010). Among her many literary awards are a Guggenheim fellowship, an O. Henry Award, a World Fantasy Award, and an award from the National Book Critics Circle for* Love Medicine.

Erdrich is a magical realist ideally gifted to mediate between the Native American world and the Caucasian world. Her use of meticulously linked stories that form novels, and individual novels that, in sequence, provide an ongoing history of a time and a place, has proven a brilliant writerly strategy for one chronicling the difficult and often tragic history of Native North Americans.

Fleur

The first time she drowned in the cold and glassy waters of Lake Turcot, Fleur Pillager was only a girl. Two men saw the boat tip, saw her struggle in the waves. They rowed over to the place she went down, and jumped in. When they dragged her over the gunwales, she was cold to the touch and stiff, so they slapped her face, shook her by the heels, worked her arms back and forth, and pounded her back until she coughed up lake water. She shivered all over like a dog, then took a breath. But it wasn't long afterward that those two men disappeared. The first wandered off, and the other, Jean Hat, got himself run over by a cart.

It went to show, my grandma said. It figured to her, all right. By saving Fleur Pillager, those two men had lost themselves.

The next time she fell in the lake, Fleur Pillager was twenty years old and no one touched her. She washed onshore, her skin a dull dead gray, but when George Many Women bent to look closer, he saw her chest move. Then her eyes spun open, sharp black riprock, and she looked at him. "You'll take my place," she hissed. Everybody scattered and left her there, so no one knows how she dragged herself home. Soon after that we noticed Many Women changed, grew afraid, wouldn't leave his house, and would not be forced to go near water. For his caution, he lived until the day that his sons brought him a new tin bathtub. Then the first time he used the tub he slipped, got knocked out, and breathed water while his wife stood in the other room frying breakfast.

Men stayed clear of Fleur Pillager after the second drowning. Even though she was good-looking, nobody dared to court her because it was clear that Misshepeshu, the waterman, the monster, wanted her for himself. He's a devil, that one, love-hungry with desire and maddened for the touch of young girls, the strong and daring especially, the ones like Fleur.

Our mothers warn us that we'll think he's handsome, for he appears with green eyes, copper skin, a mouth tender as a child's. But if you fall into his arms, he sprouts horns, fangs, claws, fins. His feet are joined as one and his skin, brass scales, rings to the touch. You're fascinated, cannot move. He casts a shell necklace at your feet, weeps gleaming chips that harden into mica on your breasts. He holds you under. Then he takes the body of a lion or a fat brown worm. He's made of gold. He's made of beach moss. He's a thing of dry foam, a thing of death by drowning, the death a Chippewa cannot survive.

Unless you are Fleur Pillager. We all knew she couldn't swim. After the first time, we thought she'd never go back to Lake Turcot. We thought she'd keep to herself, live quiet, stop killing men off by drowning in the lake. After the first time, we thought she'd keep the good ways. But then, after the second drowning, we knew that we were dealing with something much more serious. She was haywire, out of control. She messed with evil, laughed at the old women's advice, and dressed like a man. She got herself into some half-forgotten medicine, studied ways we shouldn't talk about. Some say she kept the finger of a child in her pocket and a powder of unborn rabbits in a leather thong around her neck. She laid the heart of an owl on her tongue so she could see at night, and went out, hunting, not even in her own body. We know for sure because the next morning, in the snow or dust, we followed the tracks of her bare feet and saw where they changed, where the claws sprang out, the pad broadened and pressed into the dirt. By night we heard her chuffing cough, the bear cough. By day her silence and the wide grin she threw to bring down our guard made us frightened. Some thought that Fleur Pillager should be driven off the reservation, but not a single person who spoke like this had the nerve. And finally, when people were just about to get together and throw her out, she left on her own and didn't come back all summer. That's what this story is about.

During that summer, when she lived a few miles south in Argus, things happened. She almost destroyed that town.

When she got down to Argus in the year of 1920, it was just a small grid of six streets on either side of the railroad depot. There were two elevators, one central, the other a few miles west. Two stores competed for the trade of the three hundred citizens, and three churches quarreled with one another for their souls. There was a frame building for Lutherans, a heavy brick one for Episcopalians, and a long narrow shingled Catholic church. This last had a tall slender steeple, twice as high as any building or tree.

No doubt, across the low, flat wheat, watching from the road as she came near Argus on foot, Fleur saw that steeple rise, a shadow thin as a needle. Maybe in that raw space it drew her the way a lone tree draws lightning. Maybe, in the end, the Catholics are to blame. For if she hadn't seen that sign of pride, that slim prayer, that marker, maybe she would have kept walking.

But Fleur Pillager turned, and the first place she went once she came into town was to the back door of the priest's residence attached to the landmark church. She didn't go there for a handout, although she got that, but to ask for work. She got that too, or the town got her. It's hard to tell which came out worse, her or the men or the town, although the upshot of it all was that Fleur lived.

The four men who worked at the butcher's had carved up about a thousand carcasses between them, maybe half of that steers and the other half pigs, sheep, and game animals like deer, elk, and bear. That's not even mentioning the chickens, which were beyond counting. Pete Kozka owned the place, and employed Lily Veddar, Tor Grunewald, and my stepfather, Dutch James, who had brought my mother down from the reservation the year before she disappointed him by dying. Dutch took me out of school to take her place. I kept house half the time and worked the other in the butcher shop, sweeping floors, putting sawdust down, running a hambone across the street to a customer's bean pot or a package of sausage to the corner. I was a good one to have around because until they needed me, I was invisible. I blended into the stained brown walls, a skinny, big-nosed girl with staring eyes. Because I could fade into a corner or squeeze beneath a shelf, I knew everything, what the men said when no one was around, and what they did to Fleur.

Kozka's Meats served farmers for a fifty-mile area, both to slaughter, for it had a stock pen and chute, and to cure the meat by smoking it or spicing it in sausage. The storage locker was a marvel, made of many thicknesses of brick, earth insulation, and Minnesota timber, lined inside with sawdust and vast blocks of ice cut from Lake Turcot, hauled down from home each winter by horse and sledge.

A ramshackle board building, part slaughterhouse, part store, was fixed to the low, thick square of the lockers. That's where Fleur worked. Kozka hired her for her strength. She could lift a haunch or carry a pole of sausages without stumbling, and she soon learned cutting from Pete's wife, a string-thin blonde who chain-smoked and handled the razor-sharp knives with nerveless precision, slicing close to her stained fingers. Fleur and Fritzie Kozka worked afternoons, wrapping their cuts in paper, and Fleur hauled the packages to the lockers. The meat was left outside the heavy oak doors that were only opened at 5:00 each afternoon, before the men ate supper.

Sometimes Dutch, Tor, and Lily ate at the lockers, and when they did I stayed too, cleaned floors, restoked the fires in the front smokehouses, while the men sat around the squat cast-iron stove spearing slats of herring onto hardtack bread. They played long games of poker or cribbage on a board made from the planed end of a salt crate. They talked and I listened, although there wasn't much to hear since almost nothing ever happened in Argus. Tor was married, Dutch had lost my mother, and Lily read circulars. They mainly discussed about the auctions to come, equipment, or women.

Every so often, Pete Kozka came out front to make a whist, leaving Fritzie to smoke cigarettes and fry raised doughnuts in the back room. He sat and played a few rounds but kept his thoughts to himself. Fritzie did not tolerate him talking behind her back, and the one book he read was the New Testament. If he said something, it concerned weather or a surplus of sheep stomachs, a ham that smoked green or the markets for corn and wheat. He had a good-luck talisman, the opal-white lens of a cow's eye. Playing cards, he rubbed it between his fingers. That soft sound and the slap of cards was about the only conversation.

Fleur finally gave them a subject.

Her cheeks were wide and flat, her hands large, chapped, muscular. Fleur's shoulders were broad as beams, her hips fishlike, slippery, narrow. An old green dress clung to her waist, worn thin where she sat. Her braids were thick like the tails of animals, and swung against her when she moved, deliberately, slowly in her work, held in and half-tamed, but only half. I could tell, but the others never saw. They never looked into her sly brown eyes or noticed her teeth, strong and curved and very white. Her legs were bare, and since she padded around in beadwork moccasins they never saw that her fifth toes were missing. They never knew she'd drowned. They were blinded, they were stupid, they only saw her in the flesh.

And yet it wasn't just that she was a Chippewa, or even that she was a woman, it wasn't that she was good-looking or even that she was alone that made their brains hum. It was how she played cards.

Women didn't usually play with men, so the evening that Fleur drew a chair up to the men's table without being so much as asked, there was a shock of surprise.

"What's this," said Lily. He was fat, with a snake's cold pale eyes and precious skin, smooth and lily-white, which is how he got his name. Lily had a dog, a stumpy mean little bull of a thing with a belly drum-tight from eating pork rinds. The dog liked to play cards just like Lily, and straddled his barrel thighs through games of stud, rum poker, *vingt-un*. The dog snapped at Fleur's arm that first night, but cringed back, its snarl frozen, when she took her place.

"I thought," she said, her voice soft and stroking, "you might deal me in."

There was a space between the heavy bin of spiced flour and the wall where I just fit. I hunkered down there, kept my eyes open, saw her black hair swing over the chair, her feet solid on the wood floor. I couldn't see up on the table where the cards slapped down, so after they were deep in their game I raised myself up in the shadows, and crouched on a sill of wood.

I watched Fleur's hands stack and ruffle, divide the cards, spill them to each player in a blur, rake them up and shuffle again. Tor, short and scrappy, shut one eye and squinted the other at Fleur. Dutch screwed his lips around a wet cigar.

"Gotta see a man," he mumbled, getting up to go out back to the privy. The others broke, put their cards down, and Fleur sat alone in the lamplight that glowed in a sheen across the push of her breasts. I watched her closely, then she paid me a beam of notice for the first time. She turned, looked straight at me, and grinned the white wolf grin a Pillager turns on its victims, except that she wasn't after me.

"Pauline there," she said, "how much money you got?"

We'd all been paid for the week that day. Eight cents was in my pocket.

"Stake me," she said, holding out her long fingers. I put the coins in her palm and then I melted back to nothing, part of the walls and tables. It was a long time before I understood that the men would not have seen me no matter what I did, how I moved. I wasn't anything like Fleur. My dress hung loose and my back was already curved, an old woman's. Work had roughened me, reading made my eyes sore, caring for my mother before she died had hardened my face. I was not much to look at, so they never saw me.

When the men came back and sat around the table, they had drawn together. They shot each other small glances, stuck their tongues in their cheeks, burst out laughing at odd moments, to rattle Fleur. But she never minded. They played their *vingt-un*, staying even as Fleur slowly gained. Those pennies I had given her drew nickels and attracted dimes until there was a small pile in front of her.

Then she hooked them with five-card draw, nothing wild. She dealt, discarded, drew, and then she sighed and her cards gave a little shiver. Tor's eye gleamed, and Dutch straightened in his seat.

"I'll pay to see that hand," said Lily Veddar.

Fleur showed, and she had nothing there, nothing at all.

Tor's thin smile cracked open, and he threw his hand in too.

"Well, we know one thing," he said, leaning back in his chair, "the squaw can't bluff."

With that I lowered myself into a mound of swept sawdust and slept. I woke up during the night, but none of them had moved yet, so I couldn't either. Still later, the men must have gone out again, or Fritzie come out to break the game, because I was lifted, soothed, cradled in a woman's arms and rocked so quiet that I kept my eyes shut while Fleur rolled me into a closet of grimy ledgers, oiled paper, balls of string, and thick files that fit beneath me like a mattress.

The game went on after work the next evening. I got my eight cents back five times over, and Fleur kept the rest of the dollar she'd won for a stake. This time they didn't play so late, but they played regular, and then kept going at it night after night. They played poker now, or variations, for one week straight, and each time Fleur won exactly one dollar, no more and no less, too consistent for luck.

By this time, Lily and the other men were so lit with suspense that they got Pete to join the game with them. They concentrated, the fat dog sitting tense in Lily Veddar's lap, Tor suspicious, Dutch stroking his huge square brow, Pete steady. It wasn't that Fleur won that hooked them in so, because she lost hands too. It was rather that she never had a freak hand or even anything above a straight. She only took on her low cards, which didn't sit right. By chance, Fleur should have gotten a full or flush by now. The irritating thing was she beat with pairs and never bluffed, because she couldn't, and still she ended up each night with exactly one dollar. Lily couldn't believe, first of all, that a woman could be smart enough to play cards, but even if she was, that she would then be stupid enough to cheat for a dollar a night. By day I watched him turn the problem over, his hard white face dull, small fingers probing at his knuckles, until he finally thought he had Fleur figured out as a bit-time player, caution her game. Raising the stakes would throw her.

More than anything now, he wanted Fleur to come away with something but a dollar. Two bits less or ten more, the sum didn't matter, just so he broke her streak.

Night after night she played, won her dollar, and left to stay in a place that just Fritzie and I knew about. Fleur bathed in the slaughtering tub, then slept in the unused brick smokehouse behind the lockers, a windowless place tarred on the inside with scorched fats. When I brushed against her skin I noticed that she smelled of the walls, rich and woody, slightly burnt. Since that night she put me in the closet I was no longer afraid of her, but followed her close, stayed with her, became her moving shadow that the men never noticed, the shadow that could have saved her.

August, the month that bears fruit, closed around the shop, and Pete and Fritzie left for Minnesota to escape the heat. Night by night, running, Fleur had won thirty dollars, but only Pete's presence had kept Lily at bay. But Pete was gone now, and one payday, with the heat so bad no one could move but Fleur, the men sat and played and waited while she finished work. The cards sweat, limp in their fingers, the table was slick with grease, and even the walls were warm to the touch. The air was motionless. Fleur was in the next room boiling heads.

Her green dress, drenched, wrapped her like a transparent sheet. A skin of lakeweed. Black snarls of veining clung to her arms. Her braids were loose, half-unraveled, tied behind her neck in a thick loop. She stood in steam, turning skulls through a vat with a wooden paddle. When scraps boiled to the surface, she bent with a round tin sieve and scooped them out. She'd filled two dishpans.

"Ain't that enough now?" called Lily. "We're waiting." The stump of a dog trembled in his lap, alive with rage. It never smelled me or noticed me above Fleur's smoky skin. The air was heavy in my corner, and pressed me down. Fleur sat with them.

"Now what do you say?" Lily asked the dog. It barked. That was the signal for the real game to start.

"Let's up the ante," said Lily, who had been stalking this night all month. He had a roll of money in his pocket. Fleur had five bills in her dress. The men had each saved their full pay.

"Ante a dollar then," said Fleur, and pitched hers in. She lost, but they let her scrape along, cent by cent. And then she won some. She played unevenly, as if chance was all she had. She reeled them in. The game went on. The dog was stiff now, poised on Lily's knees, a ball of vicious muscle with its yellow eyes slit in concentration. It gave advice, seemed to sniff the lay of Fleur's cards, twitched and nudged. Fleur was up, then down, saved by a scratch. Tor dealt seven cards, three down. The pot grew, round by round, until it held all the money. Nobody folded. Then it all rode on one last card and they went silent. Fleur picked hers up and blew a long breath. The heat lowered like a bell. Her card shook, but she stayed in.

Lily smiled and took the dog's head tenderly between his palms.

"Say, Fatso," he said, crooning the words, "you reckon that girl's bluffing?"

The dog whined and Lily laughed. "Me too," he said, "let's show." He swept his bills and coins into the pot and then they turned their cards over.

Lily looked once, looked again, then he squeezed the dog up like a fist of dough and slammed it on the table.

Fleur threw her arms out and drew the money over, grinning that same wolf grin that she'd used on me, the grin that had them. She jammed the bills in her dress, scooped the coins up in waxed white paper that she tied with string.

"Let's go another round," said Lily, his voice choked with burrs. But Fleur opened her mouth and yawned, then walked out back to gather slops for the one big hog that was waiting in the stock pen to be killed.

The men sat still as rocks, their hands spread on the oiled wood table. Dutch had chewed his cigar to damp shreds. Tor's eye was dull. Lily's gaze was the only one to follow Fleur. I didn't move. I felt them gathering, saw my stepfather's veins, the ones in his forehead that stood out in anger. The dog had rolled off the table and curled in a knot below the counter, where none of the men could touch it.

Lily rose and stepped out back to the closet of ledgers where Pete kept his private stock. He brought back a bottle, uncorked and tipped it between his fingers. The lump in his throat moved, then he passed it on. They drank, quickly felt the whiskey's fire, and planned with their eyes things they couldn't say out loud.

When they left, I followed. I hid out back in the clutter of broken boards and chicken crates beside the stock pen, where they waited. Fleur could not be seen at first, and then the moon broke and showed her, slipping cautiously along the rough board chute with a bucket in her hand. Her hair fell, wild and coarse, to her waist, and her dress was a floating patch in the dark. She made a pig-calling sound, rang the tin pail lightly against the wood, froze suspiciously. But too late. In the sound of the ring Lily moved, fat and nimble, stepped right behind Fleur and put out his creamy hands. At his first touch, she whirled and doused him with the bucket of sour slops. He pushed her against the big fence and the package of coins split, went clinking and jumping, winked against the wood. Fleur rolled over once and vanished in the yard.

The moon fell behind a curtain of ragged clouds, and Lily followed into the dark muck. But he tripped, pitched over the huge flank of the pig, who lay mired to the snout, heavily snoring. I sprang out of the weeds and climbed the side of the pen, stuck like glue. I saw the sow rise to her neat, knobby knees, gain her balance, and sway, curious, as Lily stumbled forward. Fleur had backed into the angle of rough wood just beyond, and when Lily tried to jostle past, the sow tipped up on her hind legs and struck, quick and hard as a snake. She plunged her head into Lily's thick side and snatched a mouthful of his shirt. She lunged again, caught him lower, so that he grunted in pained surprise. He seemed to ponder, breathing deep. Then he launched his huge body in a swimmer's dive.

The sow screamed as his body smacked over hers. She rolled, striking out with her knife-sharp hooves, and Lily gathered himself upon her, took her foot-long face by the ears and scraped her snout and cheeks against the trestles of the pen. He hurled the sow's tight skull against an iron post, but instead of knocking her dead, he merely woke her from her dream.

She reared, shrieked, drew him with her so that they posed standing upright. They bowed jerkily to each other, as if to begin. Then his arms swung and flailed. She sank her black fangs into his shoulder, clasping him, dancing him forward and backward through the pen. Their steps picked up pace, went wild. The two dipped as one, box-stepped, tripped each other. She ran her split foot through his hair. He grabbed her kinked tail. They went down and came up, the same shape and then the same color, until the men couldn't tell one from the other in that light and Fleur was able to launch herself over the gates, swing down, hit gravel.

The men saw, yelled, and chased her at a dead run to the smokehouse. And Lily too, once the sow gave up in disgust and freed him. That is where I should have gone to Fleur, saved her, thrown myself on Dutch. But I went stiff with fear and couldn't unlatch myself from the trestles or move at all. I closed my eyes and put my head in my arms, tried to hide, so there is nothing to describe but what I couldn't block out. Fleur's hoarse breath, so loud it filled me, her cry in the old language, and my name repeated over and over among the words.

The heat was still dense the next morning when I came back to work. Fleur was gone but the men were there, slack-faced, hung over. Lily was paler and softer than ever, as if his flesh had steamed on his bones. They smoked, took pulls off a bottle. It wasn't noon yet. I worked awhile, waiting shop and sharpening steel. But I was sick, I was smothered, I was sweating so hard that my hands slipped on the knives, and I wiped my fingers clean of the greasy touch of the customers' coins. Lily opened his mouth and roared once, not in anger. There was no meaning to the sound. His boxer dog, sprawled limp beside his foot, never lifted its head. Nor did the other men.

They didn't notice when I stepped outside, hoping for a clear breath. And then I forgot them because I knew that we were all balanced, ready to tip, to fly, to be crushed as soon as the weather broke. The sky was so low that I felt the weight of it like a yoke. Clouds hung down, witch teats, a tornado's green-brown cones, and as I watched one flicked out and became a delicate probing thumb. Even as I picked up my heels and ran back inside, the wind blew suddenly, cold, and then came rain.

Inside, the men had disappeared already and the whole place was trembling as if a huge hand was pinched at the rafters, shaking it. I ran straight through, screaming for Dutch or for any of them, and then I stopped at the heavy doors of the lockers, where they had surely taken shelter. I stood there a moment. Everything went still. Then I heard a cry building in the wind, faint at first, a whistle and then a shrill scream that tore through the walls and gathered around me, spoke plain so I understood that I should move, put my arms out, and slam down the great iron bar that fit across the hasp and lock.

Outside, the wind was stronger, like a hand held against me. I struggled forward. The bushes tossed, the awnings flapped off storefronts, the rails of porches rattled. The odd cloud became a fat snout that nosed along the earth and sniffled, jabbed, picked at things, sucked them up, blew them apart, rooted around as if it was following a certain scent, then stopped behind me at the butcher shop and bored down like a drill.

I went flying, landed somewhere in a ball. When I opened my eyes and looked, stranger things were happening.

A herd of cattle flew through the air like giant birds, dropping dung, their mouths opened in stunned bellows. A candle, still lighted, blew past, and tables, napkins, garden tools, a whole school of drifting eyeglasses, jackets on hangers, hams, a checkerboard, a lampshade, and at last the sow from behind the lockers, on the run, her hooves a blur, set free, swooping, diving, screaming as everything in Argus fell apart and got turned upside down, smashed, and thoroughly wrecked.

Days passed before the town went looking for the men. They were bachelors, after all, except for Tor, whose wife had suffered a blow to the head that made her forgetful. Everyone was occupied with digging out, in high relief because even though the Catholic steeple had been torn off like a peaked cap and sent across five fields, those huddled in the cellar were unhurt. Walls had fallen, windows were demolished, but the stores were intact and so were the bankers and shop owners who had taken refuge in their safes or beneath their cash registers. It was a fair-minded disaster, no one could be said to have suffered much more than the next, at least not until Fritzie and Pete came home.

Of all the businesses in Argus, Kozka's Meats had suffered worst. The boards of the front building had been split to kindling, piled in a huge pyramid, and the shop equipment was blasted far and wide. Pete paced off the distance the iron bathtub had been flung—a hundred feet. The glass candy case went fifty, and landed without so much as a cracked pane. There were other surprises as well, for the back rooms where Fritzie and Pete lived were undisturbed. Fritzie said the dust still coated her china figures, and upon her kitchen table, in the ashtray, perched the last cigarette she'd put out in haste. She lit it up and finished it, looking through the window. From there, she could see that the old smokehouse Fleur had slept in was crushed to a reddish sand and the stockpens were completely torn apart, the rails stacked helter-skelter. Fritzie asked for Fleur. People shrugged. Then she asked about the others and, suddenly, the town understood that three men were missing.

There was a rally of help, a gathering of shovels and volunteers. We passed boards from hand to hand, stacked them, uncovered what lay beneath the pile of jagged splinters. The lockers, full of the meat that was Pete and Fritzie's investment, slowly came into sight, still intact. When enough room was made for a man to stand on the roof, there were calls, a general urge to hack through and see what lay below. But Fritzie shouted that she wouldn't allow it because the meat would spoil. And so the work continued, board by board, until at last the heavy oak doors of the freezer were revealed and people pressed to the entry. Everyone wanted to be the first, but since it was my stepfather lost, I was let go in when Pete and Fritzie wedged through into the sudden icy air.

Pete scraped a match on his boot, lit the lamp Fritzie held, and then the three of us stood still in its circle. Light glared off the skinned and hanging carcasses, the crates of wrapped sausages, the bright and cloudy blocks of lake ice, pure as winter. The cold bit into us, pleasant at first, then numbing. We must have stood there a couple of minutes before we saw the men, or more rightly, the humps of fur, the iced and shaggy hides they wore, the bearskins they had taken down and wrapped around themselves. We stepped closer and tilted the lantern beneath the flaps of fur into their faces. The dog was there, perched among them, heavy as a doorstop. The three had hunched around a barrel where the game was still laid out, and a dead lantern and an empty bottle, too. But they had thrown down their last hands and hunkered tight, clutching one another, knuckles raw from beating at the door they had also attacked with hooks. Frost stars gleamed off their eyelashes and the stubble of their beards. Their faces were set in concentration, mouths open as if to speak some careful thought, some agreement they'd come to in each other's arms.

Power travels in the bloodlines, handed out before birth. It comes down through the hands, which in the Pillagers were strong and knotted, big, spidery, and rough, with sensitive fingertips good at dealing cards. It comes through the eyes, too, belligerent, darkest brown, the eyes of those in the bear clan, impolite as they gaze directly at a person.

In my dreams, I look straight back at Fleur, at the men. I am no longer the watcher on the dark sill, the skinny girl.

The blood draws us back, as if it runs through a vein of earth. I've come home and, except for talking to my cousins, live a quiet life. Fleur lives quiet too, down on Lake Turcot with her boat. Some say she's married to the waterman, Misshepeshu, or that she's living in shame with white men or windigos, or that she's killed them all. I'm about the only one here who ever goes to visit her. Last winter, I went to help out in her cabin when she bore the child, whose green eyes and skin the color of an old penny made more talk, as no one could decide if the child was mixed blood or what, fathered in a smokehouse, or by a man with brass scales, or by the lake. The girl is bold, smiling in her sleep, as if she knows what people wonder, as if she hears the old men talk, turning the story over. It comes up different every time and has no ending, no beginning. They get the middle wrong too. They only know that they don't know anything.

JEFFREY FORD
(b. 1955)

Considering the richly atmospheric "gothic" tales that are characteristic of nineteenth-century American literature—stories in this volume by Washington Irving, William Austin, Nathaniel Hawthorne, Herman Melville, and Edgar Allan Poe—it is surprising that in more contemporary times, with virtually no exceptions, the "gothic" has become peripheral to what might be called mainstream "realist" fiction.

Jeffrey Ford, a six-time winner of the World Fantasy Award, the Grand Prix de l'Imaginaire (a French award for "fantastic" fiction), and a recent winner of the Shirley Jackson Award, is one of those difficult-to-define writers whose subject matter is both "surreal" and "realistic" depending upon one's perspective, and whose finely honed prose style is of a quality one would certainly call "literary." Ford's story, "The Drowned Life," included here, is a brilliantly depicted political/ personal nightmare of a kind that transcends labels of literary taxonomy.

Born in West Islip, Long Island, in 1955, Jeffrey Ford received his BA and MA degrees in English at SUNY Binghamton where he studied with the legendary teacher and inspirer-of-young-writers John Gardner. He dropped out of the PhD program at Temple University after nearly completing all his requirements and began teaching at Brookdale Community College, in Monmouth College, New Jersey, in 1988, where he has taught early American literature, composition, and fiction writing for nearly a quarter-century. Ford is the author of eight novels including The Physiognomy *(1997),* The Portrait of Mrs. Charbuque *(2002),* The Girl in the Glass *(2005), and* The Shadow Year *(2008) as well as three story collections including* The Empire of Ice Cream *(2005) and* The Drowned Life *(2008). Ford has published over a hundred short stories in such magazines as the* Magazine of Fantasy and Science Fiction, Weird Tales, *and* Fantasy Magazine; *his work has been collected in many anthologies including* The Dark, Inferno, Naked City, *and* Supernatural Noir *(all edited by Ellen Datlow),* Stories *(edited by Al Sarrantonio and Neil Gaiman), and* New Jersey Noir *(edited by Joyce*

Carol Oates) as well as numerous editions of The Year's Best Fantasy and Horror.

Like his gothic American predecessors, Jeffrey Ford is a visionary storyteller who has transmogrified the personal into the impersonal—into an idiosyncratic and disturbing art. Of "The Drowned Life" Ford has said: "I look at America and see it moving with the speed of a freight train out of hell straight down the toilet. [Our recent political history] has been a nightmare of torture, deceit, death on a grand scale, fear, and an economy run by thieves. Where's my flag lapel pin when I need it? The grim nature of it bubbles through you and into the fiction."

The Drowned Life

1

It came trickling in over the transom at first, but Hatch's bailing technique had grown rusty. The skies were dark with daily news of a pointless war and genocide in Africa, poverty, AIDS, desperate millions in migration. The hot air of the commander in chief met the stone cold bullshit of congress and spawned water spouts, towering gyres of deadly ineptitude. A steady rain of increasing gas prices, grocery prices, medical costs, drove down hard like a fall of needles. At times the mist was so thick it baffled the mind. Somewhere in a back room, Liberty, Goddess of the Sea, was tied up and blindfolded—wires leading out from under her toga and hooked to a car battery. You could smell her burning, an acid stink that rode the fierce winds, turning the surface of the water brown.

Closer by, three sharks circled in the swells, their fins visible above chocolate waves. Each one of those slippery machines of Eden stood for a catastrophe in the secret symbolic nature of this story. One was *Financial Ruin*, I can tell you that—a stainless steel beauty whose sharp maw made Hatch's knees literally tremble like in a cartoon. In between the bouts of bailing, he walked a tightrope. At one end of his balancing pole was the weight of the bills, a mortgage like a Hydra, whose head grew back each month, for a house too tall and too shallow, taxes out the ass, failing appliances, car payments. At the other end was his job at an HMO, denying payment to people with legitimate claims. Each conversation with each claimant was harrowing for him, but he was in no position to quit. What else would he do? Each poor sop denied howled with indignation and unallied pain at the injustice of it all. Hatch's practiced facade, his dry "Sorry," hid indigestion, headaches, sweats, and his constant, subconscious reiteration of Darwin's law of survival as if it were some golden rule.

Beyond that, the dog had a chronic ear infection, his younger son, Ned, had recently been picked up by the police for smoking pot and the older one, Will, who had a severe case of athlete's foot, rear-ended a car on Route 70. "Just a tap. Not a scratch," he'd claimed, and then the woman called with her dizzying estimate. Hatch's wife, Rose, who worked 12 hours a day, treating the people at a hospital whose claims he would eventually turn down, demanded a vacation with tears in her eyes. "Just a week, somewhere warm," she said. He shook his head and laughed as if she was kidding. It was rough seas between his ears and rougher still in his heart. Each time he laughed, it was in lieu of puking.

Storm Warning was a phrase that made surprise visits to his consciousness while he sat in front of a blank computer screen at work, or hid in the garage at home late at night smoking one of the Captain Blacks he'd supposedly quit, or stared listlessly at Celebrity Fit Club on the television. It became increasingly difficult for him to remember births, first steps, intimate hours with Rose, family jokes, vacations in packed cars, holidays with extended family. One day Hatch did less bailing. "Fuck that bailing," he thought. The next day he did even less.

As if he'd just awakened to it, he was suddenly standing in water up to his shins and the rain was beating down on a strong southwester. The boat was bobbing like the bottom lip of a crone on Thorazine as he struggled to keep his footing. In his hands was a small plastic garbage can, the same one he'd used to bail his clam boat when at eighteen he worked the Great South Bay. The problem was Hatch wasn't eighteen anymore, and though now he was spurred to bail again with everything he had, he didn't have much. His heart hadn't worked so hard since his twenty-fifth anniversary when Rose made him climb a mountain in Montana. Even though the view at the top was gorgeous—a basin lake and a breeze out of heaven—his T-shirt jumped with each beat. The boat was going down. He chucked the garbage can out into the sea and *Financial Ruin* and its partners tore into it. Reaching for his shirt pocket, he took out his smokes and lit one.

The cold brown water was just creeping up around Hatch's balls as he took his first puff. He noticed the dark silhouette of Captree Bridge in the distance. "Back on the bay," he said, amazed to be sinking into the waters of his youth, and then, like a struck wooden match, the entire story of his life flared and died behind his eyes.

Going under was easy. No struggle, but a change in temperature. Just beneath the dark surface, the water got wonderfully clear. All the stale air came out of him at once—a satisfying burp followed by a large translucent globe that stretched his jaw with its birth. He reached for its spinning brightness but sank too fast to grab it. His feet were still lightly touching the deck as the boat fell slowly beneath him. He looked up and saw the sharks still chewing plastic. "This is it," thought Hatch, "not with a bang but a bubble." He herded all of his regrets into the basement of his brain, an indoor oak forest with intermittent dim light bulbs and dirt floor. The trees were columns that held the ceiling and amid and among them skittered pale, disfigured doppelgangers of his friends and family. As he stood at the top of the steps and shut the door on them, he felt a subtle tearing in his solar plexus. The boat touched down on the sandy bottom and his sneakers came to rest on the deck. Without thinking, he gave a little jump and sailed in a lazy arc ten feet away, landing, with a puff of sand, next to a toppled marble column.

His every step was a graceful bound, and he floated. Once on the slow descent of his arc, he put his arms out at his sides and lifted his feet behind him so as to fly. Hatch found that if he flapped his arms, he could glide along a couple of feet above the bottom, and he did, passing over coral pipes and red seaweed rippling like human hair in a breeze. There were creatures scuttling over rocks and through the sand—long antennae and armored plating, tiny eyes on sharp stalks and claws continuously practicing on nothing. As his shoes touched the sand again, a school of striped fish swept past his right shoulder, their blue glowing like neon, and he followed their flight.

He came upon the rest of the sunken temple, its columns pitted and cracked, broken like the tusks of dead elephants. Green sea vines netted the destruction—two wide marble steps there, here a piece of roof, a tilted mosaic floor depicting the Goddess of the Sea suffering a rash of missing tiles, a headless marble statue of a man holding his penis.

2

Hatch floated down the long empty avenues of Drowned Town, a shabby but quiet city in a lime green sea. Every so often, he'd pass one of the citizens, bloated and blue, in various stages of decomposition, and say, "Hi." Two gentlemen in suits swept by but didn't return his greeting. A drowned mother and child, bulging eyes dissolving in trails of tiny bubbles, dressed in little more than rags, didn't acknowledge him. One old woman stopped, though, and said, "Hello."

"I'm new here," he told her.

"The less you think about it the better," she said and drifted on her way.

Hatch tried to remember where he was going. He was sure there was a reason that he was in town, but it eluded him. "I'll call, Rose," he thought. "She always knows what I'm supposed to be doing." He started looking up and down the streets for a pay phone. After three blocks without luck, he saw a man heading toward him. The fellow wore a business suit and an overcoat torn to shreds, a black hat with a bullet hole in it, a closed umbrella hooked on a skeletal wrist. Hatch waited for the man to draw near, but as the fellow stepped into the street to cross to the next block, a swift gleaming vision flew from behind a building and with a sudden clang of steel teeth meeting took him in its jaws. *Financial Ruin* was hungry and loose in Drowned Town. Hatch cowered backward, breast stroking to a nearby dumpster to hide, but the shark was already gone with its catch.

On the next block up, he found a bar that was open. He didn't see a name on it, but there were people inside, the door was ajar, and there was the muffled sound of music. The place was cramped and narrowed the further back you went, ending in a corner. Wood paneling, mirror behind the bottles, spinning seats, low lighting and three dead beats—two on one side of the bar and one on the other.

"Got a pay phone?" asked Hatch.

All three men looked at him. The two customers smiled at each other. The bartender with a red bow tie, wiped his rotted nose on a handkerchief, and then slowly lifted an arm to point. "Go down to the grocery store. They got a pay phone at the deli counter."

Hatch had missed it when the old lady spoke to him, but he realized now that he heard the bartender's voice in his head, not with his ears. The old man moved his mouth, but all that came out were vague farts of words flattened by water pressure. He sat down on one of the bar stools.

"Give me something dry," he said to the bartender. He knew he had to compose himself, get his thoughts together.

The bartender shook his head, scratched a spot of coral growth on his scalp, and opened his mouth to let a minnow out. "I could make you a Jenny Diver...pink or blue?"

"No, Sal, make him one of those things with the dirt bomb in it...they're the driest," said the closer customer. The short man turned his flat face and stretched a grin like a soggy old doll with swirling hair. Behind the clear lenses of his eyes, shadows moved, something swimming through his head.

"You mean a Dry Reach. That's one dusty drink," said the other customer, a very pale, skeletal old man in a brimmed hat and dark glasses. "Remember the day I got stupid on those? Your asshole'll make hell seem like a backyard barbecue if you drink too many of them, my friend."

"I'll try one," said Hatch.

"Your wish is my command," said the bartender, but he moved none too swiftly. Still, Hatch was content to sit and think for a minute. He thought that maybe the drink would help him remember. For all of its smallness, the place had a nice relaxing current flowing through it. He folded his arms on the bar and rested his head down for a moment. It finally came to him that the music he'd heard since entering was Frank Sinatra. "The Way You Look Tonight," he whispered, naming the current song. He pictured Rose, naked, in bed back in their first apartment, and with that realization, the music went off.

Hatch looked up and saw that the bartender had turned on the television. The two customers, heads tilted back, stared into the glow. On the screen there was a news show without sound but the caption announced *News From The War.* A small seahorse swam behind the glass of the screen but in front of the black-and-white imagery. The story was about a ward in a makeshift field hospital where army doctors treated the wounded children of the area. Cute little faces stared up from pillows, tiny arms with casts listlessly waved, but as the report obviously went on, the wounds got more serious. There were children with missing limbs, and then open wounds, great gashes in the head, the chest, and missing eyes, and then a gaping hole with intestines spilling out, the little legs trembling and the chest heaving wildly.

"There's only one term for this war," said the old man with the sunglasses. "'Clusterfuck.' Cluster as in 'cluster' and fuck as in 'fuck.' No more need be said."

The short man turned to Hatch, and still grinning, said, "There was a woman in here yesterday, saying that we're all responsible."

"We are," said the bartender. "Drink up." He set Hatch's drink on the bar. "One Dry Reach," he said. It came in a big martini glass—clear liquid with a brown lump at the bottom.

Hatch reached for his wallet, but the bartender waved for him not to bother. "You must be new," he said.

Hatch nodded.

"Nobody messes with money down here. This is Drowned Town... think about it. Drink up, and I'll make you three more."

"Could you put Sinatra back on," Hatch asked sheepishly. "This news is bumming me out."

"As you wish," said the bartender. He pressed a red button on the wall behind him. Instantly, the television went off, and the two men turned back to their drinks. Sinatra sang "Let's take it nice and easy," and Hatch thought, "Free booze." He sipped his drink and could definitely distinguish its tang from the briny sea water. Whether he liked the taste or not, he'd decide later, but for now he drank it as quickly as he could.

The customer further from Hatch stepped around his friend and approached. "You're in for a real treat, man" he said. "You see that little island in the stream there." He pointed at the brown lump in the glass.

Hatch nodded.

"A bit of terra firma, a little taste of the world you left behind upstairs. Remember throwing dirt bombs when you were a kid? Like the powdery lumps in homemade brownies? Well you've got a dollop of high grade dirt there. You bite into it, and you'll taste your life left behind—bright sun and blue skies."

"Calm down," said the short man to his fellow customer. "Give him some room."

Hatch finished the drink and let the lump roll out of the bottom of the glass into his mouth. He bit it with his molars but found it had nothing to do with dirt. It was mushy and tasted terrible, more like a sodden meatball of decay then a memory of the sun. He spit the mess out and it darkened the water in front of his face. He waved his hand to disperse the brown cloud. A violet fish with a lazy tail swam down from the ceiling to snatch what was left of the disintegrating nugget.

The two customers and the bartender laughed, and Hatch heard it like a party in his brain. "You got the Tootsie Roll," said the short fellow and tried to slap the bar, but his arm moved too slowly through the water.

"Don't take it personally," said the old man. "It's a Drowned Town tradition." His right ear came off just then and floated away, his glasses slipping down on that side.

Hatch felt a sudden burst of anger. He'd never liked playing the fool.

"Sorry, fella," said the bartender, "but it's a ritual. On your first Dry Reach, you get the Tootsie Roll."

"What's the Tootsie Roll?" asked Hatch, still trying to get the taste out of his mouth.

The man with the outlandish grin said, "Well, for starters, it ain't a Tootsie Roll."

3

Hatch marveled at the myriad shapes and colors of seaweed in the grocery's produce section. The lovely wavering of their leaves, strands, tentacles, in the flow soothed him. Although he stood on the sandy bottom, hanging from the ceiling were rows of fluorescent lights, every third or fourth one working. The place was a vast concrete bunker, set up in long aisles of shelves like at the Super Shopper he'd trudged through innumerable times back in his dry life.

"No money needed," he thought. "And free booze, but then why the coverage of the war? For that matter why the Tootsie Roll? *Financial Ruin* has free reign in Drowned Town. Nobody seems particularly happy. It doesn't add up." Hatch left the produce section, passed a display of anemone, some as big as his head, and drifted off, in search of the deli counter.

The place was enormous, row upon row of shelved dead fish, their snouts sticking into the aisle, silver and pink and brown. Here and there a gill still quivered, a fin twitched. "A lot of fish," thought Hatch. Along the way, he saw a special glass case that held frozen food that had sunk from the world above. The hot dog tempted him, even though a good quarter had gone green. There was a piece of a cupcake with melted sprinkles, three

French fries, a black Twizzler, and a red and white Chinese take out bag with two gnarled rib ends sticking out. He hadn't had any lunch, and his stomach growled in the presence of the delicacies, but he was thinking of Rose and wanted to talk to her.

Hatch found a familiar face at the lobster tank. He could hardly believe it, Bob Gordon from up the block. Bob looked none the worse for wear for being sunk, save for his yellow complexion. He smoked a damp cigarette and stared into the tank as if staring through it.

"Bob," said Hatch.

Bob turned and adjusted his glasses. "Hatch, what's up?"

"I didn't know you went under."

"Sure, like a fuckin' stone."

"When?" asked Hatch.

"Three, four months ago. Peggy'd been porking some guy from over in Larchdale. You know, I got depressed, laid off the bailing, lost the house, and then eventually I just threw in the pail."

"How do you like it here?"

"Really good," said Bob and his words rang loud in Hatch's brain, but then he quickly leaned close and these words came in a whisper, "It sucks."

"What do you mean?" asked Hatch, keeping his voice low.

Bob's smile deflated. "Everything's fine," he said, casting a glance to the lobster tank. He nodded to Hatch. "Gotta go, bud."

He watched Bob bound away against a mild current. By the time Hatch reached the deli counter, it was closed. In fact, with the exception of Bob, he'd seen no one in the entire store. An old black phone with a rotary dial sat atop the counter with a sign next to it that read: FREE PAY PHONE. NOT TO BE USED IN PRIVACY!

Hatch looked over his shoulder. There was no one around. Stepping forward he reached for the receiver, and just as his hand closed on it, the thing rang. He felt the vibration before he heard the sound. He let it go and stepped back. It continued to ring, and he was torn between answering it and fleeing. Finally, he picked it up and said, "Hello."

At first he thought the line was dead, but then a familiar voice sounded. "Hatch," it said, and he knew it was Ned, his younger son. Both of his boys had called him Hatch since they were toddlers. "You gotta come pick me up."

"Where are you?" asked Hatch.

"I'm at a house party behind the 7-Eleven. It's starting to get crazy."

"What do you mean it's starting to get crazy?"

"You coming?"

"I'll be there," said Hatch, and then the line went dead.

He stood at the door to the basement of his brain and turned the knob, but before he could open it, he saw way over on the other side of the store, one of the silver sharks, cruising above the aisles up near the ceiling. Dropping the phone, he scurried behind the deli counter, and then through an opening that led down a hall to a door.

4

Hatch was out of breath from walking, searching for someone who might be able to help him. For ten city blocks he thought about Ned needing a ride. He pictured the boy, hair tied back, baggy shorts and shoes like slippers, running from the police. "Good grief," said Hatch and pushed forward. He'd made a promise to Ned years earlier that he would always come and get him if he needed a ride, no matter what. How could he tell him now, "Sorry kid, I'm sunk." Hatch thought of all the things that could happen in the time it would take him to return to land and pick Ned up at the party. Scores of tragic scenarios exploded behind his eyes. "I might as well be bailing," he said to the empty street.

He heard the crowd before he saw it, faint squeaks and blips in his ears and eventually they became distant voices and music. Rounding a corner, he came in sight of a huge vacant lot between two six-story brownstones. As he approached, he could make out there was some kind of attraction at the back of the lot, and twenty or so Drowned Towners floated in a crowd around it. Organ music blared from a speaker on a tall wooden pole. Hatch crossed the street and joined the audience.

Up against the back wall of the lot, there was an enormous golden octopus. Its flesh glistened and its tentacles curled, unfurled, created fleeting symbols dispersed by schools of tiny angel fish constantly circling it like a halo. The creature's sucker disks were flat black as was its beak, its eyes red, and there was a heavy, rusted metal collar squeezing the base of its lumpen head as if it had shoulders and a neck. Standing next to it was a young woman, obviously part fish. She had gills and her eyes were pure black like a shark's. Her teeth were sharp. There were scales surrounding her face and her hair was some kind of fine green seaweed. She wore a clam shell brassiere and a black thong. At the backs of her heels were fan-like fins. "My name is Clementine," she said, "and this beside me is Madame Mutandis. She is a remarkable specimen of the Midas Octopus, so named for the beautiful golden aura of her skin. You see the collar on the Madame and you miss the chain. Notice, it is attached to my left ankle. Contrary to what you all might believe, it is I who belong to her and not she to me."

Hatch looked up and down the crowd he was part of—an equal mixture of men and women, some more bleached than blue, some less intact. The man next to him held his mouth open, and an eel's head peered out as if having come from the bowels to check the young fish woman's performance.

"With cephalopod brilliance, nonvertebrate intuition, Madame Mutandis will answer one question for each of you. No question is out of bounds. She thinks like the very sea itself. Who'll be first?"

The man next to Hatch stepped immediately forward before anyone else. "And what is your question asked the fish woman?" The man put his hands into his coat pockets and then raised his head. His message was horribly muddled, but by his third repetition Hatch as well as the octopus got it—"How does one remove an eel?" Madame Mutandis shook her head sac as if in disdain while two of her tentacles unfurled in the man's direction. One swiftly wrapped around his throat, lurching him forward, and the other dove into his mouth. A second later, the Madame released his throat and drew from between his lips a three-foot-long eel, wriggling wildly in her suctioned grasp. The long arm swept the eel to her beak, and she pierced it at a spot just behind the head, rendering it lifeless. With a free tentacle, she waved forward the next questioner, while, with another, she gently brushed away the man now sighing with relief.

Hatch came to and was about to step forward, but a woman from behind him wearing a kerchief and carrying a beige pocketbook passed by, already asking, "Where are the good sales?" He wasn't able to see her face, but the woman with the question, from her posture and clothing, seemed middle-aged, somewhat younger than himself.

Clementine repeated the woman's question for the octopus. "Where are the good sales?" she said.

"Shoes," said the woman with the kerchief. "I'm looking for shoes."

Madame Mutandis wrapped a tentacle around the woman's left arm and turned her to face the crowd. Hatch reared back at the sudden sight of a face rotted almost perfectly down the middle, skull showing through on one side. Another of the octopus's tentacles slid up the woman's skirt between her legs. With the dexterity of a hand, it drew down the questioner's underwear, leaving them gathered around her ankles. Then, wriggling like the eel it removed from the first man's mouth, that tentacle slithered along her right thigh only to disappear again beneath the skirt.

Hatch was repulsed and fascinated as the woman trembled and the tentacle wiggled out of sight. She turned her skeletal profile to the crowd, and that bone grin widened with pleasure, grimaced in pain, gaped with passion. Little spasms of sound escaped her open mouth. The crowd methodically applauded until finally the object of the Madame's attentions screamed and fell to the sand, the long tentacle retracting. The fish woman moved to the end of her chain and helped the questioner up. "Is that what you were looking for?" she asked. The woman with the beige pocketbook nodded and adjusted her kerchief before floating to the back of the crowd.

"Ladies and gentleman?" said the fish-woman.

Hatch noticed that no one was too ready to step forth after the creature's last answer, including himself. His mind was racing, trying to connect a search for a shoe sale with the resultant...what? Rape? Or was what he witnessed consensual? He was still befuddled by the spectacle. The gruesome state of the woman's face wrapped in ecstasy hung like a chandelier of ice on the main floor of his brain. At that moment, he realized he had to escape from Drowned Town. Shifting his glance right and left, he noticed his fellow drownees were still as stone.

The fish-woman's chain must have stretched, because she floated over and put her hand on his back. Gently, she led him forward. "She can tell you anything," came Clementine's voice, a whisper that made him think of Rose and Ned and Will, even the stupid dog with bad ears. He hadn't felt his feet move, but he was there, standing before the shining perpetual motion of the Madame's eight arms. Her black parrot beak opened, and he thought he heard her laughing.

"You're question?" asked Clementine, still close by his side.

"My kid's stuck at a party that's getting crazy," blurted Hatch. "How do I get back to dry land?"

He heard murmuring from the crowd behind him. One voice said, "No." Another two said, "Asshole." At first he thought they were predicting the next answer from Madame Mutandis, but then he realized they were referring to him. It dawned that wanting to leave Drowned Town was unpopular.

"Watch the ink," said Clementine.

Hatch looked down and saw a dark plume exuding from beneath the octopus. It rose in a mushroom cloud, and then turned into a long black string at the top. The end of that string whipped leisurely through the air, drawing more of itself from the cloud until the cloud had vanished and what remained was the phrase *322 Bleeter Street* in perfect, looping script. The address floated there for a moment, Hatch repeating it, before the angel fish veered out of orbit around the fleshy golden sac and dashed through it, dispersing the ink.

The fish-woman led Hatch away and called, "Next." He headed for the street, repeating the address under his breath. At the back of the crowd, which had grown, a woman turned to him as he passed and said, "Leaving town?"

"My kid ..." Hatch began, but she snickered at him. From somewhere down the back row, he heard, "Jerk," and "Pussy." When he reached the street, he realized that the words of the drowned had crowded the street number out of his thoughts. He remembered Bleeter street and said it six times, but the number....Leaping forward, he assumed the flying position, and flapping his arms, cruised down the street, checking the street signs at the corners and keeping an eye out for sharks. He remembered the number had a 3 in it, and then for blocks he thought of nothing but that last woman's contempt.

5

Eventually, he grew too tired to fly and resumed walking, sometimes catching the current and drifting in the flow. He'd seen so many street signs—President's Names, different kinds of fish, famous actors and sunken ships, types of clouds, waves, flowers, slugs. None of them was Bleeter. So many store fronts and apartment steps passed by and not a soul in sight. At one point, tiny starfish fell like rain all over town, littering the streets and filling the awnings.

Hatch had just stepped out of a weakening current and was moving under his own volition when he noticed a phone booth wedged into an alley between two stores. Pushing off, he swam to it and squeezed himself into the glass enclosure. As the door closed, a light went on above him. He lifted the receiver, placing it next to his ear. There was a dial tone. He dialed and it rang. Something shifted in his chest and his pulse quickened. Suffering the length of each long ring, he waited for someone to pick up.

"Hello?" he heard; a voice at a great distance.

"Rose, it's me," he screamed against the water.

"Hatch," she said. "I can hardly hear you. Where are you?"

"I'm stuck in Drowned Town," he yelled.

"What do you mean? Where is it?"

Hatch had a hard time saying it. "I went under, Rose. I'm sunk."

There was nothing on the line. He feared he'd lost the connection, but he stayed with it.

"Jesus, Hatch...What the hell are you doing?"

"I gave up on the bailing," he said.

She groaned. "You shit. How am I supposed to do this alone?"

"I'm sorry, Rose," he said. "I don't know what happened. I love you."

He could hear her exhale. "OK," she said. "Give me an address. I have to have something to put into MapQuest."

"Do you know where I am?" he asked.

"No, I don't fucking know where you are. That's why I need the address."

It came to him all at once. "322 Bleeter Street, Drowned Town" he said. "I'll meet you there."

"It's going to take a while," she said.

"Rose?"

"What?"

"I love you," he said. He listened to the silence on the receiver until he noticed in the reflection of his face in the phone booth glass a blue spot on his nose and one on his forehead. "Shit," he said and hung up. "I can take care of that with some ointment when I get back," he thought. He scratched at the spot on his forehead and blue skin sloughed off. He put his face closer to the glass, and then there came a pounding on the door behind him.

Turning, he almost screamed at the sight of the half gone face of that woman who'd been goosed by the octopus. He opened the door and slid passed her. Her Jolly Roger profile was none too jolly. As he spoke the words, he surprised himself with doing so—"Do you know where Bleeter Street is?" She jostled him aside in her rush to get to the phone. Before closing the door, she called over her shoulder, "You're on it."

"Things are looking up," thought Hatch as he retreated. Standing in the middle of the street, he looked up one side and down the other. Only one building, a darkened storefront with a plate glass window behind which was displayed a single pair of sunglasses on a pedestal, had a street number—621. It came to him that he would have to travel in one direction, try to find another address and see which way the numbers ran. Then, if he found they were increasing, he'd have to turn around and head in the other direction, but at least he would know. Thrilled at the sense of purpose, he swept a clump of drifting seaweed out of his way, and moved forward. He could be certain Rose would come for him. After 30 years of marriage they'd grown close in subterranean ways.

Darkness was beginning to fall on Drowned Town. Angle-jawed fish with needle teeth, a perpetual scowl and sad eyes, came from the alleyways and through the open windows of the apartments, and each had a small phosphorescent jewel dangling from a downward curving stalk that issued from the head. They drifted the shadowy street like fireflies, and although Hatch had still to see another address, he stopped in his tracks to mark their beautiful effect. It was precisely then that he saw *Financial Ruin* appear from over the rooftops down the street. Before he could even think to flee, he saw the shark swoop down in his direction.

Hatch turned, kicked his feet up and started flapping. As he approached the first corner, and was about to turn, he almost collided with someone just stepping out onto Bleeter Street. To his utter confusion, it was a deep sea diver, a man inside a heavy rubber suit with a glass bubble of a helmet and a giant nautilus shell strapped to his back, feeding air through two arching tubes into his suit. The sudden appearance of the diver wasn't what made him stop, though. It was the huge gun in his hands with a barbed spear head as wide as a fence post jutting from the barrel. The diver waved Hatch behind him as the shark came into view. It hurtled toward them with a dagger-toothed lunge, a widening cavern with the speed of a speeding car. The diver pulled the trigger. There was a zip of tiny bubbles, and *Financial Ruin* curled up, thrashing madly with the spear piercing its upper pallet and poking out the back of its head. Billows of blood began to spread. The man in the suit dropped the gun and approached Hatch.

"Hurry," he said, "before the other sharks smell the blood."

6

Hatch and his savior sat in a carpeted parlor on cushioned chairs facing each other across a low coffee table with a tea service on it. The remarkable fact was that they were both dry, breathing air instead of brine, and speaking at a normal tone. When they'd both entered the foyer of the stranger's building, he hit a button on the wall. A sheet of steel slid down to cover the door, and within seconds the sea water began to exit the compartment through a drain in the floor. Hatch had had to drown into the air and that was much more uncomfortable than simply going under, but after some extended wheezing, choking, and spitting up, he drew in a huge breath with ease. The diver had unscrewed the glass globe that covered his head and held it beneath one arm. "Isaac Munro," he'd said and nodded.

Dressed in a maroon smoking jacket and green pajamas, moccasins on his feet, the silver-haired man with drooping mustache sipped his tea and now held forth on his situation. Hatch, in dry clothes the older man had given him, was willing to listen, almost certain Munro knew the way back to dry land.

"I'm *in* Drowned Town, but not *of* it. Do you understand," he said.

Hatch nodded, and noticed what a relief it was to have the pressure of the sea off him.

Isaac Munro lowered his gaze and said as if making a confession, "My wife Rotzy went under some years ago. There was nothing I could do to prevent it. She came down here, and on the day she left me, I determined I would find the means to follow her and rescue her from Drowned Town. My imagination, fired by the desire to simply hold her again, gave birth to all these many inventions that allow me to keep from getting my feet wet, so to speak." He chuckled and then made a face as if he were admonishing himself.

Hatch smiled. "How long have you been looking for her?"

"Years," said Munro, placing his teacup on the table.

"I'm trying to get back. My wife Rose is coming for me in the car."

"Yes, your old neighbor Bob Gordon told me you might be looking for an out," said the older man. "I was on the prowl for you when we encountered that cutpurse leviathan."

"You know Bob?"

"He does some leg work for me from time to time."

"I saw him at the grocery today."

"He has a bizarre fascination with that lobster tank. In any event, your wife won't make it through, I'm sorry to say. Not with a car."

"How can I get out?" asked Hatch. "I can't offer you a lot of money, but something else perhaps."

"Perish the thought," said Munro. "I have an escape hatch back to the surface in case of emergencies. You're welcome to use it if you'll just observe some cautionary measures."

"Absolutely," said Hatch and moved to the edge of his chair.

"I take it you'd like to leave immediately?"

Both men stood and Hatch followed through a hallway lined with framed photographs that opened into a large space, like an old ballroom with peeling flowered wallpaper. Across the warped wooden floor scratched and littered with, of all things, old leaves and pages of a newspaper, they came to a door. When Munro turned around, Hatch noticed that the older man had taken one of the photos off the wall in the hallway.

"Here she is," said Isaac. "This is Rotzy."

Hatch leaned down for a better look at the portrait. He gave only the slightest grunt of surprise and hoped his host hadn't noticed, but Rotzy was the woman at the phone booth, the half faced horror mishandled by Madame Mutandis.

"You haven't seen her, have you?" asked Munro.

Hatch knew he should have tried to help the old man, but he thought only of escape and didn't want to complicate things. He felt the door in front of him was to be the portal back. "No," he said.

Munro nodded and then reached into the side pocket of his jacket and retrieved an old fashioned key. He held it in the air, but did not place it in Hatch's outstretched palm. "Listen carefully," he said. "You will pass through a series of rooms. Upon entering each room, you must lock the door behind you with this key before opening the next door to exit into the following room. Once you've started you can't turn back. The key only works to open doors forward and lock doors backward. A door can not be opened without a door being locked. Do you understand?"

"Yes."

Munro placed the key in Hatch's hand. "Then be on your way and Godspeed. Kiss the sky for me when you arrive."

"I will."

Munro opened the door and Hatch stepped through. The door closed and he locked it behind him. He crossed the room in a hurry, unlocked the next door and then, passing through, locked it behind him. This process went on for twenty minutes before Hatch noticed that it took less and less steps to traverse each room to the next door. One of the rooms had a window, and he paused to look out on some watery side street falling into night. The loneliness of the scene spurred him forward. In the following room he had to duck down so as not to skin his head against the ceiling. He locked its door and moved forward into a room where he had to duck even lower.

Eventually, he was forced to crawl from room to room, and there wasn't much space for turning around to lock the door behind him. As each door swept open before him, he thought he might see the sky or feel a breeze in his face. There was always another door but there was also hope. That is until he entered a compartment so small, he couldn't turn around to use the key but had to do it with his hands behind his back, his chin against his chest. "This has got to be the last one," he thought, unsure if he could squeeze his shoulders through the next opening. Before he could insert the key into the lock on the tiny door before him, a steel plate fell and blocked access to it. He heard a swoosh and a bang behind him and knew another metal plate had covered the door going back.

"How are you doing, Mr. Hatch?" he heard Munro's voice say.

By dipping one shoulder Hatch was able to turn his head and see a speaker built into the wall. "How do I get through these last rooms?" he yelled. "They're too small and metal guards have fallen in front of the doors."

"That's the point," called Munro, "you don't. You, my friend are trapped, and will remain trapped forever in that tight uncomfortable place."

"What are you talking about? Why?" Hatch was frantic. He tried to lunge his body against the walls but there was nowhere for it to go.

"My wife, Rotzy. You know how she went under? What sunk her? She was ill, Mr. Hatch. She was seriously ill but her health insurance denied her coverage. You, Mr. Hatch, personally said *no*."

This time what flared before Hatch's inner eye was not his life, but all the many pleading, frustrating, angry voices that had traveled in one of his ears and out the other in his service to the HMO. "I'm not responsible," was all he could think to say in his defense.

"My wife used to tell me, 'Isaac, we're all responsible.' Now you can wait, as she waited for relief, for what was rightly due her. You'll wait forever, Hatch."

There was a period where he struggled. He couldn't tell how long it lasted, but nothing came of it, so he closed his eyes, made his breathing more steady and shallow, and went into his brain, across the first floor to the basement door. He opened it and could smell the scent of the dark wood wafting up the steps. Locking the door behind him, he descended into the dark.

7

The woods were frightening, but he'd take anything over the claustrophobia of Munro's trap. Each dim lightbulb he came to was a godsend, and he put his hands up to it for the little warmth it offered against the wind. He noticed that the creatures prowled around the bulbs like antelopes around waterholes. They darted behind the trees, spying on him, pale specters whose faces were masks made of bone. One he was sure was his cousin Martin, a malevolent boy who'd cut the head off a kitten. He'd not seen him in over thirty years. He also spotted his mother-in-law, who was his mother-in-law with no hair and short tusks. She grunted orders to him from the shadows. He kept moving and tried to ignore them.

When Hatch couldn't walk any further, he came to a clearing in the forest. There, in the middle of nowhere, in the basement of his brain, sat twenty yards of street with a brownstone situated behind a wide sidewalk. There were steps leading up to twin doors and an electric light glowed next to the entrance. As he drew near, he could make out the address in brass numerals on the base of the banister that led up the right side of the front steps—322.

He stumbled over to the bottom step and dropped down onto it. Hatch leaned forward, his elbows on his knees and his hands covering his face. "That's not me," he said, "it's not me," and he tried to weep till his eyes closed out of exhaustion. What seemed a second later, he heard a car horn and looked up.

"There's no crying in baseball, asshole," said Rose. She was leaning her head out the driver's side window of their SUV. There was a light on in the car and he could see both their sons were in the back seat, pointing at him.

"How'd you find me?" he asked.

"The Internet," said Rose. "Will showed me MapQuest has this new feature where you don't need the address anymore, just a person's name, and it gives you directions to wherever they are in the continental United States."

"Oh, my God," he said and walked toward Rose to give her a hug.

"Not now Barnacle Bill, there's some pale creeps coming this way. We just passed them and one lunged for the car. Get in."

Hatch got in and saw his sons. He wanted to hug them but they motioned for him to hurry and shut the door. As soon as he did, Rose pulled away from the curb.

"So, Hatch, you went under?" asked his older son, Will.

Hatch wished he could explain but couldn't find the words.

"What a pile," said Ned.

"Yeah," said Will.

"Don't do it again, Hatch," said Rose. "Next time we're not coming for you."

"I'm sorry," he said. "I love you all."

Rose wasn't one to admonish more than once. She turned on the radio and changed the subject. "We had the directions, but they were a bitch to follow. At one point I had to cut across two lanes of traffic in the middle of the Holland Tunnel and take a left down a side tunnel that for more than a mile was the pitchest pitch-black."

"Listen to this, Hatch" said Ned and leaned into the front seat to turn up the radio.

"Oh, they've been playing this all day," said Rose. "This young woman soldier was captured by insurgents and they made a video of them cutting her head off."

"On the radio, you only get the screams, though," said Will. "Check it out."

The sound, at first, was like from a musical instrument, and then it became human—steady, piercing shrieks in desperate bursts that ended in the gurgle of someone going under.

Rose changed the channel and the screams came from the new station. She hit the button again and the same screaming. Hatch turned to look at his family. Their eyes were slightly droopy and they were very pale. Their shoulders were somehow out of whack and their grins were vacant. Rose had a big bump on her forehead and a rash across her neck.

"Watch for the sign for the Holland tunnel," she said amid the dying soldier's screams as they drove on into the dark. Hatch kept careful watch, knowing they'd never find it.

HA JIN
(b. 1956)

"Most fiction writers think of short fiction as a minor form, but for me it's the most literary form."

Born in Liaoning, China, the son of a military officer, Ha Jin (pen name of Jin Xuefei) has lived in the United States since 1985 and considers himself a "Chinese American writer"—one who writes in English of Chinese subjects. (Jin's books are banned in China.) The author's focus upon the short story is unusual among writers who have achieved success in both the short story and the novel; Jin has published four collections of stories, Ocean of Words *(1996, winner of the PEN/Hemingway Award),* Under the Red Flag *(1997, winner of the Flannery O'Connor Award for Short Fiction),* The Bridegroom *(2000), and* A Good Fall *(2009), and his stories have appeared in numerous distinguished anthologies—the* Pushcart Prize: Best of the Small Presses, The Best American Short Stories, *and the* O. Henry Awards. *In addition, Jin is the author of several books of poetry including* Facing Shadows *(1996) and* Wreckage *(2001), and six acclaimed novels,* In the Pond *(1998),* Waiting *(1999, winner of the National Book Award and the PEN/Faulkner Award),* The Crazed *(2002),* War Trash *(2004, winner of the PEN/Faulkner Award),* A Free Life *(2007), and* Nanking Requiem *(2011).*

Of the writers included in this volume, no one has led a more varied and more tumultuous life than Ha Jin, whose childhood coincided with the notorious Culture Revolution in China—the closing of schools and universities for a decade, the demotion of educated and professional classes to manual labor, a protracted and self-sabotaging "purging" of individuals thought to be counterproductive to the Communist Revolution. With the breakup of his family, Ha Jin joined the People's Liberation Army at the age of fourteen and remained in the army for six years during which time he read and educated himself as he could: among the first books he tried to read were Cervantes's Don Quixote *and Walt Whitman's* Leaves of Grass. *After leaving the army he entered Heilongjiang University where he earned a BA degree in English;*

then, he earned a master's degree in Anglo-American literature at Shandong University. Having emigrated to the United States, Ha Jin worked as a custodian and in restaurants and libraries; he preferred the job of night watchman since it gave him time to read. He was on a scholarship at Brandeis University at the time of the 1989 Tiananmen Square massacre, which precipitated Ha Jin's decision to reside permanently in the United States and to write in English "to preserve the integrity of his work."

Jin's initial intention was to become a translator and a scholar/teacher, but a serendipitous meeting with the American poet Frank Bidart turned Jin into a poet, a writer of short fiction, and a novelist now on the faculty at Boston University. Jin has said movingly of his background: "In China the individual is treated as a screw or a cog in the revolutionary machine. I wanted to be a being with a voice."

Ha Jin's sparely written, anecdotal but trenchant "Children as Enemies" carries the never-predictable immigrant experience forward into the second and third generations.

Children as Enemies

Our grandchildren hate us. The boy and the girl, ages eleven and nine, are just a pair of selfish, sloppy brats and have no respect for old people. Their animosity toward us originated at the moment their names were changed, about three months ago.

One evening the boy complained that his schoolmates couldn't pronounce his name, so he must change it. "Lots of them call me 'Chicken,'" he said. "I want a regular name like anyone else." His name was Qigan Xi, pronounced "cheegan hsee," which could be difficult for non-Chinese to manage.

"I wanna change mine too," his sister, Hua, jumped in. "Nobody can say it right and some call me 'Wow.'" She bunched her lips, her face puffed with baby fat.

Before their parents could respond, my wife put in, "You should teach them how to pronounce your names."

"They always laugh about my silly name, Qigan," the boy said. "If I didn't come from China, I'd say 'Chicken' too."

I told both kids, "You ought to be careful about changing your names. We decided on them only after consulting a reputable fortune-teller."

"Phew, who believes in that crap?" the boy muttered.

Our son intervened, saying to his children, "Let me think about this, okay?"

Our daughter-in-law, thin-eyed Mandi, broke in. "They should have American names. Down the road there'll be lots of trouble if their names remain unpronounceable. We should've changed them long ago."

Gubin, our son, seemed to agree, though he wouldn't say it in our presence.

My wife and I were unhappy about that, but we didn't make a serious effort to stop them, so Mandi and Gubin went about looking for suitable names for the children. It was easy in the girl's case. They picked "Flora" for her, since her name, Hua, means "flower." But it was not easy to find a name for the boy. English names are simple in meaning, mostly already empty of their original senses. Qigan means "amazing bravery."

Where can you find an English name that combines the import and the resonance of that? When I pointed out the difficulty, the boy blustered, "I don't want a weird and complicated name. I just need a regular name, like Charlie or Larry or Johnny."

That I wouldn't allow. Names are a matter of fortune and fate—that's why fortune-tellers can divine the vicissitudes of people's lives by reading the orders and numbers of the strokes in the characters of their names. No one should change his name randomly.

Mandi went to the public library and checked out a book on baby names. She perused the small volume and came up with "Matty" as a choice. She explained, "'Matty' is short for 'Mathilde,' which is from Old German and means 'powerful in battle,' very close to 'Qigan' in meaning. Besides, the sound echoes 'mighty' in English."

"It doesn't sound right," I said. In the back of my mind I couldn't reconcile "Matty" with "Xi," our family name.

"I like it," the boy crowed.

He seemed determined to contradict me, so I said no more. I wished my son had rejected the choice, but Gubin didn't make a peep, just sitting in the rocking chair and drinking iced tea. The matter was settled. The boy went to school and told his teacher he had a new name—Matty.

For a week he seemed happy, but his satisfaction was short-lived. One evening he told his parents, "Matty is a girl's name, my friend Carl told me."

"Impossible," his mother said.

"Of course it's true. I asked around, and people all said it sounded girlish."

My wife, drying her hands on her apron, suggested to our son, "Why don't you look it up?"

The book on baby names was not returned yet, so Gubin looked it up and saw "f. or m." beside the name. Evidently Mandi hadn't seen that it could be both female and male. Her negligence or ignorance outraged the boy all the more.

What should we do? The eleven-year-old turned tearful, blaming his mother for giving him a name with an ambiguous gender.

Finally my son slapped his knee and said, "I have an idea. 'Matty' can also come from 'Matt.' Why not drop the letter 'y' and call yourself Matt?"

The boy brightened up and said he liked that, but I objected. "Look, this book says 'Matt' is a diminutive of 'Matthew.' It's nowhere close to the sense of 'amazing bravery.'"

"Who gives a damn about that!" the boy spat out. "I'm gonna call myself Matt."

Wordless, I felt my face tightening. I got up and went out to smoke a pipe on the balcony. My wife followed me, saying, "My old man, don't take to heart what our grandson said. He's just confused and desperate. Come back in and eat."

"After this pipe," I said.

"Don't be long." She stepped back into the apartment, her small shoulders more stooped than before.

Below me, automobiles were gliding past on the wet street like colored whales. If only we hadn't sold everything in Dalian City and come here to join our son's family. Gubin is our only child, so we'd thought it would be good to stay with him. Now I wish we hadn't moved. At our ages—my wife is sixty-three and I'm sixty-seven—and at this time it's hard to adjust to life here. In America it feels as if the older you are, the more inferior you grow.

Both my wife and I understood we shouldn't meddle with our grandchildren's lives, but sometimes I simply couldn't help offering them a bit of advice. She believed it was our daughter-in-law who had spoiled the kids and made them despise us. I don't think Mandi is that mean, though beyond question she is an indulgent mother. Flora and Matt look down on everything Chinese except for some food they like. They hated to go to the weekend school to learn to read and write the characters. Matt announced, "I've no need for that crap."

I would have to force down my temper whenever I heard him say that. Their parents managed to make them attend the weekend school, though Matt and Flora had quit inscribing the characters. They went there only to learn how to paint with a brush, taking lessons from an old artist from Taiwan. The girl, sensitive by nature and delicate in health, might have had some talent for arts, but the boy was good at nothing but daydreaming. I just couldn't help imagining that he might end up a guttersnipe. He wouldn't draw bamboos or goldfish or landscapes with a brush; instead, he produced merely bands and fines of ink on paper, calling them abstract paintings. He experimented with the shades of the ink as if it were watercolors. Sometimes he did that at home too. Seeing his chubby face and narrow eyes as he worked in dead earnest, I wanted to laugh. He once showed a piece with some vertical lines of ink on it to an art teacher at his school. To my horror, the woman praised it, saying the lines suggested a rainfall or waterfall, and that if you observed them horizontally, they would bring to mind layers of clouds or some sort of landscape.

What a crock was that! I complained to Gubin in private and urged him to pressure the children to study serious subjects, such as science, classics, geography, history, grammar, and penmanship. If Matt really couldn't handle those, in the future he should consider learning how to repair cars and machines or how to cook like a chef. Auto mechanics make good money here—I know a fellow at a garage who can't speak any English but pulls in twenty-four dollars an hour, plus a generous bonus at the end of the year. I made it clear to my son that a few tricks in "art" would never get his kids anywhere in life, so they'd better stop dabbling with a brush. Gubin said Matt and Flora were still young and we shouldn't push them too hard, but he agreed to talk to them. Unlike Gubin, Mandi aligned herself with the children, saying we ought to let them develop freely as individuals, not straitjacket them as they would back in China. My wife and I were unhappy about our daughter-in-law's position. Whenever we criticized her, our grandchildren would mock us or yell at us in defense of their mother.

I have serious reservations about elementary education in the United States. Teachers don't force their pupils to work as hard as they can. Matt had learned both multiplication and division in the third grade, but two months ago I asked him to calculate how much seventy-four percent of $1,586 was, and he had no clue how to do it. I handed him a calculator and said, "Use this." Even so, he didn't know he could just multiply the amount by 0.74.

"Didn't you learn multiplication and division?" I asked him.

"I did, but that was last year."

"Still, you should know how to do it."

"We haven't practiced division and multiplication this year, so I'm not familiar with them anymore." He offered that as an excuse. There was no way I could make him understand that once you learned something, you were supposed to master it and make it part of yourself. That's why we say knowledge is wealth. You can get richer and richer by accumulating it within.

The teachers here don't assign the pupils any real homework. Instead they give them a lot of projects, some of which seem no more than woolgathering, and tend to inflate the kids' egos. My son had to help his children with the projects, which were more like homework for the parents. Some of the topics were impossible even for adults to tackle, such as "What is culture and how is it created?" "Make your argument for or against the Iraq War," "How does the color line divide U.S. society?" and "Do you think global trade is necessary? Why?" My son had to do research online and in the public library to get the information needed for discussing those topics. Admittedly, they could broaden the pupils' minds and give them more confidence, but at their tender age they are not supposed to think like a politician or a scholar. They should be made to follow rules; that is, to become responsible citizens first.

Whenever I asked Flora how she was ranked in her class, she'd shrug and say, "I dunno."

"What do you mean you don't know?" I suspected she must be well below the average, though she couldn't be lower than her brother.

"Ms. Gillen doesn't rank us is all," came her answer.

If that was true, I was even more disappointed with the schools. How could they make their students competitive in this global economy if they didn't instill in them the sense of getting ahead of others and becoming the very best? No wonder many Asian parents viewed the public schools in Flushing unfavorably. In my honest opinion, elementary education here tends to lead children astray.

Five weeks ago, Matt declared at dinner that he must change his last name, because a substitute teacher that morning had mispronounced "Xi" as "Eleven." That put the whole class in stitches, and some students even made fun of the boy afterward, calling him "Matt Eleven." Flora chimed in, "Yeah, I want a different last name too. My friend Reta just had her family name changed to Wu. Some people couldn't pronounce 'Ng' and called her 'Reta No Good.'"

Their parents broke out laughing, but I couldn't see why that was funny. My wife said to the girl, "You'll have your husband's last name when you grow up and get married."

"I don't want no man!" the girl shot back.

"We both must have a new last name," the boy insisted.

I burst out, "You can't do that. Your last name belongs to the family, and you can't cut yourselves off from your ancestors."

"Baloney!" The boy squished up his face.

"You mustn't speak to your granddad like that," his grandmother butted in.

Mandi and my son exchanged glances. I knew they saw this matter differently from us. Maybe they had been planning to change their children's last name all along. Enraged, I dropped my bowl on the dining table and pointed my finger at Mandi. "You've tried your best to spoil them. Now you're happy to let them break away from the family tree. What kind of daughter-in-law are you? I wish I hadn't allowed you to join our family."

"Please don't blow up like this, Dad," my son said.

Mandi didn't talk back. Instead she began sobbing, wrinkling her gourd-shaped nose. The kids got angry and blamed me for hurting their mother's feelings. The more they blabbered, the more furious I became. Finally unable to hold it back anymore, I shouted, "If you two change your last name, you leave, get out of here. You cannot remain in this household while using a different last name."

"Who are you?" Matt said calmly. "This isn't your home."

"You're just our guests," added Flora.

That drove both my wife and me mad. She yelled at our granddaughter, "So we sold everything in China, our apartment and candy store, just to be your guests here, huh? Heartless. Who told you this isn't our home?"

That shut the girl up, though she kept glaring at her grandma. Their father begged no one in particular, "Please, let us finish dinner peacefully." He went on chewing a fried shrimp with his mouth closed.

I wanted to yell at him that he was just a rice barrel thinking of nothing but food, but I controlled my anger. How could we have raised such a spineless son?

To be fair, he's quite accomplished in his profession, a bridge engineer pulling in almost six figures a year, but he's henpecked and indulgent with the kids, and got worse and worse after he came to America, as if he had become a man without temper or opinions. How often I wanted to tell him point-blank that he must live like a man, at least more like his former self. Between his mother and myself, we often wondered if he was inadequate in bed; otherwise, how could he always listen to Mandi?

After that quarrel, we decided to move out. Gubin and Mandi helped us fill out an application for housing offered to the elderly by the city, which we'll have to wait a long time to get. If we were not so old and in poor health, we'd live far away from them, completely on our own, but they are the only family we have in this country, so we could move only to a nearby place. For the time being we've settled down in a one-bedroom apartment on Fifty-fourth Avenue, rented for us by Gubin. Sometimes he comes over to see if we're all right or need anything. We've never asked him what last name our grandkids use now. I guess they must have some American name. How sad it is when you see your grandchildren's names on paper but can no longer recognize them, as though your family line has faded and disappeared among the multitudes. Whenever I think about this, it stings my heart. If only I'd had second thoughts about leaving China. It's impossible to go back anymore, and we'll have to spend our remaining years in this place where even your grandchildren can act like your enemies.

Matt and Flora usually shun us. If we ran into them on the street, they would warn us not to "torture" their mother again. They even threatened to call the police if we entered their home without permission. We don't have to be warned. We've never set foot in their home since we moved out. I've told my son that we won't accept the kids as part of the family as long as they use a different last name.

Gubin has never brought up that topic again, though I'm still waiting for an answer from him. That's how the matter stands now. The other day, exasperated, my wife wanted to go to Mandi's fortune cookie factory and raise a placard to announce: "My Daughter-in-Law Mandi Cheng Is the Most Unfilial Person on Earth!" But I dissuaded my old better half. What's the good of that? For sure Mandi's company won't fire her just because she can't make her parents-in-law happy. This is America, where we must learn self-reliance and mind our own business.

LORRIE MOORE
(b. 1957)

Born in Glens Falls, New York, Lorrie Moore received a BA from St. Lawrence University in Canton, New York in 1978. She lived in New York City for two years, working as a paralegal in a law firm, and then entered the MFA writing program at Cornell, from which she graduated in 1982. For more than a quarter-century Lorrie Moore has lived in Madison, Wisconsin, where she is Professor of English and where, in a succession of exemplary prose-fiction works, she has finely calibrated a unique "Midwest" sensibility—one that informs much of her strongest writing, including her most recent novel A Gate at the Stairs.

Social awkwardness, emotional indeterminacy, hesitations and missteps of all kinds—Lorrie Moore is the very Jane Austen of the ill-at-ease and the inept. Her characters are not tragic figures but painfully recognizable seriocomic portraits of individuals who suffer from excruciating loneliness, or its opposite; who move from tension to tension, which is "where the story is" (to quote Moore); who fail at relationships for lack of confidence, or as a consequence of knowing too much. The author is much admired for her brilliantly inventive word-play and for her methodical, minute examinations of just-slightly-bizarre situations in which individuals, nearly always women, innocently and fatefully find themselves, as in stories with such titles as "How to Become an Other Woman," in Moore's debut story collection Self-Help *(1985) and "You're Ugly, Too," included in* The Best American Short Stories of the Century *edited by John Updike.*

Lorrie Moore is the author as well of the acclaimed collections Like Life *(1990),* Birds of America *(1998), and the* Collected Stories of Lorrie Moore *(2008), as well as the novels* Anagrams *(1986),* Who Will Run the Frog Hospital? *(1994), and* A Gate at the Stairs *(2009). Her children's book is* The Forgotten Helper *(1987). She has guest-edited* The Best American Short Stories 1994 *and her work appears often in the* New Yorker, *the* New York Review of Books, *the* Best American Short Stories, *and the* O. Henry Prize Stories; *in 2006, she was inducted into the American Academy of Arts and Letters.*

"How to Become a Writer" is quintessential early–Lorrie Moore: droll, funny, touching, and memorable.

How to Become a Writer

First, try to be something, anything, else. A movie star/astronaut. A movie star/missionary. A movie star/kindergarten teacher. President of the World. Fail miserably. It is best if you fail at an early age—say, fourteen. Early, critical disillusionment is necessary so that at fifteen you can write long haiku sequences about thwarted desire. It is a pond, a cherry blossom, a wind brushing against sparrow wing leaving for mountain. Count the syllables. Show it to your mom. She is tough and practical. She has a son in Vietnam and a husband who may be having an affair. She believes in wearing brown because it hides spots. She'll look briefly at your writing, then back up at you with a face blank as a donut. She'll say: "How about emptying the dishwasher?" Look away. Shove the forks in the fork drawer. Accidentally break one of the freebie gas station glasses. This is the required pain and suffering. This is only for starters.

In your high school English class look only at Mr. Killian's face. Decide faces are important. Write a villanelle about pores. Struggle. Write a sonnet. Count the syllables: nine, ten, eleven, thirteen. Decide to experiment with fiction. Here you don't have to count syllables. Write a short story about an elderly man and woman who accidentally shoot each other in the head, the result of an inexplicable malfunction of a shotgun which appears mysteriously in their living room one night. Give it to Mr. Killian as your final project. When you get it back, he has written on it: "Some of your images are quite nice, but you have no sense of plot." When you are home, in the privacy of your own room, faintly scrawl in pencil beneath his black-inked comments: "Plots are for dead people, pore-face."

Take all the babysitting jobs you can get. You are great with kids. They love you. You tell them stories about old people who die idiot deaths. You sing them songs like "Blue Bells of Scotland," which is their favorite. And when they are in their pajamas and have finally stopped pinching each other, when they are fast asleep, you read every sex manual in the house, and wonder how on earth anyone could ever do those things with someone they truly loved. Fall asleep in a chair reading Mr. McMurphy's *Playboy.* When the McMurphy's come home, they will tap you on the shoulder, look at the magazine in your lap, and grin. You will want to die. They will ask you if Tracey took her medicine all right. Explain, yes, she did, that you promised her a story if she would take it like a big girl and that seemed to work out just fine. "Oh, marvelous," they will exclaim.

Try to smile proudly.

Apply to college as a child psychology major.

As a child psychology major, you have some electives. You've always liked birds. Sign up for something called "The Ornithological Field Trip." It meets Tuesdays and Thursdays at two. When you arrive at Room 134 on the first day of class, everyone is sitting around a seminar table talking about metaphors. You've heard of these. After a short, excruciating while, raise your hand and say diffidently, "Excuse me, isn't this Bird-watching One-oh-one?" The class stops and turns to look at you. They seem to all have one face—giant and blank as a vandalized clock. Someone with a beard booms out, "No, this is Creative Writing." Say: "Oh-right," as if perhaps you knew all along. Look down at your schedule. Wonder how the hell you ended up here. The computer, apparently, has made an error. You start to get up to leave and then don't. The lines at the registrar this week are huge. Perhaps you should stick with this mistake. Perhaps your creative writing isn't all that bad. Perhaps it is fate. Perhaps this is what your dad meant when he said, "It's the age of computers, Francie, it's the age of computers."

Decide that you like college life. In your dorm you meet many nice people. Some are smarter than you. And some, you notice, are dumber than you. You will continue, unfortunately, to view the world in exactly these terms for the rest of your life.

The assignment this week in creative writing is to narrate a violent happening. Turn in a story about driving with your Uncle Gordon and another one about two old people who are accidentally electrocuted when they go to turn on a badly wired desk lamp. The teacher will hand them back to you with comments: "Much of your writing is smooth and energetic. You have, however, a ludicrous notion of plot." Write another story about a man and a woman who, in the very first paragraph, have their lower torsos accidentally blitzed away by dynamite. In the second paragraph, with the insurance money, they buy a frozen yogurt stand together. There are six more paragraphs. You read the whole thing out loud in class. No one likes it. They say your sense of plot is outrageous and incompetent. After class someone asks you if you are crazy.

Decide that perhaps you should stick to comedies. Start dating someone who is funny, someone who has what in high school you called a "really great sense of humor" and what now your creative writing class calls "self-contempt giving rise to comic form." Write down all of his jokes, but don't tell him you are doing this. Make up anagrams of his old girlfriend's name and name all of your socially handicapped characters with them. Tell him his old girlfriend is in all of your stories and then watch how funny he can be, see what a really great sense of humor he can have.

Your child psychology advisor tells you you are neglecting courses in your major. What you spend the most time on should be what you're majoring in. Say yes, you understand.

In creative writing seminars over the next two years, everyone continues to smoke cigarettes and ask the same things: "But does it work?" "Why should we care about this character?" "Have you earned this cliché?" These seem like important questions.

On days when it is your turn, you look at the class hopefully as they scour your mimeographs for a plot. They look back up at you, drag deeply, and then smile in a sweet sort of way.

You spend too much time slouched and demoralized. Your boyfriend suggests bicycling. Your roommate suggests a new boyfriend. You are said to be self-mutilating and losing weight, but you continue writing. The only happiness you have is writing something new, in the middle of the night, armpits damp, heart pounding, something no one has yet seen. You have only those brief, fragile, untested moments of exhilaration when you know: you are a genius. Understand what you must do. Switch majors. The kids in your nursery project will be disappointed, but you have a calling, an urge, a delusion, an unfortunate habit. You have, as your mother would say, fallen in with a bad crowd.

Why write? Where does writing come from? These are questions to ask yourself. They are like: Where does dust come from? Or: Why is there war? Or: If there's a God, then why is my brother now a cripple?

These are questions that you keep in your wallet, like calling cards. These are questions, your creative writing teacher says, that are good to address in your journals but rarely in your fiction.

The writing professor this fall is stressing the Power of the Imagination. Which means he doesn't want long descriptive stories about your camping trip last July. He wants you to start in a realistic context but then to alter it. Like recombinant DNA. He wants you to let your imagination sail, to let it grow big-bellied in the wind. This is a quote from Shakespeare.

Tell your roommate your great idea, your great exercise of imaginative power: a transformation of Melville to contemporary life. It will be about monomania and the fish-eat-fish world of life insurance in Rochester, New York. The first line will be "Call me Fishmeal," and it will feature a menopausal suburban husband named Richard, who because he is so depressed all the time is called "Mopey Dick" by his witty wife Elaine. Say to your roommate: "Mopey Dick, get it?" Your roommate looks at you, her face blank as a large Kleenex. She comes up to you, like a buddy, and puts an arm around your burdened shoulders. "Listen, Francie," she says, slow as speech therapy. "Let's go out and get a big beer."

The seminar doesn't like this one either. You suspect they are beginning to feel sorry for you. They say: "You have to think about what is happening. Where is the story here?"

The next semester the writing professor is obsessed with writing from personal experience. You must write from what you know, from what has happened to you. He wants deaths, he wants camping trips. Think about what has happened to you. In three years there have been three things: you lost your virginity; your parents got divorced; and your brother came home from a forest ten miles from the Cambodian border with only half a thigh, a permanent smirk nestled into one corner of his mouth.

About the first you write: "It created a new space, which hurt and cried in a voice that wasn't mine, 'I'm not the same anymore, but I'll be okay.'"

About the second you write an elaborate story of an old married couple who stumble upon an unknown land mine in their kitchen and accidentally blow themselves up. You call it: "For Better or for Liverwurst."

About the last you write nothing. There are no words for this. Your typewriter hums. You can find no words.

At undergraduate cocktail parties, people say, "Oh, you write? What do you write about?" Your roommate, who has consumed too much wine, too little cheese, and no crackers at all, blurts: "Oh, my god, she always writes about her dumb boyfriend."

Later on in life you will learn that writers are merely open, helpless texts with no real understanding of what they have written and therefore must half-believe anything and everything that is said of them. You, however, have not yet reached this stage of literary criticism. You stiffen and say, "I do not," the same way you said it when someone in the fourth grade accused you of really liking oboe lessons and your parents really weren't just making you take them.

Insist you are not very interested in any one subject at all, that you are interested in the music of language, that you are interested in—in—syllables, because they are the atoms of poetry, the cells of the mind, the breath of the soul. Begin to feel woozy. Stare into your plastic wine cup.

"Syllables?" you will hear someone ask, voice trailing off, as they glide slowly toward the reassuring white of the dip.

Begin to wonder what you do write about. Or if you have anything to say. Or if there even is such a thing as a thing to say. Limit these thoughts to no more than ten minutes a day; like sit-ups, they can make you thin.

You will read somewhere that all writing has to do with one's genitals. Don't dwell on this. It will make you nervous.

Your mother will come visit you. She will look at the circles under your eyes and hand you a brown book with a brown briefcase on the cover. It is entitled: *How to Become a Business Executive.* She has also brought the *Names for Baby* encyclopedia you asked for; one of your characters, the aging clown–schoolteacher, needs a new name. Your mother will shake her head and say: "Francie, Francie, remember when you were going to be a child psychology major?"

Say: "Mom, I like to write."

She'll say: "Sure you like to write. Of course. Sure you like to write."

Write a story about a confused music student and title it: "Schubert Was the One with the Glasses, Right?" It's not a big hit, although your roommate likes the part where the two violinists accidentally blow themselves up in a recital room. "I went out with a violinist once," she says, snapping her gum.

Thank god you are taking other courses. You can find sanctuary in nineteenth-century ontological snags and invertebrate courting rituals. Certain globular mollusks have what is called "Sex by the Arm." The male octopus, for instance, loses the end of one arm when placing it inside the female body during intercourse. Marine biologists call it "Seven Heaven." Be glad you know these things. Be glad you are not just a writer. Apply to law school.

From here on in, many things can happen. But the main one will be this: you decide not to go to law school after all, and, instead, you spend a good, big chunk of your adult life telling people how you decided not to go to law school after all. Somehow you end up writing again. Perhaps you go to graduate school. Perhaps you work odd jobs and take writing courses at night. Perhaps you are working on a novel and writing down all the clever remarks and intimate personal confessions you hear during the day. Perhaps you are losing your pals, your acquaintances, your balance.

You have broken up with your boyfriend. You now go out with men who, instead of whispering "I love you," shout: "Do it to me, baby." This is good for your writing.

Sooner or later you have a finished manuscript more or less. People look at it in a vaguely troubled sort of way and say, "I'll bet becoming a writer was always a fantasy of yours, wasn't it?" Your lips dry to salt. Say that of all the fantasies possible in the world, you can't imagine being a writer even making the top twenty. Tell them you were going to be a child psychology major. "I bet," they always sigh, "you'd be great with kids." Scowl fiercely. Tell them you're a walking blade.

Quit classes. Quit jobs. Cash in old savings bonds. Now you have time like warts on your hands. Slowly copy all of your friends' addresses into a new address book.

Vacuum. Chew cough drops. Keep a folder full of fragments.

An eyelid darkening sideways.
World as conspiracy.
Possible plot? A woman gets on a bus.
Suppose you threw a love affair and nobody came.

At home drink a lot of coffee. At Howard Johnson's order the cole slaw. Consider how it looks like the soggy confetti of a map: where you've been, where you're going—"You Are Here," says the red star on the back of the menu.

Occasionally a date with a face blank as a sheet of paper asks you whether writers often become discouraged. Say that sometimes they do and sometimes they do. Say it's a lot like having polio.

"Interesting," smiles your date, and then he looks down at his arm hairs and starts to smooth them, all, always, in the same direction.

DAVID FOSTER WALLACE
(1962–2008)

Born in Ithaca, New York, and raised in Champagne, Illinois, where his father was a professor of philosophy at the University of Illinois at Urbana-Champagne, David Foster Wallace received a BA degree in English and philosophy (with an emphasis upon modal logic and math) from Amherst College in 1985; he received an MFA degree from the University of Arizona in 1987 and began Ph.D. graduate studies in philosophy at Harvard, then dropped out, and for a while taught at Emerson College in Boston. In 1992, Wallace began teaching at Illinois State University, and at the time of his premature death in Claremont, California, he was on the faculty of Ponoma College, where he had been Professor of Creative Writing and English since 2002.

A brilliantly inventive, ceaselessly curious, and often self-reflexively playful writer in the mode of Sixties experimentation—Thomas Pynchon, John Barth, Donald Barthelme are predominant influences—Wallace is one of the most original writers of a generation that includes Jonathan Franzen, Michael Chabon, and Jennifer Egan. His subjects are numerous but linked: underlying his narratives are the theme of addiction, of which Wallace, congenitally predisposed to severe depression, had firsthand experience; and the theme of the mind's deracination from the objects of its perception, a bifurcation of the self that results in spiritual paralysis. As a counter to this stasis of the soul, in his later work Wallace was exploring the possibilities of salvation through intellectual discipline, attentiveness, duty, and compassion for living things.

Though somewhat difficult of access, Wallace's much-admired novels The Broom of the System *(1987), the massive* Infinite Jest *(1996), and the posthumously published* The Pale King *(2011) have acquired cult status; considerably more accessible are Wallace's several story collections* Girl With Curious Hair *(1989),* Brief Encounters with Hideous Men *(1999), and* Oblivion: Stories *(2004). Wallace's essay collections, which in their verve, idiosyncrasy, and self-reflexive perspective recall the political-memoirist essays of Norman Mailer, are* A Supposedly Fun Thing I'll Never Do Again *(1997) and* Consider the Lobster *(2005). Wallace's work appeared frequently in an unusual variety of magazines*—Science, Playboy, Esquire, *the* New Yorker, Paris Review, Conjunctions, Harper's.

In mid-career at the time of his self-inflicted death, Wallace had already received numerous awards: the O. Henry short story prize, the Aga Khan Prize, and a MacArthur Foundation fellowship. "Good People," included here, is notable for its sobriety, straightforward narration, and relative detachment from the author, in contrast to the author's more characteristic hyperbolic style.

Good People

They were up on a picnic table at that park by the lake, by the edge of the lake, with part of a downed tree in the shallows half hidden by the bank. Lane A. Dean, Jr., and his girlfriend, both in bluejeans and button-up shirts. They sat up on the table's top portion and had their shoes on the bench part that people sat on to picnic or fellowship together in carefree times. They'd gone to different high schools but the same junior college, where they had met in campus ministries. It was springtime, and the park's grass was very green and the air suffused with honeysuckle and lilacs both, which was almost too much. There were bees, and the angle of the sun made the water of the shallows look dark. There had been more storms that week, with some downed trees and the sound of chainsaws all up and down his parents' street. Their postures on the picnic table were both the same forward kind with their shoulders rounded and elbows on their knees. In this position the girl rocked slightly and once put her face in her hands, but she was not crying. Lane was very still and immobile and looking past the bank at the downed tree in the shallows and its ball of exposed roots going all directions and the tree's cloud of branches all half in the water. The only other individual nearby was a dozen spaced tables away, by himself, standing upright. Looking at the torn-up hole in the ground there where the tree had gone over. It was still early yet and all the shadows wheeling right and shortening. The girl wore a thin old checked cotton shirt with pearl-colored snaps with the long sleeves down and always smelled very good and clean, like someone you could trust and care about even if you weren't in love. Lane Dean had liked the smell of her right away. His mother called her down to earth and liked her, thought she was good people, you could tell—she made this evident in little ways. The shallows lapped from different directions at the tree as if almost teething on it. Sometimes when alone and thinking or struggling to turn a matter over to Jesus Christ in prayer, he would find himself putting his fist in his palm and turning it slightly as if still playing and pounding his glove to stay sharp and alert in center. He did not do this now; it would be cruel and indecent to do this now. The older individual stood beside his picnic table—he was at it but not sitting—and looked also out of place in a suit coat or jacket and the kind of men's hat Lane's grandfather wore in photos as a young insurance man. He appeared to be looking across the lake. If he moved, Lane didn't see it. He looked more like a picture than a man. There were not any ducks in view.

One thing Lane Dean did was reassure her again that he'd go with her and be there with her. It was one of the few safe or decent things he could really say. The second time he said it again now she shook her head and laughed in an unhappy way that was more just air out her nose. Her real laugh was different. Where he'd be was the waiting room, she said. That he'd be thinking about her and feeling bad for her, she knew, but he couldn't be in there with her. This was so obviously true that he felt like a ninny that he'd kept on about it and now knew what she had thought every time he went and said it—it hadn't brought her comfort or eased the burden at all. The worse he felt, the stiller he sat. The whole thing felt balanced on a knife or wire; if he moved to put his arm up or touch her the whole thing could tip over. He hated himself for sitting so frozen. He could almost visualize himself tiptoeing past something explosive. A big stupid-looking tiptoe, like in a cartoon. The whole last black week had been this way and it was wrong. He knew it was wrong, knew something was required of him that was not this terrible frozen care and caution, but he pretended to himself he did not know what it was that was required. He pretended it had no name. He pretended that not saying aloud what he knew to be right and true was for her sake, was for the sake of her needs and feelings. He also worked dock and routing at UPS, on top of school, but had traded to get the day off after they'd decided together. Two days before, he had awakened very early and tried to pray but could not. He was freezing more and more solid, he felt like, but he had not thought of his father or the blank frozenness of his father, even in church, which had once filled him with such pity. This was the truth. Lane Dean, Jr., felt sun on one arm as he pictured in his mind an image of himself on a train, waving mechanically to something that got smaller and smaller as the train pulled away. His father and his mother's father had the same birthday, a Cancer. Sheri's hair was colored an almost corn blond, very clean, the skin through her central part pink in the sunlight. They'd sat here long enough that only their right side was shaded now. He could look at her head, but not at her. Different parts of him felt unconnected to each other. She was smarter than him and they both knew it. It wasn't just school—Lane Dean was in accounting and business and did all right; he was hanging in there. She was a year older, twenty, but it was also more—she had always seemed to Lane to be on good terms with her life in a way that age could not account for. His mother had put it that she *knew what it is she wanted,* which was nursing and not an easy program at Peoria Junior College, and plus she worked hostessing at the Embers and had bought her own car. She was serious in a way Lane liked. She had a cousin that died when she was thirteen, fourteen, that she'd loved and been close with. She only talked about it that once. He liked her smell and her downy arms and the way she exclaimed when something made her laugh. He had liked just being with her and talking to her. She was serious in her faith and values in a way that Lane had liked and now, sitting here with her on the table, found himself afraid of. This was an awful thing. He was starting to believe that he might not be serious in his faith. He might be somewhat of a hypocrite, like the Assyrians in Isaiah, which would be a far graver sin than the appointment—he had decided he believed this. He was desperate to be good people, to still be able to feel he was good. He rarely before now had thought of damnation and Hell—that part of it didn't speak to his spirit—and in worship services he more just tuned himself out and tolerated Hell when it came up, the same way you tolerate the job you've got to have to save up for what it is you want. Her tennis shoes had little things doodled on them from sitting in her class lectures. She stayed looking down like that. Little notes or reading assignments in Bic in her neat round hand on the rubber elements around the sneaker's rim. Lane A. Dean, looking now at her inclined head's side's barrettes in the shape of blue ladybugs. The appointment was for afternoon, but when the doorbell had rung so early and his mother'd called to him up the stairs, he had known, and a terrible kind of blankness had commenced falling through him.

He told her that he did not know what to do. That he knew if he was the salesman of it and forced it upon her that was awful and wrong. But he was trying to understand—they'd prayed on it and talked it through from every different angle. Lane said how sorry she knew he was, and that if he was wrong in believing they'd truly decided together when they decided to make the appointment she should please tell him, because he thought he knew how she must have felt as it got closer and closer and how she must be so scared, but that what he couldn't tell was if it was more than that. He was totally still except for moving his mouth, it felt like. She did not reply. That if they needed to pray on it more and talk it through, then he was here, he was ready, he said. The appointment could get moved back; if she just said the word they could call and push it back to take more time to be sure in the decision. It was still so early in it—they both knew that, he said. This was true, that he felt this way, and yet he also knew he was also trying to say things that would get her to open up and say enough back that he could see her and read her heart and know what to say to get her to go through with it. He knew this without admitting to himself that this was what he wanted, for it would make him a hypocrite and liar. He knew, in some locked-up little part of him, why it was that he'd gone to no one to open up and seek their life counsel, not Pastor Steve or the prayer partners at campus ministries, not his UPS friends or the spiritual counselling available through his parents' old church. But he did not know why Sheri herself had not gone to Pastor Steve—he could not read her heart. She was blank and hidden. He so fervently wished it never happened. He felt like he knew now why it was a true sin and not just a leftover rule from past society. He felt like he had been brought low by it and humbled and now did believe that the rules were there for a reason. That the rules were concerned with him personally, as an individual. He promised God he had learned his lesson. But what if that, too, was a hollow promise, from a hypocrite who repented only after, who promised submission but really only wanted a reprieve? He might not even know his own heart or be able to read and know himself. He kept thinking also of 1 Timothy and the hypocrite therein who *disputeth over words*. He felt a terrible inner resistance but could not feel what it was that it resisted. This was the truth. All the different angles and ways they had come at the decision together did not ever include it—the word—for had he once said it, avowed that he did love her, loved Sheri Fisher, then it all would have been transformed. It would not be a different stance or angle, but a difference in the very thing they were praying and deciding on together. Sometimes they had prayed together over the phone, in a kind of half code in case anybody accidentally picked up the extension. She continued to sit as if thinking, in the pose of thinking, like that one statue. They were right up next to each other on the table. He was looking over past her at the tree in the water. But he could not say he did: it was not true.

But neither did he ever open up and tell her straight out he did not love her. This might be his *lie by omission*. This might be the frozen resistance—were he to look right at her and tell her he didn't, she would keep the appointment and go. He knew this. Something in him, though, some terrible weakness or lack of values, could not tell her. It felt like a muscle he did not have. He didn't know why; he just could not do it, or even pray to do it. She believed he was good, serious in his values. Part of him seemed willing to more or less just about lie to someone with that kind of faith and trust, and what did that make him? How could such a type of individual even pray? What it really felt like was a taste of the reality of what might be meant by Hell. Lane Dean had never believed in Hell as a lake of fire or a loving God consigning folks to a burning lake of fire—he knew in his heart this was not true. What he believed in was a living God of compassion and love and the possibility of a personal relationship with Jesus Christ through whom this love was enacted in human time. But sitting here beside this girl as unknown to him now as outer space, waiting for whatever she might say to unfreeze him, now he felt like he could see the edge or outline of what a real vision of Hell might be. It was of two great and terrible armies within himself, opposed and facing each other, silent. There would be battle but no victor. Or never a battle—the armies would stay like that, motionless, looking across at each other, and seeing therein something so different and alien from themselves that they could not understand, could not hear each other's speech as even words or read anything from what their face looked like, frozen like that, opposed and uncomprehending, for all human time. Two-hearted, a hypocrite to yourself either way.

When he moved his head, a part of the lake further out flashed with sun—the water up close wasn't black now, and you could see into the shallows and see that all the water was moving but gently, this way and that—and in this same way he besought to return to himself as Sheri moved her leg and started to turn beside him. He could see the man in the suit and gray hat standing motionless now at the lake's rim, holding something under one arm and looking across at the opposite side where a row of little forms on camp chairs sat in a way that meant they had lines in the water for crappie—which mostly only your blacks from the East Side ever did—and the little white shape at the row's end a Styrofoam creel. In his moment or time at the lake now just to come, Lane Dean first felt he could take this all in whole: everything seemed distinctly lit, for the circle of the pin oak's shade had rotated off all the way, and they sat now in sun with their shadow a two-headed thing in the grass before them. He was looking or gazing again at where the downed tree's branches seemed to all bend so sharply just under the shallows' surface when he was given to know that through all this frozen silence he'd despised he had, in truth, been praying, or some little part of his heart he could not hear had, for he was answered now with a type of vision, what he would later call within his own mind a vision or *moment of grace*. He was not a hypocrite, just broken and split off like all men. Later on, he believed that what happened was he'd had a moment of almost seeing them both as Jesus saw them—as blind but groping, wanting to please God despite their inborn fallen nature. For in that same given moment he saw, quick as light, into Sheri's heart, and was made to know what would occur here as she finished turning to him and the man in the hat watched the fishing and the downed elm shed cells into the water. This down-to-earth girl that smelled good and wanted to be a nurse would take and hold one of his hands in both of hers to unfreeze him and make him look at her, and she would say that she cannot do it. That she is sorry she did not know this sooner, that she hadn't meant to lie—she agreed because she'd wanted to believe that she could, but she cannot. That she will carry this and have it; she has to. With her gaze clear and steady. That all night last night she prayed and searched inside herself and decided this is what love commands of her. That Lane should please please sweetie let her finish. That listen—this is her own decision and obliges him to nothing. That she knows he does not love her, not that way, has known it all this time, and that it's all right. That it is as it is and it's all right. She will carry this, and have it, and love it and make no claim on Lane except his good wishes and respecting what she has to do. That she releases him, all claim, and hopes he finishes up at P.J.C. and does so good in his life and has all joy and good things. Her voice will be clear and steady, and she will be lying, for Lane has been given to read her heart. To see through her. One of the opposite side's blacks raises his arm in what may be greeting, or waving off a bee. There is a mower cutting grass someplace off behind them. It will be a terrible, last-ditch gamble born out of the desperation in Sheri Fisher's soul, the knowledge that she can neither do this thing today nor carry a child alone and shame her family. Her values blocked the way either way, Lane could see, and she has no other options or choice—this lie is not a sin. Galatians 4:16, *Have I then become your enemy*? She is gambling that he is good. There on the table, neither frozen nor yet moving, Lane Dean, Jr., sees all this, and is moved with pity, and also with something more, something without any name he knows, that is given to him in the form of a question that never once in all the long week's thinking and division had even so much as occurred—why is he so sure he doesn't love her? Why is one kind of love any different? What if he has no earthly idea what love is? What would even Jesus do? For it was just now he felt her two small strong soft hands on his, to turn him. What if he was just afraid, if the truth was no more than this, and if what to pray for was not even love but simple courage, to meet both her eyes as she says it and trust his heart?

PINCKNEY BENEDICT
(b. 1964)

Born in Ronceverte, West Virginia, Pinckney Benedict grew up on his family's dairy farm north of Lewisburg. He graduated from Princeton University *magna cum laude* in 1986 with a BA in English, and received his MFA from the Writers' Workshop of the University of Iowa in 1987. After an appointment to the Hill School, his alma mater in Pottstown, Pennsylvania, Benedict spent two years on the Creative Writing Faculty of Oberlin College. He has subsequently taught at Davidson College and at Southern Illinois University at Carbondale, where he is now a professor of English.

Pinckney Benedict's first short story collection, *Town Smokes* (1987), revised from his senior thesis at Princeton University, received the Nelson Algren Award for the short story. Benedict has subsequently received a literary fellowship from the National Endowment for the Arts and a fiction grant from the Illinois Arts Council. Among his publications are the story collections *The Wrecking Yard* (1992) and *Miracle Boy* (2010), and the novel *Dogs of God* (1995), which was awarded the Steinbeck Award. Benedict has edited, with his wife Laura Benedict, the *Surreal South* fiction anthology.

One of the most gifted American writers of his generation, Pinckney Benedict writes primarily of rural subjects, with an emphasis upon his distinctive West Virginia background. His poetically rendered yet jarringly graphic stories are models of seemingly effortless storytelling; in Benedict's most characteristic work, as in "Mercy," included here, protagonists and their landscapes are deeply bonded. Suspense is generated out of a potentially tragic clash of personalities—or traditions. One never knows how a story by Pinckney Benedict will end until the very last, perfectly rendered line.

Like a number of other writers in this volume, including Sherwood Anderson, Eudora Welty, Flannery O'Connor and Louise Erdrich, Pinckney Benedict raises "regional" writing to a transcendental level.

Mercy

The livestock hauler's ramp banged onto the ground, and out of the darkness they came, the miniature horses, fine-boned and fragile as china. They trit-trotted down the incline like the vanguard of a circus parade, tails up, manes fluttering. They were mostly a bunch of tiny pintos, the biggest not even three feet tall at the withers. I was ten years old, and their little bodies made me feel like a giant. The horses kept coming out of the trailer, more and more of them every moment. The teamsters that were unloading them just stood back and smiled.

My old man and I were leaning on the top wire of the southern fenceline of our place, watching the neighbor farm become home to these exotics. Ponies, he kept saying, ponies ponies ponies, like if he said it enough times, he might be able to make them go away. Or make himself believe they were real, one or the other.

I think they're miniature horses, I told him. Not ponies. I kept my voice low, not sure I wanted him to hear me.

One faultless dog-sized sorrel mare looked right at me, tossed its head, and sauntered out into the thick clover of the field, nostrils flaring. I decided I liked that one the best. To myself, I named it Cinnamon. If I were to try and ride it, I thought, my heels would drag the ground.

Horses, ponies, my old man said. He had heard. He swept out a dismissive hand. Can't work them, can't ride them, can't eat them. Useless.

Useless was the worst insult in his vocabulary.

We were angus farmers. Magnificent deep-fleshed black angus. In the field behind us, a dozen of our market steers roamed past my old man and me in a lopsided wedge, cropping the sweet grass. They ate constantly, putting on a pound, two pounds a day. All together like that, they made a sound like a steam locomotive at rest in the station, a deep resonant sighing. Their rough hides gleamed obsidian in the afternoon sun, and their hooves might have been fashioned out of pig iron.

The biggest of them, the point of the wedge, raised his head, working to suss out this new smell, the source of this nickering and whinnying, that had invaded his neighborhood. His name was Rug, because his hide was perfect, and my old man planned to have it tanned after we sent him off to the lockers in the fall. None of the other steers had names, just the numbers in the yellow tags that dangled from their ears. Rug peered near-sightedly through the woven-wire fence that marked the border between his field and the miniature horses', and his face was impassive, as it always was.

The teamsters slammed the trailer's ramp back into place and climbed into the rig's cab, cranked up the big diesel engine, oily smoke pluming from the dual stacks. The offloaded horses began to play together, nipping at one another with their long yellow teeth, dashing around the periphery of the field, finding the limits of the place. Cinnamon trailed after the others, less playful than the rest. Rug lowered his head and moved on, and the wedge of heavy-shouldered angus moved with him.

Another livestock van pulled into the field, the drivers of the two trucks exchanging casual nods as they passed each other. I was happy enough to see more of them come, funny little beggars, but I had a moment of wondering to myself how many horses, even miniature ones, the pasture could sustain.

More of the midgets, my old man said. What in hell's next? he asked. He wasn't speaking to me exactly. He very seldom addressed a question directly to me. It seemed like he might be asking God Himself. What? Giraffes? Crocodiles?

This valley was a beef valley from long before I was born. A broad river valley with good grass, set like a diamond in the center of a wide plateau at twenty-four hundred feet of altitude. For generations it was Herefords all around our place, mostly, and Charolais, but our angus were the sovereigns over them all. My grandfather was president of the cattlemen's association, and he raised some trouble when the Beefmasters and Swiss Simmentals came in, because the breeds were unfamiliar to him; and my old man did the same when the place to our east went with the weird-looking humpbacked lop-eared Brahmas. But they got used to the new breeds. They were, after all, beefers, and beef fed the nation; and we were still royalty.

Then the bottom fell out of beef prices. We hung on. Around us, the Charolais and Simmentals went first, the herds dispersed and the land sold over the course of a few years, and then the rest of them all in a rush, and we were alone. Worse than alone. Now it was swine to the east, and the smell of them when the wind was wrong was enough to gag a strong-stomached man. The smell of angus manure is thick and honest and bland, like the angus himself; but pig manure is acid and briny and bitter and brings a tear to the eye. And the shrieking of the pigs clustered in their long barns at night, as it drifted across the fields into our windows, was like the cries of the damned.

Pigs to the east, with a big poultry operation beyond that, and sheep to the north (with llamas to protect them from packs of feral dogs), and even rumors of a man up in Pocahontas County who wanted to start an ostrich ranch, because ostrich meat was said to be low in fat and cholesterol, and ostrich plumes made wonderful feather dusters that never wore out.

The place to our west wasn't even a farm anymore. A rich surgeon named Slaughter from the county seat had bought the acreage when Warren Kennebaker, the Charolais breeder, went bust. Slaughter had designed it like a fortress, and it looked down on our frame house from a hill where the dignified long-bodied Charolais had grazed: a great gabled many-chimneyed mansion that went up in a matter of months; acres of slate roof, and a decorative entrance flanked by stone pillars and spear-pointed pickets that ran for three or four rods out to each side of the driveway and ended there; and gates with rampant lions picked out in gold. That entrance with its partial fence made my old man angrier than anything else. What good's a fence that doesn't go all the way around? he asked me. Keeps nothing out, keeps nothing in.

Useless, I said.

As tits on a bull, he said. Then: Doctor Slaughter, Doctor Slaughter! he shouted up at the blank windows of the house. He thought her name was the funniest thing he had ever heard. Why don't you just get together and form a practice with Doctor Payne and Doctor Butcher?

There was no Doctor Payne or Doctor Butcher; that was just his joke.

Payne, Slaughter, and Butcher! he shouted. That would be rich.

The horses started testing the fence almost from the first. They were smart, I could tell that from watching them, from the way they played tag together, darting off to the far parts of the pasture to hide, flirting, concealing their compact bodies in folds of the earth and leaping up to race off again when they were discovered, their hooves drumming against the hard-packed ground. They galloped until they reached one end of the long field, then swung around in a broad curve and came hell-for-leather back the way they had gone, their coats shaggy with the approach of winter and slick with sweat. I watched them whenever I had a few moments free from ferrying feed for the steers.

I would walk down to the south fence and climb up on the sagging wire and sit and take them in as they leaped and nipped and pawed at one another with their sharp, narrow hooves. I felt like they wanted to put on a show for me when I was there, wanted to entertain me. During the first snow, which was early that year, at the end of October, they stood stock still, the whole crew of them, and gaped around at the gently falling flakes. They twitched their hides and shook their manes and shoulders as though flies were lighting all over them. They snorted and bared their teeth and sneezed. After a while, they grew bored with the snow and went back to their games.

After a few weeks, though, when the weather got colder and the grass was thin and trampled down, the horses became less like kids and more like the convicts in some prison picture: heads down, shoulders hunched, they sidled along the fence line, casting furtive glances at me and at the comparatively lush pasturage on our side of the barrier.

The fence was a shame and an eyesore. It had been a dry summer when it went in, five years before when the last of the dwindling Herefords had occupied the field, and the dirt that season was dry as desert sand, and the posts weren't sunk as deep as they should have been.

They were loose like bad teeth, and a few of them were nearly rotted through. I was the only one who knew what bad shape it was getting to be in. My old man seldom came down to this boundary after the day the horses arrived, and nobody from the miniature horse farm walked their border the way we walked ours. We didn't know any of them, people from outside the county, hardly ever glimpsed them at all.

It wasn't our problem to solve. By long tradition, that stretch was the responsibility of the landowner to the south, and I figured my old man would die before he would take up labor and expense that properly belonged with the owners of the miniature horses.

Cinnamon, the sorrel, came over to me one afternoon when I was taking a break, pushed her soft nose through the fence toward me, and I promised myself that the next time I came I would bring the stump of a carrot or a lump of sugar with me. I petted her velvet nose and she nibbled gently at my fingers and the open palm of my hand. Her whiskers tickled and her breath was warm and damp against my skin.

Then she took her nose from me and clamped her front teeth on the thin steel wire of the fence and pulled it toward her, pushed it back. I laughed. Get away from there, I told her, and smacked her gently on the muzzle. She looked at me reproachfully and tugged at the wire again. Her mouth made grating sounds against the metal that set my own teeth on edge. She had braced her front legs and was really pulling, and the fence flexed and twanged like a bow string. A staple popped loose from the nearest post.

You've got to stop it, I said. You don't want to come over here, even if the grass looks good. My old man will shoot you if you do.

He surprised me watching the horses. I was in my usual place on the fence, the top wire biting into my rear end, and he must have caught sight of me as he was setting out one of the great round hay bales for the angus to feed from. Generally I was better at keeping track of him, at knowing where he was, but that day I had brought treats with me and was engrossed, and I didn't hear the approaching rumble of his tractor as it brought the fodder over the hill. When he shut down the engine, I knew that I was caught.

What are you doing? he called. The angus that were following the tractor and the hay, eager to be fed, ranged themselves in a stolid rank behind him. I kicked at Cinnamon to get her away from me, struggled to get the slightly crushed cubes of sugar back into my pocket. Crystals of it clung to my fingers. He strode down to me, and I swung my legs back over to our side of the fence and hopped down. It was a cold day and his breath rolled white from his mouth.

You've got plenty of leisure, I guess, he said. His gaze flicked over my shoulder. A number of the miniature horses, Cinnamon at their head, had peeled off from the main herd and were dashing across the open space. What makes them run like that? he asked. I hesitated a moment, not sure whether he wanted to know or if it was one of those questions that didn't require an answer.

They're just playing, I told him. They spend a lot of time playing.

Playing. Is that right, he said. You'd like to have one, I bet. Wouldn't you, boy? he asked me.

I pictured myself with my legs draped around the barrel of Cinnamon's ribs, my fingers wrapped in the coarse hair of her mane. Even as I pictured it, I knew a person couldn't ride a miniature horse. I recalled what it felt like when she had thrust her muzzle against my hand, her breath as she went after the sugar I had begun bringing her. Her teeth against the wire. I pictured myself holding out a fresh carrot for her to lip into her mouth. I pictured her on our side of the fence, her small form threading its way among the stem gigantic bodies of the angus steers. I knew I would be a fool to tell him I wanted a miniature horse.

Yes sir, I said.

He swept his eyes along the fence. Wire's in pretty bad shape, he said. Bastards aren't doing their job. Looks like we'll have to do it for them.

He shucked off the pair of heavy leather White Mule work gloves he was wearing and tossed them to me. I caught one in the air, and the other fell to the cold ground. You keep the fence in shape then, he said. The staples and wire and stretcher and all were in the machine shed, I knew.

Remember, my old man said as he went back to his tractor. First one that comes on my property, I kill.

On the next Saturday, before dawn, I sat in the cab of our beef hauler while he loaded steers. There were not many of them; it would only take us one trip. I couldn't get in among them because I didn't yet own a pair of steel-toed boots, and the angus got skittish when they were headed to the stockyard. I would have helped, I wanted to help, but he was afraid I would get stepped on by the anxious beeves and lose a toe. He was missing toes on both feet. So he was back there by himself at the tailgate of the truck, running the angus up into it, shouting at them.

Rug was the first, and my old man called the name into his twitching ear—Ho, Rug! Ho!—and took his cap off, slapped him on the rump with it. Get up there! he shouted. I watched him in the rearview mirror, and it was hard to make out what was happening, exactly, because the mirror was cracked down its length, the left half crazed into a patchwork of glass slivers. The other angus were growing restive, I could tell that much, while Rug balked.

My old man never would use an electric prod. He twisted Rug's tail up into a tight, painful coil, shoving with his shoulder, and the big steer gave in and waddled reluctantly into the van. The truck shifted with his weight, which was better than a ton. The rest followed, the hauler sinking lower and lower over the rear axle as they clambered inside. My old man silently mouthed their numbers, every one, as they trundled on board, and he never looked at their ear tags once. He knew them.

When they were all embarked, when for the moment his work was done, his face fell slack and dull, and his shoulders slumped. And for a brief instant he stood still, motionless as I had never seen him. It was as though a breaker somewhere inside him had popped, and he had been shut off.

I made my daily round of the southern fence, patching up the holes the horses had made, shoveling loose dirt into the cavities they carved into the earth, as though they would tunnel under the fence if I wouldn't let them break through it. They were relentless and I had become relentless too, braiding the ends of the bitten wire back together, hammering bent staples back into the rotting posts. The sharp end of a loose wire snaked its way through the cowhide palm of the glove on my right hand and bit deep into me. I cursed and balled the hand briefly into a fist to stanch the blood, and then I went back to work again.

The field the horses occupied was completely skinned now, dotted with mounds of horse dung. Because the trees were bare of leaves, I could see through the windbreak to the principal barn of the place, surrounded by dead machinery. I couldn't tell if anyone was caring for them at all. I don't believe a single animal had been sold. Their coats were long and matted, their hooves long untrimmed, curling and ugly. A man—I suppose it was a man, because at this distance I couldn't tell, just saw a dark figure in a long coat—emerged from the open double doors of the barn, apparently intent on some errand.

Hey! I shouted to him. My voice was loud in the cold and silence. The figure paused and glanced around. I stood up and waved my arms over my head to get his attention. This is your fence!

He lifted a hand, pale so that I could only imagine that it was ungloved, and waved uncertainly back at me.

This is your fence to fix! I called. I pounded my hand against the loose top wire. These here are your horses!

The hand dropped, and the figure without making any further acknowledgment of me or what I had said turned its back and strolled at a casual pace back into the dark maw of the barn.

Most days I hated them. I cursed them as they leaned their slight weight against the fence, their ribs showing. I poked them with a sharp stick to get them to move so that I could fix the fence. They would shift their bodies momentarily, then press them even harder into the wire. The posts groaned and popped. I twisted wire and sucked at the cuts on my fingers to take the sting away. I filched old bald tires from the machine shed and rolled them through the field and laid them against the holes in the fence. The tires smelled of dust and spider webs. This was not the way we mended fence on our place—our posts were always true, our wire stretched taut and uncorroded, our staples solidly planted—but it was all I could think of to keep them out. The horses rolled their eyes at me.

And I tossed them old dry corn cobs that I retrieved from the crib, the one that we hadn't used in years. The horses fell on the dry husks, shoving each other away with their heads, lashing out with their hooves, biting each other now not in play but hard enough to draw blood. I pitched over shriveled windfallen apples from the stunted trees in the old orchard behind the house. I tried to get the apples near the sorrel, near Cinnamon; but as often as not the pintos shunted her aside before she could snatch a mouthful.

You know why we can't feed them, don't you? my old man asked me. We were breaking up more of the great round bales, which were warm and moist at their center, like fresh-baked rolls. The angus, led not by Rug now but by another, shifted their muscular shoulders and waited patiently to be fed. I could sense the miniature horses lining the fence, but I didn't look at them.

They'd eat us out of house and home, he said. Like locusts.

Behind me, the hooves of the horses clacked against the frozen ground.

One morning, the fence didn't need mending. It had begun to snow in earnest the night before, and it was still snowing when I went out to repair the wire. The television was promising snow for days to come. Most of the horses were at the fence, pressing hard against it but not otherwise moving. Some were lying down in the field beyond. I looked for the sorrel, to see if she was among the standing ones. All of them were covered in thick blankets of snow, and it was impossible to tell one diminutive shape from the next. Each fence post was topped with a sparkling white dome.

I walked the fence, making sure there was no new damage. I took up the stick I had used to poke them and ran its end along the fence wire, hoping its clattering sound would stir them. It didn't. Most of them had clustered at a single point, to exchange body heat, I suppose. I rapped my stick against the post where they were gathered, and its cap of snow fell to the ground with a soft thump. Nothing. The wire was stretched tight with the weight of them.

I knelt down, and the snow soaked immediately through the knees of my coveralls. I put my hand in my pocket, even though I knew there was nothing there for them. The dry cobs were all gone, the apples had been eaten. The eyes of the horse nearest me were closed, and there was snow caught in its long delicate lashes. The eyes of all the horses were closed. This one, I thought, was the sorrel, was Cinnamon. Must be. I put my hand to its muzzle but could feel nothing. I stripped off the White Mule glove, and the cold bit immediately into my fingers, into the half-healed cuts there from the weeks of mending fence. I reached out again.

And the horse groaned. I believed it was the horse. I brushed snow from its forehead, and its eyes blinked open, and the groaning continued, a weird guttural creaking and crying, and I thought that such a sound couldn't be coming from just the one horse, all of the horses must be making it together somehow, they were crying out with a single voice. Then I thought as the sound grew louder that it must be the hogs to the east, they were slaughtering the hogs and that was the source of it, but it was not time for slaughtering, so that couldn't be right either. I thought these things in a moment, as the sound rang out over the frozen fields and echoed off the surrounding hills.

At last I understood that it was the fencepost, the wood of the fencepost and the raveling wire and the straining staples, right at the point where the horses were gathered. And I leaped backward just as the post gave way. It heeled over hard and snapped off at ground level, and the horses tumbled with it, coming alive as they fell, the snow flying from their coats in a wild spray as they scrambled to get out from under one another.

The woven-wire fence, so many times mended, parted like tissue paper under their combined weight. With a report like a gunshot, the next post went over as well, and the post beyond that. Two or three rods of fence just lay down flat on the ground, and the horses rolled right over it, they came pouring onto our place. The horses out in the field roused themselves at the sound, shivered off their mantles of snow, and came bounding like great dogs through the gap in the fence as well. And I huddled against the ground, my hands up to ward off their flying hooves as they went past me, over me. I knew that there was nothing I could do to stop them. Their hooves would brain me, they would lay my scalp open to the bone.

I was not touched.

The last of the horses bolted by me, and they set to on the remains of the broken round bale, giving little cries of pleasure as they buried their muzzles in the hay's roughness. The few angus that stood nearby looked on bemused at the arrivals. I knew that I had to go tell my father, I had to go get him right away. The fence—the fence that I had maintained day after day, the fence I had hated and that had blistered and slashed my hands—was down. But because it was snowing and all around was quiet, the scene had the feel of a holiday, and I let them eat.

When they had satisfied themselves, for the moment at least, the horses began to play. I searched among them until finally I found the sorrel. She was racing across our field, her hooves kicking up light clouds of ice crystals. She was moving more quickly than I had ever seen her go, but she wasn't chasing another horse, and she wasn't being chased. She was teasing the impassive angus steers, roaring up to them, stopping just short of their great bulk; turning on a dime and dashing away again. They stood in a semicircle, hind ends together, lowered heads outermost, and they towered over her like the walls of a medieval city. She yearned to charm them. She was almost dancing in the snow.

As I watched her, she passed my old man without paying him the least attention. He wore his long cold-weather coat. The hood was up, and it eclipsed his face. He must have been standing there quite a while. Snow had collected on the ridge of his shoulders, and a rime of frost clung to the edges of his hood. In his hand he held a hunting rifle, his Remington .30-06. The lines of his face seemed odd and unfamiliar beneath the coat's cowl, and his shoulders were trembling in a peculiar way as he observed the interlopers on his land. I blinked. I knew what was coming. The thin sunlight, refracted as it was by the snow, dazzled my eyes, and the shadows that hid him from me were deep.

At last, the sorrel took notice of him, and she turned away from the imperturbable angus and trotted over to him. He watched her come. She lowered her delicate head and nipped at him, caught the hem of his coat between her teeth and began to tug. His feet slipped in the snow. Encouraged by her success, she dragged him forward. I waited for him to kill her. She continued to drag him, a foot, a yard, and at last he fell down. He fell right on his ass in the snow, my old man, the Remington held high above his head. The sorrel stood over him, the other horses clustered around her, and she seemed to gloat.

The Remington dropped to the ground, the bolt open, the breech empty. Half a dozen bright brass cartridges left my old man's hand to skip and scatter across the snow. The hood of his coat fell away from his face, and I saw that my old man was laughing.

JHUMPA LAHIRI
(b. 1967)

Born in London, England of Bengali Indian immigrants, Jhumpa Lahiri grew up in Kingston, Rhode Island where her father works as a librarian at the University of Rhode Island. Lahiri received several degrees from Boston University: an MA in English, an MFA in creative writing, an MA in comparative literature, and a PhD in Renaissance studies. She has been a fellow in the Provincetown Fine Arts Work Center and has taught creative writing at Boston University and the Rhode Island School of Design.

Though Lahiri has said that her finely honed short fiction was rejected by magazine editors for many years, her first collection, Interpreter of Maladies *(1999), was awarded a Pulitzer Prize and the PEN/Hemingway Award, a rare distinction for a story collection. Lahiri is the author of the acclaimed novel* The Namesake *(2003), which was made into a successful feature film, as well as a second collection of stories,* Unaccustomed Earth *(2008), which debuted as the number one fiction bestseller on the* New York Times *bestseller list, a yet more rare distinction for any short story collection. Lahiri publishes frequently in the* New Yorker *and has had many stories anthologized in the yearly* Best American Short Stories *and* O. Henry Awards. *She has had a Guggenheim fellowship and is the 2008 winner of the Frank O'Connor International Short Story Award and the 2009 Asian-American Literary Award.*

Lahiri, who lives in Brooklyn with her husband and young children, describes herself as an American citizen, though the subjects of her beautifully rendered fiction are likely to be Indian immigrants and their families. She aspires to a finely wrought but distinctly unshowy "plainness" of style and has been described by literary journalists as a "miniaturist"—a "microcosmologist"—and a "transnational" (one for whom displacement and a dual cultural citizenship are the status quo). Her most characteristic fiction is distinguished by an intense, unhurried, and methodical inwardness, a seeming aversion to dramatic crises and developments of plot; her models are classic nineteenth-century writers—Chekhov, Tolstoy, Thomas

Hardy—and her older contemporaries William Trevor, Alice Munro, and Mavis Gallant.

As in the short stories and plays of Anton Chekhov, whose work Lahiri's most resembles, a seemingly static surface of domestic ordinariness can crack open to reveal something very different, very disturbing, and profoundly moving. "Hell-Heaven" is an ideal entry into Jhumpa Lahiri's distinctive world.

Hell–Heaven

Pranab Chakraborty wasn't technically my father's younger brother. He was a fellow Bengali from Calcutta who had washed up on the barren shores of my parents' social life in the early seventies, when they lived in a rented apartment in Central Square and could number their acquaintances on one hand. But I had no real uncles in America, and so I was taught to call him Pranab Kaku. Accordingly, he called my father Shyamal Da, always addressing him in the polite form, and he called my mother Boudi, which is how Bengalis are supposed to address an older brother's wife, instead of using her first name, Aparna. After Pranab Kaku was befriended by my parents, he confessed that on the day we met him he had followed my mother and me for the better part of an afternoon around the streets of Cambridge, where she and I tended to roam after I got out of school. He had trailed behind us along Massachusetts Avenue and in and out of the Harvard Coop, where my mother liked to look at discounted housewares. He wandered with us into Harvard Yard, where my mother often sat on the grass on pleasant days and watched the stream of students and professors filing busily along the paths, until, finally, as we were climbing the steps to Widener Library so that I could use the bathroom, he tapped my mother on the shoulder and inquired, in English, if she might be a Bengali. The answer to his question was clear, given that my mother was wearing the red and white bangles unique to Bengali married women, and a common Tangail sari, and had a thick stem of vermilion powder in the center parting of her hair, and the full round face and large dark eyes that are so typical of Bengali women. He noticed the two or three safety pins she wore fastened to the thin gold bangles that were behind the red and white ones, which she would use to replace a missing hook on a blouse or to draw a string through a petticoat at a moment's notice, a practice he associated strictly with his mother and sisters and aunts in Calcutta. Moreover, Pranab Kaku had overheard my mother speaking to me in Bengali, telling me that I couldn't buy an issue of *Archie* at the Coop. But back then, he also confessed, he was so new to America that he took nothing for granted and doubted even the obvious.

My parents and I had lived in Central Square for three years prior to that day; before that, we lived in Berlin, where I was born and where my father had finished his training in microbiology before accepting a position as a researcher at Mass General, and before Berlin my mother and father had lived in India, where they were strangers to each other, and where their marriage had been arranged. Central Square is the first place I can recall living, and in my memories of our apartment, in a dark brown shingled house on Ashburton Place, Pranab Kaku is always there. According to the story he liked to recall often, my mother invited him to accompany us back to our apartment that very afternoon and prepared tea for the two of them; then, after learning that he had not had a proper Bengali meal in more than three months, she served him the leftover curried mackerel and rice that we had eaten for dinner the night before. He remained into the evening for a second dinner after my father got home, and after that he showed up for dinner almost every night, occupying the fourth chair at our square Formica kitchen table and becoming a part of our family in practice as well as in name.

He was from a wealthy family in Calcutta and had never had to do so much as pour himself a glass of water before moving to America, to study engineering at MIT. Life as a graduate student in Boston was a cruel shock, and in his first month he lost nearly twenty pounds. He had arrived in January, in the middle of a snowstorm, and at the end of a week he had packed his bags and gone to Logan, prepared to abandon the opportunity he'd worked toward all his life, only to change his mind at the last minute. He was living on Trowbridge Street in the home of a divorced woman with two young children who were always screaming and crying. He rented a room in the attic and was permitted to use the kitchen only at specified times of the day and instructed always to wipe down the stove with Windex and a sponge. My parents agreed that it was a terrible situation, and if they'd had a bedroom to spare they would have offered it to him. Instead, they welcomed him to our meals and opened up our apartment to him at any time, and soon it was there he went between classes and on his days off, always leaving behind some vestige of himself: a nearly finished pack of cigarettes, a newspaper, a piece of mail he had not bothered to open, a sweater he had taken off and forgotten in the course of his stay.

I remember vividly the sound of his exuberant laughter and the sight of his lanky body slouched or sprawled on the dull, mismatched furniture that had come with our apartment. He had a striking face, with a high forehead and a thick mustache, and overgrown, untamed hair that my mother said made him look like the American hippies who were everywhere in those days. His long legs jiggled rapidly up and down wherever he sat, and his elegant hands trembled when he held a cigarette between his fingers, tapping the ashes into a teacup that my mother began to set aside for this exclusive purpose. Though he was a scientist by training, there was nothing rigid or predictable or orderly about him. He always seemed to be starving, walking through the door and announcing that he hadn't had lunch, and then he would eat ravenously, reaching behind my mother to steal cutlets as she was frying them, before she had a chance to set them properly on a plate with red onion salad. In private, my parents remarked that he was a brilliant student, a star at Jadavpur who had come to MIT with an impressive assistantship, but Pranab Kaku was cavalier about his classes, skipping them with frequency. "These Americans are learning equations I knew at Usha's age," he would complain. He was stunned that my second-grade teacher didn't assign any homework and that at the age of seven I hadn't yet been taught square roots or the concept of pi.

He appeared without warning, never phoning beforehand but simply knocking on the door the way people did in Calcutta and calling out "Boudi!" as he waited for my mother to let him in. Before we met him, I would return from school and find my mother with her purse in her lap and her trench coat on, desperate to escape the apartment where she had spent the day alone. But now I would find her in the kitchen, rolling out dough for luchis, which she normally made only on Sundays for my father and me, or putting up new curtains she'd bought at Woolworth's. I did not know, back then, that Pranab Kaku's visits were what my mother looked forward to all day, that she changed into a new sari and combed her hair in anticipation of his arrival, and that she planned, days in advance, the snacks she would serve him with such nonchalance. That she lived for the moment she heard him call out "Boudi!" from the porch and that she was in a foul humor on the days he didn't materialize.

It must have pleased her that I looked forward to his visits as well. He showed me card tricks and an optical illusion in which he appeared to be severing his own thumb with enormous struggle and strength and taught me to memorize multiplication tables well before I had to learn them in school. His hobby was photography. He owned an expensive camera that required thought before you pressed the shutter, and I quickly became his favorite subject, round-faced, missing teeth, my thick bangs in need of a trim. They are still the pictures of myself I like best, for they convey that confidence of youth I no longer possess, especially in front of a camera. I remember having to run back and forth in Harvard Yard as he stood with the camera, trying to capture me in motion, or posing on the steps of university buildings and on the street and against the trunks of trees. There is only one photograph in which my mother appears; she is holding me as I sit straddling her lap, her head tilted toward me, her hands pressed to my ears as if to prevent me from hearing something. In that picture, Pranab Kaku's shadow, his two arms raised at angles to hold the camera to his face, hovers in the corner of the frame, his darkened, featureless shape superimposed on one side of my mother's body. It was always the three of us. I was always there when he visited. It would have been inappropriate for my mother to receive him in the apartment alone; this was something that went without saying.

They had in common all the things she and my father did not: a love of music, film, leftist politics, poetry. They were from the same neighborhood in North Calcutta, their family homes within walking distance, the facades familiar to them once the exact locations were described. They knew the same shops, the same bus and tram routes, the same holes-in-the-wall for the best jelabis and moghlai parathas. My father, on the other hand, came from a suburb twenty miles outside Calcutta, an area that my mother considered the wilderness, and even in her bleakest hours of homesickness she was grateful that my father had at least spared her a life in the stern house of her in-laws, where she would have had to keep her head covered with the end of her sari at all times and use an outhouse that was nothing but a raised platform with a hole, and where, in the rooms, there was not a single painting hanging on the walls. Within a few weeks, Pranab Kaku had brought his reel-to-reel over to our apartment, and he played for my mother medley after medley of songs from the Hindi films of their youth. They were cheerful songs of courtship, which transformed the quiet life in our apartment and transported my mother back to the world she'd left behind in order to marry my father. She and Pranab Kaku would try to recall which scene in which movie the songs were from, who the actors were and what they were wearing. My mother would describe Raj Kapoor and Nargis singing under umbrellas in the rain, or Dev Anand strumming a guitar on the beach in Goa. She and Pranab Kaku would argue passionately about these matters, raising their voices in playful combat, confronting each other in a way she and my father never did.

Because he played the part of a younger brother, she felt free to call him Pranab, whereas she never called my father by his first name. My father was thirty-seven then, nine years older than my mother. Pranab Kaku was twenty-five. My father was a lover of silence and solitude. He had married my mother to placate his parents; they were willing to accept his desertion as long as he had a wife. He was wedded to his work, his research, and he existed in a shell that neither my mother nor I could penetrate. Conversation was a chore for him; it required an effort he preferred to expend at the lab. He disliked excess in anything, voiced no cravings or needs apart from the frugal elements of his daily routine: cereal and tea in the mornings, a cup of tea after he got home, and two different vegetable dishes every night with dinner. He did not eat with the reckless appetite of Pranab Kaku. My father had a survivor's mentality. From time to time, he liked to remark, in mixed company and often with no relevant provocation, that starving Russians under Stalin had resorted to eating the glue off the back of their wallpaper. One might think that he would have felt slightly jealous, or at the very least suspicious, about the regularity of Pranab Kaku's visits and the effect they had on my mother's behavior and mood. But my guess is that my father was grateful to Pranab Kaku for the companionship he provided, freed from the sense of responsibility he must have felt for forcing her to leave India, and relieved, perhaps, to see her happy for a change.

In the summer, Pranab Kaku bought a navy-blue Volkswagen Beetle and began to take my mother and me for drives through Boston and Cambridge, and soon outside the city, flying down the highway. He would take us to India Tea and Spices in Watertown, and one time he drove us all the way to New Hampshire to look at the mountains. As the weather grew hotter, we started going, once or twice a week, to Walden Pond. My mother always prepared a picnic of hard-boiled eggs and cucumber sandwiches and talked fondly about the winter picnics of her youth, grand expeditions with fifty of her relatives, all taking the train into the West Bengal countryside. Pranab Kaku listened to these stories with interest, absorbing the vanishing details of her past. He did not turn a deaf ear to her nostalgia, like my father, or listen uncomprehending, like me. At Walden Pond, Pranab Kaku would coax my mother through the woods, and lead her down the steep slope to the water's edge. She would unpack the picnic things and sit and watch us as we swam. His chest was matted with thick dark hair, all the way to his waist. He was an odd sight, with his pole-thin legs and a small, flaccid belly, like an otherwise svelte woman who has had a baby and not bothered to tone her abdomen. "You're making me fat, Boudi," he would complain after gorging himself on my mother's cooking. He swam noisily, clumsily, his head always above the water; he didn't know how to blow bubbles or hold his breath, as I had learned in swimming class. Wherever we went, any stranger would have naturally assumed that Pranab Kaku was my father, that my mother was his wife.

It is clear to me now that my mother was in love with him. He wooed her as no other man had, with the innocent affection of a brother-in-law. In my mind, he was just a family member, a cross between an uncle and a much older brother, for in certain respects my parents sheltered and cared for him in much the same way they cared for me. He was respectful of my father, always seeking his advice about making a life in the West, about setting up a bank account and getting a job, and deferring to his opinions about Kissinger and Watergate. Occasionally, my mother would tease him about women, asking about female Indian students at MIT or showing him pictures of her younger cousins in India. "What do you think of her?" she would ask. "Isn't she pretty?" She knew that she could never have Pranab Kaku for herself, and I suppose it was her attempt to keep him in the family. But, most important, in the beginning he was totally dependent on her, needing her for those months in a way my father never did in the whole history of their marriage. He brought to my mother the first and, I suspect, the only pure happiness she ever felt. I don't think even my birth made her as happy. I was evidence of her marriage to my father, an assumed consequence of the life she had been raised to lead. But Pranab Kaku was different. He was the one totally unanticipated pleasure in her life.

In the fall of 1974, Pranab Kaku met a student at Radcliffe named Deborah, an American, and she began to accompany him to our house. I called Deborah by her first name, as my parents did, but Pranab Kaku taught her to call my father Shyamal Da and my mother Boudi, something with which Deborah gladly complied. Before they came to dinner for the first time, I asked my mother, as she was straightening up the living room, if I ought to address her as Deborah Kakima, turning her into an aunt as I had turned Pranab into an uncle. "What's the point?" my mother said, looking back at me sharply. "In a few weeks, the fun will be over and she'll leave him." And yet Deborah remained by his side, attending the weekend parties that Pranab Kaku and my parents were becoming more involved with, gatherings that were exclusively Bengali with the exception of her. Deborah was very tall, taller than both my parents and nearly as tall as Pranab Kaku. She wore her long brass-colored hair center-parted, as my mother did, but it was gathered into a low ponytail instead of a braid, or it spilled messily over her shoulders and down her back in a way that my mother considered indecent. She wore small silver spectacles and not a trace of makeup, and she studied philosophy. I found her utterly beautiful, but according to my mother she had spots on her face, and her hips were too small.

For a while, Pranab Kaku still showed up once a week for dinner on his own, mostly asking my mother what she thought of Deborah. He sought her approval, telling her that Deborah was the daughter of professors at Boston College, that her father published poetry, and that both her parents had PhDs. When he wasn't around, my mother complained about Deborah's visits, about having to make the food less spicy, even though Deborah said she liked spicy food, and feeling embarrassed to put a fried fish head in the dal. Pranab Kaku taught Deborah to say *khub bhalo* and *aacha* and to pick up certain foods with her fingers instead of with a fork. Sometimes they ended up feeding each other, allowing their fingers to linger in each other's mouth, causing my parents to look down at their plates and wait for the moment to pass. At larger gatherings, they kissed and held hands in front of everyone, and when they were out of earshot my mother would talk to the other Bengali women. "He used to be so different. I don't understand how a person can change so suddenly. It's just hell–heaven, the difference," she would say, always using the English words for her self-concocted, backward metaphor.

The more my mother began to resent Deborah's visits, the more I began to anticipate them. I fell in love with Deborah, the way young girls often fall in love with women who are not their mothers. I loved her serene gray eyes, the ponchos and denim wrap skirts and sandals she wore, her straight hair that she let me manipulate into all sorts of silly styles. I longed for her casual appearance; my mother insisted whenever there was a gathering that I wear one of my ankle-length, faintly Victorian dresses, which she referred to as maxis, and have party hair, which meant taking a strand from either side of my head and joining them with a barrette at the back. At parties, Deborah would, eventually, politely slip away, much to the relief of the Bengali women with whom she was expected to carry on a conversation, and she would play with me. I was older than all my parents friends' children, but with Deborah I had a companion. She knew all about the books I read, about Pippi Longstocking and Anne of Green Gables. She gave me the sorts of gifts my parents had neither the money nor the inspiration to buy: a large book of Grimm's *Fairy Tales* with watercolor illustrations on thick, silken pages, wooden puppets with hair fashioned from yarn. She told me about her family, three older sisters and two brothers, the youngest of whom was closer to my age than to hers. Once, after visiting her parents, she brought back three Nancy Drews, her name written in a girlish hand at the top of the first page, and an old toy she'd had, a small paper theater set with interchangeable backdrops, the exterior of a castle and a ballroom and an open field. Deborah and I spoke freely in English, a language in which, by that age, I expressed myself more easily than Bengali, which I was required to speak at home. Sometimes she asked me how to say this or that in Bengali; once, she asked me what *asobbho* meant. I hesitated, then told her it was what my mother called me if I had done something extremely naughty, and Deborah's face clouded. I felt protective of her, aware that she was unwanted, that she was resented, aware of the nasty things people said.

Outings in the Volkswagen now involved the four of us, Deborah in the front, her hand over Pranab Kaku's while it rested on the gearshift, my mother and I in the back. Soon, my mother began coming up with reasons to excuse herself, headaches and incipient colds, and so I became part of a new triangle. To my surprise, my mother allowed me to go with them, to the Museum of Fine Arts and the Public Garden and the Aquarium. She was waiting for the affair to end, for Deborah to break Pranab Kaku's heart and for him to return to us, scarred and penitent. I saw no sign of their relationship foundering. Their open affection for each other, their easily expressed happiness, was a new and romantic thing to me. Having me in the backseat allowed Pranab Kaku and Deborah to practice for the future, to try on the idea of a family of their own. Countless photographs were taken of me and Deborah, of me sitting on Deborah's lap, holding her hand, kissing her on the cheek. We exchanged what I believed were secret smiles, and in those moments I felt that she understood me better than anyone else in the world. Anyone would have said that Deborah would make an excellent mother one day. But my mother refused to acknowledge such a thing. I did not know at the time that my mother allowed me to go off with Pranab Kaku and Deborah because she was pregnant for the fifth time since my birth and was so sick and exhausted and fearful of losing another baby that she slept most of the day. After ten weeks, she miscarried once again and was advised by her doctor to stop trying.

By summer, there was a diamond on Deborah's left hand, something my mother had never been given. Because his own family lived so far away, Pranab Kaku came to the house alone one day, to ask for my parents' blessing before giving her the ring. He showed us the box, opening it and taking out the diamond nestled inside. "I want to see how it looks on someone," he said, urging my mother to try it on, but she refused. I was the one who stuck out my hand, feeling the weight of the ring suspended at the base of my finger. Then he asked for a second thing: he wanted my parents to write to his parents, saying that they had met Deborah and that they thought highly of her. He was nervous, naturally, about telling his family that he intended to marry an American girl. He had told his parents all about us, and at one point my parents had received a letter from them, expressing appreciation for taking such good care of their son and for giving him a proper home in America. "It needn't be long," Pranab Kaku said. "Just a few lines. They'll accept it more easily if it comes from you." My father thought neither ill nor well of Deborah, never commenting or criticizing as my mother did, but he assured Pranab Kaku that a letter of endorsement would be on its way to Calcutta by the end of the week. My mother nodded her assent, but the following day I saw the teacup Pranab Kaku had used all this time as an ashtray in the kitchen garbage can, in pieces, and three Band-Aids taped to my mother's hand.

Pranab Kaku's parents were horrified by the thought of their only son marrying an American woman, and a few weeks later our telephone rang in the middle of the night: it was Mr. Chakraborty telling my father that they could not possibly bless such a marriage, that it was out of the question, that if Pranab Kaku dared to marry Deborah he would no longer acknowledge him as a son. Then his wife got on the phone, asking to speak to my mother and attacked her as if they were intimate, blaming my mother for allowing the affair to develop. She said that they had already chosen a wife for him in Calcutta, that he'd left for America with the understanding that he'd go back after he had finished his studies and marry this girl. They had bought the neighboring flat in their building for Pranab and his betrothed, and it was sitting empty, waiting for his return. "We thought we could trust you, and yet you have betrayed us so deeply," his mother said, taking out her anger on a stranger in a way she could not with her son. "Is this what happens to people in America?" For Pranab Kaku's sake, my mother defended the engagement, telling his mother that Deborah was a polite girl from a decent family. Pranab Kaku's parents pleaded with mine to talk him out of it, but my father refused, deciding that it was not their place to get embroiled. "We are not his parents," he told my mother. "We can tell him they don't approve but nothing more." And so my parents told Pranab Kaku nothing about how his parents had berated them and blamed them, and threatened to disown Pranab Kaku, only that they had refused to give him their blessing. In the face of this refusal, Pranab Kaku shrugged. "I don't care. Not everyone can be as open-minded as you," he told my parents. "Your blessing is blessing enough."

After the engagement, Pranab Kaku and Deborah began drifting out of our lives. They moved in together, to an apartment in Boston, in the South End, a part of the city my parents considered unsafe. We moved as well, to a house in Natick. Though my parents had bought the house, they occupied it as if they were still tenants, touching up scuff marks with leftover paint and reluctant to put holes in the walls, and every afternoon when the sun shone through the living-room window my mother closed the blinds so that our new furniture would not fade. A few weeks before the wedding, my parents invited Pranab Kaku to the house alone, and my mother prepared a special meal to mark the end of his bachelorhood. It would be the only Bengali aspect of the wedding; the rest of it would be strictly American, with a cake and a minister and Deborah in a long white dress and veil. There is a photograph of the dinner, taken by my father, the only picture, to my knowledge, in which my mother and Pranab Kaku appear together. The picture is slightly blurry; I remember Pranab Kaku explaining to my father how to work the camera, and so he is captured looking up from the kitchen table and the elaborate array of food my mother had prepared in his honor, his mouth open, his long arm outstretched and his finger pointing, instructing my father how to read the light meter or some such thing. My mother stands beside him, one hand placed on top of his head in a gesture of blessing, the first and last time she was to touch him in her life. "She will leave him," my mother told her friends afterward. "He is throwing his life away."

The wedding was at a church in Ipswich, with a reception at a country club. It was going to be a small ceremony, which my parents took to mean one or two hundred people as opposed to three or four hundred. My mother was shocked that fewer than thirty people had been invited, and she was more perplexed than honored that, of all the Bengalis Pranab Kaku knew by then, we were the only ones on the list. At the wedding we sat, like the other guests, first on the hard wooden pews of the church and then at a long table that had been set up for lunch. Though we were the closest thing Pranab Kaku had to a family that day, we were not included in the group photographs that were taken on the grounds of the country club, with Deborah's parents and grandparents and her many siblings, and neither my mother nor my father got up to make a toast. My mother did not appreciate the fact that Deborah had made sure that my parents, who did not eat beef, were given fish instead of filet mignon like everyone else. She kept speaking in Bengali, complaining about the formality of the proceedings, and the fact that Pranab Kaku, wearing a tuxedo, barely said a word to us because he was too busy leaning over the shoulders of his new American in-laws as he circled the table. As usual, my father said nothing in response to my mother's commentary, quietly and methodically working though his meal, his fork and knife occasionally squeaking against the surface of the china, because he was accustomed to eating with his hands. He cleared his plate and then my mother's, for she had pronounced the food inedible, and then he announced that he had overeaten and had a stomachache. The only time my mother forced a smile was when Deborah appeared behind her chair, kissing her on the cheek and asking if we were enjoying ourselves.

When the dancing started, my parents remained at the table, drinking tea, and after two or three songs they decided that it was time for us to go home, my mother shooting me looks to that effect across the room, where I was dancing in a circle with Pranab Kaku and Deborah and the other children at the wedding. I wanted to stay, and when, reluctantly, I walked over to where my parents sat, Deborah followed me. "Boudi, let Usha stay. She's having such a good time," she said to my mother. "Lots of people will be heading back your way, someone can drop her off in a little while." But my mother said no, I had had plenty of fun already and forced me to put on my coat over my long puff-sleeved dress. As we drove home from the wedding I told my mother, for the first but not the last time in my life, that I hated her.

The following year, we received a birth announcement from the Chakrabortys, a picture of twin girls, which my mother did not paste into an album or display on the refrigerator door. The girls were named Srabani and Sabitri but were called Bonny and Sara. Apart from a thank-you card for our wedding gift, it was their only communication; we were not invited to the new house in Marblehead, bought after Pranab Kaku got a high-paying job at Stone & Webster. For a while, my parents and their friends continued to invite the Chakrabortys to gatherings, but because they never came, or left after staying only an hour, the invitations stopped. Their absences were attributed, by my parents and their circle to Deborah, and it was universally agreed that she had stripped Pranab Kaku not only of his origins but of his independence. She was the enemy, he was her prey, and their example was invoked as a warning, and as vindication, that mixed marriages were a doomed enterprise. Occasionally, they surprised everyone, appearing at a pujo for a few hours with their two identical little girls who barely looked Bengali and spoke only English and were being raised so differently from me and most of the other children. They were not taken to Calcutta every summer, they did not have parents who were clinging to another way of life and exhorting their children to do the same. Because of Deborah, they were exempt from all that, and for this reason I envied them. "Usha, look at you, all grown up and so pretty," Deborah would say whenever she saw me, rekindling, if only for a minute, our bond of years before. She had cut off her beautiful long hair by then, and had a bob. "I bet you'll be old enough to babysit soon," she would say. "I'll call you—the girls would love that." But she never did.

I began to grow out of my girlhood, entering middle school and developing crushes on the American boys in my class. The crushes amounted to nothing; in spite of Deborah's compliments, I was always overlooked at that age. But my mother must have picked up on something, for she forbade me to attend the dances that were held the last Friday of every month in the school cafeteria, and it was an unspoken law that I was not allowed to date. "Don't think you'll get away with marrying an American, the way Pranab Kaku did," she would say from time to time. I was thirteen, the thought of marriage irrelevant to my life. Still, her words upset me, and I felt her grip on me tighten. She would fly into a rage when I told her I wanted to start wearing a bra, or if I wanted to go to Harvard Square with a friend. In the middle of our arguments, she often conjured Deborah as her antithesis, the sort of woman she refused to be. "If she were your mother, she would let you do whatever you wanted, because she wouldn't care. Is that what you want, Usha, a mother who doesn't care?" When I began menstruating, the summer before I started ninth grade, my mother gave me a speech, telling me that I was to let no boy touch me, and then she asked if I knew how a woman became pregnant. I told her what I had been taught in science, about the sperm fertilizing the egg, and then she asked if I knew how, exactly, that happened. I saw the terror in her eyes and so, though I knew that aspect of procreation as well, I lied, and told her it hadn't been explained to us.

I began keeping other secrets from her, evading her with the aid of my friends. I told her I was sleeping over at a friend's when really I went to parties, drinking beer and allowing boys to kiss me and fondle my breasts and press their erections against my hip as we lay groping on a sofa or the backseat of a car. I began to pity my mother; the older I got, the more I saw what a desolate life she led. She had never worked, and during the day she watched soap operas to pass the time. Her only job, every day, was to clean and cook for my father and me. We rarely went to restaurants, my father always pointing out, even in cheap ones, how expensive they were compared with eating at home. When my mother complained to him about how much she hated life in the suburbs and how lonely she felt, he said nothing to placate her. "If you are so unhappy, go back to Calcutta," he would offer, making it clear that their separation would not affect him one way or the other. I began to take my cues from my father in dealing with her, isolating her doubly. When she screamed at me for talking too long on the telephone, or for staying too long in my room, I learned to scream back, telling her that she was pathetic, that she knew nothing about me, and it was clear to us both that I had stopped needing her, definitively and abruptly, just as Pranab Kaku had.

Then, the year before I went off to college, my parents and I were invited to the Chakrabortys' home for Thanksgiving. We were not the only guests from my parents' old Cambridge crowd; it turned out that Pranab Kaku and Deborah wanted to have a sort of reunion of all the people they had been friendly with back then. Normally, my parents did not celebrate Thanksgiving; the ritual of a large sit-down dinner and the foods that one was supposed to eat was lost on them. They treated it as if it were Memorial Day or Veterans Day—just another holiday in the American year. But we drove out to Marblehead, to an impressive stone-faced house with a semicircular gravel driveway clogged with cars. The house was a short walk from the ocean; on our way, we had driven by the harbor overlooking the cold, glittering Atlantic, and when we stepped out of the car we were greeted by the sound of gulls and waves. Most of the living-room furniture had been moved to the basement and extra tables joined to the main one to form a giant U. They were covered with tablecloths, set with white plates and silverware, and had centerpieces of gourds. I was struck by the toys and dolls that were everywhere, dogs that shed long yellow hairs on everything, all the photographs of Bonny and Sara and Deborah decorating the walls, still more plastering the refrigerator door. Food was being prepared when we arrived, something my mother always frowned upon, the kitchen a chaos of people and smells and enormous dirtied bowls.

Deborah's family, whom we remembered dimly from the wedding, was there, her parents and her brothers and sisters and their husbands and wives and boyfriends and babies. Her sisters were in their thirties, but, like Deborah, they could have been mistaken for college students, wearing jeans and clogs and fisherman sweaters, and her brother Matty, with whom I had danced in a circle at the wedding, was now a freshman at Amherst, with wide-set green eyes and wispy brown hair and a complexion that reddened easily. As soon as I saw Deborah's siblings, joking with one another as they chopped and stirred things in the kitchen, I was furious with my mother for making a scene before we left the house and forcing me to wear a shalwar kameez. I knew they assumed, from my clothing, that I had more in common with the other Bengalis than with them. But Deborah insisted on including me, setting me to work peeling apples with Matty, and out of my parents' sight I was given beer to drink. When the meal was ready, we were told where to sit, in an alternating boy-girl formation that made the Bengalis uncomfortable. Bottles of wine were lined up on the table. Two turkeys were brought out, one stuffed with sausage and one without. My mouth watered at the food, but I knew that afterward, on our way home, my mother would complain that it was all tasteless and bland. "Impossible," my mother said, shaking her hand over the top of her glass when someone tried to pour her a little wine.

Deborah's father, Gene, got up to say grace, and asked everyone at the table to join hands. He bowed his head and closed his eyes. "Dear Lord, we thank you today for the food we are about to receive," he began. My parents were seated next to each other, and I was stunned to see that they complied, that my father's brown fingers lightly clasped my mother's pale ones. I noticed Matty seated on the other side of the room and saw him glancing at me as his father spoke. After the chorus of Amens, Gene raised his glass and said, "Forgive me, but I never thought I'd have the opportunity to say this: Here's to Thanksgiving with the Indians." Only a few people laughed at the joke.

Then Pranab Kaku stood up and thanked everyone for coming. He was relaxed from alcohol, his once wiry body beginning to thicken. He started to talk sentimentally about his early days in Cambridge, and then suddenly he recounted the story of meeting me and my mother for the first time, telling the guests about how he had followed us that afternoon. The people who did not know us laughed, amused by the description of the encounter, and by Pranab Kaku's desperation. He walked around the room to where my mother was sitting and draped a lanky arm around her shoulder, forcing her, for a brief moment, to stand up. "This woman," he declared, pulling her close to his side, "this woman hosted my first real Thanksgiving in America. It might have been an afternoon in May, but that first meal at Boudi's table was Thanksgiving to me. If it weren't for that meal, I would have gone back to Calcutta." My mother looked away, embarrassed. She was thirty-eight, already going gray, and she looked closer to my father's age than to Pranab Kaku's; regardless of his waistline, he retained his handsome, carefree looks. Pranab Kaku went back to his place at the head of the table, next to Deborah, and concluded, "And if that had been the case I'd have never met you, my darling," and he kissed her on the mouth in front of everyone, to much applause, as if it were their wedding day all over again.

After the turkey, smaller forks were distributed and orders were taken for three different kinds of pie, written on small pads by Deborah's sisters, as if they were waitresses. After dessert, the dogs needed to go out, and Pranab Kaku volunteered to take them. "How about a walk on the beach?" he suggested, and Deborah's side of the family agreed that that was an excellent idea. None of the Bengalis wanted to go, preferring to sit with their tea and cluster together, at last, at one end of the room, speaking freely after the forced chitchat with the Americans during the meal. Matty came over and sat in the chair beside me that was now empty, encouraging me to join the walk. When I hesitated, pointing to my inappropriate clothes and shoes but also aware of my mother's silent fury at the sight of us together, he said, "I'm sure Deb can lend you something." So I went upstairs, where Deborah gave me a pair of her jeans and a thick sweater and some sneakers, so that I looked like her and her sisters.

She sat on the edge of her bed, watching me change, as if we were girlfriends, and she asked if I had a boyfriend. When I told her no, she said, "Matty thinks you're cute."

"He told you?"

"No, but I can tell."

As I walked back downstairs, emboldened by this information, in the jeans I'd had to roll up and in which I felt finally like myself, I noticed my mother lift her eyes from her teacup and stare at me, but she said nothing, and off I went, with Pranab Kaku and his dogs and his in-laws, along a road and then down some steep wooden steps to the water. Deborah and one of her sisters stayed behind, to begin the cleanup and see to the needs of those who remained. Initially, we all walked together, in a single row across the sand, but then I noticed Matty hanging back, and so the two of us trailed behind, the distance between us and the others increasing. We began flirting, talking of things I no longer remember, and eventually we wandered into a rocky inlet and Matty fished a joint out of his pocket. We turned our backs to the wind and smoked it, our cold fingers touching in the process, our lips pressed to the same damp section of the rolling paper. At first I didn't feel any effect, but then, listening to him talk about the band he was in, I was aware that his voice sounded miles away, and that I had the urge to laugh, even though what he was saying was not terribly funny. It felt as if we were apart from the group for hours, but when we wandered back to the sand we could still see them, walking out onto a promontory to watch the sun set.

It was dark by the time we all headed back to the house, and I dreaded seeing my parents while I was still high. But when we got there Deborah told me that my parents, feeling tired, had left, agreeing to let someone drive me home later. A fire had been lit and I was told to relax and have more pie as the leftovers were put away and the living room slowly put back in order. Of course, it was Matty who drove me home, and sitting in my parents' driveway I kissed him, at once thrilled and terrified that my mother might walk onto the lawn in her nightgown and discover us. I gave Matty my phone number, and for a few weeks I thought of him constantly, and hoped foolishly that he would call.

In the end, my mother was right, and fourteen years after that Thanksgiving, after twenty-three years of marriage, Pranab Kaku and Deborah got divorced. It was he who had strayed, falling in love with a married Bengali woman, destroying two families in the process. The other woman was someone my parents knew, though not very well. Deborah was in her forties by then, Bonny and Sara away at college. In her shock and grief, it was my mother whom Deborah turned to, calling and weeping into the phone. Somehow, through all the years, she had continued to regard us as quasi in-laws, sending flowers when my grandparents died and giving me a compact edition of the *O.E.D.* as a college-graduation present. "You knew him so well. How could he do something like this?" Deborah asked my mother. And then, "Did you know anything about it?" My mother answered truthfully that she did not. Their hearts had been broken by the same man, only my mother's had long ago mended, and in an odd way, as my parents approached their old age, she and my father had grown fond of each other, out of habit if nothing else. I believe my absence from the house, once I left for college, had something to do with this, because over the years, when I visited, I noticed a warmth between my parents that had not been there before, a quiet teasing, a solidarity, a concern when one of them fell ill. My mother and I had also made peace; she had accepted the fact that I was not only her daughter but a child of America as well. Slowly, she accepted that I dated one American man, and then another, and then yet another, that I slept with them, and even that I lived with one though we were not married. She welcomed my boyfriends into our home and when things didn't work out she told me I would find someone better. After years of being idle, she decided, when she turned fifty, to get a degree in library science at a nearby university.

On the phone, Deborah admitted something that surprised my mother: that all these years she had felt hopelessly shut out of a part of Pranab Kaku's life. "I was so horribly jealous of you back then, for knowing him, understanding him in a way I never could. He turned his back on his family, on all of you, really, but I still felt threatened. I could never get over that." She told my mother that she had tried, for years, to get Pranab Kaku to reconcile with his parents, and that she had also encouraged him to maintain ties with other Bengalis, but he had resisted. It had been Deborah's idea to invite us to their Thanksgiving; ironically, the other woman had been there, too. "I hope you don't blame me for taking him away from your lives, Boudi. I always worried that you did."

My mother assured Deborah that she blamed her for nothing. She confessed nothing to Deborah about her own jealousy of decades before, only that she was sorry for what had happened, that it was a sad and terrible thing for their family. She did not tell Deborah that a few weeks after Pranab Kaku's wedding, while I was at a Girl Scout meeting and my father was at work, she had gone through the house, gathering up all the safety pins that lurked in drawers and tins, and adding them to the few fastened to her bracelets. When she'd found enough, she pinned them to her sari one by one, attaching the front piece to the layer of material underneath, so that no one would be able to pull the garment off her body. Then she took a can of lighter fluid and a box of kitchen matches and stepped outside, into our chilly backyard, which was full of leaves needing to be raked. Over her sari she was wearing a knee-length lilac trench coat, and to any neighbor she must have looked as though she'd simply stepped out for some fresh air. She opened up the coat and removed the tip from the can of lighter fluid and doused herself, then buttoned and belted the coat. She walked over to the garbage barrel behind our house and disposed of the fluid, then returned to the middle of the yard with the box of matches in her coat pocket. For nearly an hour she stood there, looking at our house, trying to work up the courage to strike a match. It was not I who saved her, or my father, but our next-door neighbor, Mrs. Holcomb, with whom my mother had never been particularly friendly. She came out to rake the leaves in her yard, calling out to my mother and remarking how beautiful the sunset was. "I see you've been admiring it for a while now," she said. My mother agreed, and then she went back into the house. By the time my father and I came home in the early evening, she was in the kitchen boiling rice for our dinner, as if it were any other day.

My mother told Deborah none of this. It was to me that she confessed, after my own heart was broken by a man I'd hoped to marry.

JUNOT DÍAZ
(b. 1968)

Born in Santo Domingo, Dominican Republic, Junot Díaz lived with his mother and grandparents until he was reunited with his father in Parlin, New Jersey, as a teenager. (There, Dias has said, he and his father lived "less than one mile from one of the largest landfills in New Jersey.") Díaz has a BA degree in English from Rutgers College in New Brunswick (1992) and an MFA from Cornell University (1995). He has been a Millet Writing Fellow at Wesleyan University and has participated in Wesleyan's Distinguished Writers Series; he has taught at MIT and has been fiction editor of the Boston Review.

Díaz's career, still in its ascendency, has been greeted with much acclaim and too many awards to enumerate. Though he has published just two books—the story collection Drown *(1996) and the novel* The Brief Wondrous Life of Oscar Wao *(2007)—he has been awarded the Pulitzer Prize, the Rome Prize from the American Academy of Arts and Letters, the 2002 PEN/Malamad Award for the Short Story, the National Book Critics Circle Award, the Anisfield-Wolf Book Award, the John Sargent Sr. First Novel Prize, and the Dayton Literary Peace Prize for Fiction. Díaz has also been listed in the* New Yorker *as one of the top twenty young writers for the twenty-first century. His work has appeared in* The Best American Short Stories *and* The O. Henry Awards: Best Short Stories of the Year *as well as, frequently, in the* New Yorker.

Stalled for more than five years with his first novel after the publication of his story collection Drown, *Díaz has written with painful frankness of the misery of what is commonly called "writer's block": "A writer is a writer because even when there is no hope, even when nothing he does shows signs of promise, he keeps writing anyway." This identification with protracted struggle and failure has allowed Díaz to write, ironically, such beautifully understated short fiction as the story included here, aptly titled "Edison, N.J."*

Edison, New Jersey

The first time we try to deliver the Gold Crown the lights are on in the house but no one lets us in. I bang on the front door and Wayne hits the back and I can hear our double drum shaking the windows. Right then I have this feeling that someone is inside, laughing at us.

This guy better have a good excuse, Wayne says, lumbering around the newly planted rosebushes. This is bullshit.

You're telling me, I say but Wayne's the one who takes this job too seriously. He pounds some more on the door, his face jiggling. A couple of times he raps on the windows, tries squinting through the curtains. I take a more philosophical approach; I walk over to the ditch that has been cut next to the road, a drainage pipe half filled with water, and sit down. I smoke and watch a mama duck and her three ducklings scavenge the grassy bank and then float downstream like they're on the same string. Beautiful, I say but Wayne doesn't hear. He's banging on the door with the staple gun.

At nine Wayne picks me up at the showroom and by then I have our route planned out. The order forms tell me everything I need to know about the customers we'll be dealing with that day. If someone is just getting a fifty-two-inch card table delivered then you know they aren't going to give you too much of a hassle but they also aren't going to tip. Those are your Spotswood, Sayreville and Perth Amboy deliveries. The pool tables go north to the rich suburbs—Livingston, Ridgewood, Bedminster.

You should see our customers. Doctors, diplomats, surgeons, presidents of universities, ladies in slacks and silk tops who sport thin watches you could trade in for a car, who wear comfortable leather shoes. Most of them prepare for us by laying down a path of yesterday's *Washington Post* from the front door to the game room. I make them pick it all up. I say: Carajo, what if we slip? Do you know what two hundred pounds of slate could do to a floor? The threat of property damage puts the chop-chop in their step. The best customers leave us alone until the bill has to be signed. Every now and then we'll be given water in paper cups. Few have offered us more, though a dentist from Ghana once gave us a six-pack of Heineken while we worked.

Sometimes the customer has to jet to the store for cat food or a newspaper while we're in the middle of a job. I'm sure you'll be all right, they say. They never sound too sure. Of course, I say. Just show us where the silver's at. The customers ha-ha and we ha-ha and then they agonize over leaving, linger by the front door, trying to memorize everything they own, as if they don't know where to find us, who we work for.

Once they're gone, I don't have to worry about anyone bothering me. I put down the ratchet, crack my knuckles and explore, usually while Wayne is smoothing out the felt and doesn't need help. I take cookies from the kitchen, razors from the bathroom cabinets. Some of these houses have twenty, thirty rooms. On the ride back I figure out how much loot it would take to fill up all that space. I've been caught roaming around plenty of times but you'd be surprised how quickly someone believes you're looking for the bathroom if you don't jump when you're discovered, if you just say, Hi.

After the paperwork's been signed, I have a decision to make. If the customer has been good and tipped well, we call it even and leave. If the customer has been an ass—maybe they yelled, maybe they let their kids throw golf balls at us—I ask for the bathroom. Wayne will pretend that he hasn't seen this before; he'll count the drill bits while the customer (or their maid) guides the vacuum over the floor. Excuse me, I say. I let them show me the way to the bathroom (usually I already know) and once the door is shut I cram bubble bath drops into my pockets and throw fist-sized wads of toilet paper into the toilet. I take a dump if I can and leave that for them.

Most of the time Wayne and I work well together. He's the driver and the money man and I do the lifting and handle the assholes. Tonight we're on our way to Lawrenceville and he wants to talk to me about Charlene, one of the showroom girls, the one with the blow-job lips. I haven't wanted to talk about women in months, not since the girlfriend.

I really want to pile her, he tells me. Maybe on one of the Madisons.

Man, I say, cutting my eyes towards him. Don't you have a wife or something?

He gets quiet. I'd still like to pile her, he says defensively.

And what will that do?

Why does it have to *do* anything?

Twice this year Wayne's cheated on his wife and I've heard it all, the before and the after. The last time his wife nearly tossed his ass out to the dogs. Neither of the women seemed worth it to me. One of them was even younger than Charlene. Wayne can be a moody guy and this is one of those nights; he slouches in the driver's seat and swerves through traffic, riding other people's bumpers like I've told him not to do. I don't need a collision or a four-hour silent treatment so I try to forget that I think his wife is good people and ask him if Charlene's given him any signals.

He slows the truck down. Signals like you wouldn't believe, he says.

On the days we have no deliveries the boss has us working at the showroom, selling cards and poker chips and mankala boards. Wayne spends his time skeezing the salesgirls and dusting shelves. He's a big goofy guy—I don't understand why the girls dig his shit. One of those mysteries of the universe. The boss keeps me in the front of the store, away from the pool tables. He knows I'll talk to the customers, tell them not to buy the cheap models. I'll say shit like, Stay away from those Bristols. Wait until you can get something real. Only when he needs my Spanish will he let me help on a sale. Since I'm no good at cleaning or selling slot machines I slouch behind the front register and steal. I don't ring anything up, and pocket what comes in. I don't tell Wayne. He's too busy running his fingers through his beard, keeping the waves on his nappy head in order. A hundred-buck haul's not unusual for me and back in the day, when the girlfriend used to pick me up, I'd buy her anything she wanted, dresses, silver rings, lingerie. Sometimes I blew it all on her. She didn't like the stealing but hell, we weren't made out of loot and I liked going into a place and saying, Jeva, pick out anything, it's yours. This is the closest I've come to feeling rich.

Nowadays I take the bus home and the cash stays with me. I sit next to this three-hundred-pound rock-and-roll chick who washes dishes at the Friendly's. She tells me about the roaches she kills with her water nozzle. Boils the wings right off them. On Thursday I buy myself lottery tickets—ten Quick Picks and a couple of Pick 4s. I don't bother with the little stuff.

The second time we bring the Gold Crown the heavy curtain next to the door swings up like a Spanish fan. A woman stares at me and Wayne's too busy knocking to see. Muñeca, I say. She's black and unsmiling and then the curtain drops between us, a whisper on the glass. She had on a t-shirt that said *No Problem* and didn't look like she owned the place. She looked more like the help and couldn't have been older than twenty and from the thinness of her face I pictured the rest of her skinny. We stared at each other for a second at the most, not enough for me to notice the shape of her ears or if her lips were chapped. I've fallen in love on less.

Later in the truck, on the way back to the showroom Wayne mutters, This guy is dead. I mean it.

The girlfriend calls sometimes but not often. She has found herself a new boyfriend, some zángano who works at a record store. *Dan* is his name and the way she says it, so painfully gringo, makes the corners of my eyes narrow. The clothes I'm sure this guy tears from her when they both get home from work—the chokers, the rayon skirts from the Warehouse, the lingerie—I bought with stolen money and I'm glad that none of it was earned straining my back against hundreds of pounds of raw rock. I'm glad for that.

The last time I saw her in person was in Hoboken. She was with *Dan* and hadn't yet told me about him and hurried across the street in her high clogs to avoid me and my boys, who even then could sense me turning, turning into the motherfucker who'll put a fist through anything. She flung one hand in the air but didn't stop. A month before the zángano, I went to her house, a friend visiting a friend, and her parents asked me how business was, as if I balanced the books or something. Business is outstanding, I said.

That's really wonderful to hear, the father said.

You betcha.

He asked me to help him mow his lawn and while we were dribbling gas into the tank he offered me a job. A real one that you can build on. Utilities, he said, is nothing to be ashamed of.

Later the parents went into the den to watch the Giants lose and she took me into her bathroom. She put on her makeup because we were going to a movie. If I had your eyelashes, I'd be famous, she told me. The Giants started losing real bad. I still love you, she said and I was embarrassed for the two of us, the way I'm embarrassed at those afternoon talk shows where broken couples and unhappy families let their hearts hang out.

We're friends, I said and Yes, she said, yes we are.

There wasn't much space so I had to put my heels on the edge of the bathtub. The cross I'd given her dangled down on its silver chain so I put it in my mouth to keep it from poking me in the eye. By the time we finished my legs were bloodless, broomsticks inside my rolled-down baggies and as her breathing got smaller and smaller against my neck, she said, I do, I still do.

Each payday I take out the old calculator and figure how long it'd take me to buy a pool table honestly. A top-of-the-line, three-piece slate affair doesn't come cheap. You have to buy sticks and balls and chalk and a score keeper and triangles and French tips if you're a fancy shooter. Two and a half years if I give up buying underwear and eat only pasta but even this figure's bogus. Money's never stuck to me, ever.

Most people don't realize how sophisticated pool tables are. Yes, tables have bolts and staples on the rails but these suckers hold together mostly by gravity and by the precision of their construction. If you treat a good table right it will outlast you. Believe me. Cathedrals are built like that. There are Incan roads in the Andes that even today you couldn't work a knife between two of the cobblestones. The sewers that the Romans built in Bath were so good that they weren't replaced until the 1950s. That's the sort of thing I can believe in.

These days I can build a table with my eyes closed. Depending on how rushed we are I might build the table alone, let Wayne watch until I need help putting on the slate. It's better when the customers stay out of our faces, how they react when we're done, how they run fingers on the lacquered rails and suck in their breath, the felt so tight you couldn't pluck it if you tried. Beautiful, is what they say and we always nod, talc on our fingers, nod again, beautiful.

The boss nearly kicked our asses over the Gold Crown. The customer, an asshole named Pruitt, called up crazy, said we were *delinquent*. That's how the boss put it. Delinquent. We knew that's what the customer called us because the boss doesn't use words like that. Look boss, I said, we knocked like crazy. I mean, we knocked like federal marshals. Like Paul Bunyan. The boss wasn't having it. You fuckos, he said. You butthogs. He tore us for a good two minutes and then *dismissed* us. For most of that night I didn't think I had a job so I hit the bars, fantasizing that I would bump into this cabrón out with that black woman while me and my boys were cranked but the next morning Wayne came by with that Gold Crown again. Both of us had hangovers. One more time, he said. An extra delivery, no overtime. We hammered on the door for ten minutes but no one answered. I jimmied with the windows and the back door and I could have sworn I heard her behind the patio door. I knocked hard and heard footsteps.

We called the boss and told him what was what and the boss called the house but no one answered. OK, the boss said. Get those card tables done. That night, as we lined up the next day's paperwork, we got a call from Pruitt and he didn't use the word delinquent. He wanted us to come late at night but we were booked. Two-month waiting list, the boss reminded him. I looked over at Wayne and wondered how much money this guy was pouring into the boss's ear. Pruitt said he was *contrite* and *determined* and asked us to come again. His maid was sure to let us in.

What the hell kind of name is Pruitt anyway? Wayne asks me when we swing onto the parkway.

Pato name, I say. Anglo or some other bog people.

Probably a fucking banker. What's the first name?

Just an initial, C. Clarence Pruitt sounds about right.

Yeah, Clarence, Wayne yuks.

Pruitt. Most of our customers have names like this, court case names: Wooley, Maynard, Gass, Binder, but the people from my town, our names, you see on convicts or coupled together on boxing cards.

We take our time. Go to the Rio Diner, blow an hour and all the dough we have in our pockets. Wayne is talking about Charlene and I'm leaning my head against a thick pane of glass.

Pruitt's neighborhood has recently gone up and only his court is complete. Gravel roams off this way and that, shaky. You can see inside the other houses, their newly formed guts, nailheads bright and sharp on the fresh timber. Wrinkled blue tarps protect wiring and fresh plaster. The driveways are mud and on each lawn stand huge stacks of sod. We park in front of Pruitt's house and bang on the door. I give Wayne a hard look when I see no car in the garage.

Yes? I hear a voice inside say.

We're the delivery guys, I yell.

A bolt slides, a lock turns, the door opens. She stands in our way, wearing black shorts and a gloss of red on her lips and I'm sweating.

Come in, yes? She stands back from the door, holding it open.

Sounds like Spanish, Wayne says.

No shit, I say, switching over. Do you remember me?

NO, she says.

I look over at Wayne. Can you believe this?

I can believe anything, kid.

You heard us didn't you? The other day, that was you.

She shrugs and opens the door wider.

You better tell her to prop that with a chair. Wayne heads back to unlock the truck.

You hold that door, I say.

We've had our share of delivery trouble. Trucks break down. Customers move and leave us with an empty house. Handguns get pointed. Slate gets dropped, a rail goes missing. The felt is the wrong color, the Dufferins get left in the warehouse. Back in the day, the girlfriend and I made a game of this. A prediction game. In the mornings I rolled onto my pillow and said, What's today going to be like?

Let me check. She put her fingers up to her widow's peak and that motion would shift her breasts, her hair. We never slept under any covers, not in spring, fall or summer and our bodies were dark and thin the whole year.

I see an asshole customer, she murmured. Unbearable traffic. Wayne's going to work slow. And then you'll come home to me.

Will I get rich?

You'll come home to me. That's the best I can do. And then we'd kiss hungrily because this was how we loved each other.

The game was part of our mornings, the way our showers and our sex and our breakfasts were. We stopped playing only when it started to go wrong for us, when I'd wake up and listen to the traffic outside without waking her, when everything was a fight.

She stays in the kitchen while we work. I can hear her humming. Wayne's shaking his right hand like he's scalded his fingertips. Yes, she's fine. She has her back to me, her hands stirring around in a full sink, when I walk in.

I try to sound conciliatory. You're from the city?

A nod.

Where about?

Washington Heights.

Dominicana, I say. Quisqueyana. She nods. What street?

I don't know the address, she says. I have it written down. My mother and my brothers live there.

I'm Dominican, I say.

You don't look it.

I get a glass of water. We're both staring out at the muddy lawn.

She says, I didn't answer the door because I wanted to piss him off.

Piss who off?

I want to get out of here, she says.

Out of here?

I'll pay you for a ride.

I don't think so, I say.

Aren't you from Nueva York?

No.

Then why did you ask the address?

Why? I have family near there.

Would it be that big of a problem?

I say in English that she should have her boss bring her but she stares at me blankly. I switch over.

He's a pendejo, she says, suddenly angry. I put down the glass, move next to her to wash it. She's exactly my height and smells of liquid detergent and has tiny beautiful moles on her neck, an archipelago leading down into her clothes.

Here, she says, putting out her hand but I finish it and go back to the den.

Do you know what she wants us to do? I say to Wayne.

Her room is upstairs, a bed, a closet, a dresser, yellow wallpaper. Spanish *Cosmo* and *El Diario* thrown on the floor. Four hangers' worth of clothes in the closet and only the top dresser drawer is full. I put my hand on the bed and the cotton sheets are cool.

Pruitt has pictures of himself in his room. He's tan and probably has been to more countries than I know capitals for. Photos of him on vacations, on beaches, standing beside a wide-mouth Pacific salmon he's hooked. The size of his dome would have made Broca proud. The bed is made and his wardrobe spills out onto chairs and a line of dress shoes follows the far wall. A bachelor. I find an open box of Trojans in his dresser beneath a stack of boxer shorts. I put one of the condoms in my pocket and stick the rest under his bed.

I find her in her room. He likes clothes, she says.

A habit of money, I say but I can't translate it right; I end up agreeing with her. Are you going to pack?

She holds up her purse. I have everything I need. He can keep the rest of it.

You should take some of your things.

I don't care about that vaina. I just want to go.

Don't be stupid, I say. I open her dresser and pull out the shorts on top and a handful of soft bright panties fall out and roll down the front of my jeans. There are more in the drawer. I try to catch them but as soon as I touch their fabric I let everything go.

Leave it. Go on, she says and begins to put them back in the dresser, her square back to me, the movement of her hands smooth and easy.

Look, I say.

Don't worry. She doesn't look up.

I go downstairs. Wayne is sinking the bolts into the slate with the Makita. You can't do it, he says.

Why not?

Kid. We have to finish this.

I'll be back before you know it. A quick trip, in out.

Kid. He stands up slowly; he's nearly twice as old as me.

I go to the window and look out. New gingkoes stand in rows beside the driveway. A thousand years ago when I was still in college I learned something about them. Living fossils. Unchanged since their inception millions of years ago. You tagged Charlene, didn't you?

Sure did, he answers easily.

I take the truck keys out of the toolbox. I'll be right back, I promise.

My mother still has pictures of the girlfriend in her apartment. The girlfriend's the sort of person who never looks bad. There's a picture of us at the bar where I taught her to play pool. She's leaning on the Schmelke I stole for her, nearly a grand worth of cue, frowning at the shot I left her, a shot she'd go on to miss.

The picture of us in Florida is the biggest—shiny, framed, nearly a foot tall. We're in our bathing suits and the legs of some stranger frame the right. She has her butt in the sand, knees folded up in front of her because she knew I was sending the picture home to my moms; she didn't want my mother to see her bikini, didn't want my mother to think her a whore. I'm crouching next to her, smiling, one hand on her thin shoulder, one of her moles showing between my fingers.

My mother won't look at the pictures or talk about her when I'm around but my sister says she still cries over the breakup. Around me my mother's polite, sits quietly on the couch while I tell her about what I'm reading and how work has been. Do you have anyone? she asks me sometimes.

Yes, I say.

She talks to my sister on the side, says, In my dreams they're still together.

We reach the Washington Bridge without saying a word. She's emptied his cupboards and refrigerator; the bags are at her feet. She's eating corn chips but I'm too nervous to join in.

Is this the best way? she asks. The bridge doesn't seem to impress her.

It's the shortest way.

She folds the bag shut. That's what he said when I arrived last year. I wanted to see the countryside. There was too much rain to see anything anyway.

I want to ask her if she loves her boss, but I ask instead, How do you like the States?

She swings her head across at the billboards. I'm not surprised by any of it, she says.

Traffic on the bridge is bad and she has to give me an oily fiver for the toll. Are you from the Capital? I ask.

No.

I was born there. In Villa Juana. Moved here when I was a little boy.

She nods, staring out at the traffic. As we cross over the bridge I drop my hand into her lap. I leave it there, palm up, fingers slightly curled. Sometimes you just have to try, even if you know it won't work. She turns her head away slowly, facing out beyond the bridge cables, out to Manhattan and the Hudson.

Everything in Washington Heights is Dominican. You can't go a block without passing a Quisqueya Bakery or a Quisqueya Supermercado or a Hotel Quisqueya. If I were to park the truck and get out nobody would take me for a deliveryman; I could be the guy who's on the street corner selling Dominican flags. I could be on my way home to my girl. Everybody's on the streets and the merengue's falling out of windows like TVs. When we reach her block I ask a kid with the sag for the building and he points out the stoop with his pinkie. She gets out of the truck and straightens the front of her sweatshirt before following the line that the kid's finger has cut across the street. Cuídate, I say.

Wayne works on the boss and a week later I'm back, on probation, painting the warehouse. Wayne brings me meatball sandwiches from out on the road, skinny things with a seam of cheese gumming the bread.

Was it worth it? he asks me.

He's watching me close. I tell him it wasn't.

Did you at least get some?

Hell yeah, I say.

Are you sure?

Why would I lie about something like that? Homegirl was an animal. I still have the teeth marks.

Damn, he says.

I punch him in the arm. And how's it going with you and Charlene?

I don't know, man. He shakes his head and in that motion I see him out on his lawn with all his things. I just don't know about this one.

We're back on the road a week later. Buckinghams, Imperials, Gold Crowns and dozens of card tables. I keep a copy of Pruitt's paperwork and when the curiosity finally gets to me I call. The first time I get the machine. We're delivering at a house in Long Island with a view of the Sound that would break you. Wayne and I smoke a joint on the beach and I pick up a dead horseshoe crab by the tail and heave it in the customer's garage. The next two times I'm in the Bedminster area Pruitt picks up and says, Yes? But on the fourth time she answers and the sink is running on her side of the phone and she shuts it off when I don't say anything.

Was she there? Wayne asks in the truck.

Of course she was.

He runs a thumb over the front of his teeth. Pretty predictable. She's probably in love with the guy. You know how it is.

I sure do.

Don't get angry.

I'm tired, that's all.

Tired's the best way to be, he says. It really is.

He hands me the map and my fingers trace our deliveries, stitching city to city. Looks like we've gotten everything, I say.

Finally. He yawns. What's first tomorrow?

We won't really know until the morning, when I've gotten the paperwork in order but I take guesses anyway. One of our games. It passes the time, gives us something to look forward to. I close my eyes and put my hand on the map. So many towns, so many cities to choose from. Some places are sure bets but more than once I've gone with the long shot and been right.

You can't imagine how many times I've been right.

Usually the name will come to me fast, the way the numbered balls pop out during the lottery drawings, but this time nothing comes: no magic, no nothing. It could be anywhere. I open my eyes and see that Wayne is still waiting. Edison, I say, pressing my thumb down. Edison, New Jersey.

AUTHOR INDEX